Shirley Conran Strips Away
the Silken Veils of Civilization in . . .

SILVANA: The cold, elegant wife of the retiring company president, she was once a bewitching, sensual beauty. Now, on the island of Paui, she will fight to the death to survive . . .

SUZY: A voluptuous, sexy social climber, she believed money could buy safety. Now she must confront her darkest fears . . .

PATTY: A California blonde, she ran miles every day, trying to forget her past. On Paui her physical strength is the women's greatest asset, but her violent temper is a danger to them all . . .

CAREY: The only one with her own career, she drowned her fears in champagne at company parties. Now, cut off from civilization, she finds a surprising strength—and an unexpected weakness . . .

ANNIE: Sweet-natured and shy, she was tormented by powerful sexual yearnings. Trapped in a nightmare world, she teeters between utter despair and extraordinary courage . . .

Books by Shirley Conran

Crimson
Lace
Lace 2
Savages

Published by POCKET BOOKS

SHIRLEY CONRAN

SAVAGES

POCKET BOOKS, a division of Simon & Schuster, Inc.
1230 Avenue of the Americas, New York, N.Y. 10020

Copyright © 1987 by Shirley Conran Ltd.
Cover photo copyright © 1988 Herbert Photography

All rights reserved, including the right to reproduce

POCKET BOOKS

New York   London   Toronto   Sydney   Tokyo   Singapore

This book is a work of fiction. Names, characters, places and incidents are either the product of the author's imagination or are used fictitiously. Any resemblance to actual events or locales or persons, living or dead, is entirely coincidental.

POCKET BOOKS, a division of Simon & Schuster Inc.
1230 Avenue of the Americas, New York, NY 10020

ISBN: 0-671-72719-2

First Pocket Books printing July 1988

10 9 8 7 6 5 4

POCKET and colophon are registered trademarks of Simon & Schuster Inc.

Printed in the U.S.A.

To do is to be.

—John Stuart Mill

CONTENTS

CONTENTS

BOOK ONE

THE GOLDEN TRIANGLE

THURSDAY, OCTOBER 25, 1984

Slowly, silently the door swung open. That was odd, thought Lorenza, because since that silly kidnap threat, the invisible security precautions at home had been rigorous. She pushed at the blackened, heavy medieval door. She had known its weathered vertical ridges all her life; her great-grandfather had brought this wooden door, along with the rest of the manor house, from the Cotswolds across the Atlantic to Pennsylvania. For twenty-three years—all her life—she had seen daydream pictures in the door's wizened indentations as she waited for it to be opened.

"Where *is* everybody?" she called, as she stepped onto the old York stone of the entrance hall and kicked off her scarlet pumps.

Nobody answered. The echoes of the bell died away.

In stockinged feet, Lorenza walked back outside the front door and glanced beyond her red Ferrari Mondial, carelessly parked askew at the bottom of the steps. She gazed around the quiet parkland that fell away on all sides from the house to distant woods and the Ohio River, but she saw nobody.

Once again, Lorenza gave the bell three peremptory tugs, then walked over to one of the ancient stone lions that stood at the top of the steps. She patted its stone head, as she always

3

did when she came home, then pulled off her sable coat and draped it over the lion; it was warm for the end of October.

She wandered back into the hall and looked up at the life-size Sargent portrait of her great-grandmother. "Robbed? Raped? Kidnapped? Where do you think they all are, Great-grandma?"

Lorenza had the same abundant but wispy russet hair as the anxious-looking lady in the pale-gray satin ballgown, but she didn't have the same twenty-inch waist; Lorenza was chubby, like her mother, especially now. *At last* she was pregnant! She'd married Andrew sixteen months ago, in June 1983, and since the day she'd returned from her honeymoon her mother had looked hopeful. Lorenza had only to watch her mother stroke her six black cats—sinuous, small panthers—to know that she loved with her hands and longed for a grandchild to cuddle.

In her stockinged feet, Lorenza padded to her right, through a suite of reception rooms linked by double doors; there was no sign of anyone in the morning room, the salon, the library or the ballroom, beyond, which ran the full depth of the house and led into the orangery.

As she returned through the library, Lorenza noticed her mother's reading glasses lying by a scatter of papers on the silver-gray carpet. So her mother was around *somewhere*, she thought. Idly, she picked up two invitation cards, a newspaper and a travel brochure. She looked with interest at the travel brochure, on the cover of which was pictured a tropical beach; palm trees waved against an aquamarine sky, above which scarlet words promised: "Paradise can be yours on Paui." Lorenza flicked open the brochure and saw photographs of a low modern hotel, tropical gardens, black women with pink flowers stuck behind their ears, trays of flower-decorated drinks; young, clean-cut, bronzed white couples smiled into each other's eyes as they dined under the stars, swam in an azure pool, swung golf clubs and tennis rackets or enjoyed a champagne picnic on a deserted beach. "Just north of Australia and south of the equator, you can reserve a slice of paradise

4

for yourself," the brochure suggested. "Toll-free reservations 1-800-545-PAUL."

Lorenza threw down her mother's papers, returned to the hall and shouted again up the ancient stairs. Her voice echoed around the oak-paneled minstrel's gallery, but once more there was no response. She pattered to the back of the hall and peered through the double doors onto the terrace, where three fountains were linked by flowerbeds, the whole neatly framed by rows of box hedge. Although the Grahams employed three gardeners, her mother was often to be found weeding the formal Italian garden, beyond which the lawn sloped down to the Ohio River. Today there wasn't a soul in sight.

Lorenza headed to her left, down the passage that led past the dining room and her father's study to the staff quarters. No one in the kitchen . . . No one in the pantry . . . No one in the staff sitting room . . . No one in the flower room. But this house contained a butler, a cook, three Filipino housemaids and her mother's personal maid. Where *were* they all?

The linen room was off the staff sitting room. In front of a pile of unfolded sheets, a shapeless woman in a white smock was slumped in a rocking chair, her sleeves rolled up over skinny arms with sinews that stood out like a man's. On the back of each hand was a delta of thick blue veins.

Lorenza tiptoed over, tickled the woman's ear and bawled into it, "*Ciao*, Nella!"

With a shriek the woman leaped to her feet, clutching her breast. "Oh! You very bad girl, Miss Lorenza!" As Lorenza hugged her, Nella added in a muffled voice, "You give me the heart attack, then nobody to cook for the family." Nella had been transplanted from Rome when Lorenza's mother had first arrived in Pittsburgh as the new Mrs. Arthur Graham.

Lorenza yelled, "Where's Mama? And where's everyone else?"

Nella was deaf and had to be bawled at. She used her deafness as a convenient excuse for not hearing anything she did not wish to discuss. If pressed, she would thump the square of white fabric that jutted out between her flat breasts and hid her

5

old-fashioned box hearing aid, saying, "This thing no damn good again, needs fixing."

Nella said, "Your mama give staff free afternoon, because us all work late tomorrow night for your papa's birthday party. Your mama, she gone shopping."

"What for?"

"Clothes."

"But Mama always buys her clothes in Rome."

Nella looked uncomfortable. "Well, maybe not clothes, but is a secret."

"Aw, come on, Nella."

Nella looked furtive, but what Italian cook can keep a secret? "Your mama go shopping with the decorator to choose things for your apartment upstairs. Your mama have your rooms redone, because of the baby."

"But Andrew and I live in New York, and the baby will live there with us, not here."

"Your mama say, just in case."

"Just in case of *what?*"

Lorenza's attention was distracted as she heard an engine softly hum in the distance. She pushed open a diamond-paned window, hung out and waved at the white Van den Plas Jaguar as it moved sedately up the gravel drive. She said, "Mama must be the only person in the world who drives a six-cylinder Jaguar fifteen miles an hour."

"Your mama have plenty accident in her cars. Your mama not fast, but not careful. Always she think about other things, always some other place in her head. Your papa want she have some man to drive her, but your mama, she say too much trouble, is just someone else to organize."

But Nella was talking to the air. Lorenza had rushed off to meet her mother.

Silvana Graham hurried up the steps, dropped two gift-wrapped packages at the top and hugged her daughter. "Put your shoes on, darling! Mustn't catch cold, it's bad for the baby." She had a low, lilting voice like a flock of doves, a voice not unusual in Rome, but rare in Pennsylvania. This soothing quality of Silvana's voice permanently irritated her husband, because it sounded as if she were trying to calm him down, and therefore reminded him of his high blood pressure.

Lorenza kissed her mother on the lips. It was Silvana's bewitching mouth that had captivated Arthur Graham the first time he saw her, laughing in a seaside café at Santa Margherita, on the Italian Riviera, in 1956. Sophisticated, cosmopolitan Arthur had been surprised by his own reaction to the sensuality and insouciance of the big-breasted, cheerful seventeen-year-old with the loud laugh. Twenty-eight years later, only Silvana's mouth remained the same. The big dark eyes had lost their sparkle, the heavy black hair no longer tumbled around her shoulders but was tamed back in a tight, graying French twist.

The two women moved toward the library. Shoeless Lorenza waddled with pregnant self-importance; her mother's slow, regal carriage just offset a heaviness that threatened to turn into bulkiness, but even her upright head could no longer disguise the start of a double chin. Women thought Silvana Graham elegant but unapproachable; men thought she was over the hill, twenty-five pounds too heavy and not worth making a pass at. Silvana moved through life in a lethargic dream, propelled forward only by timetables. "Mustn't keep the servants waiting" had been the constant admonishment in the small palazzo in Rome, near the Borghese Gardens, where Silvana was born, and where her parents still lived.

In the library, Lorenza picked up the tropical island brochure. "What's this about, Mama? Are you escaping at last?"

Silvana laughed at their old joke. "No, it's a business trip. We're leaving next week for Australia. Nexus is holding the annual conference in Sydney this year. After that, we're having the usual top-brass working holiday. Your father has chosen Paui because he's never been fishing there, and apparently there are plenty of sharks. He's never caught a shark."

"There's something to be said for being president of a corporation." Lorenza threw herself on the silver brocade sofa, propped her feet up and started to discuss her pregnancy with the obsessive concentration of a five-months-pregnant first-timer, who little realized how bored she would be by the subject in two months' time. Although her baby wasn't due until late February, Lorenza now looked at her life as if down the wrong end of a telescope: it had shrunk to a circle that included only her husband and this blurry-faced sexless baby. Silvana listened to her daughter's self-important chatter. "Andrew feels . . . Andrew knows . . . Andrew wants me to give up my job . . . Andrew thinks he should look after my money. It's one of the things I want to talk to Papa about. Andrew says it's ridiculous to have someone else invest my money, when he's a broker . . . Andrew says . . ."

Silvana said, "Why give up your job? I thought you enjoyed it. Although I never understood why you took a job in the first place."

"Don't you remember? Gran said it would give me an interest." Lorenza remembered that Arthur's mother had also implied she didn't want Lorenza to follow her mother's aimless path, padding her life out with trivia in order not to notice that she was merely marking time until she died. Gran had always had eccentric ideas.

Lorenza laughed. "It's just an itsy-bitsy job at Sotheby's. Andrew says I haven't learned as much about pictures as Gran expected, and I don't *use* my history degree. I'm polite to people on the phone, help someone else to catalogue the paintings and occasionally take telephone bids at auctions. . . . I'll have plenty to do at home, looking after Andrew and the baby."

Silvana lifted the heavy silver coffeepot from the tray that Nella had just placed in front of her. "Nella's sister is coming from Varese to be your nanny. You'll have plenty of staff. You're luckier than most women. You'll have time to do something, to continue to be somebody."

Lorenza looked surprised. "Mama! That's sixties Women's Lib talk!" She laughed affectionately. "It's taken you twenty years to catch up."

"No, it's taken me twenty years to notice."

"Notice what?"

Silvana rubbed her pearl necklace against her cream silk collar, a sign of mild agitation. Hesitantly she said, "Few women are as happy after marriage as they expected to be."

"What are you *talking* about, Mama?" Don't say you and Papa are going to split, she thought. She asked in alarm, "Aren't *you* happy? Haven't you got everything that you could possibly want?"

Everything except what matters most, thought Silvana.

"What more could you possibly want, Mama?"

"To feel that I exist."

So it was only that. Lorenza stretched out one arm and gently pulled Silvana's hand toward her pink Fiorucci maternity overalls, so that Silvana could feel the hard little belly beneath. "Of course you exist, and so does that."

Silvana said, "I hope it's a boy." She hesitated again, then added, "I meant what I said about your job. I don't want your life to be eaten up without your noticing it. One day you look up and think, Where did it go, my life?" She shook her head. "Don't laugh, Lorenza. The people you love can swallow up your life, if you let it happen. You won't notice it's happening or how it happens—and if you do notice, you won't know how to stop it."

"Darling Mama, don't worry." Lorenza's indulgent voice didn't quite hide her irritation. "I have total faith in Andrew."

Silvana shrugged, remembering that she had once had total faith in Arthur. She recalled the angry scene with her father when she had carefully, casually told her parents over breakfast—one warm autumn day like this, years ago in Rome—that she wanted them to meet an American friend. Yes, a man. No, she had met him on the beach. (Because husky, blond Arthur had followed her from the café to the sand.) Her father had turned the page of his newspaper and said sharply that well-brought-up girls did not pick up boys on the beach, and *he* certainly did not wish to meet a young beach bum. So seventeen-year-old Silvana blurted out that Arthur was *not*

9

young—he was quite old, thirty-four, and she was going to marry him!

The result had been like pushing a flaming rag into a jar of kerosene. Her father smashed down the paper, leaped out of his chair and yelled, "When is it due?" Her mother said, "Tulio, lower your voice or the servants will hear." She then looked reproachfully at Silvana and asked, "When is it due?"

Amused at being taken for a parvenu, Arthur (whose girlfriend had flown back to New York after a quarrel, leaving him alone on vacation) had taken care to get Silvana pregnant as soon as she had explained that she was—sort of—engaged to be married, to the son of the family whose beautifully tended estate in Tuscany bounded theirs. Without a word Arthur had turned down the next country lane, stopped the car and thrust himself upon her. Silvana had willingly thrust back, then and subsequently, in the backs of hired cars, under hedges, in vineyards, legs waving from the bottom of a motorboat, and once behind a village bakery. Silvana had been thrilled at being made a proper woman by a proper man—not a boy. She thought that Arthur had all the sophistication, vitality and glamour of the U.S.A., a country that Silvana knew only from the movies and the advertising pages of *Life* magazine, a country which seemed glamorous and as distant as Mars from shabby postwar Italy, where an unmarried girl meekly obeyed her father.

After her father stormed from the breakfast room, followed by her mother repeating, "At least she says he's a Catholic, Tulio," the weeping Silvana had been examined by a strange physician—not the family doctor—then locked in her bedroom while her parents argued angrily. Nella, the kitchen maid who brought her meals, took Silvana's note to Arthur, who read the sad, crumpled letter, grinned, then telephoned his mother in Pittsburgh.

Not astonished by his news, but astounded that this time Arthur actually intended to marry a girl he'd gotten pregnant, Mrs. Graham had sighed, telephoned Nexus Tower and told the office to book her a seat to Rome. After the eighteen-hour flight, during which she had plenty of time to realize that she would, as always, be unable to dissuade her only son from doing what he wanted, Mrs. Graham stepped into the waiting maroon Rolls-Royce, thinking, Well, at least she's a Catholic.

Upon arriving at her usual suite at the Grand, Mrs. Graham wrote a short letter of invitation to Silvana's parents, which was delivered by hand to the crumbling Palazzo Cariotto just off the Borghese Gardens.

Count Cariotto went alone to meet the tragically widowed Mrs. Graham, who wore a navy Mainbocher dress, one long string of 16-millimeter pearls—she liked the fact that it never occurred to people that they were real—and her engagement ring, which was the biggest diamond the Count had ever seen. He found his eyes repeatedly drawn to it as they talked, with formal delicacy, of the inexorably approaching event. Eventually it was agreed that their lawyers should meet to discuss the suggested, generous marriage settlement upon Silvana, and the Count returned home to tell his wife that it could have been worse, at least the mother was a lady.

The engagement party was held on a starlit September evening in the interior courtyard of the Palazzo Cariotto, where careful spotlighting drew eyes away from the decay. White satin streamers fell from tubs of dark-green yew trees; marble statues were hung with garlands of white flowers; the many servants wore livery with waistcoats striped in the dark green and yellow Cariotto colors. All the delicious buffet food—the trout, the huge hams, the smoked delicacies, the fruit and the wine—had come from the Cariotto estate in Tuscany. Although the Count's business schemes invariably failed— someone he trusted always let him down—his farms ran as smoothly as they had always run, administered by the land agent who had inherited the job from his father, to whom it had been handed down by *his* father.

As swiftly as was decent, the engagement party was followed by the wedding—the bridegroom had business commitments, the Countess explained to her friends, who nodded understandingly. Following the elaborate Roman ceremony,

Silvana and Arthur flew to India for their honeymoon. Thirty minutes after the Karachi stopover, Silvana had the first of her miscarriages. This had upset the food service and sanitary facilities in the first-class cabin, but music was played to drown the noise of her pain and an ambulance was waiting at Delhi, where she spent a depressing three weeks in King George Hospital, before being flown in cautious stages back to Pittsburgh.

Silvana had now seen that Arthur was wonderful in a crisis, and fell even more deeply in love with him. "Arthur says . . . Arthur thinks . . . Arthur wants me . . . Arthur insists . . ." she told her mother over the long-distance calls that grew increasingly frequent. Her mother, correctly diagnosing homesickness, dispatched young Nella to help Silvana settle down in Arthur's family mansion in Sewickley, but Silvana never felt really happy away from the cheerful noise of Rome or the serenity of the Tuscan countryside where she had grown up, and flew back regularly to visit. Twice a year she observed her mother and father growing smaller, thinner and grayer. At first she clung to Arthur, seeking the support and security of his enfolding arms, but those strong, blond-haired, muscular arms enforced as well as enfolded. Silvana soon found out that she could do anything she wanted—unless Arthur wanted something else.

Arthur's mother had moved out of the English manor house in Sewickley before Arthur and his bride returned from India. Happily she commissioned Philip Johnson to build her a long, low house of glass, high in the hills, which is what she had always wanted, rather than that gloomy pile of thirty rooms with diamond-paned windows that never let in enough light and heavy carved furniture—much of it supposedly sixteenth-century—faded tapestries, brocade upholstery in several dingy shades and heavy, dark velvet curtains.

While Silvana recovered from her first miscarriage, she lay in her four-poster bed and scribbled notes about her pending transformation of the gloomy house. But when, one morning, she casually told Arthur what she was doing, he stopped dressing and looked at her sharply, tie tack in one hand, its stud in the other. "This is one of the best houses in Pennsylvania," he had said. "I grew up here and I don't want *anything* changed. You can replace things when necessary, but the replacements are to be just that—not changes."

Silvana tried to protest, she even made the mistake of saying that most of the expensive furniture was fake—or, if not, then *greatly* repaired. Arthur listened in cold silence, turned his ice-blue eyes toward her without moving his head and observed, "At least it doesn't have to be propped up with somebody else's money." A large part of Silvana's settlement had been "loaned" to repair the Palazzo Cariotto. For a week after that, Arthur did not speak to her. In bed, he treated her as if they had not been introduced. They made up, but things were never the same again.

In romantic fiction, which Silvana loved, the hero is always permanently obsessed by the heroine, whereas in real life, once passion fades, a woman always comes second to a man's career. Silvana never came to terms with the fact that her romantic ideas were unrealistic, so without noticing it she gradually became permanently depressed—a condition that evinced itself in weariness.

By the time Silvana managed to carry a baby to term, she had been married for four years and had been pregnant, sick or recovering from a miscarriage for almost all of that time. Arthur no longer found Silvana's pink, moist mouth a novelty, and his interest in her had dissolved like the morning mist that rose from the river at the foot of their estate. The twelve evenings that followed the birth of their daughter were spent by Silvana alone (so that she could rest, Arthur had said). On the thirteenth evening, Silvana realized that Arthur must be doing all those wonderful things to somebody else. She tried to discuss this with him, but if Arthur didn't want to talk about something, then it wasn't discussed. His job at Nexus Mining International—the firm started by his great-grandfather—was an excuse for any absence. If Silvana telephoned him at his downtown office in Nexus Tower, then he was at the plant, or

vice versa. On his frequent trips to the Nexus offices in New York or Toronto, Arthur was absent all day, and in the evening he left orders at his hotel that he was not to be disturbed.

But, although Arthur didn't bother to hide his lack of interest from Silvana, he seemed to want to hide it from Pittsburgh. He was never seen with another woman, and he and Silvana made regular public appearances, at which he insisted that Silvana be exquisitely dressed. However, it was noticed that the couple rarely talked to each other when they were seated in the cream-and-crimson velvet Graham box at Heinz Hall, waiting to listen to the Pittsburgh Symphony Orchestra or watch the Pittsburgh Ballet Company.

By that time, Silvana found that she could no longer speak up for herself—the words would not come. She had been frightened of asking Arthur for the truth, but now she was frightened of being told it. She was terrified that one day Arthur would divorce her. She would wake up in the dark with the words *Then what?* whispering in her ears. She felt panic at the thought of being without a husband, of being sent home to Rome like some export reject, of hearing her father say, "I told you so." So, after a few timid attempts at discussion had been expertly turned aside by Arthur, Silvana shut her eyes to her marital unhappiness. After all, passion never lasted longer than two years, did it?

But in Arthur's case, passion had not been replaced by affection. He simply disregarded his wife. Increasingly, Silvana felt insignificant and without hope. She trembled when spoken to, and to speak was a great effort. To outsiders she appeared vague, absentminded or aloof. She felt that real life was on the other side of a glass wall, but she could never decide whether she was looking into the aquarium, or looking out. She confided her humiliation to no one, feeling that pity would render it intolerable.

She clung to her baby, chubby Lorenza who blew bubbles and dribbled down fragile clothes that had been embroidered by Italian nuns. Everyone at Nexus knew that Arthur had returned to his bachelor habits and was once again using his old apartment below the hotel penthouse that was permanently reserved for visiting Nexus VIPs. But, surprisingly, he had felt possessive pride as soon as he saw his baby daughter's red, screwed-up little face and heard her yell. "She takes after you," said Silvana, and he beamed.

Within three months of Lorenza's birth, Arthur's old nursery suite of four rooms had been redecorated in pale pink, and from that moment Silvana knew she could have anything she wanted, provided that it was for the benefit of Lorenza. Anything, that is to say, except money.

Arthur allowed Silvana no cash. Everything had to be charged. Arthur's secretary paid the travel bills to Rome, the accounts from Valentino, the bills from Elizabeth Arden on Fifth Avenue, where Silvana bought all her Christian Dior lingerie. Not that Arthur was cheap. If Silvana wanted a new car, she had only to say so in September, when Arthur ordered his next year's models. Schooled by his mother, Arthur had good taste in jewelry and loved to buy it, so Silvana had plenty of everything—emeralds, pearls, sapphires and diamonds (not rubies, Arthur thought them vulgar). However, Silvana never had any *cash*.

Arthur knew that cash meant freedom. With even a little stash, flight would be possible. If Arthur didn't want Silvana to stay, he also didn't want her to go. The fact of Silvana's existence prevented Arthur's mistresses from being too demanding, because Arthur always made it clear that, as he was a Catholic, there could never be a divorce. So Silvana was not allowed the one thing that might have powered her flight from humiliation—she was dependent upon her husband's whim and her husband's money. How could she leave him, with no self-confidence and no cash? Silvana felt ashamed of her powerless situation and dealt with her timidity and insecurity by withdrawing from the world. She tried to become nothing, so that nothing could hurt her. Her body was present, but she was not, and Arthur didn't want her body. Biologically, Silvana was alive, but emotionally she felt dead—she went through the motions of living like a languid sleepwalker, and at all times, behind her exquisite manners, she suppressed her rage toward her husband.

Except on one occasion.

The Grahams kept a ten-berth yacht at Monte Carlo and generally spent the month of June cruising the Mediterranean with a few friends. One starlit night in 1968 the party went ashore at Cannes to dine at the Carlton and Arthur drank too much Laphroaig malt whiskey after dinner. As they were returning through the moonlight in the launch, he made the mistake of telling Silvana that everyone knew she'd married him for his money.

Silvana, in strapless emerald satin, jumped to her feet— dangerously rocking the launch—and cried, "My father called you a beach bum, and as far as I knew, that's what you were. *This* is what I care about your money!"

She pulled off her emerald earrings and flung them overboard.

In the stunned silence that followed, Silvana tore off her emerald bracelet and tossed it into the black, lapping waters. As the launch droned on slowly toward the yacht, Silvana licked her finger—she had put on weight and her rings were now tight—and yanked off her huge emerald engagement ring. She held it up in the moonlight and asked, "How much did you pay for *that,* darling?" Over the side it went, as Silvana laughed.

One of the male guests grabbed Arthur as he lunged toward Silvana, and the sailor at the wheel yelled *"Attention!"* as they nearly rammed the stern of another boat. Silvana was the first to climb aboard their yacht. Heedless of her guests, she scrambled below to her stateroom, locked the door and with trembling fingers opened her safe. Because of her agitation, she had to dial the combination twice. Carefully she withdrew the green Moroccan-leather jewel box and hurried back up the companionway to the deck.

Holding up a pearl collar that had belonged to Catherine the

Great, Silvana yelled, "How much did this cost you, Arthur?" She threw it overboard—as far as she could.

It now took two male guests to restrain Arthur. "Now, Arthur . . . Careful . . . Arthur, get a grip on yourself."

A diamond necklace flew among the stars, then fell into their reflection. "How much did *this* set you back, *caro?*" Silvana shouted. She held up a set of Edwardian diamond star brooches.

Sleepy voices called from neighboring yachts, requesting silence in varying degrees of politeness, as Silvana, with surprising speed and relish, flung all her jewelry into the silver and black Mediterranean. Then she yawned, stretched and tripped off to her stateroom, feeling physically lighter and exultant—her humiliation had dissolved like sea-mist at sunrise.

Inside her stateroom, Silvana hesitated, then double-locked the door. Her ebullience drained away as she sat slumped on the end of the bed. For the first time, she seriously considered leaving her husband, but she realized that would also mean leaving her small daughter. She knew that Arthur's lawyers would, by expensive, legal and ruthless methods, gain custody of Lorenza for him.

Eventually, Silvana curled into an unhappy mound of crushed emerald satin and fell asleep, resigned to the continuation of her empty life. She had completely forgotten about the jewelry, now settling into the black silt of the harbor.

By four in the morning, Arthur had located two professional scuba divers. Abruptly sobered, he had first telephoned his broker in New York (where it was still only 10 P.M.) to check the insurance situation; he had then wakened the harbor master, and subsequently the Mayor of Cannes. Before first light, a rope cordon was bobbing around the Graham yacht (curious onlookers thought that someone must have drowned), and within two days every item of jewelry had been recovered. Apart from her emerald engagement ring, Silvana had never again worn any of the jewelry except at Arthur's specific request. She had inherited from her grandmother a row of exquisite but discolored sixteenth-century pearls, and it was these she now fingered in the pale-gold autumn light that flooded the library.

By the time Lorenza left home, her mother had lost her nerve and wouldn't have dared face life alone—didn't even dare wonder why not. As for Lorenza, she had never thought to wonder whether her mother was happy. Her mother was just . . . *there*.

Lying on the silver brocade couch in the library, Lorenza pulled a pillow toward her and fitted it under the small of her back. She held a sheet of paper—a typed guest list for her father's birthday party, which celebration was the reason for her trip home.

Lorenza skimmed the list. "What a bunch of bores! Isn't there going to be *anyone* here who's not Nexus?" She peered closer at the list. "Hey, I thought you said you were never again going to invite Suzy the Blond Bimbo, after the way she behaved last time."

"Your father wouldn't like you to use that word. And I suppose that anyone can accidentally fall into a pool at a party."

"Into the *shallow* end, of course. And in a white dress with nothing under it—as we had all noticed *before* she fell into the pool. Don't you remember Suzy standing up, dripping like Raquel Welch in one of her Grade B movies. And how every man in sight rushed to help her out, poor thing."

"Your father particularly wanted me to invite Suzy because the other wives aren't nice to her."

Lorenza yawned. "They hate her guts. With good reason."

"Lorenza, you must remember that Suzy is a distant relative."

"She's married to my second cousin by marriage. That's pretty distant." Suddenly Lorenza sat up. "I hear Papa's car. He's back early, isn't he?"

"He knew you were coming."

Something about his ice-blue eyes told you that, just like

his forebears, Arthur Nimrod Graham watched for the main chance. Although Nexus was no longer entirely a family-owned business, Arthur merited his place as its president, because he was as shrewd, tough and implacable as his ancestors. Arthur's suits may have been hand-tailored by Huntsman, the Royal tailor in London's Savile Row, but the man who filled those suits was an old-fashioned Yankee entrepreneur, whose family motto was WHAT WE HAVE WE HOLD. Arthur believed that the best form of defense was to be the first to kick the other guy where it hurt, and everybody of any importance in Pittsburgh knew this. He was sixty-two years old, silver-haired and chunky, but still fighting fit as he walked into the library. He paused, beamed and held his arms wide to Lorenza.

"How's my girl? Not driving too fast, I hope. There's my grandson to consider." He chuckled. "How's Andrew? Taking good care of my girl, I hope."

Arthur wasn't aware of the sharp edge of his joviality, as his arms enfolded the only person in the world that he loved. He wasn't saying she was perfect, in fact he knew she was a little scatterbrain, but his daughter was full of energy. He would agree that she wasn't beautiful, but you had to admit that Lorenza had irresistible charm—the bright blue eyes and the little white teeth always seemed to be smiling with infectious delight, as if you were the only person in the world she wanted to see, as if she trusted you completely, as if you and she were conspirators in a secret world. Arthur didn't realize that it was easier to have such magical charm if you were not distracted by life's exasperating realities, such as waiting in the rain for a bus, carrying groceries, arguing with repair men or paying their bills with money you can't afford.

To date, nothing worse than a toothache had gone wrong in Lorenza's life and Arthur was going to make damn certain that nothing ever did. As Lorenza in her Brussels lace wedding dress had waited with her father for the "Wedding March" to start, he had turned to her and said, "Don't forget, my darling, that if you ever have any problems you don't want to discuss with Andrew, you tell your papa! Andrew must see you're not dependent on him."

"Why shouldn't I be, Papa?"

"Because dependency destroys self-confidence, my darling."

Charmingly, Lorenza had lifted her veil and kissed the tip of her father's nose. "Darling Papa, you worry too much."

After the ceremony Arthur had taken his new son-in-law aside and said amiably, "Take care of my little girl, now." His eyes had added, "Or I'll break your neck."

"I love her as well, sir." Andrew had smiled politely. "You can have her on alternate weekends," he added softly to himself as Lorenza pulled him through a shower of rose petals toward the helipad at the side of the house, where the Nexus helicopter waited to sweep them to the airport, where the Nexus Lear waited to whisk them to Belle Rêve, the Nexus island in the Caribbean.

As she waved at the helicopter growing smaller and smaller, Silvana had worn her indulgent-mother smile, but she had felt left out of life, forgotten.

She still did.

"Where am I? Who *is* this person in bed beside me?" Annie's heart was constricted, her forehead was sweating, she was breathing hard and she felt nauseous. Beside her, in the pearl-gray light of dawn, Annie's husband mumbled in his sleep. She touched his warm back for comfort. Of course. She was in her own bed, in her own house, and Duke was lying beside her.

So why had she woken in a panic?

Then she remembered that tonight was Arthur's birthday party. In the dim light she could just see the clock; the alarm wasn't due to sound for another hour. Beside the glass of water and the copy of *Time* magazine (which she always read right through, to keep up), she could see the silver-framed color photograph of her family that had been taken at Lorenza's wedding. Had the photographer taken two hours, in-

stead of two minutes, he couldn't have achieved a more perfect example of the all-American family. Annie, wearing blue
silk, stood in the middle of the group, obscuring Silvana's
Corot seascape on the wall behind her. Annie's left hand
rested on the shoulder of fourteen-year-old Rob, the brightest
and noisiest of her four sons, who looked ill at ease in his first
adult suit. On Rob's left—solid, rugged and reliable—stood
Annie's husband, Duke. She thought he looked like John
Wayne in his prime, only not so tall and of course he carried a
bit more weight. Annie would be lost without her husband,
because Duke looked after everything. Annie didn't even
know where the insurance forms for their house were. (The
gracious antebellum house with the pillared porch had been a
wedding gift from Duke's parents and was singularly inappro-
priate for the noisy, sporty lives led by its owners.) Annie
didn't *want* to know where the insurance forms were, she had
had enough of filing documents when she was Duke's secretary.

In the photograph, next to Duke, grinned Fred, the eldest of
their four sons; he never looked tidy in a suit, God bless him.
Fred was a mathematician, doing graduate work at the University of Pennsylvania and still, thank heaven, living at home.
Annie dreaded the day when all her sons were gone from
home and there would be nothing to do in her silent house
except empty the ashtrays. To Annie's right, in front of one of
Silvana's pianos, stood Bill, unsmiling, with his hands in his
pockets. Bill, the Romeo of the family, was still at college.
The girls couldn't leave him alone—Annie and Duke had had
to give him his own telephone when he was fourteen. Next to
Bill was Dave, who, at nineteen, was the best-looking of the
boys, although of course they were all attractive in their own
ways. Gazing at her sons, Annie thought that at least she had
done something right. Four sons was exactly what Duke had
wanted—in fact they often behaved like five brothers together. That reminded her, she'd better get the banister fixed
again. . . .

They were a football family, as the local glazier could testify. There was also a baseball diamond at the end of the yard, their pool had a proper diving board and they'd had a basketball hoop fixed in the ballroom, which was really only used for table tennis. When Annie's sons weren't horsing around or training or playing, they were watching other people play, as they cheered on the Pirates, rooted for the Steelers and howled at the ref on behalf of the Penguins. Dinner-table talk tended to center on what should have happened during the last game and what had better happen at the next one.

Annie was going to feed them all earlier than usual tonight, because it was the maid's night off and Annie hadn't wanted to ask her to change nights. But it didn't matter. Before she dressed, she would fix hot dogs and hamburgers. The boys wouldn't mind a snack, just this once, instead of a meal.

At the thought of the party, panic set in again. Annie's head felt as if something was squeezing it, and she was short of breath. She hoped she wouldn't drop anything this time. At Silvana's last party, the one where poor Suzy had ruined her dress in the pool, a canapé had simply *collapsed* in Annie's fingers and dripped cheese sauce down her white satin formal. She hoped she wouldn't make a fool of herself tonight. But if she said nothing, then Duke would throw her one of his looks, and if, obediently, Annie jerked out a few words, then—in spite of *Time* magazine—people tended to look surprised by what she said. So the perspiration would start beneath her arms, her hairdo would sag and she would quickly disappear into the bathroom. However, there was a limit to the number of trips and the amount of time she could spend in the bathroom, or else Duke would growl on the way home, "For Chrissake, you've known all these people for *years! You grew up here!* You yak-yak for hours on the telephone, then you can't open your mouth at a party, in front of all my colleagues."

She knew that Duke wished she were a better hostess and felt it would help his career if she were, but she was too timid even to try. She forgot or mixed up people's names. *She* could never stand, calm and gracious, at the entrance to her ballroom saying one charming (and *different*) sentence to two hundred people in turn, as Silvana could.

Silvana made Annie feel dowdy and clumsy. She was always so elegant and remote, and her flower-filled house always looked as if she were expecting the *House and Garden* photographers any moment. Of course, Silvana had plenty of help—but then, so did Annie.

Running her family seemed to take up all of Annie's time. She didn't know how other women found the hours for outside interests—proper intellectual interests, not stuff like fund-raising or doing needlepoint covers for the dining chairs, any-one could do that sort of thing. Sadly Annie wondered if the Labrador pup had found her needlepoint, because it had dis-appeared again. That reminded her, she had to phone Father O'Leary before ten, about the kneeling pads she was working on. In turn, this reminded her that it was her responsibility to do the flowers this Sunday at St. Paul's, in Oakland, where she'd worshipped all her life. Annie had once bought a self-help book called *How to* Make *Time!*, but after two months she still hadn't found the time to read it, then the Labrador ate it.

Unfortunately, needlepoint kneeling pads and church flower arrangements didn't seem to interest Duke's business asso-ciates. Sometimes, after an evening of business entertaining, Duke would simply sigh, and they would drive back to Fox Chapel in silence. Sometimes, Annie would timidly say she was sorry and Duke would yell, *"For Chrissake, stop apolo-gizing!"* Whereupon Annie would sit there beside him, mak-ing herself as small as possible and wondering if she should take that course in dynamic self-projection that Duke had once suggested.

She couldn't help feeling apologetic toward Duke, because he'd never really *chosen* her, he'd been stuck with her. Annie's dad had been the Company Coordination executive at Nexus, and after junior college he'd sent her to take a secretar-ial course at Mrs. Parker's, then pulled strings to get her a job at Nexus, to give her something to do until she got married.

Annie had been Duke's temporary secretary for one whole summer. During the first few weeks she had regarded him with never-diminishing awe. She saw him through his own eyes, and with the same self-importance. Anxious to please him, she sprang to take his dictation, fill his water carafe, check the office bottle of Wild Turkey and anticipate all his other needs—so much so, that after they'd been working late one night Duke wasn't surprised to find himself humping that pretty little red-headed temp on the office carpet. He'd had no idea that this was her first time until weeks later when, looking even whiter than usual, she had told him that they had a problem. Well, if you had that sort of problem in Pittsburgh in 1952, you got married, especially if the girl's father was your boss.

The warm mound next to Annie grunted in his sleep and turned over, causing the quilt to slip to the floor. Carefully Annie slipped out of bed, tiptoed around the four-poster, picked up the quilt and replaced it, covering Duke's shoulders. She was so proud of him. If Duke were only ten years younger, he would be taking over from Arthur as president. There would be no question about it. But it was just as well that he wasn't trying for the job.

One thing Annie had to admit was that Duke was *not* a good loser—in fact it was one of the things that made Duke's Irish temper blow like a volcano. Of course, he wasn't physically violent, and he had never laid a finger on Annie in his life— well, hardly ever, if you didn't count that time she'd forgotten to video the Pirates' play-off, but then he didn't realize what he was doing until he saw the bruises on her arm the next day. The boys always kept well out of sight when their father was in one of his moods; they could spot the buildup and take cover, and they knew that he was always sorry afterward. The entire family was aware that certain subjects, ranging from Commies to Gay Lib to bad school marks, were certain to cause a rage, and so Annie would try to watch for them in conversation and attempt to sidestep a whole stream of topics before they came up. If she failed to do so, she would placate her husband by agreeing with him.

They always knew his mood as soon as he came in the house in the evening by the way he shut the front door—the degree of slam acted as a barometer. There had been a bad time, a few years after they were married, when Duke had been passed over for promotion. Every night before he came home Annie would find herself short of breath, then she'd get this feeling of panic. She'd hurry the kids to bed early and make sure that there were no skates or baseball bats around for Duke to fall over—because if there were, he would—and then she would just wait, heart thumping and stomach knotted, for the hurricane to hit. She always went to church the day afterward, because it calmed her agitation and helped her to stop feeling distressed and frustrated because she hadn't been able to soothe his rage.

The boys had never discussed their father's temper with her. They'd grown up with it, so they accepted it as part of their lives, but they were all silently ashamed of his rages and simply disappeared if, when he came home, the door slammed fit to shake the house.

Annie was also ashamed of it. She had never talked to anyone about Duke's terrible temper, except for her mother, who sighed and said that lots of men didn't realize that they were bullies, and women just had to put up with it . . . At least Duke was a good provider.

That had certainly proved to be the case, because Duke was now VP Comco—and Vice President of Company Coordination Worldwide was a very great responsibility.

In his sleep, Duke flung an arm up and again dislodged the quilt. Again Annie slid out of bed and replaced it, tucking it around his shoulders. Accidentally she backed into his bedside table and one of the silver picture frames fell on the rug. She picked it up and looked at the grinning redheaded skier in a pale blue suit, flicking through the slalom poles. Harry had taken that picture of her shortly after he'd joined Nexus, the year before she'd married Duke. She'd be seeing Harry again next week and she couldn't help feeling nervous about it. Harry became *more* of a problem, not less, as the years went by.

As Annie tiptoed around to her side of the bed, she caught sight of herself in the full-length mirror. In the ghost light of dawn, in her crumpled white nightgown, she looked pleasantly pale, rather than colorless and skinny. You couldn't see the hollows in her collarbone; her white, freckled forearms were covered with fine, gold down, her once-red hair looked golden, instead of faded ginger. But as the sun rose and light flooded the room, Annie clearly saw her unprepossessing reflection and, for the first time, felt dubious about what she'd planned to do that day.

Again Annie's heart constricted with fear. She told herself not to be so gutless. She was determined to try—just for one night—to look as stunning as Suzy. Suzy was so full of life, she had such impact and if her clothes were a little flamboyant at times, well, Suzy was always a knockout.

No, *this* evening, Annie wouldn't have a thing to worry about. She had been planning her appearance for weeks, and Suzy had been helping her. Suzy had picked the outfit, Suzy had arranged for a professional makeup and this morning she was going to Suzy's hairdresser.

This evening, just for once, Annie was going to make Duke *proud* of her!

Two miles away, another woman also lay in bed, watching the hands of her bedside clock move toward six in the soft light. Thinking about Arthur's party, Patty had bitten her thumbnail to the quick without realizing it.

Patty slid out of bed, taking care not to wake her husband, Charley, who was vice president of the Legal Department and corporate counsel at Nexus. Quickly she wriggled into her navy jogging suit and crept quietly downstairs, because their son, Stephen, wasn't supposed to wake for another hour.

She let herself out of the massive oak front door, heavily embedded with knockers, studs and other bits of ironwork that looked as if they'd been made by the early settlers and contrasted oddly with the three, supposedly burglarproof, chrome locks.

This was the only part of the day that belonged to Patty. She took her pulse, then started to warm up with slow stretches against the door for her hamstrings and calves, followed by toe rises on the doorstep. After that she did two splits on the lawn before setting off.

Jogging slowly along the deserted streets, passing one neat grass patch after another beneath maples turning autumnal shades of russet, she wished that, after all, she'd bought a new dress for the party. But they needed every spare penny for the trust fund, and saving was like dieting—you couldn't allow yourself "just one" anything. But of course the wife of the future president of Nexus would play the same sort of role as an ambassador's wife, and being well dressed was part of that job. As she rounded the first corner, she wondered whether Silvana got an official dress allowance from the company to cover all those Valentino numbers.

Patty quickened her stride. The first five minutes were usually the worst. After that she hit her rhythm and it got easier. She liked *fartlek*, running steadily but varying the pace —fast, slow, medium. It was a good technique for long-distance runners . . . Damn it, why hadn't she bought a new dress—she should be doing *everything possible* to help Charley get the promotion. Everybody said that her husband was the best corporate counsel Nexus had ever had, and at forty-five he was just the right age—he'd be forty-eight by the time Arthur had shepherded him into the job and retired. Charley would have fourteen good years ahead of him before it was his turn to pick his own successor.

Of course, Arthur hated the thought of *anyone* taking over the helm, as he jovially put it, but everyone knew that he'd been pressed by the Board to make his final decision before the end of the year. Undoubtedly the Paui trip was going to be decisive, unless Arthur decided to bring in someone from outside. But Charley had told her this only happened when a

27

company wasn't doing well—which wasn't the case. The Board wanted someone who'd been with Nexus a long time and who had worked with the top-level staff in the various Nexus-affiliated companies around the world.

Maybe she should reconsider her clothes for the convention next week, Patty thought. Maybe a little spending at this stage was really an investment. Because the next president would undoubtedly be decided on this trip. Arthur was playing his cards close to his chest, but his successor *had* to be one of the guys on the Paui trip. The group was far smaller than usual this year. Why? So that Arthur could make a final selection, that was why. And the reason he was taking so long about it was because he wasn't only handing over his job, he was also choosing the person who would be responsible for his family fortune, that large slice of Nexus Mining International which was still owned by the Grahams.

Patty checked her watch. Time to slow down.

Perhaps she'd better not have coffee at breakfast today, not with her nervous stomach. She didn't want to feel ill at the party. She'd scrap her afternoon reading session with Stephen and meditate instead. Immediately she felt guilty but pushed the thought aside, because tonight it was important that she behave like the *perfect* president's wife. And by God, when her time came she'd do a better job than that snotty, standoffish Silvana. Just because she'd been brought up in a palazzo, that woman could hardly bring herself to talk to ordinary mortals! Sure, she managed a word or two, and a gracious smile from the receiving line, but Silvana didn't really *care* about Nexus. Patty intended to make it clear that she was *concerned* about the company. She wasn't going to interfere, of course —but she'd certainly be one hundred percent supportive. Charley needed someone to talk to when he came home, someone who was rooting for him, who understood the stresses of his job but was also interested in the job itself, someone who would help him carry that huge responsibility but nevertheless keep it in perspective. Because Charley must never forget that his first responsibility was toward their son.

They shared that responsibility (Doctor Beck had warned her never to call it *guilt*).

Patty checked her heart rate, which was a bit higher than usual. She'd continue slow.

Well, her gown might not be anything to write postcards about, but her figure was better than Silvana's. Served her right for eating all that pasta! Probably the reason why Silvana was faithful to that lecherous Arthur was because she didn't dare let a lover see her naked. Even at her own pool parties, Silvana was never seen in a swimsuit. She had an endless wardrobe of shapeless silk muumuus from Hawaii. By God, Patty thought, if I had a cook . . . *when* I have a cook . . . She'd take advantage of it. Having a cook was the one sure, long-term way to get it off and *keep* it off. All the First Ladies lost weight as soon as they stepped into the White House. Apparently the current chef still had Jacqueline Kennedy's menus. Orange juice, poached egg, bacon and black coffee for her breakfast, total 240 calories; for lunch a cup of consommé, a small bowl of salad with French dressing and a grilled hamburger (without the bun), total 250 calories; a cup of tea with a slice of lemon at five o'clock left Jackie 500 calories in hand for the evening. She could manage a good meal and a glass of red wine on 500 calories. For instance, artichokes Provençale, leg of lamb marinated with coriander, cucumber salad and peaches in wine. Of course, Jackie only ate a teaspoon of *any* sauce, but look at all the years she'd kept to that diet and how it paid off. Oh, it was easy enough to be disciplined if you had somebody else to measure the food out and put it on a plate in front of you.

Patty jogged past the elegant Corinthian columns of the next house. It was only half past six, but already two of Annie's huge, jock sons were throwing a football around the front lawn. Patty just wouldn't bother having windows in a house with four of those hulks inside it. Annie never disciplined them, so they all followed that noisy, extrovert Duke's example. In the eight years she'd known Annie, Patty had watched them treat her as a short-order cook and errand runner—but that was just as much Annie's fault as theirs. She behaved like a doormat, so it wasn't surprising that they walked all over her. No self-image, that was Annie's problem. She was perennially apologetic, a professional worrier. DID I TURN THE LIGHTS OFF? would be carved on Annie's tombstone. Although Patty had to admit that being "just a housewife," as Annie always described herself, was probably a full-time survival job in *that* family.

Patty reached her halfway point and turned back toward home. As she ran, now with a medium pace, she passed other joggers, and few of them could resist throwing her a sideways look. She was as near perfect a human specimen as you were likely to find. Her tall, lean, athletic figure had a natural grace that most plodding joggers lack, her profile had the nervous tension of a greyhound waiting for the trap gates to open, her white-blond straight hair was cut like a boy's, with a side part, and her blond eyebrows were a straight line above a narrow, elegant nose. The short upper lip and wide mouth with chiseled outer edge to it might have been sculpted by Michelangelo.

Patty was a California baby and had grown up in Tiburon, the little peninsula with a fine view of Alcatraz, that jutted out into San Francisco Bay. She had started jogging when she was at Stanford, where she used to race around those yucky pink-brown, Spanish-style buildings every morning before school, when everyone else was still yawning or asleep. You had to be bright, not just rich, to get into Stanford. Patty had been a good student because she had a photographic memory, but she had been impatient and lacked concentration, so she was easily attracted by fast solutions; she'd been a natural for TM and est. Charley had refused to do est, and before Nexus functions he made Patty promise to keep quiet about her how-to-get-anything-done-in-ten-minutes philosophies. Apart from that enthusiasm, Charley adored Patty and could find no fault with her.

It was ironic that Patty, the perfect specimen, the bronzed health nut, should have given birth to a baby with spina bifida, for which there was no cure, and for which endless patience was required. There was nothing wrong with Stephen's brain—in fact he had turned out to be an unusually bright child, which made his physical state all the more frustrating for him. Because of congenital malformation of his spinal cord, Stephen had been born with deformed limbs and would always be helpless and incontinent. Dr. Beck had told them that there was no reason why Stephen should not grow to manhood and lead a useful life, but he would never be normal.

Charley had been wonderful. They had clung to each other in that small, cheery, primrose hospital room and Charley had told Patty that there was no reason for either of them to feel that it was their fault. It wasn't such a phenomenon, the incidence was 1.5 percent of births.

Clutching her baby, Patty refused to consider putting him in a home, even before Charley had been able to explain the advantages. Stephen was *their* child. His beautiful face looked up at Patty with soft, blue-eyed trust. The only home that Stephen would know, Patty had instantly decided, would be his parents'. They had formed him and brought him into the world as he was. To care for him themselves was the least they could do to make up for the terrible accident of his birth.

In the eight years since Stephen's birth, Patty's care had been constant and the medical bills had been endless. Because of the enormous expenses, it had been hard to start the trust fund, which had been set up to look after Stephen; he would need round-the-clock care for the rest of his life. It was unlikely, but possible, that Stephen might outlive Patty and Charley. Of course, both parents carried heavy life insurance, but they had set up the trust in case their son should need a large sum of money while they were still alive. And there were tax benefits.

The birth of Stephen delivered a blow to Patty's self-confidence from which she was still reeling. She felt that, in some unknown way which she didn't understand, she must have done something terrible to deserve such a punishment. She must be guilty of *something*, although she didn't know what. So she punished herself, without realizing it.

Puffing slightly, Patty rounded the final corner, from where she could see Judy, the housekeeper, turning her car into their drive just as the night nurse was leaving. A few minutes later Patty could see her home, a Tudor-style farmhouse with diamond-paned windows and that huge over-scaled front door. She would just have time for a quick shower before it was time for Stephen's breakfast.

She slowed to a walk over the gravel drive, then pulled her navy sweatband from her hair and checked her pulse. She had pushed it further today. Patty had no patience with women who let themselves get out of shape, then had hysterics and rushed to fat farms when they hit thirty. She intended to keep herself in good condition.

Patty didn't need a new dress tonight to hide *her* body—although she had to admit that Suzy had a pretty good body, and Suzy never did *one* minute's exercise, the bitch. Suzy would have a new dress tonight, Suzy *always* had a new dress. She had nothing to spend her money and time on except herself. Personally, Patty couldn't stand wasting an entire day at the hairdresser, the manicurist, the masseur, the suntan parlor and so on—but then, Suzy made a career of maintaining her appearance.

Patty stopped abruptly, struck by a sudden nasty thought. No, Charley would never look at another woman. But maybe she would have just *one* cup of coffee for breakfast. Without cream or sugar, of course . . .

◄ **2** ►

FRIDAY, OCTOBER 26, 1984

"I'm sorry, Mr. Douglas, but Mrs. Douglas is in conference." The secretary's voice sounded tinny over the telephone.

"Could you perhaps tiptoe into her office and ask whether I'm *really* needed at this party tonight? Something's cropped up at my office."

"I'm sorry, I can't interrupt this meeting. But it's Mr. Graham's birthday party tonight, Mr. Douglas. I don't think . . ."

Roddy sighed. "Okay, okay, I'll dust off my dancing shoes. But maybe you should remind Mrs. Douglas that although she only has to walk three blocks, she's going to be late for the party if she doesn't get moving soon. She's usually home by now."

"Mrs. Douglas is never late, Mr. Douglas."

The secretary was right. Isabel kept her watch ten minutes fast. Roddy put down the red telephone and looked from the penthouse window at the spectacular view of the river and the russet, tree-covered hills beyond. He glanced again at his watch. It was a steel Rolex Oyster, waterproof and automatic, with a steel expansion bracelet. It had been an eighteenth birthday present from his parents, in 1965, and although Isabel had offered to buy him an expensive gold watch, he refused to let her replace it.

Roddy poured himself a drink and headed for his bathroom.

He was in the shower before realizing that his shampoo bottle was almost empty, so, dripping wet, he padded to the storeroom for a replacement.

Isabel had fixed adjustable shelves in one of the spare bedrooms to hold all supplies, from lipstick to Drano. She ordered by the dozen, and checked her lists four times a year. The shelves also held a dozen spare white shirts, underwear and socks for Roddy, together with Isabel's travel bag, which was always repacked as soon as she returned from a trip. Isabel never took suitcases on business trips, because retrieving them wasted time at airports and the airlines often lost them, so she traveled only with hand luggage—a briefcase and a light seven-section zippered bag which held seven changes of underwear, seven blouses, three no-crush silk-jersey dresses, a white jumpsuit for visiting mines, nightwear, a bathing suit, a pair of pants to match her travel jacket, shoes, toiletries, small makeup bag (Isabel used only one lipstick) and a spare pair of prescription glasses. Her travel suits hung in the storeroom, ready to go. Isabel traveled in a soft wool suit of either black or scarlet, a black raincoat and a pair of sturdy black walking shoes. She could be out of the house and heading for the airport within ten minutes of a phone call.

After showering and dressing, Roddy poured himself another drink and picked up *Publishers Weekly*. He lay with his feet up on the sofa, flipping through the news about books.

He never heard his wife enter. Isabel stood in the doorway, thinking that Roddy really looked wonderful in a tuxedo, the Nexus bunch would look like penguins beside him. He might easily be some Italian film star—tall and lithe, with dark curly hair and friendly brown eyes behind wire-rimmed glasses. He was in good shape, too. He'd won the Eastern Division squash championship in his age group last year. Isabel knew she was lucky that he was so protective and proud of her. A lot of men would feel threatened or resent the sort of success that she'd had. She had fought a hard and bitter battle for her job as VP Corporate Development of Nexus—that's what it was called, but what she really did was look around for acquisitions, spin-offs and general expansion grabs. She'd come into Nexus on the marketing side, right after graduating from Harvard Business School, and after three years she'd moved over to Administrative Finance, then became assistant to the VP Corporate Development, who not long afterward was poached by RTZ. She didn't kid herself that one of the reasons for her promotion had been because Nexus wanted a token woman on the Board, although this was always denied.

Within a month of her joining the company, Roddy realized that Isabel was determined to be president of Nexus. He'd never laughed at her, although he teased her gently about her lists, her note-taking and the pile of reports that was always stacked on her side of the bed. Isabel knew that she was lucky not to encounter resentment, because Roddy also loved *his* job, as district manager of a national bookstore chain.

Isabel walked toward Roddy on the sofa and said proudly, "We got a *great* deal today on the Columbus project. Now I can tell you all about it." Her dark blue eyes glowed with triumph. She was small, with tiny bones and a mass of thick dark hair that was cut short. Four times a year her hairdresser came to the apartment to cut it.

Roddy looked up and blew her a theatrical kiss. "That's terrific. No wonder you're seven minutes late. I almost called the hospital."

As she showered and dressed, Isabel told him about the Columbus deal, then she asked Roddy what sort of a day he'd had.

"Checking our autumn order list. Listen to this." Roddy leaned against the bedroom door and read aloud from the trade magazine. "'From a man so rich that he never gets a full accounting, to a vicious vixen who vows to take a man's head.' Guess the title."

"Something new by Harold Robbins?"

"No, it's the Bible, entering a new era of hype. But then it's still an expanding market, it did over a hundred and ten million dollars last year."

Isabel laughed as she pulled on her cream silk-jersey dress.

It had only one sleeve, leaving the other shoulder bare. She'd chosen cream rather than white because, unless it was cotton and could be washed, white was always a dry-cleaning headache.

"Roddy, would you mind fetching me some Perrier while I do my face?"

Roddy was walking toward the kitchen when the telephone rang. Isabel automatically answered the bedroom extension.

"Leonore *who?* . . . Talk of the Trade? . . . How do I feel about *what?* . . . Oh, delighted, of course . . . Yes, of course I'm delighted . . . I'll get him."

But Roddy had already picked up the phone in the kitchen. Isabel listened in and her quick mind immediately realized why Roddy hadn't yet told her that he'd been promoted; because it would mean relocating to Minneapolis, that was why.

Roddy appeared in the doorway. "I'm sorry, I didn't want to tell you until we had a quiet moment. I can't think how the hell Leonore found out so fast."

"Honey, I'm thrilled. Of course, I'm sorry you didn't discuss it with me before accepting, but at least we'll both be in adjacent time zones."

Roddy had been prepared for this, but he hadn't expected her to attack within thirty seconds. He said lightly, "We'll be in the same *town*, Isabel. It's my turn now."

"I can't possibly leave Pittsburgh, and you know it! If you want to live in Minneapolis, then you can live in a hotel apartment and come back home on weekends."

"I have never met anyone so selfish!"

"Don't shout at me. What's selfish about not wanting to give up my career?" But Isabel knew what was coming next.

"Cinderella, you're thirty-seven years old, and time is running out. I want kids before I have to wear bifocals and see them close up."

"When I agreed to stop work at thirty, we didn't know that I was going to do so well."

"I'm not doing too badly myself."

They glared at each other.

Finally Isabel said, "Maybe just one. Maybe I could manage to take just a couple of months off."

"We've been through that before. I want at least two kids and I want them to have a proper mother, not a boardroom organizer. I've seen other women try to juggle kids, a job and a husband and it can't be done. You can only do two things properly. Most women—"

"Most women don't realize that they have choices in life, until it's too late and the opportunities are gone."

"When we got married—"

"When we got married, the empty nest syndrome didn't exist. I don't want to give up an exciting job with great prospects to raise a couple of kids who'll leave home at sixteen without a backward glance."

"Plenty of other women rejoin the work force late."

"Not at age fifty, and not at my level. You're asking me to give up my *life.*" Isabel glared at him and then burst out with what she'd never said before. "Roddy, I don't *want* to have kids. Once I thought I did, but now I don't."

"Well, I *do*. And you agreed, and *I* can't have them for you."

Isabel knew that they were going to be late for the party.

Carey had been kept at the office because the plans for the alterations to the Silverman lake house were needed for the following morning. Finishing a job properly, not losing interest, not even in the tiresome little details, was the hardest part of her job, but Carey knew it was the mark of a professional. Now she was belting her Volkswagen GTI too fast toward Upper St. Clair. She couldn't help being late, but she really was sorry, because Ed had particularly asked her to be on time for gruesome Arthur's party tonight.

Carey was an assistant architect in a small partnership that specialized in modern homes which blended the building with the landscape. Everyone in the office dreamed of one day building a house for themselves like Falling Water, the Frank Lloyd Wright place at Laurel Highlands; the sandstone house was poised over the tumbling falls, surrounded by laurels, rhododendrons and wildflowers, with the forest beyond it. It must be great to be lulled to sleep by the splash of . . . Oops! She had taken that bend a bit close. She'd better slow down. Ed wouldn't want to take a corpse to Arthur's party.

Normally, Ed didn't care if his wife was a little late, he was easygoing and so was she. She wasn't the Superwoman type and didn't want to be. She was just a woman doing a job and trying to hang on to her identity, as well as raise a family— she didn't want to be a female man like Isabel. But this morning, Ed had asked her to be on time, and made a point of telling her how important she was to his image at the moment. He seemed to have entirely lost his sense of humor since the question of replacing Arthur had arisen. Carey supposed that they'd have to wait for the appointment of a new president before Ed could get it up again. Ed attributed the problem to the fact that he felt threatened by what he called Carey's quest for identity. (Sometimes Carey would like to pick Ed's shrink up by the neck and rattle him.)

But Ed's real threat was Charley, Nexus's corporate counsel. Ed wasn't used to being frustrated. This executive cat-and-mouse game had been going on for months, and the more tense Ed became, the limper grew their love life. Carey was grateful to whoever had invented the missionary position, because Ed couldn't seem to manage anything else at the moment, and only that once or twice a month. What was playing havoc with their sex life was Ed's undischarged anxiety.

She wished Ed would talk to her about his worries instead of pretending that everything was fine and normal, but Ed saw himself as the strong, silent type. Why couldn't men admit their vulnerability? Carey would like, just for once, to be told what was going on inside Ed's head, instead of guessing.

She swerved to avoid a squirrel, glanced in her mirror to check that it hadn't been harmed and then grinned at her reflection. She was a big tawny blonde, who was often told that she looked like Princess Diana, although in fact she took after her grandmother who lived in Stockholm.

Because she was a big woman, few people realized that
Carey found it difficult to stand up for herself. She couldn't
seem to hit the right balance. She could argue without hesitation over some architectural point that she felt was important,
but she was a gutless wimp when it came to dealing with
salespeople and hairdressers or complaining to the plumber
that his bill was twice what he'd said it would be. So Carey
was hustled into shoes that were too small for her ("You have
such *big* feet, madam"), dresses that didn't suit her ("Horizontal stripes will make you look *smaller,* madam") and clothes
that cost more than she'd intended to spend ("Well—sniff—if
you want something *cheap* . . .").

Carey's fear of disapproval wasted hours of agonized
thought, as well as a lot of money, and she would go to extraordinary lengths to avoid the curled lip, raised eyebrow,
scornful gaze or pained hauteur of someone who was waiting
to be tipped—some stranger who could, at a glance, make her
feel contemptible. How did they manage it? Did they go to
night school? Could you major in pained expression? Was it
possible to get a degree in disdain? Carey knew that she
should have gone to the hairdresser before tonight's big party,
but she'd ducked it rather than go through the tipping ordeal.
Now, of course, she regretted it, because all the other women
would have spent hours preparing to look their best.

She sighed as she swung the car off the road and up the
avenue of tall auburn trees, but she cheered up a few minutes
later when her house came into view. She always loved this
first view of the eighty-year-old white clapboard farmhouse,
as well as everything else about it. She loved the high ceilings
and was gradually collecting Shaker furniture for the entire
house. Their water was piped in from a spring up the hill.
They owned all the land which surrounded the house, so nobody overlooked them, and the house felt peacefully rural.
But if Ed said, "Let's see who's playing at the Stanley this
evening," it took them only half an hour to get there, so they
hardly ever missed a jazz performance.

Ed was standing on the porch, looking like Carey's mother used to, when she had gotten home after midnight.

Carey said, "Look, I'm sorry. It won't take me ten minutes to get ready." She flung her left arm around Ed and kissed his unyielding cheek. It was like kissing a cigar-store Indian.

She hurried through the square hall and started up the stairs. Ingrid and Greta were hanging over the top banister, looking like reproachful, bespectacled, russet-haired mice: they both looked like Ed's sister. Together the little girls said, "You're *late*. Daddy's mad."

Sometimes Carey could see why Ed's first wife had left him, although she couldn't say so, because Carey had also been married before. College madness. After six months he'd turned into a flower child and left her to go to India and study yoga. It was pretty humiliating, but nevertheless a great relief. One moment she'd been married to a football quarterback, the envy of all, and the next thing he was wearing saffron robes and chanting *om* at five in the morning. The entire dorm had complained.

Carey grinned as she climbed the stairs. "Hi, kids. How's the house going?"

Last weekend she'd shown her daughters how to build their dreamhouse, with a red Tinker Toy set of miniature scaffolding.

"*Booooooooring.*"

"It takes *soooo looooong*."

"We gave a doll's tea party instead."

"You've been playing with Mummy's makeup again." Now she was close enough to see the luridly applied and not-quite-scrubbed-off signs.

"No, no, it was our paintbox . . . well, *almost* all of it. We were playing Avon ladies."

She'd brought them every masculine and intellectual toy, from a tool set to Rubik's cube, but they were a living reproach to the Women's Movement. Sometimes Carey thought she'd done all that campaigning for nothing, at college, way back, when her heroine was Gloria Steinem.

Carey would have liked to have had a boy as well, but she didn't want to risk another duplicate of Ed's sister and, to be serious, she didn't think she'd be able to manage three kids and hang on to her job without going out of her mind. She'd had a surprise to find that two kids were twice as much work as one, and she'd had postnatal depression after both children, which had magically cleared up as soon as Greta had turned five and Carey had returned to work. (She'd decided to go back to work on the day she found herself cutting all the food on her own plate into itsy-bitsy, child-size pieces.) Carey loved working with real grown-up people who knew words of more than two syllables, but maybe her daughters wouldn't be playing at Avon ladies if Carey were there to see that they didn't grow up frightened of a screwdriver.

Carey felt a flicker of guilt as she scrambled in and out of the shower. These days you felt guilty if you stayed at home, and guilty if you left it.

Ed appeared in the bedroom doorway; he was still wearing his pained expression. "How much longer are you going to take?"

"Almost ready, if you'd just do up the zipper."

He hadn't noticed that she'd bought a new Bill Blass for the occasion. Severely simple, in black piqué with huge sleeves, it was cut low and flat at the front and even lower behind; Carey thought she looked like a Spanish *infanta* in it. She quickly fastened her pearl choker, while Ed tugged crossly at her back.

The zipper broke.

"Ed, why did you have to tug so goddamn hard?"

"Don't swear at me. If you'd gotten home earlier, you wouldn't have been rushed."

"Look, why do *I* have to go to this party? You know I hate white wine and babble. None of the men listen if I talk sense, all the wives think I'm a homespun crank and you're speaking to me as if you had a wooden upper lip. I don't expect *you* to come to *my* office parties."

"I merely expect your support," Ed said through stiff lips.

"Is that too much to ask?" He turned away from her and shoved his hands in his pockets.

"Did anyone ever tell you you look gorgeous when you're mad?" she teased as she wriggled out of her dress, then sat on the bed and worked at the zipper with her eyebrow tweezers. Ed was really good-looking—nearly six feet and well built, with dark red hair like the kids, pale skin, gray eyes and a cleft chin. It wasn't like him to pick a fight. He was on edge about this damn promotion. He'd never minded about her job before—he was abroad so much as VP Overseas Expansion that he was glad she had independent interests.

Carey suddenly hoped that Ed wasn't getting as grouchy as this at the office. He was a quietly popular man, known to be a brilliant negotiator and easy to work for. He got a lot of respect because he was so good at his job and looking after his people. Ed's background was geology, and he had the instinct of a truffle hound for nosing out what Nexus was looking for. It was uncanny; he'd brought off some of the company's biggest coups. And, except for the last few months, he was also a loving husband, and crazy about his daughters. Carey had read somewhere that the average American father spent an average of only twelve minutes a day with his children, whereas Ed was really involved with his family—when he was home. What more could she ask for?

They'd been really happy, in a jogging-along, peaceful way, until Arthur announced his retirement, whereupon Ed had started to twang. Ed said that stress was a part of success, but Carey knew that too much of it could kill you; she wondered what the statistics were on executives who dropped dead from heart attacks and strokes. She found herself hoping that Ed *didn't* get the damned job, because just the prospect of it seemed to be upsetting the whole family.

Furthermore, Carey knew without being told, that her own job was at risk. There was a constant stream of Nexus vice presidents from all over the world who expected to be entertained by the president and his wife when they visited Pittsburgh. That was why Ed had been behaving in such a furtive manner—although he hadn't suggested that she might have to quit her job. Outwardly, of course, he'd approved of her going back to work after the girls were in school, she had a right to her own life, blah, blah . . . But nobody in the family took her job seriously, and sometimes she felt that Ed resented her lack of total attention to himself. He could be quite a subtle, closet tyrant. His other uncanny instinct was for knowing someone's weak point and pressing on it in seeming innocence. Why else would she defend her job, when Ed hadn't suggested she give it up?

As she hurried down the stairs toward Ed waiting in the hall, Carey's stomach rumbled loudly. She said, "Hang on. I didn't have time for lunch today, I'll get a few cookies and eat them in the car."

"They'll spoil your appetite and you won't eat your dinner. Silvana has probably gone to a lot of trouble. Just don't drink before we eat. You know how you get."

"Okay, okay."

As the black Lincoln headed silently toward Sewickley, Ed said, "Guess I need a holiday." It was the nearest he'd get to saying "Sorry."

Carey patted his knee. "I hope it *is* going to be a holiday, not just a week-long executive conference around a pool on this tropical island."

"There'll be a certain amount of discussion, of course."

Suddenly Carey saw that Ed was going to return to Pittsburgh even more tense than when he left. She sighed and said, "Ed, do you *really* want me along on this trip? I mean, isn't it foolish to use up half my year's vacation time to go to some coral island where *I'll* be stuck with a bunch of Nexus wives, and *you'll* be stuck with the men, all wearing Hawaiian shirts and sunglasses but behaving as if they're still in Pittsburgh's Golden Triangle." She turned toward Ed and stroked his arm. She said softly, "What's the point, Ed, when the Silverman lake house needs daily site visits? I have to coordinate the landscaping, we're in the middle of planting and it *must* be done before the end of October. It's fine for all the other

43

wives, they don't have jobs, but this is the most exciting project I've ever worked on."

"Most wives would think this holiday was fun." Ed shrugged her hand off his arm.

"Fun? Watching Arthur indulge his macho fantasies? Watching him fight sharks like a Hemingway hero on some half-developed tropical Disney World for jaded businessmen that looks adventurous but is really no more dangerous than sailing a duck in a bathtub?" Carey snorted and settled back in her seat.

"Paradise Bay isn't half-developed, it's *newly* developed," Ed said. But she'd scored on the rest. Paui's first luxury resort had been planned as a new experience for the superrich seeking thrills; it offered adventure in a safe location. You could fish either from a dugout canoe or the most up-to-date power-boat.

Carey lit a cigarette and returned to the attack. "If Arthur wants to fish, why can't we go to someplace like Fiji or Kenya or Mauritius again?"

"Stop being difficult, Carey. You know we hold the annual conference in a different trading area each year. This year it's Australia, and Paui is just off the northwest coast. And Nexus people like to visit new places."

"You mean *Arthur* likes to visit new places. Thank heaven there's no deep-sea fishing at the North Pole, or we'd all be dragged there for our summer holidays." She inhaled deeply, then added, "I've never *heard* of this place, Paui, as a resort. I've only heard about the copper mine and that revolution they had last year."

"It was only a *riot,* and only in Queenstown. Riots are no longer rare. They even have riots in England." Ed carefully kept his voice low and reasonable. Carey was chain-smoking again, and he didn't want her in her assertive mood tonight; let her get it out of her system now, before the party.

Softly he said, "I need you there, Carey, because *I* know that you're president's-wife material, even if you refuse to see it. You're a good organizer and you get on well with everyone. I want Arthur to see that, and this trip will give him the opportunity. You've got so much more to contribute than Patty, that neurotic greyhound who's married to Charley." He glanced toward her and said softly but firmly, "This trip is going to be important to our future, and *this* year that's more important than your vacation time."

Carey sat in stony silence.

"This is my chance to outshine Charley," Ed continued. "I know more about the people and the mining possibilities on Paui than anyone else in Nexus. This is one round that Charley's going to lose."

"You don't need a situational advantage to show that you're better than Charley."

Reluctantly Ed said, "Okay, I'll tell you the real reason, but I don't have to tell you to keep it to yourself. Our mining concession in Paui runs out in June '85 and the new government hasn't been easy to negotiate with. They want to meet the Nexus top chief, and they won't be fobbed off with Harry Scott, because they know he's only top chief of Nexus, *Australia*. The President of Paui wants to meet Arthur. In person. But if Arthur flew to Paui to meet the President, then Nexus would lose face."

"So this is really a kind of unofficial state visit?"

Ed nodded. "The first round of the new concession talks."

To his surprise, Carey started to laugh. "I can't help thinking of those photographs you brought back from your first trip—all those naked natives with painted faces and feathered headdresses. Does Arthur have to dress up to negotiate?"

"No, they mostly wear Western clothes in Queenstown." But Ed started to laugh as well and patted Carey's knee.

So she decided not to tell him about what he'd said in his sleep.

A howl of joy rose from the stadium, echoed by approving grunts from the darkened living room. Annie's four sons, draped over sofas or sprawled on the floor, never took their eyes off the television as Annie handed around the supper trays of hot dogs and hamburgers, to a background staccato rattle. . . . *With three down and four to go inside the Raiders ten, the Steelers are running out of chances here . . .*

Annie's hair was tied up in a scarf, she was wearing her wrapper over her outfit, and because of the gloom, the boys hadn't noticed her makeup. She'd spent two hours this afternoon lying flat on her back on a sort of operating table. Stan, Suzy's *visagiste* (as he called himself), had stared at her face in silence for about five minutes, then, leaning down close enough to make Annie feel uneasy, dabbed at the little pots of color that he kept in a toolkit tray, mixed shades on the back of his hand and painted Annie's face with delicate strokes from sixteen different brushes. Afterward he'd said she could get up now, as if she were at the dentist. He'd looked faintly smug as he handed Annie the mirror, and when she looked into it, Annie understood why. Because she looked seventeen again.

Suddenly Annie had also *felt* seventeen again; she felt all the anxieties, the uncertainties, the sudden absolute conviction that she'd done the wrong thing, the mortification and the blushes—it all rushed back to her, and she longed to scrub her face. Instead she had said, "Why, thank you, that's amazing," and had written the check.

"Wow, you look like an old Rita Hayworth movie," Suzy had said as she handed Annie a pair of earrings, to each of which a fresh pink camelia had been wired.

Annie said uncertainly, "It doesn't feel like *my* face. I feel like somebody else."

"Ain't that the whole point? Anyway, you look *terrific!* Let's hook you into the outfit, I want to check the flowers against it."

Back in Annie's room, Suzy had lifted poppy-splashed pink silk from the dress box and white tissue had fluttered to the floor. Dubiously Annie had said, "Are you *sure* that it's okay to wear pants, Suzy?"

"Evening pajamas, not pants," Suzy said as she helped

Annie into the outfit. "It's a Saint Laurent, honey. You know you can't go wrong if you buy a designer outfit." Suzy then stepped back and screwed her eyes up, as she examined Annie. "It needs something more . . . if you're going to really knock 'em dead." She snapped her fingers. "No! I must be losing my touch; it needs something *less*. Take off those pants, I mean pajamas."

"Take the pants off?" Defensively, Annie clutched at the waistband.

"Yeah, the outfit isn't sexy enough. It's snappy all right, but the high neck with those gypsy violinist sleeves . . . I mean, you've got to show *something*." Suzy urged, "Go on, try it. That tunic top comes down way past your knees."

"But there's a gap on both sides, from my armpits to the hem," Annie protested.

"Yeah, but with those little pink silk straps they can't open. You'll be okay."

Reluctantly, Annie removed the pajama bottoms.

"Now your pantyhose and underpants, because they show at the waistline." Suzy was inexorable.

"Suzy, I can't go to Arthur's party *naked*."

"Aw, you're showing less at the sides than the rest of them will be showing at the front, *and* you'll be able to keep your sandals on better without pantyhose." Suzy glanced down at the thin silver straps that crisscrossed Annie's ankles.

"Suzy, I *can't*."

"Annie, stand up, forget you're an old married lady and look in the mirror!" Suzy pushed Annie in front of her antique cheval glass.

Annie looked at herself, blinked, looked again and slowly smiled. Then she looked dubious. "I don't know what Duke will think."

"Don't tell him—show him! You'll take his breath away!"

Now, serving food to the boys, Annie felt safe with her wrapper around her.

* * *

There's the handoff and it looks like a sweep around the right end, but no, they didn't make it . . .

The communal groan of the crowd at the Three Rivers Stadium was echoed in Annie's TV room. Her sons groped like sleepwalkers for their hamburgers, without taking their eyes off the screen.

"Are you guys okay now? Is there anything else I can get you?"

Bill said, mildly, "Mom, how can we hear what's going on if you keep talking?"

Dave inspected his hamburger. "Hey, you know I don't like mustard."

The other two merely grunted, as if in a trance, so Annie scuttled upstairs to fix the camelias on her ears.

Annie heard the front door bang, then the bar door bang, but not too loud. Sounded as if he'd had a good day, thank God for that. She'd left a pitcher of martinis ready on top of the bar. She felt a sudden, unusual flash of resentment that her happiness this evening was going to depend upon whether anyone had irritated Duke at the office that afternoon, but she pushed this disloyal thought to the back of her mind. She'd wait until he'd probably poured his second martini, then she'd walk downstairs, stand in the TV room doorway, smile and say, "I'm ready when you are."

So that's what Annie did.

Duke was watching the screen and didn't hear her. Annie said it louder, sounding a bit squeaky, and Duke turned around. He stared incredulously.

"My God, Annie, what have you done to your hair?"

"I went to the beauty parlor. For the party."

"You can't go to my boss's home looking like you fell into a wind tunnel." Duke had to shout to be heard above the TV commentary. "Go comb it out and fix it like you always do, with the headband."

Annie hesitated, then moved toward Duke's chair so that she wouldn't have to shout. Duke's eyes slowly moved from

48

Annie's hem upward. He leaped forward and turned the TV off, amid protesting yells.

"What the hell do you think you're doing, Annie? Go and put some decent clothes on."

"But this is from Yves Saint Laurent."

"I don't care if it's from St. Peter. Take it off."

"Take it off! Take it off!" Dave guffawed, but shut up when his father glared at him.

The boys all melted out of the room as Annie started to cry. She was ruining her eye makeup—and Stan had spent an hour of his life sticking those individual eyelashes on. Wordlessly, she ran out of the room.

At the top of the stairs she noticed a pile of dirty, smelly football clothes. *Why* couldn't they drop them down the laundry chute, it was only at the end of the hall? With her pretty silver sandals she kicked the grubby heap.

As she stooped to pick up the dirty shirts and socks, she heard fourteen-year-old Rob behind her. "I think you look *great*, Mom. It's just that you don't look like . . ."

"A mom," Annie added bitterly.

"Dad's kind of old-fashioned, I guess."

Annie thought, Suzy wouldn't have done it on purpose . . . Or would she?

At seven o'clock that evening, Patty called her mother in Florida.

"How's the pacemaker, Mom?" Patty always asked, although it had been two years since her mother's operation.

"Fine, fine." The voice was frail but full of vim; all the residents of Silver City sounded that way. "I was just getting into my new western outfit—red with white fringe, Stetson and cowboy boots. You'd love it. I bet you never thought I'd be a cheerleader, Patty. Silver City's playing the Sarasota Over-Sixties Club tomorrow."

Patty burst into tears.

The frail voice turned grim. "What's he done now?"

Patty brushed the cornflakes out of her hair with one hand as she sobbed, "I'm at the end of my rope."

"I *knew* it! I dreamed last night that you were being sucked into a black hole. Dr. Manheim says . . ."

Patty yelled, "I don't want to hear that Jungian mumbo-jumbo."

"That's no way to speak to your mother. And it's not Jungian, it's Freudian. I do wish *you'd* try an analyst, dear."

"I do not need *psychiatric* help. Stephen is a *practical* problem."

"No need to be defensive, dear, this is your mother you're speaking to. You may be taking responsibility to the level of obsession. It could become compulsive and lead to clinical depression."

"How dare you discuss me with Dr. Manheim!"

"I was afraid you were getting like your father's Aunt Ella."

"Mom, she's *senile*. I'm only thirty-three." Patty shook the milk from her green wool sleeve. "My problem is simply that my child is handicapped, so now and again it naturally depresses me, and I need a little verbal chicken soup."

The frail voice sounded weary. "Sympathy is easy to give, dear, but you know it isn't constructive. Stephen is normal enough to lead you by the nose."

"How can you *say* these things about a child who's going to spend his life in a wheelchair?"

"Wherever he spends it, Stephen is not an idiot. Remember that high IQ under those golden curls. He knows exactly what he's doing when he throws these tantrums. And the rest of the time he sits in that wheelchair watching television all day and using what strength he's got to throw everything he can get his hands on. He takes his anger out on you because nobody else would put up with his kicking and screaming. Stephen knows exactly how to manipulate you, honey, and because you feel guilty, you let him get away with it. If he was with other handicapped children, he wouldn't be able to indulge his self-pity and rage."

"Stephen doesn't *like* being with other children. You know what happened when we tried group physiotherapy."

"Patty, you're making him an emotional cripple too. He must learn to rely on himself where he can, otherwise he'll *always* be a bad boy."

"No, he won't."

"Yes, he will. He'll grow up dependent, resentful and vindictive. I'm sorry to say this, but that child has no aim or purpose in his life. He's merely sorry for himself, so he's either spiteful or plays for sympathy."

Patty started sobbing again.

"Do you want me to pay you a visit, Patty?"

"No!"

"Honey, I'm only saying this because I'm your mother. I don't like to see you with no time for a life of your own. You hardly ever go out. You're making a pointless sacrifice and you're not being fair to yourself, or to Charley, or to Stephen."

"It's what I *choose* to do."

"What would Stephen do if anything happened to you *and* Charley? I mean, nobody ever imagines that *they're* going to have an auto accident . . . I know you've got the insurance, dear, but I'm thinking about his emotional needs. He *must* learn to come to terms with himself."

"I am not putting Stephen in a home."

Her mother sighed again. "You always were stubborn. I mean fixated. That's extra stubborn."

Patty heard the crash of china behind her and said, hastily, "Momma, I've got to go. I'll call you tomorrow, same time, to hear how Silver City made out."

Patty could hear high-pitched screaming as she rushed back to Stephen's room, which had once been their living room but now was decked out like a hospital playroom and contained Stephen's special bed.

Judy, the housekeeper, stood in a pool of water in the middle of the cheerful yellow linoleum; she was surrounded by purple and white chrysanthemums.

From the wheelchair Stephen yelled, "She hit me! Judy hit me!"

Patty knew it wasn't true, it never was. Judy was the one person who had been able to handle Stephen since he was born. *She'd* been born in the Hill district, in a black slum (these days it was called a depressed neighborhood), so Judy understood what it was like to feel anger against the world. However, she wouldn't allow Stephen to manipulate her. She was as firm with him when his parents were around as when they weren't. She ignored all his cries of "I'll die, *then* you'll be sorry."

"Don't you worry, Mrs. Silver." Judy wiped the blood from her forehead. "He's in a bad mood tonight, that's all."

Patty rushed for the first-aid box to background yells of "I didn't ask to be born."

After treating Judy's forehead, Patty telephoned for a cab to take her to the hospital. It wasn't a bad cut, but Patty didn't want to take chances. Next, she dialed the nursing bureau for a babysitter that evening, before the night nurse. The bureau had a list of nurses who knew Stephen, who got double rates for daytime work, treble for evenings. Neither Patty nor the agency liked to send anyone along cold.

From the moment Patty said goodbye to her mother on the phone until the moment Charley's Mercedes could be heard drawing up outside the front door, Stephen never stopped screaming.

Wet-fringed, big blue eyes looked up as Charley entered and his son softly said, "Momma's sad."

Charley looked at Patty, who had collapsed white-faced in an armchair; he noticed that her suit had dark stains.

"It's been that bad today?" Charley put his suitcase down, sat on the arm of the chair and kissed the top of her head. Patty snuffled into his sleeve. Charley kissed her hair again and whispered, "Three little words."

Patty snuffled harder. "We'll be late."

Charley shook his head, and his eyes said, "I love you."

Stephen noticed and looked surly.

Apologetically Patty said, "But we *are* going to be late. The nurse can't get here for another hour."

"It doesn't matter. We needn't go at all, if you don't feel up to it. I'll put Stephen to bed. You fix yourself a drink, take it up to the bathroom and get into a warm tub."

Stephen said, "Daddy, Daddy, she hasn't given me my supper."

No sooner was Patty in the tub than Judy returned with a bandage across her forehead. "I wouldn't have gone to the hospital if Mrs. Silver hadn't insisted."

Charley looked at her and said, "Thank you." Both he and Judy knew that he was thanking her not only for tonight but for the past eight years.

Judy said, "Maybe I'll ask Ben again if we can move in here."

Charley went up to Patty's bathroom. She was lying in the beige fiberglass Jacuzzi and staring at the leaded, diamond-paned windows. She hadn't touched her glass of white wine.

"Charley, I don't think I should go on this trip. Judy can't handle him by herself for two weeks."

Charley sat on the edge of the tub. "It'll do *you* good to get away for two weeks. You can't go on like this. It's bad for him and it's bad for you."

"That's what Mom just told me."

"I don't know why you talk to her about Stephen, you know it upsets you." He picked up Patty's glass and sipped the wine. "You both have firmly opposing views, but you *will* discuss it. It's like sticking your tongue against a sore tooth."

"She said I needed a shrink!"

"She's only recommending therapy because it helped *her*. My point is that you could have some life of your own too, Patty." He put the glass down on the dressing table. "I've wondered if you'd like to go back to work? Maybe part-time? We could afford a daytime nurse for Stephen."

Patty looked up sharply, panic on her face. "No! I'm totally out of touch!"

Before they married, Patty had been a sportswear coordinator at I. Magnin. She knew it could be very tough and very lonely in the competitive world outside her home. Now, Patty had no intention of competing with women ten years younger than herself. She didn't want to stand alone, she didn't want the criticism and she didn't want to risk being fired.

"No," she said firmly. "That's a helpful, caring suggestion, Charley, but *no.*"

"Whatever you want."

"Hand me a towel, Charley. I feel fine now. Let's get ready for the party. I'm looking forward to it."

Suzy yawned the way a cat yawns—in a long, luxuriant stretch. She'd had a nap after going around to check that Annie-the-doormat wasn't going to back out.

Slowly Suzy sat up, naked between beige satin sheets in the circular, king-sized bed in her huge beige bedroom. Annie had really looked fabulous, Suzy thought—she'd have all the other wives green with envy this evening! Annie's nearly-auburn hair had been pulled back at one side and rippled forward on the other. Stan had really paid attention to her eyebrows, which most women ignored. But you only had to look at before-and-after photos of Marilyn Monroe to see how important eyebrows were. Annie had still looked pale, but not pasty, more like a magnolia blossom (Stan never altered anything, he just emphasized it), and her eyes looked enormous in their thick fringe of lashes. When she'd taken the pajama bottoms off, she looked slim instead of scrawny. Yeah, she'd really cause trouble tonight.

Suzy glanced at the gold and claret enamel traveling clock that stood on the bedside table; on the dial were the words Cartier-Paris. She'd put one in every bedroom—in different colors, of course.

Suzy yawned again. They'd all be climbing into their formals about now. Slowly she stretched, picked up the intercom and asked the maid to bring her another cup of coffee. They didn't really need a full-time maid, but what the hell? They didn't need a house this size, either.

Suzy looked at herself in the mirrored wall opposite the bed, with some satisfaction. She hadn't done badly for a high school dropout who had been raised (if you could call it that) in a falling-down house shared by three families on the North Side, off Sherman Avenue. It was now a yuppie redevelopment area; the sagging gingerbread houses had been propped up and painted in sugar-almond colors and the trees had been carefully clipped. Suzy refused to go near the North Side, no matter how much they gussied it up. She guessed her pa had been moved out, but she hadn't seen *him* since the day they buried her mom, thank God.

Suzy slipped out of bed and stretched seductively again in front of her reflection. After they'd bought the house in Shadyside she'd told the decorator that she liked a lot of mirrors, creamy marble, gilt and those cute little French antique chairs with the curved legs. She couldn't see why Brett's mother didn't care for the results. The old girl tried hard to act as if she liked her daughter-in-law, but Suzy knew that she didn't. Not many women liked Suzy. She knew that the Nexus bunch called her the Venus flytrap. Brett sometimes called her his pocket Venus, but mostly Brett called her his mermaid, when nobody was around. When he did, Suzy knew that she could get anything out of him, she had only to ask. And she always did.

Suzy stretched again, enjoying the sight of her perfect small body. Her breasts were a bit too big, but that never did a girl any harm. She turned around and looked over her shoulder to check her rear view; she had a wonderful ass, which sort of shivered when she ran as she had taught herself to, in a helpless way with her knees tight together. Suzy turned to front view again and wondered if she should have her bush bleached to match her hair.

She'd ask Stan.

Suzy ran her hands through her carefully tousled, white-blond hair and looked critically at her face. Her eyelids covered the top of her pale green irises, giving her a sleepy look. As a result, since she was twelve years old Suzy hadn't been

55

able to ask a man to pass the salt without his reading a sexual invitation into the words. Suzy had looked seventeen since she was twelve, she still did at twenty-seven, and she intended to continue doing so. She sauntered into the bathroom and started to shave her legs, which she did every evening without fail.

Above the whirr of the electric razor she heard a soft knock at the door.

"Okay, Nora, put the coffee by the bed. And get Alfie to put the hardtop of my Mercedes on, willya!" Suzy yelled from the bathroom in her cheery, rough, natural voice, which she rarely used unless she was mad. When she was still trying to make it as an actress in New York, she'd had voice training, from a coach in the Village, who'd softened it to a sort of slow, Persian-kitten purr. It had been worth every hard-earned penny it had cost from Suzy's earnings as a cocktail waitress. She hadn't made it as an actress, but she lied about her age and got a job as a stewardess with Eastern Airlines, which was how she met Brett.

She had snapped him up on sight, ten miles south of Boston and thirty thousand feet up. Suzy remembered the very moment. She'd seen a sandy head bent over an expensive maroon calf briefcase, a freckled hand with a gold signet ring on the pinkie and a wafer-thin gold watch with a black crocodile strap. As she bent over him to ask if he'd like a drink, Suzy could swear that she really *smelled* old money; it was a mix of laundry starch, eau de cologne, big shaggy dogs, barn straw, speckled brown eggs, worn leather, thick tweed, canvas straining in the wind and foam on the sea. Afterward, it turned out that Brett had borrowed some other guy's talc at the squash club. Suzy had never been able to discover which brand it was.

Brett had looked up into Suzy's pale green eyes, which glistened like peeled grapes. Suzy saw straight sandy eyebrows above big brown eyes, a firm square jaw and a wide mouth. A Brooks Brothers type, kinda British-looking, kinda cute. Suzy had found out on their first date that Brett also came from Pittsburgh, but it wasn't until a lot later that she'd realized he was the anxious type and the square jaw was deceptive.

Suzy carefully rubbed moisturizer into her legs, then climbed back into the satin sheets to drink her coffee. Nora had put out her clothes for this evening. The dress was a really hot number from Saint Laurent; she'd spotted it when she went shopping with Annie. Suzy never wore anything without a designer label. It was insurance; that way she could choose sexy numbers and still be sure of being a class act. Brett's mother had looked sort of *pained* last week when Suzy arrived at her dinner party in a new Christian Dior gown of black organza, close-fitted right to the ankle, with swirls of silver sequins and short, white-mink sleeves. But it *had* said formal on the invitation.

Brett breezed through the door. "Still in bed, baby? Shouldn't be late tonight."

Suzy yawned. "I *intend* to be late, Brett. I'm not gonna get dressed for another half hour."

"In that case . . ." Brett moved hopefully toward the bed.

"No. You'll muss my hair."

A string quartet was playing in the rear of the hall, which Silvana had turned into a bower of white flowers for the evening. Passing through the library on her way to her ballroom, Silvana heard snatches of conversation from the small groups of men. "Measured ore reserves . . . Concentrator expansion program . . . Peripheral drainage . . . Heavy equipment reconditioning . . . Long-term effects of tailings disposal . . . Cleaner circuit modification costs . . ." Silvana had heard it all before, without interest then or now.

In the ballroom, Silvana gave a final check to the sixteen tables for eight that had been set up; Silvana believed that conversation flagged around tables for six, and that twelve people around a table were too many for general conversation. Silver and glass gleamed among the flowers on the pale blue damask cloths, and laurel leaves wound around the marble columns at the far end of the candlelit room. On the buffet table were huge silver platters containing salmon mousse, potted rabbit with plums, sturgeon, roast duck, Westphalian ham, an assortment of pâtés and terrines, clams in a cream sauce tinted with curry, cold pasta salads with basil, artichokes, asparagus, leeks vinaigrette and bowl upon bowl of green salads and dips. That was the first course; once everyone was seated, the dinner would be served by waiters.

Beyond the ballroom Silvana could see the curved tops of the row of French windows in the tree-filled orangery, which was where they would dance after dinner; outside, at the end of the floodlit terrace, was the Olympic-sized, heated swimming pool; it was faced in dark-green glass mosaic, because everybody had aquamarine pools.

The evening was colder than Silvana had expected, so she decided that the orangery doors should be closed. After all, this wasn't a big party where you had to watch the temperature the whole time in case the rooms became too hot.

She swooped back to the entrance hall, moving swiftly past her beautifully dressed guests, bestowing a smile here, a word there. She had been receiving for over an hour when Carey arrived.

"Hi, Silvana. This all looks *wonderful*. How's Arthur?"

"Arthur's looking forward to being a grandfather, but he isn't too thrilled about being married to a grandmother." It was the seventh time Silvana had laughingly said that this evening. She nervously stroked her subtle silver dress, which hung heavy and straight from the shoulders. Turning to Lorenza, she said, "Look who's here, darling—Carey!"

As they started talking, both women flicked a look at the other's dress. Lorenza was wearing a Zandra Rhodes, pale blue chiffon printed with a swirling green pattern. Unnoticed, she could have given birth to twins beneath it. In contrast, Carey looked as tall and lithe as an Amazon ballet dancer in her simple, tight-waisted black dress and low-heeled bronze sandals.

Carey said, "That's the sort of dress Mrs. Ricketts always

wore. Did you have her for art history?" Carey and Lorenza had both been at the same Eastern college, though several years apart.

"Sure." Lorenza imitated a high, squeaky voice. "'Only the boring are bored. You live in a most fascinating world, girls.'" Both women laughed.

"I wonder if they still have those mixers?" Carey asked curiously. You wore a fancy formal to the party and carried a little purse for your lipstick and drugs. Freddie-the-lookout drove you there in a Volvo station wagon and, at dawn, Freddie would come looking for you, gently pry you from your date and help you stagger back to the station wagon.

Lorenza said, "Sure, they still have the mixers and Prune-face still has that sour expression when she lets you back in." They both laughed again.

A man who had just arrived said to Carey, "I hear you're married to Ed Hope. He's quite a globe-trotter, isn't he? What do *you* do with yourself when he's away?"

One of those. Bored if you talked about your home and children, indulgent if you talked about your job, and embarrassed if you talked about your business; the sort who were accustomed to talking to women at parties with a handful of well-worn clichés. He would be speechless if you didn't give the ritual response. So they both said the obvious things about Reagan's chances of getting reelected next month, and Carey escaped as soon as she could, to talk to Arthur's mother, whom she really liked.

Mrs. Graham was a steel heiress. Everyone, even Silvana, called her "Mrs. Graham." She was tall, elegant and vague, and she always said exactly what she thought and did exactly what she wanted, so she had a local reputation for eccentricity. When the rich do unconventional things, they are labeled eccentric; when the rest of us do, we are called mad, thought Carey.

Mrs. Graham had made her glass house in the hills a veritable museum; ancient, carved masterpieces from all over the world coexisted comfortably with ultramodern pale-gray suede

59

sofas. Mrs. Graham was on the advisory board of the Frick, but her heart was really with the Museum of Art at the Carnegie Institute in Oakland, which was going to get all the masterpieces after her death, on condition that they saw to it that she had a sea burial. Mrs. Graham didn't want to end up moldering in the earth or displayed in an urn.

Mrs. Graham said, "Chitter chatter, chitter chatter, what *are* they all talking about?" Her straight silver hair was cut like a helmet, and she wore as plain a dress as a black dress could be. On one shoulder a large *real* ivy leaf was casually pinned with a diamond stud the size of a jellybean.

Carey said, "The hot rumor is that next year's Rand McNally will rate Pittsburgh the best place to live in America."

"Well, of course it is, or the Grahams wouldn't have settled here."

The first Arthur Nimrod Graham had been a major in the King's Fourteenth Dragoon Guards. In 1758 the Guards had been stationed at Fort Pitt, at that time the largest and most elaborate frontier outpost in North America. Major Graham had been much intrigued by the operation of the trading post in the fort. Indians brought fur and venison to trade for blankets, kettles, knives and gunpowder. The rate of exchange was one male deerskin, or buck; one buck was worth two does, four foxes or six raccoons; a blanket cost four bucks, a tin kettle cost three bucks, one buck got you four sharp knives.

Invalided out of the army by the loss of his leg, which had to be amputated after an Indian arrow wound, Major Graham decided to stay in the charming pioneer village, rendered even more charming by a young redheaded widow whose late husband had left her a parcel of land between the future Cherry Street and Smithfield Street and four hundred acres of farmland on the south bank of the Monongahela River. The week after his marriage, the Major sent back East for a thousand blankets, kettles and knives.

Those who settled in the village of Pittsburgh were fortunate, for the rich land provided more food than they could eat. By 1802 they were exporting ham, dried pork, corn and butter downriver to New Orleans. The villagers grew their own flax and cotton for bed linen and clothes; the huge surrounding forests supplied logs to build homes and charcoal with which to forge iron; local limestone and sand meant that they were able to make their own glass—it was ruinously expensive to haul it from the East. There was iron ore with which to make nails and farming implements, and abundant coal in the surrounding hills for Pittsburgh's infant industries. A century later, the logical result of this rural cornucopia was to be U.S. Steel, Westinghouse and H. J. Heinz.

However, there was one grave disadvantage in the prosperous town of Pittsburgh: the smoke. In 1804, Arthur Nimrod Graham II, one of the city councilmen, had tried unsuccessfully to promote smoke-control regulations, but most of his fellow councilmen were against it, on the grounds of cost.

After the dreadful winter of 1940, Arthur Nimrod Graham VII had been among a small group of city fathers who put forth antipollution, flood control and slum clearance programs to save the city. But to little avail. By 1945, at the end of World War II, Pittsburgh was so filthy with soot and smog that streetlights had to burn at midday and the rivers that surrounded the town were polluted by the waste of over a hundred industries.

Forty years later, Pittsburgh was still an industrial town, but Smoke City had been transformed into a clean city surrounded by green hills. The triangle of land upon which Fort Pitt once stood, hedged on two sides by rivers and on the third by a steep hill, is now known as the Golden Triangle. One of the highest of the silver-gray skyscrapers that stands in the Triangle is Nexus Tower, from the penthouse of which the present Arthur Nimrod Graham ruled over Nexus.

It was hard to believe that Arthur had ever *needed* a mother, Carey thought. What she said was, "I love the picture you gave Arthur for his birthday present."

"The little Breughel-school battlefield? I've given up trying to think of what he wants, and now I just give him things I would like myself. If he doesn't like them, he gives them back to me for *my* birthday. It's a very satisfactory arrangement. Of course, it would be more logical if, on a child's birthday, the *mother* were given the gifts."

The decibel level rose as guests discussed the abrupt departure of André Previn as musical director of the Pittsburgh Symphony, construction progress on the new medical institute, whether Steeler Mark Malone was playing well enough and whether Stallworth should stay. However, the evening's hot topic was an unusual local homicide case. The previous August, a male Turkish student had been shot to death and another one knifed, supposedly by two girls who had picked the men up at the Three Rivers Regatta. The girls had supposedly attacked the men next day in a secluded part of the airport. Two days later they had surrendered in Virginia Beach, and were still awaiting trial. What was different from the average humdrum homicide case was that the *women* seemed to have been the aggressors. Or were they defending themselves? Everyone had a different opinion, but they all agreed that it was viciously unnatural, that there must be something very wrong with these women. They were probably lesbians.

Suddenly the twitter faltered. Carey glanced over her shoulder toward the entrance. Suzy stood in the doorway; she wore a long-sleeved, high-necked dress of iridescent blue lace that was so tight she must have been sewn into it. An enormous blue taffeta bow perched on her hip, and from the crotch to the knee she was swathed in electric-blue taffeta; below her knees, iridescent lace frothed above peacock satin pumps.

"She looks like a mermaid on a Saturday night," murmured Mrs. Graham.

Suzy, holding her head high, looked slowly around the room. She spotted the greyhound silhouette of Patty, who was wearing her black and white taffeta *again!* No wonder Charley was playing around with that redhead in Research. Silvana was dressed in a silver number that looked like chain mail; plump women should stick to dark colors. Standing by the windows at the back of the room, Isabel couldn't avoid looking like a company executive, even though she was wearing a sexy, clinging dress with one bare shoulder. Suzy would, of course, tell Isabel that she looked great. She was always careful not to irritate Isabel.

As Suzy's eyes swept around the room, she noticed that spoiled little brat Lorenza, who looked like a lampshade in that maternity dress. Although you *had* to admire anyone of her age who could call up a Lear jet just by lifting a phone. She was talking to Carey—and no wonder Suzy hadn't spotted Carey before! That black dress was really *dull*, Carey should have given it a lift with lots of jewelry—and she might have *tried* to do something with her hair. Tall girls should always pay attention to their hair, because that was what stuck out above the crowd. She really should tell Carey about Stan, the *visagiste*. On the other hand, what had Carey ever done for her? Ah, there was Annie . . . Why, Annie had chickened out! She was wearing that dreary blue thing she'd gotten for Lorenza's wedding, so she looked as dull as she usually did. Really, why bother to help people?

Looking around, Suzy didn't move until she'd counted to ten, then she swayed forward. You can't help moving voluptuously if your knees are almost bound together, and you move slowly.

"No wonder we're all jealous of her," Carey sighed.

"Envious," corrected Mrs. Graham. "Jealousy is wanting what someone has; envy is not wanting her to have it."

Silvana stepped toward the doorway. "Suzy, I'm *so* glad you could make it. Brett, I've been longing to know what's been arranged for the wives on this trip. Arthur doesn't seem to have the vaguest idea, but I suppose you've organized a packed program as usual?"

"Sure," said Brett, who was VP Public Relations. "The Sydney visit will concentrate on the sophistication of the city

—fashion shows, nightclubs, concerts. When we get to Paui, everything will be much more informal; we've arranged sailing, scuba diving, tennis and golf. Or you can just lie by the pool and tan."

In the library a group of Nexus executives clustered around their host, who stood with his back to the spluttering log fire. Arthur said, "I suppose Paui *is* safe?"

Ed, who was Vice President of Exploration and Planning, said, "Of course. Harry Scott flew up from Sydney only last week, and I've been there twice myself since the coup. It's a damn sight safer than most of Manhattan. If we didn't think Paui was safe, we wouldn't be negotiating with the government."

Thin-lipped, skinny Jerry Pearce, who was VP Corporate Finance, said, "We *aren't* negotiating with them."

"That's only because they won't negotiate with Harry," Ed said impatiently. "They didn't go to Harvard Business School, and they don't understand corporate structure. As far as they're concerned, Harry's not the top man—he's only the president of Nexus, Australia. The President of Paui will talk only to Arthur, otherwise he loses face. That doesn't matter to us."

Jerry Pearce said, "What's important to us is that they understand that the deal has virtually been completed. They must understand that Arthur's final offer *will* be our final offer, and that our deadline is Arthur's departure time."

"In my opinion," Ed said, "we'll clinch it at the last minute, maybe even at the airport."

"This last-minute drama shouldn't be necessary," Arthur said irritably. "The review of our agreement was scheduled to start four months ago, in June '84. They've been more than happy with results since start-up in 1970."

"With good reason," Jerry agreed. "Our Paui turnover last year was $474 million. We produced 43 percent of their exports, contributed 73 percent of internally generated government revenue and 80 percent of our work force are Paui citizens."

Ed sipped his Chivas Regal. "They're aware of that, but the 1970 agreement only covers the North Queenstown mine, and it only covers copper rights. If we want to tie up all mining rights to the whole island, it isn't just a question of sticking a new date on the old agreement."

Brett, who had just joined the group, said tentatively, "Isn't an all-rights deal unusual?"

"Sure," said Ed, "but there always has to be a first time. We were heading smoothly toward an all-rights deal with the previous government."

Jerry Pearce explained, "If the price is high enough, then an all-rights deal might be tempting for a President who figures that his period of power will be short—who wants to get as much as he can, as fast as he can, into a Swiss bank, then quit while he's still ahead."

Ed sighed. "The last bunch were a damn sight easier to deal with than this new bunch of woolly-minded liberals."

"Are they worried about environmental problems?" Brett asked. "Is that it?"

Everyone looked oddly at Brett, who wished he hadn't spoken.

Jerry said, "People only bring in environmental problems to jack the price up. And they always hit us for it *after* the contract has been agreed on, otherwise we would have made a lower offer."

Ed said, "Anyway, we always keep environmental disturbances to the minimum, and they have to be weighed against the benefits. What we mine is essential to modern industry. And, they benefit from the infrastructure."

Arthur nodded. "We provide them with employment and factories, as well as a number of fringe benefits. They didn't even have a road or a landing strip, let alone a hospital, on Paui before we moved in."

Jerry said, "I still don't like the idea of Arthur going there. It's a weak move."

"That's why it's important to have this trip look like a vacation," Ed argued. "Then, in their eyes, we can't lose face."

When Jerry shrugged, Ed said, "Look, I have to put up with all sorts of shit in every so-called 'developing' country that we're involved with. If *we* want what *they've* got, then we've got to know their rules, and play by their rules."

Brett tried again to take an intelligent part in the conversation. "You don't think they might back off? You're sure we're offering enough protection payment for the concession agreements?"

As soon as he spoke, Brett knew that he'd again said something wrong.

For an exasperated moment, Arthur wished his mother could have heard her protégé make this double gaffe. Why couldn't the family lame duck have stayed with that marketing firm. Because Brett's mother wanted him in a firm that wouldn't fire him. Because of his disability, goddammit . . .

"We *never* make protection payments," Arthur said sharply. "Although special arrangements are sometimes necessary. Please also remember that the phrase 'concession agreement' is most offensive to developing countries. We refer to 'heads of agreement,' or 'basic agreement' or 'intent to treat,' which is an unusual term, but one that Ed likes to use. If you have a spare hour he'll tell you why."

Brett flushed.

To cover the awkward pause, Jerry said quickly, "Brett, this situation is not unusual or unreasonable. It's simply that they don't want a foreign company to mine their metals and minerals—even though Paui hasn't got the money, the machinery or the know-how to do it for themselves."

Ed nodded. "Fifty years ago those islanders were Stone Age savages, they'd never seen a *wheel*, let alone a Jeep. The first college-educated citizens of Paui are the ones who've just taken over. So we should be patient."

Arthur grunted in agreement. "It's merely unfortunate for us that they didn't take over two years later, then we'd have been doing this deal with Raki. There's a lot to be said for a predictable, reasonable crook. Now let's stop talking shop and circulate, it's nearly time to eat."

* * *

Flushed-faced, Carey was telling Annie about her private game, the one that kept her awake at Nexus parties. She imagined each man present as a plundering Viking, complete with horned helmet, leather jerkin and thonged leggings. Carey giggled. "It's even more hilarious if the guy's wearing glasses." Annie laughed politely.

As Carey accepted another glass of champagne from a passing waiter, Ed appeared behind her shoulder.

"Carey, I thought you said you weren't going to drink before dinner. You know how you get."

Carey twisted around to face him. "No, darling, *you* said I wasn't going to drink before dinner." As she spoke, she lost her balance. She staggered and fell against Annie, spilling her champagne down Annie's blue gown. Ed looked thunderous.

Annie said, "Look, it doesn't matter."

Carey said, "It's very hot in here. I don't feel well."

"Pie-eyed," Ed said grimly.

Annie put her glass on a side table. "Maybe you'd like to come upstairs and help me sponge this off, Carey?"

Carey mumbled, "I think I'm going to be . . . Oh, dear."

Annie took Carey by the arm. She hurried her through the hall, up the massive oak staircase, along the minstrel's gallery and past the bathrooms that the other guests were using. They turned into the passage that led to Lorenza's apartment, where they wouldn't be disturbed.

Annie led Carey into the bathroom, held her head over the washbasin, grabbed a washcloth and slapped cold water over the back of her neck.

Carey gasped, "Okay, okay. Will you please let up, Annie?"

"I've been with you since you got here, Carey. You haven't drunk much. When did you last eat?"

"Yesterday evening. I didn't have any breakfast."

"Well, what can you expect?" Annie led Carey into the bedroom. "Lie down on the couch. I'll get you something to eat. Look, there's a jar of cookies beside the bed."

"Granola. Yuck."

67

"Eat them."

Annie sponged her dress, then sat with Carey until remorse had replaced nausea.

Carey sat up on the couch and wailed, "I just made a fool of myself in front of Ed's colleagues!"

"No, you didn't. Nobody noticed. And it doesn't matter. You're among friends."

Still tipsy and verbose, Carey said, "Oh, Annie, we're none of us friends; we're line-toeing, loyal, pushed-around company wives. Not real friends. We're just polite and agreeable . . . why, we *never* disagree." Then she giggled. "Gee, I'm looking forward to the trip to Paui."

Outside the ladies' bathroom, Suzy leaned over the banister and watched the guests below as they moved toward the ballroom, where supper was laid out. She'd wait until they were all seated before she went down.

Until then, Suzy would play her own, private party game, which was sorting out the new-rich from the old-rich. Old money didn't wear jewelry in the daytime, and when they *did* wear their rocks, they didn't go for plunging necklines. Old money were always beautifully groomed and wore beautifully finished, dull-colored clothes. They never wore very high heels and their shoes were never scuffed, although their purses often were. But they were always really good quality, even when they were beat-up; if you wanted to look like old money, the thing to do was to buy some cracked, old crocodile purse from a Palm Beach thrift shop. Old money always had good posture, because they had been endlessly told to sit up straight by their governesses and British nannies. Sometimes Suzy felt like asking Mrs. Graham what year she'd been at West Point.

Suzy studied the people in the lovely hall below; she always picked up a few good tips from a visit to this house. Brett would never have this sort of money, damnit. He wasn't a Graham, he was Arthur's mother's childless sister's husband's nephew. That was another thing about old money, they always expected you to be able to follow immediately when they came up with the family tree bit about their relations—whom they called relatives.

Suddenly, to her annoyance, Suzy saw her husband hurrying toward the staircase. How dare Brett come to get her!

Then she noticed that Brett was hanging on to the banister as he slowly climbed the stairs. Jeez, what a time to choose for one of his attacks. Especially since he hated people to notice them. They had to have latex pillows and synthetic bedcovers because Brett was allergic to feathers and lint; they couldn't have pets, because of animal dander; the house had to be spotlessly clean, not a speck of dust; and the mattress had to be cleaned once a week to avoid fluff. When Brett felt a bronchial asthma attack coming on, he'd suddenly feel a tightness in his chest and start wheezing. Breathing out was especially difficult; Suzy had to reassure him that he wasn't suffocating, it merely *felt* as if he were. But the Ventolin spray made all the difference, provided Brett used it at the first sign of an attack.

In her tight dress, Suzy hobbled quickly to the top of the stairs. "Brett, *where's your spray?*"

"I left it in my coat pocket," he gasped, holding up a blue ticket.

Suzy snatched it. "You sit here. I'll go get it."

Brett staggered to a fragile, carved oaken chair, which wasn't supposed to be sat on. Suzy kicked her shoes off, and awkwardly wiggled to the men's coat room. She grabbed Brett's coat from the maid and located his asthma spray, which was the size of a large cigarette lighter. She ran back to Brett as fast as she could, in her constricting dress.

Brett breathed out, held the spray to his mouth, breathed in and held it for ten seconds.

A manservant came up to them, but Suzy waved him away. "He'll be okay, this happens all the time. The spray always fixes it . . . Hey, could you get me a drink? It usually takes him about twenty minutes to get over these attacks. I'd like some champagne."

BOOK TWO

PARADISE

FRIDAY, NOVEMBER 9, 1984

"Well, now, isn't that thoughtful of them." Roddy inspected the orchid corsage that had arrived on his breakfast tray with the compliments of the Regent Hotel, Sydney. He picked up a large envelope. "This entitles me to a free facial and hairdo, plus a mudpack and a massage in the hotel beauty parlor! A special treat because it's the last day of the conference."

Sitting up against the pillows, studying her papers, Isabel looked over the tops of her horn-rimmed glasses and laughed. "I got a free necktie last time I traveled on the Concorde."

Roddy had noticed that Isabel didn't receive any of these daily breakfast-tray gifts. He also noticed that she kept aloof from the other women in their party; she was a top Nexus executive and wasn't going to risk being treated like a wife. On the other hand, she wore jackets that were too large for her and big glasses that were always slipping off her little nose, which somehow made a guy feel protective. Isabel liked to have it both ways. She wasn't averse to feminine luxury. She enjoyed the pale flowers that were massed in every room (even the bathroom), the courtesy makeup and toilet articles supplied by the hotel, the wicker basket of assorted bath fragrances and shell-shaped soaps in different colors, the small sewing kit and the thick white terry-cloth robe in her bathroom.

As she ate her croissant, Isabel studied her typewritten notes for the speech she was going to make that morning to two hundred senior managers. She had been hard at it ever since she stepped off the plane. When everyone else flopped with jet lag, Isabel, crisp and efficient, had a long meeting with Harry Scott, the boss of Nexus, Australia. Isabel avoided jet lag because on the plane she never drank alcohol, which dehydrates you even more than the air conditioning. As soon as she stepped into the cabin, she switched to arrival time. She ate only three small high-protein snacks (at arrival mealtimes), she slipped a mask over her eyes and took a sleeping pill at 10 P.M. by her wristwatch, so she woke up (at arrival wake-up time) fresh and ready to go, whereas most of the other passengers were feeling as crumpled as they looked.

Early in life, Isabel had learned to be economical with time and money. Her mother had been a legal secretary before marrying a Navy petty officer, who died when Isabel was seven. Her mother stretched a sailor's pay by dressmaking for her neighbors. Most of Isabel's clothes had been made by her, and she used to be lulled to sleep at night by the whirr of her mother's old-fashioned, pedal-driven sewing machine. Her mother had died of pneumonia the week after Isabel's tenth birthday. Ever since, Isabel had been slightly afraid of totally loving anything, in case it was taken away from her.

Isabel put her notes aside and poured a second cup of coffee. She picked up *The Australian* and leaned back against the pillows.

Roddy nuzzled her bare shoulder. "What's on your agenda today?"

"A lecture on media communication by the editor-in-chief of the *Sydney Daily Telegraph*. She's a glamorous blonde called Ita Buttrose."

"Isn't Brett speaking today?"

"Yes, on Nexus being a Caring Company. After that, we have Ed on the exhaustion of nonrenewable resources. You'll be glad to hear that the world isn't going to run short of any

74

major elements before the year 2050. But this afternoon is free, for all the delegates."

Roddy's fingertips crept tentatively up her arm, in a little dance which they both recognized as his invitation. "How about exhausting a nonrenewable husband before leaping along to the conference theater?" He kissed the hollow of her neck.

"Honey, I haven't put my diaphragm in. And there isn't time."

"Okay, okay. I'll give myself a mudpack instead."

Naked, Roddy slid from the sheets and ambled to the luxurious bathroom. Almost immediately, he returned to the bedroom and pulled open the doors to the balcony, which overlooked the spectacular view of Sydney Harbor twenty stories below.

"Isabel, darling." Roddy held something up in the air.

Isabel looked up. "Hey, is that my diaphragm?"

"It was." Roddy flung it off the balcony high into the air.

"How *dare* you!"

"Oh, it was easy. You're going to have a baby whether you like it or not, Isabel, and we're going to start practicing right now."

Lying in bed, Brett watched Suzy in her red lace bra and string bikini. As she danced to the radio he felt lust rise again. He could watch her brush her teeth and it would excite him— and she knew it. He didn't give a damn whether his friends or family accepted Suzy, all he cared about was whether any other man liked her too much. He had observed that when other men were present—whether it was a ten-year-old kid or an eighty-year-old grandfather—Suzy's actions were subtly different from when she was alone with him. He'd come to the conclusion that she was unaware of the electricity she was creating; it must be unconscious, because she never *seemed* interested in any man other than Brett. He had been mesmerized by Suzy since the moment he first set eyes on her, and he was terrified that one day she might get bored and just walk out. Brett knew there would be another guy at her side before she'd walked ten steps. Brett couldn't very well lock his wife out of sight, but that's what he felt like doing.

Paradoxically, he also loved to see Suzy admired, and he loved to see Suzy enjoying herself, as she was on this trip. She always liked traveling, especially by air; she liked being the one who was bent over, instead of doing the bending.

Now, in the pale-gray hush of the hotel suite, Suzy, with one leg up behind her and arms extended like a skater, cheerily asked, "Hey, Brett, d'you think I'm fucking Arthur?"

It was this tough, unexpected, straightforward quality in her that Brett found irresistible. He said, "I must admit that it had crossed my mind." In fact, he couldn't figure out why else a relatively junior exec had been included on the exclusive Paui trip.

"Well, I'm not."

As he hurled himself out of bed toward her Suzy thought, Not yet. She had no intention of being screwed by anyone she wasn't married to. Temptation was the ace up her sleeve. She'd landed Brett with that old-fashioned weapon, but her next marriage was going to be, if not to Arthur, to somebody with Arthur's money and power—the boss.

Although Silvana was accustomed to luxury, she was enjoying the quiet peace of the Royal Suite in one of the most elegant hotels in the world. The restful pale color scheme, the discreet lighting, the personal butler—all contributed to the feeling of calm order and remoteness from the world. Silvana murmured, "I think I'll stay up here and read quietly today."

"You read too much," Arthur said. "It's not healthy to shut yourself away all the time with a book. I suppose you're feeling all right? Do you need anything?"

Had Silvana said, "No, I'm not all right, I've been emotionally lonely for years and what I need is a *mate*," Arthur would simply have stared in astonishment and told her to get a medical checkup when they returned to Pittsburgh.

Restlessly, Arthur paced their suite. It was not divided into rooms but consisted of one big interior, in which different areas were grouped: the dining area, the two desk areas and the huge central seating area, where four beige leather sofas were arranged around a low marble table. They had arrived to find champagne, vodka, Beluga caviar and exotic fruits awaiting them on that table.

In such surroundings, Silvana had decided to enjoy a co-cooned day of service, and the luxury of not being responsible for the smooth functioning of this cushioned ease.

Ed was reading his speech in front of the mirror. Carey, wearing an orange nightshirt, sat cross-legged on the bed and listened carefully.

"'. . . so the world can continue to supply mankind with all the resources needed by industry, if we assume reasonably stable political conditions, absence of energy crises, sufficient capital and the successful location of new sources of material.'"

Carey thought that was a lot to assume, but she didn't say so.

Ed continued, "'. . . and providing that no other cartels are formed—such as that which produced the oil crises—to hold the world to ransom for materials which come mainly from one country.'"

Carey clapped encouragingly as Ed went on, "'I'm thinking of materials such as platinum, gold and chromite from South Africa, cobalt from Zaïre and Zambia. We all know that after the 1978 rebel invasion of Zaïre, cobalt prices went quickly from eleven dollars a kilogram to over one hundred and twenty, although this was mainly as a result of panic buying. Should South Africa ever withhold its chromite from the rest of the world . . .'"

Carey sat up. "Ed, can't scientists find substitutes for those sorts of raw materials?"

"Carey, can't you wait until I've finished? I lose my train of thought if you interrupt."

"Sorry. But can't they?"

77

"No, we can't produce substitutes in adequate supply. That's why the one-source countries might be able to hold up the rest of the world for ransom one day. Now for Crissake, let me finish. I'm supposed to deliver this speech to two hundred people in an hour."

Ten minutes later, Ed looked earnestly into the mirror as he summed up. "'My main theme today has been what's going to happen to world natural resources, which of them are likely to run out and what strategy should be adopted, considering the projected variations of demand against increases of supply through successful exploration, sufficient research and development, and improved technology.'"

"Ed, I really think that last sentence is a bit of a mouthful."

"SHUT . . . UP!"

"Sorry."

In the early morning sun, the lone figure of Arthur reclined on a lounge chair at the side of the rooftop swimming pool. Arthur wrongly believed that you always got complete security by the pool. Whereas you never knew who could hear you in a restaurant. Arthur was talking to Pittsburgh on two telephones. There was a fifteen-hour time difference; conveniently, 8 A.M. on Friday morning in Sydney was 5 P.M. on Thursday in Pittsburgh, just before the working day ended. On one of his poolside tables stood ham and eggs, orange juice and coffee. His maroon Cartier Le Must briefcase lay on the other table.

Arthur slid a hand under his turquoise swimming trunks and scratched. "Okay, Joe, I'll take two thousand shares at twenty-three ten. G'bye . . . Delia, you still there? . . . Okay, put him on." All Arthur's calls were routed through his confidential secretary, Delia, using the Pittsburgh office switchboard. Arthur liked lying by the pool and scratching his belly in the sun while he made people jump through hoops in their offices, and Delia recorded every conversation.

As he sipped his orange juice, he negotiated a land purchase and short lease on a building on Cherry Street, then had an argument with his insurance agent.

"Don't *but* me, Syd, I want the figures by Monday." Arthur crashed the phone down, wiped the sweat from his sunglasses and nodded to the bellboy, who held out a silver salver on which lay the 8 A.M. news summary from the hotel wire.

While Arthur finished his scrambled eggs, he made a quick call to New York to inform Municipal Allied that he was prepared to go ahead, provided they accepted his nominee for the board; he then telephoned his contact on the city desk of the *New York Times* to leak a story about Municipal Allied.

After confirming with Delia that all calls had been recorded, he drank a final cup of coffee and direct-dialed someone to check whether she'd gotten his roses. He smiled briefly as her squeals of joy were transmitted over thousands of miles from Pittsburgh.

Arthur checked his eighteen-karat-gold perpetual calendar Breguet watch, which showed the phases of the moon, could withstand a dive to 2,000 feet underwater and had set his mother back $25,000 on his sixtieth birthday. He frowned slightly at the memory of his more recent birthday. You were as young as you felt, the doctors all said. At sixty-two, Arthur was as fit as a man ten years younger. He didn't enjoy this business of choosing his successor, but the Board had been pressuring him for two years, so he had finally agreed to let them have his decision by the new year. That way, the next president would be seen as Arthur's choice.

Again, he glanced at his watch. The others weren't due for two minutes; he had time for another call.

Harry Scott stepped out of the elevator into the soft morning sun. In the distance he could see Arthur lying by the pool, but the boss could wait for a couple of minutes while Harry looked at the splendid view that he loved. He pushed his sunglasses up into his dark, curly hair and narrowed his gr y eyes. As a boy he had been teased at school because of his curly black eyelashes, but it had stopped when Harry grew taller and huskier than the other boys in his class. A nose

broken by a cricket bat made him look tougher and more aggressive than he was, as did his high cheekbones and sunken
cheeks. He was too thin, because he wasn't very interested in
food and frequently forgot to eat.

To Harry's left was the Harbor Bridge; on his right, the
soaring white shell shapes of the Opera House and, all around
them, yachts and ferryboats danced on the blue waters of Sydney Harbor. This spot was where Australia had started,
thought Harry. His country was about the same size as the
United States, but more than two hundred years after Captain
James Cook sailed into Botany Bay in 1717, there were still
only fifteen million people in Australia.

Soon after Cook's discovery, the American Revolution was
lost by the British, which forced them to look for somewhere
else to dump their convicts. Australia was chosen for the new
open prison; by 1868, when transportation ended, one in every
nine Australians was of convict origin, although it was considered an insult to refer to this in any way.

Harry's grandfather, Andy Scott, had sailed as a deckhand
from Inverness, in Scotland, to try his luck in the first Australian gold rush of the 1850s. Along with thousands of others,
Andy Scott hadn't panned any gold, but when his money ran
out he'd taken a job in a silver mine, and so had been in at the
start of the Australian mining industry. By 1870, when Andy
Scott II was a mining supervisor at Southern Star Mining,
Australia was exporting copper, lead, silver and zinc, and
James Scott was two years old. James stayed with Southern
Star. In 1952 his son, Gordon, became the financial controller
of Nexus, Australia, and their geologists discovered huge deposits of coal, bauxite and iron ore. By 1960 oil, nickel and
manganese had been found, and Gordon's twenty-one-year-
old son, Harry, had been awarded the Nexus development
scholarship. Shortly after Harry first joined the Sydney office
as a junior accountant trainee, the world's largest undeveloped
area of uranium had been located in the Northern Territory,
and Australia had become one of the world's leading mining
countries.

The Scotts were not one of the Australian families that had torn a vast fortune out of the ground, somehow it had always eluded them, but they were a family that had lived with the excitement of mining since the industry started, and rarely was anything else (except cricket) discussed over their breakfast table in Cronulla, the pleasant Sydney suburb where Harry Scott had been raised.

To the pride of his parents, Harry was now responsible for all Nexus activities in Australia, and they were considerable. Nexus mined nickel, iron ore and bauxite in Western Australia, more bauxite and copper in Queensland, more copper and coal at the Woodongolla mine in New South Wales and manganese in the Northern Territory.

In the early morning sun, as Harry Scott walked around the deserted hotel swimming pool, Ed and Charley, casually dressed but carrying briefcases, stepped from the elevator and joined their boss. Harry wondered which of those two blokes he'd be reporting to in the future; both were valuable men in their different ways. Nothing ever seemed to go wrong when that notoriously efficient lawyer Charley was involved, but Ed, a geologist, was equally efficient and *he* had the rare quality of exciting people; anyone who worked on one of Ed's projects was always devoted to it—and to Ed.

Arthur pulled a Hawaiian shirt over his head and greeted the lean, tanned newcomer. "Everything fixed, Harry?"

"Exactly as we hoped. On Saturday morning we fly from Sydney to Paui in the Lear. It's a two-thousand-mile trip, so we'll arrive around three in the afternoon and helicopter to the hotel. On Sunday morning we all go swimming—as if it's the start of a lazy holiday. On Sunday afternoon we take a relaxed sightseeing trip around the island, again by helicopter. You'll be sitting behind the pilot, Arthur. Ed will be sitting next to you and he'll point out all the beauty spots. When we get to our proposed sites, he'll rub his nose, once for cobalt, twice for uranium."

Ed thought, And when I take off my sunglasses, that means chromite.

Charley asked, "Is this cloak-and-dagger stuff really necessary?"

Harry said, "The pilots are real gossips, and it's surprising what they pick up." He thought, The speculative price is high enough, but if anyone knew what was there, the price would soar, *and* it would take years to get an agreement. The favorite Paui sport was bargaining.

Arthur said, "Get on with the briefing." A summary wasn't really necessary; a ninety-two-page written report was locked in his briefcase and all prices and payments had already been secretly agreed, but this meeting had been arranged in case of last-minute changes in plan.

"On Monday we all go deep-sea fishing, still relaxing," Harry said. "On Tuesday morning the helicopter collects us to fly to Queenstown. Ostensibly, we're inspecting the mine. A car will be waiting at the airport, but before we visit the mine we will, of course, pay a courtesy call at the Presidential Palace, which is just south of Queenstown. When we arrive, only Arthur will get out of the car. He will be kept waiting—I don't know how long, ten minutes should be sufficient for status purposes—but if he's kept longer than thirty minutes, then Arthur leaves. However, that won't happen. The President will offer coffee, which Arthur will accept. No business will be discussed. Arthur will leave when the President stands up."

"How long should the meeting be?" Charley asked.

"Allow twenty minutes. When Arthur reappears, the Nexus party drives off to visit the mine, which is twenty-seven miles north of Queenstown."

"And after that?" Charley asked.

"On Wednesday morning the President will send his personal helicopter to collect Arthur. I'll go with him. We'll meet with the President and the Minister of Finance. Arthur will then make our first offer, which will be refused, whereupon Arthur and I will return to the hotel and go fishing.

"On Thursday, Arthur and I again visit the palace, and again we will be kept waiting before seeing the President.

This time we'll see him alone and he will be prepared to cede all mineral and mining rights on Paui to Nexus, but he'll ask for a higher price than our first offer. Arthur then makes our second offer, which will be refused. Arthur and I then leave and have lunch at the Queenstown Hotel.

"After lunch a messenger will arrive from the Finance Minister to take us to his office. He will agree to a price slightly above our second offer and we will sign the Heads of Agreement. We'll have to make their private payments to Switzerland before the final agreement is signed, but that's Charley's department."

Charley said, "That's some charade you've organized."

Ed said, "You're getting off lightly. If you treat with certain tribes in Papua New Guinea, you're obliged to lick the chief's armpit as a sign of goodwill." He shrugged his shoulders. "Things would have been a lot easier if the Nationalists hadn't been kicked out just as we were about to renegotiate. With Raki, it would have been merely a question of how much, where and when. But these Democrats are left-wing idealists. The guys in charge see themselves as the Kennedy boys of Paui."

"What happens if they don't agree to our second offer?" Charley asked.

"Then Arthur leaves, looking unconcerned, and goes fishing. They may well choose to make it a tight deadline—in fact, that's what I expect. We may find ourselves negotiating at the airport, right up to takeoff. But Arthur must *not* deviate from his timetable, or Nexus will lose face."

Charley said, "You're sure that the President doesn't know what we know?"

"You can never be *sure,* Charley. But nobody in Nexus knows, except us four," Harry said. "And if there's a leak, then Brett is on the spot, ready to be briefed. *He* can defuse anything, or red-herring the press."

Charley said, "Has there been any more trouble with General Raki?"

"Sure," said Harry. "He's holding court at the Port Moresby

Travel Lodge in Hunter Street, doing his best to convince me that he's still an influential bloke on Paui and whingeing because we stopped his payments. All the other Nationalist ministers were either killed, jailed or thrown off Paui eighteen months ago when the Democrats took over."

"So Nexus is not returning Raki's calls?"

Harry nodded. "And he hasn't received any special payment, not since his party lost power."

That afternoon, Annie and Duke, Ed and Carey sailed in Sydney Harbor in Harry's eleven-meter racing yacht. After a week spent in the hotel conference hall, the men were enjoying the spring sunshine of November and the feel of the wind on their faces. The two American men wore new casual clothes, picked out for the trip by their wives, but Harry wore jeans and a battered navy windbreaker.

Harry warned Carey, who'd never been sailing before, "Duck when we come about or the boom will hit you. Ready about? . . . Lee-o."

The *Sea Witch* swung out on the opposite tack, sailing past Fort Denison, where convicts used to be imprisoned, and made for the Heads at the entrance to the harbor.

"Feel like taking over?" Harry offered. He knew that Duke would want to take the wheel, and preferred to let him handle the *Sea Witch* inside the harbor, where he couldn't do much harm. She was only carrying a mainsail and a number two jib, which shouldn't get him into any trouble.

"Only thing to watch out for is the Sow and Pigs, that reef in the middle of the harbor," Harry warned as Duke took the helm. Although it was clearly marked, people always forgot the Sow and Pigs. He added, "And watch out for the rock on the southeast side of the reef." Apart from that, there weren't any obstructions in this part of the harbor. When they reached the entrance, Harry would again take the wheel.

Annie knew why Harry had handed the wheel of his beloved boat to Duke with such alacrity.

Harry moved forward to take Duke's place beside Annie. He whispered, "You've been avoiding me."

The sun seemed to flicker red sparks from Annie's hair as she shook her head. Harry thought, I don't know what she's done to herself, but she looks just like she used to.

Of course I've been avoiding you, Annie thought. Harry never stopped putting the pressure on her, whenever they met. Thank heaven Duke had no idea. It was so unfair of Harry. After all, he'd only kissed her *once*, years ago. Most men would have forgotten that.

It had happened when Harry was working in Pittsburgh and spending the Christmas vacation with Annie's family at their ski chalet in the Alleghenies.

When they took him skiing, Harry turned out to be a natural. Annie still remembered that first day, when she had yelled at him to bend his knees more and lean out from the hill, and he had asked at what angle. When they all told him how good he was, Harry had just shrugged his shoulders and said that the gravitational situation was pretty similar to riding a motorcycle. He'd done a red run on his first day out and was doing blacks by the end of the week, after which, suddenly, all the girls in the resort had noticed this dazzling new skier. But Harry never returned their interest.

He and Annie had been skiing alone one day when, on their last run, it started to snow. Annie took a fall, and she heard the crunch of Harry's skis as he pulled up beside her. He held out his pole and pulled her up out of the snow. Then he leaned forward and gently kissed a snowflake from Annie's nose. They looked at each other without speaking, and Harry took her in his arms. Annie's mitts, still clutching the ski poles, were also clutching the back of his parka. Her knees seemed to give way, she lost her balance and they both fell in the snow, lying wrapped around each other.

Annie still couldn't understand how she could have felt such searing passion when she'd been wearing about three layers of underclothes, a woolen hat and a scarf that went up to her nose. She remembered hoping that her skis wouldn't come off, because there was no other way of getting down the mountain. And then she'd ceased to care whether or not she reached the bottom of the mountain.

They'd stopped, dazed, only when Harry's ski came off. Luckily, the leather strap around his ankle had held. They both realized that the light was nearly gone and they had to move. Annie had never skied so badly, or felt so exalted, as on that twilight run, racing down the quiet, white mountain behind Harry.

That night she hadn't been able to sleep. Crossly, in the middle of the night, her sister had complained, "Annie, will you quit bumping around for water and climb back into your bunk. Honestly, this is like sharing a cabin with a *bear*."

The next morning Annie had a temperature of 104 degrees and she spent the rest of the holiday in her bunk with influenza, feverishly worrying whether she could be in love with two men at the same time. Her mother stayed in the chalet until Annie recovered, and by the time she got back to Pittsburgh, Annie had missed twice (she'd hoped that the skiing would fix it), and had no choice as to which man she loved. Her eldest son was on his way.

Water hissed softly against the hull of the *Sea Witch*. Annie's hair blew in the harbor breeze as she sneaked a sideways look at Harry. He wasn't a man you'd notice in a crowd, he wasn't obviously attractive. Below that knobbly broken nose was a wide mouth that lifted to the left; his high cheekbones and sunken cheeks had made Annie's mother want to fatten him up. Harry wasn't bold or thrilling, Harry had no wild romantic gestures, but he was thoughtful, kind and caring—a really nice guy. If he hadn't been so persistent in his ridiculous obsession, Annie would probably have forgotten him long ago, or so she always told herself. She wanted to forget how she'd felt when, a few years ago, one Easter, Duke had unexpectedly brought Harry home to visit and Annie's heart had turned over. Her whole body had trembled, as it had so long ago on that snowy mountainside. Annie had been horrified by this physical treachery. *Nothing* was going to upset her marriage, she told herself. So she had taken Harry aside, walking him to the end of the garden, ostensibly to show him the new Cunningham Whites that she'd planted in the shrubbery, but really to tell him he ought to stop this nonsense. Harry was a dynamic, international businessman and should forget this teenage stuff.

Harry had nodded. "You're right, Annie," he said. "For years I've been telling myself all that you've just said. Believe me, I've tried everything I can do, but it won't go away. I'm stuck with the way I feel about you. It seems to be a part of me, whether I see you or not."

"But that's ridiculous!"

"Don't tell *me*."

"You're wasting your time, Harry. Nothing can ever come of it."

Harry had given her an odd look and said, "I've told myself that for years. And I've never said a word against Duke to you. But I would *care* for you, Annie. And your boys are nearly grown." He had then taken a step toward her, and she'd fled back to the house.

Waves slapped against the hull of the *Sea Witch*. To Annie's left rose Sydney's skyscrapers, a dramatic background to the yachts tacking across the sheet of blue water. The harbor was so large that you couldn't see the end of it, or grasp the shape of it. Harry was sitting close enough to Annie to touch her, and she was conscious of his shoulder, his arm and his lean thigh against hers. She moved away slightly but so did Harry. Annie quickly looked toward the bow. But no one was watching; Carey and Ed were gazing at the undulating foothills and creeks of North Sydney.

"You've been avoiding me," Harry repeated softly.

"If you don't stop," Annie whispered crossly, "I'm going to tell Duke."

"There's nothing to tell," whispered Harry. "That's my complaint."

The *Sea Witch* came about and headed toward the harbor entrance.

"Do you think you'd like to live here, Annie?" Harry asked.

Annie jumped at the seemingly innocent question, thinking, *Please,* Harry, don't start this again. Her feelings hadn't changed since Harry had first brought this up, years ago. Annie was a happily married woman, with a family that she loved dearly, and she couldn't help it if she was the first and only girl that Harry Scott had ever fallen for. She refused to be held responsible for Harry's embarrassing devotion. Of course she was fond of Harry—he'd been a part of her girlhood—but she didn't want him to upset her, or worse, upset Duke. Duke always had a lot of work at these conferences, and he needed a few days' rest afterward, before returning to the rigors of his job and the Pittsburgh winter.

"Can't I see you alone, Annie?"

"No. You know I *always* say no, and I *always will!* Now if you don't stop this nonsense, I'll go up and sit with Ed and Carey. You're spoiling what's been a wonderful week."

"What's been so wonderful about it?" He took off his windbreaker, and wasn't wearing a shirt. He was still as lean as ever, she couldn't help noticing.

"I hadn't expected Australia to be so glamorous," Annie said. "It's like California, but more vigorous and friendly. The people we've met here have such a zest for living."

"Where have you been?" His knee was touching hers, so again she moved slightly.

"We spent Monday morning at the surfing beaches north of Sydney." Annie remembered the Pacific thundering against cliffs carved by the sea. "Then we went on to the Hawkesbury River." She remembered that beautiful area of tranquil inlets and rugged bushland, quiet except for the birds. "We visited an old town that's just as it was a hundred years ago. You could see what the life of the river must have been like as the new country got going." She could feel Harry's bare arm against hers, and again she edged sideways; at this rate, she'd soon be overboard.

Annie saw Duke beaming at her from the wheel. It was so *unfair* that she should feel guilty, when she'd done *nothing*.

"Stop touching me, Harry, and behave yourself," she whispered. Couldn't he see that she was exasperated, and anxious that he shouldn't make trouble for her? Annie's whisper was almost inaudible but determined. "If you don't get away from me, Harry, I'm going to jump off this boat, and you can explain *that* to Duke."

Harry grinned. "Sharks in the harbor." He couldn't understand why it excited him to play this little game, to see Annie react to his slightest movement. Just to check that she really did, he stretched his lean, brown arm along the gunwale behind her back.

Annie jumped.

Harry smiled.

Duke called out, "What are you two whispering about?" He grinned at them, a captain-at-the-tiller, the-outdoors-man-in-control sort of grin.

Harry called back, "Annie's just telling me what she's been up to all week."

Harry was so close that she could smell his body.

Then Annie looked at him with consternation. Something had just happened inside her head. The boat, the harbor, the sky, everything had become part of a new, disastrous reality —disastrous because Annie didn't want it, and she couldn't control it. This new sensation was stupid, it was impossible, but it was *real*, and it was swamping her senses. There had been some sort of invisible explosion inside her body, and it was physically apparent. She was hot and trembling. Surprised and shocked, Annie recognized her rising heat as passion.

More than anything else in the world, Annie wanted to touch those fine gold hairs on Harry's brown forearm.

This was terrible! Annie's mind whirred around, trying to escape from this frightening new situation. She whispered, "Harry, this has *got to stop!*"

From the bow, Carey casually turned her head back toward

Annie. "Didn't you like the Blue Mountains, Annie? That was *my* favorite trip of the week."

On Friday, the Nexus wives had been helicoptered to the huge national park west of Sydney; the spectacular hazy blue mountain ranges covered with rain forests had made Carey feel an awe which she had only previously felt when she climbed down the Grand Canyon. It was a hushed, solemn feeling, as if you were in a soaring cathedral, as if you were in the presence of God.

Harry again edged toward Annie. This time she didn't move away as she felt the hard warmth of Harry's thigh. She longed to hurl herself into his arms, as she felt a warm, strange sensation, which she hadn't felt for years. It was like remembering something wonderful that had happened long ago, or like inhaling a long-forgotten perfume.

To Annie's horror she suddenly found herself imagining, in great detail, what it would be like to go to bed with Harry. Wildly, she jerked her head around to look at Duke, then jerked it back again, as though he could read her thoughts. She thought, Thank God for the privacy of your head.

Carey said, "But I couldn't stand the Jenolan caves—they were really eerie." The black, echoing caves had been illuminated, but they were so vast that you couldn't see the black backs or the tops of the intricate, lacelike limestone formations. Notorious bushrangers used to hide in them; Carey couldn't understand how anyone could stay long in those caves, she'd felt instant claustrophobia. She'd started to sweat and tremble violently as she thought of the oppressive weight of the thousands of tons of earth and rock above her. Carey had never been able to stand caves.

Annie took no notice. She could feel the length of Harry's lean body hard against her, gently persistent.

With joy and wonderment and thrilling horror, Annie realized she was in love with Harry.

No! This was not love, this was lust. She mustn't prettify it. It was sordid, this sudden obsessive desire—this feeling of being driven beyond control, heedless of logic and safety.

Within seconds, in her head, Annie had been seduced by Harry, confessed to Duke, destroyed her husband's manly pride in himself and his confidence in her. Now things would never be the same again between them. She had wrecked her happy family and her marriage, and was on the verge of suicide, another mortal sin.

Harry said, "Would you like a drink?"

"*No!*"

Harry was surprised by Annie's vehemence.

She couldn't risk being with Harry for another week, Annie thought. Duke would be bound to notice. She couldn't understand why she always felt, after these occasions, that somehow she'd been leading Harry on, enjoying her power over him.

Annie turned to look into Harry's gray eyes. He looked amused. She said, "Harry, would you do something for me?"

"Sure. Anything. What?"

"Do you *have* to come to Paui?"

"Of course."

For the past six months he'd looked forward to being with Annie for six whole days. He said, "The Paui trip is my responsibility, it's on my territory. Please don't ask me not to come."

"Harry, if you really do feel . . . the way you say you do about me . . . *please* don't come! You'll be able to think of some excuse. *Please.*"

Harry, a professional bargainer, quickly calculated how many hours he might see Annie next week. He remembered the frustrations of never seeing her alone, never being able to touch her, unless he cornered her, as he had today.

"*If* I don't come to Paui," he said finally, "will you come skiing with me—alone—for a *whole* day, next time I get to Pittsburgh?" If so, it would be the best chance he'd ever get to try to persuade her. That corn-fed tub of lard she'd married didn't ski.

Annie hesitated, then said, "Okay, it's a deal." Anything.

Carey turned her head toward them again. "It sure is hot. Got anything to drink, Harry?"

"Fosters or Coke?"

Everybody chose soft drinks, and Harry went below to fetch them from the cabin.

Still in his Hemingway-at-the-helm mood, Duke was tacking toward South Head when he caught sight of Lady Jane, the famous nude beach.

Duke-the-macho-sailor altered course and cut across the harbor to get a better look at the girls. A group of glistening golden bodies were playing volleyball like a *Playboy* photograph come to life.

Suddenly there was a tearing, scraping noise, as if the bottom of the boat was being torn off, and everyone was thrown across the deck.

Harry flung down the drinks and scrambled onto the outboard end of the boom. As he swung from it, he yelled, "Duke, let go the mainsheet! Everyone else move over here and sit over the side, putting your weight outboard."

Harry's weight threw the boom outboard, toward the reef. The added weight of the entire party helped to tip the boat over at an even greater angle, which lifted the keel away from the reef.

The boat shuddered.

Slowly, very slowly, the current carried them off the reef.

Harry said, "Maybe I'd better take over."

Arthur, his bathrobe still limp from the sauna, turned the key in the door of his suite. It had been a successful week and he was looking forward to . . . He stopped abruptly.

A man—quite small, black and very thin—was lying comfortably on one of the beige leather couches, his crossed feet resting on the central marble table. His shoes were pale ostrichskin; the shoelaces were made of gold thread and studded at every inch with a two-karat blue-white diamond.

Arthur barked, "What the hell are you doing here? Who let you in?" He grabbed the telephone to call Security, but the man on the sofa didn't seem perturbed. He slithered to his feet and extended a thin, black hand.

"I flew from Port Moresby only to see *you,* Mr. Graham," the stranger said. "General Raki, of the Paui Nationalist Army." He spoke English with the American twang of the Philippines, rather than with the guttural accent of Paui.

"Ah." Arthur ignored the hand, but replaced the receiver. "Good afternoon, General. Perhaps you would be good enough to telephone the Nexus office on Monday morning. I believe you deal with Harry Scott."

"That is exactly what I wish to discuss, Mr. Graham." The whites of his eyes were faintly yellow. "I want to speak to you alone, on a personal level, because I have received no payments via Mr. Scott since July of last year. This is contrary to our agreement."

"Nexus only deals with the government in power, General Raki."

"That was not mentioned in our agreement, Mr. Graham. The Nexus agreement was that my payments should be made regularly, so long as there was no holdup in production at the mine."

"General, I'm sorry, I can't discuss these matters." There *had* been a holdup at the mine, but if Arthur pointed that out, then he would start another argument. "I'll show you the way to the elevator, General."

"You *are* aware, then, that this money is being withheld from me."

The little bastard was implying that Harry might have kept Raki's payments for himself. Grimly, Arthur opened the door to the hallway.

"I had expected a more friendly welcome, Mr. Graham."

"I can't think how you got in here."

"As you should know, Mr. Graham, money unlocks all doors. I came because I wanted to find out whether you, personally, knew that my payments had been stopped."

Arthur gave a brief nod. He wanted the General out of his suite as fast as possible. He wouldn't want this encounter to be reported as a secret meeting, jeopardizing the Nexus deal with the new government of Paui.

The General stood up and flexed his fingers. "In that case, I have no news for you. I hear that next week you start talks with the President of Paui. I'm sure you'll get a wonderful welcome. No doubt they will pull out all the stops. Fireworks and so forth." His eyes—cold and brutal—contradicted the friendly words. He bowed politely. His body seemed boneless as he sauntered down the hallway. Arthur slammed the door.

94

day of tea for coffee, a tray for coffee, a bowl of fruit and a jar of cookies. Everything was checked twice daily and replenished if necessary. There were fresh orchids in the bathroom and in pots on the terrace. Every evening the beds were turned down and the little, pale blue pillows scattered with purple frangipani. The chambermaids moved with calm dignity and grace; they walked like queens, for they were sturdy, but their facial features finely molded. Each woman tucked a flower behind one ear, which had to be removed before returning home at night to their village, for only the village chief was allowed to wear flowers on his hair.

Upon their arrival, Carey had looked around at the suite, flopped into and the children screamed, "Where's the pool, Mummy?"

SUNDAY, NOVEMBER 11, 1984

How pleasant it would be not to have to go to work tomorrow on a Monday morning, thought Carey. Yesterday, when they had landed on Paui, she'd been immediately enticed by the drowsy languor, the indifference to time. She was lying on a wicker chaise longue in her private flower-scented patio and enjoying the early morning sun. The only sound was the soft splash of the waves on the sandy beach.

The guest villas at the Paradise Bay Hotel were thatched, so that the exteriors resembled a tribal chief's hut. The huts were carefully spaced at the back of the beach; privacy was provided by hedges of pink, vanilla-scented oleander, and each hut had its own patio.

Virtually a self-contained house, each hut had two bathrooms, a makeup area, a dressing room and a kitchen leading off the huge main room, but the color scheme was different in each apartment. Carey's walls were cream and the pitched wooden ceiling had dark beams; the dark, tiled floor was covered by a huge pale blue rug, which matched the covers on the two double beds. There was lots of rattan furniture, and the walls were hung with native ceremonial cloths, woven in geometric abstracts of chestnut and black.

On each bedside table stood a balloon glass and a small bottle of brandy, and in the kitchen was a fully stocked bar, a tray of tea things, a tray for coffee, a bowl of fruit and a jar of cookies. Everything was checked twice daily and replenished if necessary. There were fresh orchids in the bathroom and in pots on the terrace. Every evening the beds were turned down and the huge, pale blue pillows scattered with purple frangipani. The chambermaids moved with calm dignity and grace, they walked like queens; their bodies were stocky, but their facial features finely molded. Each woman tucked a flower behind one ear, which had to be removed before returning home at night to their village, for only the village chief was allowed to wear flowers in his hair.

Upon their arrival Carey had looked around at the palm-fringed bay and the blue sky beyond, then cried, "This really is Paradise!"

She had entered her blue-tiled bathroom and turned on the cold-water faucet. It came off in her hand. She screwed it back and turned it again, but could get no water. Carey tried the hot-water faucet. After a few moments a resentful trickle of cold water fell into the tub.

Okay, she'd settle for a shower.

Carey turned the temperature-control dial to cold and was rewarded with a jet of scalding water. She screamed and jumped out of the stall.

Ed appeared in the doorway, looking startled, until he saw that Carey was unharmed.

"Yours too?" He grinned. "Don't try to use the bidet."

That useful French contribution to civilization had been installed parallel to the bathroom wall, so that only a one-legged woman could sit on it. Ed had said, "I suppose you can't expect them to rocket from the Stone Age to the bidet overnight."

Now, Ed lazed on the patio in the early morning sun while Carey read aloud to him from a tourist leaflet.

"'North of Australia, in the Arafura Sea, the island of Paui nestles into the coastline of Irian Jaya. At its southernmost tip, Paui is only seventy-two miles distant from Pulau yos Sudarsa. Covering approximately fourteen thousand square miles, the island is two hundred fourteen miles long and seventy-four miles wide. The population is estimated to number fifty-one thousand two hundred people.'"

"Accurate but not riveting," Ed murmured.

"'Largely tropical, the temperature is rarely above eighty-five degrees during the day and seventy-three at night. The wet season is from early December to early March.' We'll just miss it," Carey said. "'Much of Paui is mountainous; a great deal of the island is covered by sandalwood forest. The volcanic Central Mountains dominate the west coast, the Victoria Highlands lie to the east, while the mountains of Stanley Heights almost cover the southern tip of Paui, which consists mainly of high cliffs and virgin forest, and is sparsely populated by fisherfolk. There is some pearl diving. Queenstown, the capital city, is situated on the northeast coast at the mouth of the St. Mary River. Queenstown is the main port and the seat of government.'"

Ed yawned. "Honey, I know all this stuff. I've lost count of the number of times I've visited this island."

Traveling was a part of Ed's job, and a part of his ambition. He aimed to be the best-known man in the Nexus worldwide empire. Right after he'd qualified, Ed had started working with a survey team in northern Ontario; he still remembered his bursting pride when he'd been made head of that team. Euphorically, he'd repeatedly bought drinks all around, until one of the older geologists had grunted over his fourth whiskey, "Team manager's no big deal. Quit acting as if you were head of the goddamn survey section."

Ed had looked at the man, and in that moment, Ed's ambition was sparked. Years later, when Ed was made head of Survey, he'd invited that guy around to his impressive office for a fifth whiskey.

But Ed's ambition wasn't satisfied then, nor was it when he became responsible not only for Survey but also for Mapping, Research and Sample Analysis, or when he had finally been made Vice President Exploration and Expansion. Ed had always avoided thinking seriously about the urge that drove him on. At first, it had seemed the natural exercise of his competitive streak, then it had developed into a quiet hunger to get things done, then a positive greed, and now Ed's driving force was a carefully hidden lust for power.

Carey had stopped reading to watch a finch dive onto the breakfast tray debris and carry off a crumb. She settled back on her chaise longue and again lifted the guidebook. "'The island is known for its many unique species of butterflies and beautiful birds; there are more than thirty species of birds of paradise.'" She broke off. "Hey, Ed, stay awake, I'm getting to your bit . . . 'Twenty-seven miles north of Queenstown, copper is mined at Mount Ida together with some manganese.'" She stretched for her glass of orange juice. "Hey, Ed, is *this* true? It says that there are no roads suitable for automobiles! 'Air transport is widely used but is expensive, because of the unpredictable weather, the rugged mountains and the rough landing strips.' Why does that make it expensive, Ed?"

"Because it's damned dangerous to be a pilot around here. One of the Nexus planes crashed only last week, but it's not so much a problem for the little Bell helicopter."

Carey continued to read. "'The inhabitants of the island number at least seventeen different tribes, each with its own distinct language as opposed to dialect. Melanesian Pidgin is the lingua franca.'"

Ed yawned. "Pidgin can be picturesque. They call a helicopter 'mixmaster belong Jesus Christ,' and any unfit person or machine is a 'buggerupem.'"

Carey smiled at him then read again. "'Ownership is in kinship groups, as opposed to individuals. Village leaders are elected on the basis of achievement, wealth and the provision of lavish feasts; they can only keep their status by continuing to produce food and gifts for their clan . . .'"

"You stop giving, they kick you off the throne."

"'. . . and personally leading their men into battle. Outside Queenstown, the Australian Catholic missionaries are still in charge of the only available education.' Hey, listen to *this*, Ed! To hunt, the islanders still use a bow and arrow, an ax or a club. Wow! It's a pity we've come here to fish, not hunt. I'd love to see Arthur heaving a club."

"Quit that."

Carey continued. "'Local currency is the *kina* . . . '"

Ed yawned, "*Kina* means 'shell.' They used to trade in shells, then they used coins, and now they use paper, like everyone else."

"'. . . Or else wealth is reckoned in pigs.' *Pigs*, Ed?"

"Sure. Pigs and wives—to work—are signs of wealth. Meat is scarce and only the men are allowed to eat it. They kill the pigs at the end of November. It's a very important village festival."

"Let's hope we miss it." Carey continued to read. "'Relics from the Second World War are still seen in beaches and in forests along the coast.' What sort of relics, Ed?"

"Rusty pieces of trucks, landing craft, lots of submerged airplanes—anything the natives couldn't unbolt. There are also a great many plane wrecks in the jungle. Only the skeletons are left, of course."

Carey shivered. "'In 1947, when the islands of the South Pacific area assumed independent status, Paui became part of the Independent Federation of Islands in the Territory and was administered by Australia until 1975, when it was declared independent, under the protection of the United Nations. The Australian administration brought the vicious intertribal wars under control.' Why did they have vicious tribal wars, Ed?"

"Because if a man from tribe A gets drunk and insults a man from tribe B, then the whole of tribe B is automatically pledged to avenge Mr. B. Naturally, Mr. A is supported by the whole of tribe A, so you only have to call a man a *soppo*—that means a bastard—and you have a small tribal war on your hands. Retribution is called 'the Payback,' and it's always savage." Ed sat up and stretched. "Unfortunately, the fighting started up again as soon as the Aussies left, and there was also a lot of looting in Queenstown. Feel like another swim?"

"Am I boring you, then?"

"Yes."
"*Soppo.*"

Patty didn't want to go on the helicopter sightseeing tour. In a daisy-patterned sundress, she stood looking at the beguiling, twelve-foot-high pink frangipani bushes that surrounded the big outdoor swimming pool. A few people were already splashing around and a scraggy Englishman on a floating mattress had already ordered his first *mai-tai* from the pool bar.

Patty wanted to stay *here*, she didn't want to go on a smelly, noisy trip in a helicopter. She'd like to go for another run up that white deserted beach before it got too hot, then maybe swim to that small island about a mile out. She'd swum there yesterday evening, before dinner. There had been nothing to see except unkempt undergrowth. It was very different from Paradise Bay, which didn't have a leaf out of place, she'd thought as she swam back toward the low line of thatched huts that stretched along the shoreline on either side of the main hotel building.

After last night's swim she'd gone for a run along the deserted beach while everyone else was dressing for dinner, then she'd jogged around the perimeter of the hotel grounds. Beyond the six-foot-high wire fence, the boundary lights already had been switched on; they illuminated a rough-cleared strip of ground, beyond which writhed the sinister blackness of the jungle, alive at night with the noise of insects and the sharp calls of unknown creatures.

Patty had shivered as she jogged back to her hut, not because it was cold—it was still hot and humid—but because she had noticed that the clever lighting around the grounds of the hotel not only spotlit the beauty of the gardens but also guaranteed that no one could steal through the grounds unnoticed. Somebody had obviously paid a great deal of attention to security.

Patty turned her back to the now sunlit garden and said, "I don't think I'll come on the sightseeing trip, Charley, if you don't mind."

Charley took off his sunglasses; his eyes looked anxious. "Are you feeling all right? You don't think you're coming down with the same trouble as Harry?"

"Harry's trouble was a bad oyster at dinner. It hardly ever happens, and you can't tell at the time, although you sure know all about it afterward. If I'd had a bad oyster, I'd have been doubled up in bed yesterday morning, like Harry." She hitched up the strap of her dress. "Nothing's wrong. But we've only just arrived, and I'd like to have a quiet laze around the beach, unless you really want me along."

"You do whatever you want. I want you to get a real rest on this trip."

Patty said softly, "There's something spooky about this place . . . Don't laugh at me, Charley. I *know*, I can feel it. It's something to do with the hotel staff." She frowned in thought. "I sense resentment behind those smiles. It reminds me of that trip we took to Fiji, where everyone said how charming and helpful the natives were and they burned down the hotel the day after we left. Just because you've built a luxury hotel in a place doesn't change that place, Charley."

Through ten years of marriage, Charley had learned to respect Patty's intuition. He said, "The average income on this island is under two hundred U.S. dollars a year, and a whole family lives on that. I can see that an islander might feel resentful if he serves a breakfast that cost seven dollars to some white tourist who doesn't bother to finish it. Maybe that's what your antennae are picking up."

Patty said, "Maybe they don't really like tourists. Maybe the islanders feel that it's humiliating to be forced to sell their hospitality for foreign currency, be looked upon as a human zoo by teeming crowds of pink-faced people who say, 'Aren't the natives friendly?' Maybe tourism *doesn't* promote international goodwill, but international resentment. Maybe it only *adds* to racial prejudice, and makes them hate our guts."

"Honey, you're on vacation. Don't *make* problems." Charley put his arms around Patty and kissed the top of her smooth blond hair.

101

Her head against the safety of his chest, Patty persisted. "You're sure it's safe here, Charley? Have you seen the fence? We're in a luxury concentration camp. Why?"

Charley murmured into her hair, "Back home in the U.S. someone is murdered every twenty-three minutes, a woman is raped every six minutes and something is stolen every four seconds. I don't know where 'safe' is, but I expect you're as safe as you can get, right where you are." Again he kissed her silk-soft hair, then checked his watch. No, he was due at the helipad in seven minutes.

There was a sharp rap at the door.

The man standing outside wore white shorts and a white shirt, dappled by the early sun that shone through the trees. He was thin, blond and bronzed, with a pink, peeling nose. He looked beyond Charley to Patty and said, in a strong Australian accent, "Beg pardon, but are *you* the lady who did the fast swim to the island yesterday evening?" His eyes were aquamarine, with sandy lashes under sandy brows.

"Yes, that was me." Patty looked pleased.

"Well, you were bloody lucky to get there, and even luckier to get back. We'll be shark fishing in that water tomorrow. Please understand that there'll be no swimming from *my* vessel." He nodded curtly. "Good morning," he said, and turned around and disappeared into the trees.

After the helicopter trip, Isabel and Roddy had arranged to play tennis with Patty and Charley. Isabel swung her racket as she strolled toward the tennis courts in the late afternoon sun. The green lawns were bordered with fifteen-foot-high, mauve and white flowered shrubs.

Isabel had enjoyed the flight. The island looked beautiful from the air, particularly as they followed the coast, skimming over the thick aquamarine band of water around green jungle. From above, the jungle looked impenetrable. The pilot explained that faults and folds in the limestone meant abrupt plunges in the terrain—sometimes from as much as six thousand feet to sea level—which was one of the reasons the island was so difficult to traverse by land. Mountains on the side of a ravine were called razorbacks—apparently, you could stand on one razorback and throw your pack to the next one, but then take a whole day to walk down and up the other side. During the cyclone season the whole side of a hill might be torn away, while sudden swollen river torrents roared down the narrow gorges. The Nexus party would, of course, be gone before the Long Wet, which didn't start until December 1. You could almost set your watch by the start and finish of the cyclone season, it was the only predictable thing about Paui, the pilot said.

For once, the annual trip was really interesting, thought Isabel, as she waved her tennis racket in greeting to Patty and Charley, who were waiting at the court, immaculate in white. Isabel wished that Roddy hadn't worn cutoffs and a T-shirt. Isabel figured that Charley would be the next president. In many ways Charley resembled Arthur—the entire Board was cool, fast and tough—but Charley had the killer instinct. Isabel had seen it time and again.

Isabel's train of thought was distracted by Billy, the hotel's pet goat, who appeared from behind a palm tree and tottered forward on slim, trembling legs, a little silver bell tinkling from his leather collar. As Isabel stopped to stroke the white, silky head she felt the bony cranium beneath the soft skin and touched the delicate silky ears. The kid nuzzled at her hand, licking it hopefully, with abrupt movements. It was hard to believe that this charming little creature was going to grow into an aggressive animal that would devour anything it came across.

Isabel said, "I wonder what they'll do with Billy when he gets big enough to be a nuisance?"

"Goat stew," Roddy said.

How pleasant it was to stroll instead of hurry, Isabel thought, to have nothing to do but enjoy the beautiful beach or the pool, which was what most of her friends imagined Isabel did when she traveled abroad.

In fact, Isabel's foreign travel was generally about as exciting as catching a bus to work. Basically, her job was to locate the need for future Nexus acquisitions, find them and arrange for their purchase. In the course of doing this, Isabel moved around the world a great deal. The travel was both tiring and demanding, and it exasperated Isabel that every time she went abroad everyone behaved as if she were going on a vacation.

Isabel prepared for her trips by reading reports on individual companies and talking with bankers and executives to pinpoint their acquisition needs. After they had identified a target and formulated a strategy, Isabel would travel to the country in which the target business was located, then start negotiating. She always took her own lawyer, and also hired an English-speaking local lawyer. She often worked with Ed, especially in countries where they wouldn't negotiate with a woman, of which Paui was a perfect example. Of course, all that would change in time, and, at thirty-seven, Isabel still had a lot of time—at least another thirteen years before she made her play for the top job.

Roddy always felt particularly affectionate when he and Isabel were about to play tennis. He'd fallen in love with her the first time they'd played together, when they were still in college. He'd seen those big blue eyes and that determined little frown across the net and he kept giving her shots that she *just* might get . . . if she really ran for them. Roddy played well but he played for fun. He didn't have the instinct to go for the jugular, and he didn't want it.

In spite of all Charley's private lessons, Roddy and Isabel won the tennis game. Afterward, looking at Charley's sweating, grim face, Isabel remembered that this was the man upon whom her future promotion would probably depend. Maybe she should have lost the game; Roddy realized what Isabel was thinking, he recognized the calculating little frown.

As they stripped to shower, Roddy yelled, "You want Charley to want you on his side, Isabel, but remember he's only going to pick winners, not losers, for his team."

He turned the shower dial to Cold and stepped beneath the

spray, then angrily leaped away from the scalding jets of water. "*What* are they trying to do, kill us?" he shouted.

Crash!

Suzy sat up abruptly. "Brett?" It was still dark.

Brett called from the bathroom, "It's okay, honey. Sorry if I woke you. I was looking for a replacement asthma spray and I knocked a bottle off the bathroom shelf."

Brett threw the empty spray can toward the wastepaper basket, but it missed the basket and clattered over the floor. Later, the chambermaid retrieved it and put it neatly with the other toilet accessories beside the washbasin.

Suzy snuggled down but couldn't get to sleep again. Brett was so weird about that spray. He hated to admit a weakness and tried not to mention his asthma, because it didn't fit the correct Nexus macho image. Everyone knew about it, but they pretended not to, because Brett was so sensitive on the subject. He hadn't even told Suzy about it until after they were married. He'd had virus pneumonia seven years earlier and bronchial asthma was the result. The first time Suzy had seen him having an attack, she'd been terrified by Brett's white face and blue lips, by the gasping and wheezing sounds that came from his mouth, until he inhaled from the spray. Brett had an asthma attack if he got overanxious or if he caught a cold. The doctor had explained that it was due to a spasm of the bronchial tubes, which worsened if the tubes were further blocked by mucus. Apparently, before asthma had been diagnosed, a cold could knock Brett out of action for as long as three months.

As Brett tiptoed toward the door, Suzy said sleepily, "You must be crazy to get up this early on vacation. I can't understand what you see in fishing."

"It's exciting," Brett said, apologetically, but Suzy had drifted back to sleep.

In the faint pearl glow of dawn, Brett could just see the path to the beach, still spotlit at ground level. Although he was wearing a windbreaker, he shivered as he hurried toward the sound of the sea. He wished he could explain to Suzy what fascinated him about fishing. The thrill of hooking a big fish is the thought that only a rod and a fine line join you to it. Through the rod, you can feel every move the fish makes—in fact you can predict the next move from the last one. When the fish starts to fight, you know it has total confidence in its strength. After a while, when it realizes it can't shake you off, you can feel its self-confidence has been shaken, you can sense it ebbing, you can feel fear in the movements of the fish, so far below.

Then the fish panics. When the fish has exhausted itself, the battle turns in the favor of the fisherman. By then, the fisherman's whole body might be aching; his back muscles, thigh muscles, arms and hands—all might have been put under pressure by that big fish, perhaps for several hours. Fighting a fish can be as physically exhausting as wrestling.

Once you feel the fish start to crack, you reel in your line as often as possible, pulling it toward you—maybe only an inch at a time—but as the inches grow into yards, you're pulling it closer. And the closer the fish comes to you, the closer it is to death.

Brett could now see shadowy figures waiting at the jetty, a rough wooden platform that stretched twenty feet out to sea from the middle of the beach.

Brett hurried past the wooden structure where big fish were hung to be photographed with the proud fishermen who had just caught them. He nearly tripped over the leg of the blackboard, on which was chalked the weight of the catch. Beyond it, the white fishing boat looked gray in the half-light.

A muscular arm steadied Brett as he jumped into the thirty-eight-foot Commander Sport Sedan.

The skipper said, "Glad you're not late. Life jackets are in the cabin. So's the coffee. Don't know if they've left any for you." He spoke with an Australian twang and slurred some of his words, pronouncing "you" and "your" as "yer," "late" as "lite" and "don't know" as "dunno."

The crowded cabin smelled of fish and diesel oil, while the

heads, opposite the tiny gallery, stank of urine. Carey poured the last of the hot coffee from a thermos into a plastic cup. "Brett, I hope this doesn't taste as bad as it smells. Sugar?"

Brett shook his head to the proffered screw-top jar, sat on one of the blue bunks and nodded hello to Arthur, Ed and Charley. The engine started and the hull began to vibrate.

Slowly the boat left the jetty behind and moved toward the open sea. Behind him, Brett could see the island coming awake, in smudged, irregular bands of gray, like a Chinese watercolor. A sleepy security guard dragged himself across the empty beach. The dark smudges of the hotel buildings hardly showed against the burnt-sienna strip of palm trees behind them. As the background mountains shrank in the distance, the grays grew lighter, until the darkly wooded peaks were almost the same pale gray as the sky above them.

Sipping his coffee, which tasted of tacks, Brett looked around the cabin. In the bow was a pile of equipment: fishing tackle, bait box, a battered toolbox, a couple of buckets, a neatly rolled sheet of plastic, a box of old sneakers in assorted sizes and what looked like a pile of mosquito netting. It was the usual fishing boat equipment, which always looked like a heap of junk to anyone who wasn't fishing.

A head appeared upside down in the cabin entrance; the skipper asked, "Everyone comfortable?"

Everybody nodded. Charley had recognized the aquamarine eyes, toffee-colored hair and sandy eyebrows ("There'll be no swimming from *my* vessel"). Not a lady's man. A maverick, who was old enough to have knocked about a bit, the kind of guy who doesn't stay in any job or place for long, because he gets bored and moves on when *he* decides it's time to go. Charley recognized the type.

The skipper said, "My mate's had to get back to Darwin— his mother's poorly. But I reckon we can manage with just the fisherboy. He's a sharp lad."

From the deck, the skipper climbed up to the wheelhouse, sat beneath the canvas awning and pushed the throttle forward. They'd be quiet below for a bit, they weren't really awake.

He headed out to sea, listening to the comfortable smack of water against the bow, feeling the soothing rhythm of the diesel.

The sky was golden and the water was no longer oily black but gray. The skipper looked down at the stick-thin native boy on deck, who wore only a tattered pair of khaki shorts. He shouted, "Winston, wipe the chairs and get the rods ready, lad."

With fluid movements, the boy reached for a cloth, wiped the dew from the blue plastic seats of the deck benches, then swabbed the three white, fiberglass, swivel fishing chairs in the stern. They were fixed to the deck, the central chair further astern than the others. Whistling, the boy set out seven fiberglass fishing rods, each about eight feet long. He satisfied himself that rods, reels and lines were in order, then turned his attention to the tackle box and selected traces, swivels, clips and hooks. He fitted four rods into their sockets, on either side of the hull, then got to work on the mackerel baits. When all the rods were baited, the boy called, "Skipper is okay."

"Come up here and take the wheel."

The boy scrambled up the short ladder to the canvas flying bridge and proudly sat on the high stool at the wheel, which needed almost no attention. The skipper checked the lines and let out the three at the stern; he watched the baits plane and jump in the wake of the boat, then disappear as the lines ran out. The skipper moved forward to the cabin and stuck his head through the door.

"We're three miles out and it's fine fishin' weather."

To protect them from the sun, they all wore cotton trousers, long-sleeved shirts and floppy hats. Arthur moved to the central chair and waved Ed and Charley to the ones on either side of him; Brett and Carey sat on the benches. They all grinned at each other. They were fishing.

Carey tested the grip of her rod; it was covered with cork, so that it couldn't slip in a wet or sweaty hand. The heavy rod had enough give to play the fish but was stiff enough to stand up to the water drag without bending, and to firmly embed the hook into the flesh of whatever was thrashing far below, trying to shake off that agonizing hook. A properly balanced rod should not break when bent at an angle under 70 degrees; the flexible rod acts as a shock absorber when the fish makes a sudden desperate plunge to rid itself of the line which is inexorably controlling it. Carey's reel carried six hundred yards of non-stretch braided nylon line; it was a simple, center-pin reel, the revolving spool fitted with a braking gear to stop it from spinning too fast if it had a heavy fish on it—any amateur fisherman could use it without trouble.

Ed felt a strike almost immediately. His reel screeched briefly, until he tightened the brake. As the boat stopped, the other fishermen reeled in their lines, to prevent theirs from tangling with Ed's or with whatever he had hooked. Everyone longingly watched as Ed carefully pulled the fish nearer the boat. It fought hard but came up quickly, and was obviously not a big one.

Minutes later the boatboy gaffed a medium-size tuna, and flung it, blue-green and thrashing, onto the deck behind them.

"'Bout fourteen pounds. Better luck next time," muttered the skipper. "Something bigger. A real fish." He meant shark. Every tourist wanted to land a shark, especially the Germans. They'd rather catch a small shark than a big barracuda. If the shark was longer than the fellow that caught it, and the skipper had his camera ready when they got back to the weigh-in at the jetty, then the skipper always got a really good tip.

Ed stood up and offered his chair to Carey. After you had a catch, you always gave your seat to someone who was waiting. This point of fishing etiquette was broken only by Arthur, who always stayed in the central chair whenever the fish were running well.

Nothing happened for the next half-hour. Then they ran into a school of tuna. Two hours later, when everyone paused for breath, fourteen more fish were gasping and flapping on deck.

The skipper looked at the gleaming scales, at the staring,

black, pop eyes as each newly caught fish seemed to gather its strength for one last mighty effort to leap into the air, then subside, quivering, on the slippery dying fish beneath. He said, "I reckon you got near two hundred pounds there. Ain't caught so much so fast before, in these waters."

It was now half past eight and the sun was hot, but there was no humidity at sea, and a slight breeze was blowing under the canvas awning. Limp cheese sandwiches were handed around for breakfast by Winston, who, Carey had discovered, was twelve years old.

There was hardly any swell; the slight rocking, the heat and the steady rhythmic throb of the engine combined to make Carey feel drowsy. She enjoyed thinking that it was overcoat weather in Pittsburgh.

For the next two hours they all sat, waiting hopefully. By midday, the hull had long been too hot to touch and the skipper had distributed calamine lotion for noses; they all wore dark glasses and brimmed sun hats, but your face could burn from the reflection of the sun on the water, and the nose was especially susceptible.

Carey asked the boatboy to draw up a bucket of seawater to throw over her, to cool her, but he shook his head and grinned. Once seawater dries, each grain of salt acts as a lens, magnifying the harmful rays of the sun.

She could feel the heat striking through her cotton shirt and slacks, and she hoped she wasn't burning. Nearly all the soft drinks were gone from the refrigerator, although there was still plenty of beer. The skipper also kept gin, whiskey and vodka in one of the lockers, but he could see that this lot wanted to fish, not drink.

The skipper said, "If fish suddenly stop biting when the moon's in the first quarter and the tide's in flood, then it means only one thing—shark." He slowed the engine almost to idling and called to the boy to hang a bag of mackerel and tuna overboard. As the boat drifted, it left behind a trail of fish oil and blood.

The boat moved gently ahead on the sea for nearly another

hour, without any action. Their attention wandered. The boat kept going because unless you are moving, your lures will sink below the surface, and a big fish will only take a moving lure. Shark and tuna swim near the surface because there's more to eat there than in the depths.

Suddenly Carey's rod was almost jerked from her hand. Instantly she was wide awake again. Her line was reeling out fast.

The skipper called down from the wheel, "Looks like you've got a big 'un. Let him run for a bit, then strike hard to drive that big hook home. Everyone else, reel in your lines, please."

The skipper scrambled down the ladder and stood behind Carey, squinting at the wake. Winston nipped up the ladder to take the wheel.

"Better get the shoulder harness on you." The skipper opened a deck locker under the bench seat and pulled out several harnesses. He held up a stained soft leather vest with several dangling straps. Cautiously, Carey released her left hand and slipped her arm into the vest, then her right arm. Two straps dangled down her back. She lifted each buttock and the skipper pulled the straps up between her thighs. Two more straps were pulled over her breasts, then all the leather straps joined to a pad that held a rod socket firmly against her stomach: this gave her more control and pulling force over her taut rod.

The line went slack.

The skipper muttered, "He's running towards the boat. Reel in fast, don't give him slack line or you'll lose the hook."

Carey pulled her rod up carefully, reeling in with her right hand as fast as she could.

The line tugged again, and she let it run out.

The line slackened, and she reeled in again.

Suddenly the line was yanked away, and she nearly lost it.

Every man in the boat instinctively leaned toward her as she pulled her rod firmly down in the socket and let the line run out—faster this time.

Shirley Conran

"Watch that line, you don't want to lose it," the skipper warned.

They all watched the wake of the boat.

The line went slack again and Carey reeled in fast, hoping that her arms would hold out. She'd never imagined feeling anything as strong as this at the end of a rod. It was as if the line were attached to a runaway horse; her shoulders were hurting already.

The line pulled again, so suddenly that Carey's sunglasses fell to the deck, but she barely noticed, because she was concentrating so hard on the fish she was fighting. She reeled in fast. The men watched her big, lithe Amazon frame, silhouetted against the sparkling sea.

Arthur said, "It's too big for you, Carey. Why don't I take over?"

"That's okay, Arthur. I'm fine," Carey said firmly.

There was a pause, and then Ed said, "Carey, maybe it would be better if Arthur took over."

"Ed, this is my fish, whether I land it or lose it."

"Carey . . ."

"Ed, this is *my fish*." The line pulled again and Carey let it out.

"Let her play it, Ed." Arthur's voice sounded unconcerned.

Oh, fuck, Ed said to himself.

Seventy-three minutes later, Carey brought in a 192-pound gray reef shark. As the shark had repeatedly tried to break free, she'd hung on fighting her invisible opponent until its will suddenly snapped, exhausted by the violent fight for its life.

The skipper, who had stood behind Carey quietly advising her, yelled to Winston to put the engine into neutral and get out the big gaff.

When the shark was nearly beaten, the skipper pulled on a pair of old leather fishing gloves. He leaned over the side and rammed the gaff behind the shark's malevolent eye. As the shark twisted and thrashed, trying to rid itself of the heavy

112

hook and get away, the needle-sharp hook at the end of the heavy wooden pole sank into its leathery hide.

With some difficulty, the skipper and Winston slipped a rope noose around the tail, and eventually heaved it aboard.

"Watch out," warned the skipper. "Even if you think he's dead, keep away from a shark in a boat, because if he isn't, you can lose your foot."

Everyone drew back from the huge, dark, glistening bulk of this awesome creature in front of them. A shark, you had to respect it.

Winston jumped forward with a heavy hammer from the wheelhouse and smashed it hard against the shark's nose, low on the head and between the eyes, where the brain is situated.

Until they returned to harbor, Carey stayed down in the cabin shaking with exhaustion. Her clothes were wet with sweat as if she'd fallen into a tub. Her shoulders, her back, her thighs and her stomach ached as they had never ached before. She almost cried because of the pain in her arms, and she couldn't move her chafed hands or wrists.

But she'd won. And she hadn't only been fighting the shark. She'd also been fighting Arthur. Strange that she could stand up to Ed and Arthur, but not to a hairdresser or a head-waiter, she thought.

Nobody came down to congratulate her, except the skipper, whose upside-down head in the doorway grinned and whispered, "Good on yer."

In the privacy of their beach hut, Ed yelled at the exhausted Carey.

"Why do you have to draw attention to yourself? Don't you realize that your aggressive behavior is standing in the way of my promotion?" He grabbed the miniature bottle of brandy from his bedside table and emptied it into the balloon glass. "Why can't you be like the other wives and talk about kids and clothes? Why do you want to fish, for heaven's sake?"

"For the same reason that Arthur wants to fish." Carey lit a cigarette, as Ed knocked back the brandy. "If you'd hooked that shark, would you have handed your rod to Arthur?"

Ed truly didn't know. He walked round to Carey's bedside table and poured her bottle of brandy into his glass. "Oh, for Christ's sake," he said.

"Ed, what's more important, your wife and family, or the company?"

"Don't be dramatic."

"I'm *not* being dramatic. I don't think you realize how Nexus is sucking you up. If you get to be president, I don't suppose we'll *ever* see you at home."

"You're exaggerating, as usual."

"I'm just hoping that this Christmas isn't going to be like last Christmas. Except for Christmas Eve and New Year's Day, you were working in the lab until the early hours of the morning for six solid weeks. Too tired to do anything . . ."

Ed turned his back on her and stared out at the trees and shrubs, neatly groomed like green poodles.

Carey added crossly, "If I hadn't known about the chromite find, I'd have thought you had a girlfriend."

"What did you say?"

Carey looked up from rubbing lotion into her raw hands. "I said, if I hadn't known that you found chromite on Paui . . ."

Ed whispered, "How do you know anything about chromite?"

"When you're tired, you talk in your sleep."

"This looks like a goddamn funeral parlor." Arthur looked around his vast beach hut. White lilies stood on every surface. With gawky angularity, the lily stalks thrust up from the vases; the rust stamens hung from the inverted white trumpet petals, like miniature, menacing chandeliers.

"It also *smells* like a goddamn funeral parlor." With distaste, Arthur sniffed the cloying, oversweet odor which hung oppressively over the room.

Lying on the couch, Silvana languidly looked up from her book. Arthur hadn't mentioned his catch, and she knew better than to ask. "It's the standing order. I'll have them taken away." Whenever Silvana was booked into a hotel, two hundred dollars' worth of white flowers were automatically ordered for her suite. It is impossible, even for a hotel florist, to make white flowers look garish.

Arthur took the book from her hands. *"Elective Affinities.* Catchy title."

"I think I'll have a drink," said Silvana. She moved to the bar and poured a large scotch for Arthur.

Half an hour later the lilies had disappeared and Arthur lay on the wicker chaise longue in the patio, draining his second, enormous scotch. As he put the empty glass down he said, "I've decided to pick Charley as my successor. He's got that go-for-the-jugular quality that's needed to run a multinational."

Silvana thought, It's called ruthlessness. She said, "Why not Ed?"

"A man who can't control his own wife can't control a company." He hoped that hit home—and got back to Ed, via the wives.

"Would you have considered Isabel, if she were a little older?" Silvana knew better than to mention it more directly, but prior to Arthur's appointment, three presidents had died within seven years, which was why the board was insistent that Arthur choose a reasonably youthful successor.

"For God's sake, she's still a child, in company terms," Arthur snorted. "And anyway, I'd never choose a woman. When it comes to the crunch, they duck responsibility."

Silently, Silvana went inside and poured him another scotch.

◄ **5** ►

TUESDAY, NOVEMBER 13, 1984

After breakfast on Tuesday, Ed walked alone along the dirt road that led from the hotel grounds to the airstrip. He had told no one except Arthur about the chromite strike. If Arthur found out that Carey knew, it would seriously count against Ed in the struggle for the presidency. So Ed decided not to tell Arthur, and hoped to God that there hadn't been any other leaks, as he mentally reviewed the events that had brought them to this island.

Immediately after being awarded the first mining concession on Paui, Nexus had sought permission to prospect elsewhere on the island. For years, not even Raki had been able to get permission from the Nationalist president of Paui to prospect anywhere except on the northeast tip of the island, for the President hadn't wanted to upset the network of powerful tribal chiefs who held him in power, and wanted no whites in their area. Finally, in 1981, Nexus had been allowed to send a small team into the Central Mountains, where, for two years, they had found nothing particularly exciting. However, when they were working on a strip of mountain about twenty miles inland from the northwest coast, on almost the same line of longitude as the Mount Ida mine, the survey leader (for none of the right reasons, as it later turned out) had ordered the team to concentrate their search in an area of nondescript hills called, because of their humped shape, the Turtlebacks. As usual, the survey team had cleared vegetation, bored holes and taken samples of the topsoil and the rock beneath, as well as the sand and gravel of streambeds. The samples had been sealed in canvas sample bags, each labeled with a coded map reference, flown out by helicopter and dispatched to the Pittsburgh laboratories, together with the film of all aerial photographs of the survey site. In due course, Ed had received the lab report, the survey site map and the aerial photographs.

After reading the lab report on the Turtlebacks survey, Ed took it straight to Arthur. They both canceled their plans for the weekend, which they spent closeted in Arthur's study, except for brief pauses for fresh air, when, wrapped in scarves and overcoats, they trudged along the chilly bank of the Ohio River, which bordered part of Arthur's estate.

As expected, the samples showed copper. They also showed uranium, but the concentrate level was not high, and these days, after Three Mile Island, you could hardly give away uranium. Nevertheless, Nexus had been prospecting unsuccessfully in Australia's Northern Territory, which contains the highest undeveloped uranium deposits in the world; perhaps this Paui strike would now provide competition for Mary Kathleen, Australia's only uranium mine. When he reached that part of the report, Arthur nodded with satisfaction, then muttered, "But an ore grade of only five percent and the price is going through the floor."

Arthur read on, then looked up sharply. "This cobalt concentrate! There are very few cobalt deposits with a concentrate of forty percent. Remember what happened in Zaïre."

Ed nodded. In 1973, OPEC had raised the price of oil; the energy crisis and worldwide inflation were the result. Not surprisingly, there had been great anxiety as to whether other cartels might form, whether other producers of such necessities to Western industry as copper or bauxite might collude to form a monopoly and then raise their prices to a level at which whole industries and whole countries would suffer.

In early 1978 the African nation of Zaïre—which produced

over half the world's cobalt supply—reduced cobalt allotments to their customers by 30 percent. The rebel invasion of Zaïre in May 1978 was followed by a minor panic, because the world's cobalt supply was expected to be drastically reduced. The price of cobalt quickly jumped from $11 to $25 per kilo, and by December (because of panic buying) the price had jumped to $120. Vast fortunes had been made—and probably would be made again, for cobalt resources were expected to be exhausted by the year 2065.

During the mid-1970s, soaring prices of other raw materials started a worldwide rush to buy new mines; this overinvestment resulted in an oversupply of raw materials and consequent low prices, at a time of world recession. This was one of the reasons that Nexus, together with the entire global mining industry, had been in a slump for several years.

Ed said, "Read on, Arthur. It gets even better."

Arthur read on. Suddenly he sat up and looked at Ed.

Ed nodded. "Yes, the real find is chromite." All the different, treble-checked tests had shown that the samples contained evenly distributed, high-concentrate chromite.

In the bleak November light, the two men stared at each other. Provided they handled it carefully, the chance of a lifetime might lie beneath the dark-green jungle canopy of the Turtlebacks.

Wonderingly Arthur said, "Not only chromite, but this *very* high concentrate?"

"Seven to ten. That equals the best in South Africa."

"We could use a little good luck, for a change," Arthur said softly. "How many people have seen this report?"

"I brought it straight to you," Ed said.

"South Africa will be after it."

Ninety percent of the world's chromite reserves were in South Africa, so that country was in a position to hold up the rest of the world for ransom. Chromite alloy is used to make stainless steel for the automobile, aircraft and spacecraft industries. If South Africa, for political reasons, decided to withhold its chromite, the result would be a sudden, world-wide recession.

Arthur tapped the report. "If this news gets out, we'll never get the Paui mining concessions, because South Africa will pay whatever is asked for them. They'll *have* to outbid Nexus, to protect their own position."

"No question."

"This survey has cost us a helluva lot of money. Why hand them the report on a platter?"

Ed nodded. Together with many senior officials, the Paui Minister of the Interior and Natural Resources had been paid his secret fee, after which permission to survey the whole of the north coast had been given. As was customary, Nexus had also agreed to let the minister read the survey report.

After a brief pause, Arthur added softly, "I think you'd better lose a page or two of this report, Ed."

Ed looked apprehensive but resigned, for he had expected the suggestion. It meant that he would be aiding and abetting an illegal operation. However, few mining prospectors have the scruples of an archbishop when it comes to staking, registering, purchasing, or in any way hanging on to their claim.

Ed said, "You mean we only mention copper and uranium in the survey report that we show the President, but we hold out for an all-minerals-and-all-metals contract. Of course that will arouse their suspicions. So we allow them to . . ."

". . . find out about the cobalt. You have to sacrifice a goat to get a tiger."

"Naturally they won't expect us to tell the whole truth."

"It never pays to be straight with the crooked. They can't understand it, it bewilders them," Arthur said.

"So we plant a red herring for them to discover—and then not mention?" Ed thought a moment, then said, "At least two people in the lab must know that we're on to chromite—the analyst concerned, and the chief analyst. But of course the samples were coded as usual—so ultimately, Arthur, only you and I know where they came from."

Arthur waved at the 150-page report on the sofa, which

included the maps and photographs. "Get the file copy of the report from Records. Ask Records for all the other copies, then send Records a memo telling them to book everything out to you. Get the negatives and all prints from the studio."

Ed thought, *I'll* be the only person responsible for concealing, falsifying and possibly destroying documents. He said, "Will do."

"Keep the report locked in your safe at home, Ed, not in the office safe. See that the rock samples are dumped as junk."

"Sure, Arthur."

"And of course, the Paui negotiations are now top priority. Tell Harry Scott to handle it personally. It won't look unusual, will it, if he goes along with the man from his Contracts Department to negotiate with them?"

"Not at all unusual. In fact, Third World presidents sometimes insist on *only* doing business with the head of an organization, for status reasons."

They both knew that after a series of meetings with the President and his Minister of Finance and Natural Resources, the Nexus men would hammer out a mining rights contract which would include a profit-participation percentage for the Paui government (which already owned 20 percent of Paui-Nexus Mining Ltd.). Of course, they would also have to make private payments to the Credit Suisse in Zurich, into the accounts of the President and the two ministers concerned—who might go barefoot in their home villages but were pretty sophisticated when it came to Swiss banks.

The special payments would not be mentioned in the contract or at the meetings. Only once would they be allusively referred to, at a one-on-one, short meeting for coffee in the private house of one of the ministers concerned. Eventually, after a certain amount of stilted conversation over coffee, the Heads of Agreement would be signed by everyone concerned, after which it was up to the lawyers to write a contract that would be agreeable to all parties.

In the dusk, Arthur tapped the survey report. "Pity there's been a change of government." Unfortunately, in November

1983, Raki had been out of power for several months, and negotiations with the new government had produced no results.

Now, almost a year later, the President of Paui had at last agreed to talk to the president of Nexus, which is why the Nexus top executives were on the island, wearing tropical suits and open-necked shirts, strolling along to the Paradise Bay airstrip, hoping to take the biggest step that Nexus had ever taken. . . .

As Ed turned the bend in the road to the airstrip, he heard running footsteps behind him.

Brett was panting on Ed's heels; he'd been halfway to the airstrip before he realized that once again he'd forgotten his asthma spray.

"Broke a shoelace," Brett said.

Scarlet creepers framed the door of the modest bungalow on the hotel grounds, in front of which the skipper of the *Louise,* wearing blue jeans and a white shirt, was kissing his wife. He'd met her when he went to her dad's place to purchase supplies for his boat, and they had been married shortly afterward. Louise was small, slim and dark, with yellow-speckled hazel eyes that slanted up at the corners like a cat's; people thought she was South American or perhaps Greek, but she was Anglo-Indian, and there was a trace of her Indian mother's pedantic lilt in her voice.

"Curry tonight, Louise?" He pulled down her turquoise sarong and kissed the top of her breast.

"My goodness, we don't eat home tonight." She drew back and pulled her sarong up to a respectable height. "Tuesday night is beach barbecue night and tonight's going to be the last of the season, with tribal dancing afterwards. So make sure you get those tourists back to me in time for it. We light the bonfire at seven o'clock sharp. And no flirting tonight."

This was their private joke. Female hotel guests often made overtures to the wiry, bronzed skipper, but he saw tourists only as a means of paying for his boat. He didn't dislike them, they probably deserved their holiday. He was always polite, but he kept his distance and never became involved with them, never accepted any evening invitations.

"And the same to you, Lou." Louise's official title was Entertainments Manager, which meant that she sat at a desk in the reception area of the Paradise Bay Hotel and arranged all outings, trips, tennis court and golf bookings. The male guests were as much of a hazard for Louise as the female ones were for her husband.

Rather than sitting around being affable with strangers tonight, he would prefer to be snug in his own crib, thought the skipper as he set off down the poinsettia-lined path toward the jetty, but it was no use arguing with Lou. Outwardly submissive to him, she had a mind of her own and he always seemed to do as she wanted, even if it was being agreeable to a bunch of noisy strangers rather than having a quiet dinner at home. Their bungalow had hardly any furniture, because Lou liked to go barefoot indoors and sit cross-legged on the beautiful rugs her grandfather had sent them as a wedding present. The only Western furniture they possessed was a big brass bed that the skipper had bought cheap in Queenstown from a missionary who'd had enough of Paui.

At the bend in the path, the skipper turned again to wave goodbye. He laughed. That bloody goat was chewing her sarong again.

Louise bent down, parted the little pink jaws and gently prized the turquoise cotton from them.

She called out, "Billy wants his breakfast. Goodbye, darling."

" 'Bye, Lou." As he set off down the path toward the beach, he could not know he was saying that to her for the last time.

The women climbed aboard the boat with stiff little movements, afraid of losing their balance. As the skipper helped Carey aboard, he noticed her gloved hands and said, "Sore? Well, that was a good catch yesterday. You'll find the tackle box down below, if you care to try your luck today."

He shot out a brown arm to steady Suzy, who had jumped down from the jetty and landed off-balance. She wore a pink halter top, skin-tight pink shorts, white wraparound sunglasses with slits like a ski racer's, and high-heeled white sandals.

The skipper said, "There's a box of tennis shoes in the cabin, ma'am. Those heels'll ruin my deck."

Suzy said, "Is it okay if I go barefoot?"

The skipper nodded, then helped Silvana aboard. She stumbled against him, climbed down awkwardly to the deck and straightened her black cotton Valentino jumpsuit, which had been cleverly cut over the behind.

Slowly, the boat moved from the quay. Roddy, in brief yellow swimming trunks, waved them off. He firmly intended to stay by the pool for the entire day. The women waved back to him. In the bow, Suzy tied up her long blond hair in a pink scarf and settled down carefully to anoint every visible inch of her flesh with suntan oil.

Patty went below to check the snorkeling equipment. "You got spear guns. Great."

The skipper looked at her short-sleeved navy shirt and white shorts. "There's a pile of long-sleeved cotton shirts in that end locker, and cotton jungle hats and straw sun hats in the corner. You'll get a bad sunburn if you stay all day in short sleeves. Please tell the other ladies." Except for Carey, they were all the same, he thought, no hats, short sleeves, shorts that left their legs bare and hardly covered their bums, and they expected a pair of snappy sunglasses and a suntan spray to protect them from the tropical sun. They'd all get bad burns if he didn't nurse them.

Carey poked her head out of the cabin and called, "I can't find the tackle box, there's such a lot of stuff down here."

The scrawny black boatboy jumped from the upper deck, landed like a cat and joined her in the cabin.

"Why isn't all this stored away?" Carey waved at the heap of gear at the back of the cabin.

"Hotel visitors want many things. No room in lockers." He

pointed to the lockers beneath the bench seats on either side of the cabin. Carey tried to open one, but it was locked.

The boy said, "Guns in locker."

"Guns?"

The skipper poked his head into the cabin. "I keep a rifle in there, in case someone tries to steal the boat or I have to go ashore in strange country. Winston stores a machete there, for the same reason. We lock 'em up because I don't want my passengers to accidentally chop their hands off or blow each other's heads off." He turned to the boy. "Get up to the wheel, Winston, and keep her heading out to sea until we're level with the headland. Then call me."

Carey said, *"None* of these lockers open."

"No," the skipper said. At least one of them's properly dressed, he thought. Carey wore a loose, long-sleeved blue cotton shirt and matching pants. "Lockers are for locking, to keep people away from the contents. We store emergency rocket flares and mini-flares in the first locker. The far locker is the ship's paint store."

Carey looked at the heap of gear in the back of the cabin and asked, "Why do you need mosquito nets and a flashlight to fish?"

"It's an underwater flashlight, and it ain't for fishing. Sometimes you want to get under your boat and see what's happening to the keel. And if you ever had to sleep aboard around here, you'd know why I keep the mozzie nets handy." He fumbled beneath the mosquito netting. "Here's the tackle box. Now let's decide what you're going to use today." Squatting, he picked among the brilliantly colored plastic lures.

In the stern, Annie tucked her pale green sleeveless shirt into her dark green slacks and said to Carey, "Isn't this wonderful weather? I love these company trips." She had firmly pushed thoughts of Harry out of her mind, but at night her body betrayed her.

"You're *meant* to love them," Carey said idly, her eyes on their wake. "These trips are meant to keep us all in line. Once a year, all wives of executives are whisked off to some exotic place, waited on hand and foot, offered tall drinks and orchids, and are expected to forget what they had to put up with during the past year, thanks to the company."

"You don't really *mean* that, Carey." Annie looked around nervously to check that Silvana wasn't listening.

"I mean that the first rule of big business is women and children last," Carey said, firmly. "I'm supposed to sympathize, not complain, if Ed's exhausted because of jet lag, expense-luncheon lag or entertaining-Arabs-at-the-Playboy-Club lag."

"Keep your voice down, Carey," Annie urged.

Carey ignored her. "I'm not supposed to mind if our plans are canceled at the last minute, or if I only see Ed in the evenings at some dreadful business banquet with a smile plastered on my face."

"That's part of being a loyal company wife," Annie chided, "and the company *does* care about a man's family obligations."

"The company is very careful to be *seen* to care, because that's good business sense."

"Don't be cynical, Carey," Annie said. "Think of those personalized Christmas gifts to all the kids."

"Takes no time to tap them out on the computer," Carey pointed out. "Then even the *kids* are rooting for the company. We've all been brainwashed, Annie." Carey jerked her head up as her line went tense. But she hadn't got a bite. "At the last Nexus picnic I met a poor soul whose husband is in Overseas Development. She'd had to move sixteen times in eighteen years."

"She's obviously a loyal company wife."

Carey snorted. "Do you know what being a loyal company wife is? It's being a dumb woman. And to think that Ed wonders why I hang on to my job."

There was silence on board as they rounded the southern headland. Carey was fishing, Suzy was sun-bathing and the three other women were gazing hypnotically at the brilliant green strip of shore that was slowly moving past their eyes.

They didn't speak much. Although their manner was friendly, these women had nothing in common. An amicable veneer of politeness covered Annie's timidity, Patty's anxiety, Carey's cynicism, Suzy's defensive hostility and Silvana's languid indifference. Because Silvana was Arthur's wife, the other women felt slightly ill at ease.

"You'll all need these," said the skipper firmly, and distributed the shirts.

NEXUS was printed in black letters on the doors of the yellow Toyota minibus moving slowly through the crowded main street, heading for the Presidential Palace on the other side of town.

The Nexus VPs had flown to town in two loads, because the mine only had one four-passenger helicopter. Usually a mine wouldn't have even that, because helicopters are only used to search for mine sites and haul in building materials when an operation is being set up. But a helicopter was the only practical way to travel around the difficult terrain of Paui. Nexus also used the Bell to fly executives and key technicians to and from Queenstown Airport and the Mount Ida airstrip, and as a medical vehicle, to get people from the mine to the hospital as fast as possible.

The pilot, an uncommunicative New Zealander, was a pilot-engineer, which meant that no technician was needed for the Bell. She carried normal running spares; otherwise, spare parts had to be flown in from the mainland on the once-a-week Air Niugini flight.

The custom-built, air-conditioned interior of the minibus was a relief after the heat of the airport. As they moved through the town, Arthur peered through a window. There seemed to be one hell of a lot of police around. They wore black boots and camouflage uniforms and across their chests were strips of white tape on which the word POLICE had been scrawled in ballpoint pen.

The mine manager said, "There are always a lot of police around, sir." As soon as the Australians left, in 1975, the colonial-style constabulary had been transformed into a para-military police force, and within a few months that force had transmogrified into the Paui Defense Force, the PDF.

"Seems as if the whole town is on this road today," joked Arthur. Everybody in the bus laughed with him.

"This is the center of town, the poor part," the manager explained, as the yellow bus threaded its way through a vibrant mess of stalls, bars, clubs blaring native music and shifty-looking mongrels. There was not a white person in sight.

On either side of the broken, potholed road were gutters full of garbage. The road was lined with small shops, closed at night by rusting iron gates. The shops were painted (or had once been, by their Chinese owners) bright pink, orange or pale blue and were crammed with men wearing what looked like brilliantly colored nightshirts. Occasionally, the line of shops was broken by a peeling, concrete building, not so much of modern design as of no design whatsoever. Invariably, the tiny windows were heavily barred.

As the smartly painted bus bumped slowly over the rusting ironwork of the single-lane St. Mary Bridge, the occupants glanced below at the sluggish khaki waters of the St. Mary River. Safely across, the bus swerved to avoid a bicycle and nearly hit a peeling, turquoise shack with GREAT UNIVERSAL SUPERMARKET painted on the corrugated tin roof. Tacked to the wall was a sign that read BEWARE VERY BAD DOG.

The bus passed through a less congested area, after which it bumped by the side of a street market, where black women bent speculatively over dusty pyramids of yellow and rust-colored vegetables piled on leaves in the road.

As the bus crawled on, the manager said apologetically, "This is the only road to the palace. I'm afraid we always have this problem."

Arthur looked at the manager; he had a chunky sunburned body and ears that stuck out from an unmemorable round face, like a toasted muffin.

"Build another road," said Arthur.

"Certainly. I'll see to it this afternoon, sir."

The road had widened, and there were fewer people on it; the shacks and shops had been left behind. The bus passed two-story houses with wooden verandas or corrugated tin porches, then these houses gave way to even grander ones, of colonial design with once-white painted balconies.

Gradually the houses petered out, and on both sides the dark green jungle spilled over the buckled surface of the road, which could be described as potholes linked by tarmac, and might well have been the result of earth tremors. Brett clung to the seat in front of him as, time after time, the bus threatened to leave the road, but miraculously jerked back on course.

As the bus turned the next corner, the driver slammed on the brakes.

On the stretch of road ahead, a group of naked blacks were fighting with spears; on either side of the road stood more blacks, pointing drawn bows at each other.

"Heads down, everybody," said the manager sharply.

The bus driver leaned on his horn, languidly motioned to the natives to clear off the road and moved slowly ahead.

Surprisingly, the mob of scuffling men parted and moved to either side of the road, except for one man who lay motionless. Angrily, the driver banged on his horn. Two spear-carrying natives moved forward. One took an arm and the other a leg, and they dragged the man out of the route of the bus.

As soon as the bus had passed, the naked warriors started to fight again.

"Just a routine tribal battle," the manager explained.

Charley said, "I'm glad you told us to duck."

Brett said, "That man on the road looked dead to me."

"He probably was," the manager agreed. "They're a blood-thirsty lot. There are some odd traditions around here."

"Such as?" Brett asked. He was still shaken by the sight of the body on the road but hoped that nobody would notice, if he continued to talk.

"Most visitors find the Cargo Cult pretty odd," the manager

said. "The islanders believe that all Western manufactured goods are sent from God and should be shared equally. Instead of which, white men keep the lot. So, there's a small group called the Cargo Party; their politicians offer death to all whites, followed by speedy salvation and reward."

"Does anyone take any notice of them?" Brett asked nervously.

"There's always a bit of anxiety at election time, because of these extravagant promises, but Cargo politicians are a disorganized bunch. None of them is what you'd call a born leader. There's no one in the party with charisma."

"What if a dynamic leader were to appear?" Brett asked.

The manager laughed. "Charisma wouldn't be enough. He'd also need to be rich, well organized and well disciplined, with well-equipped troops. But if a guy like that did appear, he'd be able to reach into the hearts and beliefs of every villager in the country, and we might be in for trouble. However, there's nobody like that on Paui." He pointed ahead. "Look, that's the palace."

There, two miles south of Queenstown, stood the ramshackle Presidential Palace. It had been built in 1975, as soon as independence had been declared, but the contractors' fee had been eaten away by bribery, so the building had been flimsily constructed and soon fell into decay.

The yellow bus drove toward a high wall, in the center of which was a once-imposing concrete arch; beyond, the passengers could see a group of two-story, mauve-washed buildings. All the window apertures were heavily barred.

The bus stopped at the arch. The manager climbed out to present his pass to the armed guards, and held the door open for Arthur.

"That's the most beautiful beach I've ever seen!" Annie said.

The skipper nodded. "I often bring tourists here. It's the best beach on this part of the island, but the natives never come here."

The *Louise* was heading into a small lagoon that looked about a mile wide and was surrounded by a ring of coral, except for a small gap. The beach was backed by high, black cliffs, parted on the left by a waterfall that shimmered in the sun. It wasn't a sheer drop; although rocky, the cliff sloped gradually down to a wide rock pool about fifteen feet above the beach, after which it continued its descent to the sand. On top of the cliff, luxuriant foliage soared on either side of the waterfall.

"Hang on tight," called the skipper from the flying bridge. "I'm taking her through the reef."

As the *Louise* drew nearer to the line of white foam that delineated the reef, the passengers could see the waves breaking against it; the sound was like distant thunder as the surf hurled against the invisible coral, just below the surface. As the *Louise* surged toward the gap, none of her passengers were aware of the delicate seamanship involved in getting the boat through that narrow channel in the coral reef. Over millions of years the skeletons of minute sea animals had built up from the bed of the ocean, to form the rocklike accumulation of limestone which had gradually formed the reef. It was razor-sharp, and should a swimmer be dashed by the sea against the coral, he would instantly be slashed to pieces, head pulverized, body torn to a bloody pulp before the sharks could get to it.

"Is it safe to swim here?" Patty asked, looking ahead at the calm aquamarine waters of the bay.

The skipper nodded. "Sure. Big predatory fish don't come over the reef, it's like an underwater fence."

"Why not?" Patty asked.

"Dunno. Maybe it looks like a trap to a shark. You'd better stay in the southern end of the lagoon, because there's a current on the north side, where the waterfall joins the sea, and there's quicksand beyond that, where the mangroves come down to the water. So don't go beyond the waterfall."

The skipper waited for a high wave to enter the lagoon. The *Louise* surged in with the wave, which provided the boat with the deepest possible water at the shallow entrance to the lagoon.

They dropped anchor about thirty feet out from the beach. Winston started to load up an inflatable dinghy with insulated picnic bags, parasols and cotton mats to sit on. Just as the *Louise* was the skipper's pride, the inflatable dinghy was Winston's joy; he loved every inch of her gray rubberized fabric. Although only ten feet long, the dinghy had a 20-horsepower outboard engine and could be used for water skiing. When deflated, it could be packed back in its little bag and stowed in the trunk of a small car, a trick that always intrigued Winston. The outboard fired immediately, which was lucky because it was a temperamental old engine. The skipper intended to get a new one, as soon as he had a bit of spare cash.

The women made a wobbly descent into the dinghy. Winston took them ashore in two trips. He carried the provisions to the shade of the palm trees at the back of the beach. The ground there was littered with palm fronds, fallen coconuts and brittle, dead leaves.

It was blistering hot on the beach, so they decided to walk to the waterfall and take a natural shower before lunch. The women changed into swimsuits and trailed after the skipper, beguiled by the soft caress of the sea, the palms stirring in the slight breeze and the splashing of the waterfall, which grew louder as they approached, until it swelled into a persistent roar.

Patty pointed. "Look. There's a path up the side of the waterfall."

A narrow, overgrown path meandered in a ragged zigzag between blackish rocks to the top of the cliff.

"Don't go up the cliff and into the jungle," the skipper warned. "You never go into the jungle without a compass, because it all looks the same. You'd lose your bearing within five minutes and never find your way out."

"Do you have a compass on you?"

"Sure." From under his shirt he pulled out a hand-bearing compass suspended from a leather thong around his neck.

Patty said, "Then *you* can take us into the jungle. Just a little way. Just so that we can say we've been in the jungle."

"Maybe after lunch. Let's have a swim now."

"Why only maybe?" Patty persisted.

"The natives don't like anyone to go up there. It's a taboo area. There are taboo areas all over this island, which is why I never move around without a native."

"Why is it taboo?"

"I expect there's an abandoned village somewhere up there. When the soil is worked out in one place, the inhabitants move on and build a village someplace else, but the bones of their ancestors stay buried around the abandoned village. The natives don't believe that the dead are gone, they reckon they've merely left their bodies, but they're still here. The invisible dead always continue to live where they lived when they had a body."

"Yuk! How creepy!" Suzy gave a pretty shudder.

Patty said, "It looks as if there's a rock pool about fifteen feet up the cliff. Can we at least go up to the pool?"

"Sure," said the skipper. "That's a very pretty pool. I always take visitors up there."

They climbed up the path to the pool. Four of the women plunged in and frolicked in the spray at the side of the fall. They were careful not to get under it, because the weight of the water might have hurt them.

Suzy, in a pink bikini, sat on a rock, her legs dangling in the water. In answer to a surprised look from the skipper, she shook her head. "I can't swim."

The skipper squatted beside her. "Then you'll have a grand-stand view of Winston's little trick. It came about because I gave him a penknife, and a month or so ago he dropped it in this pool. The lads on this island will do anything for a pen-knife, it's a real treasure, so Winston wasn't going to say goodbye to it. He's a real good diver—he'd find a contact lens in the bottom of the lake—and when he was diving for his knife down there, he found a cave under the surface of the pool; the entrance was hidden by a rock overhang."

Suzy was fascinated. "Have you been in it? How big is it? How could he breathe?"

"No, I've never been in it, sailors don't like getting their feet wet. Winston says there's an underwater tunnel, and at the end of it there's a cave with fresh air. It must be there, otherwise he couldn't do his little trick."

Suzy said, "That's amazing."

"Not really. Underground limestone caves aren't unusual in this part of the world. Though there's nothing on Paui as big as the one in East New Britain—she's six hundred yards long and twenty yards high in the central cavern, and there's an underground stream running right through her. The natives keep quiet about these caves, they don't like whites to know about them."

Below them, in the pool, Winston rolled his eyeballs, let out a shriek and disappeared below the surface. The reaction of the swimmers was everything he could have hoped for.

"Help!"

"He must have gotten a cramp!"

"Did some animal pull him under?"

"Should we dive for him?"

Carey waved urgently to the skipper, then cried, "Why are you two laughing? Something's happened to Winston. He's been gone for over two minutes."

Patty spluttered. "I'm going down for him."

She was just about to duck-dive, when the skipper called out. "Winston's *okay*. This is his parlor trick. Usually he takes bets on how long it will be before he comes up again. He'll be gone at least five minutes. I don't want you to worry." He explained again about the cave.

Sure enough, five minutes later, Winston surfaced, the grinning center of attention.

The women laughed and scolded him for giving them such a fright. The skipper ruffled his black fuzzy hair and said, "You're a game little lad."

This attention went to Winston's head. He jumped up and down on his broad, flat feet and wriggled his splayed toes. "Winston not believe in waterfall spirits. Winston not bloody savage." He waved his skinny arms. "Winston is good Christian. Jesus is strong magic. There is no other God but Him."

The skipper gave him a friendly cuff. "You can tell he's been to the Queenstown mission school."

Winston led the way back to the picnic site with the bow-legged, bent-kneed, steady lope of a jungle dweller. While he spread the cotton rugs and unpacked the picnic, the women went for a swim in the warm blue water of the lagoon.

Silvana jerked through the water, keeping her neck held high so that her hair didn't get wet. She stayed in for only a couple of minutes, then changed as fast as possible out of her one-piece black swimsuit with the supposedly slimming cut into her figure-concealing black jumpsuit.

Annie, in a pale blue, one-piece suit, ran dripping up to the picnic rugs. She threw herself down in the shade. "Gee, I'm thirsty. Oh, isn't there anything to drink but beer? No Perrier?"

There wasn't, so Winston went to fetch a bucket of water from the waterfall.

A splendid Amazon figure in a flowered bikini, Carey ran up the beach from the lagoon, her long, taffy-colored hair streaming down her back. But Patty wasn't back and the skipper had to go to the water's edge to yell for her to come out before she got sunstroke. Head down, Patty plowed in a racing crawl across the lagoon and didn't seem to hear him. The skipper bellowed, "Come out of the water, or I'll have to come and get you."

Reluctantly, Patty headed for shore. She waded from the water shaking her short, blond, boyish-cut hair and tugging at the bottom of her navy Speedo tank suit, with white stripes down the side and the straps cut inward so they didn't chafe her shoulders when she swam fast. She flung herself down in the shade and took a sandwich.

"You'd think that they could give us something better than chicken sandwiches," Suzy complained.

Carey started to laugh. "The chef has put up a *fishing* picnic!" Fishing picnics consist of a great many cans of beer and a few thick sandwiches easily held in the mouth or thrown to the deck should the fishermen get a bite while eating.

"Well, it's too hot to eat anyway," said Patty, slapping at the sand flies that attacked her legs. It was too hot to walk barefoot on the beach, she'd burned the soles of her feet just now, and she could feel a headache coming on—although she wasn't going to say so, because that bossy skipper had warned her that she might get a touch of the sun if she swam too long. What a great place! Too hot to sit on the beach, and if you went in the water you got sunstroke. Patty slapped the midges off her legs again, then watched Suzy putting her lipstick on with a little brush.

"I suppose Winston learned English at the mission school," Patty said. "I can understand *him* perfectly, but I can't understand a word the other natives say, although they seem to expect me to."

"They're speaking Pidgin," the skipper said. "It's basically Melanesian and English, with a bit of Malay, Chinese and German thrown in. There are only thirteen hundred words in the language, there's no grammar and no plural, but you can translate thousands of English words into it. Some think it's ugly, I think it's ingenious. My favorite word is 'engine,' which can mean anything from a can-opener to a bulldozer. A table fork is 'engine belong kau-kau,' which means 'eat.' "

"None of it sounds like any sort of English to me," Patty said.

"It's difficult to understand because the natives can't pronounce *f* or *v;* so 'fish' is 'pish,' and 'every' is 'ebry.' And they use *s* for *ch*, so 'church' is 'surch.' 'Ebry Mary go surch' is 'every woman goes to church.' "

He taught Patty a few words of Pidgin, but then she lost interest. It was too hot.

The wind dropped, and the afternoon grew hotter.

In the shade of the palms, it was humid and sticky. Silvana —the only one who had brought a book—lay stretched out, reading.

Patty turned to the skipper. "When it gets cooler, can we waterski?"

"Matter of fact, I'm having a spot of trouble with the outboard, so I'd prefer you didn't use the dinghy." He didn't want to get them all excited about water skiing and then have the outboard pack up.

Patty swore under her breath. She wanted a distraction, because she definitely felt a headache coming on; the back of her head was throbbing like crazy.

The sun exhausted them.

Nobody talked until Suzy, who couldn't stand silence and thought that the picnic was about as cheerful as a funeral parlor, looked over Silvana's shoulder and said, "Hey, what's the book?"

"*Jane Eyre.*"

"The book of the movie? I saw it on TV one afternoon. A golden oldie with Joan Fontaine, about some orphan girl who married her boss. Kind of sentimental."

"I wouldn't say so," Silvana said. "It's a rather aggressive Cinderella story. Jane starts out as a poor governess who falls in love with her rich employer, but by the end of the book he is blind and utterly dependent on her. No other woman can make a play for him, because he can't see anyone, so Jane is in total control of the situation." Power without responsibility, she thought. Arthur would say that was every woman's dream.

Suzy watched Carey wading into the water, fully dressed in pale blue shirt and pants plus snorkel mask. Annie was dozing. What a dreary sight she looked in that bilious green shirt and the baggy dark green slacks! Patty was holding her head in her hands. Jeez, what a bunch of fun people, Suzy thought. She decided she'd go and look for shells.

She wandered along the beach, amusing herself with a

mental image of Arthur shuffling around like a bear, with his eyes bandaged, but it was unlikely that Arthur would go blind, they'd graft on some new corneas or something. It was more likely that Arthur's tragedy would be to fall for some young girl. He was the right age to make a fool of himself, and Suzy had seen it happen before. After the divorce from Silvana, Arthur marries the young girl, but she doesn't want to stay at home, she wants to party. So there's the old guy, working all day at the office, whooping it up in the evening and fucking his brains out all night, until he has a heart attack in some nightclub at three in the morning, and at the funeral the young girl looks wonderful, in black with crimson touches at the collar, like Elizabeth Taylor stealing the scene at Richard Burton's memorial service. So this young girl ends up with all the old guy's money and lives happily ever after. That's the stuff that modern Cinderella stories are made of . . .

Suzy tugged at her left foot, but her sneaker sank in the gritty sand. Her right sneaker started to squelch, and her left foot sank completely beneath the surface. It was boggy here, she thought, not sandy like the rest of the beach. The ground was slushy, with tufts of coarse grass.

Again Suzy tried to pull her left foot free. The shoe made a sucking, squelchy noise, but she couldn't heave her foot out.

This was ridiculous! Exasperated, she jerked her knees, trying to release her feet, then crossly bent down to untie her shoelaces.

Behind her, Suzy heard someone yelling. She turned her head. The skipper, followed by Winston, was running along the beach. He called, "You're in the quicksand, lady. Don't move."

It didn't occur to Suzy to be frightened. So she'd stepped in the quicksand. So they were coming to get her out. She'd forgotten, was all. Sure, she'd splashed through that little rivulet in the sand between the waterfall and the sea, even though she'd been warned. No big deal. It wasn't a crime. They were supposed to be looking after her, weren't they? Why hadn't anyone called out earlier?

The skipper panted up to the edge of the coarse grass. He was about fifteen feet from Suzy, and he kept moving around, because the sludge was sucking at the soles of his sneakers. Winston scuttled to the back of the beach, where he pulled dead branches from the debris beneath the trees. He dragged the branches back to the skipper, who had taken off his shirt and torn it into strips. The skipper knotted bits of cotton and used them to lash two branches together, to form one longer branch. Winston, who weighed far less than the man, lay on his stomach at the edge of the quicksand; slowly, he pushed the elongated branch toward Suzy, whose ankles were now submerged.

Suzy now realized that she was in danger. Her whole body was rigid and trembling.

The branch didn't reach her, short by about six feet.

The scene seemed sharp but unreal to Suzy, like a surrealist painting. It looked exactly the same as it had before lunch — the little waves still hit the beach with a friendly slurp, the sun still shone on the azure sea. But as she felt herself sinking deeper into the bog, she started to whimper. Soon, it would still look exactly the same, except that Suzy would be gone.

"Crouch down, Suzy," the skipper called. "Now, *very slowly,* try to crawl on your hands towards me. Don't try to move your feet, you'll only sink further. Throw yourself forward with your arms spread out. I want you horizontal."

White-faced, Suzy did so, but still she couldn't reach the branch. Covered in muck, sand in her mouth, she lay with her arms outstretched, but the branch was still two feet beyond her reach.

The skipper pulled back the spread-eagled Winston by his ankles — it wasn't fair to push the boy farther — then, swearing softly, he spread his arms and legs. He started to snake his hips toward Suzy, pushing the branch before him.

Lying in the muck, and whimpering, Suzy desperately

twitched her fingers, trying to reach the branch as he shoved it toward her. Eventually, her fingertips touched it, but she could only grasp the weak ends of the palm fronds.

The skipper dared go no farther, but he shoved the bound branches as far as he could, beyond his reach. Suzy was able to get a good grip on it, but now the skipper couldn't reach it.

"Hang on, Suzy." If he could go that far, then Winston could go a bit farther. He snaked backward until he was clear. He told Winston to crawl onto the bog again and get a grip on the branch. Winston knew the danger, but without a word he lay down and edged onto the slush, until he was about two feet inside the quicksand area. The skipper crawled behind him. "Okay, Winston, when I say one, two, three, *pull*, you and Suzy hang on to the branch, and I'll pull you out. *Stop sniveling, girl, and concentrate!*

"One, two . . . *three!*"

Nothing happened. Winston felt as if he were being torn in two.

"Again," said the skipper. "One, two, three . . . *pull!*" As he wriggled backward off the quicksand, he pulled Winston toward him. Winston hung on firmly to the branch.

"My arms! Oh, my arms!" gasped Suzy through a mouthful of sand. "I can't hold on anymore."

"Suzy, you're moving! You're coming out! Hang on, girl!" The sinews on the skipper's arms trembled with the effort, but he was now clear of the treacherous sand and Suzy's muddy bare feet were clear of the ground. The sneakers would never be seen again.

Inch by inch, Winston was pulled clear, heaving the palm branch with him.

Finally, Suzy was dragged from the swampy sand.

"You can stand up, Suzy, you're clear now."

But Suzy couldn't. She was shaking and whimpering with fright; the skipper had to help her to her feet. It was no longer possible to see that she wore a pink halter top and shorts.

Except for the blond crown of her head, every bit of her was caked in khaki mud.

As they staggered toward the sea to clean themselves, the rest of the party could be seen half a mile up the beach; Carey was still snorkeling, Silvana was still reading, Annie was still dozing and Patty was sitting cross-legged with her head bowed; she was meditating.

White is a status symbol in mining. Mine supervisors always wear white hard hats, and the Queen of England is always zipped into a white jumpsuit before her occasional trip down a mine. As soon as they arrived at the Mount Ida mine, the visitors from Pittsburgh were all issued white hard hats and white jumpsuits. At the top of the grimy mineshaft, looking like soap powder ads, they were greeted by an enthusiastic cheer from a crowd of grinning mineworkers. The beige shirts and shorts of the workers were stained with sweat, their heavy boots flopped, with laces undone, and their yellow hard hats were pushed to the back of the head. Charley noticed that some of the hard hats had been painted with face designs that resembled the mask in his beach hut.

As always, Charley hated that very fast elevator and the bone-shaking crash landing at the bottom, after forty people had been lowered down the vast shaft in as many seconds. Most copper mines are open cast; suddenly, Charley wished that this Mount Ida mine was not underground.

The bottom of the mine was well lit, like a subway, and forced air sent a steady draft through it. Trucks and other vehicles were clustered around the base of the shaft; everything visible had been cleaned or polished, while all dirty machinery had been shoved out of the way for this important visit. The little party in dazzling white climbed into the battery powered jeep and drove a mile along the twenty-foot-wide tunnel to the mine face.

Charley felt now as he always felt when he was down a mine. Scared. All the time you're in a mine, you're conscious of that mass of earth poised above your head, and you can't help wondering what's to stop it falling on you. Charley turned his head away whenever the jeep passed old sections of the mine where the earth had caved in and the floor had heaved up.

As they approached the mine face, the dust increased and the noise became intolerable; the compressed-air drills made more noise than pneumatic drills used in road repair. The deafening roar reverberated in the confined space.

At the end of the tunnel, the demonstration team was waiting to start a drill for blasting at the face.

With carefully appreciative faces, the Pittsburgh party watched the demonstration. Because this was the umpteenth time Arthur had seen this operation, his attention wandered back to that morning's interview with the President of Paui. Everything had happened more or less according to Ed's briefing, except that after he'd handed over the report (which Ed had redrafted to include uranium, but with no mention of cobalt or chromite), the President had looked him straight in the eye and said, "Are there cobalt expectations?"

So much for secrecy. Let's hope the red herring works, thought Arthur as, blank-faced, he had replied, "No, sir." He had added, "The President is, of course, aware that even if cobalt were to be found, the price fell abruptly in 1980 due to the world oversupply. Demand is now starting to rise again and prices are expected to level out at around twenty dollars a kilo by 1985, but we have no reason to hope for a cobalt find, Mr. President."

The President had chuckled, "Oh, but which of us can know the future, sir?"

"Whatever we find, Mr. President, Paui will receive a considerable share of it."

Arthur's reverie was cut short by an abrupt change in the yowling of the drills. The white-clad group at the mine face was suddenly enveloped in swirling dust. There was a roar of high-pressure air escaping. One of the bright orange air lines whipped dangerously above the visitors, moving so fast that it seemed to be a fan of orange, as in an action photograph.

An air-line coupling had come apart, Arthur realized immediately. Nobody had time to move. Thick as a man's wrist, the air line twisted and flayed the roof of the shaft, smashing the flameproof overhead electric light. They were plunged into claustrophobic darkness. In that second, every man present was not only conscious of the shrieking, whipping air line, but also of the pressure of the thousands of tons of black earth above them.

Upstream of the air line, the spring-loaded pressure sensor had immediately snapped shut and closed the valve that led to the air line. As soon as the air pressure dropped, the writhing metal snake fell to the ground. With a final hiss, it lay still in the darkness. But the panicking men in the dark at the mine face did not know this.

Charley could hear screaming, close at hand. He had been standing by the emergency telephone that dangled from the wall at the face and connected directly to the shift safety crew. Coughing and choking, Charley felt along the wall for the phone but couldn't locate it.

The lights on their white hard hats cut dim, erratic beams through the dust as the party of distinguished visitors gasped for breath but inhaled dust. Dust clogged their nostrils and stung their eyes. They choked and could not escape it.

Farther along the tunnel was a faint circle of light. The little group realized that by following the undamaged string of overhead lights, they would be led back to the elevator, then up to the safety of the surface.

They scrambled back toward that faint halo of light, and away from the dust, the darkness and the terror of what might happen next.

But one man didn't run. Ed yelled, "There's an injured man back here! Call the safety team to come with a stretcher!" But nobody heard him, and he groped his way in the dark toward the moans.

The choking dust was thicker than a Newfoundland fog, but as it settled, Ed could see by the beam from his hard hat that a pale, bearded man—the man who had been drilling—was writhing on the ground and screaming. His hat and glasses had disappeared, and his right leg was bleeding badly. The loosened coupling at the end of the air hose had pulverized his knee joint.

At the top of the shaft, the three-man safety crew had been playing poker when the alarm sounded. Wordlessly they had thrown down their cards and scrambled into the medical jeep that waited, permanently, outside their hut. Within twenty-five seconds of the alarm, they were moving down the shaft.

Normally, the driver of the medical jeep would have driven faster, but, without realizing it, he slowed down. He didn't want to run over all those important executives. So the jeep moved at not much more than a running pace down the mile-long tunnel.

Activated by the pressure differential valve, an alarm had also rung in the control office. The on-shift supervisor had immediately leaped into his jeep and followed the medical vehicle, hoping that the problem was only a broken air line, as had been indicated on the alarm panel. He nearly shunted the medical jeep when it stopped abruptly near the mine face.

The spotlight and headlights of the medical jeep homed on a crowd of filthy, gasping, choking men, trying to recover under the first overhead light they had reached. Beyond these spluttering men, someone was groaning and someone else was yelling for help.

The paramedic driver jumped out of his seat and threaded his way through the group. He headed down the tunnel toward the point where Ed's hat light shone a faint beam onto the wounded operator, who was still crying; it was a gurgling, low moan.

The paramedic knelt down, and shone his lamp on the mangled leg. "Amputation, poor bugger," he muttered, and yelled for the rest of his team.

They hurried up. One man held an oxygen mask to the wounded man's face, while the other jabbed morphine into his arm, after which they loaded him onto the stretcher and hurried him to the medical jeep. The medical party was now alone, except for Ed. The inspection party had been ferried back to the elevator by the on-shift supervisor.

While the paramedics were tending the wounded man, Ed jumped onto the jeep and maneuvered the spotlight around the dusty scene, to make sure that nobody else had been injured.

The pale beam picked up a crumpled, white-clad figure lying in the shadow of the big excavator.

Ed yelled, "Stretcher needed over to the left." He climbed down from the jeep, dashed over to the figure that lay against the wall and pulled him on his back.

"Oh, my God! It's Brett," Ed said.

When everyone had stampeded in the dark, Brett had probably run into the heavy excavator—or maybe he'd been accidentally pushed into it.

Ed yelled, "Stretcher! Oxygen! Fast!"

Two paramedics hurried over. The first one knelt, shoved a tube down into Brett's trachea, then attached it to the oxygen cylinder. But there was no response. It is very difficult to force air down blocked bronchial tubes.

When the second paramedic lifted Brett's wrist to feel his pulse, the blue aerosol spray fell from his limp fingers. The paramedic lifted the spray and shook it. "This thing's empty!" he said.

In the dim light of the mineshaft, the paramedic gave Brett an intravenous injection of steroids. There was no response from the patient.

It had taken twenty-five seconds for the medical team to get into the jeep, six minutes to get down the mile-long tunnel, another three minutes to ascertain that the choking executives were not at risk, and two minutes to attend the injured drilling operator. About twelve minutes had elapsed since the alarm bell rang. The medics looked at each other in the artificial twilight. One shrugged his shoulders. They both knew that this man was dead.

"Poor bugger," said the first paramedic. It was their all-purpose expression of condolence.

Neither of them could have known that if the hotel maid hadn't picked Brett's empty spray from the bathroom floor and put it carefully back on the shelf, next to the new one, so that he took it by mistake, Brett might have been able to save his life, instead of desperately pressing the button while he choked to death . . .

◀ 6 ▶

"Sit well down in the boat, please, ladies."

The skipper maneuvered the *Louise* through the gap in the coral reef, heading straight into the waves and riding out on the swell. On either side of the gap an incessant boom could be heard as the sea hurled itself against the submerged banks of coral and flung spray into the air.

The *Louise*, on a northwesterly course, headed back to Paradise Bay. The sun lost its fierce intensity, and a light breeze started to blow.

The skipper hoped the women would soon perk up a bit. Suzy sat hunched in the airless cabin, still weepy after her quicksand ordeal; Annie, the quiet one, was pouring another vodka and tonic.

The other women on the beach had looked up in alarm when Suzy, Winston and the skipper, all covered in mud and sand, had staggered back to the picnic site. Annie and the big woman, Carey, had helped the trembling Suzy to the water's edge, where they had pulled off her filthy clothes, washed her and dressed her in a clean blue fishing shirt. The plump one, Silvana, had wanted to get back to the hotel, but the boyish blonde had objected. Why the hell spoil their day, Patty had said, when Suzy had been warned not to go near the quicksand?

The skipper watched Carey fish from the stern. They were all wearing fishing shirts, like he'd told 'em. Most tourists never listened, they always thought they knew best. He always told them to take the sun carefully at the start of the holiday—to swim in long pants and a long-sleeved shirt, and not to sunbathe—but they always wanted to prance around in the fancy new swimsuits they'd brought. They forgot they were in the tropics. He'd found out, after two seasons at the Paradise Bay Hotel, that it was no use insisting, because the tourists always thought him interfering, if not insolent. Too late, they realized what the skipper meant, when the pain and swelling immobilized them for the next three days and they lay sobbing as the hotel nurse delicately applied calamine lotion to their scorched skin. Then, when the burned skin fell away, like a snakeskin being sloughed off, they worried whether the raw pink flesh beneath was going to stay that color for the rest of their lives.

The skipper stifled a yawn. The tourist season was nearly over; the wet season would start on December 1. He turned from the wheel and looked back over his shoulder at the deck below.

Carey had just reeled in a small tuna—about six pounds, he reckoned—and she was squatting on the deck, rebaiting her line. Winston was helping her.

The skipper was really pleased with that lad. He swam like a trout and dived like a dolphin; he was worth every grain of the two sacks of flour a year for which his father leased him out. The skipper could swear that Winston preferred the sea to dry land. On land he was an excitable, skinny twelve-year-old, but in the water he was amazingly mature, a calm, fast thinker who never wasted a movement. But that shouldn't be surprising, since he came from a local pearl-diving family. This afternoon he'd been a bloody marvel in that quicksand. Winston had saved the little blonde's life. He'd get two extra sacks of flour for that.

Perched on the transom, Winston had just finished reciting the names of his ten older brothers and sisters to Annie, who was seated in a fishing chair. Annie's sleeveless pale green shirt kept working loose from the waistband of her baggy green slacks. She listened to Winston's stories about Father Winston Churchill Smith, the missionary who had baptized him, who had taught him at the mission school and who had given him the white rosary beads that he proudly fished from the pocket of his torn khaki shorts. "Bible Prize," Winston said proudly. "Winston good Christian. Winston eat body of Jesus and drink blood of Jesus and take strength of Jesus thereby. Winston not bloody savage. Jesus good strong magic. Winston not believe God-Kilibob."

"Cut it out, Winston," the skipper called. "Get up here and take the wheel."

Winston shinned up the ladder, and the skipper jumped down on deck for a beer.

"What did he mean, God-Kilibob?" asked Annie.

"It's a sort of religion, the Cargo Cult," the skipper explained. "The old native ways ain't changed much, not even in Queenstown. Ordinary villagers still live like their ancestors lived, except they maybe use a few Western goods—anything from a can of soup to a teakettle. They don't believe that stuff is made by human beings. They reckon all the jeeps, and mine machinery, and tins of instant coffee are made by a god, and delivered to earth by the spirits of the dead, for the benefit of everyone." He took a swig of beer. "All Western goods are called Cargo. They're supposedly sent by God-Kilibob."

Suzy laughed. "You mean, they think your Swiss army knife, and that can of beer, and this boat were sent from heaven?"

"Yes. It ain't surprising, considering that none of 'em have ever seen a factory." He looked around at the bright pink, interested faces. "Some of 'em also reckon the missionaries misled 'em. Christianity hasn't given 'em the secret of amassing Cargo. But they can see the missionary johnnies know the secret, because they've got plenty of Cargo goods."

"But the natives seem friendly enough," Annie protested.

"If an islander thinks a whitey will tell him the Cargo secret, then he'll be *very* friendly. Be careful about giving 'em gifts—even small things, like that penknife I gave Winston."

"What do you mean, *careful?*" Suzy asked sharply.

"Don't expect gratitude," the skipper said. "An islander reckons the gift is his share of Cargo, something he's entitled to. Don't let 'em think you've lots of stuff, or they'll reckon *you're* responsible for stealing the Cargo that God-Kilibob sent to earth for them."

"But surely not all of them feel that way? Winston doesn't believe in God-Kilibob. He just said so," Annie remonstrated.

The skipper laughed. "That's because he *does* believe it. A few years of mission school don't wipe out a lifetime spent in a tribal village where every man jack offers their prayers, their food and their flowers to God-Kilibob." He didn't mention the human sacrifices.

"What sort of Cargo do they want?" Annie asked.

"Some of 'em pray for axes, cloth, knives. The really aggressive ones want military Cargo—airplanes and warships— to drive the whites off the island."

Carey said, "So you've got a gun aboard because there's a *real* possibility that your boat might be stolen."

"Aw, I ain't never had any trouble. Out here, they don't blame welfare for what they ain't got, they blame the whites for withholding it, or their medicine men for getting the ritual wrong. They reckon they must've used the wrong dances, the wrong chanting or the wrong sacrifices, but if they keep at it, they figure one day they'll get it right. Then the spirits of their dead ancestors will give 'em amazing stuff, like this can of Fosters and your lipsticks."

Carey said, "So they expect goods in return for prayers?"

The skipper nodded. "A real reward, in this life, not a promise in the next." He turned his head sharply, like a dog pointing. Did he detect a slightly different note in the engine?

No, it was his imagination. He added, "Tough tribesmen being ferried to some workplace by plane start to cry with terror if they fly over a Cargo-worship village. They know that, down below, the villagers are casting spells to make the plane crash and hoping that it's carrying refrigerators and beer."

Again the skipper lifted his head. Now he was sure that the engine was losing power. Gradually the engine revolutions fell away, until it was just ticking over.

He scrambled up to the bridge and checked the fuel. It was a bit low, but nothing to worry about. Maybe water in the diesel fuel. He topped up the tank, which emptied his jerry can.

To his relief the engine suddenly picked up and they started moving again. Funny, he'd never had that problem before, but then the boat wasn't serviced regularly, because it meant taking her around to Queenstown and losing valuable charter days during the season.

As the crimson sun fell toward the sea, the dark water looked streaked with blood.

Suzy, who seemed to have forgotten already that she had nearly died so recently, held open the neck of her oversized shirt and peered inside at her sunburned skin. "Aw, look at these marks! I won't be able to wear a strapless dress tonight."

"The beach barbecue's always informal," the skipper said. "The ladies usually wear a cotton frock, maybe a light jacket. It can get chilly after sunset watching them native dances, even when you're sitting round the campfire."

Suzy decided she would wear her white strapless Calvin Klein, but with bare feet and no jewelry; she'd do her hair in a braid and stick a yellow orchid behind one ear. She'd cover the top of her body with bronze Cover-up of the Stars. She looked at her wristwatch. It was nearly five forty; they were due back at six.

The skipper saw Suzy glance at her watch. "Nearly home. Paradise Bay's just around the next point."

"Will the dancers wear native dress?" Carey asked, remembering some of those weird photographs that Ed had brought home.

"They used to dance stark naked, but now they wear a little rattan skirt for the sake of decency. And feather headdresses two feet high." As he spoke, the skipper's head jerked around. Again, he heard that different note in the engine. Damn, it couldn't be fuel, but she was certainly dying on him again.

The engine quickly faded, until there was no power. The boat stopped moving forward.

"Sorry about this, ladies. Would you mind moving to the cabin? The engine's under the deck. I'll just take a look at her."

The skipper could see nothing obviously wrong with the engine. A diesel engine will go pretty well forever, but if she stops, then it generally means there's something seriously wrong. Why couldn't the old girl have waited just a little bit longer, until they were safely back in Paradise Bay?

Only a small crimson arc was now visible above the horizon. The sea was slashed in irregular bands of red and orange fanning toward the *Louise*.

Five minutes later the skipper yelled, "Try her now, Winston."

Winston pressed the starter, which reluctantly coughed.

"Okay, stop it. I reckon I know what's the trouble." The skipper's fingers moved skillfully over the engine, but he could find nothing wrong with it.

"Try her again, Winston."

Nothing happened.

Swiftly, at three minutes past six, the sun fell under the dark line of the horizon, and almost immediately the glaring red streaks on the water paled to gold, glittering on the heaving surface of the black water. There is almost no dusk in the tropics; within ten minutes of sundown it is dark.

Sweating and red-faced, the skipper said, "I'll radio the hotel and tell 'em what happened."

"Get them to send another boat for us," Silvana told him.

"There ain't another boat with an engine. The little thing they use for waterskiing is under repair; the only other craft are monosails or dinghies."

The skipper radioed the hotel and explained their position. "Yeah, we're on the other side of the peninsula . . . What'll I *do?* Leave my fisherboy on the boat and take the ladies ashore in the dinghy. She only holds four people, but two trips'll do it. I'll bring 'em back by the path across the neck of the peninsula, so send a couple of boys with torches to meet us . . . Got no choice, it's only a couple of miles . . . They'll *have* to walk, if they want to get to the barbecue. If not, they'll have to stay aboard all night . . . Look, they've been lying about on a bloody beach all day, two miles ain't going to kill 'em . . . Yeah, tell their husbands we'll be a little late and ask Lou to hold up the start of the barbecue, will you? If the suckling pigs have been cooking all day, a few minutes longer won't hurt 'em . . . No, she ain't due for an overhaul for another month. . . . Yeah, bound to be something simple, I just wish I bloody knew what."

He climbed down the ladder and explained the situation.

Silvana was vexed. "I'm surprised they haven't got other boats."

"We only need boats for waterskiing and fishing, ma'am. This boat costs five hundred dollars a day to hire, and some days she ain't booked out. So it'd be a waste of money to have two of 'em."

The engine coughed and started. Winston's face wore a beam as wide as a slice of coconut flesh. "She go, boss. Winston pressa titty. She go!"

The engine coughed again and stopped.

"*Shit*. Beg pardon, ladies," said the skipper. "Let's get you all to shore before it gets dark. You stay with the boat, Winston. Don't let anybody board her, you understand? I'll be back in a couple of hours."

He went below, and returned with his rifle.

"Hey," cried Suzy. "If it's just a short walk, why do we need a gun?"

"We don't. It's for Winston. This boat is big Cargo."

"But Winston's only twelve years old!"

"He was only eleven when I took him on, and the first thing I taught him was how to blow a hole in a man's chest, if anyone tries to steal my boat. Now, ladies, please get sneakers from the box in the bow. Your shoes weren't made for jungle walking."

Just before half past six, all the women, wearing ill-fitting sneakers, were standing on a soggy, rocky strip of beach. They watched the skipper drag the dinghy up the sand; he kicked a hole to bury the anchor, then covered it with sand. "Not that she'll need it, tide's going out." He tucked his white shirt back into his blue jeans. "Let's go, ladies."

The light was fading fast as the women followed the skipper up the sandy, shrub-covered slope at the back of the beach.

Suzy slipped and tumbled back a few feet. "My fingernails!" she shrieked.

Annie went back and helped her scramble up the last few yards to where the rest of the party waited.

"Hurry *up!*" Patty called impatiently. She could see they were in for slow progress. Silvana had heaved herself up that twenty-foot slope like a baby elephant.

Suzy cried, "Something just stung me! Oh! Oh! Oh!" She brushed the stinging flies from her legs and arms. "Ants in my sneakers!" She hopped from one leg to the other. "Jeez, what a picnic!"

Silvana thought, Serves her right for wearing those tiny shorts and skimpy halter. Silvana was glad she'd worn her jumpsuit.

The skipper said, "You stay here. I'll find the path." He disappeared, leaving them standing in knee-high, coarse grass.

At the beach, where they'd had the picnic, there had been silence, except for the sound of the waterfall and the gentle lap of waves on the sand, but here, the jungle was noisy with the sounds made by wild creatures after sunset—the hum of cicadas rubbing their back knees together, buzzing, rustling and high-pitched, irregular gurgles.

The women all jumped as a wild shriek shot through the night.

The skipper reappeared. "Only a parrot. The path's about

ten feet away. It's more a track than a path; natives move sideways along 'em." His light illuminated the track.

They trudged into the jungle, where it was far darker.

The skipper said to Carey, "You go at the end. Nobody lose sight of the person in front."

The women started to move along the winding track; it was covered with damp and decaying vegetation, swarming with insects. Overhead, they could hear the rustle of leaves as unseen creatures leaped from branch to branch, unseen mouths and beaks hooted and moaned, chattered and yelled.

"This is like being stuck in a goddamn zoo," Suzy complained.

"It's so thick and scratchy," Silvana muttered. "I can't see the branches and the damn things seem to claw at me as I pass."

"This path has been cleared through secondary jungle," said the skipper over his shoulder.

"What's secondary jungle?" Patty asked, thinking that the other women were making a ridiculous fuss.

"It's where primary jungle was cleared for cultivation, then abandoned after the soil was exhausted. When jungle reclaims the land, you get this thick undergrowth."

"Couldn't we wait at the next village?" Silvana suggested. "While you go to the hotel and bring lights?"

"Best keep moving," said the skipper firmly. "We ain't got far to go."

The women were tired and fractious, grumbling like children up long past bedtime.

Suzy started to whimper. "How much longer?"

"Not far," the skipper said. "If you keep closer to me, you can see the way by my light."

They stumbled on, tripping over slimy stones, exposed tree roots and tangled brush. In their ludicrously large, ill-fitting sneakers, they shuffled forward, arms bent over their eyes to protect their faces from the twisted, hanging creepers.

Silvana gasped as some creature started from under her foot; she felt a warm, furry limb briefly touch her bare ankle.

Annie jumped as a bat fluttered in front of her face and brushed by her hands. Carey scolded herself as she would a child afraid of the dark. Patty crossed her fingers. Suzy whimpered.

The women were no longer petulant. Their confident assumption of safety had evaporated. Although they all knew that there was no reason to be frightened, they all were.

A scream of agony shrilled through the air. The women stopped abruptly.

"Don't tell me *that* was a parrot," Suzy snapped.

"Stay here," said the skipper uneasily. "I'll see what that noise was. Don't move." He sensed their rising panic. "Back in five minutes." He plunged ahead and a moment later the small dancing circle of light had disappeared, leaving the women in the dark.

Five minutes later, Silvana heard a rustle. She jumped back into Annie, who cannoned backward into Patty.

They heard the skipper whisper, "It's only me. There's a native village ahead, to the left, and they're punishing a thief. Let's move on fast."

Suzy sobbed, "No. I'm going to that village and I'm paying them to take me back to the hotel. And I'm going to get Brett to take me off this fucking place *first thing* tomorrow!"

"You ain't *none* of you going to that village," the skipper said firmly. "They're maybe a little overexcited."

"What do you mean?"

The skipper had moved up to the fishing village. By the light of the bonfire he had been able to see a man forcibly held to the ground while village elders hammered at his right hand with a heavy wooden club. They were breaking all the bones in that hand, which would maim him and mark him as a thief forever—if he didn't die of infection.

The skipper repeated, "I'm sorry, you mustn't go to that village."

Suzy didn't insist. She had noticed the worried note in his voice.

Patty said, "But won't they hear us?"

"Don't matter if they do. They ain't going to leave their village after sunset. They're all scared of the night—it belongs to the spirits of the dead. The living are supposed to keep out of the way."

The little party stumbled on. They lifted their feet high, but still tripped over the fetid tangle of vegetation on the path.

Suzy stopped again. She spoke in a childish, mulish voice. "I can't go on. I'm staying *here!*"

"Can't think where them guys with torches are," the skipper said. "But the hotel ain't more'n ten minutes ahead. We're almost at the boundary fence. Do you want me to go ahead and check?"

"No!" Suzy sobbed. *"Don't* leave us again!"

Patty checked the luminous dial of her watch. They had started walking at six twenty; it was nearly seven twenty.

It had been the longest hour of her life. So far.

The silent Nexus executives in their pale cotton tropical suits sat in wicker chairs on the patio outside the hotel bar. The strip of beach in front of them was surrounded by flaming kerosene torches on six-foot poles, which cast shuddering shadows over their white faces. The phosphorescent sea glittered, treacle-dark beyond the torches. Arthur listened to the soft hiss of waves advancing up the beach and the sucking sound as they were torn back by the sea and white foam spread like lace on the dark sand.

Arthur looked at his watch. Seven twenty. Oh, God, they'd be back soon. He had been told that the boat party had been delayed and were returning overland. When they reappeared, it would be his job to break the news of Brett's death to Suzy.

The beach barbecue had been abruptly canceled. The tables laden with food had been carried back from the beach. The huge bonfire was gradually dying down. As it was the end of the season, there were hardly any guests: only the Nexus group, two Japanese businessmen, a middle-aged Englishwoman who never spoke to anyone and her angular, stooping, sandy-moustached husband, who spent most of his time in the bar.

Arthur finished his whiskey. As well as breaking the news to Brett's wife, he would also have to tell Brett's mother. Maybe it would be better if he got *his* mother to do that. He'd telephone her in the morning, then leave the decision to her. Women knew best about that sort of thing.

Arthur hoped that by tomorrow the telephone would be back in service. As soon as they'd returned to Paradise Bay, Arthur had tried to phone the Sydney office but the local line was down. They'd been on Paui four days, and during that time the line had been out of action *twice!* Still, Arthur had done what he'd come to do. Ed had been wrong, the President hadn't procrastinated that morning; he'd briskly said, "Let us not go beating about this bush, Mr. Graham. Let us conduct our business in the Western way, quick as you like, with speed."

Speed!, Arthur had thought, recalling the months of fruitless negotiations. The President had carefully alluded to cobalt, then briskly suggested the percentage of shares to be held by the Paui development company, the flat fee payable annually, the percentage of profits and the amount on the check to be made out in his name and paid to Credit Suisse in Zurich before the Heads of Agreement could be signed. Surprisingly, these amounts were only slightly more than Arthur's planned first offer.

Without a word, Arthur had produced the check, already made out and drawn on a Nexus holding company in Switzerland. He had merely to fill in the amount.

"A pleasure to do your business," the President had said, inclining his head.

Arthur had returned, well satisfied, to the Nexus minibus, which had then bumped through Queenstown toward the mine. . . .

In the flickering light of torches on the beach, Arthur turned to Charley and said, "Think you could get me another scotch? I don't know where the hell the waiters are this evening."

Usually a three-piece calypso band played on the dance floor, but tonight there was no music. The darkened swimming pool was similarly deserted. The flaming torches mocked the conspicuous lack of gaiety.

Charley came back from the bar. "I couldn't find a waiter," he said, "but the girl at the reception desk said she'd bring us drinks."

Charley sat down. Nobody spoke. Accidents are not rare in the mining business, but the fact that they'd been in a jovial holiday mood that morning, and that Brett's pretty little wife would shortly appear, cheerful and smiling, left the small group depressed.

Looking like an exotic stewardess in her maroon hotel uniform, Louise laid a tray of glasses and bottles before the little group. "I thought I'd better bring the bottle, sir, as the barman is temporarily absent."

"Everybody seems temporarily absent." Gloomily, Charley poured the drinks.

Arthur lifted his head and frowned at the sea. "What's that noise?"

"Outboard motor. They're back at last!" Ed said with relief.

"Odd that there aren't any lights," Arthur said.

"I can hear more than one engine," Charley said.

"Let's go meet them." Arthur stood up. Everybody else stood up.

Eyes peering into the black night, the Nexus party walked slowly down the beach toward the water.

In the darkness before them, darker shapes appeared.

"Something's wrong!" Ed cried. "Three boats. No lights. *Get back to the hotel!*" He grabbed Isabel by the arm and turned to run up the beach.

Ed nearly collided with Louise, who had run barefoot behind them, holding her shoes in her hand. "I can't find *anyone.*" She sounded frightened. "Everyone's disappeared. There are soldiers getting out of trucks in front of the hotel. *What's happening?*"

Three outboards cut out, and three black, inflatable assault craft glided toward the beach. Black men wearing helmets and black combat clothes waded ashore, carrying assault rifles. Quickly, they fanned over the beach.

"Terrorists! Get off the beach!" Ed yelled, grabbing Louise. Dragging the two stumbling women, he ran back toward the hotel, then stopped abruptly.

"Oh, my God!" Isabel cried.

A line of similarly dressed soldiers had emerged from the hotel. With rifles at the ready, they slowly advanced.

Patty lifted her head sharply. "What's that noise?"

"Probably fireworks," said the skipper. "Louise has them for the beach barbecue. Hey! Look, ladies! The boundary fence!"

The bedraggled little group cheered up and limped faster toward the wire fence hung with electric lamps that surrounded the hotel grounds.

Suzy said, "I've gotta do something about my face before we go any further." She hobbled to the nearest light and fumbled in her purse for a comb.

Carey had never seen Suzy look such a mess. Wearily she said, "My face can wait. But I sure do need a cigarette," and fumbled in her white beachbag.

Annie halfheartedly searched her green raffia tote bag for her makeup kit, but she knew she was beyond repair. She needed total immersion in a warm tub with a bottle of shampoo before she would feel halfway human.

Silvana said impatiently, "Let's not hang around. The men must be worrying."

Suzy gave a little yelp as she peered into her hand mirror and saw her scratched, filthy, mascara-streaked face. "Can't we sneak in without being seen? I can't *possibly* let anyone see me like this."

"Okay," the skipper said, relieved that in a few minutes this spoiled bunch of Sheilas would be off his hands. "I'll take you to your huts by the back path, the one the staff uses."

"Let's hurry." Patty zipped her navy canvas shoulder bag, which told the world that she loved San Francisco.

The small, exhausted group stumbled along the wire fence until they reached the gate.

"Hey, there should be a guard on this gate," the skipper said. "I'd better report it." A missing guard was a serious matter. Should thieves get into the grounds, within minutes the entire contents of a hut could be missing.

"I can see the beach torches!" Suzy said, cheering up, as they walked over the clipped grass of the hotel grounds.

The skipper halted. "Something odd seems to be happening. Keep quiet and listen." He had heard the cocking of a weapon.

In the distance they heard a sharp command, followed by two shots.

Someone screamed, then there was silence, then more screaming. They heard another shot, then silence.

The skipper turned and whispered, "Don't any of you move. I'm going ahead to see what's happened." He moved forward in a crouch.

Anxiously, the women watched his white shirt recede among the dark trees.

Suzy looked around nervously. "I'm not going to stay here alone," she whispered. "I'm going after him."

Everyone nodded in agreement.

Using the numerous shrubs as cover, the women scuttled behind the skipper as he crept toward the beach in the semi-darkness.

Carey caught up with the skipper as he took cover in the shadow of an oleander bush, beyond range of the beach torches. The vanilla smell of oleander filled Carey's nostrils.

The skipper whispered, "You shouldn't have followed. Go back."

Carey did not hear him. She could not believe what she saw. There must have been about eighty silent soldiers on that beach, all wearing black combat fatigues, all clutching rifles. In front of the patio bar stood Arthur, Duke, Ed, Charley and

Roddy, with their hands behind their backs. Ed's face was covered with blood. Isabel and the girl from the hotel recreation desk stood about six feet away, also with their hands behind their backs. The Japanese were being tied up by soldiers, while the English couple lay still upon the sand.

Carey jumped as she felt a hand on her shoulder, but it was Patty. She groaned, "Charley, Charley . . ."

"*Shut up!*" Carey hissed.

The girl from the recreation desk yelled, "You can't *do* this! These are American citizens and Japanese citizens! They are guests of the hotel. They have *passports.*"

A soldier stepped forward and casually smashed the girl's face with his rifle butt. She pitched to the sand and lay still.

The skipper gasped. "That's Louise, my wife. I've got to get her out." He turned to Carey. "You're in charge. Get these women back to the jungle double-quick, and *no talking!*" He thrust the flashlight into Carey's hand and crouch-ran away to the right, into the dark circumference of the grim scene before him.

Frozen with shock, Carey couldn't believe what she was seeing. It had the unreal quality of a nightmare, she had that same sense of being eerily apart, that heart-thumping feeling of menace and dread. She couldn't obey the skipper's orders; she was incapable of movement. As if hypnotized, she watched Ed yell to an officer who held a machine gun, "What have you done with our wives?"

The man grinned. "Nothing. Yet. But I want you to see what we will do."

Ed yelled, "Where *are* they?"

Charley said, "Careful, Ed."

Several voices yelled at once, so Carey couldn't hear what was said.

One of the Japanese men called, "We are nothing to do with these Americans. Please release us."

The other Japanese called, "The women went on a boat this morning. I saw them."

The officer turned to him. "Where did the boat go, my friend?"

"I don't know."

Arthur called out, "We will pay whatever you want, we will give you helicopters, ships, gold—anything—if you release us."

The officer sauntered over and stood in front of Arthur. "You will ask for your life on your knees."

As Arthur clumsily maneuvered himself onto his knees, Carey could see that his hands were bound behind him. Then the officer calmly drew his pistol and shot Arthur in the groin. He screamed. The officer fired again, this time in the stomach. Arthur pitched forward head first onto the sand, kicked for a moment, and died.

Behind Carey, Silvana gasped in incredulous disbelief. As if in a nightmare her entire body felt leaden and immovable.

Carey heard Charley shout, "Do you realize that you've just shot an *American citizen*? You'll never be able to hush this up!"

The officer said, "Yes, we will, my friend. You will be taken out to sea, beyond the shark net. The CIA will not investigate down there."

"What do you want?" Charley cried desperately. "Whatever you want we'll *give* it to you."

There was a cry, then a scuffle, as the two Japanese broke loose and dashed for the trees, leaving two terrorists howling with pain on the sand.

A sharp order was followed by a staccato burst from a submachine gun. One of the Japanese fell and lay groaning, while the second man staggered on.

There was another burst of fire. Very slowly, the Japanese dropped to his knees, slithered onto his face and lay whimpering.

Ed was praying aloud as they shot Charley in the stomach. Then they shot Ed. Then Roddy. Then Duke. After that, they shot the skipper's wife as she lay unconscious on the ground.

They didn't shoot Isabel. As Carey watched what they did

to her, she vomited into the oleander bush. Patty started to shake uncontrollably. The two women clutched each other's hand and tore back across the hotel grass, the way they had come. They were followed by Annie, who dragged Suzy. Silvana puffed along behind, tears coursing down her face in the darkness, her lip bitten through with the effort of keeping silent.

Sobbing and gasping for breath, the women ran through the gate in the wire fence and hurled themselves back into the jungle.

BOOK THREE

PANIC

◄ 7 ►

Patty, the fastest runner, was the first to reach the black comfort of the jungle, but after a few paces she had to stop, because she could see nothing in the dark. *Where* was that
goddamn skipper? Behind Patty, Carey bumped into her. The
two women clung to each other, wet with sweat and shaking
with fear, as they waited for the others to catch up.

In the dark, dense undergrowth, the five women felt less
exposed and vulnerable. Suzy started to cry.

"Shut up, Suzy!" Carey whispered. "We don't dare make a
noise. Let's get as far away as possible."

They moved as fast as they could along the narrow track.
Now they were heedless of shaking legs, ants in their shoes,
creepers that lashed against their faces, thorns that tore at their
arms and legs and clothes. The sharp tang of their own sweat
mixed with the musty, fetid night smell of the jungle. Ankle
deep in the mushy filth of the track, they stumbled after each
other, tripping over tree roots and dead branches that cracked
beneath their feet and scratched their legs.

With one arm held in front of her face, Carey, in the lead
with the light, was forcing a path through the undergrowth
when she heard an urgent whisper.

"*Stop!*" It was Annie. "Silvana isn't behind me anymore."

"We can't stop," Patty hissed. "If Silvana can't keep up, that's her problem. If we stop, we'll all be caught."

They stumbled on, then stopped abruptly. Carey had taken a wrong turn, and they were facing an impenetrable wall of twisting, black vegetation.

The women shuffled back until they located the path, after which they moved along it with more caution.

Suddenly Carey went rigid and switched off the flashlight. She could hear what sounded like a large animal panting in front of her. No big cats on the island, it had said in her little guidebook, no predatory creatures. But this hoarse panting sounded like . . .

"Dio mio," came a fearful sob from ahead.

It was Silvana, who had not taken the wrong route, and was now ahead of them.

Carey switched on the flashlight, cautiously played it over the path ahead and spotlit the dirt-streaked Valentino jumpsuit and grubby sneakers.

Silvana sobbed, "Oh, thank God, I thought I'd lost you."

"If any of us gets left behind and found by those soldiers, they'll know that the rest of us are ahead," Carey said. "So we'll have to stick together. Patty had better take the flashlight and lead, with Silvana behind her. I'll go in the rear."

Unfortunately, Patty moved fast. It was relatively easy for her to do so, because she was holding the flashlight. Carey, bringing up the rear, could see nothing. With one hand, she clung to Annie's shoulder. Ahead of them, Suzy continually stumbled and fell, tripping the women behind her. Each time they fell, they were immediately bitten by insects in the rotting vegetation of the path. When they scrambled to their feet for the fourth time, Patty and the light were nowhere to be seen.

"That bitch! That selfish bitch!" Suzy cried. "She's just left us without any light!"

They stumbled on, blind. Annie was now in the lead, one arm protecting her eyes, the other groping ahead. A thorn spray tore at her cheek, and she stopped. "I can't see a thing. Perhaps we'd better get off this track and simply hide."

There was a rustle ahead.

Patty, with the flashlight, had returned for them. "For God's sake, don't fall behind again. Pull your shirttails out and let's hang on to them. This is the last time I'm coming back."

"Give me back that flashlight," Carey demanded.

"No, you can damn well keep up."

"Patty, can't we stop just a few minutes? I've got a terrible stitch in my side," whimpered Suzy.

"We . . . don't . . . stop!" Patty whispered fiercely. "A stitch in your side is nothing compared to what they just did to Isabel. Just think of that and keep going."

After the first, frantic, headlong flight of panic had subsided, the women moved forward more easily, although Patty, in the lead, still fought imagined horrors. Her whole body had been scratched by thorns and branches, and every bit of bare flesh agonizingly bitten by insects. Patty was sure one had gotten into her vagina, she could feel it itching inside. Didn't insects like moist, warm places? Hadn't she heard some story about an insect that buried itself into somebody's ear and burrowed right across her brain? It was an American female ambassador to some filthy part of Africa. How *fast* could insects travel up your vagina? Deep breathing, that was what she had better do, to stop this panic.

To her right, Patty heard the sharp bark of a dog and realized that they must be near the native fishing village, where they'd heard the scream earlier.

Better steer clear of *that* place, too. For the next few hundred yards, Patty slowed down, in order to move as silently as possible.

Suzy's cramp subsided. As she stumbled through the black, torturous brambles and leaves, hanging on to Annie's shirt, it slowly dawned on Suzy that Brett had not been among the men who'd been shot on the beach.

No, she definitely hadn't seen Brett.

If Brett had escaped from that bunch of black murderers,

then he might still be alive. Perhaps there *was* hope. Perhaps Brett would be able to rescue them. Brett knew that the women had gone for a picnic along the coast, so he knew roughly where to look for them. As soon as he could get to a phone he'd call up the nearest American embassy, he'd tell them to send in the Marines.

Patty stopped. Above the small circle of light, her voice whispered back to the women behind her. "Can you hear the sea? It sounds close. I think we're nearly at the beach. I'm going to have a look. You guys stay here."

She returned almost immediately. "You can't get through that stuff, it's impenetrable jungle. Let's move on."

But within five minutes, they suddenly found themselves moving through knee-high coarse grass. They could see the stars again, they could make out one another's heads against the black night sky. They could smell the sea and hear the beguiling invitation of the waves.

Silvana whispered, "Be careful, Patty. You don't want to fall down that cliff."

"I think we've come too far. I think we've passed the boat. I'll go see. Stay here." Cautiously Patty moved ahead.

A few minutes later she rushed back excitedly. "I saw lights at sea! It's the boat!"

Small sighs of relief. At last, in this suddenly bewildering world, the women had a reference point.

They followed Patty to the edge of the cliff. To their right, they could see the lights of the boat—one high white speck, plus a bright light in the cabin. They were only about two hundred yards away from it.

Hopefully, the women scrambled down the scrub-strewn slope and once again found themselves on the stony beach. Surprisingly, they located the dinghy with no difficulty. Five pairs of hands tore at the sand that buried the anchor.

"Shouldn't we wait for the skipper?" Carey whispered.

"Are you *crazy*?" Patty hissed. "They probably shot him as well."

They all dragged the dinghy down to the water and with the

last dregs of their energy they shoved her into the sea. Standing knee-deep in the ocean, Patty held the light while Carey held the boat steady. The other three women flung themselves aboard. As she scrambled in, Carey whispered to Patty, "How do we know that there aren't soldiers aboard? How do we know that Winston's still alive?"

Patty said, "It's worth taking the risk."

"Shouldn't only one of us go to the boat?"

"There's no noise. If there were terrorists aboard, wouldn't we hear them?" Patty swung the outboard into place and climbed aboard. She knew how to start an outboard and, once the engine was turning over, she steered toward the *Louise*.

Then Patty thought, My God, maybe Winston will shoot at us. She cut the engine and whispered urgently, "Winston . . . Winston . . ."

A voice quavered, "Skipper?"

"No. We're the American women."

"White ladies?" The voice was clearly fearful of the dark.

Patty started the engine again.

As the dinghy bumped alongside the *Louise*, Carey fumbled with the painter, then flung it up to Winston. One by one, the women scrambled aboard. Temporarily, they were safe. Now, in their filthy, torn clothes, their bodies started to tremble and their fingertips tingled. Suzy headed straight for the refrigerator and pulled out the vodka bottle. She grabbed a paper cup and filled it. She passed the bottle to Carey, who took a swig.

Patty said, "That stuff'll only make you thirsty and drunk. Are there any soft drinks left, Winston?"

"Soft?"

"Lemonade. Coca-Cola."

"No, only water."

Thirst overcame fear for a few minutes, and they all drank the water greedily. Patty said, "If only this boat hadn't broken down . . ."

Carey said, "If it hadn't, we'd have been at the beach with the rest of them."

Winston said, "Boat not buggerupem."

"No, the boat's not broken," Patty said, "but the engine is."

"Engine is okay. Winston fix engine."

"You mean the engine works?"

In the dim cabin light, Winston grinned and nodded. He scampered onto the bridge and pressed the starter. The engine turned over.

Carey spoke fast. "Let's get out to sea straight away. Let's get as far away as we can." She swung up the ladder and stood beside Winston. "Take us out to sea! *Right now,* Winston."

Winston looked bewildered, then frightened. Maybe they were stealing the boat? Where was his master? He said, "Winston no . . . can . . . no . . . ."

"But you just fixed the engine!" said Suzy. "Surely you can drive the fucking boat?"

Winston looked helpless.

Patty said, "Winston either can't or won't. So let's figure out how this thing works."

From the black waters of the bay, a voice rose above the engine. "Winston!"

Winston jumped and looked terrified. Maybe water spirits stronger than Jesus Christ.

The voice from the water urged, "Winston, for God's sake, let the ladder down before a shark gets me."

Winston raced to the rail and lowered the ladder.

Dripping wet, the skipper climbed aboard.

"Glad to see you all made it," he grunted.

Wordlessly, Suzy held out the vodka bottle but, gasping for breath, he shook his head. "Any beer left? What the hell did you do to the engine, Winston? She sounds fine."

"I check 'im slow time, boss. From fuel tank to injectors in engine. Pressa titty, boss, no problem."

"Good work, m'lad," the skipper said. According to the fuel gauge, there was still plenty of fuel, so maybe the filter in the tank was slightly blocked and the fuel pump wasn't strong enough to suck fuel past it. That would explain why the engine had stopped, and it would explain why it could start again a couple of hours later, because enough diesel would have seeped past the blockage to fill the injection system. Now, she'd probably go fine, until the filter blocked again.

Can of beer in hand, the skipper looked at his passengers. Suzy had pulled on a white fishing shirt; her scratched legs were streaked with blood. The shoulder of Silvana's black jumpsuit had been torn away. Annie looked as if she'd slept for months in her sleeveless green shirt and baggy pants. Patty's white shorts and navy shirt were in tatters. Carey's pale blue shirt and pants were the only clothes that weren't badly torn, but her long tawny hair had been mercilessly snagged by branches, and she looked like a crazed hillbilly. Their hair was tangled, their faces dirty and bleeding.

He said, "I counted over eighty of them bastards on the beach."

"What happened to you?" Patty asked.

"Crawled halfway round the back of the beach—wanted to surprise one of 'em from the rear and get his gun. I was going for one of the machine guns but there didn't seem much point after the shooting. They killed my wife along with the others. So I crawled back, found you'd scarpered and followed you back to the boat. Wasn't easy without a flashlight."

Silvana said, "Thank God you got here. Now take us out to sea. Radio for help. Call the police in Queenstown."

The skipper man shook his head. "Three assault craft are beached in front of the hotel. That means at least one fair-sized ship offshore, probably armed. If I radio, they'll know where we are. As it is, they're going to come looking for us, because they know we're out here somewhere. Seems a pity to tell 'em exactly where. Probably catch us within twenty minutes."

"Well, for God's sake, let's just *go!*" Silvana urged.

"Where to? We'll be in danger soon as we poke our nose beyond the point. Even if we head south, they'll probably hear us. Noise travels far over calm water."

"But we can't just stay here!" Silvana said. "We must get to Queenstown, to the police!"

"We don't know what the hell is happening in Queenstown.

They might be fighting those bastards at this minute, or maybe the bastards have taken over the town." He drained his beer. "On my way back, I was thinking what to do. Reckon the safest thing we can do for the moment is to stay here."

"But you said they'll come looking for us." Silvana was frantic.

"Won't bother to look if they think we're already dead. Reckon I'll put you ashore with enough gear to keep us alive. Winston and I'll take the boat out to sea, scatter your swimsuits around, then blow the poor old girl to pieces."

"But what will happen to you and Winston?" Carey asked.

"Just before the *Louise* goes up, we'll head for shore in the dinghy. With any luck they won't spot us. If they do, they'll likely think we're the only survivors. I reckon nobody saw us back on the beach. They were concentrating on other things."

For a long moment, they remembered seeing their menfolk brutally killed. All energy drained from the women and all eyes filled with tears, including those of the skipper. They felt without hope, they experienced a physical heaviness that made movement impossible. As they sobbed with sorrow, each woman's misery was also tinged with regret and fear.

Annie thought wildly, How can I manage without Duke? Our boys are all at the age when they need a man to guide them.

Silvana thought, Now Arthur never *will* be a grandfather. Thank God Lorenza is married. At least we won't be a family of women, we'll have Andrew to look after us.

Patty knew that she would never be able to cope with Stephen without her husband's loving support. After all these years of solicitous care, Stephen would have to be institutionalized. And how could *she* manage without Charley?

Carey felt deeply sorry that after being so near to it, Ed would never be president of Nexus. He had wanted that prize so much, and had striven so hard for it.

Although Suzy was crying tears of rage, she was the only woman who wasn't grieving for her man. In her heart she felt a *certainty* that Brett was still alive. She *hadn't* seen him on the beach. And in her magazine stories, the heroine was never *really* left stranded, the man was never *really* killed, there was always some good reason that he was absent, and he always turned up in the last chapter to save the girl.

"Can't have this," the skipper snuffled through his own sobs. "Time for grief when we get out of here. I'll get the dinghy ready."

"But you said the dinghy's outboard was unreliable!" Patty said.

The skipper shrugged. "If she conks out on us, we'll just have to row."

Patty said tartly, "You don't seem to have much luck with your engines."

"Don't seem to have much luck with anything at the moment." First he'd lost his wife, now he was going to lose his boat, and on top of that he had this load of useless Sheilas on his hands.

Carey said, "But what then? How are we going to get off the island?"

"We'll hide out in the jungle for a few days, then I'll send Winston to scout around. When things are quiet enough, three of us can escape at night in the dinghy. She won't take more than three, not with provisions."

Carey nodded. The dinghy had been low in the water when the five women returned to the *Louise*.

The skipper said, "I go in the dinghy, Winston stays to look after you. Carey stays because she can fish; Suzy stays because she can't swim. The others can toss for two seats in the dinghy."

Reluctantly Silvana said, "It's my responsibility to stay, that's what Arthur would want."

The skipper said, "It's only about seventy miles by sea from the southern tip of Paui to Irian Jaya."

"Where's that?" Suzy asked.

"The mainland. Once it was called Dutch New Guinea. Now it's called Irian Jaya and ruled by Indonesia."

Patty said, "If it's only seventy miles to safety, isn't it worth the risk to make a dash for it in *this* boat tonight?"

"Don't think I ain't considered that," the skipper said. "But we don't know what's going on, or where those murdering bastards came from, or how many ships there are out there. Them three big landing craft set out from a sizable vessel, and she's probably got radar and guns that could blow us out of the water as soon as we put to sea. . . . By the way, did you hear what they called the bloke who was giving the orders on the beach?"

Her voice choking, Suzy said, "Ed called him Rocky."

Carey started to cry.

"Not Rocky. My guess is it's Raki," the skipper said. "He used to be head of the army, under the Nationalists, but when they got kicked out, about eighteen months ago, Raki went into exile. So, if he's landing with troops, this might be a Nationalist countercoup. If I'm right, they're probably slugging it out in Queenstown at this very moment, and they'll certainly have the landing points covered from the sea. You can bet your life there are other ships out there in the dark."

Patty and Silvana started to cry.

The skipper said, "I know how you feel. Christ, I just lost my wife. But we can't afford to think about it now. We've got to get enough stuff off the boat to keep us alive. We're going to need every plastic container on this boat for the trip to the mainland."

Annie asked tentatively, "If you went alone, wouldn't there be more space for your water?"

"I'll need a lookout for when I sleep," the skipper said. "And I'm going to need at least one of you ladies for proof of what I'm claiming. Otherwise, how can your State Department insist on a search? Another thing, if anything happens to me, the lives of the rest of you will depend on whoever else is in that dinghy."

Suzy snapped, "Oh, for God's sake, let's stop talking and *do* something."

"Best figure things out first," the skipper said. "Winston'll help you get the stuff off the boat. I'll unscrew the bridge ladder. When we get it ashore, we'll throw the awning over it, tie the supplies on top and carry it, like a stretcher, till we find somewhere to hide."

Patty said, "Where will we go?"

"As far south as we can get before dawn. Tide's still going out, so we'll go round the coast at sea level. The dinghy will go with us, filled with supplies. We'll head into the jungle at dawn. Winston can find a hideout for us."

Suzy said, "What if—"

"Look, I can't tell you exactly what we're going to do," the skipper said. "We'll have to wait and see what happens. But I've worked out a timetable for our next move. It's nine thirty now. By ten o'clock we'll have unloaded. Winston and me'll be ready to go. Ought to be back by eleven. We'll trek till dawn, around six o'clock. That's seven and a half hours of hard walking, so get something in your stomachs, while I tell Winston what to take ashore."

Carey shared out the leftovers from the despised picnic. The women were all very hungry; they attacked the curling chicken sandwiches and they gobbled up every crumb.

While they ate, the skipper threw their bathing suits up to the bridge. He started to unscrew the eight-foot-long aluminum ladder that led from the deck to the bridge. Unsuccessfully, he tried to wrench off the binnacle that housed the ship's compass. He grabbed the sextant and the chronometer and handed them down to Winston, who had already unlaced the canvas awning over the bridge and folded it. Winston then scurried around the boat, fetching the supplies to be taken ashore.

Suzy watched the heap of equipment pile up on deck. "What the hell do we need all that for? What are we going to do with it when we get ashore?"

The skipper called, "Shut up, Suzy. I've no idea how fast we can get off this island, but it ain't going to be tomorrow. I'd rather we took too much than too little. And once the *Louise* is gone, it'll be too late to get more."

Patty took the dinghy to the beach on its first trip; it carried Silvana and Suzy, the canvas awning, the fishing tackle, the toolbox, three mosquito nets and the two wicker picnic baskets, which had been stuffed with sneakers, fishing shirts and four pairs of leather fishing gloves.

When Patty returned, Carey whispered from the rail, "He says you mustn't use the outboard, it's too noisy. You'll have to row."

Patty rowed back to shore. This time she took the fishing rods, the tackle box, the gaff and two fishing nets. In the plastic garbage pail were some waterproof matches, two metal cans used for bait, one battered metal bucket and two plastic ones, eight gutting knives, Winston's machete, the ladder, four rocket flares, a bundle of mini-flares and six life jackets.

Patty whispered to the shadowy figures who met her on the beach, "He says you have to put the life jackets on straight away, so that we don't have to carry them."

On the dinghy's third trip, it was laden with two spear guns, six spears, two pairs of black swim fins and underwater masks, an empty five-gallon jerry can and the ax. Patty carefully hugged the ICOM portable marine radio as she waited for Carey to climb aboard.

Carey whispered over the side, "Hey, catch this. I nearly forgot it." She threw down the first-aid kit.

In the dark, the heavy box hit Patty on the head and nearly knocked her overboard. Wildly she waved her arms to regain her balance and dropped the ICOM. It gave a little plop as it hit the water and sank into the black depths.

Patty whispered up, "I'm sorry, but I just dropped the radio overboard. Tell him."

"*Shit!*" Carey knew this meant that once the *Louise* put to sea, there was no way for the skipper to let the little party on shore know what was happening to him.

Carey whispered down, "Well, don't drop this, it's the rifle." Then she and Annie slipped down into the dinghy. Patty cast off. As the gray rubber craft headed for shore, there was no sound except for the soft lapping of water against the hull and the creaking of the oars.

In the cabin the skipper reached for six empty Perrier bottles from the bar and unlocked the paint stores locker. He took out four half-gallon cans of white paint, a gallon of white spirit in a plastic container and a can of paraffin, which was used for the lights. He dragged two five-gallon jerry cans on deck, one containing gasoline, the other oil. The two-stroke outboard on the dinghy ran on a mixture of gasoline and oil. The *Louise* ran on diesel fuel, which doesn't burn if you heat it. She wasn't supposed to carry gasoline, because it was a fire hazard, but some paying customers liked to waterski all day and the dinghy had to be refueled.

It is not difficult to make a gasoline bomb; every Belfast urchin knows how to do it. The skipper carefully poured gasoline into the Perrier bottles, which he didn't completely fill; he added a handful of sugar from the jar in the galley, then lightly screwed back the tops of the bottles. He prized open the can of white paint with difficulty, using a metal spoon because by that time the toolbox had already been taken ashore. He checked his mini-flares and slipped the pack into the pocket of his shorts.

As Winston and the skipper removed their sneakers—they didn't want to swim in them—they heard Patty row the dinghy alongside. The skipper handed down both pairs of sneakers, climbed down into the dinghy and rowed Patty back to shore. Normally he would have let Winston do this, but at that moment the dinghy was their most precious possession and Winston *was* only twelve years old.

The skipper put Patty ashore, whispered, "Atta girl, see you soon," and rowed quickly back to the *Louise*, where Winston was showing the port and starboard lights to guide him. Once the skipper was aboard, Winston extinguished the navigation lights. The skipper poured the four cans of white paint, the white spirit and the paraffin over the deck; he doused the deck with the remains of the five gallons of gasoline and five gallons of oil. That should be enough to set fire to an aircraft carrier.

Winston scrambled down into the dinghy, stowed the empty jerry cans and climbed back to the sticky deck.

With lights doused, the skipper started the engine. Obediently, the *Louise* chugged north, toward the invisible tip of the Paradise Bay peninsula. The skipper reckoned that guards would undoubtedly have been posted there. Just before they passed the tip he said, "Winston, get into the cabin and lie on the floor until I tell you to come up again."

Obediently Winston squelched over the deck and went below, his black splayed feet covered in white paint.

On the bridge, the skipper lit one of the paraffin-powered navigation lights.

Nothing happened.

The boat chugged slowly on, rocking from side to side in a soothing, lullaby rhythm.

The skipper heard a whistle, immediately followed by an explosion, which hurt his ears. At last the lookout had noticed them.

The skipper immediately extinguished the light and headed out to sea at full speed. Now they'd be wondering whether they'd really seen anything, they'd be straining their ears to hear the engines. But he didn't want to go too far from the shore, because he'd be picked up on a radar screen, or maybe even crash into the side of some troop carrier, so he cut the engine.

"Winston, get into the dinghy. Prepare to untie the painter, *fast*."

The skipper carefully handed the six Perrier bottles down to the boy. He pulled out his mini-flare pack, unclipped the flare gun, screwed it into a flare and withdrew it, cocked the flare gun, pointed the gun at the deck of the *Louise*, pressed the trigger, then flung himself overboard and into the dinghy as fast as he could.

Quickly, Winston rowed farther out to sea, to a position where the *Louise* was between the dinghy and the shore.

Above the gunwale of the *Louise*, which was about twenty-five feet distant, the skipper could see a faint glow. Thank God for that, he thought. He wouldn't have liked to go back and do it again.

"Okay, Winston, ship the oars and get into the bow. And keep your head down."

The skipper unscrewed the first glass bottle, hurled it toward the deck of the cruiser and crouched low in the dinghy.

The bottle fell short, landing harmlessly in the sea.

The skipper unscrewed the second bottle, hurled with greater strength than before, then quickly ducked.

The bottle hit the side of the *Louise*, then fell into the sea.

"Take her closer, Winston."

The third bottle fell onto the deck, but the skipper didn't hear the glass break. Was the bottle rolling around the deck? Had he remembered to unscrew the top?

The skipper unscrewed the fourth bottle and stood up to throw it, but before he could do so the cruiser disintegrated in a spectacular manner. Flames leaped up into the sky, and debris flew over the dinghy.

Another explosion followed fast upon the first one. The black night was lit with yellow flames.

As the *Louise* seemed to explode in his face, the skipper lost his balance and stumbled backward. As Winston scrambled toward his boss, the dinghy capsized and they were both hurled into the water.

When the skipper surfaced, he could clearly see the black shape of the upturned dinghy silhouetted against the yellow flames. He swam up to it, heaved himself on top and fumbled for the understrap that stretched beneath the dinghy.

He stood up and immediately lost his footing on the slippery, rubberized fabric. He fell back into the water.

Once again, he heaved himself on top of the upturned dinghy. This time he moved more carefully.

He hitched one foot beneath the understrap and leaned forward. With both hands, he grabbed the other end of the strap and leaned backwards, pulling with all his weight away from the dinghy.

Righting the inflatable wasn't as easy as it is supposed to be; the skipper had to struggle for some time before he was successful.

Success hurled him back into the black, heaving water—but the dinghy had been righted. No chance now of getting the outboard started, the prolonged immersion would have finished off those spark plugs he'd been meaning to replace. He'd better ditch the outboard.

Quickly he heaved himself up over the side of the dinghy. In a hoarse whisper he called, "Winston, Winston." As he called, the skipper patted the inside of the inflatable to check that the oars were still clipped into place. Yes, they were.

Was it his imagination, or was the hull less taut?

"Winston, where the hell are you?" he called softly.

"Boss! Boss!" The cry came from astern.

Swiftly, the skipper unclipped the oars and started to row, softly calling, "Winston?"

In the dark they had only their voices to guide them to each other. The skipper was worried, because they should have been well clear of this area by now. He must have been rowing for three minutes.

He called again, "Winston?"

"Here, boss." In the blackness, the voice seemed astern and a little to port.

There was a slight bump, then a scratching on the hull and some splashing.

"You hit me, boss."

Thankfully, the skipper shipped the oars. Kneeling, he felt carefully over the side, along the inflated curve of the hull. Yes, she was definitely wrinkling, which meant that she was leaking somewhere. Something from the explosion had holed her. What filthy luck, he thought.

His fingers touched cold wet flesh, and the skipper grasped

Winston's hand. "Gotcha! Good boy, Winston. Give me your other hand and I'll pull you in."

There was a shrill scream from the water and the small wet hand was torn from his grasp. Another agonizing scream ended abruptly in a gurgle.

In the dark, the waves slapped softly against the smooth hull of the dinghy.

SAVAGES

◀ **8** ▶

Patty was down on the beach with a flashlight, somewhere near the pile of stores, but the rest of the women had scrambled up the steep incline and were hiding in the secondary jungle at the top. The solid green wall of vegetation that surrounded them was so thick that they had great difficulty burrowing into it; you might be a yard away from a terrorist, and neither of you would know. The women hadn't been able to endure sitting down, because of the ants and the spiders, so they squatted, shivering in spite of the hot night. In the dark, Carey sniffed the damp, sour stink of rotting vegetation—an unmistakable smell, and one that she'd been told by Ed was ineradicable. He could never get the smell of the jungle off his clothes when he returned from a tropical field trip.

At the thought of Ed, Carey put her hands over her mouth to stifle a sob, but she couldn't stop the tears welling from her eyes. She had heard snuffles and gulps from all the others, although not one of the women had yet spoken of the massacre on the beach.

Carey said, "I wish I could have just one cigarette."

"Well, you can't, because someone might smell the smoke," Suzy said. "Here, try this." She had brought a bottle of vodka from the boat.

Down on the dark beach, Patty too was shivering. It was all

184

right for the rest of them, they were *together* up there, but *she* was alone down here, and she was sure she'd heard a heavy gun fired, about twenty minutes ago.

Without warning, the sky to Patty's right lightened momentarily over the peninsula; the noise of an explosion quickly followed.

They'd done it!

Good for the skipper! They were now all officially dead. Patty imagined Carey's flowered bikini floating on the black surface of the bay, then she started to calculate how long it would take the skipper to get back to shore in the dinghy. Patty didn't want to waste the flashlight battery, and she didn't want to risk being seen. She'd count to twenty minutes, then start to flash the light. If you said "hippopotamus," that took one second. Hippopotamus one, hippopotamus two, hippopotamus three . . .

Patty felt very sleepy. Counting hippopotami obviously had the same effect as counting sheep. Maybe she'd sit down. If the light was a couple of feet lower, it wouldn't make any difference. She felt exhausted. . . .

The skipper had managed to get the nine-foot, slowly deflating dinghy around the point of the peninsula, but it was still half a mile to the beach. He shipped his oars again and felt for the string attached to the bailer. Now the bitch was leaking as well as deflating fast.

The nearest shore seemed to be a mangrove swamp, or that's what it smelled like; he could faintly hear water sucking at the mangrove roots, making a sloppy, chuckling noise. If he went ashore into that, God knows how he'd get back to the beach.

Arms aching, he threw down the bailer, picked up the oars and started to row as hard as he could. His shoulder joints felt as if they were being wrenched out of their sockets. The dinghy seemed to sigh; with his backside, he felt that she was getting lower in the water. She was definitely going under, he could feel her slack beneath him. He tensed his buttock muscles, willing the dinghy to keep afloat but, once again, the wooden stern dipped. He relived what had happened to poor Winston, and put his aching back into his rowing. He willed himself not to think of sharks. God knows what would happen to those poor cows if he didn't make it to the beach.

Just before he'd rounded the peninsula, he'd seen a patrol boat approach the wreckage. Well, he hadn't actually seen it, the vessel had played her searchlights over the wreckage-strewn water. Thank God she'd hove to—presumably to retrieve wreckage. She had then cruised around the bay, probably looking for survivors. She'd also shone her searchlights over the shoreline. Thin, white fingers of light had probed the pale line of beach and the black trees beyond.

Water started to flood over the stern. He'd already cut the line that attached the oars to the inflatable. Now he moved forward as fast as he could. He sat with a leg on either side of the hull and used one oar like a canoe paddle, dipping it into the sea, first on one side and then on the other, trying not to think about the fact that this bay wasn't protected by a shark net.

It was no good. The water was sucking at the dinghy—not that he could call her that now, she felt like a kid's swimming ring, once you'd pulled the plug out. She just wasn't moving forward anymore.

No use letting the bloody thing sink under him. He'd just have to swim ashore, pushing an oar in front of him, and longing for a third hand to protect him down below.

Trying to make as little splash as possible, he slid into the black water and hoped he was swimming in the right direction.

When he finally scrambled out of the water, still hanging on to the oar because it would be a giveaway, there was no sign of a light. Was this the right beach? Maybe he'd gone too far down the coast. No, that wasn't possible. Maybe those idiot women had had some brilliant idea of their own. Or maybe they'd already been picked up by terrorists. . . . They had to be terrorists. Decent soldiers didn't behave like that.

Creeping cautiously along the beach, he crashed over a warm lump. He thought at first that he'd fallen over an animal, then it swore at him.

"Why the hell weren't you flashing the light for me?"

"Sorry," Patty said. "I fell asleep."

"Keep your voice down! Where are the rest?"

"Hiding at the top of the cliff," she whispered. "Shall we start loading the dinghy? Where's Winston?"

"Winston won't be back. The dinghy sank."

"But how can we escape without the dinghy? How can we get the equipment down the coast? How can . . . *What do you mean, Winston won't be back?"*

"Keep quiet! Why don't *you* think of something for a change. I'm bushed." He collapsed on the sand, and immediately felt the sand flies attack. This woman must have the skin of a rhinoceros to be able to sleep on the beach. Or else she was really whacked.

"What happened to Winston?" Patty persisted.

"Shark, poor little bugger."

Patty started to cry.

The skipper said, "I feel the same way."

They were both silent, then the skipper said in a tired voice, "We'll hide out now, and decide what to do in the morning. I'll steal a boat from a native village or something."

"Where are we going to hide?"

"I don't bloody know. If those soldiers weren't Filipino mercenaries, then they're from Paui—local lads. They'll ferret us out in five minutes if they find any trace of us tomorrow."

Patty said hesitantly, "What about hiding in that cave? The cave that Winston found under the waterfall? We saw some caves in Australia where bushrangers hid out for months."

The skipper considered this suggestion. "Waterfall Bay's about fifteen miles away. It's just turned midnight. We'd have to travel over two miles an hour, along the shore path, or we wouldn't get there before daylight. That ain't impossible." Strolling along a country walk you'd cover three miles an hour, and there was nothing like fear to make you walk faster. "Why not?" he said.

"Can't we leave the equipment here?"

"No. If them terrorists don't spot it, then the local natives will. If we don't take the equipment, we'll never see it again." Wearily, he stood up. "The sooner we go the better, so let's find the others."

He sniffed disapprovingly. "Have you ladies been drinking?"

Carey said, "Suzy brought some vodka off the boat. Want some?"

"Give it here. Last thing I need is a bunch of tipsy women, and the last thing *you* need to survive in the jungle is liquor."

"To hell with you," Suzy said.

"Honest, liquor ain't a good idea. Even on Arctic survival trips, they don't take liquor. Forget those stories about St. Bernard dogs with little barrels of brandy strung around their necks. Alcohol gives you a false sense of warmth and a false sense of security—and it dulls your wits. If I'm to get you out of here, I want you in full working order and obeying my instructions. Is that clear? That bottle will be thrown away, or I'm leaving."

Reluctantly, Suzy handed over the bottle. The skipper pulled off the cap and emptied it onto the grass. "Let's not waste any more time," he said. "Get down to the beach, and I'll tell you what we're going to do."

Only the skipper knew what their walk would entail, because only he knew the coastline. It was mostly sandy beaches, with rocky headland between them. They would have to cut behind the muddy estuaries, which was where the estuarine crocs were—some of them up to twenty feet long.

They would also have to avoid the poorly drained, saline swamps, where the gnarled mangroves clustered. The trees were often over a hundred feet high; their twisting, thick roots were tough enough to withstand the battering of the wind and the daily rise and fall of the tide. The only way to make progress through the mangroves was at low tide, when you could climb over the gnarled entanglement, taking care not to step on a scuttling crab in the mud, or the mangrove's breathing roots, which stuck up like twisted nails and could tear through light shoes.

The skipper decided to divide their equipment into six packs; they'd try to carry them on the ladder, used as a stretcher, with the canvas awning of the wheelhouse on top of it. Both those items were very heavy. If they couldn't manage the stretcher, then they'd dump the ladder and awning and each carry a load.

He slipped into the jungle and returned with some lengths of what looked like brownish-greenish, thin rope. "It's rattan," he told the women. "Grows everywhere in the jungle. Tarzan swung on vines, but he could have swung across them gorges on rattan."

The moon had risen, which made it easier to assemble their load. The skipper made three sacks from the three mosquito nets, threading rattan around the perimeter and then pulling it taut. They loaded what they could into these net bags and everything else went into the two picnic baskets and the plastic garbage pail, all of which were carefully tied on the stretcher.

The skipper picked up the rifle, the flares, the matches and the machete. He stuck three fishknives in his belt and two handfuls of fish hooks in the pockets of his shirt and pushed the underwater flashlight down his shirtfront, where the charts were drying out against his skin. He was carrying the most valuable items, including the navigational instruments, and they would be the last things to be dumped.

He said, "Let's go. Anyone who can't keep up will have to be left behind. Understand? There ain't no alternative."

The skipper led the way. Behind him, the women took turns carrying the stretcher. The first part of their journey lay along the track that led south from the hotel. By following this track through the jungle, they would avoid walking around another peninsula. The skipper didn't want to risk being seen on the open beach so near Paradise Bay.

As they trudged along the narrow, leaf-covered track, the skipper mentally assessed the strengths and weaknesses of the women he was leading. They were clearly all soft, pampered, used to being looked after, like children. The skipper reckoned that Carey was going to be most help to him; she was a big, strong girl, and she'd fought that shark, calmly and bravely, for hours. She obviously had a lot of stamina and determination, qualities that might just get them out of this mess.

Patty, too, appeared self-disciplined and physically strong; she was also a first-rate swimmer. But there was something about Patty—a nervous tautness, a neurotic overanxiousness —that made the skipper feel uneasy. She was the sort that seemed dependable but might crack when you were least expecting it—and could least afford it.

Now that wouldn't apply to little Suzy. She was thoughtless, she snapped, she had a short fuse, she liked to make a fuss and she was clearly aggressive. But undoubtedly she had a gutsy streak; a lot of women would have made a helluva lot more fuss than she did after that quicksand incident, but Suzy had merely looked him in the eye and said, "You and Winston saved my life. Thanks." It wasn't much—but the earnest way she said it made it enough. He had the feeling that Suzy was tougher than she looked, and a survivor.

He also had the same feeling about the quiet one—Annie. She was timid, conciliatory, and hardly said a word, but *she* was the one who had jumped to her feet and briskly dealt with Suzy after the quicksand incident. The skipper sensed that she was practical and reliable in an emergency.

He wasn't so sure about the plump one in the black jumpsuit—Silvana. She was certainly the slowest mover of the group—she'd seemed languid and disengaged all day, even when she'd taken her nose out of that book. He reckoned that Silvana was going to be more of a hindrance than a help.

Once in the jungle, the little party no longer had the faint light of the stars and moon to light the way, and it was a hard job to concentrate on their footing. As they panted along the narrow track, Suzy asked wearily, "Can't we dump some of the stuff on this stretcher?"

"Sure," said the skipper. "What do you want to dump? Think carefully, because your life might depend on your choice."

"The canvas awning is the heaviest thing," Suzy said.

"If we can't get a boat, we'll have to make a raft. We'll need that canvas for the underside, to hold the thing together —for insurance. You wouldn't want to be at sea on a raft that's coming to pieces under you."

Dragging their feet, knowing that anyone who dropped out would be left in the jungle, the women struggled through the night; they fell into a sort of mental hibernation, a weary, stoic apathy, a suspension of awareness until they could bear to think again. This was the only way they could endure the sticky heat, the arm-aching weight of the stretcher and the onward shuffling of their exhausted legs, which trembled with the strain. Hoping to hasten the progress, the skipper decided to carry the back end of the stretcher and took over from Suzy, who was the smallest of the group. He gave her the flashlight and the machete.

Suzy played the flashlight over the two-foot-long, wickedly sharp blade. "I don't know how to use this thing."

"You will if you have to," the skipper said.

Suzy whimpered, "I'm frightened of snakes."

"And they're frightened of you. Even the most deadly snake will get out of your way if it hears you coming—except for the king cobra, and there ain't any of them in this part of the world." He added, "Snakes only attack if you alarm them, or corner them or tread on them—just like human beings."

The other women took turns carrying the front of the stretcher, because the track was too narrow to allow more than one person at a time. Suzy moved slowly ahead, picking out the track with the light. She moved with care, for she didn't want to take another dead end, as Carey had done. She knew that if she made a mistake, the flashlight would be taken away from her and she'd have to go back to carrying that damn stretcher.

Suddenly Suzy gave a shriek. The faint line of light that preceded her had disappeared. The rest of the party stopped abruptly.

Nobody moved. They tried not to breathe. They heard the by-now familiar sound of Suzy sniveling.

The skipper whispered, "What's up?"

From ahead, Suzy snuffled, "There's something big in the way. I walked smack into it and fell down. I dropped the light."

The skipper put down the stretcher and picked up his rifle; he moved to the front of the line, feeling before him with his toes before taking each step. His foot prodded the soft bundle that was Suzy. He grunted, "Get up, girl, and look for that light."

He shifted his rifle to his left hand, squatted on his haunches and ran his fingers through the long grass to his right, hoping nothing would bite his hand.

He saw a faint glow. The flashlight hadn't gone out, it had rolled under an enormous dead tree that had crashed across the track, creating a barrier before them. He retrieved the light and played it over the huge tree trunk, which was about five feet high and very thick.

"We'll have to climb over her," he said. "I'll go over first. Carey, give Suzy a leg up, then the rest of you follow. Before you start climbing, unload the stretcher and throw the stuff over to Suzy. Take your life jackets off and throw 'em over first; it'll be easier to climb that thing without 'em."

"Can't we walk round it?" Suzy asked.

"No. We've no idea how long it is and it's not possible to move more than six inches into the jungle on either side of this track."

Carey held the flashlight as he clambered up the deadwood; it flaked beneath his foothold, and he fell back to the ground. He said, "Kneel down, Carey. I'll have to get on your back."

Gingerly, Carey knelt down in the rotting vegetation of the

path; ants immediately ran over her hands and ankles. She felt a jolt when the skipper's foot used her spine as a springboard, but he was quickly on top of the tree trunk and sitting astride it. Carey frantically brushed the insects from her hands.

After the man's weight, it wasn't too bad having Suzy stand on her back as the skipper hauled her up onto the tree and helped her to slither down the other side.

Annie wasn't much heavier, but when Silvana stood on her back Carey gasped, "I can't stand any more." Her elbows gave way and both women collapsed onto the track. Carey hissed, "You're not supposed to *stand* on me! You're supposed to put *one* foot on me, to help you jump up on the tree." As she said it, Carey could hardly believe she was using that tone of voice to the wife of Ed's boss.

"Shut up!" the skipper growled, and groped down for Silvana's hand.

It took several attempts, but eventually Silvana lay on her stomach on top of the tree trunk with her plump legs dangling on one side and her arms hanging over the other. The skipper helped her into a sitting position, forcing the path they were about to follow. "Now jump, Silvana," he urged.

"I can't! I can't!"

So he pushed her off, then turned back to Carey. "You'd better hand the equipment up, then jump up next. The last one over should be the lighter."

Patty knelt down in the filth; with a nimble step on her back, Carey jumped up. She sat astride the tree trunk, facing the skipper, then they both leaned down to Patty and hauled her up onto the tree like a sack of potatoes.

On the other side of the dead tree, the skipper encouraged his little party as again they donned their life jackets. "We ought to hit the coast soon, then we'll walk by the shore route. That bloody tree lost us fifteen minutes, so try to move faster."

Half an hour later Suzy, still in the lead, hissed, "Stop!" She turned to the skipper. "The track's disappeared, and I can hear water."

He took the flashlight from her and cautiously moved forward.

"It's only a stream, and there's stepping stones. There's a bit of a current running, so I'll go over first to check it. I'll shine the light back, so Patty can see where she's going." He had noticed that Patty was the only woman who wasn't dragging her body, completely exhausted.

The stepping stones were slippery, and some were a few inches underwater, but he and Patty managed to get to the other side.

The skipper said, "I'll go back and get the others. You hold the light. Then we'll both go back for the gear."

Suzy called anxiously, "I can't swim."

"You won't need to," he reassured her. "And remember, you're wearing a life jacket." He returned to where the women waited, then he firmly grasped Suzy's hand and coaxed her across the stepping stones in the faint light of the flashlight. Patty had to concentrate hard to direct the light on the next stone to be stepped on.

When it was Silvana's turn to take the skipper's outstretched hand and jump, she missed the first stone, waved her free hand wildly, clutched the skipper's fingers and pulled them both into the turgid waters of the stream.

As they waded toward the opposite bank, the skipper said in disgust, "Strewth, it's only a couple of feet deep! Would have been easier and safer to wade across her, instead of hopping on them slippery stones."

He and Patty waded back for the bundles of equipment. Afterward, they rested, exhausted, while the other women reassembled the stretcher. Patty thought, I sure wish he hadn't poured out Suzy's vodka.

About twenty minutes later they reached another stretch of water, wider than the previous stream. The skipper said, "There are rivers and streams all along the coastline, they drain down from the mountains."

This time there were no stepping stones, and the water was deeper. The skipper tied a length of rattan around his waist and fastened the other end around Patty's middle; he told Suzy to shine the light ahead.

"How do we know it's not out of your depth?" Patty asked, watching the circle of light dance on the swirling, sludge-brown water.

"We're on a much-traveled highway. This is the local Fifth Avenue," he said. "If it was too deep, they'd have built a bridge across it."

Wading waist-deep, they seemed to be walking on an even surface of grit and sand. Then, abruptly, Patty's foot stepped on nothing. She lost her balance and fell forward into the muddy water. She immediately started to swim, but was tugged back by the rope around her waist.

The skipper cried, "Don't swim! Stand up, it's okay. The riverbed dropped suddenly, I nearly went over myself."

Patty found that she could stand, although the water was up to her armpits and her soggy, sucking sneakers did little to protect her feet from the knobbly stones that now formed the riverbed.

Exhausted, Patty scrabbled up onto the bank. She squatted on the ground and held the flashlight as the skipper waded back to the other women. As he carried Suzy over, piggyback, Patty thought crossly, Some people certainly have the knack of getting the best deal. First she gets to hold the light, then she gets carried across the river; it sure pays to be small and look helpless.

When the other women had forded the river, Carey, who was easily the tallest, helped the skipper carry the equipment over; her hands, which had been sore from fighting the shark, were now raw and bleeding. All equipment was transported on their heads, except for the garbage pail, which was too big and unwieldy, so they each took a handle to carry it across. Wearily, they picked themselves up and continued on along the track.

Suzy stopped again. "Listen. The *sea!*"

As they listened to the distant roar of the surf, the tired little party cheered up; they straightened their tortured backs and ignored their blistered hands. At least they'd soon be out of this putrid, steaming black nightmare and back in the moonlight. Their steps quickened, their blistered feet in the overlarge, squeaking wet sneakers lifted higher as they moved toward that beguiling sound. Now they could see the stars overhead, beyond the black canopy of the forest.

The skipper ordered ten minutes' rest. He unpacked the stretcher and cleared an area free of leaves. He unfolded the canvas and spread it on the ground, to protect them from insects. The women collapsed on it, thankful that they hadn't ditched it.

A moment later Carey yelled and jumped to her feet. "Aaah! Slimy things on my leg!" She rolled up her pale blue pants and screamed again as the skipper shone the light on her legs. About fifteen black, two-inch-long, sluglike creatures were clinging to her skin.

"Leeches," he said. "Must have picked them up when we was fording the river."

Carey panicked. She couldn't get away from her own legs, and she couldn't bear to touch those foul things. She jumped up and down, screaming.

"Don't touch them," said the skipper. "Don't try to brush them off, because their teeth will stay in your skin and infect it."

By now the other women had felt their legs; leeches clung to all of them. They all jumped off the canvas as if it were red hot.

"Stop that noise," growled the skipper. "They don't hurt. You've only just noticed them. Anyone got a cigarette?

Carey was shaking with loathing, as she rummaged in her shoulder bag for cigarettes; she was trembling too much to light one, so the skipper took the pack from her. He lit a cigarette and knelt down in front of her. Holding the flashlight in one hand and the cigarette in the other, he gently touched each glistening black creature with the lighted cigarette end, whereupon it dropped off.

After the last leech had fallen from Suzy's inner thigh, the women slowly calmed down.

"Ain't any of you seen *The African Queen?*" the skipper grumbled, "Katharine Hepburn didn't make a fuss like you lot. Hopping about like bloody grasshoppers! I don't know where you get the strength."

He looked at their dirty, frightened faces. "You been doing fine up to now. Take five more minutes, then we must get going again. It's just past two, and we've got another ten miles to cover before dawn—six o'clock. If they're going to come looking for us, that's when it will be."

Five minutes later he called, "On your feet. Time to rest after sunrise."

Annie and Suzy, who had fallen asleep, were shaken awake. Wearily, they plodded on, with fingers that were almost too stiff to grasp the stretcher. With the skipper now in the lead, they moved, one behind the other, through thigh-high grass toward the sound of the sea, until they found themselves standing at the top of the steep incline, about forty feet above the ivory-pale line of the beach below.

They slipped and slid down the slope to the beach. On the descent, the load on the stretcher became dislodged, so the skipper picked it up and repacked it.

They stumbled off again, heading south along the shoreline.

As they plodded on, their spirits lifted. In spite of their aching arms and legs, their clothes were almost dry and they were making much faster progress than before. A slight breeze blew off the sea, smelling of salt and seaweed, refreshing on their faces and cleansing their nostrils of the rotting stench of the jungle.

Occasionally someone stumbled over a stone. Once Annie slipped on seaweed and the stretcher fell in the sand, but for the next two hours the little party made good progress as it trudged around headlands and across long stretches of beach, under the starlight and the moon, always to the soothing rhythm of the sea.

At about four in the morning, they crossed a beach and

found themselves facing a steep headland, which fell straight into the sea. Looking at it, the skipper reckoned that they'd either have to retrace their steps or swim around it. However, when he waded into the sea, he found that he was able to move around the point in waist-level water, although the rocks beneath his feet were slippery.

Once again, the stretcher was unloaded and the contents distributed among the women. Suzy asked exasperatedly, "Why do we have to keep packing and unpacking this god-damn stretcher all the time?"

Patty thought, What nerve, she isn't even carrying it.

"It's the easiest way to carry a lot of stuff," the skipper explained. "If we don't unpack it, we risk wetting the equipment. We couldn't have burnt off them leeches if Carey's cigarettes had been wet." One slimy rock underfoot could make the stretcher bearers slip, and then the whole load would be soaked. He said, "I don't like it any more than you do. Stay behind if you want to. I ain't going to argue with you. You can argue with them terrorists."

Grumbling and tearful, Suzy waded into the water, and the little party started to circumnavigate the cliff. Halfway around, Suzy yelled and dropped the flashlight and the mos-quito-net bag she was carrying. She hopped around, clutching her foot.

Exasperated, the skipper said, "Give me your bundle, Annie, and get that flashlight. Suzy probably stepped on a sea urchin, and if she keeps hopping around, she'll step on some more."

Annie groped in the water for the flashlight. She could see the beam of light, so, although she had to duck her head underwater, the flashlight wasn't difficult to retrieve. She shone it where Suzy was standing. "I can see a lot of brown balls as big as fists down here. They're covered with spikes."

"Sea urchins, like I said. I'll have a look at her foot later. If a spike's gone into her foot, she'll have a septic wound. Right now, Annie, you keep hold of that flashlight and find us a path that ain't covered in sea urchins. Suzy can go to the rear."

There was an air of smugness among the others as Suzy, in disgrace, splashed to the rear of the line. Slowly, they all waded after Annie, then plodded along yet another blackened beach.

As the sky lightened, Annie anxiously asked, "Are we nearly there?"

"Sure," the skipper reassured them, as they trudged along. In fact, he had no idea where they were; he wouldn't be able to get his bearings until it was light enough to see properly. But there was no point in disheartening them, it would only slow them down.

The sky brightened, until it was a stripe of pale gray above a strip of dark gray. Quite suddenly, the jungle noises ceased; the only sound was the soft swish of the feathery palm tops, moving slightly in the breeze blowing off the sea.

"Okay. Take five minutes' rest. This is our last breather," the skipper said. "Spread the canvas, or you'll get bitten by sand flies."

"I'm so thirsty," Suzy grumbled.

"You ain't the only one. But we'll soon be at that waterfall, then you can drink all you want." Maybe he had been wrong about Suzy. Maybe she was a complainer—always whinge-ing. None of the other women were making a fuss, but maybe the poor creatures didn't have the strength to do so, they were all being sensible and saving their strength.

Leaving the women huddled on the canvas, the skipper walked to the water's edge and turned to look at the beach, trying to imagine it as he would have seen it before—from the sea. Might Waterfall Bay be the next blasted beach on their route? He looked around. No, it wouldn't, because Waterfall Bay had mangroves to the north of it, and there weren't any on the next headland. He'd have to take his little party inland when they reached those mangroves; no one carrying this sort of load could get around those grabby roots, twisting like ar-thritic fingers above and below the water.

He walked back to the women. "Just a *bit* further. Go as fast as possible, because after sunrise we'll have to move into the trees, so that we're under cover if a boat comes round the headland. And *that* means walking on soft sand, so hurry on this hard stuff while you can. Remember we're nearly there. Soon you can all shower in the waterfall, have a bite to eat and a good sleep."

Carey said, "We haven't got anything to eat."

"I've got a little treat tucked away. Now, on your feet. It's nearly five o'clock."

As they rounded the next headland, the horizon was pale yellow with the orange curve of the sun just above it. The skipper was always surprised at the speed with which the sun reared up from the horizon; three minutes and she was clear of it.

If they were going to send a search party, the buggers would be setting off about now, so he'd have to get these women off the beach in ten minutes. Then he'd let them sleep for an hour. The poor wretches deserved it. By that time, the search party would either have passed or it wouldn't be coming. He had hoped that they'd have reached the waterfall by now, but you couldn't time this sort of lark like a royal wedding.

Under the palm trees, well back from the beach, the women wearily spread the still-damp canvas awning, which seemed to have grown six times heavier during the night. They huddled against each other, which felt odd, because none of them had cuddled up like this against another female since they were children. Damp and sweating, aching and uncomfortable, they curled up on the canvas and were all asleep within two minutes.

Forty minutes after the women had left the beach, the skipper heard the drone of an outboard motor, coming from the north. He rolled over onto his stomach and cautiously lifted his head. A large, black, inflatable landing craft was zipping past the beach. It was over twenty feet long and could probably hold twenty men. He could see the glint of metal helmets and binoculars as the boat moved in close to check the shoreline. That craft certainly moved fast. Lucky the women were off the beach, they might not have had time to hide, and they'd certainly have had to drop all their gear on the sand; might as well have stuck up a signpost and a red flag.

He watched the landing craft disappear around the southern headland.

Well, they couldn't stay here hoping the buggers wouldn't show up again; they might zip up and down all day. Even if they weren't looking for this lot, the terrorists might well be paying friendly calls on the villages along the coast in their steel helmets, with their AK-47's at the ready.

He shook Patty awake, made her stand up and gave her the rifle.

"I'm off to check what's round the next headland. Patty, *don't* sit down before I get back. If a boat passes, lie low. If anything nasty happens, point that gun at the sky, slip back the safety catch, and pull the trigger. I'll be back as fast as I can."

Terrified into wakefulness, Patty stood rigid, nervously cradling the rifle in her arms.

Thirty minutes later, the skipper returned. "On the far side of this bay there's another big beach; the southern headland is a mass of mangroves. I reckon the beach beyond is Waterfall Bay. Pity we can't walk along the shoreline a bit longer, but we've made pretty good time, considering everything." He nodded toward the little group huddled like puppies on the canvas. "Wake 'em up."

There were groans and curses. It was impossible to wake Carey, until the skipper said in her ear, "We just had visitors, a boat patrol passed half an hour ago."

Then they all sat up, looked at him with frightened eyes from sleep-pale faces, and slowly scrambled to their feet.

The skipper took out his compass, the women picked up their hated load and they headed inland, along the coastal track that led to the east. Shortly afterwards, the skipper realized that they'd struck it lucky for a change because they were clear of secondary jungle. Primary jungle—virgin, tropical rain forest—was easy to move in.

Their path led beneath high trees, well over a hundred years old and ten feet wide at the base. They soared up sixty feet, forming a dense canopy under which the light was dim and gloomy green. The whole forest was festooned with creepers and vines, and there was little noise except for the gentle rustling of leaves. It was comparatively easy to walk through, not much more difficult than the redwood forests of her California girlhood, thought Patty, perking up.

They left the path. Following his compass, the skipper led them on a bearing that would bypass the swampy mangrove area and, with any luck, lead them to the river that fed the waterfall. He counted his footsteps aloud, and Carey double-checked the tally. Every two thousand paces was roughly a mile.

After nearly two miles, they reached an almost sheer ravine about forty feet wide. Shrubs clung to both rocky sides, and sixty feet below was a fast-flowing torrent, probably on its way to the waterfall. All they had to do was follow it to the sea.

The going wasn't difficult, and they made good progress. After covering about half a mile, Patty whispered to the skipper, "What's that?" She nodded toward three ropes that crossed the ravine.

"Might as well have followed the bloody path," he said glumly. "It's a Burma bridge."

The rope bridge was alarmingly basic: the lower rope was knotted at close intervals; the two ropes above it, at armpit level, were each attached to the foot rope by lengths of rattan.

The skipper said, "You get across by moving one foot in front of the other and angling your feet outward like a ballet dancer. You feel along the notches of the bottom rope with the arch of your foot and you hitch your elbows over the top ropes and pull yourself along with your hands."

Silvana said faintly, "You're not expecting *us* to go over that thing?"

"It's easier than it looks, but I don't think we need to cross it. We'll follow this side of the ravine, and maybe cross at the waterfall if the current ain't too strong. Let's push on, we're nearly there."

By now their feet had been rubbed raw by the wet sneakers. Each of the women only kept going because the others were still moving. The skipper sensed this and hoped to God that Suzy wouldn't crack, because if she stopped, they'd all fall down.

Silvana was conscious of some maddening bird repeatedly singing C sharp, G, E flat. Suddenly, as she staggered under the weight of the stretcher, her legs crumpled under her. Carey, who was holding the other end, found it jerked from her bleeding hands as it crashed to the ground.

Silvana's shoulders sagged. "It's no use, I can't go any further." She burst into tears and collapsed on the ground. "I give up."

"Get *up*, you spoiled bitch!" Suzy kicked Silvana's plump rump. "We haven't come all this way just to let *you* decide that we're not going on."

The skipper said, "Suzy's right. If you don't get up, we'll have to leave you."

"I don't care, I don't *care*," Silvana sobbed. "I can't go on."

Suzy yelled, "If you stay here and you're found, they'll know we're somewhere ahead." She nudged Silvana again.

The skipper said, "No use shaking your head, no use thinking you won't give us away. They'll torture you and you'll tell—you won't be able to help it. And after that, they'll kill you anyway."

Patty said, "You saw what happened to Isabel."

"I don't care! I don't care! I can't move," Silvana sobbed.

"Stop that, Suzy," Annie said wearily. "Silvana, we must both go on. I've got my boys to think of, and you've got Lorenza."

Silvana was helped to her feet by the skipper. The little party staggered forward.

Ten minutes later Patty lifted her head and said, "Listen!"

Above the splashing of the river below, they could hear a noise in the distance.

Patty cried, "The waterfall!"

The sound gave extra strength to the thirsty, tired women and they moved a little faster. The sound grew steadily louder. The path had led down into the ravine, and now they were only about ten feet above the river. Excitement grew.

Carey craned her neck. "I can see the sea! Through the trees ahead!"

Within minutes they could all see the black boulders at the top of the cliff and the sparkling aquamarine sea beyond. Below them lay the sandy beach; to the left was the tumbling, sparkling torrent of the waterfall, curving over the cliff.

The skipper warned, "Don't get too excited . . . and *don't get careless!* Don't move out of the cover of these trees. We don't know if there's anyone up there. Everyone stay here while I move forward and look around. Silly to get captured now, after that walk."

His cautionary words effectively dampened their excitement and feeling of achievement. The women once again unpacked the hated canvas awning and once again slumped onto it. The skipper crawled forward to reconnoiter.

He reappeared within minutes. "It looks clear ahead. Now listen to me. I'm going to dive for that cave, but I don't swim anywhere near as good as Winston, so if anything happens to me, then Carey is in charge. No particular reason, but someone has to be. In the meantime, you stay here, because you might be seen in the open." He looked at Patty. "Get the flashlight out of the picnic hamper, and let's you and me have a swim."

Quickly, he took off his yellow life jacket, unbuttoned his shirt and took out the coastal charts, which were still soggy. He emptied his pockets onto the canvas: a few *kina* and other coins, a key ring, the red Swiss army knife, his miniature compass on a thong and another small, two-inch-diameter compass. He picked up the underwater flashlight, pulled a set of fins and a diving mask from the garbage pail and gently pulled Patty to her feet.

Together, on legs that shook with exhaustion, Patty and the skipper scrambled down the black rocks to the rock pool below, in which—only yesterday—they had cheerfully splashed with Winston.

Twenty minutes later, the skipper surfaced for the seventh time. Spluttering and coughing, he was too exhausted to climb from the pool; he clung to a rock, his weightless body floating behind him. He gasped, "I can't find it. I can't stay under long enough."

Patty said, "I do yoga. Maybe I can hold my breath longer than you. Let me try." She stood up, stripped to her underwear and kicked off the damned sneakers. She pulled on fins and mask and slipped into the water.

The water soothed her sore muscles and sticky skin; she swam around for a few minutes, easing the stiffness from her body. Then she took fifteen seconds to exhale, tightening her solar plexus until she'd expelled all the air from her lungs. She took twenty-five seconds to inhale, carefully inflating her lower belly. She pulled her knees up to her chest, pulled her arms apart and duck-dived beneath the surface.

Down, down she went, until she reached the bottom of the pool, a murky mass of silt and debris. It wasn't difficult to see the rock face through her diving mask, although it was a little dim.

Slowly, Patty allowed herself to float to the surface. There were as many rocks below the water as there were above it. She had seen no gap in them, no crack or hole. She'd have to search the pool systematically, working from right to left.

By her fourteenth dive, Patty's lungs felt about to explode; on the way up, she gasped for air too soon and took in water. She coughed and spluttered, just as the skipper had. She didn't want—she *couldn't*—dive again.

But she knew that the cave was down there *somewhere*.

Yesterday, with her own eyes, she'd seen Winston disappear for far longer than a human being could hold his breath. Patty felt furious and frustrated. She *knew* that the damn cave was down there! She'd even had a light to help her. Poor Winston had had no flashlight.

Exasperated and exhausted, she resumed her search, this time exploring the pool from left to right.

◀ **9** ▶

WEDNESDAY, NOVEMBER 14, 1984

From the depths of the waterfall pool, Patty surfaced again, gasping for breath and white with exhaustion. Although she couldn't speak, the skipper could tell by the triumphant look on her face that she'd found the cave. Clumsy with fatigue, she swam a weak breaststroke to where the skipper sat on a flat rock.

Patty gasped, "It's down there, all right."

"Good on you, girl. What's she like?"

"You'd never find it unless you knew it was there." She paused to catch her breath. "It's about fifteen feet down. I couldn't find it at first, because I was searching from right to left. You can only see the entrance if you're looking from the left, then you notice the fissure behind a slab of rock."

"Sounds safe. The cliff path's on the south side of the waterfall, so're these rocks." He patted the flat stone slab on which he sat. "So anyone exploring the pool would search as you did at first—from the south side of the waterfall, from the right."

Patty gasped, "I'm going to get my wind back, then go in."

"Only one of us can dive," the skipper warned. "You got the light. But I'll be worrying. Just see if there's a dry space in there, then come straight back. Don't hang around inside."

Patty swam back to the north side of the pool; she took a

series of deep breaths, in order to expel the carbon dioxide and get the maximum oxygen into her lungs. Then she jack-knifed below the surface, impeded slightly by her flashlight. The greenish, rocky sides of the pool receded past her face, until she reached the entrance to the cave, which was hidden by a vertical slab of limestone.

She pulled herself behind the limestone and swam through the black hole behind it; she kicked her way into it, feeling the slimy sides of the tunnel with her right hand, holding the flashlight with her left. She was terrified. She didn't want to swim on into that sinister blackness. She wanted to double up in a ball, roll around to reverse direction, glide out of that cave and shoot through the surface of the pool before her lungs burst. But by the time this urge gripped her, Patty knew she hadn't enough time to go back. She hovered on the edge of terror, she wanted to scream, as her instinct told her to retreat but her reason told her to go forward.

Patty's absence seemed endless to the skipper, who was checking her time on his watch. So much depended on Patty's diving ability. Only she could quickly get the exhausted women to safety. He hadn't liked telling them why it wasn't safe to go on, and anyway, those poor Sheilas had no strength left. Funny that everything now depended on Patty, when she was the only woman he'd thought might snap in a crisis. Now, she was his only hope.

Nine minutes after Patty disappeared, her head again broke the surface of the water. She gasped, "There *is* a passage. It's about twenty-five feet long and the entire length is under-water. It's very narrow, not much wider than my shoulders, and the passage slopes up quite sharply. I kept bumping my head." She shivered. "It's scary. I only kept going because I knew that Winston must have surfaced in there somewhere, and the passage was too narrow to turn around. I was just about to panic, when I surfaced." She grimaced. "It smelled foul. The tunnel continued ahead of me, above water. It looked to be quite a wide cave, and very high. I didn't climb out because I wanted to get back fast and tell you."

"Let's have a look at it." The skipper slid off the rock and into the water. "You know the way, so I'll hang on to your belt and follow you."

"Okay . . . what's your name, by the way?"

"Jonathan Blackwood."

"Okay, Jonathan, let's go. Let's time this trip."

The descent was no less fearful this time. With a gasp, Patty resurfaced in the cave. She looked at the luminous dial of her black Swatchwatch. "Fifty seconds."

"Gawd, it seemed like half an hour," said Jonathan, puffing beside her.

Patty shone her light around the cave. "Jonathan, look about six feet ahead—the floor of the cave rises above the water. We can crawl out there."

The two dripping figures emerged from the black water; they picked their way carefully along the cave, which wound back, a dark tunnel. The light shone on stalactites hanging from the limestone roof; they were like candle drips dangling from upended crystal chandeliers and sparkling with rainbow colors.

"It's like a fairy grotto," Patty whispered. She looked at the soaring ceiling, iridescent in the beam of light. The pale ray traced the delicate structures, too enormous, ambitious and fragile for any earthly sculptor to attempt to carve. They glittered silently in the light, like crumbling Gothic arches sprayed with confectioner's sugar.

From the dark floor of the cavern, sparkling stalagmites soared upward, rich and strange, a silent crystal fantasy.

Jonathan said, "Water's done that, continually dropping on the same spot, one drop at a time, for centuries."

Patty whispered, "What's that noise?"

Above the quiet drips of water from the roof of the cavern they could hear a faint sound—a piercing, high squeak.

"Bats," Jonathan said, looking upward and seeing nothing, but knowing that they must be there. "And the powdery stuff underfoot is bat shit."

"I wish you hadn't told me," Patty said. "Hey, it's cool in here, it's like air conditioning."

"Must be an air vent somewhere, because the air is breathable. And the bats must get out at night when they hunt. But we'll explore later. We'd better go back and get the others in here as fast as possible. S'truth, I don't fancy the journey back."

In the muggy heat of the forest at the top of the waterfall cliff, the four waiting women were curled on the canvas awning, asleep. During the day the forest was silent. Around the sleeping women, creepers and vines trailed gracefully from the high trees to the ground; yellow butterflies trembled in the air and yellow orchids wound around the creepers. Although it was three hours since sunrise, the women lay in green gloom, for only an occasional ray of sunlight pierced the jungle canopy.

It was undeniably beautiful, but Patty and Jonathan were too weary to notice. Without speaking, they shook the women awake. Slowly the sleepers sat up, their eyes dazed, their faces filthy and pale from lack of sleep, their hair tangled. Beneath her grubby yellow life jacket, Suzy's legs, in pink shorts, had been unprotected; now they were encrusted with bloody scratches, as though wild animals had clawed them.

Patty said, "We've found the cave!"

The chorus of approval was unanimous, except for Suzy, who had been dreading this moment. How can I swim, she wondered, what will I do if they leave me? Fighting down her panic, Suzy mumbled, "I'm thirsty." The water bottles were empty.

"Can we drink from that river?" Carey asked, pointing to the rushing water below.

"No, it might be polluted," said Jonathan. "But there are water vines all around us."

The water vines hung from trees. Jonathan showed the women how to cut the top of the vines, which were as thick as a garden hose; if you cut the bottom, the water ran out before you could drink it. This charming trick seemed magic to the thirsty women.

"Got another treat for you," Jonathan said. "Breakfast." From his pocket he pulled a small round tin of lemon drops. Gratefully, each woman took a piece of candy.

As Patty told the others about the cave, Jonathan looked around at the forest. They'd have to hide this heap of equipment, but not here, this was virgin jungle and there was no cover. Better bury the stuff on the beach; they could carry it down the cliff in two loads.

Annie said apologetically, "I'm afraid I can't stand up. My legs just won't support me."

Jonathan said fiercely, "After we've come all this way!" He meant, After I've blown up my boat. "You can either sit around passive-like and wait to get killed—or you can get off your fannies and use what guts you've got to get out of here alive." One by one, he put his hands under each woman's armpits and grimly tugged her to her feet. They stood there in their torn clothes and grubby yellow life jackets, limp and hopeless, arms dangling at their sides like rag dolls', too tired to cry.

"Only *one* more effort," Jonathan encouraged.

Carey started to sniffle. Jonathan looked at her reproachfully. Suzy started to cry hard.

Silvana muttered to herself, "Thought be the harder."

"What did you say?" Jonathan asked.

Slightly louder, Silvana whispered, "Thought be the harder, the heart the keener, courage be the greater as our strength grows less."

"That's the spirit," Jonathan said. "Whoever said that had the right idea."

"He was an eleventh-century Anglo-Saxon warrior."

"Well, you think of him, love, and let's get down to that beach. We'll soon be where no one can find you."

Through her tears Suzy said bitterly, "We're dying on our feet and Silvana spouts medieval poetry at us."

Jonathan and Carey reassembled the equipment. He said,

"Patty, carry my gun and the flares. Carey, take the ladder, if you can manage it with those hands. I'll carry the tarpaulin."

In turn, he lifted each of the three mosquito-net bundles and dumped them in the arms of Annie, Suzy and Silvana. "You three get down the cliff with this lot. Dig a hole on the beach, while Patty, Carey and I come back for the garbage bin and the picnic baskets."

There was no means of getting the bundles across the waterfall to the path on the other side, so the women slithered and slid down the north side of the waterfall, where it was steep and there was no path. Annie tripped over a rock and fell, skinning her elbows and knees; wearily she picked herself up, retrieved her bundle and staggered down after the others.

From the bottom of the waterfall, a shallow channel of water ran through the white, gritty coral sand to the sea. A strange miasma hung over this part of the beach. It stank like Jonathan's bait box after a day in the sun; it smelled of seaweed, green slime and primeval mud. Shining black rocks dotted the sand; the small ones looked like frogs, and the big ones looked like basking seals. Tiny crabs scuttled to the sea, and a few small brown birds, which looked like sandpipers, hopped on frail legs at the edge of the water, while white seagulls screamed above them.

Jonathan chose a spot at the back of the beach, which was littered with rotting palm leaves and old coconuts. He said, "We'll dig a hole, bury our stuff, then pull some débris over it."

"What do we dig with?" asked Annie, always practical.

"Two metal bait cans and two buckets; you can scoop the sand out with those. I want a six-foot trench, like a grave. And for God's sake hurry, because there ain't no cover on this beach. If a boat comes by, we'll be spotted immediately."

By the time the second load had been brought down the cliff to the beach, a shallow indentation had been scooped out of the sand. Jonathan spread the canvas over it, followed by the ladder, then the rest of the equipment, except for the coil of rope, the goggles, the flippers and the rifle. He wrapped the rifle in the plastic garbage bag that he'd intended for the outboard and tucked it under the canvas. They all knelt and, with weary hands, scooped the sand back, then camouflaged the spot with dead branches.

They waded through the channel of water to the other side of the waterfall, so that they could use the cliff path to climb up to the pool. Jonathan brought up the rear, erasing their tracks from the area around the excavated sand where they had buried their equipment. He retreated backward, sweeping with a palm frond as he went.

"Okay," said Jonathan when they reached the pool. "Now for the cave." He looked at the exhausted faces of the women and felt at a loss. He no longer knew how to urge them on. He had coaxed and pushed, bullied and threatened them. What now?

He said, "In a few minutes you'll all be safe. Patty'll take you down. We've both been in there, so we know *you* can make it. Patty'll have the light. Whoever's swimming behind her must hold on to her waistband. When you get inside, take off your goggles and flippers as fast as possible. Patty'll loop them over her arm and swim back for the next woman."

He looked around at the dazed, grubby faces. "Carey, you go in first. You'll be alone in the dark until Annie gets there. Just hang on. And *don't move*. I don't want anyone with a busted ankle. Okay now?"

Carey thought, I'll never be able to do it. He doesn't know what happens to me. I tried to get over it—only last week— by confrontation, in those Australian caves, and it didn't work. "I get claustrophobia," she said.

"Right now, you can't afford to get claustrophobia," Jonathan retorted.

In spite of the heat, Carey started to shiver. She said miserably, "I know."

"Hop in then."

Reluctantly Carey put on the flippers and goggles. She and Patty each took an end of the rope, then they swam to the north side of the pool and dived. With a splash of flippers, both women disappeared.

Carey clung to Patty's belt, and they descended deep into the black waters. Thank God this was only going to last about a minute, her hands were agonizingly painful. The fact that she had to swim distracted her, and at first she wasn't overwhelmed by the enveloping black water as she followed the dim, green beam of Patty's flashlight.

But when their heads broke the surface of the water and Patty flashed the light around the black cave, terror rose, like vomit, in Carey's throat.

"Don't leave me!" Carey clung to Patty's wet body.

"Cut it out, Carey! I've got to get back and help the others in here." Patty wriggled away from Carey and swiftly slipped back into the water.

Left alone, Carey started to shake. She started to scream. She shut her eyes. It didn't help. She screamed and screamed.

Patty resurfaced. "Annie next," she gasped, "then Silvana."

Patty and Annie surfaced in the cave to the terrifying, echoing sound of Carey's screams. They scrambled out of the water and stumbled to where Carey was huddled on the slimy floor of the cave, her head thrown back, her mouth gaping.

"What *happened*?" Annie gasped.

"Like she said, she's claustrophobic," Patty explained. "You look after her. I've got to go back for the others."

Annie crouched beside Carey, put her arms around the other woman's shoulders and soothed her as she would a frightened child, stroking her tangled hair and rocking her to and fro.

When it was Suzy's turn to dive, she quietly said, "I *can't*. I *can't*." She was overwhelmed by terror. "I can't go down there. *I can't swim.*"

Jonathan said, "Suzy, if they get you, they'll kill you."

Patty thought, Jesus, not another one! She pushed up her mask. "You don't have to swim, Suzy. You just have to hang on to my waistband and take a deep breath. I'll *pull* you through. You won't have to do a thing."

After five minutes of encouragement, coaxing and threats, Suzy still refused to get into the water.

Exasperated, Patty said, "It's an *irrational* fear, Suzy. You know in your mind that there's nothing to be afraid of, you *know* you can hang on to my belt and hold your breath for fifty seconds."

Suzy glared at her. "Stop being so goddamned condescending. You don't understand. *I can't move.*"

Patty looked at Jonathan, who shook his head. It was no use suddenly pushing Suzy in, she'd scream and gulp water, then they'd have to pull her out. Or she'd panic, clutch Patty around the neck and pull her under; then they'd both be in trouble. He called to Patty, "You a life saver?"

"Yes."

He thought, So she knows how to knock out someone in the water. But after that, you were supposed to keep their head above water, you didn't shove it under for fifty seconds. He fished in a pocket of his shorts and pulled out the tin of lemon drops. "This is all I can give you, Suzy. If you won't come with us, you'd better move on. If they find you here, they'll discover the rest of us. You'll put us all in danger if you stay here. So move on to the next bay, will you? I'm almost sure there's a village."

"Don't leave me! Don't leave me!" Suzy begged.

"I've got the rest of them to think about. Goodbye, Suzy." He jumped off the rock, swam toward Patty and took the goggles and flippers from her.

"Don't leave me!"

Patty and Jonathan never looked back as they swam toward the north side of the little pool.

"Come back!"

They swam on.

"I'll come!"

Jonathan turned around in the pool. He called, "You get one chance, Suzy. If you change your mind, we'll have to leave you. It's getting late."

Both swimmers returned to the shivering Suzy, crouched on the flat rock.

Jonathan said, "Do everything slowly. Patty and I'll each take one of your wrists. Let yourself into the water; we won't pull you. Take a deep breath and shut your eyes when I tell you." He looked at her terrified face. "And relax. It'll all be over faster than a visit to the dentist."

Suzy held her wrists toward the swimmers.

Jonathan said, "Okay, let yourself fall in."

Fists clenched and rigid with fright, Suzy fell into the water. The other two each supported her with one arm and steered her toward the spot where they were going to dive.

Jonathan spat out water. "Okay, Suzy, when I say three, take a deep breath and hold it. Slowly count to a hundred and twenty. Here we go. One . . . two . . . three . . ."

They dragged her under as fast as they could.

Suzy's lungs were burning, her eyes were aching and she had never been conscious of such bodily pain. Because all the muscles of her body were taut—even her teeth were clenched —her lungs were constricted; as they began to pump, Suzy felt a singing in her ears. She fought panic in the swirling dark water but was hauled onward by Patty's strong hand, which gripped her wrist like a manacle. As dizziness overtook her, Suzy opened her mouth to scream, gulping water into her lungs.

"Help her out!" Patty gasped as she surfaced in the cave. She'd had to swim with her feet alone, holding the flashlight in her right hand and the struggling Suzy with her left hand. She didn't have the energy to give Suzy that final push.

Patty shone the flashlight on the shadowy figures of the other three women as swiftly they moved forward to haul Suzy, coughing and incoherent, from the water.

It was Patty's sixth trip through the underwater tunnel and she was weary, too weary to think straight. She was fighting nausea.

Behind her, Jonathan staggered from the water. "Well, we

made it. They ain't going to find us here. Just mind that none of you ladies step on the machete."

The rocky floor of the cave was covered not only with bat shit but with small bits of razor-sharp limestone that had fallen from the stalactites above. The air was foul-smelling and humid, but nothing could have stopped any of them from immediately falling asleep.

In her sleep Patty attempted to turn over and instantly woke, her body was so stiff and painful. As she breathed the slight ammoniac odor of the cave, she suddenly remembered where she was. Cautiously, she put out one aching arm and touched a warm lump; it was breathing regularly.

Patty looked at the luminous dial of her black, plastic Swatchwatch. Three o'clock. Was it morning or evening? Had she slept six hours or eighteen or thirty? She peered closer. No, it was still Wednesday, November 14; thank heaven for a watch that told you the day as well as the time. Her body ached so much, she'd never get to sleep again. She sat up.

Suzy whispered, "Who's awake?"

"Patty."

"God, isn't this awful?" It was Carey's voice. She had clung to Annie until they fell asleep in each other's arms.

Reluctantly roused, Jonathan called, "Stop whingeing. We're alive, we're well and we're safe. Nobody's injured. We just ain't very comfortable."

In the darkness, Suzy gave a short laugh. "We couldn't be much *less* comfortable, could we?"

"Oh, yes, you could indeed." He thought not only of the killers on the beach but of the native cruelty, and the cruelty of nature; of the strange island diseases, such as the laughing death, for which there is no cure, or the trembling sickness, from which you shake to death. He thought of the sharks beyond the reef, of the twenty-foot-long salt water estuarine crocodiles and the sea snakes that were as deadly as the sharks. He said, "Things could be a lot worse."

"We'll never get out of here alive," said Carey hopelessly.

Annie tried to sound comforting. "The company will come and get us, when they find out what's happened. It's only a matter of time."

For some reason they all whispered; the whispers sounded muffled in the cave.

"*How* will Nexus know?" asked Patty. "How will *anyone* know what's happened to us?"

Suzy said, "Brett wasn't on the beach." During that terrible hike through the night, Suzy realized how much she had taken for granted, as she remembered the comfort, security and love that Brett had given her. She said, "Brett wasn't killed, was he?"

Suzy's words immediately conjured up the dreadful scene that all the women were trying not to think about. Once again, in her mind, Silvana stared at the little blood-smeared group on the beach, huddled in front of the patio bar. Once again she saw Arthur, with his hands tied behind him, clumsily kneel to beg for his life and his look of astonishment as his pale gray tropical suit suddenly turned dark with blood, his horn-rimmed glasses slid off his nose and he pitched forward onto the sand.

Once again, Patty heard Charley trying to negotiate with those bastards and then a shot ringing out, and her life fell apart into terror.

Once again, Carey inhaled the vanilla smell of the oleander bush and recoiled from the terrible sight of Ed, face covered in blood and yelling, "What have you done with our wives?" Even when he was in such danger, Ed had thought of *her*. He'd prayed aloud—Ed, who'd use any excuse to skip going to church—and then there had been a burst of machine gun fire and Ed had sort of jumped, fell heavily and never moved again.

Emblazoned in Annie's memory forever would be the sight of Duke standing with his hands bound behind his back and dazedly watching as Arthur was shot, then turning his head to Ed, then to Charley, as they yelled at the officer who was giving the orders. Duke hadn't said a word, he hadn't behaved like John Wayne, he'd just stood there and been shot—one moment alive and the next moment crumpled like a heap of dirty clothes.

Suzy repeated, "Brett *wasn't* killed, was he?"

No one spoke. Suzy heard snuffles and sobs from the darkness all around her. She said, "Well, I'm sorry, but it's *important*. Did anyone *see* Brett? Because if not, he may have escaped. And if so, he'll see that we're rescued *somehow*. Because he knows we were coming here for a picnic."

After tearful discussion, the women all agreed that they hadn't seen Brett on the beach.

Then Patty pointed out, "But we've killed ourselves! We were blown up in a fishing boat and eaten by sharks, remember? That's what Brett will hear."

Jonathan said, "We don't know what's going on out there, and we can't risk finding out. So we've got to hide here and get off the island later." His voice grew more thoughtful. "But before we discuss that, I'd really like to know why anyone should want to kill your husbands." There was no answer. "Any smart terrorist would try to avoid killing American civilians because of possible repercussions. But if you have a reason to kill someone who happens to be American . . . well, then, a revolution might seem a fine time to pay off old scores. In this part of the world, revenge is considered a *very* good reason for killing people. Payback is a big motivator on this island."

"What are you getting at?" Patty asked.

"Can any of you ladies think why *anyone* connected with this island should have a grudge against your husbands?" He added apologetically, "I'm sorry to ask you at a time like this. I'm only doing it because it might have some bearing on how hard those bastards will come looking for us."

They shook their heads and murmured that they had no idea.

Only Carey remained silent. She remembered last Christmas. Even if Ed hadn't talked in his sleep, it would have been obvious to her that he was hiding something important. When your husband insists on turning one of the spare bedrooms into a second study, which he equips with a paper shredder, then has the infrared burglary system checked and rechecked by security experts, who also install a second, hidden wall safe, then a wife doesn't have to be very smart to realize that something is going on which is too secret to keep in the office.

Carey also remembered one January morning when Ed had been late for work. He'd snatched up his briefcase from the table in the hall; there must have been something wrong with the lock, because the papers burst out all over the floor. When Carey stooped to help him pick them up, he'd yelled at her and snatched the typed sheets from her hand, but Carey couldn't help noticing that the tag line of the top sheet read "Area 7. Chromite. Grade reports/p2."

Carey knew that Area 7 was Paui.

Hesitantly Carey said, "I think that Nexus has just had an important chromite find somewhere on this island. Something really big. Ed turned green when I found out accidentally. He made me swear never to mention it." She added, "That's the real reason why we came here."

None of those mining-company wives needed to have the importance of a major chromite find spelled out for them.

Silvana said, "Arthur went to see the President yesterday, but he told me that it was just a formality, that all important visitors leave their cards at the palace."

Patty said, "A few months ago I heard Charley talking on the phone. He said something like, 'Rocky's been taken care of.' Then a few minutes later Charley said, 'Rocky can't hurt us on Paui and he can't help us on Paui, so why should we pay him?'" She hesitated. "I can't be sure of his exact words. I only noticed the name, because of those Sylvester Stallone films."

"Are you *sure* of that?" Jonathan asked.

"Well, I can't be certain that's what Charley said, but I *am* certain that he talked about someone called Rocky."

"Not Rocky," Jonathan said. "*Raki* . . . General Raki. Remember, I told you I thought those might be his troops. Until recently he was in charge of the army, when the Nationalists were in power. What you just said sounds like reason enough for Raki to want Payback."

Patty said, "If we're talking revenge, let's get back to the States as fast as possible and report what's happened to Washington and the United Nations. The UN is still responsible for these islands, isn't it?"

Jonathan said, "Yeah, but so what?"

Patty said, "Well! We're all eyewitnesses, who saw a bunch of thugs deliberately line up American citizens and shoot them."

In the darkness there was a general stirring. Indignation, rage and fury had given the women new energy.

Patty said, "How can we get off this place, fast?"

"Couldn't Jonathan get to Queenstown?" Carey asked. "He could buy a boat for us."

Suzy said, "How much does a boat cost?"

"We're wearing our engagement rings," Carey pointed out. "Silvana's emerald alone ought to buy us an ocean liner."

Silvana's twenty-one-karat emerald, mounted on an intricate twist of square-cut diamonds, was a masterpiece by Harry Winston. Carey's ring was an antique Roman intaglio head, set in a thin, eighteenth-century gold setting. Suzy had a heart-shaped cluster of diamonds. Annie's ring was a sapphire surrounded by diamonds. Only Patty had left her ring, a marquise diamond, at home.

Jonathan said thoughtfully, "If I go into Queenstown, I'm going to be seen. Everyone will know that I wasn't blown up in the *Louise*, won't they? Things get around here as fast as they would in a three-shack village."

Carey persisted. "Couldn't you buy us some dugout canoes from a native village? If we pay them really good prices?"

"A dugout takes weeks to make, and great skill," Jonathan said. "An islander wouldn't exchange a dugout for a green-glass ring. Even if he was told it was valuable, and even if he believed it, where would he sell the ring?"

"Queenstown," Patty said.

"Exactly, so the authorities would know about it within an hour. And remember that, by now, the authorities might be the Nationalists again. That'd mean Raki would come looking for you faster than you could launch a canoe."

Annie said timidly, "What have we got that's valuable to the natives? What about your gun? Would that buy us a canoe?"

Jonathan hesitated. "Almost everything we've just buried is valuable to a native. But these isolated fishing villages on the southwest coast aren't always friendly." He hesitated again. "Why should they barter for something, when they could just take it from us for nothing?"

Alarmed, Suzy said, "You mean they'd steal our stuff?"

"Yes."

"Then why have we left it unguarded, if it's the only stuff we have of value? How do we know the natives aren't digging it up right now?"

"No native will touch this beach."

"Why not?"

"Because it's *itambu*—taboo."

"So what?"

"Nothing would happen to you while you are in the taboo area, but you would have disturbed the spirits of their ancestors."

"So?"

"So they'd kill you as soon as you'd left it."

For breakfast, they cupped their hands and drank gritty water from the cave, then they each took another lemon drop, which they sucked slowly, trying to make it last as long as possible.

Jonathan said, "The air in this cave ain't getting in through the underwater entrance, so it must be coming in farther back. Carey, come have a look with me. We'll take the light. Patty, see that nobody moves until we get back. You can't break a leg in the dark if you don't move."

Carey started to tremble. "Why me?"

"I reckon you're the least tired. And, you know, you got to get over it. We may be here some time."

Carey said, "I don't feel too good."

"None of us do. On your feet."

By the dim beam of the flashlight, Carey and Jonathan moved cautiously back along the tunnel. Jonathan walked ahead, first checking out the filthy floor of the cave for two strides, then pausing to play the flashlight over the pale, and strangely beautiful, formations on either side of them.

Carey shivered. "They're awesome, aren't they?"

"Yeah. Reckon that's why the natives don't dare come inside. These caves are powerful magic."

Carey felt sick. She'd had a queasy feeling since they came in here, and now it was overpowering her. And that noise didn't help. The continual, almost painfully high-pitched sound consisted of thousands of beeps that were synchronized with the breathing of the bats overhead. It was like shrill Morse code. It was driving her crazy; she wanted to scream.

Every few steps Jonathan had to stop and clean the flashlight, because small flying creatures kept flinging themselves at the light. "They're mostly moths," he said hopefully as he dodged a barrage of wings.

He turned abruptly at a sudden gasp from Carey. She shrieked, *"Something's clawing at me!"*

Jonathan shone the flashlight on her head. The feet of a baby bat had become entangled in Carey's hair. The body of the bat was covered with brownish-pink fuzz, like moleskin, where the fur was not fully grown. Unfortunately for Carey, baby bats that cannot yet fly properly cling instinctively to anything that feels like fur, so its little feet clawed repeatedly in Carey's hair; frantically, it beat its stubby little wings, the tiny thumbs feeling tremulously for the nipple on its mother's stomach.

Carey screamed in terror.

Jonathan said, "Put your hands over your eyes and don't take them off. *Don't move!*"

Shirley Conran

With his left hand, he attempted to dislodge the baby bat, which only became more frantic.

Hearing her baby's calls of distress, the mother bat circled down and whizzed around Carey's head, homing in on her baby's piercing calls. Balefully, the mother bat dived at the flashlight.

Realizing it was useless to try to disentangle the struggling baby bat, Jonathan now whacked at it with the flashlight. It clawed even more wildly. At every tug of her hair, Carey screamed, and Jonathan whacked again.

Eventually the bat fell limp. The warm body dangled over Carey's hands, which she still held over her eyes.

Jonathan took out his Swiss army knife, wedged the flashlight under his chin and hacked at Carey's thick, toffee-blond hair until he had cut the bat from her head.

Carey flung herself, shaking and sobbing, against Jonathan's chest.

He patted her back. "There, there, girl, it was only a bat. Not even a big one. Take your shirt off and wrap it around your head so it doesn't happen again, and we'd better warn the others. I didn't think that could happen. I thought bats had some built-in sonic device that made them able to avoid obstacles in the dark."

Shivering with fright, Carey wrapped her head in her tattered blue shirt, which left her wearing a pale blue bra and her blue pants. They continued cautiously up the tunnel, weaving between the fairy-palace stalagmites and picking their feet high, above the disgusting litter that covered the floor of the tunnel.

It had been Carey's job to count their footsteps but, after the battle of the bat, she forgot to do so. She huddled behind Jonathan, holding one hand protectively above her eyes, as if against the sun's glare. She had been exhausted by terror, but now she was numbed, beyond it.

Jonathan stopped abruptly. "I can see light." He switched off the flashlight. They both peered through the dark, their eyes adjusting to it.

Ahead of them was a faint lightening of the darkness.

Jonathan switched on the flashlight again, and they moved forward. As they approached, he said, "It's a natural chimney."

Jonathan played the flashlight over the roof. They saw a roughly cylindrical hole in the rock, about two feet in diameter.

Jonathan said, "It must be covered by vegetation at the top."

Carey shrieked again and clutched at his shoulder.

Jonathan said, "What is it, girl, another bat?"

"No. Look over there!"

Jonathan turned and shone the torch where she was pointing. He said, "So we ain't the first visitors."

A yard away, propped against the wall of the cave, amid the bat shit, spiders, cockroaches, woodlice and other things that they had been crunching underfoot, lay the dusty, gray bones of a human skeleton.

Jonathan leaned forward and shone the light on the dirty rectangle that nested in the pelvic bone. "It's a camera," he said. It was an old, dented K2 Pentax with a 28mm lens. In the dim beam of light, brass showed where the black lacquer had rubbed off the corner points.

"Look!" Carey pointed. Something dangled from the skeleton's clavicle.

Jonathan squatted and shone the flashlight on a dust-covered disc that dangled from a thin chain; he rubbed it clean.

"It's gold," he said. "It's a St. Christopher's medal." He turned it over. "There's something written on it." He peered closer. "'To Nancy, love from Michael.'"

"So it was a woman!" Carey said. "How horrible."

◄ 10 ►

WEDNESDAY, NOVEMBER 14, 1984

Harry Scott heard it on the tail end of the news broadcast. Abruptly, he stopped shaving and turned up the transistor radio. Chin still pointing to the bathroom mirror, he listened to the rapid, flat Australian twang of the announcer. "Fighting broke out last night on the island of Paui with a military attack from the sea. All communications have been cut, but reliable sources report that a military coup is taking place, and that the leader of the Democratic Party, President Obe, has been deposed. Now for the cricket news. . . ."

Harry switched off the radio. So that was why he hadn't been able to get through to Arthur on the phone this morning. As always, when thinking hard, he ran his lower teeth up over his upper lip. Broad shouldered and lean, he stood naked in front of the mirror and stared unseeing into the gray eyes above high, flat cheekbones.

He picked up the wall telephone and dialed the American diplomat with whom he occasionally played tennis.

"Richard? There's been a coup d'état on Paui—fighting and no radio contact. I've got five of the Nexus board with their wives up there at the moment; they're all U.S. citizens. . . . Sure, I'm going to get up there as fast as I can. . . . Yes, of course, but as you know, the twenty-four hours that follow an attack are decisive in a coup, and in the

226

chaos anything might happen. I want to keep in touch with you, Richard, in case I need government help to get them out. . . . Of course I'll deal with your consulate in Moresby, but I'd like you to inform the State Department immediately that they may be in danger."

His next call was to the Nexus chief pilot. "Morning, Pat. Remember that group you took up to Queenstown last Saturday? Well, we've got to get them off, fast. There's rebel fighting on the island. . . . No, not tribal fighting, this sounds like the real thing. So when do we leave, and which aircraft will you take?"

At the other end of the line, the chief pilot rubbed sleep from his eyes. "This is one hell of a wake-up call, Harry." He was unable to smother a yawn. "We probably won't be able to land at Queenstown, because if there's fighting, some of it's bound to be going on at the airport. There might be rubble and wreckage on the airstrip."

"But you could land the Lear if the runway was clear?"

"If by some miracle the runway was clear, even if the control tower had been knocked out, yes, we could overfly and then go down."

"Would there be any danger of flight-path collision?"

"No. Any other aircraft would either have flown out or been burned out, they'd be unlikely to be flying around the airport. But what might easily happen, Harry, is that everything looks calm, so we land. Then rebels appear with bazookas and take the Lear from us. Maybe shoot us, Harry."

"What about landing up at Mount Ida on the mine airstrip."

"Hasn't got sand gear, so we can't land a jet."

"So what do you suggest, Pat?"

"You could fly up to Port Moresby, then hire a seaplane. Or an amphibian would be even better. You can land on the water *or* the strip."

"Okay. We'll fly up to Moresby in the Lear. Let's get there before lunch. Make sure you get an amphibian that's big enough to take them all off. We'll be collecting at least twelve people."

"We'll have to take what's available. We might have to ferry them out in two loads or more, but it's only seventy miles to the mainland, and the head-hunting season finished in June."

"The main thing is to get them out. If you have trouble hiring a plane, then buy one. I'll phone Finance before I leave. See you at the airport."

"Is this a danger-rate job, Harry?"

"Let's hope not, but I suppose so."

Harry's next call was to his bank manager, who was still tackling his breakfast grapefruit. Harry arranged to pick up one thousand five-dollar bills and $100,000 in travelers' checks from the Barclays branch at Kingsford Smith Airport.

"Debit it to my private account," Harry said. "I don't have time to route this through our Accounting Department."

The two men then arranged a simple oral code that Harry would use if he had to give further financial instructions. Harry was to use the phrase "salt of the earth," the manager was to repeat it and then Harry was to say it once again. If the code wasn't used, the bank manager would not obey instructions and would immediately report the telephone conversation to Harry's Nexus deputy, Bruce Collins.

Harry's third call was to Bruce, and his fourth was to his secretary, Jean. She had been just about to leave for the office, when she found herself rerouted to Harry's high-rise bachelor apartment.

He said, "And do some shopping on the way in, please, Jean. I'll need two bottles of Chivas Regal, some anti-malaria pills, water-purification tablets and insect repellent. And I'll need a hundred and fifty packs of cigarettes and twelve decks of playing cards."

Harry knew that no official business could be carried out on Paui without greasing the palms of any number of officials.

The bribes would range from cigarettes to large-denomination bills. Money would also be necessary to pay for the local lawyers, who would make any necessary political connections, draw up documents, monitor all proceedings and, even more important, check everybody's graft percentages and ensure that no exasperating double-crosses occurred.

Harry telephoned the restaurant in his apartment building and ordered a big "stockman's breakfast" of steak and eggs because he didn't know when he'd next get a decent meal. After that, with great reluctance, he dialed Pittsburgh. At seven in the morning on Wednesday in Sydney it was four in the afternoon on Tuesday in Pittsburgh.

Harry spoke to Jerry Pearce, who was not only Nexus VP Finance but also Arthur's deputy in his absence. After he outlined his plan, there was an expensive silence.

Finally Jerry said, "You're sure that it's a good idea to go up there, rather than supervise whatever's to be done from Sydney?"

"Believe me, Jerry, nothing *will* be done unless I get up there and see that it's done."

"Okay, Harry. We'll contact the State Department straight off, and I'll make sure that you have a clear line to any funds you need. And, Harry, I'd just like to add, on a personal level, that I think you were fucking crazy to let them go in the first place."

"If the Minister of Tourism tells you that one of the new governmental priorities is to encourage tourism, and the President personally invites your party to a government-sponsored luxury hotel, then you assume it's safe. And you know why Arthur was keen to go. The concession renewals should have been signed months ago."

Another expensive transoceanic silence.

Harry said, "Nothing you can say, Jerry, could be worse than what I'm telling myself." He slammed down the telephone.

The doorbell rang. Harry grabbed a towel to cover his nakedness and fetched his breakfast tray.

As he ate, Harry mentally ran a basic travel check. All his tropical shots were up-to-date and his passport was stamped with a permanent visa to Paui.

He finished breakfast, pulled on beige tropical shorts and

229

shirt, long beige socks and light boots. He took a lightweight jacket. He would carry a canvas, lock-up shoulder bag. No use taking more luggage; they were a light-fingered lot on Paui, and anything he let out of his sight would be stolen.

Methodically, Harry started to assemble his gear; he always dumped stuff to be packed on an old-fashioned country farmer's chair with wooden extending arms to fling your legs over after a hard day's riding. This piece of furniture stood oddly among the low beech tables and the tan leather and chrome Mies furniture in his functional and expensively furnished, but impersonal, sitting room decorated in black and cream, with a good collection of modern Australian paintings that included a self-portrait of Sidney Nolan belligerently chewing a cigar. Harry's home could be left at a moment's notice. He just handed over the spare key to the apartment manager and left for whichever trouble spot needed him.

Onto the farmer's chair were thrown six pairs of bush socks, six pairs of undershorts, one spare bush shirt, two pairs of sun-glasses, a Pidgin dictionary, a spongebag, a roll of toilet paper, Harry's passport and letters of accreditation. He bent to pick up a pair of long, tropical socks that had fallen to the floor beneath the farmer's chair, and carefully placed them back on the small pile of luggage: Harry was very neat and couldn't stand disorder in his surroundings, any more than in his thinking.

He removed his gold watch and strapped a cheap, waterproof watch to his wrist; he opened the wall safe behind a swing-out kitchen cabinet, placed his gold watch in it, and took out a snub-nosed Smith & Wesson .38 Chief's Special, which was as powerful as possible for a small revolver. He shoved it in his trouser waistband: it would be out of sight under his safari jacket.

He had pulled out his shirt and was just strapping his money belt around his waist, with the zipped pocket facing inward, when the doorbell rang. That would be Jean.

* * *

Harry leaned back in the seat of the executive Lear and allowed himself to relax, looking out of the window as the aircraft soared into the brilliant blue of infinity. Harry closed his eyes to avoid the glare, and instantly felt the pain again. It was like an old war wound that always ached, and sometimes unexpectedly hurt *hard*, as it did now.

Two important things had happened shortly after Harry's twenty-first birthday: the Scott family had moved from their bungalow in Cronulla to the more gentrified surroundings of Wahroonghah where his mother could, at last, plant an English garden, like the one she'd had as a girl; and Harry had won a Nexus scholarship. Every year ten graduates were recruited worldwide to undergo three years' training in Pittsburgh. The scholarships were recognized as a shortcut to managerial posts within the company, and the trainees rarely left Nexus.

Harry had flown to Pittsburgh, feeling shy and gauche, to find himself working in the Accounting Department, under a Mr. O'Brien, who, one warm September evening, took him home for supper. As the Oldsmobile drew up, the front door had been flung open by a redheaded girl wearing a black sweater, a wide, black elastic belt, a flared emerald-felt skirt, black stockings and ballerina flats.

Later, playing chess with Annie, watching her frowning in concentration, her pale freckled hand hovering above the board, Harry had felt sharp-edged and *alive*. He knew that he had met what his mother would have called "the right girl." He had met the love of his life.

Harry remembered his bewilderment when Annie married Duke. Of course, he'd understood the situation when the baby arrived. He had expected his infatuation to fade, although he felt like punching that complacent windbag on the nose every time Annie had another baby. But his feelings had not faded, and he resigned himself to being stuck with his obsession for life. He had never married, he had always drawn back just before the point of no return. He had been accused of lack of feeling, heartlessness and latent homosexuality, but Harry knew in his heart that he couldn't feel totally committed, couldn't love and cherish anyone who didn't match up to his memory of redheaded Annie plunging down a glacier in her pale blue ski suit, boldly taking the fall line in a way that she never seemed able to achieve again in the rest of her life.

Recently, Harry had once more started to have hopes. Social habits had changed in the past quarter of a century. Years ago, he'd assumed that Annie was lost to him forever, but as he saw the marriages of his friends crash or dissolve in the identity and relationship struggles of the seventies, he persuaded himself that there *was* a chance that he and Annie might one day be together. Bit by bit, he persuaded himself that Annie secretly felt as he did. Surely she *must*, when his feelings were so strong? Surely Annie must realize that after your fortieth birthday you had to grab what you wanted or you'd never get it?

The solidly built frame of Pat, the chief pilot, appeared from the flight deck. "We land in seven minutes, Harry. We've hired an amphibian—only a two-seater, though. Guy who owns it works for the Department of Human Biology. He's based at Goroka."

He noticed Harry's frown. "Sorry, but amphibs aren't lined up at 'Moresby in rows like Hertz cars waiting for us to hire them at two minutes' notice. Neither of the rental companies has anything suitable that's immediately available; the private-hire pilots have Cessna 185's or 336's, or twin-engined Cherokees, stuff like that. Not amphibians." He shrugged his shoulders. "My mate up at Jackson is still working on it."

Jackson's Field Airport is always jammed with travelers during the midday period, when most flights arrive and depart.

Harry sat in a stuffy private waiting room while his chief pilot checked on the seaplane. A native steward served lo-

cally-grown peanuts and fresh lemonade as Harry waited for
the radio news and wondered whether he was overreacting.

His thoughts were interrupted by a news flash. Transmis-
sion had been resumed on Radio Paui when, at midday, General Raki had announced to the nation that the Defense Force
had taken control of the island on behalf of the Nationalist
Party. The Defense Force would be temporarily in charge of
the island, led by a military council (headed by himself) until
free, democratic elections could be held. Mr. Obe, the corrupt
and depraved Marxist leader of the Democratic Party, was
dead. Life would now proceed as usual. Martial music had
followed the short speech.

Harry swore. That would really complicate the mining negotiations. Raki would make Nexus pay through the nose, to
compensate for those eighteen special payments that he hadn't
received. Damned accountants! And damn Jerry Pearce, his
penny-pinching and his unrealistic attitude toward special
payments. Had Jerry never heard of Lockheed? Did he think
that was an isolated case?

On the other hand, at least with Raki, Nexus was dealing
with the devil they knew, a devil who understood the extent of
the power and wealth that lay behind Nexus. Raki was unpredictable and unreliable, but he was undoubtedly more efficient
than anyone else on the island, which might be important to
the Nexus party at Paradise Bay.

Again, Harry wondered if he'd overreacted to the possibility of danger, as he absently listened to the current-affairs
discussion that followed the news flash. A couple of political
journalists, hastily yanked into the studio, were recalling that
over forty heads of state had been assassinated in the last forty
years and dozens of other leaders had survived attempts on
their lives. Today, being a successful politician seemed to be a
risky business. . . .

Business!

Suddenly Harry wondered whether Raki knew of the recent
Nexus finds.

Some executives operated on a system of total delegation,

but Harry wasn't one of them; this was one of the reasons why people liked to work for him, and it was also one of the reasons why Harry would never be president of Nexus. He knew this, but he could only operate in his own way. He would never be purely a boardroom executive and he didn't want to be. He liked to be in touch with everyone in his area, and to know everything that went on in it—particularly anything that was being kept from him.

Harry had his own simple method of making sure that he knew a lot more about Ed's work than Ed realized, including the chromite discovery. You couldn't keep so volatile a discovery secret in a small mining community, and, as usual, the company bush pilots had quietly reported all prospectors' gossip directly to Harry. It never seemed to occur to passengers that the pilot had two functioning ears, and a brain.

Ed probably thought that no one else could possibly know about the chromite deposits that Nexus had discovered on Paui; the analysis laboratories were on the other side of the world, and didn't know the country of origin of the samples analyzed. But Ed didn't realize how the islanders compensated for their lack of education with other mysterious abilities. Illiterates often had brilliant memories; men who knew only a few hundred words of Pidgin English were fluent in body language, and news sometimes flashed around the island by bush telegraph before it was announced by radio.

With growing unease, Harry wondered whether the timing of Raki's takeover had anything to do with the Nexus finds. At the thought that there might be a connection, Harry's bottom teeth started to slide anxiously over his upper lip.

The door to the private waiting room swung open. The chief pilot appeared, looking apologetic. "Sorry, Harry, but your plane has been delayed. She's bringing in a hospital patient from one of the outer islands; he had a hemorrhage just before they rowed him out to the plane. They haven't taken off yet."

Harry bit his upper lip again as he looked at his watch. The chief pilot knew what the delay would mean. They couldn't arrive before sunset. They would waste a day.

Harry sighed. "You sure we can't get a bigger, faster plane? Maybe fly one in?"

"Only if you give me enough time, Harry."

"No, I've got to get there as fast as possible. You're sure *you* can't fly this plane, Pat? I'd rather deal with a pilot I know. Can't we buy it?"

"No, the owner won't sell, and he won't let anyone else fly her. She belonged to his dad, who passed away last year. Anyway, I've never flown one. Bloody thing's got to be forty-five years old. A Grumman Duck, ex-U.S. Navy. But I hear the pilot's a good bloke. And the only alternative is to wait, Harry."

Harry shook his head.

The chief pilot said, "Maybe you'd better go ahead to the Travel Lodge. We're going to park the Lear here. I don't want to leave this place before I see you on your way."

That evening, over steaks in the hotel restaurant, Harry met Johno Boyd, the young owner-pilot of the amphibian. He was well over six feet tall, tanned, with curly fair hair and baby-blue eyes.

He was unusually talkative for a bush pilot. "What's happening on Paui?" he asked. "I heard a radio report, but I didn't understand it. Those political specialists always assume a bloke has complete knowledge of the area, and every politician in it."

Harry said, "When the Nationalists first took over in 1975 the Paui Defense Force was run by a geezer called General Gora, who died in a jeep accident—so we were told. That was when Colonel Raki took command of the army." Harry signaled for the menu. "Eighteen months ago, when the Nationalists were kicked out and the Democratics took over, Raki had just been flown to a Darwin hospital with peritonitis, so he missed the fun, but he was exiled anyway. He and his family lived in this hotel. Seems he's just made a comeback, on Paui."

Just outside the doors of the restaurant, a man was playing Cole Porter on the grand piano. Beyond the windows was a spectacular view of the town and the sea; the food was excellent and the service attentive. Raki's exile had been luxurious.

As Harry watched the pilot dishing out a third helping of salad, he said, "The Defense Force will go over to Raki, of course—the army always goes to the strongest leader. You done this sort of job before, Johno?"

Johno helped himself to his fourth baked potato and plastered the last of the butter on it. "Yeah, I've done several flyouts this year. The outer islands are growing rougher every day." He had asked for, and been given, a guarantee that he would be required to do nothing illegal, and the danger rate had been agreed at four times the usual daily charge, plus one hundred percent indemnity for pilot and aircraft. Times were tough.

Both men were back at the airfield before dawn. In the nacreous light they walked toward a small, ugly, silver-blue aircraft. With its huge float and splayed wheels, the aircraft looked like something out of a display at an aviation museum, a battered, scarred and oil-streaked curiosity. The old amphibian could land on land or sea, and she could refuel from the pumps at the Mount Ida mine, but the enclosed cabin only seated two people, one behind the other.

"Do they speak Pidgin on Paui?" Johno asked as they reached the plane.

"Sure." Pidgin English was first used in the sixteenth century among European and Chinese traders in the South Seas; it evolved into its present form in the nineteenth century, on the sugar plantations of northwest Queensland. Effortlessly, it spread throughout the Pacific. Some people hate the clackety sound of Pidgin, but Harry was fascinated by the way in which a few basic words were used to express complicated, modern ideas. As well as being used for whites to communicate with natives, Pidgin is used by natives from different tribes to communicate with each other.

Harry said, "Pidgin has a high prestige value on Paui, same as anywhere else in these parts; nobody can get a low-grade government job unless they speak Pidgin although of course high-level officials also speak correct English. But I hope we won't be there long enough to do much talking."

Johno unlocked the aircraft. Both men swung into their seats and strapped themselves in. Johno spread a large-scale map on his lap and started his pre-takeoff routine. His hands moved over the controls, checking indicators on the control panel. Then he cleared with the control tower and taxied to the holding point. He turned to Harry and grinned. "Okay balus leave place balus?"

Harry knew that "balus" was Pidgin for bird or airplane. He nodded and grinned.

As they flew over Port Moresby, Harry could see the modern, downtown office blocks. Sprawling along the hills above the harbor were the brilliant green, well-watered lawns of the wealthy. As they passed over the harbor, he could make out a transport ship that had been sunk by the Japs in World War II and still lay on its side, submerged.

The Duck flew up the rugged coastline, high above featureless bush country dotted with soft green scrub.

After about an hour they passed the tiny island of Daru on the starboard wing, and later, the muddy delta of the Fly River. Johno altered course and the seaplane headed toward the blue glare of the open sea. He traced their route on the map with his left index finger.

After five hours of monotonous flight over empty ocean broken only occasionally by the black smudge of a ship, Johno called over his shoulder, "There she is."

He pointed dead ahead, to a dark blob where the blue of the sea met the paler blue of the sky.

The aircraft followed the railway line inland from the small mining port of Tureka, heading west for the hilly area around Mount Ida.

Wordlessly, the pilot pointed down to the small mining settlement, half a mile to the east of Mount Ida. Beyond the mine buildings was the airstrip, and about half a mile beyond it were four rows of neat white bungalows which housed the engineers and other white mine staff. The bungalows terminated in a circle of two-story houses with beautifully tended gardens of frangipani and hibiscus—the houses of the managers and senior geologists. Behind these houses was a small street with a few shops and a garage. The amphibian was flying low enough to see that the shutters were closed over every window. There was no traffic and little sign of life.

"Ground doesn't answer my signals," Johno yelled cheerfully as he started to make his approach toward the airstrip.

They flew low over the runway. Everything seemed quiet.

"Too quiet," Johno commented. "But we can't go back, and we can't stay up here."

As he spoke, a white man in overalls appeared in the entrance of a hangar, with both arms slowly beckoning.

"No mistake," yelled Johno. "He's inviting us down to tea."

He made another circle, dropped the wheels, then landed smoothly and neatly, bringing the little plane to a standstill at the end of the runway.

Both men climbed down from the Duck into a blast of heat. They shook their cramped bodies and stretched their necks. Then they picked up their gear and started walking toward the terminal hut.

A yellow Toyota, jeep-like vehicle bumped toward them over the coarse dry grass. Harry peered at it. "That's Kerry MacDonald, the mine manager."

As the two men clambered into the cool, air-conditioned vehicle, Harry asked, "How's everything, Kerry?"

"Under control, Harry. The excitement was all in town." Kerry was small and chunky, with crew-cut hair and a round, naughty-boy face.

"What alert are you on?"

"Alert two. All Nexus personnel are under orders to keep inside their homes until further notice. We've closed the mine, we've doubled up on barbed wire and we're patrolling the perimeter."

"Have you heard from Arthur Graham?"

"No. Of course I telephoned Mr. Graham straightaway, but the telephone's on the blink, so I'm going to take the helicopter to Paradise Bay. That's why I was on the landing strip when you arrived. I'll wait until you clean up and have a meal, then we can go together."

The Toyota heaved itself onto a dirt road, and they headed for the mine office.

Kerry said, "Pity about Brett Adams."

"What about him?" Harry asked casually.

"He's dead."

"What?"

"Sorry, old chap, I thought you'd know. It happened just before the fighting. By the time I got back from the hospital, after dealing with the formalities about Brett's death, the telex wasn't working and neither was the telephone, but I assumed Arthur had phoned you."

"Well, he didn't. Tell me what happened."

Kerry quickly described the accident in the mine. As the vehicle bumped along the ruts, both men fell silent. Neither of them knew Brett well, but all miners live with danger and any death strikes close to home.

"Have you arranged shipment of the body back to Pittsburgh?" Harry asked.

"Not yet. There hasn't been time. The accident happened late on Tuesday afternoon. I was going to deal with it first thing on Wednesday, but by then we found ourselves in the middle of a mini-war, so Brett's still in the hospital morgue."

Johno said, "What exactly happened here? Who's fighting who?"

Kerry pulled the wheel over sharply, to stay in the corrugations, those deep ruts formed by countless previous wheels on the dirt road. "As far as we can make out, Raki invaded the island from the sea, just after dusk last Tuesday, with a large force of Filipino mercenaries.

"Undoubtedly the numbers have been greatly exaggerated, but I would guess he landed with about four hundred men. He claims he acted on behalf of the Nationalists, but it's starting to look like a solo performance. Raki had a Filipino grandmother, and he trained in the Filipino army, so it's not surprising that he recruited there." Again he jerked the wheel over. "Of course, Raki would have found it difficult, if not impossible, to get local people to fight after dark on Paui, because that's the time when spirits are supposed to walk, so they'd all be terrified. For that reason, I don't suppose he's met with much resistance. Apparently the first thing Raki did was to storm the radio station, which immediately surrendered. This was followed by the battle at the post office, which took ten minutes—after which Raki severed all communication with the outside world. No telephone, telegraph, telex or radio."

Harry nodded. He knew that the telecommunications system of Paui consisted of a satellite-linked radio, picked up by the relay station in Darwin from a geosynchronous satellite in orbit over the equator. In order to cut off the island from the outside world, Raki merely had to take over the recently completed electronic exchange at the post office, tell the two frightened operators to go home, then simply switch off the external radio link.

They pulled up in front of a house. From the open door a woman in a flowered cotton dress waved to Kerry. Kerry waved back, but seemed reluctant to leave the luxurious cool of the vehicle. He said, "Things calmed down pretty fast after that. As far as we can make out, everyone simply turned and ran, or else hid under the bed."

"Many casualties?" Harry asked.

"Nobody from Nexus has been hurt, so far as I know. Hardly any military casualties either. A few civilians got in the way of bullets. I'm afraid that's inevitable on these occasions. Of course President Obe is dead, and the rest of the Cabinet couldn't have had much chance of escape, unless they were able to head for a hiding place with their tribe. The Defense Force went straight over to Raki. He's always been popular. First the young officers defected, then the rest followed."

Harry said, "Are you sure things have quieted down in Queenstown?"

"Sure. I sent a couple of chaps into town at dawn this morning. They went with Mindo, so I know that the report is reliable."

"Who's Mindo?"

"He's the mineworkers' spokesman. An interesting guy; intelligent, and very well informed. Tough, but not ludicrously demanding. Always gives good reason for what the miners want." He scratched his short sandy hair, then added, "Mind you, he can be exasperating. He led our first strike last year. It got them a nine percent wage rise, but Mindo had enough sense to see our subsequent production losses and realize how badly that affected the men's end-of-year bonuses."

"So what did Mindo report from town?"

"All whites are safe. The big excitement seems to have been the storming of the Presidential Compound. Once the invaders were past the outer wall, they poured hundreds of rounds into the main building. Everyone inside stupidly fled upstairs to the roof, and there they were either shot or thrown off, or jumped of their own accord."

Harry said, "It would probably have been a different story had it happened in daylight. Was there any looting?"

"Of course. Looting started as soon as they could see, and lasted till about midday. They mainly went for the Asian shopkeepers around the harbor. They pulled off those protective grilles from the shop fronts and helped themselves to radios, watches and bicycles. They also got the town's entire supply of tinned food, makeup and bottled gas. The only shop that wasn't harmed was Mrs. Chang's sewing machine emporium; it's surrounded by broken glass and rubble, but it's untouched."

"What happened to the looters?"

"Apparently Raki shot about ten of them—and anyone that looked like a college student."

The dumpy woman in the flowered cotton dress frowned, and started down the path toward the Toyota.

Hurriedly, Kerry said, "Betty's wondering why we're sitting out here. I expect you'd like a shower and a quick meal."

But the meal wasn't quick, because the three houseboys and Cookie were saying their prayers in the little garden behind the house. Apologetically, Kerry's wife offered her guests a bowl of fruit and some apathetic potato chips.

She gave a laugh and said, "I don't dare go into the kitchen; it would upset Cookie, and he's such a gem. Really *clean,* which is so unusual for an islander. Cookie makes the houseboy scrub the kitchen every day. Kerry says you could operate on the kitchen table."

Harry asked, "Apart from the fighting, Kerry, how're things at the mine?"

"It's been pretty quiet. We're meeting our targets. The usual labor problems, but for the usual reasons."

Harry nodded. The mineworkers were tough, cheerful and full of vitality, but unpunctual and improvident. The mine had trouble keeping its staff, and deserters were frequent because once a man had a bicycle, a watch, a transistor radio and a sewing machine, he was by definition rich and it was beneath his dignity to work. He needed no other consumer goods until his machines broke down. It was not in the interest of the shops to repair goods; few of them could or would. So the man went back to the mines until he had sufficient money to buy new ones.

Kerry, who could see that Harry didn't want to chat, asked his wife, "How much longer are the kitchen staff going to be?"

"I don't know, darling. They're praying for their dead ancestors to watch over the living and keep the rioters from their village pigs. They seem to have as many conversations with the dead as with the living."

Johno stripped the last banana. "Do they *really* think the dead act as pig protectors?"

"Of course they do; no islander has doubts about his faith," Betty said earnestly from behind her ornate, blue-framed glasses. "Traditional religion is undisputed *fact* on Paui. It's as little questioned as the European medieval belief that the earth was flat."

"Weird," Johno said.

"Other people's religious beliefs often seem weird," Kerry said; "what you believe depends on where you were born. Faith can be a matter of geography: in some places, they believe that a man could turn wine into water; over here they believe in invisible pig-protectors."

Johno said, "It's pretty ludicrous that they have the most up-to-date radio station side by side with witchcraft on this island."

Kerry laughed. "The radio stations seem like witchcraft to them. So we're even."

The mine pilot pressed the starter button of the Bell. The engine whirred, the blades started to turn. When the speed and pitch were right and the noise deafening, the helicopter daintily lifted from the ground and hovered for a moment. The pilot applied full power and the Bell rose straight up fast, then went into a forward climb to a thousand feet and headed south.

Mount Ida receded behind them. Soon Harry could see the St. Mary River, undulating like a silver snake from the west until it finally spread into a muddy fan on the outskirts of Queenstown.

The pilot altered course to southwest. On a passenger aircraft you feel unconnected with the ground, but dipping along in a small helicopter you feel a part of the doll's-house details of the landscape.

From Queenstown they followed the new Plains Road,

which winds southwest between two mountain ranges. On the dirt road was a small moving trickle of black beads.

Kerry said, "Refugee women and kids, heading away from possible future fighting in Queenstown. They'll stay in their villages, either in the Central Mountains or on the west coast, where they'll be safe from bombs, unintentional bullets or intentional rape."

The Bell flew over lush green countryside, veined with small silver streams. Below them, the landscape was like a bumpy patchwork quilt lying upon a sleeping giant. Harry could see the small ragged squares of different greens that were field and pastureland clustered around a broken line of villages, behind which the gentle foothills rose to dense, high tropical forest and mountain peaks.

Sometimes the country fell steeply from the high peaks in jagged cliffs and gorges down to the swampy lowlands. The scattered patches of cultivation were separated by ravines in the highlands, stretches of almost impenetrable rain forest and, at a lower level, huge swamps into which the muddy waters of the mountain rivers debouched.

Within an hour Harry sighted the blue sea sparkling beyond the jungle greens of Paradise Bay. Minutes later the Bell touched down on the small airstrip behind the hotel.

The steamy heat was like lifting a casserole lid. The two Nexus executives ran in a crouch away from the helicopter blades, then stood up and looked around the airstrip.

"Seems quiet enough," Kerry said. "Not a soul in sight. Let's go, Harry."

The two men left the pilot with the helicopter, in case a fast takeoff was necessary. In the sweaty heat, they walked off the airstrip and turned onto the winding country track that led to the hotel entrance. They sauntered in a carefree, casual manner, but Kerry carried a handgun. As they turned a bend in the road, they saw the low, cream-colored hotel building.

Both men froze.

They were close enough to see clear traces of battle; windows were broken and the walls were pitted by an uneven line of bullet holes. The elaborately carved teak entrance doors lay smashed on the forecourt.

The only sound was birdsong and the faraway rhythmic sound of the surf as it boomed against the reef.

From the main doorway five khaki-clad, jungle-booted soldiers appeared, with rifles held at the ready.

"Don't move," Kerry said, unnecessarily.

THURSDAY, NOVEMBER 15, 1984

In the darkness of the cave, Carey looked at the skeleton and trembled. She said, "She must have fallen down the shaft into the cave and broken her pelvis. Look, you can see it's broken."

Jonathan, kneeling by the skeleton, looked up at Carey. "Maybe she has something to do with this area being taboo, if she fell down here and yelled for help. If the natives heard cries coming out of the ground and thought it was the voices of spirits, they would have been terrified."

Carey shivered.

Jonathan said, "What's important is, if she *fell* down, we ought to be able to *climb* down—and up! That means we'd have a beaut of a place to hide, without underwater torture every time." He paused. "If the natives don't know about this hole, then it's probably difficult to spot topside." He stood up. "Now let's get back to the others and tell them."

As Jonathan neared the little group of frightened women, he heard the snuffling and sobs and stopped abruptly. Suddenly he could no longer push to the back of his mind the fact that his wife was dead. His chest seemed filled with stones, he couldn't speak, he couldn't move and he couldn't face those women. Tears welled into his eyes, and he let out a sob. He wanted to sit alone in silence to mourn.

Behind him, Carey started to cry. Jonathan turned and put his arm around her. Slowly, they followed the circle of light toward the weeping women.

Sounding hoarse from suppressing his sobs, Jonathan said, "We can remember them tonight, but from tomorrow we must try *not* to think of what's happened. We must postpone our sorrow until we're safe. Otherwise, we'll never get out of this place."

The women nodded.

Jonathan sat down in the ammoniac guano, put his head in his hands and wept without restraint.

In the dark, tears streamed down Patty's face. She couldn't stop worrying about Stephen. She always tried to telephone him every day when she was away. So Stephen would immediately miss his mother's daily telephone call. The housekeeper, Judy, had been instructed to call Patty's mother if there was any problem. Mom would probably fly up from Florida, but no one understood Stephen as Patty did, so who would look after him if she didn't get out of this nightmare alive? He would be lost and terrified without her. He would be feeling exactly as his mother was feeling in this black hole. Patty wiped her swollen nose on the back of her hand and looked at her luminous watch. It was nearly seven o'clock on Thursday morning, November 15. She had cried herself to sleep, and slept for fifteen hours on this hard, rock-covered ground. Her eyes were so swollen she could hardly open them, but she could hear clearly the sound that had awakened her. Something was hauling itself from the water.

Terrified, Patty sat up. Then she spotted a dancing disc of light ahead of her. She whispered, "Did you swim outside, Jonathan?"

"Yes. Nobody around." He waded from the water, clutching his wet shirt with his left hand. "I brought back breakfast. Coconuts."

"I've never been so hungry in my life," Patty whispered, anxious not to awaken the other women.

247

He had swum outside, with only the machete for protection. After checking that there was no one in sight, he had collected four green coconuts from the back of the beach. Ravenously hungry, he had prized off the green, fibrous husk at the pointed end of each nut, then banged on the spot three times with the handle of the machete until the hard shell came away. It's hard work, opening a coconut. As a reward, he drank the sweet milk.

He hadn't liked the idea of diving down that bloody hole again, but those poor starving Sheilas inside hadn't had much to eat during the past two days. He had to admit, he hadn't heard one complaint.

By now the other women had stirred awake and were gratefully chewing hunks of moist coconut flesh. Jonathan said, "So far, we've done quite well. It looks as if we've evaded those bastards. We've got fresh water—even if it does have a few twigs and leaves in it. We have plenty of coconuts to eat. We've got enough equipment to look after ourselves. And we've found a really good place to hide."

"Sure," said Suzy. "But how will Nexus find us in here?"

"Nexus ain't coming to look for us," Jonathan said gently. "We were all blown up on the *Louise*, remember? If we wanna get off this island, we can only rely on our own efforts. That's why I reckon we have to build a raft."

"A *raft!*" Suzy shrilled.

"Yeah, I reckon we can make a raft that's big enough for all of us. We'll take off one evening after sunset and head for Irian Jaya. I've got my instruments, although I *can* navigate by the stars and the sun."

Carey said, "Why can't we just stay here and hide, until the fighting is finished and it's safe to go out?"

"From what I've seen of their fighting methods, the invaders might win," Jonathan said. "And from what I've seen of their goodwill, I don't want to risk showing my face to them."

The silence was broken by Patty. "How are we going to get anywhere without an outboard motor?"

"From October, northwest trade winds blow to the south along this coast. The current's also in our favor," he explained. "It sweeps round the southern tip of Paui toward the Torres Strait at about one knot."

"What's a knot?" Suzy asked.

"About fifteen percent more than a mile an hour. We might arrive in three days, although we'll allow longer, to cover over seventy miles."

"Three days!" Silvana gasped. "On a *raft!"*

"That's a realistic time," Jonathan said. "And the alternative is to stay here."

"That doesn't sound very fast," Patty objected. "I can *swim* faster than a mile an hour."

Carey said, "Yes, but not seventy miles nonstop."

"Will you two stop being so negative?" Annie said. "Jonathan's obviously been thinking this out for *hours*. For heaven's sake, let's listen to him!"

"We've got to get the raft made *fast,* or we'll be trapped by bad weather," Jonathan explained. "Today is November 15; the cyclone season starts December 1—regular as clockwork, and it lasts until the end of February. If we don't get off before the Long Wet, we'll be stuck here until next March. So we're in a race against time, as they say."

"That's right," Carey said. "It said in the travel brochure that the Paui tourist season is April to November."

"How long will it take to build a raft?" Suzy asked.

"Maybe twelve days, if we don't run into problems. That gives us three days' leeway. But I've always found that where there's life, there's problems."

"Surely it can't rain for three whole days?" Suzy said. "And if it does, surely we can put up with a bit of heavy rain, if it means getting off this place."

Jonathan said, "A cyclone's more than heavy rain. It flattens you." On Christmas morning, 1975, he had been in the rescue party after a cyclone destroyed Darwin. The North Australian town looked as if an atomic bomb had hit it. There were no fires, but for miles around, the trees had no leaves;

those that *looked* as if they were covered with autumn leaves were actually bearing shreds of corrugated iron from the roofs of buildings. Of twelve thousand homes, nine thousand had been flattened. Fifty-six people had been killed, and dead animals lay all over the place.

"Then surely it can't be safe to leave, if the rain is so dangerous," Suzy said.

"It ain't safe to go, and it ain't safe to stay," Jonathan said.

Patty said, "Suzy, why don't you just shut up and listen?"

"Because I want to know what I'm getting into," Suzy snapped. "And so should you. How the hell can *we* build a raft?"

"It might not be as hard as you think," Jonathan said. "All you need is trees, an ax and a knife. You don't even need rope in the jungle; we can use vines."

"Have you ever built a raft?" Suzy asked.

"No."

Suzy burst into tears of rage and misery. "*We* can't build a raft. I've never even been to camp. I can't use an ax or a knife!"

Wearily, Jonathan thought, And I bet you can't start a fire, catch a fish or pluck a bird. These women, with their long red nails, were obviously pampered bitches. He said shortly, "You can do far more than you think you can. I'll show you how to build a shelter, find food and make the raft."

There was a dubious silence.

"How come you know all this survival stuff?" Suzy asked.

"The Australian army had a battalion in Vietnam; I was with 'em for a year. Didn't like it, so I left. Didn't bother to tell anyone at the time," Jonathan said. He began to chew the last lump of coconut. That bit of food had made him realize how very hungry he was and that he'd better get them all a proper meal as soon as possible. Not for the first time, he resented thralldom to the body, to food and water at regular intervals, inexorably through life; to spending such a lot of effort just to stay alive, every single, blessed day.

He said, "We've all done well to get here. Now we've got

to keep going in the same way, until we're off this island. If you want me to be in charge, you've all got to do as I say. I warn you, I'm going to be a real slave driver. It's going to be work, sleep, work, sleep, boiled fish and coconuts, until we get to sea."

Silvana burst into tears of despair. "How can we possibly do these things? We don't know how to survive in the jungle! *We are all going to die!* How can *we* survive, if our husbands couldn't?"

This is like dealing with a bunch of kids, Jonathan thought, except that kids would love a jungle adventure. He said, "I don't want no talk of dying—that's *forbidden,* do you hear?"

In the dark, they started to snuffle again.

He said, "What's going to decide whether you survive or not is *you.* I want no tears, no apathy, no sitting down and weeping. People can easily talk themselves out of things they're capable of doing."

Patty said, "We have to be single-minded, to keep at our goal, if we're to get off this place."

Jonathan nodded. "You've got to be determined to survive, determined to see your families again."

Patty said quietly, "Determined to get those bastards who murdered our husbands."

Carey said, "That's right." She wondered whether she'd be able to stay on at the farm. Without Ed it would be lonely and perhaps dangerous. Perhaps she wouldn't be able to afford to stay there.

Annie said firmly, "I have to get back to my boys." She knew they were almost grown men, but she could never think of her sons as other than boys, in need of her love and care.

Jonathan said, "Common sense and the will to survive is all I'm asking from you. Otherwise, you ain't got a chance."

He swallowed the last shred of coconut and spat out a lump of fiber. "I can't help anyone who's going to fall out or sulk because she's got blisters on her hands or she's tired. If anyone ain't prepared to work hard without complaint, if anyone prefers to go off on her own, now's the time to say so."

Nobody moved.

"Then remember, we've agreed there'll be no moaning," Jonathan said. "That can wait until later."

Nobody spoke.

"Once you get used to the jungle, I promise you, you'll love it. It's got everything you need—food, water and vegetables. If you have fire, you could live happily here for the next ten years."

Somebody started to sob hard.

"What do we have to do?" Suzy asked.

"There's a few basic things to remember," he said. "We need a camp lookout. Each person takes it in turn to do a two-hour watch until we leave. Whoever has the watch also has the M-16, if only to warn the others. I've only got seventeen rounds, so I won't use it for hunting. If we hear a shot, then everyone drops what they're doing and heads for this cave. Everyone stays as close as possible to camp. No one goes into the jungle alone, or without a compass and matches. You'd be lost within fifty paces."

Suzy asked, "Why matches?"

"If you were lost or injured, you'd need a fire to protect yourself against animals. There's nothing really dangerous on this island except the odd wild pig, and you're unlikely to see any, because the natives eat anything that moves. But you never know."

"Won't a fire show anyone where we are? Surely they'll see the smoke?" Silvana asked.

"No, the smoke would be dissipated before it reaches the top of these high trees. The terrorists don't know we're here, so there's no reason for them to penetrate the jungle."

"But . . . ."

"No more buts," he said. "We're going to swim out of here, climb the cliff and set up camp on top. After we have a meal, we'll build a shelter. Then we'll look for the cave chimney and let a rope down it. That's our loose plan, and we're sticking to it."

"No matter what happens?" Carey questioned.

"Sure. I've found that nothing in life ever goes exactly to plan."

Silvana said hesitantly, "What about . . . sanitary matters?"

"Everyone goes ten paces beyond the camp, digs their little hole and then afterwards fills it in with earth. Don't use the fishing knives for hole digging. I'll get some big shells off the beach." Grateful for a few feeble giggles, he added earnestly, "Remember that the biggest hazard in the jungle is *you*. The wild animals will keep out of your way if you keep out of theirs and don't startle them. That goes for the sea snakes as well as the land ones." He heard a rustle of relief; snakes were what they'd all been scared of on that overnight march.

Jonathan said, "Basically, I want you to keep covered up, clean and cheerful, no matter how you feel. Depression is contagious, it generates anxiety. Anxiety can grow into fear; fear can grow into panic, and *that's* when people lose their heads and act without thinking. If you lose your head, you'll probably lose the rest of you."

Carey thought about the bat in her hair, and she saw what he meant.

Patty said, "Who does what when we get outside?"

"I hunt and fish," Jonathan said. "Patty's responsible for our shelter and the cave. Carey is in charge of the raft, as we build it. Silvana does the cooking. Annie can be camp nurse and responsible for hygiene, which includes the latrine check. Suzy's in charge of the water supplies, because she's got to get used to water. Patty can teach her to survival-float—it only takes half an hour. After that, as fast as possible, Suzy must learn to swim."

There was an immediate chorus of protest to all these demands.

Jonathan said, "I *know* you've never done it before. Now's the time to learn."

253

Anxiously, Patty persisted. "But if we *are* found, if we *are* attacked, what do we do *then?*"

Jonathan said softly, "I'll teach you how to kill."

Once outside the cave, the women blinked in the hot sun. Their wet clothes quickly started to steam as they scrambled up the path to the clifftop. It had been difficult to get Suzy to swim out, and she only did so because the alternative—being left alone with the bats in the dark—was worse than being dragged underwater once again by Jonathan and Patty.

Patty gasped. "What's *that?*"

At the clifftop, just inside the shelter of the trees, they saw nailed to the slim trunk of a eucalyptus tree a bit of rusting metal—probably the side of a kerosene tin—which bore the impression of a big black hand. Below the handprint the letters ITAMBU were crudely painted in red.

They were all rigid with fear.

"That," said Jonathan, "is our protection. *Itambu* means taboo, forbidden. No native dares to pass that sign, to tread on forbidden land."

Jonathan took his time choosing a campsite. Eventually he picked a slope that fell toward the sea, about twenty yards inland from the cliff and a hundred yards to the south of the waterfall. The small clearing was in an area of primary jungle between the dense undergrowth at the side of the river and the equally impenetrable secondary jungle that lay farther to the south. It was far enough away to avoid moisture from the waterfall seeping into the ground, and the slope was steep enough to make it unlikely that they would find themselves lying on wet earth in the middle of the night. The site was near enough to the river to fetch water.

Between the campsite and the cliff was a clump of trees with low branches that the women could reach to climb. One of these could be used as a lookout tree. It had a dense, rounded crown of feathery leaves, but no fruit or flowers; it was over sixty feet high, and its gnarled trunk and many branches provided relatively easy footholds. Jonathan thought that it might be a tamarind tree. Once you were up the tree you not only had a better view but you damn well kept awake, which was one of the reasons why Jonathan wanted them up there.

Suzy was posted first lookout. She stood under the tamarind tree with the rifle while the rest of the group went wearily down the footpath, with aching arms dug up the equipment, then lugged it up the cliff path.

The women cleared the dead and decaying vegetation off the campsite, because this could harbor ticks, ants, scorpions and spiders. Jonathan then handed out palm branches, which they used as brooms to sweep all remaining insects from the site.

It was midday by the time they had finished. In the energy-sapping heat nobody, not even Jonathan, had the strength to talk. Wordlessly he nodded to Patty, who helped him spread the canvas awning on the cleared site. They all crumpled onto it and immediately fell asleep.

Two hours later Suzy woke Jonathan. He blinked, sat up and shook his head. Then he woke Patty.

"Get down the cliff," he whispered. "Bring back some coconuts. Pick green ones, only stupid Europeans eat stale brown coconuts. I'll start the fire."

Carey and Jonathan collected fallen branches. Over a few handfuls of dried grass, he propped twigs together to form a pyramid. It took three of their precious matches to light the heap of dried grass, because Jonathan's hands were shaking with fatigue, and he dropped the first two, but eventually the little smoking pile spat into flame.

Jonathan grunted with satisfaction. "We'll take ash from the fire and draw a circle round the campsite. Ash will stop the insects crawling in."

He shook the other women awake. They drank the coconut milk and ate the meat in exhausted silence.

"I know you're all tired," Jonathan said apologetically, "but we must make a temporary shelter before nightfall or you'll get no sleep, because leaves'll fall on you and insects'll dive-bomb you."

"We should dig a drainage ditch," Carey said.

"Right. You do it." At last one of these Sheilas was waking up.

While Jonathan chopped down four saplings with the small boat ax, Carey, using an empty coconut shell, dug a small ditch on one side of the shelter site. This led downhill, so it would keep the shelter floor dry.

Annie measured out a square of earth a little smaller than their canvas awning. The others painfully dug a twelve-inch-deep hole at each corner, using coconut shells as scoopers. They protected their hands with the soft leather fishing gloves that Jonathan handed out.

Jonathan trimmed the cut saplings just above the trunk where the first branches divided to form a Y; one pair were two feet long, the other pair measured four feet. He then set the poles in the four corner holes, with the taller pair on the upper part of the slope and the smaller poles on the lower.

They heaved the canvas awning over the smaller posts and secured it with the rope that had held the awning above the bridge of the *Louise*. They rolled the tarpaulin up to the higher poles and lashed it to them. The angled awning would protect them from any wind blowing off the sea.

Jonathan said, "Tomorrow when we've got our strength back we'll make a proper house, with walls and a roof of interlaced leaves."

Carey and Suzy spread an assortment of leaves and brush over the floor of the lean-to so that they wouldn't catch a chill from sleeping on bare earth. Jonathan piled the equipment inside the shelter, then the women crawled beneath the canvas and collapsed into sleep.

Carey, who was posted as sentry, fell asleep ten minutes after the others. One moment she was standing up and trying to keep her eyes open, the next moment her knees buckled as if she were drunk and she skinned them as she hit the ground. She decided to stay there just for a minute or two. . . .

FRIDAY, NOVEMBER 16

Jonathan shook Carey awake.

"Damnit, you *must all* learn to stay awake when you're the lookout. Now take a line, wade into the sea and try to catch some fish. Don't take your shoes off, then you won't scratch your feet or get bitten by anything underfoot." He moved on to Suzy, shook her awake and said, "You're the lookout. If you go to sleep, you won't get any supper."

As he shook Patty awake he said softly, "We've got work to do, you and I. We won't be safe until we find the exit to that cave chimney. If somebody was after us, we'd never get Suzy through the water fast enough to hide."

Patty staggered to her feet and rubbed her eyes. "Okay, okay."

After a breakfast of coconuts, Jonathan took them all into the dark, damp rain forest. Birds of paradise with pink or turquoise plumage flashed high overhead under the soaring green canopy.

He held up a red berry. "The rule of the jungle is 'Never eat red,' except for ginger, persimmon or mango." He passed around the little red berry of the strychnine plant, with its deadly poisonous seeds. "Never touch brightly colored fruits or berries. Avoid anything that looks even *vaguely* like a tomato."

He plucked a hairy green fruit from a branch. "Rub off all hairs on berries or leaves. Never eat roots, fruit or vegetables with a bitter or stinging taste. Always test with yer tongue anything yer try for the first time, so yer can spit it out if necessary. Don't touch any plant, shrub or tree with a milky sap."

"What about these mushrooms?" Carey pointed at one.

"Don't risk eating *anything* that looks like a toadstool or a mushroom."

"Which plants are poisonous to touch?" Patty asked.

"Anything that makes yer flesh go red or swell or itch or blister, same as anywhere else in the world. Yer won't know till yer touch it. But nothing can kill yer."

Silvana asked, "What about snakes? I'm far more frightened of snakes than plants."

"Very few of the world's snakes are poisonous. The aggressive snakes are the cobras, kraits and pit vipers, but there's less danger from snakes in the tropics than from rattlesnakes or moccasins in some parts of America."

"I just hope the snakes have been reading the same book as you," Suzy said tartly.

"Snakes'll get out of the way if they hear yer coming," Jonathan said, "but yer mustn't disturb a snake, or frighten it, or corner it."

"I'll try not to," Suzy said.

"You won't have no problems if you walk slow and deliberate, if you watch where you're going, watch where you put your hand, and run like hell if yer see a snake."

"What about sea snakes?" Silvana asked, still nervous.

"You get venomous sea snakes in the tidal rivers and along the shore, but if you ain't stupid enough to swim into one, they won't disturb yer."

"And lizards?" Silvana persisted.

"Lizards ain't poisonous here."

The other women returned to camp, and Jonathan and Patty set off to search the jungle. They had calculated that the cave chimney lay southeast of their camp, but they found that this area was secondary jungle. Jonathan looked at the thick tangle of undergrowth and said, "Must have been a village here once. Maybe if you swim into the cave, Patty, and holler up, I'll hear yer voice." Then he shook his head. "No, even if I heard yer, I reckon it'd be almost impossible to tell where your voice was coming from."

Patty said hesitantly, "I once saw someone climb a natural rock chimney on TV. I could try going up the chimney from below, with a rope. If I got to the top, we could tie the rope to a tree and let it dangle down."

Jonathan nodded. "It makes more sense if *you* climb the shaft. I can swim out, climb the cliff and hack a path in the undergrowth towards your voice. If *I* climb up the chimney, I won't know where to start hacking my way out. You probably won't be able to see a thing from the dense undergrowth on top." He thought, I can't tell her this, but if *I* climb that chimney and fall, then they'll all die with no one to look after 'em. He added, "We *must* locate the cave exit before we pick a permanent campsite, because camp must be near our hidey-hole."

Taking the underwater flashlight and the coil of rope, Jonathan and Patty once more climbed down the cliff and dived into the cave. To protect it from bats, Patty wrapped her silver-blond hair in Jonathan's white shirt. Slowly they made their way deep into the cave until they reached the faint shaft of light that marked the chimney.

"Don't think about it. Just get up there," Jonathan urged.

Patty thought, It's all right for *him* to sound so confident. *He* doesn't have to risk falling sixty feet.

Without speaking, she coiled the rope over one shoulder and under the other arm.

"You're a brave lass. Once we've found the way down here, we'll be safe."

Patty nodded toward the skeleton. "She wasn't." She looked up at the faint circle of light. "Maybe I should practice?"

"What for? Get up there, that's practice."

She thought, Slowly but inexorably, *I'm going to reach the top*. Her heart had started to thump and her breath was shallow, so she made herself do deep breathing exercises, pushing at her abdomen as she breathed in slowly, sucking it back as she exhaled.

Jonathan said, "What are you waiting for?"

"I'm thinking myself through it," Patty told him. She must never once think of failure; she must never think of falling, of smashing her body, of dying underground in this foul-smelling darkness like that poor skeleton. She must be determined. She must not allow her thoughts to wander toward failure. She must calmly start and not stop until she reached the top. She mustn't falter at that point, she must know exactly what to do. If she distracted her imagination by counting, she wouldn't be *able* to think about anything else. If she breathed deeply all the way up, she wouldn't panic, because it is physically impossible to panic if you breathe slow, deep and easy.

"If you can go up two feet, you can go up the whole way. *Remember that,*" Jonathan said.

She moved forward and stood with her slim back pressed against the rough wall of the shaft. She lifted one leg at a time, bracing her feet against the opposite side.

Better get moving.

She pressed against the wall with her hands and moved her butt up a couple of inches. Cautiously she lifted her left foot up a couple of inches, using her other foot as a brace to stop herself from falling. She thought, I'll count to four hundred and by that time I'll either be at the top or I'll have joined that skeleton at the bottom. Without discussing it, both she and Jonathan knew that if she lost her footing, she had no way of breaking her fall.

In her navy shirt and filthy white shorts, with Jonathan's white shirt wrapped round her head, to protect it from bats, Patty started to inch her way up the shaft, shifting her rear up a few inches at a time as she pushed the earth wall with the palms of her hands. Very soon her legs started to tremble because of the need to keep them constantly braced. To focus her concentration (and keep her imagination shut in its box) she started to count aloud. Thirty-four . . . thirty-five . . . thirty-six . . .

Concentrate on deep breathing. *In* when she inched herself up with her butt, *out* as she moved her feet. Seventy-one . . . seventy-two . . .

She longed to look up to see how far she still had to go, but she mustn't break her concentration. Two hundred and one . . . two hundred and two . . . Every shaking muscle in her body shrieked in protest as she slowly edged her way up the shaft.

Her arms were trembling, her whole body was shaking and dripping with sweat. It was increasingly hard to discipline her breathing, she was panting now. Five hundred and one . . . five hundred and two . . . Maybe she would reach the top by the time she had counted to a thousand. If not, then she'd just have to go for two thousand. She'd damn well do it to get Charley's killers. . . .

Her legs were no longer trembling, they were making involuntary jerking movements. Suddenly she was terrified of cramp. What was that twinge? Idiot, don't *invite* a cramp.

Each movement of her feet became slower and shorter, each successive brace more agonizing; her navy shirt was now in ribbons and the rough stones and earth tore at her back.

She couldn't go on much longer. Six hundred and one . . . six hundred and two . . . The unaccustomed movement was tearing at the muscles of her inner thighs, while her stomach ached as if she'd just finished a fast five-mile run. She started to rasp rather than breathe. Her back, her arms and hands were bleeding and torn; she started to sob the numbers, counting in the gloom. Six hundred and fourteen . . . Breathe *in*. *Push* with her palms. *Edge* up her butt. *Slowly* let her breath out. *Bring up* left foot. *Bring up* right foot.

She longed to stop and rest but she didn't dare, because her arms might stiffen or her knees jump uncontrollably. She was keeping her knees rigid by the pressure of the soles of her feet against the earth walls of the shaft.

Pieces of earth and stone rattled down, dislodged as she climbed upward. She longed to scream, she longed to stop—

just for one minute—but she knew that she was doomed if she did so. She continued upward, upward. . . .

Sweat running into her eyes, trembling in every limb, Patty slowly realized that there was more light now, she could clearly see the filthy laces of her sneakers. She sobbed a little louder. Seven hundred and seven . . .

The worst moment was when she suddenly felt a scratching against the top of her head and realized that she had reached the foliage at the top of the shaft. Suddenly she doubted her ability to get out. She mustn't panic, she mustn't think *down*, she must think *out*.

Slowly, trembling, careful to keep both feet braced, Patty felt with her right hand through the foliage. It didn't seem very thick or tangled, she could feel that the top of her fingers were moving freely in the air above the scratchy undergrowth. She fought back the urge to grab at the foliage for support. Slow and steady, control your breathing, slowly *in* . . . slowly *out* . . .

Feeling now with her left hand, she tentatively pulled on the undergrowth above her, which immediately gave way. So she had guessed correctly, she couldn't haul herself out by hanging on to this stuff.

She slid her butt up a little more, and again inched up her legs, which were now jerking so hard they were almost out of control. With both hands she managed to clear a space above her head, then she moved her hands back so that once again the torn and bleeding palms were pushing on either side of her hips. Again, she edged herself upward, through the thicket that scratched at her face and throat.

Keep counting. Seven hundred and twenty-six . . .

She felt a beguiling air of false security. She longed to grab again at the surrounding vines, but knew they were likely to be treacherous, and break beneath her clutch.

The most difficult part was when her head and shoulders were well clear of the undergrowth and her body still submerged. She realized how much she'd counted on watching her shoelaces, to focus her concentration; now she could no longer see them.

Looking fixedly at the point where her sneakers should emerge, Patty slowly stretched each arm above the foliage. She was shaking as if she had a fever. A leaf floated onto her face and she spat it away, refusing to let it spoil her concentration.

When the upper part of her body was clear of the chimney, Patty paused again. She moved her head to the left, feeling with her left arm through the undergrowth, groping for the ground beneath, to check that it was firm, that it was unlikely to crumble and give way—to slide with her back into the chimney and hurtle to the floor of the cave.

Patty hoped she wasn't sticking her groping hand into some creature's mouth, she hoped she wasn't going to throw herself sideways onto an ants' nest.

The ground seemed firm enough. She twisted a creeper around her left hand. With her last scrap of strength, she heaved herself up and over the edge of the chimney.

She lay, trembling and nauseous, upon rotting vegetation. Red ants started to bite the flesh of her arms and legs.

Patty managed to haul herself into a crouch position; slowly she edged her way toward the nearest tree trunk, hacking at the foliage with the two fish knives that had been stuck in her belt.

It took her nearly half an hour to reach the tree and tie the rope around the silvery trunk. She scrabbled with bleeding hands for stones; cautiously, she moved near enough to throw them down the chimney. She threw three stones, which meant, "I'm up and I'm okay, and the rope is attached to the tree."

She thought she heard a cry from the shaft, but it was too faint and distorted for the words to be distinguishable. She tugged off Jonathan's shirt from her hair and wiped her sweating face with it, then crouched against the tree. She wasn't going to move from this spot. As agreed, she was going to whistle until he found her, until Jonathan hacked his way through to her with his machete. She wasn't going to move *one inch*. There might be other natural chimneys around here. If so, she didn't want to stumble into one.

Patty could hear Jonathan before she saw him. As they shouted to each other, she gradually heard the thwack of his machete, hacking a path toward her. When at last he made his final slashes through the undergrowth, Patty hurled herself against his naked sweating chest.

"That's my good girl," he said, holding her trembling body against him and stroking her short, fair hair. "We'll soon have you feeling fine again."

He half-carried, half-dragged her through the low, narrow tunnel he had cut through the undergrowth. As soon as they were clear of secondary jungle, he picked Patty up in his arms and gently carried her to the waterfall pool.

Carefully, Annie removed what remained of Patty's navy shirt. Silvana tenderly bathed her scratches and dried them with her own shirt. Softly, Annie gently rubbed antiseptic cream on the wounds.

As she watched, Suzy realized for the first time that she, like Patty, would soon be dependent on this bunch of women, whom she had never before trusted. They said they were going to teach her to swim, and Suzy didn't like the idea. She trusted the water no more than she trusted the women. Trust was alien to Suzy's nature; she loathed the idea of dependency, and was as suspicious of it as a wild animal scenting a trap.

Carey hadn't returned from her fishing trip. Jonathan went to look for her, while the four other women peeled off their clothes and bathed naked in the waterfall pool, except for Silvana, who swam in her black lace underwear.

By the time Carey joined the other women, Patty had recovered enough to help her teach Suzy to survival-float.

Patty explained, "You don't move, Suzy. You hang in the water, like a skydiver, with legs and arms apart, loose and relaxed."

Crouched on the sea rocks, Suzy snorted. It was hard to

persuade her into the water, because the entire pool was out of her depth. The two swimmers treaded water with Suzy clinging between them, an arm around each neck.

Eventually, using the empty plastic water container as a float, Suzy lay, clumsily spread-eagled, with the container bobbing beneath her stomach. As she floated by herself around the pool, flanked by Patty and Carey, she crowed with delight at her achievement.

Then came the nasty moment when the plastic container was pushed out of the way. Patty and Carey crossed their arms under Suzy's stomach while she got used to the idea of hanging in the water.

Patty said, "Try dipping your face underwater, to get used to the feeling."

Suzy's body immediately went rigid and her head jerked upward. "I can't! I won't! You can't make me!"

Patty and Carey said nothing, but waited. After a few minutes Suzy's mutinous fear subsided; she knew that this was for real. Jonathan had made it clear that he wouldn't allow her on the raft if she couldn't swim.

Within half an hour, Suzy was confidently survival-floating.

They had no soap. Annie and Silvana rubbed their bodies and hair with handfuls of sand before they dived in. Silvana had never seen another naked female adult. Embarrassed, she wouldn't remove her black lace underwear, but couldn't help shooting furtive glances at the bodies of the other women. She had thought that women were all pretty much the same shape except that some were bigger than others; but these bodies were all a different shape and the breasts differed as much as the noses of their owners. Patty's long, narrow body was lean, like that of a boy, and her breasts were small and pointed. Annie was very white and soft; her breasts were like halves of a tennis ball, with little pink stick-out nipples. Carey had large brown nipples; her body was big and solid like a Botticelli maiden, except that she still had some tan from the summer. Suzy had the legs and midriff of a twelve-year-old child, but there was nothing immature about her big breasts and small, high, dimpled backside.

While the other women larked around in the pool, Silvana felt self-conscious, as though they were looking at her. Treading water, Silvana pinched her behind; it felt as if she were digging her finger into an overripe avocado. She felt ashamed of her body and vulnerable. Although nobody was likely to do so, she felt that at any moment the others might point scornfully at her and jeer.

Afterward, as they sat on the rocks, Annie distributed their clothes; she'd soaked them to disperse the sweat. Dressed in their wet clothes, the women felt relatively cool as they scrambled up the rocks and back to their camp.

Before the swim, Carey had caught four small parrotfish. She found this a disappointing catch; she had a proper line, she knew how to fish and there seemed to be plenty of fish in the lagoon. Now Jonathan gutted the fish and they roasted them over the campfire, spiked on branches. Bits of fish were raw and bits were burned, but nobody complained.

After the fruit course—raw coconut again—Jonathan refused to let Carey smoke one of her own cigarettes. They were the only cigarettes that the small group possessed—a valuable, fast way of dispelling leeches and mosquitoes, which hate smoke. The most deadly form of animal life that threatened them was the mosquito, one female type of which carried malaria.

"Just *one* cigarette," Carey pleaded. "*Please*. I've been smoking two packs a day since I first went to college."

"Then you'd finish these in half a day, so why not pretend they're already finished?" Jonathan said.

Patty suggested, "Maybe you can find a leaf substitute in the jungle. The natives smoke a native tobacco in their long pipes; it must grow around here someplace."

"I wouldn't count on that," Jonathan said shortly.

In the searing midday heat, they slept again; it was too hot to do anything else.

Later, they built a proper campfire. Patty and Carey dug a

pit, about the size of a baby's bath, scooping up the dirt with the empty coconut shells. Jonathan trimmed a couple of saplings at the branch division until he had two Y-shaped pieces of wood each about a foot long. He buried one of these supports at either end of the little pit and across them he placed a stout stick of green wood, from which he hung a metal bucket of water.

"In the future," he said, "all our water has to be purified by boiling and then it must be filtered through my socks, to catch almost invisible bits of twig, leaf and other vegetation."

Suzy stopped laughing when she realized he was serious. She was the camp water carrier. He'd showed her how to draw water from the river, the pail tied to her waist by a long length of rattan, in case she let go of it.

"Any fast-flowing water that runs over sand will have been filtered," he explained, "but there may be a village upstream of that rope bridge, and when there's a village, there'll be rats, and where there's rats, there's rat piss, and that pollutes the water."

Jonathan and Carey followed the river upstream, until they reached a stream that ran into it. Later, Jonathan brought all the women to the edge of the wide, fast-running stream, where he taught them how to fish. Carey carefully demonstrated the techniques to the other women.

As they trudged back to camp with three small trout and a freshwater shrimp the size of a lobster, Jonathan said, "This time, you each gut your own fish."

"Yuk!" said Suzy.

After their evening meal, as they squatted around the campfire in the dark, he cut up one of the mosquito nets to make veils that tied under the chin—like beekeepers' veils—for the floppy white sun hats they'd saved from the *Louise*. They would take turns using the other two mosquito nets at night, with priority going to anyone who fell ill.

"Okay!" said Jonathan as he finished the veils. "Pretend it's Melbourne Cup Day. Hats fit to lead in the winning horse. Try 'em on for size."

"Try my mudpacks first," Annie said. She had mixed up a billycan of black mudpack, using earth and water from the riverbank. This was to be slapped on legs and ankles to protect them from mosquitoes and to soothe their sting.

On the previous night, there had been fierce arguments over the four pairs of leather fishing gloves, which could protect hands from mosquitoes. They were all grateful for the huge white cotton fishing shirts from the boat which protected the top of the body, but beneath their skimpy shorts, Suzy and Patty's legs, and everybody's ankles, had been mercilessly bitten.

Looking at one another's muddy faces, topped by the ludicrous veiled hats, the women started to laugh—for the first time since their tragedy.

Annie said, "We'll wash it off every morning when we dip."

"And after the dip you'll hold a foot inspection," Jonathan said. Their feet were going to be even more important than their hands. Sneakers were to be washed every night and dried by the fire. Feet were to be bathed every evening in hot saltwater to harden them. "And don't, for God's sake, break a blister. Once you get foot rot or jungle footsores, you probably won't get rid of them."

Patty held her head in both hands. "I need a nurse right now. I've had a headache ever since I climbed up that chimney. Isn't there any aspirin in the first-aid box?"

Although it contained a battered packet of aspirin, the first-aid box was a disappointment. The tin was rusty and none too clean, and the contents were old and used. The tube of antiseptic cream had been squeezed nearly empty, as had the tube of insect repellent. Half the calamine lotion was gone, and there was very little adhesive tape left on the roll. Nevertheless, the box contained a couple of bandages, a small pair of scissors, a tube of lip-blister cream, a tin of talcum powder, a broken thermometer, a bottle of smelling salts and a small, dirty jar of anonymous ointment.

Jonathan picked up the small jar and rubbed some brown

ointment on the center of Patty's forehead. "It's tiger balm, opium-based. Removes headaches and hangover."

Annie said, "Let's see what everyone has in their purses. Maybe there are things we can use here."

"Sure," said Jonathan. "I've always wondered what women cart around in them."

In the firelight, their purses yielded a jumble of melting lipsticks, powder compacts, mirrors, money, keys, sun cream, tissues and ballpoint pens. Annie had a packet of tampons. Carey had cigarettes, a lighter and a notebook. Patty triumphantly produced a tiny hotel free gift sewing kit, which contained another pair of scissors. Suzy had two thousand dollars in American Express checks.

Jonathan said, "Who's got a watch that isn't waterproof? Hand 'em over now, and we'll keep 'em in the lemon-drop tin, in case we need to use 'em for barter."

Suzy handed over her platinum watch, the face surrounded by diamonds. Annie removed the black silk strap of the old-fashioned, round gold watch that had been her grandmother's. Silvana didn't wear a watch, and neither did Carey when she was on vacation. The only waterproof watches were Jonathan's chrome Seiko and Patty's black plastic Swatchwatch.

Jonathan said, "Anyone who leaves camp wears the Swatchwatch."

"What about our rings?" Silvana asked wistfully.

"Can't we still wear the rings our husbands gave us?"

It was an emotional moment. Jonathan nodded. "Sure. Like I said, I don't *want* to barter anything, because it'll get traced back in no time."

Patty asked how far the taboo area extended.

"Not farther than that Burma bridge, because that's obviously a track that's in use." Jonathan said, "Stay as near to the camp as possible and there's less risk of going out of the taboo area—and on no account go near the next village."

Suzy persisted. "But why not?"

Jonathan said, "It's not safe."

"But *why* not?"

He said slowly, "I suppose you've got to know sometime. They're practicing cannibals. All the fishing villagers are."

There was a shocked silence, followed by a babble of horror.

"How revolting!"

"Disgusting!"

"You *can't* be serious!"

"I think I'm going to throw up!"

"You've *got* to be kidding!"

Suzy gasped, "But when I wouldn't swim into the cave, *you told me to go to the next village!*"

"You'd have died anyway," Jonathan said. "I had the safety of the party to consider. The natives don't talk English and you don't talk Pidgin, so you couldn't have told them that we'd hidden in the pool."

There was another shocked silence.

Jonathan said, "A lot of this island is still primitive—particularly the wild, barren bits in the south, where the fisher-folk live. Around here, you can buy a hard-working bride for a couple of axes and a pig."

Patty said, "What's that got to do with cannibalism?"

"Animals are rare and fresh meat is scarce. The natives keep pigs, but they don't kill 'em, because they're a sign of wealth. They use the pigs for barter or for paying debts. They only kill one for a special feast, and then they're only eaten by the men, not wasted on women and children. To natives, cannibalism is human ecology; they think it's a waste to bury people or burn 'em. When their own people die, they get eaten."

Patty said, "But we're not their goddamned relatives."

"Any stranger risks being considered a free pig."

Patty spoke very fast. "You must teach us all to use that gun. Now!"

"Not much to worry about *now*. Head-hunting is seasonal, in June, and they raid the *other* islands—there are nearly eight hundred islands in this area. A fast canoe-man can paddle nonstop for forty-eight hours to carry off a victim. But

270

they ain't used just as grub, human sacrifices are needed for religious and ceremonial purposes."

Carey burst out, "But *why* did you bring us to this place in your boat? *Why* did you let us picnic on a cannibals' beach? *Why* did they build a luxury hotel in the middle of cannibal villages?"

"The National Assembly wants to encourage tourism, because it provides easy money," Jonathan said, "and this island needs cash to haul itself into the twentieth century. The only sandy beaches are on this side of the island."

Silvana said, "I can't *imagine* why Arthur allowed it."

"Probably Arthur didn't know about it. Officially, all cannibalism stopped years ago. It's something that isn't discussed, but everyone knows it still goes on here, just as it does in Papua New Guinea—although PNG is teeming with tourists. Remember that millionaire's son who disappeared in the sixties? They reckon he ended up in the pot."

On the next day, Saturday, November 17, they built their house.

Jonathan cut down twelve saplings of different lengths, which Patty trimmed with one of the fish knives. Suzy gathered rattan, for use as rope and string; it sprouted, vinelike, from the ground and twisted up like ivy—thickest at the root for rope, thinner toward the tip for string. Carey found it difficult to work, because of her damaged hands, but she was able to carry rattan back to camp in her arms.

Jonathan staked out an area about fifteen feet square and sank an eight-foot Y-topped pole in each corner. He said, "We'll lash four more poles to these corner supports to form a boxlike frame about six feet high."

He propped two poles to form an A-shape at each end of the box frame. "We'll lash slimmer poles horizontally between the A-frames to form the skeleton of our hut; she'll have eaves that almost reach the ground."

Annie and Silvana had been collecting elephant's ears— huge, oval leaves up to four feet long with very thick spines. In the center of each spine they cut a slanted notch; with the leaf tip pointing up, Jonathan hooked each notch over the horizontal poles of the hut, starting at the bottom, so that each new row of elephant's ears overlapped the previous ones, on the same principle as roof tiles.

Suzy grumbled at the work. "I don't see why we can't just sleep under the canvas awning, like we did last night."

"Because it's not big enough for us to stretch out, and you're going to need proper sleep or you won't be able to work," Jonathan told her.

"I don't *want* to do this work."

He stared hard at Suzy. "When we've finished making the roof, you can dig the drainage ditch, just above and to one side of the hut. That'll keep the floor dry."

They all realized that if you complained, you were apt to get a worse job.

Their most serious problem was not snakes or sharks, it was the climate. The nights seemed even hotter than the days; except for one cool hour at dawn, there was no escape from the humidity, which was generally well above 90 percent. Their hair was always lank and soaked with sweat, their clothes were wet enough to wring out, and they felt hot, sticky and lethargic most of the time, as if they'd just had influenza and were at the stage when, no matter how thirsty you are, it is simply too much trouble to reach for a glass of water.

So in the late afternoon, Jonathan introduced a little luxury. He cut a sapling into four twelve-inch lengths and hammered them into the beaten earth floor of the new hut, to form a three-foot by six-foot rectangle. He cut some thirty-foot-high bamboo poles, chopped each into four pieces and bound them with rattan into a rectangle that could be fitted on top of the four stakes.

He grinned. "Scorpion-proof bed. Insulation against ground chill and damp at dawn." Because it was cold just before dawn, they had already suffered from indigestion and diarrhea.

Suzy immediately scrambled onto the bamboo bed, which yielded beneath her weight, then sprang back like bed springs.

"Why, it's really comfortable," she said, sitting cross-legged. "I want one."

So each woman built her own bed, which would clearly make a great difference to the comfort of their nights and also to the comfort of their afternoons, when it was too hot to move. From the moment they had beds, the spirits of the women lifted.

At last, something had improved.

Toward dusk Jonathan, carrying two pails, two spear guns, two fishing rods and two knives, was followed down to the beach by all the women except Carey. She had been posted as lookout because she already knew how to fish in the ocean, whereas the other women were about to learn.

Jonathan taught them to look along the shore for crabs, worms or insects to use for bait. He showed them how to conceal the hook in the bait, how to make hooks from large thorns or carved bits of bone and to make fishing lines from rattan or from unraveled threads of canvas, rewound counter-clockwise, to form a stronger line.

"Why do we have to make our own hooks and lines and fishing spears when we've still got the spearguns and plenty of ready-made ones?" Suzy grumbled.

"Takes time to learn to use a speargun. And you can't help losing lines and hooks—they catch on rocks or get tangled on something underwater," Jonathan told her. "And most of my tackle's too heavy for this sort of fishing. We want to save it for when we go to sea."

He showed them how to strand fish when the tide went out by piling up a wide crescent of rocks on the tidal flats from which they could scoop up any floundering fish with their nets. He taught them to use stones and loose rocks to block the natural opening of pools on the rocks, and so trapping any fish in them.

He made a fishing spear by binding his fish knife to a bamboo pole about the thickness of a thumb, then showed them how to throw the spear, aiming just ahead of the fish, in the direction in which it is moving, to allow for the refraction of the water. He showed them how to thrust the spear straight down and out of the water in one smooth swoop, so that the fish couldn't wriggle off the prong before it was netted.

He also taught them not to be discouraged if the fish didn't bite. "There are two secrets of fishing," he explained. "One is using the correct bait in the correct way, and the other is patience."

"Then how come Patty fishes so well?" Suzy asked crossly.

Wearing leather gloves, Patty and Annie searched the shore and tidepools formed by coral. The coral, exposed at low tide, wasn't a pretty pink color but dull, earthy shades from tan to black. There were many different shapes: branch, fern and brain.

"Look for clams, mussels, scallops, sea cucumbers—they look like large slugs—," Jonathan had encouraged, "and you'll also find shrimp, prickly sea urchins, crayfish and crabs." He had shown them which poisonous shells to avoid —the ones with cone-shaped or spindle-shaped shells.

Suzy and Silvana were collecting pigweed, a fleshy, reddish-green weed that grows in large patches on coral. "Tastes like watercress if you eat it fresh, and like spinach if you boil it in seawater," Jonathan had said.

Half an hour later, when they met on the sand, Patty had about a quart of shellfish.

"That's not much for six people," Suzy commented.

"We'll boil this lot up with your pigweed and have clam chowder," Jonathan promised. "Before we go to sleep, I'll make a dip net. I'll bend a little sapling into a circle and lash it to a mosquito-net bag. Tomorrow, you'll be able to go shrimping in the rock pools like a couple of kids."

All day, the women had worked hard under Jonathan's direction, like a class of students working obediently for their professor. They were still not very friendly with each other, and each was, in her own way, vying for the attention of the only man.

While they were assembling the skeleton frame of the hut,

Suzy kept dropping the poles and looking hopefully toward Jonathan; Carey kept leaping forward to help Jonathan pick them up. Every time Annie prepared a pile of elephant's ears she looked hesitantly at Jonathan and waited for his nod of approval before continuing. Every time an elephant's ear fell off of the frame of the hut, Silvana shrugged her shoulders and threw Jonathan an amused look, like a parent watching a child with its first building blocks. Patty proudly showed her first catch of shellfish to Jonathan, with the expression of a child that expects a pat on the head. However, Jonathan didn't seem to notice any of it.

Their evening meal of shellfish chowder was served in individual coconut shells, which they ate greedily using scooped leaves for spoons. For the first time, all the women felt a sense of order, if not security. As they gazed into the dying embers of the fire that kept the mosquitoes away, they also felt a sense of achievement. They felt soothed, and no longer at the mercy of a cruelty that they did not understand.

During the entire day—as they bathed in the pool, as they built their house, as they fished on the beach and played doll house in the jungle—hidden eyes were watching them from the leafy branches of a tree that grew on the far side of the waterfall. During the afternoon, at one point a soft gust of wind scattered the feathery palm leaves. In that moment, a native was revealed, motionless and unblinking. The next moment, the leaves had closed around him and nothing could be seen. The immobile, treetop spy continued to survey the women, with the cold, calculating look of a serpent.

THURSDAY, NOVEMBER 15, 1984

As the soldiers approached, Harry and Kerry slowly raised their hands. They knew that when you're looking into five rifle barrels, you don't act like a TV hero. You move slowly, with maximum prudence and an expressionless face. In particular, you do not react with schoolboy aggression, *especially* if it is invited—you do nothing provocative, which might be used as an excuse for shooting you.

One of the soldiers stepped forward, tugged at the wristwatch on Kerry's outstretched arm and ripped it off. Harry lost his cheap watch in a similar manner. The soldiers argued over Kerry's expensive gold watch, which they clearly preferred to Harry's. Both white men then felt hands thrusting in their jacket and trouser pockets. The soldiers snatched their handguns, their wallets, their small change and Harry's cigarettes. With rifles at their backs, they were marched up the steps of the hotel and roughly shoved to the right, into the manager's small office.

Against the rear wall of the office, a filing cabinet had been pulled open and its contents scattered over the floor. On top of the filing cabinet was a red plastic tray, upon which stood a coffeepot, an open carton of milk and a mug. A map of Paui was pinned to the wall above the cabinet.

In the middle of the office stood an unprepossessing

wooden desk; it was covered with opened cans and empty bottles. Behind the desk sat a soldier, whose sweat-stained tunic bore a corporal's stripes.

A small group of soldiers had been sitting in the shade on the concrete path outside the manager's office. They scrambled to their feet and crowded into the small room, which stank of stale drink and sweat. They glared at the two white prisoners with ill-contained hostility. The air was heavy with menace.

The corporal pointed to the raised wrists of the prisoners and spoke rapidly in a language that Harry didn't understand; it was obvious that he was asking what had happened to their watches.

Nobody spoke.

The corporal raised his voice with increased vehemence. He jumped up, moved around the desk, thrust his hands into the empty pockets of the two whites, then snarled to the soldiers behind them. Nobody answered him.

Enraged, the corporal went to the filing cabinet, snatched up the milk carton and flung the contents into Kerry's face. Kerry's expression did not alter as the stinking, sour milk dripped down his head and over his shirt.

It was not a very threatening act—yet a real threat might have been less sinister, Harry thought, as the soldiers started to laugh at Kerry's humiliation, looking at the two prisoners with gleeful anticipation. Harry suddenly thought, They're hot and they're bored. Perhaps they're going to torture us for a bit of fun. Perhaps we're going to die.

The corporal pushed his face close to Kerry's. He growled in English, "Why are you here?"

Kerry kept his voice expressionless. "We're looking for some important Americans. Guests in the hotel. Friends of General Raki."

The corporal stabbed his left forefinger over Kerry's shoulder, toward the beach. "All Americans are dead."

Not taking his eyes from Kerry's face, the corporal turned and swept the cans and bottles from the desk onto the floor.

The smell of stale hops rose sickeningly. He sat on the space he had cleared and swung his legs. "Americans went fishing. Boat blew up. All dead."

The corporal leaned behind the desk and pulled a bit of flowered fabric from a drawer. He held it toward Harry; it was the bottom of a flowered bikini, smelling faintly of suntan oil. Kerry could see a small white satin label with the word Jantzen on it. Of course it could have been anyone's bikini bottom, Harry thought. The corporal flung the garment back in the drawer.

"What happened?" Harry asked quietly.

The corporal turned to him and snarled, "No talking. You are both under arrest." He jumped to his feet, went behind the desk and sat down.

Behind Harry, more khaki-clad men crowded into the stuffy room. Harry and Kerry were shoved forward until their thighs were pressed against the desk. The air of anticipation in the room reminded Harry of a cockfight that he had once seen on the island. He remembered what had followed—the screaming violence, the smell of blood.

The soldiers joked and laughed, making lewd suggestions, daring one another to action, urging one another on. Until that moment, events had happened very fast. Now, adrenaline flowed into Harry's blood, with the result that everything appeared to be taking place in slow motion, as if on film.

Suddenly, to Harry's astonishment, the corporal stood up and saluted him respectfully.

Behind Harry an authoritative voice rapped an order. Harry heard the men behind him shuffling from the office, after which they were no longer jammed against the desk. His arms ached painfully, but he dared not lower them.

Another order was given. Harry and Kerry were roughly turned around to face the door.

Just outside it stood a slim man wearing neatly pressed khaki trousers and shirt, with a captain's insignia on the shoulder. With a faint American accent, not unusual in a Filipino, he asked, "Do you speak English?"

Both men nodded.

"Then what are you guys doing here? This hotel has been requisitioned. It is now an army barracks."

"May we put our arms down?" Harry asked.

"Yeah. How did you get here?"

"By helicopter." Harry rotated his aching shoulders. "We are business friends of General Raki, who will vouch for us. We are looking for a party of important Americans who were staying at this hotel."

"Ah." There was a slight pause.

The officer said, "This place was empty when *we* landed. The lights were on, but there was no staff." He shrugged his shoulders. "They probably ran away. When the islanders sense trouble coming, they scram." After a slight pause he added, "You better ask in town. Go to the chief of police. I want you out of here *immediately*. My men are disappointed there hasn't been any fighting. They're hard to control after a battle, but a lot harder to control if there hasn't been a fight. I'd better come back to the airstrip with you." He spoke rapidly to the corporal in Spanish, then jerked his head toward the hotel entrance. "Come on, let's go."

When they reached the edge of the airstrip, the officer said, "Have a good trip. Don't come back." He hesitated, then asked, "You really are friends of General Raki?"

Harry said, "Yes, business friends. We have been for many years."

The officer looked slightly worried. "The General cannot complain. Everything went according to plan."

"So I understand," said Harry. "Thanks. Let's get out of here, Kerry."

The pilot had started up as soon as he saw the group appear. Seconds after the two men scrambled into it, the helicopter swung into the air.

The pilot had been wondering whether to go for help. After hearing what had happened to them he said, "You blokes were lucky. Very lucky. *Bloody* lucky."

* * *

Kerry took two armed Nexus guards and an interpreter with him when they drove to Queenstown.

The yellow Toyota jeep, its hood heaving up and down as it crashed along the corrugations, bumped over a road that had seen better days, and that only a vehicle with a four-wheel drive could navigate.

After realizing that the Nexus party had truly disappeared, Kerry's first reaction was incredulous horror, followed by a swift guilty flash of relief that Harry, his boss, had been present at that nasty scene, so the responsibility would not be Kerry's. This thought was followed by acute anxiety. Why did it have to happen in *his* area?

Emotion would have to wait. He and Harry had bottled up their rage and grief. Both men realized that only fast thinking followed by equally fast action might trace the fate of their missing companions.

The yellow Toyota jeep jounced over unpaved streets with no sidewalks, gummed up with every sort of filth. Skinny dogs and scrawny chickens lay motionless in the sparse shade, or added to the many shriveled turds that dotted the road. The few stores at the side of the road gaped open and empty, showing smashed fixtures inside.

As they approached the rusting girders of St. Mary Bridge, an untidy crowd of frightened-looking women headed toward them, away from town. They carried cloth-wrapped *bilums* on their backs; all their possessions were in these string bags. On the far side of the bridge, a burned-out truck was crumpled against the girders, a charred corpse dangling from the driver's seat. Just beyond it, Kerry nodded toward a four-story concrete building.

"I hear the National Hotel is being used as a temporary military headquarters. A lot of the mercenaries who landed with Raki have been billeted there."

The Toyota turned to the left, toward Victoria Square. In contrast to the road they had just left, this narrow alley seethed with traffic; pushcarts, farm carts drawn by oxen and a couple of ancient trucks jostled in line. Beyond, the market square was strangely normal. As usual, the narrow alleyways around the square were jammed with haggling shoppers.

Harry said, "They don't seem to know there's a war on."

"The war was yesterday."

On the north side of Victoria Square stood the trim white Barclays Bank, a small Palladian-style building with green-painted steel shutters. On the west were the ministry build-ings—rectangular blocks of cracked concrete, the barred black windows gazing across the dusty palms to the houses of parliament and the supreme court. On the south side of the square, the police station was flanked on one side by the cus-toms office and on the other by the post office.

The only building not firmly locked and shuttered was the police station. Inside it, opposite the entrance, a police ser-geant sat on a battered desk. Behind him was a row of narrow, barred cells—each one just large enough to cage one person. Every cell was full, and the stink was overpowering. To the left of the sergeant, the wall was stacked with ammunition boxes; to his right, a small group of soldiers squatted on the floor, playing a gambling game with dried beans.

Lethargically, the sergeant drummed his booted feet against the wooden desk as the Nexus interpreter spoke.

The sergeant shook his head, stared straight ahead and con-tinued to bang his feet against the desk.

Kerry stepped forward and offered the sergeant a pack of cigarettes. The drumming stopped. The sergeant spoke to the interpreter, who turned to Kerry.

"He says we must make our inquiries at the Ministry of the Interior. But everybody there is on holiday, because of the soldiers."

"Tell him we would like to see the chief of police."

"He also is on holiday. It is best to be on holiday while the soldiers are in town. Maybe, master, you speak with him. He is a sergeant, so he can speak English, if he wants to. And more cigarettes."

Kerry stepped forward and greeted the sergeant. "Upi

noon! We seek news of some missing people, important top-brass Nexus people. Friends of General Raki."

Without a word the sergeant held his hand out.

Kerry placed two packs of cigarettes in it. The sergeant stuffed them down his tunic and again held out his hand.

Slowly, Kerry counted out two Australian five-dollar bills. Too much money could be self-defeating; if the information sought was thought to be very important, then an islander would not part with it. Kerry leaned over the desk and slid the money into the top drawer. The sergeant followed every movement of this universal language of persuasion with a blank expression.

Kerry asked, "May we speak with the chief of police?"

The sergeant shook his head.

Harry started to gnaw his upper lip. He knew that to expect logic would only increase his frustration. The priorities and reasoning of the islanders differed totally from those of a Westerner, and neither could clearly understand the other's viewpoint.

Half an hour later, it was made clear to the sergeant that the two whites had no more cash or cigarettes.

Harry felt in his pockets, which he'd restocked from his shoulder bag. He said, "How about a pack of cards?"

Card playing is illegal in Paui, because the loser at a card game often kills the winner. A pack of cards is therefore a highly desirable possession, treasured above money, because it is a steady source of income. The islanders play a gambling game called Lucky, which is impossible for whites to understand—the biggest winner is always the man who rents out the illegal pack of cards.

Slowly, reluctantly, the sergeant shook his head.

Harry produced a second pack of cards and put both packs on the desk—but not in the drawer. All three men knew that two packs of cards were worth far more than a hundred dollars; the sergeant could sell one pack for forty dollars cash, and then rent out the other pack in perpetuity.

"Maybe I fix."

Harry pushed one pack of cards toward the sergeant. "You get the other pack when I get a reply."

"Okay, I send pass to General Raki's palace guard, tell him good news. You give me two dollar for guard."

"For the last time, *no*," Harry said to Kerry as they stood outside the police station in the white glare of the sun. "We've got to split our approach. You write the report and take it up with the U.S. State Department." Kerry would work through the U.S. Consulate at Port Moresby, because Paui was in their area.

Harry added, "You also handle it officially at the local level, Kerry. Clearly I'm not going to find out anything if I'm stuck behind barbed wire at Mount Ida. So I'm staying in Queenstown. By myself. Might do a couple of things that wouldn't be officially appreciated. My aim is to see Raki face to face, and when I do, I'll be safe. Raki knows he has to deal through me if he wants to renew or expand the Nexus concession. If he *doesn't* want to deal with us, then there's nothing much I can do about it. But if he wants a fast, easy deal, with quick cash, then he'll continue our association. In which case he won't want me harmed, so that'll be some sort of protection."

"You're the boss, Harry. I'll send someone down with your gear."

"Send me another gun, and some cash and cigarettes as well, Kerry. You'd better hang on to the rest of my money. Which hotel do I stay at?"

"There's no choice. The army has taken over the National, so you'll have to stay with Ma Chang at the Hotel Independence. Make sure you ask her for the second-class price."

"Why?"

"If you pay first-class tariff, you'll get godawful colonial food—brown Windsor soup and thin slices of overdone beef in gravy, with vegetables that have been boiled to death, followed by rice pudding. If you choose the second-class menu, you'll get wonderful Chinese food."

"I don't expect fancy cookery in the middle of a military coup."

"Ma Chang wouldn't let a nuclear holocaust disturb her operation. Let's go."

Since the sixteenth century, when Portuguese navigators first sighted the island of Paui, European explorers had sailed around the coast, naming the most prominent geographical features after their kings, their queens, their politicians and themselves. As a matter of custom and inertia, these names mostly stuck; such landmarks as the Victoria Highlands and Stanley Heights continued to be so called, but Queenstown's oldest hotel, a once-white clapboard building surrounded by a wooden veranda, was particularly sensitive to political changes.

When the Dutch annexed Paui in 1828, the newly built hotel was named "The Amsterdam." When the first Christian missionary arrived, after the British took over in 1873, the hotel was burned down, rebuilt and rechristened "The Victoria." In 1914, when the Germans occupied Paui and the nearby islands, a new signboard was hastily painted to read "Der Kaiserhof." When the British returned in 1919, the board that hung over the rickety glass-paned door read "The Imperial."

In the twenties and thirties, the hotel had been a popular meeting place for the English colonials who ran the cocoa, coffee and copra plantations and supervised the gutting of the beautiful sandalwood forests that covered the Central Mountains and the Victoria Highlands. These gentlemen regularly received "pink tickets" from their wives entitling them to an evening out with the boys at the Imperial. One by one, they were beaten by the hot, humid and insect-infested climate, where books had to be fumigated every six months and tearful wives eventually gave up trying to make a cozy home. So they retired early, to a bungalow in Balmain, Sydney, a bungalow in Oxshott, Surrey, or a residential hotel in Earls Court, London, where they could fade out their lives playing bridge in an atmosphere of leisurely, if dusty, gentility that strangely resembled the dear old Imperial.

There had been no need to change the name in 1942, when the Japanese invaded Paui, but after the liberation in 1945 the hotel was rechristened the "Roosevelt Hylton." In 1963 it metamorphosed into the "Kennedy-Hylton," until in 1973 a similarly named hotel group threatened to sue. As this coincided with the Grant of Self-Government, a new signboard was swiftly painted. Mrs. Chang acquired the "Hotel Independence" in 1976. In 1984 it was still in pretty much the same condition as when she purchased it.

The two men walked up the steps to the wide, wooden-floored veranda that ran around the hotel. Inside, in the sepulchral gloom of the lobby, wicker chairs were grouped around low, dark-red lacquered tables, each with a fringed and beaded lamp hung above it. Beyond them, Harry could see a bar, which, he was later to discover, had a separate exit to the veranda, for flinging out undesirables. To the rear of the entrance lobby was the reception desk, a light-colored square on the wall behind it indicating that a picture had recently been removed.

To the right of the reception desk was a flight of wooden stairs, and beyond that Harry could see, through the open door, a deserted dining room. Like a European urinal, it had white-tiled floors and walls, and the small tables were covered by white plastic cloths. Harry could sniff the lingering aroma of Peking duck.

Just inside the hotel entrance and to the right, was a little alcove stuffed with dark, elaborately carved Victorian furniture. In the middle of it shone the jackdaw-bright, black eyes of a Chinese woman clad in violent pink satin pajamas; she might have been any age between thirty and sixty, but she certainly did not weigh under two hundred pounds. The elaborate dark furniture that surrounded her was a contrast to the bare efficiency of the rest of the building. On either side of her pink bulk stood two small tables, upon one stood a Monopoly board, upon the other was a modern ivory telephone.

"Come in, man," Mrs. Chang said sharply. "I can't think why you expected to see anybody important on a day like this; they are either dead or have hurried to visit their country estates upriver. Very prudent." She glanced at the Cartier tank watch that was strapped on her fat little wrist. "The sun is getting quite near the yardarm. I expect you would like a cocktail?" She clapped her hands briskly. "Freddy! The martini cart!"

From somewhere behind her great pink bulk appeared a handsome, shy islander, barefoot and wearing only a pair of white shorts.

"Freddy and Bobby are my secretaries." Mrs. Chang airily waved her left hand to another similarly handsome young islander. Freddy had a torso like Superman's without his leotard, and Bobby's build was almost as impressive; both men were nearly as tall as Harry. They didn't look pure-blooded islanders—they probably had an eighth Chinese blood, which meant that the natives wouldn't want them, and neither would the Chinese.

Mrs. Chang said, "Bobby handles the cash. Tell him if you wish to change money."

"We've just lost our money," Harry said ruefully.

"Ah! I also lend money. At two percent a day in unusual situations, such as this."

Mrs. Chang turned to Bobby and said, "Bugger off and fetch the cashbox." Bobby scooted off.

"Take a pew, both of you." Mrs. Chang rested her feet, in yellow satin slippers, on her red plush footstool and looked sharply at the men, alert as a thrush on a branch. Her sallow skin was stretched tight across her face, then fell in a series of dewlaps to her collarbone.

Kerry said, "I won't stay, thank you. I must get back to Betty."

Mrs. Chang hollered toward the kitchen, "Only one olive, Freddy." She turned back to Kerry and said, "I hope all is okay with your dear wife."

"She's fine. Writing a thesis on island religions. Gives her something to do."

Mrs. Chang giggled, "Oh, my goodness, a bugger of a task." Her English included phrases picked up from the English importer, as well as his lady wife whose children she had cared for long ago in Singapore.

Freddy came dashing back with a well-equipped drinks cart.

"Will you be shopping for gifts?" inquired Mrs. Chang.

Nothing had been further from Harry's mind, until Mrs. Chang added, "General Raki's wives and children all landed two hours ago to show that everything is back to normal. Business as usual." She leered at Harry. "May I suggest twice as many gifts for the new young wife and Raki's number-one wife. The old girl is the daughter of a powerful tribal chief and must be respected. I have some excellent lengths of silk."

Harry knew it was a waste of time to buy gifts for anyone's wife. On Paui a female was about as influential as a chicken. But he intended to leave no stone unturned, and that included the cultivation of the goodwill of Mrs. Chang. He suspected there was more to Mrs. Chang than met the eye.

On the sticky tarmac of Presidential Avenue the traffic thinned as Harry's Toyota reached the avenue of big mango trees that stand like sentinels on either side of the road leading to the Presidential Palace. Before 1975, the dilapidated colonial villas behind the trees had been occupied by white administrators and high-grade technicians; now, these rundown houses were heavily surrounded by barbed wire to protect the men who ran Paui.

Just before the Presidential Palace, Harry passed the former Colonial Club. In the days when it took two months by sea to get home to Britain for the six-month leave that you were entitled to every five years, the Colonial Club was where gin slings had been sipped, bridge played and foxtrots danced to wind-up gramophones; now, it was the noisy home of the new Minister of the Interior.

Whereas the rest of Queenstown was languidly lapsing into decay, the high wall that surrounded the presidential compound was in excellent order, except for the curlicued black iron gates, which had been torn off their hinges and left lying on the grass just inside the entrance.

Flies clustered, shining like black sequins, around five football-sized lumps stuck on top of five poles that had been thrust into the ground: these were the heads of the late President Obe and four of his unluckier ministers. The Minister of Finance and the Minister of Commerce and Industry had escaped in the presidential helicopter, the pilot of which had been receiving regular payments against just such an eventuality.

The Toyota jeep slowed, then stopped about fifty yards from the gate. Harry climbed down very slowly, put up his hands and cautiously walked toward the guards. They wore olive combat uniforms, soft khaki caps with hard peaks and laced, rubber-soled jungle boots.

When challenged, Harry showed his official appointment pass and also his passport, which was studied by the guards, page by page, from back to front, right way up and upside down. They were clearly illiterate, and recognized only Harry's passport photograph.

He was quickly and expertly searched. One of the guards grunted, "Cigarettes?"

More as a tip than a bribe, Harry handed over four packs. He explained that in his vehicle he also had gifts for the General. One of the guards collected the folded silks, then one by one they were unfolded to check that they concealed nothing.

Escorted by two guards, and followed by a soldier carrying the silk, Harry went along the gravel path that led to the palace. On either side of him were immaculately tended green lawns with clumps of orange lilies and fifteen-foot-high scarlet poinsettias.

The low, square, pale-mauve stucco palace had no windows at the lower level, and was surrounded at six-foot intervals by armed soldiers. Some of them squatted, some sat on the grass, leaning back against the wall with legs outstretched, some stood holding their rifles by the barrel, as if intending to use them as clubs. Although relaxed, they were obviously tough and alert.

The small party passed beneath a heavily guarded arch to an interior courtyard, about sixty feet square; this was surrounded by a covered walk. Standing in the shade of the veranda were wooden benches like traditional church pews, which looked out on a central lily pond, surrounded by trees, flowering shrubs and wild orchids.

Harry's entourage marched across the courtyard, mounted a white marble staircase and entered the palace at the second-floor level through an elaborate marble arch.

The little party turned to the right, their footsteps silenced by thick, bright-purple carpet, which lined the eight-foot-wide corridor. To Harry's right were high, shuttered windows, hung with gold brocade curtains. One window had been shattered; broken glass still littered the carpet beneath it. Funeral parlor décor, thought Harry, as they passed a niche which contained a small altar.

An order was snapped. Harry's escort stopped abruptly in front of a pair of high sandalwood doors guarded by two Filipinos. One of Harry's escort soldiers spoke softly to them, and was allowed to slip inside the doors.

Almost immediately, the sandalwood slabs opened again and the escorting soldier beckoned Harry inside. He stepped forward, felt an icy blast of air conditioning and then stopped in surprise.

Just inside the door, to Harry's right, was a wide table upon which was spread a large rectangular square of bright orange cloth with a crimson stripe running down the middle. Beside the cloth lay a peaked military cap, a revolver in a holster, a native machete and a submachine gun. This was what Harry expected. He had also vaguely imagined that General Raki, on the day after a successful military coup, would be closeted with his colonels, poring over maps, or surrounded by his new ministers, discussing overoptimistic five-year agricultural plans.

What Harry had not expected was to hear giggles, squeals, yelps and high-pitched laughter.

At first, because of the noise, Harry thought he had interrupted a children's party. In the room before him, the elaborately carved sandalwood furniture had been pushed back against the wall, leaving only an intricate Persian carpet in the center of the room. On the carpet a man in a khaki uniform, a black scarf tied around his eyes, was staggering, arms outstretched, amid a group of laughing young women. Small, coffee-colored women of Melanesian blood darted among darker Polynesians and jet-black outer-islanders. Most were naked to the waist, with bright cloths tied around their hips. One woman wore an elaborate, gold strapless Western evening gown, and another a grubby, once white, satin wedding dress. A very beautiful, very young, very black girl wore what appeared to be a white lace nightgown and scarlet Carmen Miranda platform sandals.

As the man in uniform staggered toward one or another of them, the women frisked out of his reach. They jumped like kittens to avoid his touch, then sneaked up behind him to tug his tunic, after which they ran away again with shrill cries of excited delight.

More daring than the rest, the black girl in the white lace nightgown ran up behind the blindfolded man and tugged his left ear. As he clawed the empty air, she dashed away, but stumbled on her clumsy, high sandals and almost fell. Harry saw her hands flail in the air as she struggled to regain her balance; the nails of her dark, childish fingers were varnished bright pink and sharpened to a point; ornate rings glinted on every finger and her thumbs.

Laughing, the girl scrambled to her feet and turned back to the game; as she did so, Harry glimpsed two high, round buttocks beneath the nearly transparent white lace. With a happy giggle, the girl again ran up to the left of the blindfolded man and her bejeweled hand shot up to cover his eyes.

The blindfolded man whirled around very fast and caught her by the wrist. Amid shrieks and giggles he fondled the young girl's breasts, squeezed the nipples, then shouted "Noma!"

As a relaxation from the weariness, the wariness and the responsibility of office, the victor of the Battle of Queenstown was playing blindman's buff.

Harry guessed that the other women—including an older one who squatted, sulking, in the corner and took no part in the game—were wives and bedmates not blessed by ecclesiastical wedlock, as well as their sisters, mothers, friends and servants.

One of the exotic girls suddenly noticed Harry and pointed to the glowing folds of jewellike silk that were carried by the soldier at his side. The girl called out sharply.

The women immediately stopped playing their game and surged toward Harry with much excited chatter.

General Raki whipped off his black blindfold, not a bit embarrassed at being found cavorting in this manner. As he walked forward, his diamond-studded shoelaces caught the light and sent a thousand refracted rays of rainbow-colored light toward the ceiling. Those diamonds were not there just in case the General had to flee for his life, Harry realized, nor merely as an unusually blatant example of conspicuous consumption. On Paui, the land of the light-fingered, they were a grim reminder. No one dared to steal even the shoelaces of General Raki, was the message they conveyed.

"Greetings, Mr. Scott." Yellowing eyeballs opened wider and yellowing teeth flashed briefly. He moved with the swift, neat movements of an agile man. His handshake was dry, quick and nervous.

"How do you like our new Paui flag, eh?" General Raki gestured to the bright orange rectangle with the central crimson stripe. He picked up the machete, seemed to drop it, caught it again, let it drop, then caught it again; this casual mannerism was as jocularly aggressive, as vain and dangerous, as the action of a man who twirls a loaded revolver by the trigger.

Harry said, "It's most distinguished, sir."

Raki looked at Harry. He didn't like Australians. In 1938, when Raki was born, Paui was still under tough Australian supervision. The officers of the Paui police force were white, although the men in the ranks were black. Raki's father had been a mission-trained schoolmaster, who admired the tough Australian administrators and had left his schoolroom job to join the Constabulary, where he quickly rose to the rank of sergeant. He ran his home and treated his children with the same strict discipline that was applied to his daily work, for he was determined that his elder son was going to succeed. This discipline (unusual on the free-and-easy island) bore fruit. At that time, education on Paui was still largely in the hands of missionaries, who could do little except teach the bare rudiments to the children of the island.

Harshly disciplined at home, confused and undereducated, it had nevertheless been clear that young Raki was too intelligent for village life, but would not be sufficiently trained for a skilled job unless he had more schooling. In 1949, when Raki was eleven years old, his father's adjutant had managed to get the boy accepted at the missionary-run Jesuit College at Port Moresby, on the understanding that when he finished his schooling he would follow in his father's footsteps and join the Constabulary. Coached by his father, Raki won one of the fifteen annual scholarships, which provided him with the equivalent of a U.S. high school education.

Even as a schoolboy, Raki had no intention of ass-licking the Australians, as his father did. He was a restless teenager. In 1954, when he was sixteen years old, he became involved in a brawl in a Queenstown Harbor grog shop in which he throttled a white beachcomber. His father managed to cover up for him, and bribed a place on a freighter bound for Manila. There, Raki lived with the family of his maternal grandmother, who had been a Filipino.

By 1965, when Marcos assumed power in the Philippines,

Raki was nearly twenty-seven years old, and a captain in the secret Q7 Army Corps. In 1968, when the President of Paui died, he had been replaced by President Kanta, who came from the tribe to which Raki's family belonged. Urged by his father, Raki instantly saw his opportunity. He returned to Paui and joined the Constabulary at a high level, intending to make a grab for power within the force as soon as those white *kanaka* had left his country.

In 1975, when the Australians finally retired, every man on the island was drunk for a week, after which, promotion in the Constabulary was given to those who were strong enough to grab it. By the age of thirty-seven, Raki was in charge of the Constabulary. His only regret was that his father, who had raised him to be an achiever, wasn't alive to see his son's career soar far beyond his own.

Two months later, when the ten-year contract with Nexus was signed, President Kanta got his first powerboat and Raki received his first, discreet, special payment.

In 1983, Raki was flown to Darwin with peritonitis, which kept him in the hospital for two months. During his absence the left-wing coup took place on Paui. When discharged from the hospital, Raki joined his four official wives, his mistresses and his swarms of children in Port Moresby, where he brooded and plotted. Now, triumphantly, he had returned.

The pretty girl called Noma tugged Harry's sleeve. "You have nightgowns from Sydney?"

Sharply, Raki rapped an order to his women and they faded away to the far side of the room, where they reassembled in smaller groups, clearly speculating who would get the silks that Harry had brought with him.

General Raki looked at Harry. "You want to talk to me, Mr. Scott?"

"I do, sir. A group of my associates, who were staying at the Paradise Bay Hotel, have disappeared."

General Raki held his hands up, palms outward; he lifted his eyebrows and shrugged his shoulders. "I heard this sad story. They were aboard a fishing vessel that caught fire, or blew up, or something. It is thought that one of the tourists was at the wheel. Someone may have done something foolish. Who knows? Very sad."

Harry said, *"Someone* must know exactly what happened. I would like to locate the hotel manager and his staff."

"I was told that a lot of débris was found, but sadly no survivors," General Raki said. "Of course, there are sharks beyond the reef. This is a very sad start to our infant tourist industry. I shall make it my business to see that it doesn't happen again."

Harry said, "I ask your permission to find out exactly what happened."

Idly the General played his drop-and-catch game with the machete. "Who would know? When all are dead, it is a matter for conjecture. A trip at sunset might have been pleasant, after a day of business discussion. I have no idea what happened." He shook his head sadly. "Of course, we shall offer our condolences through the usual channels. However, this unfortunate accident is definitely not my responsibility." He shrugged again. "I heard that it happened just after sunset on Tuesday, before I returned to this island. How lucky that *you* were not with them, Mr. Scott!"

There was something about the way he spat out the last words that made Harry remember that he *should* have been with the Nexus party. He said, "Sir, I am concerned about the complete lack of news about our people. The military at the hotel were not helpful. I am sure you understand that American citizens cannot just vanish without a trace."

"Nevertheless, it looks as if they have done so, Mr. Scott."

"Sir, if you are not responsible for their disappearance, then who *is* responsible?"

"The previous government, I'm afraid. I expect you saw them outside the main gate."

"The U.S. government will expect a full explanation, General Raki."

"Of *course* they will, Mr. Scott. And I shall see that they get it. I'm sorry you seem to feel that you are not getting the cooperation that you would like. What do you want me to do?"

"I would like your assurance that an official inquiry will be undertaken within twenty-four hours, and that an air search starts immediately."

General Raki looked thoughtful. "Of course I shall do these things, but I cannot do everything at once. Life is still a little unsettled here, and I have many other concerns."

"Is there any *proof* that they are no longer alive, sir?" Harry persisted.

General Raki lifted his chin and raised his voice. "This is *enough!* It is not *my* responsibility that Nexus people are on this island. Your company does not currently have my protection. It is not *my* responsibility that your people met with an accident on the day before I came to power, when *I* was still at sea."

"Sir, I would remind you of the international convention whereby the country in which an accident or crash has occurred always searches for the victims and the wreckage for a period of ten days after the accident."

"Naturally, we shall conduct an air-and-sea search." General Raki looked coldly into Harry's eyes. "And in the meantime, Mr. Scott, I hope that you will immediately return to Sydney, until, as you say, the dust has settled here. From Sydney, Mr. Scott, you will no doubt be able to arrange immediate payment of the money that is owed to me. Shall we say, at two hundred percent interest for late payment and the resultant inconvenience?"

Harry said, "As I'm sure you know, sir, that decision does not rest with me alone."

"Whoever makes your decisions is responsible for the fact that the past President of Paui was unable to come to any definite agreement with Nexus, after eighteen months of negotiation."

Harry said nothing.

General Raki said, "You know what an easy chap I am."

Again, he playfully dropped the machete and swiftly caught it before the weapon hit the ground.

Harry said, "I feel that Nexus will prefer to discuss such arrangements when we know the whereabouts of our missing executives, their wives and their possessions."

"Ah, the *possessions!*" Raki said. "Commandos, you understand, are not ladies' maids, but we shall do our best to return the suitcases and so forth. Your concern about *possessions* is entirely understandable. In Paui, we are also concerned about possessions—anything from coffee beans to uranium, from coconuts to cobalt."

Harry hadn't expected to have this whacked at him in the first five minutes—but at least you knew where you were with Raki, and that was a change, after eighteen months of exasperating inaction. The position was clear. Raki refused to take responsibility for the Nexus party, but he had agreed to an air-and-sea search, and he would do it immediately and properly, provided Harry got off the island and Raki got paid fast. Jerry Pearce could sort that out.

"You have no comment, Mr. Scott?"

"As soon as I can communicate with Pittsburgh, I'm hopeful that your conditions will be met. I appreciate your concern for my safety, but I prefer to stay here until the financial arrangements are to your liking. I would appreciate your permission to search myself, by air. The more planes that are out looking, the more chance there is of finding something."

"Certainly, Mr. Scott. I must say it is easier to do business with someone who understands conditions on the spot, rather than executives in faraway glass towers."

What followed happened so fast that later Harry was unable to say exactly what *had* happened. The ebullient little black girl in the white see-through nightgown had kicked off her noisy, high-heeled sandals. Mischievously, she crept up behind General Raki's left shoulder, her bejeweled left paw impudently upstretched to cover his eyes again.

Raki heard a slight sound from behind. In one fluid movement, he had shifted his grip on the machete and whirled around to the left.

Then the girl was screaming and the dark, chubby left hand, rings on every finger, was dripping blood on the Persian carpet.

Nobody in the room moved. The girl clutched the red spouting stump of her left arm, fainted in midscream and slumped to the floor.

Raki said sharply, "That was *her* fault. *She* did it. She should not have surprised me." He looked at the bleeding figure on the floor. "It was only her *left* hand." He turned to the guard at the door. "Wrap that hand in a cloth and take her to the hospital. Make sure you use a *clean* cloth. Tell them to sew it back on. But first take off her rings and give them to me."

He turned to glare at the silent women who huddled at the end of the room. He raised his voice. "She will have the best doctor. Absolutely. No expense spared."

He beckoned his number-one wife from the corner. "This is a valuable carpet. Get it cleaned immediately."

He turned to look at Harry. "We shall now go to my study for peace and quiet, my friend."

◀ 13 ▶

Harry was certain he had been followed back from the palace, but that was only to be expected. On principle, Raki would put a tail on him until he left the island, to see what other contacts Harry might be making—and paying.

Wearily, Harry climbed the wooden steps from the dark street to the hotel veranda.

"Could you maybe get me a waterproof watch, Mrs. Chang?" Harry asked. "I can't get one from the shops because they've either been looted or they're shuttered. I'm not going to risk buying a watch from a street merchant."

"No problem." Mrs. Chang beamed at him. "Did everything go according to plan, Mr. Scott? Did you see the General?"

"Yes." As if she didn't know.

As Harry entered the hotel, he was vaguely aware of something insistently disturbing his subconscious, like a bit of grit in a tennis shoe. It had started with that same phrase, used by the army captain in Paradise Bay. He had said, "Everything went according to plan. The General can't complain."

Why not? Harry wondered, as he trudged up the wooden staircase and walked to his room. *Why* couldn't the General complain? *What* had gone according to plan?

He stood in the doorway and looked around his room, not

much larger than a prison cell. To his left, a ragged mosquito net hung from the ceiling above a white iron bedstead that stood on bare boards. At the foot of the bed was a chair, and above it hung a naked lightbulb. The wall to his right was punctured by an uneven row of coat hooks. The window that faced Harry was covered by a gray cotton curtain that sagged from a string, and beneath it stood a washstand, with a white china bowl and jug. Underneath that was a chamber pot, standing beside Harry's overnight bag. Luckily, the bottle of Chivas Regal was still inside it.

Through the long dark night, Harry lay awake thinking over the previous day's events. Uncomfortable, frustrated and impotent, tossing under a mosquito net with holes that allowed easy access to any creature with a wingspan of less than six inches, he entertained different explanations for the disappearance of his colleagues but one by one, he had discarded them.

At dawn, on Saturday, November 17, Harry walked onto the back veranda for a breath of fresh air. Blinking his reddened eyelids in the glare of sunlight, he looked below, where the beaten earth of the hotel's backyard ran down to the St. Mary River. The small area was crisscrossed with clotheslines, on which hung drying sheets.

Beyond the lugubrious garden, Harry could see and hear the cheerful bustle on the river, surging downstream toward the St. Mary bailey bridge, beyond which it flowed into the north side of the harbor. Canoes and small barges, overladen and almost underwater, drifted past small riverside shops that faced the water. Bamboo rafts dodged between them, poled by errand boys and ferrymen.

The river was low. Thick mud glistened on either bank, and in the white heat of the sun, the water stank of ordure. It was used as a dump by the occupants of the boxlike wooden houses on stilts that crowded along the water's edge. They only had to climb down the ladder to wash their clothes or dishes or void their bowels in the river.

Harry headed for the communal bathroom at the end of the veranda. The shower was not the hard, cold, stinging down-

pour that would have woken him up. Lukewarm leaks dribbled over his body, fell into a central drain and could still be
heard after their disappearance being sucked and gargled by
some recumbent giant below the floorboards.

Back in his bedroom, Harry was pulling on his shirt when
the night watchman put his head around the door. "Pass he
come belong you, master."

Two long yellow teeth gleamed as Harry tipped him and
took the buff envelope, which had already been opened. He
drew out a flimsy sheet of paper headed MINISTRY OF POLICE,
QUEENSTOWN and quickly read the badly typed document:

Date	13 November 1984.
Time:	19.30 hours, approx.
Item:	1 (one) explosion of touristic fishing vessel "Louise," registered Queenstown.
Reasons:	Unknown.
Witnesses:	No persons.
List of Missing Persons:	

There followed twelve names—the entire Nexus party
staying at the Paradise Bay Hotel.

Harry gazed at the one name that stood out to him, as if
typed in scarlet: PATRICK, MRS ANNE. His mind refused to
accept that Annie was dead. If Annie—the one great love of
his life—was dead, then Harry's hope for life had been
crushed in one badly typed line—the hope which, for years,
had helped to drive Harry through a life in which he seemed
destined never to have a normal, caring relationship with anyone—never to have a mate. *No, he refused to accept it.* He
would *not* believe that Annie was dead—unless he saw her
body.

His sweaty shirt clung to his back as Harry hurried over the
cobblestones of Queenstown Wharf to where a scruffy vessel
was docking. Other ships were being loaded or unloaded by a

small group of wharfies, who moved as if sleepwalking. They were watched by onlookers, who squatted on the cobbles or sat with their backs against the shaded walls of the shops that clustered around the wharf. The iron grilles had been ripped from the fronts of the boxlike shops and their contents had vanished; their floors were a mess of broken glass, strewn with papers.

Behind the row of shops lay St. Mary's Hospital, conveniently close to the drinking shops of the wharf, from which, every evening, brawl casualties could be speedily heaved into the emergency ward.

Relieved to be out of the hard glare of the sun, Harry entered the door of the emergency ward. Beyond it, the empty white-tiled reception area looked strangely similar to the dining room of the Hotel Independence, although perhaps a trifle cleaner.

Looking for a receptionist, Harry walked down the corridor, turned a corner and almost bumped into a white-overalled Chinese nurse, who clutched a green clipboard. Harry asked her where he could find the casualty ward.

"The whole hospital is a casualty ward at the moment." The nurse sounded tired and under strain. "Upstairs in the main ward we still have seven military casualties. The rest have been treated and discharged. Only a few civilians are still here; most of them have either died or been treated and sent home."

"You look as if you've had a tough time," Harry sympathized.

"Oh, not bad. Not compared with 'Eighty-three, when there was *real* fighting." She looked almost regretful. "This time casualties have been light, and the soldiers behaved well afterwards. Few rapes and hardly any atrocities, except for President Obe and a few of the ministers."

"Was the man in the mining accident brought here?" Harry asked.

"The Nexus white? Yes, DOA. Came in last Tuesday, just before the fighting broke out. I was about to go off duty."

"I'm responsible for him. Where is the body?"

"Normally it would have gone in the morgue, but at the moment I can't say. Ask the hospital registrar. His office is just inside the main entrance, on the other side of the building."

Harry went to find the registrar who offered to show him the way to St. Mary's Hospital Morgue. It wasn't like the morgues that Harry had seen in TV police dramas, where corpses were covered by sheets and kept in drawers, like office filing cabinets. The St. Mary's morgue was set in the basement of the hospital and was simply a big, walk-in refrigerator, like a butcher's; on either side corpses lay on shelves. They were all black, except for Brett.

The color of an altar candle, Brett looked even more handsome now that his anxious-puppy look had been wiped way. Beneath the fair eyebrows, his eyes were closed, his neatly chiseled nose and mouth looked as if they had been carved from Carrara marble, his crisp, red-gold hair still looked alive and oddly incongruous, like a wig on a beautiful statue.

Harry had wanted to see with his own eyes what had happened to at least one of his missing colleagues. Now he stared down at the cold, tangible proof that Raki had misinformed him, and possibly lied to him. Brett couldn't have been killed twice on the same day, in two places, seventy miles apart. But Raki wouldn't have known, while crossing the ocean in his invading flagship, that there had been an accidental death at the mine.

From his pocket Harry pulled the official police report of the boat explosion at Paradise Bay. There it was, typed. BRETT ADAMS. He lifted the hospital label tied to Brett's ankle. It read BRETT ADAMS.

Of course, Raki could say that Brett's name had been accidentally typed on the list—an understandable error in view of the week's happenings. But as he looked at Brett's pale face, Harry realized what had been nagging at him. It was ludicrously unlikely that after Brett's tragic death the Nexus party at Paradise Bay would suddenly have chosen to go for a pleasure cruise at sunset. Arthur would probably have told Brett's wife. She would have been in tears. At least one of the other wives would have been comforting her. Someone would have been arranging for Suzy to fly home with the body. Probably they would *all* have decided to return to Pittsburgh. They certainly wouldn't have set off on a joyride around the bay, Harry told himself.

He gnawed his upper lip. In the last twenty-four hours events had been occurring too fast for him to think straight—the disappearance of his colleagues, Brett's death, the disturbing scene at Paradise Bay and then last night's revolting amputation.

Perhaps Raki truly didn't know what had happened, and had too much on his plate to pay attention to the Nexus disappearances. But if Harry assumed that Raki *did* know what had happened to the Nexus group, then either Raki was deliberately denying knowledge of something unpleasant because he didn't want to be held responsible for it or because, for some reason, in some way, he had deliberately arranged that disappearance. . . .

If *that* was so, had Raki tried to conceal the manner in which the Nexus group had disappeared? Suddenly, in the chill of the silent morgue, a colder chill snaked up Harry's spine as another thought occurred to him. *How had Raki known that Harry should have been one of the missing party? And why?*

If Raki had deliberately planned to kill the entire Nexus group, then he would have also expected Harry to die, and perhaps still wanted to kill him. Perhaps the Nexus group had been deliberately killed by Raki in revenge for the bribe payments that had been stopped. Payback was a more potent reason for violence on Paui than in any Sicilian vendetta. But Raki wasn't a Mafia hood. Harry told himself not to be melodramatic.

Or had Raki tried to make Harry believe that the Nexus people were dead—when they were still alive? Was Raki holding them prisoner? For ransom? Harry knew that Raki's main motivation was greed, and he also knew that running your own private army was undoubtedly an expensive hobby, but surely Raki would not have imprisoned the Nexus group for ransom money? Raki stood to gain a lot of *easy* money from Nexus.

No, if Raki was holding them prisoner, it was more likely that he had planned to hold the group hostage for barter—as insurance, in the event his revolution failed. Important Americans might be useful as bargaining chips. Harry remembered the black heads stuck on poles outside the palace gate. He couldn't guess what plans Raki might have made, but if he knew his man, there would certainly have been several contingency plans for escape in the event of failure.

Harry paused in his reasoning, and looked at Brett's peaceful face. Again, he wondered why the Filipino officer at Paradise Bay had been so keen to get Kerry and him back to their helicopter. The officer's troops had been rough, but not uncontrollable; there had been no further trouble from them after the officer had snapped an order. They had behaved like sulky hunting dogs, disappointed but obedient. He remembered the final words of the officer on the airstrip. "The General cannot complain," he had said. "Everything went according to plan."

Had that been a statement of the general situation? Had he meant that Raki had pulled off his coup, and should be happy? Or had it been a *specific* statement, referring to the landing at Paradise Bay? Or an even more precise reference to the disappearance of the Nexus party? Surely you didn't consider that everything had gone according to plan if you were in charge of the spot where the leaders of the island's biggest, richest and most important business had all disappeared? Unless *that* was exactly what had gone according to plan. Unless *that* was why Raki couldn't complain.

The white-coat registrar touched his shoulder, and Harry followed him out of the morgue. He stood in the sweltering heat of the hospital corridor as the door was locked behind him. Suddenly, Harry's back felt very vulnerable.

Swiftly, he looked over his shoulder. But, of course, there was no gunman behind him and Harry felt like a fool.

Mrs. Chang's ivory telephone smelled strongly of stale magnolia. When Harry telephoned, Kerry wasn't at the Mount Ida office, he'd been called home. Harry redialed. Kerry explained that Betty was a bit upset because she'd had a row with Cookie. She'd caught him scrubbing the fish with carbolic soap, which Kerry reckoned was overdoing the hygiene.

Harry said, "For God's sake, our top executives disappear and you chatter to me about *fish*."

Kerry said stiffly, "My wife's been under a helluva strain, Harry. You know perfectly well that I'm doing all I can. *You* should try dealing with Air Niugini, about shipping a corpse back to Pittsburgh. *You* should try filling in details in triplicate for the American Consulate in Moresby. *You* should tell Jerry Pearce what to do when he phones from Pittsburgh demanding instant action every five minutes. *You* should try running a bloody mine after a coup d'état."

"Sorry, Kerry. I guess yesterday upset us both. Now, who, unofficially, is most likely to know what's going on on this island?"

"Mindo," Kerry said instantly. "The miners' spokesman. He's just told me that the day after the invasion, small groups of militiamen with two-way radios were helicoptered all around the island, to talk to the villagers. Mindo seems pretty sure that Raki has informers all over the island. Apparently this rural grapevine has identified all the strongly Democratic supporters, and they're being taken to Queenstown for questioning, one area at a time."

"Do the militiamen take them in?" Harry asked.

"Yes, but not all of them. A few militia remain to have a quiet chat with the village elders about village needs . . . more dried milk for the toothless elders, another twelve-gauge shotgun for the *tultul*—that's the second man of the village. Until now, only the headman has been allowed to own a gun."

Harry said, "Raki obviously isn't relying only on military force."

"No, this infiltration at village level seems to be a civic effort to win over the rural population."

"So if we offer a really big reward for any information, the militia groups might be keen to earn it. We'd have an instant network combing the country for us."

Harry's next call was to his friend at the American Embassy in Canberra. Richard had plenty to tell him.

"Our procedure is always the same in these situations," Richard explained. "Contingency plans are always changing, but the first stage in any emergency that concerns vanishing Americans caught up in foreign political disturbances is to get the maximum information about the people concerned."

"What sort of information?" Harry asked. "Complete biographies, or just their reasons for being there?"

"Both," Richard said. "The next stage—provided we're not dealing with a terrorist government—is for the nearest U.S. embassy or consulate to arrange negotiations with the new government."

"When do they get around to searching?" Harry asked.

"The third step is to organize the land or sea search, in cooperation with the country in which the disappearance has taken place. As the Nationalist Party on Paui isn't a terrorist government, the U.S. Consulate at Port Moresby *can* negotiate with it," Richard said. "They'll ensure that all necessary searches and inquiries are made."

Harry said, "Sounds like slow death from strangling by red tape."

"Wrong," Richard said. "The consulate has already drawn up a plan of action." He explained it in detail, concluding, "The State Department has already set up a task force to coordinate all information from Paui sources, Nexus sources and from relatives. Apparently, the guy in charge of the task force in Washington has spent two years at our consulate in Moresby and is already acquainted with the new President of Paui."

"How do they expect the relatives to help?" Harry asked.

"By keeping out of the way," Richard said firmly. "All relatives have been advised to channel information and queries through the Nexus headquarters in Pittsburgh."

Harry said, "Yes, they've set up a special office to deal with this."

"And we understand that the Nexus office on Paui will organize its own search party which will keep in close contact with the State Department task force."

After that Harry tried, unsuccessfully, to telephone Jerry Pearce. He decided to wait for Jerry's return call in the bar of the Hotel Independence.

In the almost empty bar a couple of rickety tables were surrounded by broken, backless chairs. A planter's chair, similar to the one in Harry's living room, still had four stumps, but no extending arms to heave your legs over. Behind the bar, a broken green shade clung to the lightbulb over the fly-blown mirror, which was cracked in a thousand spiderwebs. A row of thick tumblers stood on top of the bar, but there wasn't a bottle in sight. The ceiling fan, shaped like an antique aircraft propeller, shuddered away. In spite of this slight movement, the air in the bar was hot and sticky.

"Last time the boys got playful, Ma Chang decided to leave it that way." The explanation of the decor came from a lean, bald man hunched over a barstool; he looked as if it had been some weeks since he'd removed his blue shirt and jeans. He waved toward a plump, sandy-haired man in the corner who was scribbling on a shorthand pad. "That's Sandy over there. He's the Moresby stringer for a group of Sydney newspapers. He also operates under a different name for an American newspaper group, as well as Associated Press and the BBC. So the poor bastard has to write every story four times in four different ways. Gets writer's cramp in both hands."

"You don't get writer's cramp in your hand, mate, you get it across your shoulders." Sandy stood up, stretched and scratched the Viking-red, matted hair that showed beneath his open shirt. He had the amiable but sharp look of a man who was going to charge one glass of beer, bought by somebody else, to four different expense accounts as double whiskeys.

Harry thought, I don't want him interfering, I don't want to give him any information—but just possibly this man knows what happened on this island last Tuesday evening.

Sandy looked at Harry. "You the bloke from Nexus who went to Paradise Bay yesterday?"

Harry nodded.

"Heard they turned you back."

Harry nodded again.

"You've heard about the boat explosion?"

Harry nodded.

"Is it true that all the Paradise Hotel tourists have disappeared?"

"Can't say. I don't know what happened."

"That's enough, mate." Mentally Sandy typed, "Haggard eyewitness reports impossible break military cordon surrounding luxury Paradise Bay Hotel stop utmost secrecy prevails as shark-infested waters searched stop little hope missing millionaire tourists."

The lean, bald man fiddled with a black transistor radio. After some ear-splitting static, they heard gloomy military music.

"They've been playing that bloody stuff on Radio Paui since dawn," the man grumbled, then explained to Harry, "We're waiting with bated breath for Raki's speech."

By the time fifteen cans of Fosters had been emptied at Harry's expense, Harry knew that the bald-headed man's name was Bill, that he was a planter, that he'd been born in Manchester, England, and had come out as a young lad in 1947, after reading too much Robert Louis Stevenson. Bill reckoned that RLS had shafted him. RLS must have written that wicked shit with one eye on his audience, who obviously didn't want to know the truth about the South Seas. The RLS audience wanted to hear about devoted native servants with regal bearing, who waved palm fans at moonlit beach picnics, where dusky maidens with breasts like coconuts swayed on

the sand; the RLS readers didn't want to hear about the flies
and infections, the heat that made you gasp, and maidens with
breasts like empty water wings.

Harry pushed another can toward the garrulous old blighter
and asked, "Well, why don't you go back to Manchester?"

Bill's blood was apparently too thin, he was too old and too
broke. One thing about Paui, he said, it didn't cost you much
to live and you never had a heating bill—but if that asshole
RLS were still alive, Bill would gladly strangle him.

There was an air-smashing screech from the radio as the
brass band stopped in mid-boom, and Bill couldn't relocate
the frequency.

Helpfully, the barman said, "Radio engine buggerupem.
One boy Missis Chang fix it."

As he fiddled with the dial, Bill explained, "Ronald Chang
is the only maintenance man on the island—that's one of the
reasons the Changs are so powerful. The islanders don't understand machinery, so Mrs. Chang's son is the local machine
medicine man."

Sandy nodded. "He sticks the batteries in transistors, the oil
in outboard motors, and screws the widgets back on the bicycles; otherwise, the natives'd just dump them and start saving
for a new one."

Bill relocated the brass band. "Second time round, of
course, Ronald Chang says they're unserviceable, so the islanders do a trade-in for a new bicycle or sewing machine,
then Ronald fixes up the old model and resells it to somebody
else. You might say he's in the recycling business." He
laughed.

The Sousa march stopped abruptly. Against a background
of shouts and whistles, General Raki was announced. He
spoke first to enlarge on what he'd said in his first broadcast,
which Harry had heard in Port Moresby.

Raki's radio manner was solemn, but strong; he drew out
his words in the manner of a man who would have people
think that he gazed upon the vision of a promised land rather
than a studio mike. "Justice . . . Freedom . . . Brave

soldiers . . . Cannot ignore the voice of the people . . . I therefore agree to accept . . . Office of President . . . Temporary position until democratic elections can be held . . . Social and economic reforms. . . ."

"Usual bullshit," yawned Bill the planter. He switched off the glowing picture of progress.

"Hey, I gotta listen," protested the freelance journalist.

Raki's slow but excitable voice was again switched on, in time to hear him declare that the following Sunday would be a holiday. Religious ceremonies of thanksgiving for deliverance from the degenerate Marxist, President Obe, would be followed by feasts of free pig and beer. The new President would immediately start touring the villages by helicopter, to distribute feast money. Each medicine man would receive a genuine red plastic telephone and each *luluai* would get a Mickey Mouse watch.

"Clever," said the planter. "No islander takes any notice of the Houses of Parliament, the representatives just sit there with bones through their noses and don't understand a thing. It's the headman, the *luluai*, who makes all decisions, including voting decisions. And, of course, the *luluai* is greatly influenced by the medicine man."

"For God's sake, *shut up*," implored the journalist, as Raki started to repeat his speech in English, for the sake of overseas listeners.

"Sure," said the planter, "my shout." For the first time he paid for a round of drinks. He said thoughtfully, "Raki's behaving as if he's God-Kilibob himself. First he announces Deliverance Day, and then he explains that he's going to arrive in each village from heaven, with pigs and Cargo. The Cargo symbol is generally a watch, and the medicine man uses a telephone—if he can't get a real telephone, then he uses an imaginary one—to talk to God-Kilibob. The islanders have noticed that whites consult these things before making a decision."

As though on cue, Freddy appeared at Harry's elbow. "Telephone, master."

The call was from Jerry Pearce in Pittsburgh. Condensed his urgent message to Harry was to find the missing Nexus group, dead or alive. Nexus couldn't have their executives vanish into thin air. What could Jerry say to their families? Harry could imagine the pressure he was getting. Apart from considerations of personal friendship, business friendship and the helluva problem Jerry was now having to reorganize their top line of command, it was shit-awful publicity for company recruiting. It was now up to Harry to get things moving and insist on action, goddamnit.

"Jerry, you're in a better position than I am to insist on action," Harry said. "Just because you can see Queenstown marked on a map, don't think it operates like a normal Western capital city. Queenstown is about as normal as a head-hunter at a cocktail party." Harry pictured Jerry sitting in an office stuffed with computers and secretaries who had clean hair and freshly laundered clothes.

"Jerry, you don't understand what it's like out here." Harry described the pseudo-efficiency, the bureaucratic dead ends, the cynical corruption and the official lack of interest that was lending nightmare qualities to his search. But Jerry didn't seem to comprehend it.

"Surely Kerry can handle that?" Jerry said. "That's his job."

Harry explained that Kerry was doing everything possible, short of using a cattle prod, to activate the Paui Minister of the Interior and the U.S. Consulate at 'Moresby, whose job it was to bring the mighty weight of the most powerful country in the world to bear on the new President of Paui.

"Jerry, if the president and half the board of General Motors disappeared on a remote tropical island, within twenty-four hours that island would be surrounded by U.S. aircraft carriers. The air above that island would be black with the latest helicopters containing the latest detection equipment, including infrared sweepscopes that can pick up a living object on the ground at least fifty feet in the air. And inch by inch, that tropical island would be combed by battalions of Marines."

"Just what are you getting at, Harry?"

"*You* have the power to find them, Jerry. I'm just the man on the spot."

"In that case," Jerry said, "you'd better get back to Sydney. We don't want any problems there."

Careful of his words, Harry said, "There might be other complications. You've had my telex about the special arrangements that have been requested."

"Yeah. Goddamn nonsense. There's no reason for back payments. It creates an unacceptable precedent, and it's unethical."

Harry said, "I'm not talking ethics, Jerry. Nothing gets done out here without a few favors, out here it's all strictly on a cash basis. It was a pity that we stopped those payments."

"It was a Board agreement. We were having to pay the new bunch, if you remember. And the person concerned was totally without influence at that time."

"But he's in charge now, Jerry. And it looks as if he's here to stay."

"I don't like pulling rank, Harry, but I *am* acting president," Jerry snapped. "Of course, I'll do everything I can from this end and you've just said that Kerry is doing everything that can be done on Paui. So everything that can be done will be done. But we've also got a company to run and shareholders to answer to, Harry. The stock's already gone down eight and a half points since the newspapers reported that half our Board has vanished, and Wall Street's wondering who's running the company. So get back to Sydney, where you're needed, and that's an order—and I might add that it's supported by the rest of my acting Board."

As he replaced the telephone, Jerry picked up the file labeled PAUI EMERGENCY PLANS and slammed it into one of the drawers in his desk. This drawer was marked "Pending."

Depressed, Harry returned to the bar of the Independence. As he called for a beer, he could clearly imagine them all busily sending interminable telexes to each other. He realized that unless he stayed on the spot and checked every damn thing himself, no trace of the Nexus party would ever be found.

Four beers later, Harry had decided that regardless of what Jerry Pearce said, he had to do the job himself, get out there on a freelance basis and look for Annie and the others as fast as he could. He'd keep the Duck, for it was a decidedly low-profile aircraft. Johno was an asset—he spoke Pidgin, and he was used to dealing with natives on PNG. He was also a trained medical orderly, and a sailor as well as a pilot. And he seemed eternally optimistic.

Optimism was in short supply.

Raki kept his word. With a speed that made Harry uneasy, the Paui government ordered the army to begin an immediate air-and-sea search. It started on Saturday, November 17, four days after the boat explosion.

The official list of missing persons had been amended. It now included the entertainment manager, the skipper of the hotel yacht, two other British guests and two Japanese tourists. Until Raki's announcement, the British and Japanese authorities had not realized that any of their countrymen were missing. Raki had gained himself a few points, for showing himself to be concerned and efficient.

Brett Adams' name had been removed from the list. Harry thought, So I was right! Raki had put a tail on him, who had reported Harry's visit to the morgue.

SAVAGES

◀ 14 ▶

SUNDAY, NOVEMBER 18, 1984

Their grueling work gave the women no time to think, but whenever they remembered that their husbands were dead, the tears welled up, as if their eyes were controlled independently from the rest of their body. The tears flowed silently, without sobs, whenever the women stopped concentrating on their arduous jobs.

Silvana, who had never wanted another man, now saw only the advantageous side of Arthur and yearned for the chance to forgive him his little peccadillos. Timid Annie longed to bury her head against Duke's big chest and feel the comfort of his enfolding arms. Neurotic Patty remembered how understanding Charley had always been—he'd never once reproached her about keeping Stephen at home—and he had always been supportive. Stoical Carey forgot Ed's exhausting ambition, and the lonely evenings spent at their isolated farmhouse when he was on his field trips. She remembered only his enthusiasm and energy and the awful moment when she'd seen all that life wiped out in seconds. Suzy felt increasingly contrite about her husband; she hadn't been nice enough to Brett, and she knew it. All the women now realized how very, very easy their life had been, although it hadn't always seemed that way.

Now their meals were eaten in silence and sorrow, and their lives were lived in the Valley of the Shadow of Death. They

314

SAVAGES

ignored each other's sobs, because to comment would start everyone weeping. But at night, they turned to their private thoughts, and in the few minutes before sleep overcame their exhausted bodies, they wept for their men. In their state of shock, deprivation and forced labor, those few minutes of private grief were luxury.

Every night they had nightmares. They cried softly or whimpered in their sleep, but when they woke, nobody ever spoke of the sinister dreams or the shapeless black menace of the night.

They were always exhausted by the time the sun rose. Annie, who woke most frequently at night, thought that the fears of sleep were even worse than the fears of the day. Although she mourned her husband bitterly, she sometimes couldn't prevent her mind wandering to Harry. The superstitious part of Annie half-wondered whether Duke's death had been a punishment sent from God, because of her lustful thoughts. But at least Harry was *alive*. She had saved his life by stopping him from coming to Paui.

Jonathan grieved differently from the women. The finality of being without Louise was more than he could endure, so he filled every moment of the day with work. What brought him nearest to remembering his wife was the women now in his charge. In their unhappiness and need, they were so soft and vulnerable that he developed a sort of defensive hardness toward them and resented their meek subjugation to his orders. He looked at their soft arms and knew that he would never again feel the firm, brown arms of Louise. He was frightened of forgetting what she looked like, what she felt like, what she smelled like. Sometimes this made him cruel to the women, because *they* were alive.

Dawn broke. A streak of gold flashed between the lavender sky and the sea. Gradually, the gold outshone the misty blue, which receded as the blood-orange sun climbed. There had been a heavy dew during the night, and the tall trees glistened in the first rays of sun; their green darkness was scattered with flowers of brilliant pink, soft yellow and fleshy cream. The

315

songs of birds of paradise rose clear above them, and the ferns and undergrowth rustled in the slight breeze.

Annie slowly opened her sleep-encrusted eyes. Something moved against her thigh. Sleepily, she stretched her bare arm down to scratch her leg, and her hand encountered warm fur. Her finger was sharply bitten.

Within seconds of Annie's scream, Patty was crouched with her knife in her hand and Jonathan was on his feet, clutching his rifle.

Jonathan laughed. "It's only a rat."

Annie gasped. "But it was black, and at least twelve inches long. I thought it was a cat."

"The rats are as big as cats out here. Bigger, some of 'em. I reckoned we was going to have trouble with 'em in the cave. Can't think why we didn't. Watch that bite and put antiseptic cream on it."

Except for Patty, the women crouched in a little heap, clasping each other for comfort. Astonished, Jonathan said, "You're more frightened of that rat than a forest full of terrorists, scorpions and cannibals! I'll make you slingshots after breakfast. After that, the rats will be frightened of *you.*"

As the women squatted to eat their breakfast, Jonathan said, "You lot ain't used to nature, that's why you're scared of it. I'll grant you, there's a few irritations I could do without, like the mosquitoes, the ants and the sand flies. But if you'd stop being frightened by spiders and such, life would be a lot easier for you. You ain't visitors anymore. You've been out here five days. Now you're part of the scenery."

He ran his tongue around his teeth—that was the trouble with coconut, the threads got wedged between your teeth. "Pilot I know used to fly a helicopter in Canada, he said the courts dealt with some juvenile offenders by giving 'em a short survival course, then flying 'em into the bush and dumping 'em with only a fish hook, line and a knife. My mate used to pick 'em up seven days later—they never failed to turn up, he said—and what they'd learned was how to survive by themselves. They'd learned self-confidence." He sucked his tooth again. "Now that's what's lacking in you lot, so after breakfast every morning I'm going to teach you a few things."

"What sort of things?" Suzy asked.

"Climb a rope and a tree, shoot, use a slingshot. That sort of thing."

"But why do we *all* have to learn this stuff?" Silvana objected. "I'm only supposed to do the cooking."

"Never know what you might need." No need to spell out to them that the cook might be the sole survivor. "Right now, ladies, you all need toothbrushes." He pulled from his shirt pocket some small green twigs. "Chew an end into a pulp and scrub your teeth with it. Silvana can make some cooking salt, then you can use it as an abrasive, instead of toothpaste."

"And how do I do that?" Silvana asked.

"Find a large rock with an indentation in the top. Keep a bucket of seawater nearby, and keep pouring it into the rock hollow, as the sun evaporates it. You'll be left with no water, just a handful of dirty salt."

Patty took Suzy off to practice swimming in the waterfall pool, while Silvana, with an upended palm branch, swept the leaves out of the hut. This irritating daily task was necessary because scorpions and spiders might otherwise creep beneath the debris during the day.

As Annie went off to gather rattan for their first climbing lesson, Jonathan trimmed six small Y-shaped branches to make slingshots. Carey cut up her bra and Patty's, so that the straps could provide elastic for the slingshots. The two now-strapless bras were converted into belts for Suzy and Carey, who hadn't been wearing belts on the day of the massacre. They each needed a belt in which to stick a knife and a slingshot, and from which to hang a mosquito-net bag. Although Carey and Patty were now braless, they were not topless. To protect them from the sun and the jungle branches, all the women wore big white fishing shirts over what was left of their beach clothes, and the floppy cotton sun hats and sneakers from the *Louise*.

Next, Jonathan made a rope ladder, so they could all climb

the lookout tree easily. He braided rattan until he had a thick, twenty-foot length. He attached one end to the lid of a bait can, which he threw over the lowest branch of the eucalyptus tree. Then he climbed up the doubled rope to the branch, where he twisted the rope around it in a half hitch—something that they'd all seen in cowboy films, when horses were tethered outside the saloon. Sitting astride the branch, he knotted the two lines together about every twelve inches, forming loops for footholds, to use as a rough ladder.

That would do to get them up the tree, but to go up and down the cave chimney they would need to really climb a rope. Suzy and Silvana were the only ones who hadn't learned long ago, at summer camp. Suzy, who was small and agile, quickly picked up the technique of crossing her ankles and gripping the rope between them, while she reached for a higher handgrip, then loosened the ankle grip temporarily, while she hauled herself up by her arms. Unathletic Silvana couldn't get the hang of it and swayed on the rattan rope, hanging a foot above the ground, terrified.

Perched fifteen feet high in the branches, Suzy was enjoying her new and unsuspected accomplishment. She swung from a branch by her arms. She hooked her legs over it and pulled herself up, then stood on the branch showing off her ability.

"Watch out!" Jonathan ran forward as Suzy stepped backward onto a branch and it snapped beneath her weight.

Suzy grabbed an overhead branch just in time to avoid a fall. She hung from it, groping with her toes, trying not to think of the sickening fall to the ground.

"There's a foothold to your left," Jonathan yelled, his arms outstretched, ready to break her fall.

Suzy's arms felt as though they were being pulled from her sockets, as though red-hot metal were being poured over her shoulders. Slowly, she stretched up her left foot, which stubbed the tree, but she couldn't see where she was putting it.

"Higher," Jonathan called.

Slowly, painfully, Suzy bent her left knee right up to her waist.

"You're too high," Jonathan yelled. "Feel your way straight down with your left foot; it's about six inches down."

He held his breath as Suzy's toes fumbled to feel the branch.

"Two inches further to your left!" he called.

As he looked up anxiously, Suzy found the branch and slowly transferred her weight to it.

"Now move your arms—one at a time, starting with the right one. Move towards the trunk. Don't think, just *do it!*"

Slowly, Suzy jerked her arms toward the trunk until she was able to put her right foot on a branch below, which then supported her entire weight.

Trembling with relief, Jonathan yelled, "Don't step on a branch without testing it, you stupid bitch, and *never* step backwards without looking where you're going."

"Okay, okay," Suzy yelled back tearfully.

To his surprise, she started to climb higher. He had to admit she was gutsy.

The next hour wasn't very successful. Laboriously, Annie dug her latrine hole with a coconut shell, then burst into tears as it caved in before she could use it.

Suzy, staggering back from the waterfall with a full bucket of water, tripped over a branch just outside the camp and fell, spilling it all. She swore angrily.

Silvana, cutting branches for the cooking fire, swung the ax, missed the branch and narrowly missed chopping her right ankle. She looked with disgust at her broken fingernails and threw the ax on the ground.

Behind her Jonathan said, "Pick it up and don't use it again. I'm saving that ax to build the raft."

Silvana threw him her most imperious look. Then she sighed and obediently picked up the ax.

Later that morning, Carey tore open her thumb on a fish hook, which was serious, because any scratch could lead to infection in the tropics and her hands were already in a bad state. She swore, sucked at the wound and spat out the blood.

Annie asked anxiously, "What are we going to do when we run out of antiseptic cream?"

"Use boiled seawater as a disinfectant," Jonathan said.

Patty nearly had an accident when she and Jonathan were fishing. She was thigh deep in the water, prizing a shellfish off an underwater rock with her fingers, when Jonathan pulled her hand away—just before a seemingly harmless shell snapped shut.

Jonathan said, "Watch out for clinging shellfish, the large abalone, clams and oysters. Don't gather 'em by hand; always prize 'em off with a bar or a wooden wedge, or the shell might clamp down on your fingers and hold you prisoner until the tide comes up and you drown."

When the camp was more or less in order, they had a ten-minute break. Looking around at the dispirited faces, Jonathan said, "Don't be too hard on yourselves, you're all doing pretty well. You've all seen that you can do more than you thought you could. Now we'll start the raft. We'll build her up here, between the camp and the waterfall."

Patty looked astonished. "Why not on the beach?"

"Too risky. Us or the raft might be spotted by a passing boat."

They would build the raft where the wood was—at the edge of the jungle. When the raft was completed, they'd launch her at high tide, lowering her down the natural slope of the path by the side of the waterfall. Once on the beach, it shouldn't take more than fifteen minutes to load the raft with the supplies. Then they'd float her through the gap in the reef on the outgoing tide. As the raft would be rectangular, it would head southward, in the direction of the tidal current.

"How big is it going to be?" practical Carey asked.

"Nine by twelve," Jonathan answered.

"But that's enormous!" Patty exclaimed. "Surely we don't need something that size, just to go seventy miles."

320

"Just to go seventy miles!" Suzy shrilled. "Seventy miles seems *endless* to me!"

"That's the correct size for a six-person raft," Jonathan said firmly. "If she's too big, she'll break her back on the big waves; if she's too small, you'll fall off her. A raft don't sit snug in the sea like a dinghy. A raft tips and dips and tilts and swings in maybe four different directions with every wave and you ain't got no idea which way she's going to tilt next; she changes angles every second."

Silvana said glumly, "A diving raft is nine feet square, and I've felt seasick on one of those."

"You'll also have to sleep on the raft," Jonathan said. "And we'll be carrying our food, drink and equipment. The journey shouldn't take longer than three days, but we can't count on it. And you make one mistake at sea, you're a goner. The sea has no mercy."

"How are we going to make the thing?" Carey asked.

"Cut down palm trees, trim 'em into logs, lash the logs together with rattan. No, we'd better use jungle vines—they're thinner but not jointed. We'll braid 'em; that'll strengthen 'em. Them logs'll need to be lashed tight as a tourniquet—that's going to be the longest job. We'll lash the logs to three cross members to give extra security. When we've done that, we'll caulk the logs with damit."

"With *what?*" they asked.

"A filler that stops up cracks and crevices—makes the thing waterproof. There's a resin in the jungle, a sap from certain trees, which is called damit. It's real easy to spot—just black stuff lying there in lumps on the ground at the base of trees. You can also use the stuff for fire lighters or as glue. If you want glue, you break the lumps into granules, then melt it on direct heat. The natives use it for cementing their canoes."

Suzy said, "You make this jungle sound like a hardware store."

"It's cheaper than a hardware store," Jonathan said.

321

Annie looked worried. "Are you *sure* the vines will be strong enough?"

Jonathan said, "When we gather 'em, we'll have to check we don't pick any brittle or rotten vines. We'll cut 'em to different lengths, up to ten feet long, so the joins in the braids are never all at the same place, which would weaken it."

"Will the vines be watertight?" Annie persisted.

"We rub coconut oil into them. That ought to make 'em watertight and flexible and stop 'em fraying."

"Which counter sells the coconut oil?" Suzy asked.

"Heat coconut flesh and you render it down to coconut oil. We can do it around the campfire at night."

"And we just rely on the current to guide this thing?" Patty asked nervously.

"Partly. But we'll also have bamboo paddles."

There was a dubious silence.

Patty said anxiously, "You're *sure* we couldn't buy a boat?"

"Might as well give ourselves up."

"Wouldn't we go faster if we had a sail?" Carey asked.

"I'd like a sail, but I don't know how to make a mast that would stay upright."

Suzy said crossly, *"You're* supposed to be a sailor. Why *don't* you know how to make a mast?"

"You can drive a car, right," said Jonathan. "But could you *repair* one? Let alone *build* one? I always sailed on steel tankers, before I bought the *Louise.* I've sailed boats but I ain't never *built* one before."

"You're sure it'll work?" Patty persisted.

"Only one way to find out."

It took the women the rest of the day to find a bamboo grove, to collect the damit and the jungle vines and to bring them back to the camp. Jonathan selected and started to cut down the fifteen palm trees they would need for the raft. It was hard and exhausting work. Once the tree had fallen, Patty and Carey hacked off the branches and dragged the trunk to the growing pile in the clearing; hauling the individual logs was also exhausting. Neither woman offered to chop down trees. Carey had tried once, when Jonathan was off for a pee. She lifted her arms just as he had and brought the ax down just as smoothly, but then she'd felt the most awful numbing pain shoot up her arm, as if she'd hit a tennis ball on the top of the racket; she dropped the ax.

Behind her, Jonathan had said, "That's our only ax, and I can't risk chipping a bit off the blade by teaching you to use it."

Carey was deeply relieved.

About seventy yards up the riverbank, in the bamboo grove, Annie was using the razor-sharp two-foot-long machete with growing confidence. Silvana refused to touch the evil-looking thing, so after Annie chopped the green bamboo Silvana dragged it back to camp.

Jonathan had explained that they needed bamboo to make watertight containers, which could hold dried fish or water for the voyage. "Bamboo is hollow," he said, pointing to the length in his hand, "but at every joint there's a solid center, so if you cut *below* a joint, you got a cylindrical container with a solid base. Make a second container and shave down the base, and it'll plug into the top of your first container. You can stack any number of 'em, some the size of mugs, some as big as kitchen pans."

It sounded simple, but it was amazing to each of them how hard it was to *do*, how much time it took and how many times you ended up with bleeding fingers and a broken piece of bamboo.

TUESDAY, NOVEMBER 20

By the end of their first week together, the women felt less helpless and less frightened.

The days were comfortable only in the first hour after dawn; then, a light breeze blew off the sea, the humidity seemed less intense and the sun had not yet grown fierce. So they made the most of this time.

They had quickly established a working routine—breakfast, followed by a wash, then foot inspection, after which Annie rebandaged Carey's hands. Then they had survival lessons for an hour. They worked until midday. After their meal, they lay panting on the ground until the fierce heat had subsided and it was possible to work again without fainting.

Every day, when the tide was high, Carey and Patty would interrupt whatever they were doing and scramble down to the beach to fish. If they missed the outgoing tide, they had to wait until the tide came in again or collect shellfish from the rocks and pools. Fishing was even more important than making the raft, because without food their strength and energy immediately flagged.

Every day, Jonathan gave all the women a short fishing lesson. It was important that each person be able to find her own food, independently.

Once, Patty caught an odd-looking small fish, with a slick, slimy skin.

"Watch out, that's a poisonous fish," Jonathan said. "Any fish that ain't got scales, like that feller you just caught, or any fish that's covered with bristles or spines—them buggers can make you feel real crook. Chuck 'em away fast—on land, so the buggers die." He added, "And do the same for any brightcolored fish, or anything that puffs up like a balloon when you take it from the water."

Jonathan also pointed out the fish that might scratch or sting them. These were the blue, plate-shaped stingrays that lurked in the shallows, the repulsively ugly stonefish and the sinister, jutting-jawed toadfish.

The women were still nervous about sharks, although Jonathan repeated that sharks weren't normally ferocious in the tropics, where there was plenty of food for them. And anyway, they couldn't get over the coral reef and into the lagoon, because it was too shallow.

"But I've *seen* sharks in the lagoon," Suzy insisted.

"Only baby ones. Nothing more than four feet long. And I've already told you, sharks ain't looking for trouble— they're cowards. You can usually frighten 'em off by splashing water at 'em or hitting 'em on the nose with a stick. But if you ain't bleeding and don't kick up a noise, you won't attract 'em."

"What about Winston?"

Jonathan was silent, then he said, "If you run into trouble, more likely it'll come from a barracuda; they're aggressive bastards."

Every evening before sunset at six o'clock, Jonathan checked his freshwater fish trap just above the bamboo grove, where a stream flowed into the river that fed the waterfall. Jonathan had tied permanent fishing lines to trees on either side of the bank and rebaited them daily. He had also built two underwater walls of stones; the barriers slanted toward each other but didn't quite meet. Fitted around the opening was a long bag made of mosquito netting and anchored by stones. Any fish that swam downstream automatically found itself in this net trap, but unable to fight its way out against the current. Because water circulated through it, the fish could stay there for hours. All freshwater fish were edible, and Jonathan's trap often provided huge shrimp and crayfish, with no effort on his part.

To dissuade mosquitoes, which, as soon as darkness fell, swarmed from the undergrowth, the soggy swamp patches, the riverbanks and the stagnant forest-pools, Annie always built a smoking fire of green wood and leaves.

Every evening, Silvana briskly gutted and boiled the fish. Then she stood two bamboo pots filled with cold, cooked fish in a pailful of water, so that the ants couldn't get at it, and covered the pot tops with scraps of shirt. They ate cold fish for breakfast, cold fish at midday and hot boiled fish every night.

Silvana smoked any extra fish on a little wigwam-like structure that Jonathan had built by binding together three green saplings; halfway down this, he tied a triangular grill also made of green sapling. A fire was lit beneath the grill, on which slivers of fish were laid to smoke overnight. For their sea journey the little party would need smoked fish, because that would last at least ten days in hot weather, instead of turning putrid overnight.

Silvana tried to keep the camp as clean as possible. After cooking, she scoured her bamboo pots with sand before rinsing them in the tin bucket.

As the women became less squeamish, frogs, snakes and lizards were beheaded and roasted on a stick held over the fire. Silvana preferred to boil shrimp and crabs. Her most popular dish was a chowder made with clams, mussels, snails and sea urchins, thoroughly boiled to kill the parasites. It was surprising how quickly Silvana had taken over the domestic jobs, thought Suzy, when she'd never before in her entire life so much as made a bed.

At breakfast on Tuesday, the seventh day after the beach massacre, Suzy suddenly shrieked that smelling goddamn fish all the time, and smelling *of* goddamn fish all the time, was even worse than *eating* the stuff all the time. She burst into tears, flung down her coconut shell and rushed into the jungle.

Jonathan yelled, "Come back, you stupid bitch!"

"No way!" Suzy called over one shoulder.

"Childish," Jonathan said, through a mouthful of fish. "Dangerous. Don't go after her. Silly cow."

"No, she isn't," Patty snapped. "We all feel like that."

There was silent agreement from the other women; they were all nauseated by the smell of raw fish, the taste of boiled fish and the mere thought of coconut. Although there was plenty of other food in the jungle, Jonathan didn't want to waste time looking for it, and didn't want to risk illness. So long as they lived on boiled fish and boiled water, and he didn't allow them too much green coconut juice because of its laxative effect, then they wouldn't get dysentery. He reckoned that the women could put up with the monotonous diet because, for these few days, every minute counted.

After running a short distance, Suzy stopped. She couldn't see more than a few yards in any direction; she looked at the jungle floor, littered with leaves, then looked up at the fragile silver threads that spiders had woven from tree to tree. She was frightened of being alone in the quiet, green menace. Although, come to think of it, she had *always* felt as alone as she did now. Those athletic bitches, Carey and Patty, had teamed up together to hunt, while Annie and Silvana were never apart, as they squatted around the fishpot or hacked at bamboo—give each of them a wooden spoon and an apron, and they'd hardly notice that they'd left Pittsburgh.

However, nobody seemed to want Suzy along. Fetching the water was a boring, solitary job. Suzy never thought she'd feel sorry for herself because a bunch of women were neglecting her.

The hell with them, she told herself.

Almost an hour later, a grinning Suzy appeared out of the jungle, clutching at her middle. Jonathan had already gone off to fell trees, and the other women were about to start their chores.

"Hey, look what I've brought!" Suzy popped her hand down her shirtfront and pulled out a plum-size fruit with a dusky purple skin.

"They taste great," she said. "Like a persimmon, but without a kernel."

"*Fruit!* That's wonderful," Patty cried. "I've been really worried about vitamin deficiency."

Annie said anxiously, "Are you sure it's not poisonous?"

"Sure hope not, I've eaten about six; they're delicious."

The women gathered around Suzy, who unbuttoned her shirt and laid out her fruit. The others sniffed at it and savored its peachlike smell. Unlike a peach, this fruit tasted even better than it smelled. Greedily they crammed the fruit into their mouths.

"We must save some for Jonathan." Annie sounded guilty as she reached for a third fruit. "I haven't had a craving like this since I was pregnant with Fred, and then it was cucumbers."

But by the time Jonathan had returned to see why the hell Carey hadn't followed him, only two of the purple fruits remained. The women were apologetic, and slightly ashamed. Their hands had seemed to act of their own volition, as fingers reached out for yet another fruit and stuffed the delicious, soft sweetness into their mouths.

Jonathan grunted, "Never carry tropical fruit next to your skin; you might get a rash."

"Can't you just say thank you?" Patty asked.

Suzy said she'd go back and get some more.

"No, you won't," said Jonathan irritably. "You ain't peeled them things, and you ain't boiled 'em. We don't know if they're safe. If you're going to eat anything you see, then I'd better catch a taster. There ain't no monkeys on Paui, so I'll catch a rat. If he eats the food and lives, then *you* can eat that food and live."

Shrill cries of horror greeted the thought of a cat-sized rat right in the middle of their camp. Then, chastened but unrepentant, the women went about their work.

In the faint filtered moonlight, Annie staggered out of the hut yet again, heading to the latrine area. She found Suzy lying there, retching.

Suzy said, "I think I'm dying."

"So do I," gasped Annie, then threw up again. Once more, the agonizing pain squeezed her guts, and this time she didn't have the strength to pull her underpants back on, let alone cover up the latrine hole. In fact she'd probably missed the hole. Who cared?

Annie lay gasping in the undergrowth, her head only inches from her own vomit—or was it Suzy's?—as she waited for the strength to move. She was vaguely conscious of someone else crawling around and retching. It sounded like Silvana.

Then Annie's guts were squeezed again, followed by a rush from her lower intestine, but she was too weak to move her legs.

The sound of the women retching and stumbling out of the

hut had awakened Jonathan. Taking his flashlight, he made his way to the latrine.

In the beam of light Jonathan looked at the women, crawling around in their own filth or lying in a fetal position, sobbing, groaning or retching. Lying spread-eagled, Suzy looked unconscious.

There was no point in bringing the poor cows back to foul the hut, he told himself. He'd gather elephant's ears to clean them up, as soon as it was light. Then, he supposed, he'd have to bathe them.

Their cramps had started shortly after they'd eaten Suzy's fruit. How long was this going to hold up the raft? Jonathan wondered as he trudged back to the camp. He would scrape charcoal from the charred wood of the cooking fire and boil extra pails of water, because dysentery left you in a bad state of dehydration. As soon as it was light, he'd search for young, red ginger shoots. Two permanent jungle problems were constipation and diarrhea; pawpaw seeds loosened your gut, wild ginger bunged it up. Jonathan decided he could do with a few pawpaw seeds.

After that, everyone except Silvana swam naked in the lagoon; it seemed pointless to display modesty before the man who had nursed you and wiped you, washed you, then having carried you, naked, back to the hut, had patiently spooned fish gruel into your mouth and scraped the dribble away. And Silvana needed their pants to boil, then sieve water into her growing collection of bamboo pots.

On Wednesday, November 21, the morning after Suzy brought back the fruit, Jonathan decided to take a quick dip. As he scrambled down the cliff path, he noticed that a rubber tire had been washed up on the beach. He had no proof, but he liked to think it was one of the tires he'd used as fenders on the *Louise*. He was sure that he could use it on the raft in some way, and brought it back to the camp.

As he moved toward the jungle, he heard the drone of a low-flying aircraft and dived for cover, just before a small silver-blue amphibian flew directly overhead. They had seen or heard aircraft several times, but this was the first one actually to fly over the camp.

To his horror and fury, Jonathan saw Suzy rush out onto an open patch of ground at the top of the waterfall. She jumped up and down on the black rocks waving her arms, an incongruous figure in her big man's shirt and the makeshift trousers that Annie had made her from one of the other fishing shirts, using the arms as pants legs.

Jonathan leaped out, grabbed Suzy from behind and dragged her back into cover, just before the aircraft passed overhead again.

As he glared at her, his sandy eyebrows meeting above his bright blue eyes, Suzy yelled in fright because she'd never before seen him in a rage.

"You bloody idiot!" he shouted. "Just because it's a civilian plane don't mean to say it's got civilians in it! We've seen small military craft at sea, for all we know there's still a war on, but *you . . . you* go out and *wave*, to tell 'em where we are!"

"Nexus is bound to come looking for us," Suzy said defensively. "I *know* that's what Brett will do. Nexus has probably been searching for eight days. Why, I bet that plane is looking for us. Brett may have been *in* it!" She burst into tears. "You didn't tell us *not* to wave to a plane, you arrogant bastard!"

"There's lots of things I ain't warned you about, because I don't know about 'em, but *think* before you act, you stupid bitch! Our plan is to *hide* until we get off the island. No good letting a bit of wishful thinking put everybody's life in danger."

"I don't have to do everything you say," Suzy spat. "Just because the rest of them are following you with their tongues hanging out."

"They do what I say because I know how to look after myself better than they do and I know a bit more about the jungle."

"There's more to it than that!" Suzy mimicked Jonathan's

330

flat Australian twang. "'That ain't bad, Annie' . . . 'Good work, Patty' . . . 'Couldn't have done it better meself, Carey' . . . Those stupid bitches don't do *anything* unless you tell 'em. They grovel for your goddamned approval!"

She's right, Jonathan thought. Women are all the same—bloody babies when it comes to the test. But give 'em a man—*any* man—to take the final responsibility, and they'll trot along behind him and do what he tells 'em to do—whatever it is.

He said, "That's just because I'm the only bloke around. I'm trying to encourage 'em—keep their spirits up."

"You're a goddamn *slave* driver, and we're dependent on you. And you love it, and so do they." Suzy twisted herself free and stumbled back to the hut, sobbing with rage.

As Suzy entered, Silvana said mildly, "I just swept that floor, don't mess it up again. Jonathan said nothing gives the day so bad a start as treading with your bare feet on a scorpion hiding beneath the leaves."

In a fury, Suzy mimicked her. "'Jonathan says! Jonathan says!' To *hell* with what Jonathan says!"

Suzy went outside and caught up an armful of leaves and bracken. She came back into the hut and scattered the debris over the floor, stamping and crying with fury as she did so.

Jonathan poked his head around the side of the hut. "She's just disappointed," he explained to the astonished Silvana.

"Well, so am I. She can damn well sweep the hut out by herself or she doesn't get any breakfast. Say, did you hear that plane?"

THURSDAY, NOVEMBER 22

Though they were still very weak, the women started to work again. They were building the raft on two smoothed skid logs, which would serve as rollers when the raft was pushed down the path to the beach.

In their frail state, when the women started to lash the logs together with vines, they found it unbearably heavy and exhausting work.

"I can't go on much longer," Carey panted.

Jonathan kicked at the logs that Patty and Carey had been binding. Immediately the vines could be seen to loosen.

Jonathan looked grim. "Lash it tighter, Carey. Your life is going to depend on that log, and so is mine."

"Look, I'm not qualified to do this sort of work." Carey was irritable, as an overtired child is irritable. She looked at her bandaged hands and said, "I've never done practical carpentry. I just *can't* do any better."

"None of us is qualified to do it," Jonathan said. "And you *can* do it better. Use your foot to brace yourself as you pull the vines tight. Look, I'll show you again." He thought, Trouble with women is, they won't persist, they give up at the first failure. Women ain't hardened to disappointment, as men are.

Carey wiped the sweat from her cheeks. She said apologetically, "I used to be able to do this sort of thing when I was young, but not since I had children. I'm not as strong as I used to be—and my hands are still painful."

"Oh, get on with it, or we'll never get out of here," Suzy said crossly.

Silvana, who was partnered with Suzy, said in a tight voice, "*You* should talk, Suzy. You're not even trying!" She looked up at Jonathan as he approached to kick the logs. "Suzy's only *pretending* to pull. Look at her hands, they're not blistered like *mine*. And she's careless. Just look at these logs! You can *see* that the vines are loose without even pulling at them!"

Suzy scowled. "I'm about ninety pounds lighter than you are, Silvana! *That's* why I can't pull as hard on the vines. And I expect your hands are blistered because you've never done a lick of work in your life."

In a placatory voice, Annie said, "We can't afford to be impatient or careless. We don't want this thing to come apart in the water."

332

Suzy threw down her vines and said, "Are you insinuating—"

Patty yelled, "I am, if she's not. I've been watching you!"

The basic conflict that existed between the women had lain dormant, for they had been company wives and therefore expected always to behave politely to each other.

"Suzy always shirks her work," Silvana accused.

"I'm not built like an ox, Silvana. And I don't eat more than my ration. *You* always steal food before you serve it to us."

"I have to check the taste, don't I? And I've pulled my belt in four inches since we've been here. That wouldn't happen if I were stealing food." Silvana glared and thrust out her arms. "Look at my hands! How would *you* like to gut the fish?"

"I'd rather be paddling around and catching them like Patty," Suzy snapped. "She's having a goddamned fishing vacation! And as for that hulking Amazon Carey, she's slower than I am on the raft."

Carey yelled, "That's because I'm the only one doing it right."

Jonathan raised his voice above the screaming accusations and catty backbiting. "You should all be trying to work as a team; this bleedin' raft is the most important thing in our lives. You ain't assembling this raft with love and care. You *hate* the goddamn thing."

"What the hell do you mean, work as a team?" Patty asked.

"You're working like footballers who don't know the passes, you're working as if you're playing mixed doubles with a tennis partner you ain't never met before."

Carey said, "He's right. We have to learn to cooperate, and be on the lookout for each other's weaknesses."

Trying to make peace, Annie said, "Suzy can't pull the vines hard enough, because she hasn't the strength, but she's very nimble-fingered. Her knots are good. Patty's knots aren't good, because she's impatient and that makes her careless— but she's strong, so she can pull hard. So maybe Suzy and Patty should work together."

Patty said, "Your own knots aren't that great, Annie."

The fight flared up until all five women were yelling again. Accusations and counteraccusations about bad work on the raft led to more personal attacks. Whereas none of the women could see their own mistakes and weaknesses, for years in Pittsburgh, they had all observed each other carefully, so each knew the faults of the others and, like sisters, could deftly aim verbal darts, hitting exactly where it hurt most.

They all knew that vain Suzy, who was sloppy about everything except her appearance, never allowed a dark root to show in her long blond hair. They had all seen lazy Silvana neglect her role as the president's wife. They all felt that Carey flaunted her career achievements, but cared more about the appearance of her house than the comfort of her family, who had to sit on those spindly Shaker chairs. They were all aware that Annie was so afraid of upsetting people that she let them walk all over her. And that stubborn, guilt-ridden Patty —she was so preoccupied by her role as Florence Nightingale to her child that Charley never got any peace at home. They said as much, and more.

Exasperated, Jonathan slammed on his sun hat, took his rifle and walked away into the jungle.

They continued to quarrel for about thirty minutes after his departure, by which time every woman's weakness had been bluntly pointed out, the unforgivable had been clearly stated and the limits of bitterness reached.

Suddenly Patty shrieked above the angry voices. *"What's that noise?"*

Immediately there was silence. Nobody moved. The women strained their ears.

Eventually Suzy spat, "Just Patty's goddamn nerves again."

But the women had been reminded that they lived in constant danger. Terrified, they fled back to camp. Reassured by the smoking campfire they continued to smolder with indignation and resentment, but in silence.

As their rage started to subside, each woman felt alone and unprotected, raw and naked. Each wanted to weep solitary tears of rage. For they knew that they were stuck in the jungle —and stuck with each other.

Suddenly, they heard a loud crashing noise. It grew nearer and nearer, tearing through the undergrowth.

In an instant every woman was on her feet.

Patty and Carey whipped their fish knives from their belts and crouched, tense and expectant, as they faced toward the thudding creature crashing through the undergrowth; their hearts thumped, they were conscious of each breath they drew. Silvana, who had been wearing fishing gloves, grabbed a smoldering branch from the fire to use as a weapon. Annie picked up two large stones. Suzy fled in the direction of the cave chimney.

They heard his hoarse whisper before he appeared from the bushes, hatless, and with bleeding scratches on his face.

"Run to the cave shaft . . ." Jonathan gasped for breath. "Terrorists . . . on . . . track." He fought for his words. As Silvana quickly started to douse the fire, he gasped, "Take your knives . . . Patty lead 'em . . . I'll wait here . . . Distract 'em . . . *Move!*"

◀ **15** ▶

Crouching in the dank-smelling darkness of the cave, Patty whispered nervously, "What do *you* think those natives were doing?"

"Dunno," Jonathan said. "Like I told you, there was two of 'em, just walking along as if they was out for a stroll on Sunday. Maybe they was heading for the village. Maybe their aunty lives in Katanga. Maybe they got a girl there, I dunno. But I thought we'd best be down here."

"Lucky you went off alone," Carey pointed out.

After a pause, Jonathan said, "I shouldn't've done it. I've seen you frightened and hungry, tired and sick, and I swear to God you've been great. So maybe I expected too much of you when it came to building the raft." He knew that hard work under pressure shows up a person's weaknesses, and it can be a shock. Although everybody has them, not many people know or admit their true weaknesses. And if you don't admit them, you can't conquer them. Self-knowledge is the nearest thing a person can have to real security, he reckoned.

He said, "No matter how many penthouses or pearl necklaces you lot got back in Pittsburgh, all you got here is *you*. But that's enough to get us out of here."

Patty wondered whether this was psychology or religion or Dale Carnegie. She said, "So?"

"We're going to need self-discipline to get us out. But if we build that raft properly, we'll make it. We'll maybe look a bit scruffy and we'll be pretty tired and scratched, and sick of boiled fish and ants, but we *will* get out, so long as you lot remember two things."

Oh, God, Suzy thought. Another of his pep talks!

Obligingly Carey said, "Okay, what's the first thing?"

"You must *believe* that we're going to get out. Otherwise you ain't going to give it your best try."

"And the second thing?" Carey asked.

"The stronger ones must help the weaker ones. We ain't going to abandon the injured or ill, we help 'em till the group has got its strength back. You gotta realize that *nobody's* going to get left behind. We move as a group, at the speed of the slowest person. Anyone who feels impatient must realize that *right now*. You especially, Patty. Today, Suzy was a bit slow on the knots, but tomorrow it might be *you*. No use feeling cross or sorry for yerself—because that's the way it's going to be, until we kiss this place goodbye."

"We can't make the raft if we're stuck down here," Carey grumbled.

Patty anxiously asked again, "What do you think those natives were doing on the track?"

"As soon as it's dark, I'll shin up and check," Jonathan said. "And, as I don't like thinking what might have happened if they'd come across you while I wasn't around, we're going to have a few lessons in self-defense."

"Self-defense," Silvana echoed. "But I couldn't . . . it's impossible."

"I don't see why not," Carey said cheerfully. "My girls are going to take karate classes as soon as they're old enough." Boys had boxing lessons and joined ROTC. She and Ed had decided that girls needed self-defense lessons more than boys.

"What do you mean by self-defense?" Annie asked timidly.

"You've spent a week in the jungle. You've had to kill to live. You're ready for it now," Jonathan said. "So I'm going to teach you thirteen quick, easy ways for a small woman to kill a man. You'll pick it up in half an hour. It's easy."

FRIDAY, NOVEMBER 23

The following morning after foot inspection, the women squatted around Jonathan. They couldn't sit on the ground or the ants would be at them, and after days in the jungle, squatting had become automatic.

In the same matter-of-fact voice he'd used for instructing them to fish or build a fire, Jonathan said, "You'd better realize there'll be no time for hesitation. If you don't kill him, he'll kill you. You ain't got time for scruples, you ain't got time to think, you'll only have a split second to recognize a life-or-death situation and do what I'm going to train you to do. You don't think—you *react* to the situation, as soon as you recognize it. If you don't act fast enough, if you stop to think, then some big brute is going to kill you—*and* your friend, *and* the group." He looked around the ragged circle to check the impact of his words. Everyone looked scared.

Annie said nervously, "Suppose we make the wrong decision, suppose we kill somebody by accident?"

"You'll have to plead manslaughter, but at least you'll be alive to do it," he said. "Don't take a risk, don't think 'Maybe I will,' don't think how frightened or nervous you are, or that you ain't never done it before—because that may be the *last* thought you think. If you recognize a kill situation, then you get in there and kill."

Silvana said firmly, "Killing is against the teaching of the church. I don't think I could do it."

Patty looked exasperated. "What about army chaplains? They encourage people to kill just by being in the army." She

338

added, "If you're going to go by the Bible, Silvana, then how about remembering what they did to Arthur? An eye for an eye and a tooth for a tooth."

Silvana looked sick. Jonathan noticed, but didn't comment, as he continued, "Now you can kill a man in two ways—directly, or indirectly. The easy way is to pull a trigger, or press a button. Somehow, that trigger or button puts you at one remove from the fact. It absolves you from the horror of what you're doing." He looked at the serious semi-circle of faces around him, "Button or trigger is impersonal—but when you kill a human being with your own hands, it's *very* personal. You've been taught, 'Thou shalt not kill'—and there you are, *doing* it."

Patty said, "But you've just outlined a situation in which it's morally correct."

"Justification is easy," Jonathan said. "Doing it ain't."

"Isn't killing against the human instinct?" Annie asked, dubiously. "Are you sure women can do it?"

Jonathan said, "Females will kill when necessary, without hesitation." Against a chorus of dissent he continued, "Females will kill, without a second thought, to protect their young."

There were reluctant nods of agreement.

Carey said, "If I didn't want to learn how to kill, I wouldn't be squatting here now. But what worries me is that when it comes to the point—I just won't be *able* to do it."

Jonathan said, "Man or woman, when you're put in a life-or-death situation, you instinctively fight for your life with everything you've got. And you can *always* do more than you think you can. D'you remember when Suzy couldn't swim, because she was frightened? She learnt to swim because she *had* to—to survive. So if you have to kill to survive, then you will."

Silvana said firmly, "I will *never* do such a thing."

Suzy snapped, "If it's for survival of the group, you'd better do it. You don't think I'm going to get blood on my hands for you, if you're not prepared to accept the same responsibility."

"Never!" Silvana said with conviction. "I *couldn't* bring myself to do it."

Jonathan said, "If there's anyone here who's sensitive, or squeamish, or who faints at the sight of blood, then she'd better face them feelings and deal with 'em in advance. You all saw what happened on the beach at Paradise Bay. The question you have to answer is simply this: 'If some bloke is trying to kill me, am I prepared to kill him?'"

In a low voice Patty said, "*I'll* do it—if I have to. Tell us how."

Annie was apologetic but firm. "I'm sorry, but I think I'd be too frightened by guns or painted faces. I haven't got the guts."

"You'll have the guts," Jonathan said.

"How can you be so sure?" Annie asked anxiously.

"Fear creates adrenaline, which helps you do the job. Nature thinks of everything." Annie still looked dubious, Jonathan added, "Natives paint their faces and yell to frighten the other bloke; under the feathers and the yellow paint and the hollering, they're just ordinary men—but out to kill you."

Patty added, "In their old-fashioned way, they're just psyching you out."

Jonathan nodded. "So forget being frightened or nervous or doubtful if you *can* kill, or *will* kill. Forget you ain't never done it before, forget it's a person, forget it's an enemy. It's simply a moving target and you've got to strike it fast. You must simply *act*. Be impersonal, make the decision and go into your drill—one, two, three, *wham!* And get it right the first time, because you won't get a second chance. You'll be dead."

Suzy said, "What about me? I'm so small. What chance will I have against a man? I've seen women get hit. They didn't stand a chance against a bigger man."

"That's because they didn't have a teacher," Jonathan told

340

her. "Being small can be an advantage, Suzy. You'll soon see how."

Carey said firmly, "Let's stop yakking and start the first lesson."

"You just had your first lesson," Jonathan said. "The first lesson is sorting out your moral and mental attitude. I don't want anyone at the second lesson who ain't prepared to defend herself and the group."

Before they started work on the raft, Jonathan took Silvana to one side. "I don't want the others to know," he said, "but I killed a rat this morning—knocked it out with me slingshot, then hit it on the head. He's about fourteen inches long. I'm going to try and kill a few more. We'll all work better if we eat animal flesh instead of fish. I've hung the rat behind the hut. Don't handle it until it's cold, because the fleas won't leave it until then, and fleas transmit plague."

Silvana thought she was going to be sick.

Seeing her face, Jonathan said crossly, "You're the cook, it's your job. Don't tell the others what it is. Say it's rabbit, and boil it for about thirty minutes."

"How would I know what to do with a dead rat?"

"Come round to the back of the hut and I'll show you."

Behind the hut Jonathan, wearing fishing gloves, laid the dead rat on the grass. He lifted his knife. "You cut off the head, then the paws; you make two cuts from the knees up the inner back legs to the body, then one cut straight up the belly to the throat." As he spoke he demonstrated. "From the belly, make a cut down each foreleg. Once you've slashed the belly open, all the innards will fall out."

"Do I cook them?"

"No. Maybe bits, like liver, are safe to eat, but it's safer to throw the lot away."

When Silvana rejoined them at the raft, Carey said, "Are you okay? You look awful."

Silvana laughed nervously. "We all look awful."

Carey nodded and grinned.

Within twenty-four hours of their flight into the jungle, with the exception of Suzy, the women had lost all interest in their personal appearance. They were now tanned and had lost weight, but their hands and feet were filthy, their nails were black-rimmed and torn, their clothes were limp and ragged. Every evening Annie sewed up the tears, but the thread from the hotel sewing kit had long been finished, so for thread she unraveled part of a shirt thread by thread, wound it around a twig and used a thorn as a needle.

Carey's long, honey-colored hair had been cut short, because of the heat and because the top had been such a mess, where Jonathan had hacked the bat free. Annie had done her best with the sewing-kit scissors to give Carey a boyish cut, like Patty's, but when she held up the pocket mirror Carey said gloomily, "We'd better ask Vidal Sassoon along on our next trip."

Carey wasn't suffering quite so badly now from her abrupt cigarette withdrawal. (Jonathan had used the last of her cigarettes to clear the hut of mosquitoes on the night when they had diarrhea.) Nevertheless, she was drying out some leaves on a flat rock, and after each meal she rolled a different sort of weed in a leaf and tried to smoke it without gagging.

Annie had also cut Silvana's hair. She had chopped straight across the back of Silvana's neck, and this new pageboy cut made her look ten years younger. Although she was tired, Silvana felt better and fitter than she'd felt for years. She was losing weight fast and starting to feel that, instead of being imprisoned in her body, it belonged to her, and she fitted it with ease.

The third time Annie caught Suzy sneaking a depressed look into her pocket mirror, Annie threatened to throw it away. Beneath her blond mane Suzy's black roots were showing, but she had no intention of cutting her long hair and had twisted it into two braids, which she tied with thin rattan. Suzy was also gloomy about her eyebrows, the true shape of which could now clearly be seen, shadowed above and below the thin, arched line.

More than the others, Silvana suffered from lack of privacy.

She had lived in her private shell for so many years, finding comfort in solitude as she read or listened to music. She was the only one of the group who really enjoyed being alone, and she hadn't been alone since her last shower in the luxurious bathroom of the Paradise Bay Hotel. Convent-educated in Tuscany, she had also been raised to be modest to a ridiculous degree. She could not shake off her reluctance to show herself naked, as the others did when they swam with unselfconscious freedom; Silvana envied this, but could not attain it. Normally Jonathan wore his jeans and a fishing shirt. But whenever Silvana glimpsed Jonathan's lean, muscular body, she would quickly turn her head away and rush to the canvas lean-to pretending to check her growing pile of bamboo containers, some filled with dried fish, some with filtered fresh water.

All day, in the steaming heat, they worked on the raft. Having cut and unraveled all the vines that they'd lashed and knotted the day before, the women wearily set about redoing their work; they worked slowly, more carefully and without complaining. The name-calling and accusations of the previous day seemed to have cleared the air. Their feelings were no longer disguised. They all knew exactly what they thought of each other and, surprisingly, were more at ease.

"I've found a lazy way to bind the vines," Suzy said. She demonstrated her invention to the others. "See? You bind one log to the next by winding the rope around the two of them in a figure eight; then you tighten the binding like a tourniquet, by twisting the knot with a stick."

By common consent, Suzy was given a double portion of fish that evening.

After supper, the women gathered around Jonathan for their second self-defense lesson. Patty, Carey and Suzy were eager to learn, Annie was apprehensive, but Silvana was still unwilling.

"You just remember that Jonathan was going to leave me behind to die rather than put the group in danger," Suzy warned her.

"I know," Silvana said unhappily.

"Shut up, you two," said Jonathan, and started his lesson.

Briskly he said, "Basically, what you do depends on four things—whether you're surprised by the enemy or whether you have the advantage of surprise, whether you have been attacked from the front or the rear, whether *you're* going to attack from the front or the rear, and whether there's only one of you or more."

"So what do we do?" Suzy asked eagerly.

"If your target is alert, try to distract his attention. From his rear, you can use your slingshot or throw a stone to the right or forward of him. If he looks in the direction of the stone, that's fine. But if he's been properly trained, he'll look in the opposite direction—because he'll be expecting a decoy.

"Whatever he does, quickly throw a second stone—in the opposite direction to the way he's looking. Then take him fast from the rear."

Patty said, "Suppose he's . . ."

"If your target's busy attacking one of your mates, then distract him by throwing a stone or knife at his back. We'll practice knife-throwing tomorrow morning."

"Do we use our fish knives?" Patty asked.

Jonathan nodded. "They've got an eight-inch blade, like an ordinary kitchen knife; that's long enough to reach a man's heart. Your knife mustn't have a needle point, it must be rounded, so that it slides off the rib bone and continues onwards, instead of sticking in the bone. So you'll have to file the tip of your knife."

"Does it matter if you're left-handed?" asked Patty, who was.

"No, you just reverse instructions. But there's one knifing technique that's perfect for a left-hander. I'll show you later."

Using Patty as an opponent, Jonathan then demonstrated basic methods of self-defense. In a casual, comforting voice he called out, "Don't attack him from the front, because then he's got two arms and two legs to use against you. Always try to attack from the rear, or don't bother."

He stood up and beckoned to Patty, then demonstrated as he spoke.

"Forget any rubbish about crippling a bloke by kicking him in the crotch. He'll just catch your foot and pull it upwards, then you'll be on your back. A kick in the balls is a *defense* tactic. If you're being attacked and find yourself in hand-to-hand combat, then of course you bring your knee up, as hard and fast as you can. Follow it with your foot to the same place, using all the strength of your leg to push behind the thrust of your heel."

Seeing Silvana's look of distaste, he said, "That ain't nearly so nasty as what he might be thinking of doing to you. If you're being attacked from the front and you can get one of your hands free, then pull your elbow back and with the full force of your arm behind it, *punch* the base of his nose with the heel of your palm."

"Would that really hurt him enough?" Suzy thought it sounded too easy.

Jonathan said, "If you do it right, you can knock his nose bone into his brain. You can also use the same punch aimed at his Adam's apple. It's very painful—*and* easy to do, no matter how small and frail the woman is, Suzy."

"Suppose you can't pull your elbow back?" Suzy asked.

"Push his eyeball with your thumb; push on the outside toward the nose, with the full force of your arm behind it. Bend the elbow, then straighten it fast, to *jab*. . . . " He staggered. "Hey, careful, Patty. . . . But when you're attacking him somewhere else, you *don't* look at his eyes. As with a tennis ball, you focus on what you intend to hit."

They hung the tire from the tree nearest the campfire, with the top at the same height as Jonathan's head. With fish glue, they pasted on leaves to represent eyes, nose, mouth and Adam's apple.

Vigorously, Jonathan swung the tire, explaining, "There ain't a man in this world that's gonna stand still while you push his eyeball in."

They practiced on the tire and then they practiced on Jonathan. In a surprisingly short time, they realized that fighting back was much easier than they had expected it to be. Even Silvana started to enjoy a new feeling of power.

"Why don't they teach this stuff to fourteen-year-old girls in school?" Suzy panted. "There might be less rape if guys thought *this* might happen!" She grabbed Jonathan's lips between her finger and thumb, dug her nails in, then pulled her wrists inward, twisting the lips in opposite directions.

By the end of the lesson, each woman had a favorite hold. If Annie was grabbed around the throat, she turned sideways and forced her fingers down into the hollow below Jonathan's Adam's apple. When he grabbed Carey by her shirtfront, she swiftly pushed two fingers under his earlobes while her thumbs pushed up under his cheekbones. Patty preferred punching and dutifully concentrated on punching *through* the body, rather than *at* it. She punched Jonathan's chin, aiming for the back of his head; she punched his chest, aiming for his spine.

Even Silvana found that if Jonathan had her in a headlock, with her head caught between the crook of his elbow and the side of his body, she could sink her fingers and thumb into the inside of his thigh, then pinch, twist and pull.

"Feels just like being burned," Jonathan gasped.

As Silvana released her grip, she panted, "I still don't understand why we have to learn to kill, when we'll shortly be leaving this wretched place."

"Never know when it might come in useful," Jonathan said. He didn't want to tell them that the most likely moment for a native attack, as revenge for desecrating the taboo site, would be at the moment of embarkation.

SATURDAY, NOVEMBER 24

They finished the raft at four o'clock on Saturday afternoon. Jonathan gave it a final inspection, but they all knew that he would find nothing wrong with their work. As he slowly walked around the raft, the women looked at each other and grinned.

The exhausted women gazed at the raft with surprise and pride. Under pressure, in a short time, they had tapped unsuspected strength and perseverance—which is self-control. They had learned their own capacities and limitations, and how to deal with them—which is self-confidence.

They had worked hard. The harder they pushed themselves, the more they developed self-control. Jonathan had noticed a new sense of tolerance and compassion, as well as a growing brisk toughness and confidence. Under pressure, in eleven days, the small group had learned to work together, with unsuspected ingenuity and enterprise.

Jonathan grinned and said, "Well done, lads."

Suzy whooped, Silvana clapped and they all grinned with delight at Jonathan's understated praise.

"We'll soon be leaving," Suzy crowed.

"It doesn't seem as if we've been here eleven days," Carey said.

"That's because we haven't had one spare minute," Patty said tartly. There had always been something that needed doing, something to fill each minute, so that they hardly had time to think. It was only at night that each woman had time to count the days, and the hours and the minutes—to long for the moment when they *might* be able to leave this loathsome island.

Suddenly, their hopes soared. As the sweat streamed down their dirty faces, they felt new energy surge through them; because of their unaided efforts, they were about to sail off, to leave this sinister island far behind them, and head for home.

Jonathan looked at the excited little group and suggested, "There's two hours before sunset, and high tide is at midnight. So if you ain't feeling too whacked, we could leave tonight instead of tomorrow. What do you think?"

"*Yes!*" they all said.

The sweating, exhausted women found new strength. It had

been born of hope. They all wanted to get off Paui as fast as possible. Although it was hard work, two hours should give them plenty of time to lower the heavy raft down the cliff and load it with their equipment, food and water.

After that, all they had to do was sit on the raft and wait for the tide to rise and float them out to sea.

There was a feeling of elation in the camp as, squatting around the campfire, the women ate their last "rabbit" stew.

As they finished their meal, Jonathan said, "Drink as much water as you can, and have another long drink just before we start to lower the raft. After that, both food and water will be rationed."

They all nodded. They knew that to keep fit, they needed a pint of water a day, and to keep alive they needed two to eight ounces of water a day.

Jonathan said, "Drink all you can. After that, you'll get only a mugful of water a day." He stood up. "Okay, let's go!"

Annie was responsible for hauling the six bamboo oars and the raft supplies. Silvana's job was to check that everything was cleared from the camp and the fires doused. Suzy was posted as tree lookout. She had the lightest body, so she was least useful for launching the heavy raft. This was the responsibility of Carey and Patty.

Each ragged creature ran to her task. From now on, they would try not to talk. Suzy would whistle once if they were to freeze. If she whistled twice, they were to drop everything and dash for the cave. Although she'd often been posted as lookout, this responsibility now caused her unexpected anxiety. She was also aware of the politely unverbalized general opinion that she had the easiest job—sitting up a tree—while they would all be working their butts off for the next two hours. However, they all knew the strain of sentry duty, especially at night.

Jonathan had warned them that it would not be easy to launch the heavy raft. The cliff slope was too steep to push the raft down; it would crash and break up on the beach. The easiest route was beyond the cliff path, on the southern side of

348

the waterfall, which dropped about eighty feet in a series of rocky terraces to the beach.

They were going to lower the raft to the beach on four vine ropes, one bound to each cross member of the raft. The raft would run forward on the two roller logs. Two women were needed at the top of the cliff to signal to the rope handlers, so that the raft stayed on course until it arrived on the beach. It would be like a huge, heavy tray sliding down the cliff. Unless the descent were carefully controlled, the raft might gather momentum and careen onto the lower rocks of the waterfall—which would smash it to pieces.

Controlled by Carey, the two left-hand ropes were wound twice around the lookout tree—which was the nearest tree to the clifftop. Controlled by Patty, the two right-hand ropes were wound around a second tree. The trees would take the strain of the heavy raft.

Annie and Silvana were both stationed at the clifftop, to ensure that the raft moved smoothly in the correct direction. Standing at the bottom of the cliff, Jonathan was to signal with his left hand to Annie (who was partnering Carey), and with his right hand to Silvana (who was working with Patty). The two women standing on the clifftop were able to see Jonathan on the beach, as well as the raft and the women lowering it, at the trees. If Jonathan raised his left hand, then Annie signaled to Carey to let out a foot of rope. If he raised his right hand, Silvana gave a similar signal to Patty. If he raised both his arms, both ropes were to be let out one foot. If he stood with his hands at his sides, then nobody moved.

Jonathan would have preferred to have two women hanging on to each rope, but there were simply not enough of them. Instead of having two of them on the cliff, he had considered signaling with one of the whistles from a life jacket; but to lower the raft eighty feet would require a great deal of whistling and might attract attention while they were all exposed and vulnerable.

He calculated that it would take an hour and a half to launch the raft, which would only give them fifteen minutes of daylight to load it. On the other hand, that would also cut down their chances of being seen.

For the last time, he checked the vine ropes that would control the descent of the raft, after which he carefully picked his way down the cliff path. This was no time to sprain an ankle.

At the bottom, Jonathan stood at the side of the waterfall, so that he could tilt the raft away from the water channel and onto the sand, where it would be easier to load. The timing wasn't ideal, but there would be nearly a full moon, which was lucky. And at this point, so near the cyclone season, it was a reasonable risk to take, in order to save a day.

Standing knee deep in water, he looked up.

Above him, on the clifftop, Annie and Silvana waved. They were ready.

Jonathan waved both arms.

The work went faster than Jonathan had calculated. A foot at a time, the heavy raft moved with its own momentum over the undergrowth toward the edge of the cliff. Jonathan had warned Silvana and Annie not to stand in the path of the raft in case, for some reason, Patty and Carey were unable to control its descent.

The most anxious moment was when the raft slowly tipped over the top of the cliff.

Far below, Jonathan stood well back and out of the way. Patty and Carey felt the extra weight on the thick vine ropes. After that, nobody had time to be anxious.

Foot by foot, the women lowered the heavy, palm-log raft.

At one point Carey gasped to Patty, "I'm not going to be able to carry a thing down that damn cliff, after this. I swear my arms are coming off."

The wounds on her hands had opened yet again, in spite of the heavy fishing gloves.

Slowly, the raft bumped down the cliff.

The dark shape jerked downward to the beach, until it finally bumped to a stop, with its front end resting on the sand

and its rear caught on an overhang which jutted out six feet above the beach.

The four women scrambled down the cliff. Together, they finally heaved the raft onto the sand. Their sweating faces were rapturously happy.

"Last dip in the waterfall pool," gasped Jonathan, "then we load her up."

The cool water refreshed them, and in their dripping rags they climbed the path back to the camp.

Annie directed the stream of supplies to the top of the cliff, where they were bundled in mosquito netting and carried down to the beach. Silvana doused both the fires and checked that the camp had been cleared.

With all food, water and supplies at the clifftop, Patty and Jonathan carried the ship's ladder and the black rubber tire down the cliff to the beach, then Jonathan lashed both to the center of the raft. The partitions formed by the ladder rungs and the center of the tire held the food and containers in place. The bamboo paddles were tied to the ladder, and so was all other equipment; each of the passengers who were to sit on either side of the ladder would be similarly lashed to it. The lighter women were to paddle at the front of the raft, while Jonathan and Carey would kneel to paddle at the rear. In order to avoid tripping over the ropes or falling over the side, movement on the raft was to be restricted to the minimum. If anyone complained of discomfort, she could get out and walk.

Jonathan directed the loading of the raft. "Just keep going for a bit longer, lads," he said encouragingly, as the women staggered down to him with the supplies and equipment.

They had just finished loading when the sudden tropical darkness fell. The women flopped onto the sand, too tired to feel hungry. Nobody spoke.

As they lay exhausted, waiting for the tide to rise, Jonathan —yet again—checked the raft design in his mind. How high would she ride in the water? That was what worried him. And how steady would she ride?

Just after sunset, the tide reached its full ebb and the sea started to creep up the beach. Around midnight, the tide would again turn and, with luck, sweep them out to sea. They all knew that the most dangerous part of their journey would be during the first twenty minutes, when, in the moonlight, they would either surge through the narrow channel in the coral reef or be dashed against the jagged banks and ripped apart.

Jonathan handed around slices of dried fish and some water, then said, "I want you all to take your places on the raft. We've got a few hours to sit here, before the tide lifts us off. I want you to get on the raft now and behave as if we was already at sea. Get used to having no space, get used to being careful, so you don't knock anything overboard. Get used to taking a pee without moving, get used to the idea that the raft ain't rigid."

"But what about those crossbeams?" Carey asked.

"Once we're in the water, all the logs will move a bit." It was impossible to bind the logs rigid to each other, and you wouldn't want to do it because then the raft would break up faster. Jonathan didn't know how long the thing would last; he hadn't mentioned this, because he hadn't wanted to alarm the women. He was taking the risk that they'd get to Irian Jaya before the thing disintegrated.

The women sat on the raft, feeling cramped and tired, but tense with excitement and expectation.

The moon rose.

Slowly the sea crept up the beach.

The water reached the base of the raft, sighed and withdrew.

Jonathan said, "Patty, go and bring Suzy down out of that tree. She won't want to miss the trip."

By the time Suzy and Patty had clambered aboard, the front of the raft was two inches underwater.

The women were too excited to talk. Annie and Silvana were silently praying for a safe voyage. Jonathan was worrying about the possible necessity of fast weight redistribution once she had lifted off the sand.

Quietly, the black water surrounded the raft.

Excitement mounted as they waited to lift off. Although they were clearly visible, somehow they all felt that, at this moment, they were protected by destiny. And Jonathan had the M-16 in his hands. Once they were headed for the gap in the reef, it would be Annie's job to look after the rifle, because Jonathan would have to give his whole attention to the raft.

Three birds, swift black shadows, flew across the pale moon. The sea was an endless lake of silver. The moon threw elongated shadows of the raft and its occupants across the gleaming, scimitar curve of the beach. Behind them, the cliff was a silver wall, down which the silver waterfall plunged. At the clifftop, the palm trees formed a pattern of silver and black stripes, their tips waving like feather dusters.

Over the splashing roar of the waterfall and the surf now surging gently behind them, Suzy called in a clear, excited whisper, "Jonathan, my ass is underwater, and so are my feet."

"Don't worry," he whispered back. "We may get swamped at the front, until she lifts off at the rear."

Nobody said anything. Slowly, they all found themselves sitting in water.

Jonathan said, "Maybe we should get off, give her a chance to float." He sounded worried.

They all scrambled off the raft and stood, calf-deep in the water, their sneakers sinking into the submerged sand.

Jonathan said, "Maybe she's stuck on something. Give her a shove, careful like."

They all tried to push the raft forward into the sea, but without success. It might as well have been anchored in cement.

Stunned, the little group watched as, in the silver moonlight, the raft slowly disappeared underwater.

The sea started to lap at their equipment.

"This goddamned raft *won't float!*" Suzy cried.

Carey turned to Jonathan. "I suppose you did *check* that palm trees float, Jonathan?"

The small group wearily unlashed, or cut free, their equipment and dragged it from the now waterlogged raft to the dusty, dry vegetation at the back of the beach, where the tide never normally reached.

In the moonlight, they sat down and wept.

Through her tears, Annie thought, This is the worst part so far. We shouldn't have allowed ourselves to hope—that was our mistake. On the other hand, it had been hope that had kept them going for the past few days, as they toiled beneath the burning sun with more strength and endurance than they had thought possible.

Eventually Jonathan said, "Can't sit here all night. Let's get back to camp."

In a fury, Suzy cried, "I *can* sit here all night. There's not much difference between being eaten alive down here by ants and mosquitoes or up there. And why *should* we do what you say, any longer? *You* pretended to know everything. *You* got us into this mess, Mr. Big-Mouth Philosopher."

The other women joined in a weeping, disappointed chorus.

Several times Jonathan said he was sorry, but their pain, exhaustion and disappointment flared up in recrimination.

Finally he burst out, "I did the best I could! If I hadn't blown up my boat, you lot probably wouldn't be alive. None of *you* had any ideas. Just because I'm the only man around, you expect me to know everything, take all responsibility for you and be blamed by you for every damned thing that goes wrong!"

He scrambled to his feet. "I tell you, I'm fed up with playing the father. One of *you* lot can have a go at it, see how *you* like it!"

Angrily he looked at the weeping women. "I'm resigning— as of now! Consider yourselves divorced. I'm off!" He looked briefly at the spot where the sea had slid smoothly over the raft, then he turned his back on it and stomped down the beach.

Carey sat up. "He might really mean it. Go after him, Patty. He's got a soft spot for you. God knows what'll happen to us without him."

"I'm damned if I'm going after him," wept Patty. "*He* got us into this mess!"

Annie scrambled to her feet and ran after Jonathan. The gritty sand filled her sneakers as she scurried along the beach. By the time she caught up with him, he had nearly reached the end of the sand, but was unable to go any farther because it was high tide and there were sheer black cliffs ahead of him.

As Annie caught up with him, she could sense his depression and humiliation, sense that his spirit and energy had drained away. She laid a placatory hand on the hard muscles of his arm. "*Please*, Jonathan, don't be angry. We *do* appreciate you. And we need you."

"That's for sure. But I don't need *you*," he growled. "If I hadn't been stuck with a bunch of Sheilas, I could've worked my way round the coast to Queenstown, maybe jumped a boat by now. I know I'd'a got off this place somehow—if I'd had only meself to think about."

Annie said, "We all know that."

"*I* didn't ask you lot to set me up as Superman. *You* did that! I didn't *ever* pretend to be anything I ain't. I'm just an ordinary seaman. I thought all wood floated—didn't you? Course you did—and so did all of 'em, otherwise someone would'a said something before now."

"They're disappointed, you see."

"Do you think I *ain't* disappointed? *I'm* the one that had the worry, as well as the work. But *I'm* not sitting on the sand and howling like a baby."

"What do you want us to do, Jonathan?"

"I ain't going to fall for *that* again. Superman has just resigned. It's someone else's turn. You'd better decide which one of you lot wants to be Superwoman. Then *she* can do the thinking and the figuring and the planning, and you can kick *her* when things go wrong."

"Oh, dear. Do you think Patty . . . ?"

"Patty's impatience could get you in a lot of trouble."

"How about Carey?"

"My advice is don't pin your hopes on one person, then blame that person if she's wrong, because it ain't fair." Jonathan grunted, "But sure, Carey will do. She's practical—*she* can see what it's like. *She* can take over, do the fishing, wipe your asses and blow your noses, she can do *the lot!* I'm off!"

"You did better than any of us could ever have done, Jonathan, and we all know that."

They had reached the end of the beach. In silence, they turned and headed back toward the distant, mournful little group in the shadows at the back of the beach.

Jonathan muttered, "I was raised in Brisbane . . . only been here eighteen months. Picked up a bit about this island, but I ain't no Robinson Crusoe. I ain't a walking, talking *Boys' Own Encyclopedia*. I try to keep things simple, and a lot of the time I just have to . . . guess."

Annie said, "And you guessed right, most of the time."

As Annie and Jonathan drew level with the huddled group at the back of the beach, the other women jumped up and ran toward them. Silvana threw her arms around Jonathan's neck, Carey hugged both Silvana and Jonathan, Suzy hopped up and down on the sand and whispered, "I'm sorry, I'm sorry."

Patty said softly, "We couldn't manage without you, Jonathan. We all know that."

SUNDAY, NOVEMBER 25

By eleven o'clock that morning they had hauled all their possessions up the cliff, set up camp again and buried the heavy raft. After that, too exhausted to speak, they ate some dried fish and drank water from the bamboo containers.

Annie said, "We'd better sleep for a few hours, then we'll have self-defense practice. Remember, you said you'd show us how to use a garotte, Jonathan?"

Jonathan thought, Clever little Annie, she knows just how to get me back and leading the team. Only he could teach them how to kill.

Using a yard of wire from the toolbox—it was about as thick as piano wire—Jonathan tied each end around a wooden toggle about the width of a thumb and five inches long; the toggles were to provide handgrips.

He looked at the women. "Ready? This takes ten seconds and it's a silent method. If he ain't heard you creeping up behind him, he'll never say another word. Only thing you must remember is to cross your arms before you reach him to make the wire a circle."

As he spoke, he demonstrated on Patty. "Creep up behind him, with your arms crossed and your elbows touching each other. On the count of one, you slip the wire circle over his head. On the count of two, you pull your arms apart as far as you can." He added, "This isn't a method for someone small, like Suzy, unless the enemy is small too—or he's sitting down."

After garotte practice, Annie suggested, "Let's gather some wood and see what floats."

A thunderous silence followed her words. Annie ignored it. "Let's see what we can bring back in half an hour," she said.

Jonathan stayed in the hut. He was damned if he was going to have the responsibility of picking the wood this time.

In the stream behind their camp, the women experimented with different woods. "Bamboo is easily the best," Carey said. As they squatted on the bank of the stream and watched their trial branches bobbing downstream, Jonathan said from behind them, "I've seen natives use small bamboo rafts to get down a river." He seemed to be over his fit of anger, as if the prospect of starting a new raft had revived his spirits. "The things are about two feet wide by nine feet long, and they lash 'em together with jungle vines. I thought bamboo was too flimsy for a big raft. I thought our weight would sink the thing, but let's try a quick experimental lash up. Nothing seaworthy, just to see if she floats."

"Why don't we use one of our beds?" Carey suggested.

Impatiently, they waited for night to fall. When they were swimming in the lagoon and the lookout cried a warning, they could quickly hide at the back of the beach or in the cave, but they could hardly disguise a daylight raft-launching operation.

Just before dark, they hurried down to the beach. Using the flashlight for illumination, Jonathan tied a crosspole at either end of Carey's six-by-three bamboo bed, then they all waded into the waterfall current, where there were never any stonefish.

While the other women held the raft steady, Jonathan lifted Annie onto it and handed her one of the paddles. Annie was almost as light as Suzy, and she was a far better swimmer.

Annie called, "Okay, let her go."

Anxiously, the other women watched as Annie floated off, carried by the current.

There was quiet glee on the moonlit beach, which, only twenty-four hours earlier, had been the scene of their despair.

Annie quickly managed to control the light raft and paddled toward the south of the beach. Except for Suzy, who was up the lookout tree, the rest of the party moved along the beach, keeping up with the raft, until Annie paddled into the shore.

Jonathan said, "Now for the big test. Me."

The women held the floating bamboo bed, as he scrambled on.

"Don't expect to stay dry," Annie warned.

Ten minutes later Jonathan brought the raft back to the shore. Again he set off, this time with Annie behind him. They had to position themselves carefully, and every time either one of them moved, water sloshed over the bamboo poles, but it stayed afloat.

For the next hour the little group practiced maneuvering the raft around the bay, until Jonathan was satisfied that they should build their next raft of bamboo.

"Do you all agree?" he demanded. "I ain't going to make this decision by myself."

The women nodded excitedly, then dragged Carey's bed back up the cliff.

MONDAY, NOVEMBER 26

The next morning, they all woke at dawn, with renewed enthusiasm, undiminished by the fact that Patty returned from a fishing trip with no fish and only three baby crabs.

Carey stayed to fish for an extra hour, but didn't get a single bite.

So Patty went to check Jonathan's freshwater fish trap. It was her job to check these lines every morning and evening.

But the underwater trap was empty, and the lines at the side of the river were not bending toward the water.

"Sometimes," said Jonathan, "no matter how you figure it, the fish just don't bite."

"We'll have to eat the raft supplies today," Annie said. "We had enough raft supplies to last for five days, but we've been eating them for two days."

"It's a pity I've never been any good with a fish spear," Jonathan said. "If we catch no fish tomorrow, I'll go after a rabbit. Now let's get started on the new raft."

The following morning Patty checked the fish trap and lines, which were again disappointingly empty.

Jonathan sharpened the machete on a rock near the waterfall. Then he took a sharp piece of rock in his hand and carefully nicked the blade of the machete to make a crude saw. One person could use it, two-handed.

Jonathan tried it out on a bamboo log and nodded with satisfaction.

When Carey tried the saw, he jumped forward in alarm.

359

"No! Push it *away* from you, Carey. Otherwise you might slip and saw your belly open."

Annie trimmed the lengths of bamboo and dragged the logs to the raft-building site. Patty collected vines; Silvana gathered damit. Suzy switched jobs with whoever was due on guard.

They always cut just below the bamboo joints, where the bamboo wasn't hollow, so that each log would be sealed for most of its length. For each usable log they had three or four that splintered. But with practice they improved.

By midday, when they stopped work, Jonathan was pleased with their progress. He said, "I've had another idea. We can lash two bits of bamboo together to act as a rudder. It will be like a rough paddle, and we'll lash it centrally aft. Then we'll have a bit of lateral stability."

"How will that help?" Suzy asked.

"Nobody paddles at the same rate, and we don't want to find ourselves going around in circles."

While they were resting, after a meager lunch of dried fish, they heard a low-flying aircraft approach. Immediately on the alert, everyone peered upward, although they could see nothing above the green umbrella-spread of the treetops.

Jonathan shook his head. "You all know we can't risk it. It's playing Russian roulette to wave at that plane. Remember, with any luck, we'll be off here in a couple of days." Seeing their unspoken disappointment and Suzy's brimming eyes, he said, "Back to work, lads! *Work!*" Work always helped you to forget, work never let you down and it was only work that was going to get them out of this place. They'd had no combat practice this morning; he'd get them back at work as soon as possible.

He calculated the odds once again. Today was November 27. If they finished the raft in time to embark tomorrow night, they'd have three nights and two days to cover seventy-odd miles of sea before the cyclone season started on December 1. The cyclone season started in the afternoon and was never late. He knew that he would be taking a great risk going to sea so near the Long Wet, but once it started, the Long Wet wouldn't break until March. Apart from the terrorists and the natives, the jungle would be a sinister health hazard during those three wet months. It was surprising that nobody had yet been taken seriously ill, apart from diarrhea, Carey's hands, insect bites, scratches. For instance, no sores had yet become dangerously infected. Annie had warned everyone not to scratch, and she bathed all sores morning and evening with boiled seawater. The antiseptic cream had been finished long ago.

Better get back to work, he told himself. He stood up slowly, then blinked in surprise. The strength seemed to have ebbed from his legs, and they trembled.

He sat down. He definitely felt a headache coming. There is no such thing as anti-malaria immunization, and none of them had taken their daily, anti-malaria tablets since November 13. From what seemed a great distance, he heard Annie's anxious voice. "Are you all right, Jonathan?"

His head was suddenly too heavy to lift. "No." He spoke with difficulty. "Take the equipment away from the lean-to and put me in there. Get Carey. I want to speak to her."

Hurriedly, Silvana and Suzy dragged the equipment from under the canvas, which had been removed from the palm-log raft before they buried it.

With his arms around their shoulders, Patty and Carey helped Jonathan to the lean-to; they laid him on a bed of leaves, which they had covered with fishing shirts. Annie felt his burning forehead and guessed at his temperature, for the thermometer in the first-aid kit had long been broken. She reckoned that it was 103 degrees.

Annie thought, Plenty of liquids, lots of salt, make some thick fish soup and keep feeding it to him in small amounts. That was all she could think of. Didn't you turn yellow and shake if you had malaria? Was it like measles or chicken-pox? Could you catch it from other people? No, the right sort of female mosquito had to bite you personally. Why the hell hadn't anyone put a manual in the first-aid box? She sponged

Jonathan's sweating face and chest and held a cup of water to his lips.

Carey squatted by Jonathan's head. He spoke slowly and thickly, as if drunk. "Somebody gotta be in charge, make decisions . . . Check the lookout . . . No carelessness . . . You're in charge, Carey . . . Go ahead . . ." He was silent, then with great effort he spat out the words. *"Finish the raft!"*

Jonathan's skin was wax-pale and glistened with sweat. He shivered violently and talked nonsense in his delirium.

Annie refused to leave him, so she took on all the camp duties while the others sweated over the raft. They figured it would take one more day to assemble the new bamboo raft, which was far lighter and easier to build than their first one.

This time, they couldn't use the canvas awning as a base, because it wasn't long enough, so they were going to keep the canvas folded on deck, and perhaps soak it in the seawater, to use as a shelter from the sun. The ladder would be discarded too—it was too heavy for this raft.

In the late afternoon, as Annie crouched by the campfire melting the damit, Silvana came up to her. "Jonathan must eat something more sustaining than smoked fish dunked in water. If Patty can't catch any fish, she had better try to shoot a rat. *Don't* look like that, Annie. I've often served you rat stew, and you've loved it. Jonathan's our navigator and the raft's no good without him, so we've got to keep him alive. That's our priority."

For the first time since they had known her, Silvana's voice had a crisp, sure ring of authority. Nobody dared complain at having been served rat stew.

It was Carey's turn to be lookout, so Suzy and Patty, armed with knives, slings and the ax, unwillingly set out to look for a rat to kill. They had become accustomed to seeing rats around and to slinging stones at them if they came into the camp.

Now, suddenly, there didn't seem to be a rat in sight.

They moved inland, parallel to the waterfall river, so that they would be guided back by the noise, and were less likely to lose their way.

Rats move fast. While Patty thought she *might* be able to hit a large, slow man with a gun, she decided it would be a waste of ammunition to shoot at a moving rat, and the shot might be heard. The two women had decided that their best chance of getting a rat was to stun it by stoning it, then club it to death. They were not looking forward to the task.

Slowly the two women moved through the still and silent jungle, the sound of their feet absorbed by the decaying vegetation.

"I wish we were sure of the boundary lines of the taboo area," Patty said nervously.

"We're safe on the river side until we get to William Penn," Suzy reassured Patty. "And we won't move to the south, where we're not sure of the boundary."

The women had named landmarks in the taboo area—which seemed to be the triangle formed by the river, the path and the beach—with names from Pittsburgh. The waterfall river was called the Allegheny; the path that led from the Burma bridge had been christened William Penn Place. They liked to think that they were safe in this Golden Triangle.

Suzy searched to the right, while Patty searched to the left. Suzy whispered crossly, "They practically hold *conferences* in our camp at night, but when we want one, there isn't a damned rat in sight."

Suddenly Suzy froze and put a restraining hand on Patty's arm.

In front of them, grazing the forest, was a small, dirty gray animal.

Suzy whispered, "We're in luck. That's the hotel's pet goat. See the red collar? How the hell did it get this side of the river?"

Patty stood rigid. "I can't," she said.

"You catch fish every evening," Suzy whispered. "What's the difference between killing fish and killing this thing? We'll maybe get thirty meals off that goat—it'll feed us for days. And it'll be easier to kill than a rat, because it's tame. . . ."

Patty, it's your *job*, you're our goddamned hunter. Think of Jonathan."

Slowly the goat started to move.

Suzy pulled her fish knife from her belt. "All right, you bitch, I'll do it."

Patty gulped and said, "We can't risk losing it. You move around to its rear. When I whistle, we'll both move forward. We'll both go for the collar, and whoever catches it will have to hang on while the other one whacks it."

Suzy moved in a wide semicircle to the rear of the kid, which continued to graze quietly, moving only inches from the spot where they had first seen it.

The goat stopped nibbling and lifted its head. It saw Patty, jerked back and slowly retreated from her. But by that time Suzy was only two feet behind it. She threw herself forward, her eyes fixed on the red collar, her hands grabbing for it.

The kid bleated, the bell on the collar tinkled and Suzy swore as she found herself grappling on the ground with the terrified animal. She yelled, "Hurry up, Patty!"

Patty picked up a stone and smashed it against the goat's forehead. It seemed to have no effect. The kid continued to struggle.

"Again!" Suzy yelled.

Feeling sick, Patty hit the animal and heard bone crunch beneath the stone. The kid staggered, fell, then tried to scramble to its feet again.

"Quick," gasped Suzy, "slit its throat." She pulled the kid's head back by its little silky ears.

Patty stabbed it on the left hand side of its chest, in the heart. The terrified animal made a piteous noise as it struggled.

Slowly, the goat's cries grew fainter, then stopped.

Patty threw up.

"Not over the goat!" Suzy cried.

Trembling, Patty asked, "Is it really dead, Suzy? Are you sure? It was so helpless."

Over the bloody carcass, the two women looked at each other. Patty was white and shaking, and couldn't speak.

Firmly Suzy said, "Thank God we've got something to eat We'll take turns dragging it back to camp."

Silvana quickly skinned the goat. She knew that if they didn't cook it immediately, it would be rotten within twenty four hours. While Annie boiled the bones in water to make a broth, Silvana cut the meat into chunks, skewered it onto twigs and dried it over the fire, barbecue style; the trick was to dry and harden the meat without shriveling it.

It took Silvana and Annie two hours to butcher and cook the goat. Slowly, the enticing aroma of meat filled the camp clearing.

◀ 16 ▶

TUESDAY, NOVEMBER 27, 1984

Through the clear plastic canopy of the Duck, Harry gazed
down at the feathery greens of the forest far below.

"Queenstown ahead to port," Johno called back. From
above, where you couldn't see the cracks in the concrete and
couldn't smell the stink of the streets, the reeking river or the
swirling filth in the harbor, Queenstown looked like a charming little toy town. The small port, with its modern jetty, had
grown around the natural inlet of the St. Mary River, which
breaks through the hills from the west. The hills form a protective amphitheater around the harbor. Once covered by a
sandalwood forest, they are now obscured by rising rows of
small white buildings, broken by a few dusty palm trees, the
gray spire of St. Mary's Catholic Cathedral and the green
dome of the Buddhist temple on the north shore. On either
side of the stone breakwaters that slant across the harbor entrance, the lace-edged, turquoise sea snakes up and down the
coast.

Harry was sick of the view. For the past eleven days, he had
searched the island fruitlessly.

Colonel Borda, the huge, silent islander who had been appointed director of the search-and-rescue operation, was
quick-witted and efficient. The coastline search, both north
and south of Paradise Bay, had been conducted by troops sta-

tioned at the Paradise Bay Hotel. The inshore area had been searched by a coastal patrol vessel and two police launches, while a helicopter had spent a day dipping over the offshore water. Divers had been sent down at the spot where the explosion had been reported. They had come up with an astonishingly large heap of waterlogged rubbish, much of it identifiable as the remains of the *Louise*, but without a trace of the bodies.

When Harry suggested to Kerry that they conduct their own inland search using local Nexus personnel, Kerry refused. Given the unsettled political situation, he wouldn't send his men out without official protection. Territorial rights were fiercely controlled, Kerry pointed out, and he didn't want his men eaten. It would be quicker and easier, and promise far more likelihood of success, to offer a reward for information, to tempt the soldiers on Raki's "goodwill missions" sent to villages all over the island, but this had been forbidden. Kerry had to admit that he saw the logic of this from the official point of view, which was that in a country trying to start a tourist industry, it would be a bad precedent to offer a large sum of money for missing tourists, dead or alive, even if the small print clearly stated that this offer only applied to Nexus executives, and was only open for a limited period. A reward would be tantamount to declaring an open head-hunting season on whites.

It had been made clear by General Raki that he did not welcome the presence of foreign search aircraft, however peaceable their motives. Only Nexus aircraft already on the island had been allowed to search—which meant the Duck and the Bell 206. The helicopter had a good view; sitting in that big transparent bubble, Harry could see straight down, so it was the best aircraft for low-level searching.

Harry's search party had first covered a hundred-mile square, centered on the Paradise Bay Hotel, after which they had flown over the coastline of the entire island, a distance of 554 miles. For two days, the Duck in the north and the Bell in the south followed the undulations of the shoreline, droning over the offshore coral reefs, the sandy beaches and lagoons, the rocky headlands and muddy estuaries, the salt marshes and the mangrove swamps that had been such obstacles to the Allied landings during World War II.

After the coastline search proved fruitless, they searched the lowland area, droning steadily over the savannahs and swamps, the slopes of the Victoria Highlands, Stanley Heights, and the cloud-encircled peaks of the Central Mountains, which are Paui's highest mountain range. They searched only along rivers and lakes, or over open areas. A jungle search from the air was pointless.

After the first half-hour of the day, Harry always had a hard job keeping his eyes focused on the scenery below him. Boredom combined with concentration and frustration to exhaust him. He was short-tempered and tried to say as little as possible to the irritatingly cheerful Johno. By the end of the eleventh search day, their conversation consisted almost entirely of grunts.

On the evening of Monday, November 26, by which time the international ten-day air search convention had been fully complied with, the official government search for the missing Nexus party was called off, as briskly as it had been started.

Harry knew that when the cyclone season hit, he would have to stop his own search, but he still had three days before December 1. He reasoned that fourteen days was statistically a reasonable amount of time to search for a large party. After all, Paui was not the Bermuda Triangle, where aircraft vanished without explanation or trace. Sooner, or later, some evidence would appear, a clue to the fate of the Nexus party.

It was just a question of going on until that clue turned up. . . .

In his sweat-soaked clothes, Harry climbed wearily up the wooden steps of the veranda of the Hotel Independence; he brushed away the mosquitoes that swarmed in the yellow stream of light outside the glass-paned front door. He could hear Mrs. Chang's shrill voice on the telephone.

Harry said, "Good evening," and headed for his room, but Mrs. Chang's jade-green, satin-clad arm reached out and tugged at his sleeve. "Hang on a tick, Mr. Scott," she said.

She put the telephone back in its ivory cradle and said, "I have your new watch, Mr. Scott."

The day after Harry's watch had been "liberated," Mrs. Chang had found a replacement watch, with expanding metallic bracelet, ten percent surcharge, but it had gone bugger-upem eight days later, and not even Ronald Chang had been able to repair it, so Harry had asked for a replacement or his money back.

Mrs. Chang leaned forward and dug deep into her jade satin pocket. "You want to watch that sore place on your upper lip, Mr. Scott. I will send Freddy up to your bedroom with antiseptic ointment, medical care fifteen percent extra." She pulled her hand from her pocket and said triumphantly, "You will never find a better watch than this one."

Harry stared at the gold watch in her plump palm. He snatched it up and turned it over. There was no inscription, but Harry had often seen that slim, gold circle and whenever his mind wandered at meetings, he had idly watched the tiny celestial-blue window, crossed monthly by the miniature man-in-the-moon within. It was, unmistakably, Arthur Graham's twenty-five-thousand-dollar, fully automatic, perpetual calendar, gold Breguet watch with the Turkish triple-dial face and the gold-link strap—the almost-one-of-a-kind present his mother had given him, and which he never took off.

"Where did you get this, Mrs. Chang?"

"It was brought to the shop by a street trader. It cost my Ronald two Raleigh bicycles, reconditioned but almost new—a small price for such a watch."

"I'll pay you a hundred Australian dollars to speak to the man who sold you that watch."

"Exclusive of the price of the watch? It is a timepiece of rare quality."

"Get Ron here fast, Mrs. Chang."

The watch was in perfect condition. It didn't look as if it

had done time in a shark's belly. Could Arthur's watch have been stolen by a hotel servant before the trouble started? Perhaps from a bathroom shelf? But Arthur never took it off. As he waited impatiently for Ronald Chang he thought, At least it will be easy to identify. The manufacturer's serial number will be engraved inside, so the jeweler from whom it had been purchased could be located. With any luck, their records would show the customer who had bought the watch.

Harry did not even consider telling the Paui police about the watch. As it was evidence, they would confiscate it, which meant—in this land of the light-fingered and incompetent—it would inevitably disappear again, this time for good. Details would be laboriously recorded on some stock form in triplicate; it would cost Harry time and cigarettes to get nowhere, and make him even more unpopular with the police, who not only hated interference but also hated work of any sort. They took it as a direct insult.

Ronald Chang hurried in, torn away from his evening meal, the napkin still tucked in the open-necked collar of his pale green polyester shirt. He told Harry that the street trader who had sold him the watch had bought it from a soldier—one of the new ones, a Filipino. The soldier took ninety *kinas* for the watch.

Nicely recompensed for his trouble, Ronald sauntered back to his dinner. Harry unwrapped his waterproof money belt, which *he* never removed, not even in the shower, carefully tucked Arthur's watch in it and strapped it back around his waist.

Whoever sold that watch to Ronald Chang knew what had happened to Arthur, and perhaps what had happened to Annie and the others as well.

"He shouldn't be moved", Annie said firmly. "He might die

17

WEDNESDAY, NOVEMBER 28, 1984

Patty hadn't been able to eat any of the goat meat the previous
evening. Now she refused to eat it at breakfast. "I couldn't eat
something I knew when it was alive," she said.

Annie, who was preparing broth for Jonathan, remarked,
"You eat the fish you catch."

Patty thought a moment, then said, "Fish are different. You
can't see the death agony, because it goes on underwater. And
when you land a fish, you're so excited that you caught it, that
you never give a thought to the fish, with its torn insides,
gasping as it dies."

Silvana said crossly, "I worked for two hours to cook that
goat. You *need* to eat to work properly."

Carey said, "The work's done. We should finish the raft by
lunchtime."

Once again, the argument started.

"We should get off here as fast as possible. *This evening!*"
Suzy urged.

"Jonathan told us we had to be gone by the twenty-eighth,
at the latest," Carey agreed. "And that's today."

"Jonathan's got a temperature of a hundred and three degrees, and he can't be moved," Annie said firmly. "I don't

371

think it's malaria, but it's certainly a fever, and he's improving. Can't we wait just a *little* longer?"

"He told me to go ahead with the plan," Carey insisted, "and I'm going. We could take him with us. We could tie him on the deck. Maybe we could get him to a hospital within a couple of days—if we leave."

"He shouldn't be moved," Annie said firmly. "He might die of exposure."

"We'll shelter him with the canvas awning," Carey suggested. She looked around the group squatting in the firelight and said firmly, "I'm taking him to safety, along with anyone else who wants to come. Anyone who wants to stay can rot here."

They all knew that if they didn't leave the island by evening, they had no chance of reaching Irian Jaya before the cyclone season started.

"Supposing the Long Wet is late?" Patty asked.

"Suppose it *isn't*—and the raft is swamped by high seas?" Carey replied.

Silvana said, "It's crazy to think that we can survive on that raft while Jonathan is ill. We know nothing about navigation, and less about the sea."

Endlessly, they went over the arguments for and against leaving the island, until it was eventually agreed they should finish the raft, then decide by casting votes.

Well ahead of schedule—just before midday—the last length of plaited vine was lashed around the crossbeams. Sweating but triumphant, the women stood back and looked at the raft, almost with awe—they couldn't believe that they had made this huge thing, or that it was finally finished.

Patty burst into tears. "We did it!"

"Let's *go!*" Carey cried, and swung Suzy around, both laughing with delight.

Silvana ran to tell Annie, who was up in the lookout tree. Annie, ever stubborn, called down, "I'm going to stay here with Jonathan. You can send a rescue plane for us when you land."

Both women knew she meant *if* you land.

Silvana called up, "I'm not leaving, either, until Jonathan is well enough to take charge of the raft."

They argued throughout the midday meal, and later, as they rested in the shade. Suddenly, after days of toil, they had nothing to do until just before sundown. They could rest, they could swim, they could quarrel. Nobody suggested taking the vote they had previously decided upon.

Carey and Suzy lay in the shadow of the eucalyptus tree, arguing with Patty, who couldn't decide whether she wanted to stay with Silvana and Annie or leave with Carey and Suzy. Although the sky was cloudy, the heat was grueling, and there hadn't been a breath of wind in days. The trees were silent.

Carey said, "You know we'd have far more chance with three of us than with two. And we'll have enough provisions to feed six."

"I just can't make up my mind," Patty said unhappily.

"We'll be leaving in order to save the others, as well as ourselves," Suzy reminded her.

Suddenly Patty lifted her head. "Listen! Something's different. Something's odd."

Suzy said, "I can't hear anything except the cicadas."

"That's what I mean," Patty said. "It's only two o'clock, and they don't normally start singing until half an hour before sundown."

Suzy said, "So they're playing a matinee, instead of waiting until five thirty. Why don't we simply vote now whether we leave or not?"

"Because only two of us want to leave. We'd lose if we vote," Carey said. "But I don't give a damn. *I'm* getting out of here as fast as possible. Even if I have to go alone."

"I'm coming with you," Suzy said firmly. "And we should vote by four thirty at the latest. That will only leave us an hour and a half before sundown to lower the raft and load it."

Patty said, "I don't . . . Hell, I *can't* decide! We don't know what to do if we go to sea."

"Jonathan *told* us what to do," Carey said. "We have to paddle a couple of miles to the west, until we hit the current. We're almost on the southern tip of Paui, so we should be carried beyond it, then taken around the headland to the east, toward Pulau yos Sudarsa on Irian Jaya."

Patty frowned as she looked into the jungle behind her. "I can't understand why the cicadas are making such a racket."

Carey continued, "When we see land, we paddle like hell toward it. Sure, we don't understand Jonathan's charts, but it doesn't much matter."

Patty half-turned and again peered into the trees. "There's something odd about the jungle."

"Finally it feels cooler," Suzy said. "That's all. You'd better get back up the lookout tree."

Patty said, "You guys get some rest. If you leave, you'll need it."

Both the other women noticed that she didn't say *"We'll* need it."

Since Jonathan's illness, the women had been increasingly lax about posting a guard at all times. It wasn't as if they'd always been able to have a guard when Jonathan was in charge, they argued. Somehow, they now felt safe in their camp. They knew every inch of it. It felt comforting.

As Patty swung up into the tree, the jungle started to come alive with the noise of insects. This hadn't happened since the women had been on the island; usually it was quiet during the day, especially during the torpid midday heat. Perched in the tree, Patty gratefully offered her face to a faint breath of wind that had started to blow from the sea. She wondered what it was that worried her.

By three thirty that afternoon the wind was blowing hard. Except for Patty, the exhausted women were asleep.

They all knew that after sunset it would be too late to leave the island, and they would be stuck on it for the next three months.

Annie woke up, rubbed her eyes and pattered to a small clearing in the forest, where she liked to pray. Silvana and Suzy awoke and decided to dip in the waterfall pool. Patty yawned, then crawled into the lean-to and bathed Jonathan's chest and face with cool water, wishing she knew the difference between courage and rashness.

The sky turned from white to gray, then an ominous silver-purple. The water of the bay shivered, the trees rustled, the wind blew harder.

Silvana, who had pulled herself out of the water and was sitting on the wet rocks, squinted up at the sky. "You don't think that maybe . . . ?"

A drop of water fell on her face and she wiped it off. Three drops spattered on the back of her hand. Silvana looked at the cloudy sky above, then at the lagoon. The water was a soft, milky-green color. Then, before her eyes, the surface changed to a pattern of tiny, tight waves. The entire bay seemed to tremble, then go dead flat.

Silvana heard a hiss that grew louder and louder, and a mist seemed to rise from the sea. Water suddenly fell from the skies, as if from an upturned bucket.

For a moment Silvana couldn't think, she was drenched and numbed. She shouted, "Get out of the water, Suzy. It's the Long Wet. It's arrived early."

In the pool, Suzy tried to call up to Silvana, but the noise of the rain was too great for her to be heard. The force of the water was as if they were standing in the way of a fireman's hose. They could only gasp for breath.

Protecting her face with one arm, Silvana, in her bedraggled black lace bra and torn panties, pulled the naked Suzy from the pool. They snatched up their clothes and sneakers, because the rain was slamming down far too hard for them to stop and dress.

Together, the two women clambered up the cliff path, which had suddenly become a sliding sea of mud. They slithered, they slipped and they fell, but eventually they reached the summit. Silvana turned her head seaward. She couldn't see the ocean, neither could she see the beach below. The view had disappeared.

Soaking wet and covered with mud, battling against the wind, the two women staggered into the hut.

Patty, who had almost been blown from the lookout tree, greeted them with a shriek. "I guess that's one decision less to make."

BOOK FOUR

SURVIVAL

18

WEDNESDAY, DECEMBER 5, 1984

It had been seven days since the Long Wet started.

"Now you look like a baby Grace Jones. These scissors need sharpening." In the sleeping hut, Annie finished Suzy's crew cut, then stood back and looked at her.

"Guaranteed lice- and flea-proof!" Annie said.

"Any progress with the soap?" Suzy asked hopefully. Soap was the only thing that they really needed and couldn't find in the jungle. They all longed for just one cake of Ivory every time they washed with coconut oil.

"No luck," Annie said.

Suzy laughed. "We're going to be real messes when we get back."

Annie shrugged her shoulders. Under exhausting, stressful conditions, any person can expect to age ten years within twenty-four hours, but Suzy was the only one of the group who still cared how she looked.

From her bamboo bed, Patty peered out at the rain. The hut entrance didn't face the wind that blew off the sea—thanks to Carey's architectural training. "Just as well we didn't float off on the raft," she said. "We'd have been swamped in the first downpour and sunk without trace."

"And just as well Carey did that digging," Annie said, "or we'd have been flooded out of these huts." Carey had deep-

379

ened the right-angled trench that had been cut above and to one side of the hut, in order to channel rainwater away from it.

Because their quarters were so cramped, they had built another A-frame hut in the clearing. It was neater and more securely built than the first hut, and they were all proud that Carey had planned it and they had completed it without Jonathan's supervision. When Jonathan recovered, he would share the second hut with Annie and Carey.

Heat and the moist atmosphere of the jungle resulted in rot and decay. Their huts now smelled of damp and mildew, their possessions were covered with green lines of mold, their clothes yielded even faster to rot than to wear and tear. The knees went first, followed by the seat of the pants, after which the crotch gave way and then the trouser cuffs. Shirts and jackets gave at the elbows, then at the back where they had been brushed by tree branches.

In the week since the cyclone season had started, the women had become accustomed to the pattern of the weather. The mornings were sometimes sunny, but clouds started gathering at midday, when the close air was so oppressive they felt as if the heaviness lay physically upon their shoulders, as they waited for the downpour to start.

The tropical rain always flooded down with a sudden crushing weight, like the battering of the waterfall. During the monsoon storms, it was impossible for the women to do anything but stay in their huts for a couple of hours until the rain stopped, as suddenly as it started.

Clutching the M-16, Silvana ran into the hut. Soaked and shivering, she started to strip. "I'm not going up that lookout tree again in the rain! It almost knocked me off the branch just now."

"So what else is new?" Patty yawned and threw the orange beach towel to Silvana.

Silvana threw aside the towel and flung herself down, weeping as if her heart would break.

Wordlessly, Annie picked up the towel and started to dry Silvana's back.

They all now recognized (and tried to soften) the last-straw blow. This was always some small irritation, something that suddenly made jungle life intolerable and courage snap. Demoralized, they had all cracked in different ways during that first week of December.

Patty had collapsed in tears when the side of her sneaker came off, although Annie immediately offered to bind rattan around it.

Suzy slipped in the mud around the campfire and dropped her evening meal into it. She wept inconsolably, and although the others quickly gave her bits of their fish, she could not stop crying.

When Carey found that a tiny leak in the roof had reduced her bracken pillow to a pile of wet slush, she sat on the ground and howled like a dog, although the other women quickly threw out the slush and shared their bracken with her.

When Annie, with a splitting headache, could no longer scrape a smear out of the empty jar of opium balm, she felt as if she had been abandoned by civilization, and in spite of the rain, she fled to her praying place, threw herself down in the mud and screamed to her God for help.

The women had not been *mentally* prepared for their great disappointment. They had been slammed back into the jungle —and this time, the man on whom they were dependent was unable to guide and encourage them. Like children, they had leaned on and trusted him, but suddenly he had become an added problem, an extra, unwelcome anxiety.

Their frustration and disappointment deepened into depression and the lethargy of despair.

The worst times were the wet afternoons. Overworked and exhausted, the women had fought back their feelings up to now, for they knew that tears were catching, and held up the work. But now, with empty hours to fill, images of the men they had lost, of the children and relatives and friends that they missed so much and might never see again, swirled into their minds. They would lie silently on their bamboo beds, staring up at the dull green elephant's ears of the roof and feeling drained and stunned by grief, as if by a physical blow on the head.

Each woman felt overwhelmed. The least motion took great effort, as if she were underwater and struggling against the tide. And, in her own black pit of desolation and despair, each woman knew regret. Carey's arguments with Ed had always been part of their intimacy, and their amiable quarrels had been no threat to their relationship, but now Carey wished that they hadn't occurred. Silvana regretted every minute that she had not spent with Lorenza as a child, all those luxury holidays when Lorenza had been left alone at home with Nana, because a yacht at Monte Carlo was no place for a young child. Patty wished that she hadn't been so impatient with her mother; she shouldn't have turned up her nose at the geriatric gaiety of Silver City, she should have been glad of *anything* that helped her mother after her dad had died. Now Patty wished——*how* she wished!——that she hadn't been impatient and yelled at her. Suzy swore to herself that if only God would let her off this place, she'd be nicer to Brett; she'd never say no to him again. . . .

Waiting was very hard. They all lay listlessly on their bamboo beds, watching the dripping trees beyond the hut and waiting for the rain to stop. Like prisoners, they counted the weeks, the days, the hours and the minutes until their release, knowing that each week of survival increased their chances of getting back to their families, as they battled against boredom and depression.

Each woman, not only Silvana, now also felt the lack of privacy. Theirs was an odd situation where you longed for solitude but were frightened of being alone, and felt lonely all the time in spite of never being alone.

Trying not to get in each other's way was a constant preoccupation. When steam lifted the lid of the emotional kettle, the frustration and suppressed rage that was the result of their captivity led to bickering and threats from everyone, except Annie, whom Carey crossly called Pollyanna for two days, an irritation in itself.

Carey yelled if anyone banged against her bed. Suzy, who was a light sleeper, yelled at anyone in the night who groped her way out of the hut to go to the latrine. Silvana yelled at anyone who stole food between meals, for this was a hygiene hazard, and she took great care to keep their food clean and ant-free. Patty yelled at anyone who yelled.

On the whole, Carey's practical realism was more helpful in their stressful situation than the gentle remonstration of Annie or the weary passivity of Silvana. Carey was especially useful in keeping Patty and Suzy apart—they both had very short fuses.

Sometimes the antagonism of the group was suddenly directed at only one woman: at Silvana, for having taken the minimum of trouble and making a boring meal; at Carey, for lighting up yet another foul-smelling, rolled-leaf cigarette in the hut; at Suzy, for some childish act of laziness, such as not gathering wood when it was her turn; at Annie, for being so goddamn long-suffering and saintly.

Gradually, except for Patty, they had become less fearful. As the monsoon rain fell relentlessly outside the hut and she sat watching Annie cut Suzy's hair, Patty again felt prickles along her spine. She knew the other women would be irritated if she mentioned it, but she was certain they were being watched. She could feel hidden eyes on her back. She felt shivers at the base of her neck. She suddenly found that her chest was constricted and it was difficult to breathe. . . . No, she *had* to warn them!

In a carefully controlled voice, Patty said, "Carey, I truly am *convinced* that someone is watching us."

Angrily, Carey sat up on her bed. "Why can't you dump this paranoia? We've been here for three weeks, and if anyone was going to attack us, he'd have done so by now. Can't you stop crying wolf?" She brushed the bracken from her hair and added, "Suppose you really *did* hear something? Suzy would just yawn and say, 'It's Patty's goddamn nerves again.' Nobody would take any notice."

"We have enough real problems without your goddamn imaginary ones," Suzy added.

Everyone was damp, depressed and demoralized.

As Annie started to give Patty a crew cut, she wondered aloud, "How do soldiers fighting in the jungle cope with depression and defeatism?"

"Sometimes they don't," Carey said. "I read that in Vietnam some guys just sat down at the side of the road and gave up hope. So they died."

MONDAY, DECEMBER 10

Suzy's long black eyelashes framed twin views of the grape-green water of the lagoon, the churning white line of foam that marked the reef and the grape-purple ocean glittering beyond it in the morning sun.

"Ouch!" she dropped the half-filled bucket of fish, which luckily didn't spill.

"Is it your shoulder again?" Patty asked.

Wincing, Suzy nodded.

Patty said, "You probably pulled a muscle when you stabbed that parrotfish yesterday and fell over. Shall I rub it? That helped it yesterday, didn't it? Let's go into the shade."

Both women walked over the hot, white sand to the back of the beach, where they carefully placed their fishing gear at the base of a palm tree.

Patty stood behind Suzy and gently probed Suzy's shoulder, until again she cried, "Ouch!"

Patty started to rub the shoulder softly, but every time she touched the sensitive area Suzy jumped away.

"Lie down in the shade," Patty suggested. "I'll give you a back rub to relax you before I go over that sore area."

Lying naked on the sand, Suzy started to relax as Patty's sensitive hands softly stroked the tension from her spine. She could hear the soothing sigh of the sea, feel the slight warm breeze and watch the azure sky. For the first time since they had fled into the jungle, Suzy felt fear slip away as Patty's hands, firm but gentle, soothed away her tension. The frightened child within her was comforted by the intimate, physical contact.

Patty looked down at Suzy's slim brown back and thought, It looks like a child's back. Patty was reminded of the many back rubs that she had given her son, Stephen, as she stroked Suzy's soft skin—it felt as delicate and vulnerable as that of a child. Patty was not used to touching another person's skin, other than that of her hard-muscled, hairy husband. Lightly tracing her index finger to the base of Suzy's spine to finish the massage, she suddenly understood how men were attracted by the soft, fragile vulnerability of a woman's body.

On the warm sand, Suzy shuddered involuntarily. She hesitated for a moment, then twisted onto her back. The bronze skin of her face glistened and her big green eyes glittered with an unfamiliar and feverish look; her lips parted as if to say something. They trembled but remained silent.

Kneeling naked next to Suzy, Patty suddenly sensed danger. If she touched that satin skin again, she knew that something cataclysmic was going to follow. She gazed into Suzy's brilliant green eyes, and the knowledge of what they were about to do mesmerized them both.

Softly, at the same moment, they moved toward each other.

Suzy's arms stretched up around Patty's slim back, seeking for just a few moments a refuge from the terrors of the outside world, seeking the sensual comfort that a baby seeks at its mother's heart.

With one shaking finger, Patty traced the silken line of Suzy's eyebrow. Then Suzy's arms were clinging around Patty and pulling her down. Patty's heart thudded and her whole body trembled as, slowly, conscious of each breath she took, she leaned over the childlike creature who lay below her on the sand. Suddenly they were holding each other closely. Suzy's hands felt the sharp outline of Patty's shoulder blades, then moved upward toward her wheat-blond, silken hair.

Patty was instantly excited and at the same time violently frightened of her own feelings. Her hand trembled to Suzy's breast. Suzy's back immediately arched with the first thrilling shock of stimulation.

Those first affectionate caresses escalated into arousal, which led to passion, as each woman moved more urgently, in hungry need. Tenderness mingled with sensuality, and passion intertwined with lust. Wordlessly they caressed each other's body, feeling at each soft touch and stroke a vibrant electricity that tingled from head to toe.

Slowly, Patty slid the tips of her fingers down over Suzy's ribs and over the flat belly; she traced the soft line down her belly, tentatively seeking whether Suzy's responses would be the same as hers. She discovered that they were identical.

Seeing and completely understanding the other woman's reaction, Patty shed her uncertainty and suddenly felt firmly confident, as sensual as a peach and deliriously happy. For the first time Patty knew exactly what she was doing in a sexual embrace, and exactly what it was doing to her partner. She knew this body as she knew her own. It gave her an exultant confidence to know that it was in her power to give extraordinary pleasure.

From behind half-closed eyelids, Patty watched Suzy's mounting excitement, and this excited Patty more than any man had ever excited her—this extraordinary gentleness, the sensation of sensuality, of joyful control, and the ability to give ultimate pleasure to someone she loved. Patty was amazed by her lack of anxiety, the relaxed knowledge that replaced tentative fumbling. She felt no lack of communication, no anxiety.

It was not necessary to ask, "Was it all right for you?" She knew that it was, this soft eroticism that was totally different from sex with a man.

As warmth flooded through her body, Suzy felt ecstatic,

nurtured and secure. She couldn't stand it if Patty were to stop. She wasn't sure she could stand it if Patty continued. Then a glorious glow suffused her body and lightning quivers ran to the tips of her toes and her fingers, and she thought, This can't go on. But it did, and it got better.

As Suzy arched and quivered beneath her touch, and finally gasped with pleasure, Patty felt an extraordinary delight, and Suzy started to sob with sheer happiness; she fell back against the sand and felt the blue sky tilt above her, as her body went limp. But Patty, drunk with power, would allow her no respite.

A small voice at the back of Patty's head reproached her. It's only been *four weeks* since your husband was brutally murdered. You loved him, didn't you? What kind of person are you, to be unfaithful to him so soon after his death? And being unfaithful with a woman is doubly disgraceful. You should be ashamed of yourself!

Suzy felt for Patty, gasping, "I must make you feel . . . the way you made *me* feel."

Patty whispered. "Lie still." She pulled herself up on one elbow. She had watched this body and admired it, but she had never before thought of touching it. Again, Patty's hands slid possessively over Suzy's high, satin-skinned breasts.

Suzy felt as if she were the first woman on earth, as if she'd just been created. Patty touched her with delicacy, with growing confidence and skill, until Suzy felt the heat of the day enter into her body and her body become part of the day, and of the sun, and of the heat. She was aroused in every part of her being as no man had ever aroused her. There had been in their lovemaking a more total, unspoken understanding than she had ever felt with a man. It was not necessary to say one word.

On her knees, Patty leaned over Suzy as she lay with her back against the warm sand. Suzy started delicately running her fingers along Patty's spine. Each woman could smell the scent of the other, as Patty slowly lowered herself and their bodies touched. Suzy tremulously pressed upward, feeling her body melt with passion.

They held each other tightly, gasping, lost in ecstasy, touching faces and arms, thighs and breasts with the softness of a butterfly's caress. They touched each other with the gentle charm and romance of a Marie Laurencin painting. Their embraces were gentle yet insistent, completely uninhibited. Their limbs twisted around each other like warm snakes. The fact that this warm sensuality was forbidden added a thrill to their embrace. Suzy felt as if their bodies had suddenly melted and fused in the heat.

Patty was sleepily astonished that what they had done felt so natural. Was any woman completely heterosexual, she wondered, or were they merely terrified of breaking the taboo of touching, let alone loving, others of their sex?

Patty whispered softly, "I've never done this before."

"Neither have I," Suzy whispered. "Isn't it . . . *easy?*"

There had been no seducer or seduced, no mirror of a male and female relationship, but only mutual tenderness that had gently swelled into passion. There had been no foreplay, for it was all foreplay—which is all any woman needs to bring her to fulfillment. Thoughts swirled through Patty's mind. She was surprised to find so much ease in this sensuality; there was no tension, no climax anxiety, no threat.

Above all, because of each woman's intimate knowledge of the female anatomy, their unspoken feelings were gently recognized and shared. . . .

Patty was lying on her back in a semiconscious, sensuous daze. Suzy knelt at her feet, playing with Patty's toes. She separated each one carefully, brushed the sand from it, then sucked the toe as if it were a lollipop. Her thumbs gently kneaded Patty's instep, after which she trickled her thumbnail along the sole of Patty's foot.

As Patty shrieked with pleasure, they both heard Silvana calling from the waterfall, "Where are the fish? It's going to rain any minute!"

"We were just resting," Patty called. Quickly she looked at Suzy.

Nodding her head, Suzy whispered, "Tomorrow."

Reluctantly they picked themselves up and headed for the cliff path. As she trudged up the cliff path behind Silvana, Suzy felt cherished and hopeful. For that brief half-hour, she had forgotten fear. Because it was such a seductive idea, at each upward step Suzy fell a little more in love with Patty.

Behind her on the path, the trembling Patty tried to justify what had just happened, silently answering the small voice at the back of her head. It's not so terrible, she told herself. What do you suppose happens in prisoner-of-war camps? Do you think that healthy, bored, miserable young men can control their sexuality for years and years? *All* of them? There must be an unspoken male conspiracy *never* to tell what happens anywhere where people of one sex are incarcerated.

But you *did* it, said the inner voice. Now you're a lesbian!

Was she, Patty wondered. Could you be one even if you had been married? Was it latent? Patty remembered the friendships of her girlhood, she remembered her best friend, Gina, whom she had cared for, confided in, shared with and giggled with as they grew up together. She supposed that Gina and she touched each other's body, because they used to tumble around like puppies. But at a certain point that had definitely ended. Patty thought it was when they had started to date. She could remember no erotic attraction to Gina, but she'd definitely had a crush on her; it had ended only when Gina's father had relocated to Oklahoma. Perhaps friendship was a form of love, and sex was an extension of love, a physical proof of it. Perhaps there wasn't anything *basically* wrong with her after all.

You're a *lesbian*, the inner voice said accusingly.

Damned if I'm going to be! Patty silently told the voice. Suzy had definitely started it. No way was Patty going to catch it.

By the time they got back to camp, Patty was horrified by what she'd done, disgusted by it. She was also terrified that

Shirley Conran

Suzy might tell the others what had happened on the beach, and repulsed by the thought of being anywhere near Suzy.

By the time the women squatted by the campfire for their evening meal, Patty's sudden revulsion for Suzy was clearly apparent. With a gentle smile Suzy had moved over to sit beside Patty. Patty had immediately jumped up and carried her food to the opposite side of the campfire. If Suzy spoke to Patty, Patty ignored her.

After supper, Suzy whispered to Patty, "You were so wonderful. Why are you treating me like this now?" Silently, Patty had looked at Suzy as if they had just met, as if she was threatening Suzy never to remind her of the intimacy that had existed between them on the beach. And that night, Patty left her own bed and went to the other hut, where she slept on Jonathan's bed, between Annie and Carey.

Typical male behavior after a one-night stand, Suzy thought bitterly, remembering many nights of passion followed by a similar cold lack of interest. This, in turn, reminded her of all she owed Brett, whom she had just betrayed, and she wept acrid tears.

In the dark, Silvana heard Suzy snuffling. It wasn't too hard to guess the reason. They had been feasting with panthers. This new sexual current between Suzy and Patty had not been lost on the other three women.

Silvana remembered that they had both looked flustered and red-faced when she'd gone down to the beach that afternoon to look for the fish. They said they'd been resting on the beach, but it was far hotter on the beach than in the shade of the jungle. None of the women ever *rested* on the beach. They had been feasting with panthers, Silvana thought, remembering Oscar Wilde's description of homosexuality.

Silvana couldn't help being curious about what it felt like, and what they'd actually *done* together. Silvana's idea of lesbians was large, ugly women stomping around in army surplus clothes and finding solace in each other's hairy arms because no man in his right mind would want either of them. Neither Patty nor Suzy seemed the type.

390

In the second hut, Carey was thinking about the same thing. In her experience, straight women's attitudes toward lesbianism ranged from finding it vaguely threatening to downright terror of catching it. But thinking of soft, warm little Suzy, Carey guessed that perhaps lesbians liked other women for exactly the same reasons that men liked them. Maybe she wouldn't mind trying it, so long as nobody *ever* found out.

Equally wide awake, Annie lay on her bed in the darkness. She thought irritably, As if we didn't have enough problems! She tried to understand it. Of course they had all been brutally widowed and deprived of their families. They were surrounded by violence, they were cooped up and bored, with nothing to do during the interminable downpours, in confined quarters that were just short of intolerable. And they lived in constant fear. What they all needed was maternal comfort, cuddling and protection. Naïvely, Annie supposed that was why it had happened. But it was clear, from Patty's abrupt, brutal, and obvious rejection of Suzy, that it would not happen again.

But suppose it happened with somebody else?

19

TUESDAY, DECEMBER 11, 1984

After an exhausting two weeks of nursing Jonathan, Annie was again at his side, crouched under the canvas lean-to, getting ready to spoon a bowl of fish soup into his mouth.

Jonathan opened his eyes. "Hi, Annie," he said.

She blinked, because she had become used to being called Louise. Quickly, Annie felt his forehead. It was dry and cool. She grinned at him. "Good morning. We've missed you. Welcome back."

Annie rushed out of the lean-to to tell her good news to the others, but only Carey was in the camp.

During the second week of December, there had been two more sick-bay cases—Suzy and Carey. Suzy, who always grumbled when it was her turn in the morning to sweep the leaves out of the hut, had stepped on a scorpion hidden beneath a leaf.

Annie knew that a scorpion bite was treated the same as a snake bite. *You did nothing*. Jonathan had warned them never to use massage, or cut, or bleed, or suck out the poison from a bite. The more you do that, the more the venom spreads and it is possible to die from blood loss. So Annie had washed and dried the bitten area, then applied a constricting bandage—not as tight as a tourniquet—above Suzy's wound; the first day, Annie undid it and fastened it again every thirty minutes.

She also immobilized Suzy's foot by putting it in a splint, and after twenty-four hours of high fever and delirium, Suzy was weak but recovering.

Carey's tropical ulcers had been a more serious problem. The ulcers had developed on her lower legs after she had scratched ant stings in her sleep. They all knew that tropical ulcers could lead to gangrene, amputation or death. Like an inverted boil, they could start with the smallest scratch, tiny craters developing into large putrid holes that stank. Whenever Carey went fishing, she plugged her suppurating holes with bits of boiled rag and bandaged them with a torn strip of shirt. But, one day after Suzy's scorpion bite, Carey had swellings in both sides of her groin and could hardly move. Her legs were swollen and a pinkish color, like a Walt Disney pig.

When Jonathan had told her that the islanders used maggots to clean out their sores, Carey had refused to consider it. But after a night of agony, she was willing to try anything. Annie had brought her a pile of rotten fish. Carey picked off a maggot, gulped, then slapped it into one of her sores. Maggots eat only dead tissue, Jonathan had said, so they suck the pus from wounds. This proved correct. When her sores were clean, Carey brushed off the maggots and left the sores to dry. But her ant stings kept turning into new ulcers.

Eager to tell her good news, Annie cried to Carey, "Jonathan's getting better! Where are the others?"

"The rain stopped suddenly," Carey said, "so they've gone to have a dip in the waterfall pool before the afternoon rain starts."

"That means we have no lookout!" Annie tore off to the eucalyptus.

"Watch out!" Silvana warned Suzy, pointing into the shallow water of the lagoon. "You nearly stepped on a stonefish!"

Suzy shrieked as she saw the repulsive, wrinkled, gray creature.

"Jonathan said you're not to go in over your head," Silvana reminded Suzy.

Suzy mimicked Silvana's Italian accent. "'Jonathan says. Jonathan says'. . . . I'll do as I damn well please!"

Deliberately, she waded out and started to swim.

Silvana looked around for Patty, who now avoided Suzy as if she had the plague. Patty was about a hundred yards away with her head down, plowing through the water in a racing crawl. Silvana sighed, and waded in. With her careful breast-stroke and her head held above the water, she jerked along after Suzy, who was, once again, behaving like a rebellious two-year-old.

As she drew level with Suzy, Silvana yelled, "Get back near the beach, immediately."

With her clumsy dog paddle, Suzy swam obstinately on toward the entrance to the lagoon. She yelled, "Goddamn bossy know-it-all, snobbish wop."

Silvana pulled ahead of Suzy; treading water, she blocked Suzy's progress whichever way Suzy floundered.

"Get back, Suzy. You're heading for the current."

Whether or not it was deliberate, Silvana didn't know, but with one flailing arm Suzy hit Silvana in the face, ducking her.

Silvana surfaced, gasping and furious. She remembered her old-fashioned life-saving drill, and with the palm of her right hand she banged Suzy under the chin, knocking her backwards and underwater.

As she went under, Suzy thrashed out and accidentally kicked Silvana in the stomach, making her double up in pain.

Both women surfaced and faced each other, gasping and spewing out seawater. Boiling with fury, they both lunged forward. A flailing, ineffectual water fight began.

After about five minutes of furious battle, Silvana lifted her left arm to give Suzy a real punch. Her magnificent emerald-and-diamond engagement ring flew off her finger, soared through the air and disappeared beneath the green translucent water.

Suzy's wet face froze with horror.

Silvana burst out laughing. "You see, even my fingers are now thinner," she said. "All right, Suzy. You've certainly proved you can swim, so I'll leave you alone."

Lazily, Silvana swam away from Suzy. She turned on her back and floated in the water, enjoying the sun and the soothing, warm water that lapped her body and rocked it in the soft, beguiling rhythm of the sea.

In the distance Suzy shrieked, *"Shark!"*

Silvana turned her head.

Suzy was thrashing in the water, panic on her face. She disappeared below the surface.

As the horrified Silvana started to swim toward her, Suzy reappeared and screamed again. She choked, thrashed wildly and again disappeared below the water.

As she broke the surface again and shouted in terror, Suzy coughed out the water that she had just inhaled, but this caused her to expel much of the air in her lungs. Her next gasping attempt to breathe pulled even more water into her lungs. As the inhaled water again triggered coughing, yet more air was pushed out of her lungs and again she was gasping for air, trying desperately to scream—in the suddenly menacing, warm water. Because her last intake of water increased her body weight, Suzy started to sink.

Frantic and fighting for her life, Suzy thrashed her arms and kicked. Half-conscious, she struggled up toward the unruffled aquamarine surface above her. With her lungs incapacitated, she started to flail her arms harder and gasp spasmodically.

Every time she gasped for breath Suzy repeated the cycle. As she gasped, she expelled air, and as she screamed, water swamped her open mouth. Then the struggle ceased. She lost consciousness, and her water-weighted body sank slowly toward the bottom.

When Suzy disappeared, Silvana's first thought was to swim back to the beach as fast as she could, but she managed to control her panic. The only sharks that came over the reef and into the lagoon were babies—four feet long at the most.

They could hurt you—they might even bite your foot off—but they could *not* totally consume a live human being.

Silvana yelled to Patty, but she was swimming a good distance away with her face underwater concentrating on the pleasure of sliding through the water with speed, so she didn't hear Silvana's shouts.

With her jerky, awkward breaststroke, Silvana headed for the spot where she had last seen Suzy. She took a deep breath and jackknifed into the water.

Two minutes later Silvana surfaced, gasping. She had seen nothing. She swam ten strokes farther, then dived again. This time, at the limit of her breath, Silvana saw a drifting black ball, like a huge sea urchin. It was Suzy's head.

Silvana surfaced, took a deep breath and plunged deep. The body had drifted. At first Silvana could not see it, but then she spotted the limp form, languidly surging with the tide. Silvana kicked hard toward it.

When she reached Suzy, Silvana grabbed her by one arm and kicked as fiercely as she could to the surface. Spluttering, her lungs on fire, Silvana hung on to Suzy's limp, heavy body.

Once on the surface, Silvana didn't want to let go of Suzy's arm, because she was afraid of losing her again, but she managed to maneuver her body under Suzy's, then took hold of her other arm. Swimming on her back and clutching Suzy against her breast, Silvana swam jerkily toward shore. She'd never imagined that a body could be so floppy, so difficult to maneuver.

As she swam, Silvana tried to remember how to give the kiss of life. She must have read the instructions at least a dozen times at swimming pools, but now all she could remember was that you had to take any false teeth out before you started.

Patty had left the water. She stood naked on the beach, in the "tree" position. You couldn't do yoga lying down on the beach or the sand flies bit you. Deep in concentration, eyes on the horizon, Patty was unaware of the swimming accident until the gasping Silvana had reached the shallows. She let go of Suzy, scrambled to her feet and screamed to Patty.

Patty jerked her head around, to see Silvana dragging Suzy from the water.

As fast as she could, Patty ran along the soft sand toward the two women, then she hesitated.

Silvana was still gasping for breath. "For God's sake, help me, Patty. She's dying!"

Stiff and reluctant, Patty dragged Suzy clear of the water. She pushed the limp body onto its right side and roughly lifted Suzy's right arm above her head.

Silvana gasped, "The kiss of life. Can you do it?"

"Not yet," Patty said. "First you rid the mouth of obstacles and clear the airway to the lungs." Kneeling at Suzy's waist, she massaged her stomach upward to force out the water. Dribbles trickled from Suzy's blue-tinged mouth.

Gingerly, Patty hooked her index finger into Suzy's mouth, to check that there was no seaweed or other blockage.

"*Now* the kiss of life!" Silvana wailed.

Patty felt repulsed at the thought of touching Suzy, let alone with her lips. She felt as if any contact might contaminate her.

"Get *on* with it," Silvana cried.

Patty checked Suzy's pulse but couldn't feel it. She knew that four minutes after breathing stopped, permanent brain damage occurred, but if you breathe forcefully into the mouth of a person who isn't breathing, *your* discarded breath contains enough oxygen to provide a life-support system for that person.

Patty turned Suzy onto her back, unstrapped her Swatch-watch and held the black face to Suzy's mouth. "If Suzy is still breathing," she told Silvana, "her breath will mist the face."

"*Is she still breathing? Is she?*" Silvana knelt helplessly on the sand.

Patty inspected the watch. "It's misted over."

"Then get on with it! The kiss of life!"

Carefully, Patty tilted Suzy's limp head backward to open

the airway to her lungs. She pulled the slack jaw open and closed the nostrils by pinching the nose. Then she paused again.

"For God's sake, *do it*," Silvana said. "Can't you understand? She's *dying!*"

So Patty bent and blew hard into Suzy's mouth. From then on, Patty's lungs did the breathing for Suzy's body. She counted up to four, then blew hard into Suzy's mouth again.

Suddenly Suzy retched.

Patty also retched.

Silvana cried, "Oh, Patty, *don't* stop!"

Shuddering as she did so, Patty turned Suzy on her side so she could vomit. Again she massaged Suzy's stomach in an upward motion.

Slime and water gushed from Suzy's mouth onto the white sand.

Silvana held her breath.

When Suzy again lay still, Patty turned her on her back and continued with the unpleasant task of blowing hard, fifteen times a minute, into Suzy's vomit-encrusted mouth.

"Look at her chest," Silvana whispered.

In rhythm with Patty's breath, Suzy's rounded breasts gently rose and fell. This meant that there was no obstruction in her throat.

"Blow into her mouth again!" Silvana urged. "*Quickly!*"

Hating every touch of Suzy's mouth, Patty continued to give mouth-to-mouth resuscitation—fifteen breaths a minute for several minutes—then she gasped, "How long are you supposed to do this? Can't *you* take over, Silvana?"

Frozen with anxiety, Silvana said, "I've no idea. Don't stop! You know how to do it, Patty. I don't."

Patty spat into the sand, then continued with her reluctant kisses.

"Oh, Patty, she's breathing again! Look!"

Patty stopped. She saw that Suzy's chest was rising and falling of its own accord.

Swiftly, Patty turned Suzy on her right side, in the recovery position, with her right arm above her head and her left knee bent forward.

The two women watched anxiously, kneeling naked on the burning sand.

Suzy belched. She coughed and spluttered. Then she vomited.

Silvana burst into tears.

Later in the hut, the white and trembling Silvana was treated for shock by Annie.

Annie angrily turned to Patty and said, "You were only supposed to go wash, not swim. There's been nobody in the lookout for the past two hours. Get up there!"

Sickened by what she had been forced to do, Patty felt she had been suitably punished. She loped off, wondering what would have happened to Suzy had Silvana not been present.

That afternoon the rain stopped early, so Patty went to check the fish trap in the stream, which yielded only one huge shrimp. As the lines were still unbent, she returned to the camp for her beach tackle—a bucket, a dip net, two light fishing rods and the underwater spear gun. Now that their hut had suddenly been turned into a field hospital, Patty was the only person left to hunt for food.

Clutching her fishing equipment in gloved hands, lonely, depressed, still ashamed, and wondering whether they were all going to die of stinking wounds or malaria, Patty scrambled too fast down the steep cliff path. She stumbled and nearly fell. She managed to regain her balance without dropping her heavy load of tackle, but her jungle hat had fallen off and came to rest on a rock by the edge of the waterfall, where it would take some time to retrieve. Patty decided to pick it up later, when her arms were free, rather than stop now for a job that might take twenty minutes.

Thigh-deep in water, Patty had no luck. Time after time she swung the weighted lure above her head, then hurled it out over the little waves. Doggedly, she fished on. She enjoyed feeling the balance of the fishing line in her hand, and she was seriously absorbed in her task in spite of the blasting midday heat and the sweat that dripped down between her breasts.

Eventually she decided to call it a day. She would try the river later. They generally fished the river first thing in the morning and last thing at night, because that's when fish fed —when the insects came out. Patty decided that if she had no luck she'd come back to the beach in the moonlight, although they tried to avoid night fishing—there were mosquitoes by the streams and river, while in the sea there were stingrays and box jellyfish, whose sting could kill a human being in less than a minute.

At worst, when the tide was out, Patty could try to catch some scuttling crabs. At least then, she'd have the best possible fishing bait, as well as crab soup.

Wading back to shore, Patty glanced up at the ominous, purple-black clouds overhead. As she did so, she stepped on a sharp stone, tripped, then overbalanced. As she scrambled upright she felt cold gusts of wind on her back and she could hear the spatter of water on the palm leaves. By the time Patty reached the cliff path, the rain was hissing onto the lagoon, hitting the water hard in an angry, pimpled pattern. She found it was almost impossible to stand on the beach, let alone climb the cliff path, which had turned into a torrent of mud. Annie would just have to wait for the food—serve her right for ordering Patty around like that! Anyway, nobody could attack the camp in this downpour.

Dripping wet and shivering, Patty crouched at the back of the beach, above the tideline. For two hours, the rain forced her to stay there, during which time she could see nothing. It was as if the beach had been hidden by a pale gray, mountain mist. The rain fell ceaselessly.

Almost as suddenly as it had started, the rain stopped, although a strong wind still blew. Patty tied her gear to one of the sagging palm trees. She'd need both hands to climb the now slippery cliff path—and anyway, she'd need her tackle here tonight.

She found it very hard to reach the top of the cliff. It

seemed to stretch upward as she climbed. There was always farther to go, as if some giant were pulling the top away from her.

As she lurched back into the camp, feeling giddy, Patty saw Annie running toward her, looking oddly two-dimensional.

As she ran to the staggering Patty, Annie cried, "What happened? Were you stung by a sea snake or a stonefish?"

"No hat," murmured Patty, as her knees gave way. She slumped in the mud, threw up, then fainted.

Patty's neck and back had blistered through her shirt. Where her skin wasn't bright pink, it was an angry red. She was semiconscious and burning with fever. She lay groaning face down on her bed of bracken. Annie sponged her back gently with cold water.

"Boy, look at those blisters!" Suzy said, sitting up.

Annie sat back on her heels and wearily wiped her forehead with the back of her hand. "We survived for four weeks without serious illness, except for diarrhea and Jonathan's fever. Now, suddenly, within *two days* I'm running a hospital. What *happened?*"

"Domino effect, after Suzy insisted on swimming out too far," Carey suggested. "Silvana should be well enough to help tomorrow."

WEDNESDAY, DECEMBER 12

The following morning, leaving a still white-faced Silvana on lookout, Annie checked the river fishing lines, but no luck. An exhausted Jonathan, gaunt-faced and ten pounds thinner, whispered instructions to her. She must take the machete and look for food beyond the cave shaft, which lay to the southeast of the camp. It was in secondary jungle, so there must once have been a settlement nearby, and the crops they had cultivated might still be there, though now wild.

Until now, the little group had kept as closely as possible to the area around the camp, in order to conserve their energy, to avoid getting lost and so as not to move into the undefined area—they didn't yet know the exact boundary of the taboo territory. They had only moved down the cliff path or upstream to the bamboo grove or, slightly beyond it and to the right, to the spot where Jonathan had placed his fish trap in the stream. The only occasion on which they had ventured beyond this area was on the day that Suzy and Patty had killed the goat. Their only other regular route was to the cave shaft, which they always approached by slightly different routes, in order not to establish a give-away, beaten path.

For over an hour, Annie hacked her way through the undergrowth, slashing upwards with the machete to clear her path. She made very little progress. Eventually, she retreated along her own track and circumnavigated the patch of secondary jungle, trying to look *through* it, not *at* it, which is how Jonathan had told her to develop jungle eyes. Annie decided that if she couldn't find anything to eat on the outskirts of this thick vegetation she would look for a stream. Native villages were always sited on the banks of a stream or a river—perhaps she'd be able to wade or swim along such a stream looking for food.

She found a stand of papaya trees, but unfortunately, the clusters of big yellow fruit were all at the top. The trunk of the tree was similar to that of a coconut palm—it had no low branches.

Annie wished that she'd been able to bring Suzy with her. Suzy didn't mind heights, and she was the only one of the group who could shin up a coconut palm; she encircled the tree with her hands, leaned out from her feet and walked up, agile as a monkey.

Parts of the rough tree trunk seemed to crumble beneath Annie's weight, but eventually, scratched and sweating, and not daring to look down, she could touch the fruit. With her fish knife, she hacked off as much as she could carry and loaded it into the slingbag on her back.

Her bag was made from a shirt. Unless they were going

beyond the camp the women could no longer afford to wear their shirts, because they were needed to make bags, water strainers and bandages. Except for the convent-raised Silvana, all the women were now naked from the waist up.

Back on the ground, Annie slashed open one of the green fruits and tasted it. She rubbed her fingers in the milky sap and tasted it. It was delicious.

Brushing the flies from her eyes, Annie stood up and heaved the bag of fruit onto her back. She felt exultant; she was the camp provider.

Then she felt unbearable pain in her eyes.

"Must'a got unripe pawpaw sap in her eye," Jonathan said to Silvana, who was bathing Annie's eyes. Listening to Annie's nonstop groans and occasional scream, Jonathan wondered whether she should be gagged. She was certainly a security risk.

Annie had had great difficulty in regaining camp, and by the time she did so she was in terrible pain. Now she was also blind, and they had nothing to alleviate her agony.

Eventually, Annie had to be gagged. She understood what was happening and did not resist as a strip of shirt was tied around her mouth and her hands tied behind her so she couldn't tear off the gag.

Silvana's distress at trussing up her friend was so great that Patty wondered if she was in shock again.

Jonathan sent Silvana to collect coconuts. She was to take no risk, they had plenty of water and it didn't matter if they went hungry for a bit. Silvana was to rest all she could, she wasn't to knock herself out again, because she and Suzy were now the only women on their feet. For the time being, they couldn't have a lookout, not if King Kong himself were lurking in the jungle.

Apart from gathering coconuts and fetching water, nobody was to move out of camp until he was on his feet again, Jonathan announced as firmly as he could, before falling back, exhausted, on his bamboo bed.

* * *

The next day, Annie lay slumped on a pile of leaves in the hut, wondering whether she'd ever be able to see again. She was surprised not to be more distressed. She'd always had great fear of going blind, but now that it had happened in this ludicrous way, she simply felt resigned to the loss of her sight, although she wished that the pain behind her eyelids would stop. It felt as if someone were applying lighted matches to her eyeballs, and the constant pain exhausted her.

Three days after she discovered the papaya tree, Jonathan found Annie weeping quietly. He squatted and held her hand, saying nothing.

Annie sobbed, "It's as if fate and nature have turned against us, they're stamping on each one of us in turn, then grinding us underfoot."

"Oh, no, they ain't," said Jonathan. "Fate's the same as she was last week, nature ain't interested in you and the jungle's neutral. Stop being a tragedy queen."

Only Annie and Patty were still bed-ridden, and the women were no longer hungry. Silvana had been to the bamboo grove and gathered young shoots. She peeled and sliced them like carrots, then boiled and served them with a few freshwater shrimp from the stream.

"Chinese cuisine today," Suzy commented. She had been collecting fern tops. When dark green they were too tough to eat as a salad, so Silvana boiled them like spinach. She also boiled or fried seaweed, which sometimes tasted like spinach and sometimes like savory aspic. Surprisingly, it wasn't very salty. The plant food wouldn't give them much energy, but at least it was food, and it would keep them alive.

In the afternoon, Jonathan took Silvana to the overgrown settlement where Annie had found the pawpaw tree. He located a banana plant and a breadfruit tree with fist-sized globes of fruit.

"We can't eat those," Silvana said in dismay. "The skin is covered with green spikes."

"They peel off after the fruit's been baked in the embers for half an hour." He pointed. "See that vine? The knobbly, dark-pink things? They're sweet potatoes. Oh, my word, we're going to eat well tonight."

That night, for the first time since they'd taken to the jungle, they ate until they could eat no more.

On the fourth morning of Annie's blindness, when Silvana brought her breakfast to the hut Annie sleepily looked up and yawned, "Hi, Silvana."

Silvana promptly dropped the coconut shell of mashed breadfruit, and with a show of affection such as she had not demonstrated since last seeing her daughter, she hugged Annie, crying gratitude to the saints in Italian.

For the first time in nearly three weeks, no one in the little party was incapacitated.

That evening, after the others had gone to sleep, Jonathan and Patty crouched in the moonlight, their slingshots at the ready.

Jonathan hit the first rat, and the second, too hard.

"Rabbit stew tomorrow," Patty said, looking at the corpses.

Ten minutes later Patty spotted another rat. Elated, she extended the arm that held the slingshot, placed the pebble in the elastic sling and pulled it back.

The sleek dark rat gave a yelp, jumped into the air, then lay still.

"Good girl," Jonathan approved. Wearing fishing gloves to protect his hands, he shoved the limp creature into the bamboo cage he had made that afternoon.

"Keep away from it," Jonathan warned. "Rats scratch and they bite. I don't want any infected rat bites. Nobody is to take pity on this bastard and befriend it. Push food through the

405

cage bars with a long rod. Pour drinking water from a distance, through a hollow bamboo rod."

"Are you sure it can't gnaw through the bamboo cage?" Patty asked.

"I dunno. If it does, we'll have to catch another one."

"Let's call it Sinatra."

SUNDAY, DECEMBER 16

All the women now looked fitter, and each had lost a lot of weight. Sinatra was also thriving, although they kept him short of rations so he'd be hungry on cue. Any food that he refused to eat was immediately crossed off the camp menu.

In the lagoon, Jonathan continued to teach the women to fish. "The secret of fishing is to know the area you're fishing in, and know the habits of the fish you're after, so you know what he's likely to do next."

As he spoke, Patty again felt shivers run up her spine. Suppose someone who knew this area was observing *their* habits and guessing what *they* might do next? She fought against the feeling that the little party was being observed and tried to concentrate on what Jonathan was saying.

". . . Fish feed just before dawn, just after dark, just before a storm, and at night when the moon is full or waning. They bite bait they're used to seeing around."

Patty swallowed her fear and said nothing.

After three weeks of cyclones, the women had overcome their initial depression and frustration. During the rain, they all played backgammon on a board that Carey had painted with charcoal on canvas. Annie practiced her flute, and Silvana accompanied her on a set of pan pipes that she'd made with short lengths of bamboo and damit. Carey whittled at a Madonna that she was carving for Annie's praying grove.

Suzy made jewelry from shells, and Patty taught yoga to all of them. They also prepared vegetables and fish bait.

When it was not raining, they searched for food—hunting or fishing always according to Jonathan's directions. They came to rely on him in all ways, to trust his toughness and his carefully hidden benevolence. All the women felt that he was a good man. Their feelings toward him were of gratitude and love, and they obeyed him in all things.

The rejected Suzy also felt something else for Jonathan.

One night at two o'clock in the morning, Suzy slid down the lookout tree. Cramped, she stretched and yawned. Then she noticed that Jonathan hadn't gone to bed but was sitting alone, crouched over the embers of the fire. This was unusual, because they all generally went to bed shortly after sunset.

She looked at Jonathan's sharp-edged profile as he stared into the firelight. The flickering glow played over his hard, thin torso, and his blond chest hair glinted gold against the blackness of the tropical night.

On impulse Suzy slipped off the ungainly trousers that Annie had made her from an upended shirt. She moved into the firelight; instead of squatting, she spread her trousers on the ground and sat on them, with her big tattered shirt pulled up above her knees. In a forlorn voice she said, "Sometimes I feel *so* lonely."

Jonathan looked into the fire and said, "It ain't a good idea, Suzy."

"No one would know."

"You don't stop loving a person just because she's dead."

"I'll go crazy if I don't soon feel someone's arms around me." Suzy edged a little nearer to the fire, and to the man, "Don't *you* miss it? I miss it, all the time." She sighed. "It's the way my body is. I can't help it." She put one finger out and touched the blond hairs on his wrist. "I just . . . can't help it." Her index finger moved up his forearm, feeling the strength of the muscles beneath the skin.

Jonathan turned his blue eyes to hers. She looked so small

and defenseless, with her delicate little ears sticking out from her shorn head. In some ways, she was more beautiful and tempting than before. Then he thought of Louise, and shook his head. "No," he said, "it ain't a good idea." He turned away as she burst into tears.

MONDAY, DECEMBER 17

They still had a few matches left, but nobody had yet tried to make a fire without them. They had all read about rubbing two sticks together to cause friction, but nobody actually knew how to do it, and Jonathan had heard that it was a damn sight harder than it sounded.

As they crouched that evening around the now increasingly precious campfire, the flames lit up Jonathan's face from below, throwing black shadows over his gaunt cheeks.

"When I was a boy in Brisbane, going on eight years old," he remembered, "we used to go to the Botanical Gardens on Sunday afternoon. Bored me senseless, it did. Me parents just sat on a park bench. Me ma always wore her Sunday-best dress; it was bright blue silky stuff, and she was very proud of it. One Christmas, I was given a magnifying glass with a handle—the sort of thing Sherlock Holmes had. I was fiddling with this thing one Sunday, when I found I could concentrate the sun's rays on an area of my mum's dress and make this fierce spot of brilliant light on the dress, so that the blue turned to a little brown circle. I sat there, happy and quiet, burning brown spots on her best dress, all afternoon. Got tanned later by my dad." He looked around the circle of women. "I suppose none of you got a magnifying glass in your purses?"

They shook their heads.

He said wistfully, "I had a good pair of binoculars aboard the *Louise*, but we couldn't bring everything. . . . Nobody here wears eyeglasses for reading?"

Everyone shook their heads.

"We have sunglasses," said Silvana.

"It's gotta be a thick, convex bit of clear glass."

Everyone shook their heads except Carey. She said, "Remember the skeleton at the bottom of the cave shaft? Remember her camera?"

Jonathan said, "We'll get it tomorrow morning."

At dawn the following morning Patty came tearing back from the waterfall pool, naked except for the previous night's mosquito-repellent mudpack, which was still on her face.

"Jonathan! There are things moving on the beach. Three of them! I think they're turtles!"

Jonathan grabbed the gaff and the ax and ran toward the cliff path. He had been about to wash, and wore only a loincloth made from a white shirtsleeve and a rattan cord tied around his lean waist. Scrambling down the path behind him, Patty saw how thin his fever had left him. His shoulder blades were protruding triangles, and his ribs were clearly visible. He had told her that, whatever his fever had been, it would probably recur. Patty didn't think he could afford to lose any more weight; in fact, there wasn't any to lose, she thought, as her eyes flicked over his taut buttocks and long, lean legs.

Down below, on the sand, Jonathan moved slowly and quietly up the beach to within sight of the three curved, brown lumps. He turned around and soundlessly waved Patty away, clearly telling her to go back to the camp, but she followed him, anxious to miss nothing.

Since the shell cannot be penetrated, Jonathan killed the turtle by flipping it over on its back, taking care to avoid its vicious claws, and shattering the breastplate with an ax. Underneath was the mauvish-pink, wriggling body. Then he hacked the head off with the ax, slit the body, peeled it open and pulled out the intestines, taking care not to split them. Once the guts were out, he pulled out the heart and liver from beneath the breastbone. The drawback to turtle as an entrée was that it looked like a fat, dead baby.

Jonathan looked up at Patty and scowled. "Didn't I tell you

to get away. I'm going to cut it into chunks down here, then wash it in the sea, before the others see it. Tastes like fleshy chicken, a bit like a battery hen fed on fishmeal. We need the protein. And Silvana can use the shell to cook in."

Patty gasped, "I think I'm going to throw up."

"Don't look at it. Do something else. Where there's turtles, there may well be turtle eggs. Take the gaff and look for them."

Feeling queasy, Patty moved along the beach, stabbing the sand around the turtle tracks with the gaff, a long pole with a vicious hook at one end, used for landing large fish.

Eventually, the gaff came out of the sand covered with slime.

Patty knelt down. Carefully she scraped away the sand.

She uncovered seventeen eggs.

Jonathan's shadow fell across the pile. Patty looked away as he placed the turtle shell on the sand and carefully piled the eggs into it, above the raw meat.

He said crossly, "Where do you suppose the meat at the supermarket counter comes from before it gets wrapped in plastic?"

Annie stood at the top of the cave shaft while Carey slithered down the rattan rope, the flashlight tucked in her shirt. The battery had started to run down, so they used it as little as possible.

When Carey reached the vile-smelling bottom of the shaft, she tugged the rope twice to let Annie know she was safe, then switched on the light and limped over to the gray skeleton. They all felt that she had a right to be there, and that they were interlopers in her tomb. Patty had once suggested removing the depressing sight to the dark area behind the cave chimney, but nobody had wanted to disturb her.

Carey crouched and played the dim beam over the skeleton's pelvic area. Gingerly, she stretched out her hand and fumbled in the gray dust which was all that remained of what had once been a woman's stomach.

The flashlight faded completely, and Carey was left in the dark. Shuddering, she groped among the bones until she felt the camera. Carefully, she pulled it out and placed it in the mosquito-net bag hanging from her waist.

What had been a simple if unpleasant task had suddenly turned into a dangerous one. Thank God, Annie knew she was down here. If she fell over a rock and broke her leg or knocked herself unconscious, Annie would know where to find her, thought Carey, as her claustrophobia overcame her and she shook with fear, unable to move.

It was about ten minutes before Carey's shaking subsided and she could breathe again without feeling as if someone was pressing a thick blanket against her face. She knew that she had to move fast before she had another attack.

With both arms stretched in front of her, Carey shuffled forward, an inch at a time, toward the faint lessening-of-dark that marked the cave chimney.

Crouching by the campfire, Jonathan carefully rubbed the dirt from the old, dented K2 Pentax. He unclipped the bayonet fitting of the lens and blew the remaining dust from it. He examined the black cylinder, marked with rings and numbers. The large, thick lens was of the highest optical quality. Jonathan squinted through the lens at the scarlet and yellow flames of the fire.

"Okay, let's wash her," he said.

Suzy held a half coconut shell of warm water and proffered the beach towel as Jonathan carefully cleaned and dried the lens.

In the fierce afternoon sunlight, Jonathan turned the knurled ring of the camera lens so that the inside aperture opened, allowing the full power of the sun's rays to pass through the glass.

Over ninety-three million miles away there is constant nuclear fusion on the surface of the sun. A minute quantity of this energy traveled across the wasteland of the universe, the full heat of the equatorial sun focused through the lens and

Shirley Conran

produced a powerful white point of heat a few inches below it, on the back of Jonathan's hand.

He jumped, feeling an immediate sting of pain.

"Works on me! Now let's try the tinder." He focused on the screwed-up bits of paper from Carey's precious notebook, which lay beneath the little pile of twigs.

Everybody held their breath.

The spot on the paper smoldered, then started to smoke.

They had fire!

They had comfort and protection, a means of cooking and sterilization, they had a weapon.

It seemed more of a miracle than switching on an electric light.

◄ 20 ►

That afternoon, Suzy stood obstinately at the edge of the lagoon. "It *was* a shark! If it wasn't, it was a whale. It was big *and black* and shark-shaped! I'm not going swimming again, *ever!*"

"I told you before that there ain't no sharks around here," Jonathan said.

"It *was* a shark," Suzy said.

"I ain't getting at you, Suzy. I know you're *certain* that your shark existed, but it didn't—because if it had, you probably wouldn't be here now." He turned to Silvana and added, "By the way, next time somebody yells shark, don't go to help her. Head for shore as fast as you can."

Suzy said sullenly, "It *was* a shark. It *must* have been."

"We'll go out there and check," Jonathan said. "You'll see if you nearly drowned because of an imaginary fear. You probably saw *something*, but it wasn't a shark."

"What the hell do you mean by *that?*"

Jonathan said, "When you was a kid, you used to be afraid of ghosts in the dark, right? It was an imaginary danger, but it still terrified you. However, you weren't afraid of crossing the road, because you didn't know enough to be scared; you had to learn that crossing the road was a dangerous situation, then

413

you had to learn how to deal with it. Now you all have to learn the same thing on this island."

"I'm learning fast," Suzy snapped, as she watched Silvana and Patty wade into the water. Jonathan was still too weak to swim more than a few strokes, so he stood on the beach and watched them. Both women wore snorkel masks, fins and knife belts. Patty, who carried the underwater spear, was naked, but Silvana still wore her ragged black lace underwear.

"It was around here," Silvana told Patty as they nervously treaded water in the middle of the lagoon.

They swam down into a strange aquamarine world, where silver-and-black-striped fish, parrot-green and kingfisher-blue fish swam calmly around them, seemingly unaware of the two women, unless one of them almost touched a fish, whereupon it immediately swerved and shot away, as did the rest.

Patty silently stabbed her finger ahead. Both women surfaced.

"There's certainly *something* down there," Silvana said. "And it *does* look like a gigantic, rotting shark. Let's go down again."

This time, they recognized the barnacle-encrusted wreck of an airplane. After forty years on the sea floor, the metal had crumbled away and the Beaufighter now had the organic appearance of an old sea monster—a gargantuan marine dragonfly with one wing missing, overladen by the debris of the deep.

As the women surfaced, spluttering, Patty said, "Maybe it crashed in the war. Do you think it was one of ours or a Jap?"

"Doesn't matter, does it? Do you think there's anything down there that we could use? Anything that hasn't rotted or rusted? A first-aid kit, with glass bottles of antiseptic, maybe? They didn't have plastic then, did they?"

"Let's go look."

Repeatedly the two women dived, moving silently with the fish around the ghostly, crumbling machine and peering through the jagged edges of the holes torn in what remained of a famous fighter, once known as "Whispering Death."

When they surfaced, Patty spluttered, "Absolutely nothing there."

"We ought to take something back as proof for Suzy, or she'll never be convinced. I'm going down once more." Silvana's black fins splashed the surface of the lagoon as she dived.

After a few moments Patty followed her, streaking down into the glittering depths, powered by the soft movements of her fins.

Below her, Patty saw Silvana. She seemed to be struggling with something in the wreck. Her head was out of sight, thrust into a hole in the fuselage, while her legs were kicking furiously against the rusting metal and her arms beat wildly at the aircraft—as if inside the skeleton aircraft a living thing clutched her in its grip.

Patty's heart jumped as she thought, *Sea snakes!* There might be a huge Moray eel down there, making its home inside that wreck. We should have thought of it. Patty whipped out her knife.

As she touched Silvana's foot it lashed out against her and Patty nearly dropped her knife.

Silvana was clearly trapped, but why were her arms moving so strangely, both jerking behind her back? Could some sea creature be gripping her by the hair?

Suddenly Patty saw that what had trapped Silvana was the back of her own bra, which had caught on one of the jagged, protruding twists of black metal around the gaping hole into which Silvana had tried to swim.

Quickly, Patty leaned forward and with her knife cut through the back of the bra. Then she ran out of air and shot upward, her only thought to reach the surface before her lungs burst.

Behind her, Silvana's head broke the water.

When both women had recovered their breath, Silvana said,

"I dropped my knife in that hole and went after it. That's how I got caught."

Patty grinned. "At last you're topless, like the rest of us."

WEDNESDAY, DECEMBER 19

Silvana's near-death had altered the attitude of the group, in that they now realized that they might actually die there—casually. The next morning, Jonathan—now recovered—started to teach the women all he knew as fast as he could. As they practiced self-defense and jungle craft, nobody complained because they all realized that each woman was being taught to survive—*on her own*.

The first thing he taught them was how to move properly in the jungle. They all knew how easy it was to get lost because, as soon as you stepped into it, wherever you looked the jungle was a mass of endless, seemingly identical forest. If you didn't have a compass you didn't go into the jungle because you couldn't see the sun above the towering treetops which met sixty feet overhead and only filtered down a greenish, permanent twilight. The women learned the special technique for moving through the jungle, slipping sideways, weaving their way through the trees—turning their shoulders, shifting their hips, bending their bodies, concentrating on slipping through. Trying to crash through the jungle face forward only led to noise, bruises, scratches and frustration.

Jonathan also taught them how to keep track of where they were going. When the track came to a fork, they always took the path which looked the more traveled. When two paths crossed, they broke a twig to mark the track they had just left, so that they would be able to find their way back.

Suzy protested, "But you told us not to go out of this area, Jonathan. You told us not to go beyond William Penn."

"When we land on Irian Jaya we may have to track through jungle," Jonathan pointed out.

The next day they visited the abandoned village where they had found wild bananas. Taro roots and bananas were particularly popular foods, because the carbohydrate satisfied hunger in a way that leafy greens and shoots could not. They found an avocado tree, but the fruit was not yet ripe, a guava and one lone, twisted, wild lime tree. Gazing at it, Suzy said, "If we make a bamboo still, we can brew our own vodka."

Food had become of the greatest importance to their lives, because they were deprived of any other pleasures. But the searching for roots and fruit, the hunting and the fishing seemed endless. They were all surprised by the time it took to gather food for six people, day after day after day.

Although Jonathan enjoyed well-cooked food, he quietly suppressed any hint of domesticity, which could curb the natural aggression that the women might need in order to escape. When he saw Silvana arranging yellow orchids in a bamboo pot, he immediately threw them away. Before Silvana had time to argue, he told her to clean out the rat cage.

Every new potential edible was fed to Sinatra in the evening, and no matter how delicious it looked, they never tasted the food until the following morning.

Four days before Christmas Suzy staggered into camp clutching a brownish globe about the size of her head; it was covered with greenish spikes. She said, "This thing was lying under a tree between the bamboo grove and William Penn."

"My word," said Jonathan, "Sinatra will go crazy. You've found a durian. It's a bit early, we don't usually get them around here until after Christmas."

"What's a durian, and how do you open it?"

"Great delicacy in this part of the world. It's called the honeymoon fruit, and offered at bridal banquets." He looked strangely at Suzy. "When you smell it, you'll understand why." He plunged his knife into the earth to clean it, then cut a slice from the durian. Beneath the greenish spiked shell lay a creamy-colored, soft fruit.

Suzy sniffed a familiar perfume. She grinned. "Why, it smells like . . . private parts."

"Exactly," said Jonathan. "The native women say, don't pick a bridegroom who don't like the smell of durian."

"What does it taste like?"

"Delicious, a wonderful thick cream custard, the best thing you've eaten in your life. We'll go hunting tonight; I'll try to get something special to eat with the durian."

Carey and Patty had already been hunting with Jonathan in the forest, but apart from rats, they had not been very successful. They never managed to down a bird with their slingshots, except for one tough and tasteless parrot which was very hard to pluck. They followed wild pig tracks and occasionally glimpsed a dingo, but they never got near enough to one to take aim. And the bra elastic in their slingshots had started to sag.

As soon as darkness had fallen, Jonathan and Carey went frog hunting. They located the frogs by their croaks, shone the flashlight on them, then clubbed the hypnotized frogs to death with heavy sticks.

Back at the camp, Carey triumphantly upended the bagful of dead frogs in a heap by the campfire.

Annie immediately turned away, retching.

Carey was indignant. "You'd eat them in a French restaurant. Why not here? Come over and help us skin them or you won't get anything to eat."

What Suzy called the ultimate yuk experience happened the following morning when Patty was looking for a new latrine area.

On the jungle path ahead of her, Patty spotted what she at first thought was a circular pile of yellowish-brown and black leaves. Suddenly realizing what it was, she hurled a stone at it. The snake uncoiled in a leisurely manner.

Patty had pulled a pebble from the pouch that hung from her belt. As soon as she could see its head, she aimed at the snake with her slingshot. The snake went limp.

Hypnotized with loathing, Patty didn't dare approach the snake. Instead, she ran back to Jonathan, dropping pebbles in her path as she fled through the forest, as in the Hansel and Gretel fairytale.

Jonathan grabbed his machete and the two of them hurried back, following the pebbles to the snake, which Patty had half-expected to disappear.

Jonathan threw a couple of stones which hit the snake, but it didn't move.

Cautiously he moved forward and gave a quick swipe with his machete. The snake head sprang, severed, into the air.

Jonathan said, "You was lucky to get it in one shot. Python. Not very big."

"Not very big! It's about eight feet long!"

"A python can be thirty feet long." Jonathan dangled the dead snake over one shoulder and carried it back to the camp.

When she saw the limp, glistening snake, Silvana's face froze. "I hope you don't expect me to cook *that!*"

"I'll show you how." Jonathan was delighted. "Snake steaks for supper tonight! Tastes sort of like pork. Delicious!"

He showed the reluctant Silvana how to skin the snake.

"Looks like you got a new belt, Patty."

Patty looked pleased. "Three belts, maybe four."

"Why not just one, with matching shoes and purse?" Silvana suggested grimly.

As Christmas approached, although nobody mentioned it, they all thought sorrowfully about home. Instead of dwelling on the horrific fate of their husbands, their thoughts were constantly with their families in Pittsburgh. Patty hoped that her mother wouldn't take Stephen to Silver City for the holidays; he'd hate being surrounded by well-intentioned geriatrics whooping it up in paper hats. She hoped her mother would fly up to Pittsburgh and she and Stephen would have a quiet time at home.

Suzy was frankly relieved that she wouldn't have to stay on her best behavior among the ancient, blue-blooded relatives that her mother-in-law always gathered around her for Christmas.

Carey hoped that Ingrid wasn't having trouble with her throat. Sweating in the jungle, it was hard to remember that by now Pittsburgh was covered in snow. Ingrid had suffered from infected tonsils for almost three months last year. The first specialist had been against an operation, and so had the second, so they had decided to wait.

When Annie thought of Christmas, she became very quiet and her mouth turned down. Fred would, of course, organize everything. The good thing about having an athletic family was that there was always *something* going on to stop you from thinking. But the problem with the boys was that they never really talked to each other. Their only conversation was monosyllabic exchanges on the order of what-time's-the-game-start?

As Silvana cooked, she recalled the elaborate preparations that started weeks before Christmas in her home, and the self-importance that Nella assumed as she prepared for the festivities. While tears fell into the chowder she was preparing, Silvana told herself firmly how lucky she was that Lorenza had married before this happened, and to such a nice, suitable boy.

Silvana was the only woman who didn't now look gaunt. The skin of the other women was slack over visible sinews. Silvana had lost weight everywhere except her breasts, the nipples of which showed clearly through her shredded black jumpsuit. Her silhouette hadn't looked so good since the time she'd spent a whole month at the Golden Door.

All the women now had infected, pus-filled sores on their arms and legs. They all had nits or fleas. They were all weaker than they'd been when they built the rafts; they couldn't lift heavy weights, they moved more slowly and there was no spring in their steps.

Suzy's hair was now a black crew cut. Annie wore her hair in braids, like an eight-year-old. Her pale green shirt had long ago been used for straining water, so she wore only a pair of tattered dark green slacks and much-repaired sneakers. Patty's short platinum hair stuck up around her head like a punk halo. She wore a once-white, tattered fishing shirt with one sleeve missing and a cotton loincloth, made from the missing sleeve. Her sandals had inner-tube soles, held on with just a strip of canvas.

The afternoon rain slammed down outside the hut. Suzy was wearing a wreath of yellow orchids because today was December 23, her birthday. "Let's have a drink, huh?" She waved her arm expansively. "My treat."

"Double martini on the rocks with a twist," Carey said. "Patty, you *can't* have Perrier again."

"Then I'll have plain tomato juice with lemon. Somebody's got to carry you home, Carey."

"Line up the Fosters for me," Jonathan called from his bed, where he lay recovering from a second bout of fever. His pale, glistening skin stretched taut over his cheekbones, he was now an angular maquette of a man.

"Hot chocolate," Annie ordered, "with whipped cream."

"Pink champagne," Suzy decided.

Silvana said, "You'll all have fresh lime juice, because I've just made a jugful to celebrate Suzy's birthday." She lifted her head. "Listen, the rain's stopping."

"I'll have a triple martini," Carey giggled. "Two *double* triples for me."

Suzy sat up and sniffed sharply. "What's that stuff she's smoking?"

"Oh, my Gawd." Jonathan also sat up, then fell back against the bracken. "I was wondering when she'd get to it."

"Get to what?" Annie was perplexed.

"Marijuana. It grows like crabgrass out here."

"Sure does. I've been drying this for weeks. So pretty when I picked it . . . Delicate green shoots . . . Delicatessen . . . Wanna eat green shoes . . . Wanna eat something fast. I'm *staaaarving*."

Jonathan swung his legs over the side of his bed. "Give that to me, Carey."

Carey smiled foolishly. "Goin' get summa t'eat." She fell out of bed on all fours and crawled out of the hut into the churning mud beyond.

"It sure acts fast," said Annie, amazed.

Jonathan looked worried. "Go after her, Patty. Bring her back."

Suzy reported with delight, "There's another reefer on Carey's bed, and a bamboo lid with some fine, green powder in it. She's been rolling it up in dried leaves."

"Don't you touch that, Suzy!" Jonathan tried to yell, but his voice was too weak to rise above a croak.

"It's only *pot*—as smoked on campuses across the country."

"*Suzy!* Bring it to me!" Jonathan ordered. "I don't want anyone else out of their skull, understand? You can smoke the stuff till you're stupid once you get home, but you can't afford to smoke it in the jungle."

He tried to stand up, but his legs gave way and he fell back on the bed. "Patty, I told you to bring Carey back. Get out there!"

"Are you kidding? I'm not going to argue with someone that size when she's stoned," Patty said. "Hey, she's standing up now, sort of . . . She's taken her shirt off . . . Kicked her boots off . . . There go her pants . . . Now . . . trying to put her boots back on . . . Hey, she's fallen over . . . She's rolling in the mud . . . Lucky the fire's gone out because she just fell into it . . . Now she's got one boot on, but she can't seem to tie it."

All the women moved forward to peer out of the hut at the

rain-soaked scene. Suzy said enviously, "She sure seems to be having a good time."

Jonathan said, "Get her back in here at once."

Nobody took any notice of him.

Jonathan insisted, "If she tries to leave camp, you've got to stop her. *All* of you must stop her. Suzy can sit on her head—I mean it! Get out there and tie her hands behind her, then rope her to a tree, until she comes to her senses again."

Ignoring him, Patty continued to report, "Now she's at the mangoes . . . No, Silvana, leave her be, we can pick them up later. No use your going out there now. She's prancing around like a blond gorilla in army boots."

There was a crash from beyond the hut. "That was the smoking tepee," Patty called. "Now she's tearing at a mango covered with mud."

"Her or the mango?" Suzy asked.

"Both."

Jonathan muttered, "God help us when she discovers the coca shrub."

Suzy turned and looked at him sharply. "You mean there's cocaine out there as well?"

"There's a patch of it growing wild at the old settlement. Those five-foot canes with pale, sage-green leaves. The natives stir the leaves in a pot over a fire, then dry them and pound them into a powder mixed with ash, according to the strength required. During long trips at sea, the men'll go for days without sleep or food."

"Sounds just what we need," said Suzy.

"Naw, it wouldn't suit you, Suzy. You'd end up listless and resigned, a give-up sort of person. Then we'd never get out of here."

From beyond the huts came a crash.

"That was the bucket of crabs for this evening. Just as well Silvana's already boiled them," Patty reported. "No, don't go out there, Silvana, we can wash them later."

Silvana said, *"Porca miseria,* she'll wreck the camp. How long does this effect last?"

Jonathan said crossly, "Up to three hours depending how strong it is, and how much she smoked. *Put that down, Suzy.*"

Silvana said, "This is ridiculous! I'm going to get her back here before she wrecks the camp. She can lie down and sleep it off." She dashed from the hut.

Hanging around the hut entrance, Suzy reported, "Carey's hugging Silvana . . . That stuff sure makes you horny . . . No, I think Carey's trying to waltz with her . . . Silvana's just belted her . . . Now they're both down in the mud . . . Gee, mud wrestling, we should be selling tickets and making bets . . . Silvana just walloped her again . . . Boy, is Carey a mess! . . . They're down again . . . I think Silvana's going to knock her out . . . Silvana's standing up, she looks real mad . . . She's yelling at Carey in Italian and Carey's just lying there laughing . . . Now Silvana's stamping her foot; she's had enough, looks as if she's going to the pool."

Jonathan asked sharply, "What's Carey doing now?"

"She's heading up by the river, toward William Penn."

Jonathan pulled himself up from the bed and leaned on one elbow. "Patty, bring her back. You know damn well I can't."

"Are you kidding? After what she just did to Silvana?"

Jonathan yelled, "She's a menace to herself and a menace to the camp. Now get out there—*all* of you—and bring her back."

Suzy said pertly, "You only taught us to kill, not to mud-wrestle."

"Bring her back!"

Grumbling and laughing, the three women ran out into the dripping green forest.

Ten minutes later Annie, wiping the mud from her shoulders, returned to the hut. "Suzy and Patty are shadowing her. I forgot I was lookout, sorry. Are you sure you're okay on your own, Jonathan?"

"Sure, I'm fine, just wishing I was back at sea." Jonathan saw the sea as a friendly opponent, a constantly changing enigma, a challenge. It was something to be wary of, something to be survived.

Annie looked at his face and said wistfully, "I feel the same way about the snow. You'll soon be back at sea again."

"Not until we're damned sure that the Long Wet's over. You never take a chance with the sea, she's an unforgiving bitch."

By the riverbank the late afternoon sun stabbed through the high green canopy of leaves dappling the iridescent wings of giant butterflies and the peacock and emerald wings of birds of paradise—and the glistening mud that covered Carey's body as she crashed through the jungle, naked except for her boots.

Following her, Suzy panted, "Boy, is she going to have that morning-after feeling. Slowly remembering, then wishing you didn't."

Patty said, "She's getting badly scratched."

"We can't stop her, Patty."

The women carried rattan ropes. They had decided to jump Carey from behind, when they had the chance.

Carey loved to stand upriver of the waterfall, to edge her way through the undergrowth to a certain spot on the bank where she could listen to the chuckle and hiss of the water as it rushed toward the cliff. She liked to watch the malachite fronds of creepers, twined with butter-yellow orchids, that hung over the water's edge and were reflected in the rippling surface of the river. Now, as Carey crashed happily toward her favorite spot, she started to yodel.

Patty whispered to Suzy, "We'll have to do something, quickly. She'll have the entire Paui army here in no time."

Cautiously the two women started to move forward.

There was a noise like a spring snapping.

As the peacock wings of startled birds beat frantically above her, Carey stopped singing and stared lazily in front of her, at the few inches of ground between her feet and the river.

On the leaf-strewn bank lay a large blue-feathered bird, its gleaming wings tipped with a darker blue. There was an arrow through its throat.

* * *

All the women huddled in the darkness of the hut, shivering with fear and unable to sleep.

Once again Jonathan reassured them, "You're safe if you stay in the taboo area."

"But where does it *stop?*" Silvana whispered.

"I don't know exactly."

"Exactly. That's what's so frightening."

"It was only a warning," Jonathan said. "If they wanted to shoot Carey, they'd have done it, and serve her damn well right. Shooting a bird isn't taboo. In fact, ghost-granny is probably eating a ghost-bird for supper this very minute. But shooting Carey on this site would have polluted it forever."

MONDAY, DECEMBER 24

As she padded after Jonathan through the jungle, Patty thought that she'd never have imagined a Christmas Eve like this. For a moment her concentration wavered, then she firmly pushed all thought of Pittsburgh from her mind. She dare not think of home. And she dared not think of yesterday. She concentrated on the dank-smelling track ahead of her.

They were out because Jonathan was determined to have something better than roast rat for Christmas dinner.

Holding her club and her knife, Patty lifted her nose and sniffed, but although her sense of smell had greatly improved since being in the jungle, she could not smell whatever it was that Jonathan had sniffed.

Ahead of her, slowly and quietly, Jonathan moved to the right. He was circling the animal, getting upwind of the slight breeze blowing from the sea. The animal that Patty couldn't see was probably feeding. Maybe it was a wild pig.

Jonathan started to move forward. Patty followed ten paces behind, thinking, If he doesn't watch out, he'll hit William Penn. Then she realized that this was Jonathan's intention. He was going to move, fast, along William Penn Place, then quietly approach the animal from upwind.

Patty decided to stay where she was, so if the pig were alarmed and crashed her way, she could move forward and, with luck, drive it back into the path of Jonathan's gun.

Within minutes, to her horror, Patty heard someone moving to her left along William Penn—someone in boots, someone who was taking no precautions to walk silently.

Patty moved one step sideways, to hide behind a sandal-wood tree, and froze. Into her line of vision came a lone, brown-skinned, uniformed soldier.

Patty waited. Anyone accompanying him would be close on his heels. She counted thirty seconds, then started to move parallel to the soldier on the jungle path. Several possibilities whizzed through her sharpened mind as she moved, still concealed by the brush, shadowing the soldier. Was Jonathan on the track ahead? Was he hidden? Wherever he was, he'd be concentrating on that damned pig, he wouldn't be thinking about his safety—that was her job. If this agile, mean-looking little guy saw Jonathan, would he want to harm him? Would he try to capture him? Would he . . . ?

Patty had her answer when she saw the soldier stop abruptly, glance quickly behind him, then to either side. Reassured, he lifted his rifle.

She pulled her knife from her belt, knowing she had only a couple of seconds to act. As she moved onto the path, she was three yards behind him.

The soldier moved his head to his right shoulder to rest against the stock of his rifle. As he squinted along the barrel at the sight, Patty's only thought was, He's got a rifle and he's taking his time, so he's probably about to shoot Jonathan in the back.

Should she merely try to divert him, or should she take her knife by the handle and fling it at his back? But he was wearing a backpack. Anyway, suppose she missed?

She was now so near the soldier that it would have been easy to jump him from the rear, which would have guaranteed

427

a diversion. He wore a jungle hat, no helmet and, thank God, he was right-handed. By moving his head to the right to aim his rifle, the soldier had left the left side of his neck exposed.

The heart is slightly to the left of the body. If a knife with an eight-inch blade is plunged down to the hilt into the hollow in the left collarbone, with a left-handed thrust that goes straight down and slightly inward, then the knife will reach the heart because there is no bone or cartilage in the way, nothing to stop the knife blade.

Patty thought not of danger, nor of the consequences. She only thought, This is a number eight training situation. One, two, *strike!* With her knife in her left hand, she leaped at the man's back, raising her arm.

As she struck down into the man's neck, blood spurted from the wound and drenched her hand. The man gave a gasping cry, stumbled, dropped his gun and crumpled beneath her. Reacting in a frenzy of terror, Patty thrust again and again with the knife.

Hearing the noise, Jonathan came charging back along the jungle path.

He found Patty sprawled on top of a limp khaki figure and blood gushing onto the track. Quickly, Jonathan kicked aside the man's rifle and roughly pulled Patty off him. He flicked the man over and slit his throat. Then, M-16 in hand, he stood on the path, his head moving from side to side as he listened for any movement.

Eventually he whispered hoarsely, "You all right, Patty?"

"I think so," Patty said, and scrambled to her feet. She was covered in blood. It even dripped from her eyelashes.

Nothing in the jungle moved as Jonathan jerked Patty's knife from the man's body, wiped it swiftly on the grass and handed it back to her.

He whispered, "I think he was alone. Let's get his backpack off, drag him off the track and bury him. You take one foot and I'll take the other. Then we'll get back and clear up the path."

Patty didn't move, because she was staring at the man. She

was thinking that she'd just killed a human being. She was horrified and revolted.

Jonathan also stared at the body. He saw an AK-47 rifle, a khaki uniform; a soft-peaked cap, a long-sleeved shirt, a tee-shirt beneath it, a vestcoat, covered with zippered pouches, and a bottle hanging from a webbing belt.

Jonathan touched Patty's shoulder and whispered, *"Boots!"*

They dragged the body into the jungle. Then they cleared up the path, although Jonathan knew that any native would be able to tell in ten seconds that someone had just been killed on that spot.

They stripped the skinny brown body, shoved it into the vegetation and covered it with debris from the jungle floor. Again, Jonathan knew that anyone who was looking for the soldier would find the body very quickly.

Sitting back on his heels, Jonathan said, "If he was aiming to kill me, then the bastards must still be on the rampage." He checked the backpack. It contained twenty-five rounds of ammunition, two one-day ration packets, four packs of local cigarettes, six boxes of matches, a small glass bottle of crème de menthe and a length of flowered pink cotton. "Looks as if he was heading for Katanga with Christmas gifts. Oh, yes, it's also a holiday on Paui. The missionaries started it."

Jonathan stood up and looked thoughtfully at Patty. "So long as we stick inside the Golden Triangle and don't get caught on William Penn, we're reasonably safe from the natives. If terrorists come from the sea, then we've time to hide in the cave. But if they come overland from Paradise Bay, they'll have to cross the Burma bridge. So I'm going to show you how to sabotage it; it'll only take thirty seconds to slash through the two top ropes. It's not to be done except in an emergency, if we think they've deliberately come looking for us, because once we've done it, they'll know we're here."

MONDAY, DECEMBER 24, 1984

There was nobody in sight on the trail behind him. Harry pushed up his ski goggles, screwed up his eyes against the brilliant sun and looked across at the jagged white peaks which surrounded the valley. This wasn't how he'd planned to spend Christmas Eve, but within the miserable situation, he felt cheerful for the first time in weeks.

The early arrival of the cyclone season had stopped the search on Paui, not only from the air but also on land. If the downpours didn't wash tracks away, then they caused landslides which blocked the tracks. The multitude of streams and small rivers that flowed from the hill to the sea became muddy, foam-flecked torrents. During the Long Wet, the whole of Paui was impassable.

Dejected, Harry had flown back to Port Moresby on November 29. On the evening of Monday, December 3, he caught the Qantas 6:30 P.M. flight to Honolulu, then on to San Francisco. On the morning of Tuesday, December 4, the badly jet-lagged Harry rode the elevator up to the thirty-sixth floor of Nexus Tower. Seated in a pigskin swivel chair at the vast zebrano table in the hushed, understated luxury of the boardroom, he reported to the acting board.

When Harry finished, Jerry Pearce leaned forward and flicked off his cigar ash. He said, "We're currently operating here on two assumptions: one, our people will turn up; two, they won't." Being chief executive clearly suited Jerry Pearce. Behind rimless eyeglasses, the brown eyes were alert, but relaxed. He wore a superbly tailored dark-gray suit and looked handsomely crisp and immaculately dynamic, but somehow he remained as unconvincing as some male model who was acting the part of a corporate president for a *Fortune* ad. But Jerry was about to get a surprise, Harry thought. Perhaps, after all, Jerry would have to vacate that seat at the head of the table which fitted him so snugly.

Jerry said, "As you know, Harry, we're keeping in close contact with the State Department. We're doing everything we can, and no doubt they are, but we want it to be *seen* that we're giving this top priority, and that one of our top guys is handling it. As soon as you can, Harry, get back to Paui. Search again. Take a month if you have to."

Harry blinked. When he'd been on Paui, Jerry had ordered him to leave. Harry said, "I've already explained that *you* are the people who have the power to get a proper search going. That's why I've come here, to discuss it with you and the group in Washington. This can't be handled properly from Paui."

"Nonsense! Spend whatever's necessary, Harry," Jerry said firmly. "Within reason, of course. If they aren't alive, then we'll need proof of death. Here in the States, death can't legally be assumed until seven years after a disappearance. So the insurance companies won't pay up for seven years, unless we find some trace of them."

Somebody added, "By which time the money might have devalued by nearly fifty percent if inflation averages out at nine percent a year."

The man on Jerry's left said, "Charley and Patty between them were carrying more life insurance than the average passenger list of a Boeing 747."

"Plus the usual Nexus executive cover," Jerry added. "And Isabel's husband was also well covered by his company policy."

The man on Jerry's left said, "The total insurance figure will probably be an eight-figure sum. If they aren't coming back, their next of kin will be instant millionaires."

Harry said, "I expect they'd prefer not to be."

"Well, sure," Jerry said. "While you're here, Harry, we want you to visit all the families. That personal touch will reassure them that everything possible is being done. It's already been arranged. Your driver is waiting, and he has your schedule. Remember that to them you represent *hope*, Harry."

"I came here to get some action, not to pay social calls," Harry said.

A manservant appeared, wearing a white coat and black trousers; coffee was served in gold-rimmed white Wedgwood cups. Jerry Pearce shook a sugar substitute into his cup. He said, "Of course. We'll discuss that after you've seen the families. And when you return to Paui, finalize the contract with President Raki as fast as possible."

"He's still sore."

"The protection payments have been brought up to date," Jerry said. "We've also paid the extortionate interest he demanded."

"Raki's greedy," Harry said. "I hear he hasn't yet paid his army's wages. And he's been humiliated by us, as he sees it. We can expect problems."

"What sort of problems?" someone asked.

"He'll make appointments, then refuse to see me. He'll cat-and-mouse me. He'll ask for a specific sum, then as soon as I've agreed to it, he'll increase it. I suspect he wants more money than we've ever imagined."

"He's in your area, Harry," Jerry said. "He's your responsibility. Keep seeing Raki and stay friendly. Keep reminding him that, providing he makes a deal, our price will beat anyone else's. Remind him how much we've paid so far to Credit Suisse. Get on good terms, and make the deal as fast as you can."

"That's a tall order," Harry said.

"Now Harry . . ."

"I'd better tell you his new price."

After he'd spoken, there was silence around the table.

"He says that once we've dug it up, it's gone," Harry explained. "And he asked me to remind you that Nexus isn't mining for the sake of Paui."

Jerry said, "I'm tired of hearing Third World countries squawk that the multinationals are ruthlessly gobbling up their raw materials and exploiting them, when they're being paid a fortune for mining rights—plus those unethical special arrangements."

Harry said, "They don't see bribery as unethical."

Everyone winced.

Harry said, "Bribes are part of their system of operation, part of any deal. If you want to operate in some tribe's area, then you pay protection money to the headman. If you want some powerful person to use his influence to get you a contract, then you pay him for his power and he'll use part of the money for little payoffs all down the line, to see you have no problems."

"Bribery is legally forbidden," someone said irritably.

"East of Suez, they've been operating that way for thousands of years," Harry said. "And they don't see why they should stop buying power with money, just because the U.S. power-purchasing system is called 'union bargaining' or 'trade embargoes' or 'sanctions' . . . or whatever Lockheed called it." Harry looked at the tough faces around the table and thought, You can always find a civilized reason to excuse an uncivilized action.

"Will this new price get us the deal we want?" Jerry Pearce asked. "*All* mining rights on Paui for the next ten years?"

Harry shook his head. "Same deal as before, only it'll cost you more."

Jerry said, "We must insist on an all-rights deal."

So Jerry too knew about the cobalt and chromite deposits.

Jerry confirmed this later over lunch in the quiet mahogany surroundings of the Nexus Club. "Ed submitted ludicrously high security bills for his home on his expense sheet, but

Arthur okayed them. Clearly something was up. I checked Ed's trips and called for copies of the relevant lab reports. Couldn't get a copy of one of them, so I double-checked the dates against expenditures, and the only report that wasn't accounted for was Paui."

Harry said, "There are other things unaccounted for on Paui," then went on to tell Jerry of Brett's death and his doubts about the boat explosion. He felt in his pocket for Arthur's watch. Jerry recognized it instantly.

"Have you told Washington?" Jerry asked.

"If we tell Washington, nothing else may ever come to light. Raki likes the idea of a nice clean yacht explosion. He's decided that the *Louise* was overdue for service. He doesn't want anyone questioning his findings. He'd clamp down on further searching."

"What do *you* hope to find?"

"I don't know. Anything. Maybe another personal effect that can't be explained away."

Jerry nodded. "Give me that watch. I'll establish whether it's been in seawater. It doesn't look like it."

"I'd rather keep it," Harry said, returning the watch to the safety of his pocket.

"I'd rather you gave it to me," Jerry said. "It will be safer with me."

"I'd rather hang on to it for the time being, Jerry."

"Give me that watch, Harry."

Surprised, Harry stalled. "I want to check it out with Arthur's mother." Perplexed, he wondered why Jerry wanted the watch so badly.

"Well, I suppose . . . Okay, Harry, but after that, it goes in the office safe. That watch is our only proof."

"Sure, Jerry." Harry changed the subject. "Can you let me have the insurance lists of their personal valuables, including the women's jewelry? In case any of them turn up at Mrs. Chang's."

* * *

The golden-haired boy in the wheelchair roared, "You smell *old!* You *stink!*"

"Now, Stephen, that's no way to talk to your grandmother." Mildred Blauner briskly pushed up the sleeves of her scarlet jumpsuit. "Old people don't smell if they floss their teeth; you only have to sniff the floss to see why." Mrs. Blauner tapped the checkerboard between them. "You only say that because you're losing the game. If you're going to be a bad boy, I won't play with you."

No longer was Stephen called "difficult" or "frustrated" or "overstimulated." The adjectives used by his grandmother were "good" or "bad," as applicable.

Judy put her head around the door. "There's a Mr. Scott to see you. Shall I make coffee?"

Mrs. Blauner nodded. "Show him in here, please. He'll want to talk to Stephen."

The yellow-floored room looked like a cross between a gym and a toy shop, Harry thought as he looked at the expensive exercise appliances and the wall lined with shelves stacked with toys.

Beneath the short, blond curls of a Watteau cupid, large blue eyes stared at Harry. A rosebud mouth opened.

"*When are they going to find my mom?*" Stephen yelled.

"Mr. Scott won't speak to you if you shout," Mildred said in a mild voice. She put both hands on her knees to ease herself off a leather stool that was shaped like an elephant. "Nice of you to drop by, Mr. Scott."

Harry ducked as the checkerboard whizzed past his ear, followed by a hail of checkers.

"That child is a full-time job," Mildred said as she offered coffee to Harry. "Dr. Beck—that's Stephen's own doctor—is arranging for him to go into a private clinic where he'll have the same standard of care as he does at home. But he'll be with other kids, so he'll have to watch himself. They won't put up with his tantrums."

Harry looked sympathetic. "Dr. Beck said it should have been done long ago." His grandmother continued. "In a children's clinic, Stephen will be among other children who are similarly handicapped, so he won't be allowed any self-pity. He'll have to use the brains that the good Lord gave him, instead of brooding about what he hasn't got. If his parents don't come back, it's the only thing to do—and if they *do* come back, it will still be better for everyone."

Harry nodded.

She said in a low voice, "His *own* doctor says it's the right thing. Silver City is no place for a child—the people there have poodles, not children. And I'm not so young as I was. But I never expected to feel so bad about doing it."

Mrs. Blauner carefully placed her untouched cup of coffee on the small table beside her chair. Beneath her perfect makeup a sad, sagging face looked at Harry. "I thought Patty was only punishing herself by having Stephen at home. Now that I have to make the decision, I can understand how poor Patty felt."

"Why in hell do *we* have to see him?" Bill asked his brother above the staccato excitement of the football commentary.

"Jerry Pearce wants to show he's leaving no frigging stone unturned." Fred, the eldest, lay with his feet up on the flower-patterned sofa. "Why? You got a date tonight?"

"Maybe."

"Bill always has a date." Sprawled on the floor, nineteen-year-old Dave didn't take his eyes off the game. "What's happened to dinner?"

"Good old Harry is taking us out for a meal," Fred said.

"Why does *he* want to see *us*?" Bill asked.

"I told you. Nexus bullshit." Fred emptied the can of peanuts and threw it at Bill, who put up an arm, caught the can and slammed it back across the room. His brother hurled it back again.

Fourteen-year-old Rob said, "I think he has the hots for Mom."

His brothers laughed.

"No, I mean it. A couple of winters ago, Dad asked him to eat with us one Sunday," Rob explained. "Mom and I were breaking the ice on the pond in the front yard so the birds could drink. When Harry got here we were hidden behind the laurels. Mom saw him walking to the front porch and threw a snowball at him. Hit him in the back of his neck."

"So what proof is that?" Fred yawned noisily.

"He turned around, ready to murder, then saw it was Mom. So he just stood there, with this asshole grin on his face."

The doorbell rang.

"That'll be good old Harry," Fred said. "Toss me another beer."

Why couldn't they make decent coffee in Chinese restaurants, Harry wondered. The meal had been a series of uncomfortable silences. Harry sensed the dejection and depression beneath the tough-guy, monosyllabic conversation. The youngest brother, Rob, whose pale face and flaming hair reminded Harry of Annie, seemed the most forlorn.

Harry said, "What're you guys doing for Christmas?"

"Hadn't thought."

"Staying here."

"Nothing special."

"Dunno."

Fred finally said, "We've all been invited places but we'd rather stay here, together."

"That's what Mom would like," Rob explained.

Dave said, "Dad's sister asked us to Cleveland."

"Shit, who wants to go to Cleveland?" Fred asked.

"And anyway, fuck Christmas." Bill drained his beer. "It's overcommercialized, overrated and depressing."

Dave nodded. "Suicide rate soars at Christmas."

Harry said, "It wouldn't be Christmas without a few disappointments. But would you like to ski?" On a skiing trip there was always something to think about and talk about: skiing.

"No," Bill said. "We just want to stay here."

"We don't want to go anyplace," Dave said.

Harry said, "You *do* ski?"

"Sure, but not often," young Rob answered.

Harry looked at the three strapping young men and their teenage brother. "This is one Christmas you shouldn't spend at home. Get away where nobody knows what's happened and do something that takes all your concentration so you won't be able to think about anything else."

There was a pause.

"What the hell. Why not?" said Fred. "Anything's better than this."

On the morning of Wednesday, December 5, Jerry Pearce, whistling cheerfully, stepped out his front door into the early morning sun. His uniformed driver saluted and turned to open the door of the waiting black Lincoln.

Jerry nodded in acknowledgment, climbed inside and picked up the newspaper that lay waiting for him.

No way he was going to give up all this, he told himself.

He had reason to know that every other newly promoted acting vice president on the temporary Board felt the same way about *his* new position. He had sounded them all out, separately. Naturally, nothing had been *said*. The test had been at the previous day's Board meeting, where Jerry had certainly felt that everyone present was solidly behind him. What best served their purpose was to have a full-scale search, but Jerry had sensed they were all trusting him to make sure it didn't succeed.

What the hell, he thought. It was 99.9 percent certain they were dead by now anyway, watch or no watch.

Harry followed the black-coated butler past perfectly proportioned Chinese antiques, past full-sized fig trees, past modern sofas upholstered in subtle silks handwoven by Jack Lenor Larsen. They entered the conservatory, lush with orchids. The atmosphere was muggy and the smell of the earth was damp and rich and strong; it reminded Harry of Paui.

Mrs. Graham's pale gray gardening gloves matched her
pale gray gardening apron. She was eighty years old, and all
her life had been carefully looked after and given the best of
everything. She had not gone to school but had been taught by
a governess. In due course, her nurse had been replaced by a
personal maid. Her first car had been a dark green Bugatti.
She had been dressed by Mainbocher until his firm closed,
and she still had all those clothes, as well as her prewar
Schiaparellis and Balenciagas and her Paulette hats. They
were packed in tissue and stacked in boxes in the attic. Diana
Vreeland wanted them for the Metropolitan.

"It was good of you to come." Mrs. Graham held out her
elegant, thin hand. "Would you care for a martini before
lunch, Mr. Scott?"

Harry said, "I'd prefer scotch, please." He rarely drank at
midday and knew better than to accept one of Mrs. Graham's
legendary lethal martinis.

Harry's scotch was served with water imported from the
Grahams' own Highlands spring. No Perrier for her. They ate
in the breakfast room, through which ran a small stream.

Mrs. Graham looked out at the landscape. She said, "I hope
we hear some good news soon; Lorenza's baby is due in February and she's had an unpleasant pregnancy." Lorenza had
been with her grandmother when they heard of her parents'
disappearance. "It's not fair," Lorenza had sobbed again and
again. "It's not fair!"

Harry, who had heard about the scene, thought, Spoiled
women are like spoiled children; real life comes as a dreadful
shock to them, and they refuse to accept reality. But until they
do, such women remain children. You're never too old to
grow up, Harry thought, as he said, "I'm sorry to hear she's
taking it so badly."

As she carefully peeled a leaf from the artichoke on her
yellow Meissen plate, Mrs. Graham said, "I'd rather be old
than young again. Things aren't so painful when you're old.
You are no longer quite so surprised by life's unpleasant little
ways."

The butler removed the carpaccio plates and placed tiny individual cheese soufflés before them. The soufflés were followed by kumquats, nestling on vine leaves.

Selecting her fruit, Mrs. Graham said, "This President Raki, has he done everything possible to search?"

"He appears to have done everything reasonable."

"Not quite the same thing, is it?" Mrs. Graham peeled her kumquat with a malachite-handled silver fruit knife that bore the Russian imperial crest.

"No. But he's virtually a dictator, so he only sees his own point of view. That's his definition of 'reasonable.'"

Mrs. Graham said, "It is unreasonable to expect the unreasonable to be reasonable."

"You're saying we should circumvent dealing with Raki? If he doesn't stick to the rules, then we needn't? But I don't dare offend him. He could stop us from searching."

"Who doesn't dare doesn't win," Mrs. Graham said.

Never had Harry felt so hungry after a four-course meal.

Wearing identical hand-smocked pink dresses, the two little girls sat upright on Shaker chairs in the family room. Ingrid, who was eight, snuffled again; she always had trouble with her throat in winter. She asked, "Will you find them in time for Christmas?"

"I'm sorry, but I don't know." Again Harry wondered why these painful visits had been forced on him, when he had so little time in Pittsburgh. Five-year-old Greta looked as if she was about to cry again.

Swiftly Carey's sister said, "Have another cookie, Greta?"

"No, thank you, Aunt Ruth."

"Then thank Mr. Scott for coming to see you. Now hop upstairs to your baths."

Together the two little girls stood up, dejected but polite. They shook hands with Harry, then trailed from the room hand in hand.

Carey's sister said apologetically, "They don't usually cry. They don't do anything. They just sit around the house or

SAVAGES

stand hand in hand in the yard. I don't know what to do with them. In a way, not knowing is worse than bad news, because it prolongs the suspense. Their wounds can't start to heal until they're sure they've been wounded."

"Where will they spend Christmas?" Harry asked.

"I'm planning on staying a couple weeks until they've finished this school term, then I'm taking them back to Seattle. My three kids might cheer them up."

Harry doubted it.

"Be reasonable, Harry," Jerry Pearce said again, drumming his fingers on the zebrano table. The two of them were alone in the boardroom; the office staff had gone home long ago.

"I might say that to you," Harry retorted.

Jerry Pearce shrugged his shoulders. "We've done all we can, but now we must concentrate on running the company. A lot of people depend on us for their jobs. Shareholders won't stand for us sitting around wringing our hands forever. It's sad, it's tough, but it's happened. You've got to accept that, Harry."

Slowly, Harry said, "You don't *want* me to galvanize Washington into action, do you? You've kept me busy visiting the grief-stricken relatives—to get me out of the office and waste my time. The Board is using me to make everyone believe a thorough search is being made. What would suit you, Jerry, is a long-drawn-out, incompetent search, during which you establish your ability to run this company. The longer you're acting president, the greater chance you have of showing that you can do the president's job and should keep it if those missing men are never found. And there will be no criticism from the Board of the way this search is being conducted, because it isn't in their interest to have those people found. Those acting vice presidents all want to be *permanent* vice presidents, don't they?"

Jerry looked at Harry, who was standing at the huge uncurtained windows, his hands in his pockets, against a background of the starlit winter sky. Jerry said, "We've all been

441

very impressed by your efforts, Harry, but we feel there's nothing further to be done. Forget this Boy Scout nonsense and get back to business. Stop this wild-goose chase and concentrate on tying up on the contract with Raki as fast as you can. We all know he's a bastard, but then so are a lot of people, and you know how to handle him."

Harry thought, It's a good thing I didn't let Jerry have Arthur's watch. It would have turned out *not* to belong to Arthur and then, somehow, it would have been misplaced or stolen, conveniently lost forever.

Jerry looked at Harry's angry face and said, "Perhaps this is a little premature, but there's a strong feeling around here that *you* should have a seat on the Board. Think of what goes with *that*, Harry. The stock options, the prestige, the money. Now is the time for you to concentrate on your career. This could be your great opportunity."

Harry felt like smashing Jerry's glasses into his skull. Did Jerry think he was stupid, didn't know he was being bought off? At that moment Harry realized that the most important thing in his life was finding Annie. And if Annie was still alive, he'd never let her go again. What the hell, he could always get another job.

Harry said, "Sure, I'll go back to Paui as soon as I can— but I'm going to keep on looking for them. And you can't stop me, Jerry. Because I've got that watch! And that's proof that there's something to search for!"

As he strode out he slammed the door. It felt great.

On Thursday morning, December 6, Harry flew from Pittsburgh to Los Angeles. As there were no seats on a Qantas flight, he caught the Pan Am 2:30 P.M. flight to Sydney, where he arrived at 4:20 on Saturday afternoon, having lost Friday by passing over the international dateline. He spent the next two weeks working almost nonstop in his office.

He heard on the Nexus grapevine that Arthur's daughter had given birth to a boy, two months premature on December 12.

On Saturday, December 22, Harry again caught his favorite

Qantas 6:30 P.M. flight from Sydney to San Francisco. The Boeing 747 landed on the West Coast at 6:20 P.M. Harry caught the night flight to Pittsburgh, where a limousine waited at the airport to drive him the last sixteen miles of his journey to Annie's home where he would meet her boys and take them away for Christmas.

Harry took Annie's boys to the place in the Allegheny Mountains where he had skied with their mother. Of course Wisp had changed a lot in twenty-five years, though there were no plush condominiums or four-star restaurants. People came here to ski. Instead of a few wooden cabins and a single tow rope, the ski resort now had a base lodge and three chair-lifts, a T-bar, and Poma lift and there were now sixteen trails. Parts of the "Face" had the toughest moguls you'd find any-where; "Possum" and some of the other trails meandered gently from summit to base, which gave them plenty of choice. Harry had learned never to trust a person's own judg-ment of his skiing ability, and maybe Annie's boys didn't ski as well as they thought.

Harry had reserved a six-person apartment in the lodge. Annie's boys banged into it in their heavy ski boots and threw their gear on the bunks.

Harry said, "Before we start, I'd like to suggest that, until we get back to town, no one talks about anything but skiing."

"Immersion amnesia," Fred grunted.

Harry nodded. "Skiing takes all your concentration. That's why we came here."

Again, Harry turned to look behind him, where the trail curved down from the pine woods. Still no sign of young Rob. When they got back, Harry would have to speak to the boys about waiting for him. He'd also have a word with that crazy Dave. Just after lunch, Harry had seen him going for a fifteen-foot jump off a cliff onto a flat landing. Harry had yelled to him to stop. Dave had given a rebel yell and taken no notice. He went over, almost in free fall, and landed so hard that his skis went down eighteen inches and his poles were

almost buried in the snow. Dave had struggled his way out of
the snow, scowled back up at Harry and his brothers, then
continued down the mountain, too fast and clearly out of control.

"We all have different ways of showing grief," Harry had
said, grim-faced, to the others. "But smashing yourself up on
skis seems pretty pointless. Your mother wouldn't like it."

Now, in the late afternoon, Harry looked up at the sky. The
sun had disappeared behind pale clouds. Again he looked back
along the trail.

The small figure of fourteen-year-old Rob appeared between the pines, moving at a snail's pace in graceless, tense
jerks. By the time the boy reached him, Harry realized that he
was terrified.

"What happened, Rob?"

Rob's teeth were chattering. "I lost you just before the trail
hit the trees. I fell on the snowfield, above the crevasse. I
knew the crevasse was there, because I saw it on the last run
down."

Harry nodded. The crevasse plunged straight down about a
hundred and fifty feet onto rocks. "You must have been too far
over to the left."

Rob shivered. "I started to slide. The snow was frozen and I
couldn't stop, I couldn't get a grip with my skis. I just slid *on*
and *on* toward the crevasse. I thought I was going over."

"But you *didn't* go over."

"I hit a snow ledge, and it stopped me. Can we rest here a
bit longer?"

Harry shook his head. "Best be getting down. It's getting
late, and look at that sky. We'll go slowly."

A look of panic crossed the pale, freckled face. "I don't
think I can manage it, Harry."

"Let me rub you warm." Harry pulled off his own cap and
crammed it on the flame curls. He started to rub Rob's arms,
toward the heart, to improve his circulation.

Rob collapsed in a heap on his skis. "I *can't* move any
further."

"Quit that," Harry said. "I can't carry you, Rob, and it's not fair to get a stretcher up the mountain in the dark, when you don't need it. Just get up and do it."

Shivering, Rob shook his head.

Harry held out his ski pole. "Hang on." He pulled the reluctant Rob to his feet and brushed the snow from him. "Now we're going down slowly, Rob. Stick behind me. Try to see everything around you, not just the bump ahead. Widen your focus, relax and let your skis take you down."

Slowly they skied down the mountain.

In their heavy boots they clumped through the lodge door into a blast of heat and light. They could smell hot rum punch and hear recorded sleigh bells and carol singing. "God rest you merry gentlemen, let nothing you dismay . . ."

"Hot showers and hot drinks," Harry said to Rob as he took off the exhausted boy's boots.

As they approached their apartment, they could hear the noise from down the corridor. A door opened and a woman in curlers yelled out, "Any more noise and I'll call the manager."

When Harry opened the door, a pillow hit him in the face. It had been thrown by Fred, the eldest, at his two brothers, who were struggling with each other. Their bodies banged first against the bunks, then against the couch. There was a sound of splintering wood as the two of them fell onto a chair.

Harry dropped the ski boots. He leaped forward and tried to tear the two six-footers apart. All three landed on the floor, a mass of flailing arms and legs.

"Rah-rah-rah!" Fred yelled from the window and threw a half-empty can of beer into the fray. It hit Rob on the ear, and beer frothed over the floor.

Rob slammed the door shut and stood with his back to it. He yelled, "Fred, you bastard, you're drunk again."

"Fucking tired of setting a good example," Fred shouted. "Fucking tired of fucking Christmas. What have *we* got to celebrate?" Fred looked exactly the way Duke had in photographs taken when he was young. Huge and craggy.

Rob rubbed his ear and yelled, "You keep away from *me!*"

But he wasn't really angry, he'd just been taken by surprise. Poor Fred had taken it harder than his brothers. As the eldest, Fred had had to deal with the lawyers and all that shit, and his math degree didn't seem to be much use when it came to dealing with the family finances. For some reason Fred wasn't allowed to use his parents' bank account, but how else could he pay the maids and the gardener?

Bill and Dave had been irritated by Fred's sudden overprotectiveness and anxiety. Rob wished Fred would stop drinking.

Fred flung another pillow at the struggling group on the floor. The pillow split and feathers flew through the air like a snowstorm in a glass paperweight.

Rob felt tears coming. He rushed into the bathroom, slammed the door and locked it. Someone had been sick on the green tile floor.

Rob leaned against the door and told himself that only kids cry. He was the only one of the four brothers who refused to believe their parents were dead. It was too frightening to think they were dead, that they'd been snatched away from him. He was so scared that he couldn't stand it much longer. He felt the way he'd felt when he was little and Mom would walk ahead of him talking to one of the others and he would yell, "Wait for me!" He remembered the anguish of being a small child abandoned by the adult who meant safety. But she'd always turned, and smiled and waited.

This time she hadn't. This time, she'd abandoned him. Softly Rob cried, "I'm *frightened*." Primitive terror overcame him again, as it had during the afternoon on the ski slope. He slid to the floor and wept.

Harry eventually succeeded in separating Bill and Dave. Dave lay slumped in an armchair, while Harry held back the snarling Bill.

Bill felt as if he were a piece of elastic that was being slowly stretched to snapping point. He was not numb with disbelief like Fred. He was simply furious. He was angry with his parents for dying. He felt cheated. He was angry with

Nexus for not paying the wages of their household staff, for sending his father to that dangerous place and *sending his mother as well*—needlessly. He was angry with anyone who sympathetically asked, "Any news?" or who said, "Gee, Bill, I was sorry to hear . . ." They could keep their fucking sympathy to themselves.

Dave leaned forward, put his elbows on his knees and buried his face in his hands. Dave thought he never should have told Bill how he felt.

As Bill snarled and snapped at him, Dave felt he'd been pushed to the wall. He wanted to blame *someone* for the death of his parents; he wanted to attack, smash, destroy *someone*. Why not himself? He hadn't even *asked* if the Paui trip was dangerous. He hadn't done anything. Self-hatred gnawed at him.

Harry finally released Bill and said, "Give me a beer, Fred. No, don't throw it, mate." He put up one hand and caught the viciously thrown can.

"Don't call me mate." Fred knew that all his brothers felt the same way, they all resented this semi-stranger who presumed to share their sorrow.

Harry said quietly, "Where I come from, it's what you call a good friend."

"What makes you such a good friend? We hardly know you."

"I'm a friend of your mother's," Harry said, pulling open the can of beer as he moved to the bathroom door. He called, "Come out, Rob, there's a good lad. I want a hot shower. And you can't stay there all night."

Harry's feelings were intense and confused. *If* Annie were alive and *if* they ended up together, then his love for her would have to include feeling at least friendly and concerned about these four hulks. No, that wasn't fair. Rob was a gutsy, good lad. But having the other three around was going to be far more difficult, by about a million percent.

Rob unlocked the bathroom door and stood there pale and unsmiling. "They're not always like this," he said sadly to

Harry, looking beyond him to the wreckage in the apartment. "They weren't like this before. They're great guys, really." Silently he added, Like you.

Harry nodded. He didn't say anything, but they all knew he was grieving as well. Like them, he had been raised tough, not to show emotion, not to speak about his feelings.

He could see that the four brothers simply couldn't escape from their bereavement. The sadness seemed to fill them and weigh them down and paralyze them.

Harry turned to them. He said, "All I'm going to say is that your mother wouldn't like this. Your mother loved you, she put her life into you and she wouldn't want you to quit on it like this." He paused. "And there's one other thing I want to tell you. No matter what you idiots do, I'm going to be in your corner."

They all knew why.

◄ 22 ►

WEDNESDAY, DECEMBER 26, 1984

Instead of being horrified at killing the native soldier, Patty merely said, "It wasn't as bad as killing the hotel goat," and then refused to talk about it.

"I never thought that guilt-ridden sissy had it in her," Carey said to Annie as they gathered firewood. "That wasn't the gutless wimp I remember back in Pittsburgh."

"She wasn't that bad," Annie said.

"She *always* made mountains out of molehills," Carey reminded her.

"Only sometimes," Annie argued.

Carey snorted. "She always had a good reason for never helping anyone out—too busy!"

Annie's bundle of firewood started to fall apart. Carey said, "If we tie two bundles of wood in the middle, you can loop the rattan around your neck and carry two loads instead of one. Let me show you."

As she retied their bundles, Carey said, "How about the difference in Silvana? Back in the old days she never lifted a finger."

"The camp would be far less comfortable if it wasn't for Silvana," Annie agreed.

"Remember what a snob she was? Now she's the maid and

449

a really good cook." Carey stood up and hung the two bundles of wood around Annie's neck.

Annie said, "Maybe we've all *always* been tougher and smarter than we thought we were."

That night Carey couldn't get to sleep. She had been bitten on the eyelid by a mosquito and the irritation kept her awake. On one side of Carey's bed, Silvana muttered in her sleep. On the other side, Suzy was mercifully quiet.

While Jonathan was feverish, he had slept in the lean-to and Patty had slept on his bamboo bed. When he recovered, Patty, who still treated Suzy as if she had the plague, refused to move back into the hut where Suzy slept, so Carey had moved in with Suzy and Silvana.

Suddenly Suzy started to whimper. Carey sighed. She knew what would happen next. Suzy, who hadn't even been present when Patty knifed the soldier, seemed to have been most affected by the killing.

Suzy started to scream.

Carey rolled off her bed and shook Suzy awake. "It's all right, it was only a dream." She cradled Suzy in her arms and stroked her. "There, there, baby, it's all *over*," Carey whispered.

"I can't . . . *can't* stand violence," Suzy wept.

"Then you came to the wrong Club Med."

Suzy continued to cry—partly because she was furious with herself. She'd always prided herself on being street-tough, but when Jonathan and Patty had suddenly appeared in camp covered in blood after burying the soldier, Suzy recalled the childhood dread she had felt when she heard the heavy shuffle of her father's boots coming up the stairs. Since the killing, Suzy's nightmares had been filled with shuffling boots and knives and blood.

Now, as she clung to Carey, Suzy remembered clinging to her mother in the top apartment of the rickety, peeling house on Shadyside. During the day Pa worked in the clerical department of one of the big steel mills; at night he got drunk.

He didn't hit Suzy as much as he hit her mother. He didn't beat them every evening, but often enough, so that both the fear and the anticipatory dread dominated her childhood. When put to bed, she never fell asleep immediately. As soon as her mother had tucked her in and kissed her goodnight, Suzy, in her Mickey Mouse pajamas, jumped up and stood in the crib, her ear to the living-room wall. She listened anxiously in the dark—which frightened her—for sounds of what frightened her far more. She could never hear what her parents were saying, but from the tone of their voices—her father's rising, her mother's pleading—she could judge whether an interruption might avert violence. When she became more terrified of staying than of going, she would run into the living room to ask for a glass of water—anything. Sometimes it worked.

Anticipation was far worse than injury. By the time she was five, Suzy had been broken in and was slightly contemptuous of physical pain. You simply had to think of something else while he was doing it. You had to distance yourself mentally from the scene, you had to watch it from the ceiling and just wait, stoically, until it was over.

There was never any conversation in that home. The less she said, the less likely she was to say the wrong thing, whatever *that* was on a given evening. She learned to judge his mood from the way he walked up the stairs; she learned to will herself to be invisible, to hide and to lie. She learned to live with the humiliation, the impotence and the guilt of knowing that she could do nothing for her mother, that she had to submit to the bull rage and then repair the damage when it was over—wash off the blood, kiss the bruises, carefully feel the battered nose and decide whether or not to head for Emergency, where she'd tell some lie about walking into the bathroom door in the dark. But she never admitted to the shame of what had really happened, because public humiliation would be even worse than private self-disgust.

Suzy could never understand why her cowed mother hadn't left, hadn't gotten a divorce. She couldn't understand why, on those occasions when they had managed to escape into the street in their nightclothes and run to the police station, nobody did anything except scratch their heads and say, "Family dispute." Nor could Suzy understand why, on the day when her mother had finally summoned up the courage to leave, her father had broken down and wept, begged her not to go, saying he needed her, *he loved her.* Suzy's mother, more terrified of going than of staying, had fallen into his arms and stayed. Whereupon the same old cycle had started again within a week. Suzy felt baffled, impotent rage, unable to understand their mutual dependency.

So, in a way, Suzy had never really been a child. Almost as soon as she could walk, she had learned to associate the word *man* with tyranny, violence and fear. She had never had a genuine relationship with a man, not even with good-natured, besotted Brett. If you had any power at all, Suzy had reasoned, then you used it to protect yourself, to acquire necessities, then luxuries—and you never let your guard down. When you were old enough to get the hell out, you did—in spite of your shame at deserting your mother, in spite of being haunted by your final sight of her reproachful, uncomplaining face. You never once called her. You only wanted to get away from that whole scene, to erase it from your memory.

Suzy had made herself into an entirely different person. She thought she had left behind all traces of the terrified little girl cowering in her Mickey Mouse pajamas against the bars of her crib. But she had never been able to run away from that feeling of apprehension and dread in the face of violence, so whenever she thought something threatened her she became as tense and prickly as a sea urchin. "Touchy," Brett had called her. She trembled, couldn't speak and stood rooted to the spot, ready, once again, to dissociate herself from physical abuse as she had done so long ago.

In the dark, Carey stroked the top of Suzy's head. "Poor baby. Where's your mother now, Suzy?"

"Just a few months after I ran off, she fell down the stairs and hit her head. Eight days in a coma and then she was a goner. Haven't seen *him* since the funeral. Couldn't speak to him." With the back of her hand, Suzy wiped her nose. "I never want to see the skinny little bastard again," she sobbed.

"Poor baby," Carey said comfortingly.

THURSDAY, DECEMBER 27

Carey was picking pieces of cold shrimp from the turtleshell and giving them to Suzy, who smiled happily.

"Why should Suzy have all the best parts," Patty complained.

"Shut up, Patty," said Carey, "or I'll give you the slap you deserve for the way you treat her."

Silvana and Annie looked at each other and decided to keep out of it.

Patty glared at Carey but said nothing.

Silvana gazed up at the velvet blackness of the night sky. The starlight was far brighter, the stars far bigger, than in the West. When she looked up, enveloped by the night, she felt at peace. She often woke at three in the morning and would creep out to the clifftop and wait for dawn, watching the dark sky lighten first to primrose, then to flame, as the sun heaved itself over the horizon.

After her morning dip in the pool, Silvana would stand on the edge of the cliff watching the birds and looking down on the aquamarine water of the lagoon, turning her head from the cliffs at the southern point to the lush dark mangrove trees on the northern tip. Then she would scramble down the cliff path and run toward the sea.

She scrunched the still cool sand between her toes as she walked among the tufts of weeds that grew on the sand. If the big boulders were uncovered at low tide, she would jump from boulder to boulder, oblivious to the danger of slipping on the slimy surface. All the time, she was aware of the hypnotic sound of the sea lapping at the rocks to its own rhythm— tempting and dangerous. Silvana felt its bounty was offered by an invisible provider—mother earth.

During the day, Silvana didn't mind the wet, sultry oppressiveness of the jungle nearly as much as the others. Now slim and lithe, she slipped through that thick green tangle like a snake, relishing the dim, luminous light of the forest, where she felt a savage sort of welcome extended to her. She felt happily at peace when the rain stopped and every leaf shone and sparkled, when the raindrops dazzled like diamonds.

Silvana, who had never felt at home in Pittsburgh, now felt at home on Paui. She felt that she belonged here, in this place. Here she was at peace.

Silvana made a decision: she wasn't going to leave.

"Not leave Paui!" the others exclaimed that night. They were squatting around the campfire, waiting for the moon to rise.

"Not leave the Pacific," Silvana corrected them. "I'm going back to Fiji, and maybe try and do something useful there. When we were fishing there, two years ago, I fell and sprained my ankle. Every day until we left, the district nurse visited me at the hotel. That nurse was in touch with all the babies she had delivered. She watched them grow up. I remember thinking how wonderful it must be, to spend your life helping people—being *really* needed. So last night I decided that after we get back, I'm going to fly to Fiji and find that nurse and see if there's anything I can do to help her. She'll know what's needed. I might build a small hospital for children."

"But what about Lorenza?" Annie exclaimed.

"Lorenza is a married woman, she's not my baby anymore," Silvana said, with a new briskness. "It's almost as easy to direct-dial New York from Fiji as it is from Pittsburgh. I'll fly back home twice a year, and Lorenza can bring her children to Fiji. Imagine visiting with your grandmother on a Pacific island!"

"But your lovely home!" Suzy exclaimed.

Silvana shrugged. "I've never felt at ease in it. I want no more elaborate social obligations, but simple, real ones."

Suzy was shocked. "But all your lovely things . . ."

Silvana said, "The more you have, the more you want. I suspect that you're the most content when you limit your possessions to necessities."

"But these places are *uncivilized*," Patty said.

"I'm starting to believe those people who say that anxiety is a disease that you catch from civilization. I could never again live as I did before. I want to take control of my own life and lead it in a more satisfying way. Power is having choices, and this is what I choose to do."

Eventually Jonathan broke the stunned silence. "First we've got to get you all back to Pittsburgh."

As the end of February approached, an air of anticipation could be felt in the jungle camp. It could be seen in the way the women threw off their apathy. No longer did they drag their steps between the campfire and the lookout tree—just a few steps, but a journey that had nevertheless drenched them in sweat.

Now that they were about to leave it, they had all become more conscious of the languorous beauty and bounty of the island.

At dawn, they now saw what Silvana saw—that the sky was like the soft gleam of pearls against velvet, that the thick tangle of the tropical forest was enigmatic and awesome. At night around the campfire all the women were less conscious of the hovering mosquitoes and more aware of the heavenly starlight bathing the dark edge of the rain forest. No longer were the night sounds sinister as they listened to the soft wind in the trees and the deep roll of the sea as it roared over the reef.

TUESDAY, FEBRUARY 26, 1985

As suddenly as it had started, the rain stopped. The sun shone all day.

"So the Long Wet's stopped two days early," Jonathan said. "We'll wait another two days to make sure, then we'll launch the raft on March first, an hour before high tide, at ten o'clock that night."

"Why can't we launch at dusk, like last time?" Suzy asked. "We don't want to load in the dark. We're bound to slip on that steep path down to the beach."

Jonathan didn't answer immediately. Then he said, in the reassuring voice which they now recognized as meaning "trouble ahead," "We gotta assume them villagers down the coast are hostile because we've polluted their sacred site. They wasn't expecting us to leave before, but they know we'll try to leave as soon as the Long Wet's over. I don't want a fight in the lagoon, or just beyond the reef. Once we're outside . . . well, we got two rifles."

He looked at their resigned faces. "Sure, launching in the dark ain't ideal, but it's more important not to be seen. They won't suspect we'll launch at night, and with any luck they'll all be stoned to the gills, celebrating the end of the Long Wet."

FRIDAY, MARCH 1

The hours passed very slowly until nightfall. Hidden under the trees at the top of the slope, the thirty-foot bamboo raft waited, ready to be eased on log rollers down the slope of the cliff.

All that day the women worked quietly at the slow but

steady pace which they had learned was most effective in the heat.

Once again they packed their belongings in their belt bags. Once again they sharpened their fish knives, filled the bamboo water containers, checked the dried-fish containers, piled fruit and coconuts into the rattan string bags and neatly stacked all their provisions in the first hut in order of embarkation.

From dusk onward they waited, their senses heightened by guarded anticipation and watchfulness. Nobody listened to the symphony of the night.

At nine o'clock Jonathan said softly, "Okay, let's go. Get up the lookout tree, Suzy. The rest of you get the provisions down to the beach."

At the entrance to the hut, Silvana swiftly and silently loaded up the other four women who were doing pack-horse duty. It was Silvana's job to see that they carried as much as possible as safely as possible as they struggled down the cliff path in the moonlight.

At ten o'clock the women took up their launch positions. Suzy was in the lookout tree, around which the rope was half-hitched, with Carey beneath her, ready to pay the rope out slowly. Patty's rope was hitched around a neighboring eucalyptus.

On the cliff, Annie acted as Carey's lookout; Silvana was signaling to Patty.

Jonathan checked the launch logs, then whispered, "Okay, get ready to go."

He scrabbled down the cliff path and took his place at the edge of the waterfall rocks. Because it was high tide, he had to stand much nearer the cliff than he had done at the first launch, and it was harder for him to see the women. Ankle-deep in water, he tilted his head back. He could just see Annie and Silvana, silver-and-black figures on top of the cliff.

Annie saw Jonathan raise both his arms. Annie raised her left arm, and Carey let out a foot of rope. Simultaneously, Silvana raised her right arm and Patty let out a foot of rope. The raft slithered forward and jerked to a stop.

After one minute Jonathan again raised both his arms. Again, the raft slithered forward and jerked to a stop. It would be slow progress, but the cliff was steep, and it was important to let the ropes out evenly or the raft would swing from side to side.

After fourteen minutes of tension, as he was raising his arms for the fourteenth time, Jonathan suddenly heard a click that sounded like metal on metal. Feeling naked and vulnerable, conscious that he made a clear target in the moonlight, he dropped both his arms.

Above him, Annie and Silvana dropped both their arms. Obediently, Carey and Patty stopped letting out their ropes.

There was a rustle in the lookout tree. "What's the matter?" Suzy whispered down.

"Don't know."

Anxiously the women waited.

After two minutes had passed without incident, Jonathan raised both hands. The raft, out of sight on the slope above him, rolled forward on its carefully controlled descent.

In the tree, Suzy twisted around to watch. Thoughtless in her excitement, she stepped backward onto a branch that she hadn't tested.

With a crack like a rifle shot, the gnarled branch gave way. Both the branch and Suzy crashed to the ground.

They fell on Carey, who jumped and screamed—and let go of the rope.

As Carey's rope unraveled around the tree, her side of the raft crashed forward, then slewed around, pitching its full weight suddenly and unexpectedly on Patty's rope, which sliced through Patty's grip, burning both her palms. In agony, she let go.

The raft swung back in the opposite direction, then crashed out of control down the slope, heading like a deadly toboggan toward the clifftop.

Annie managed to jump out of the way just before the raft careened past. Although it was far lighter than the first raft that they'd built, this raft *was* thirty feet long and gathering speed as it bumped down the steep slope.

With a final crash, it lurched over the top of the cliff.

On the beach below Jonathan heard a scream and saw Annie disappear. We've been attacked! he thought.

Then he saw the raft hurl over the clifftop, blotting out the stars. Frozen with disbelief, he watched it drop toward the waterfall, bounce off the rocks at the bathing pool, launch itself into the air and fly toward him.

He thought, She'll smash to pieces on these rocks if I don't do something. Then the sharp edge of the raft caught him on the right side of his head near the temple. The force knocked him backward and his head crashed against a boulder, fracturing his skull. He died instantly.

Dangerously fast, Carey hurled herself down the side of the cliff, followed by Suzy. Below them, the raft crashed into the water and swirled out into the black lagoon on the waterfall current.

Scratched and bleeding, Carey reached the sand, raced across it and hurled herself into the sea, determined to retrieve the raft—their only hope of escape—before it was swept out to sea. There were six vine ropes trailing from the raft. If she could catch just one of them, she could haul herself aboard.

Carey ran through the shallows, took a deep breath and dived in. Inhale on stroke four, inhale on stroke six . . . She swam faster than she ever had before.

By the time Suzy scrambled onto the beach, Carey was halfway to the raft. It was nearing the gap in the reef, where the coral waited, razor-sharp.

From the water's edge, Suzy called in horror, "Come *back*, Carey! Sharks beyond the reef!"

Even if Carey managed to haul herself aboard the raft, without paddles she would be at the mercy of the current, and without food or water, she would soon die.

Head down, unable to hear, Carey headed for the raft.

that they'd built, this raft was thirty feet long and gathering
speed as it bumped down the steep slope.

With a final crash, it lurched over the top of the cliff.

On the beach below Jonathan heard a scream and saw
Annie disappear. We've been attacked, he thought.

Then he saw the raft hurl over the clifftop, blotting out the
stars. Frozen with disbelief, he watched it drop toward the
waterfall, bounce off the rocks at the bathing pool, launch
itself into the air and fly toward him.

He thought, She'll smash to pieces on these rocks if I don't
do something. Then the sharp edge of the raft caught him on
the right side of his head near the temple. The force knocked
him backward and his head crashed against a boulder, fracturing his skull. He died instantly.

Dangerously fast, Carey hurled herself down the side of the
cliff, followed by Suzy. Below them, the raft crashed into the
water and swirled out into the black lagoon on the waterfall
current.

Scratched and bleeding, Carey reached the sand, raced
across it and hurled herself into the sea, determined to retrieve
the raft — their only hope of escape — before it was swept out
to sea. There were six thin ropes trailing from the raft. If she
could catch just one of them, she could haul herself aboard.

Carey ran through the shallows, took a deep breath and
dived in. Inhale on stroke four, inhale on stroke six . . . She
swam faster than she ever had before.

By the time Suzy scrambled onto the beach, Carey was
halfway to the raft. It was nearing the gap in the reef, where
the coral waited, razor-sharp.

From the water's edge, Suzy called in horror, "Come back,
Carey! Sharks beyond the reef!"

Even if Carey managed to haul herself aboard the raft,
without paddles she would be at the mercy of the current, and
without food or water she would soon die.

Head down, unable to hear, Carey headed for the out

BOOK FIVE

PERIL

◀ **23** ▶

Racing after the raft in the lagoon, Carey suddenly realized her danger and started to fight her way out of the waterfall current that was carrying her toward the narrow, coral-fanged channel, beyond which lay the ocean.

Carey knew that it was useless to try to swim against the current, so she turned south and concentrated on swimming parallel to the beach, fighting sideways out of the current until she was clear. Then she made another right-angled turn and headed back toward the sand.

While Carey fought for her life in the moonlit water, Annie had slithered down the cliff behind Silvana—far too fast for safety. Together, they dragged Jonathan from the water, knowing all the while that he was not unconscious but dead.

For half an hour Patty administered the kiss of life to Jonathan, while Carey lay exhausted and panting, her head in Suzy's lap, on the bone-white beach. Moonlight brushed the scene in black and silver.

Patty finally sat back on her heels and said, "It's no use." She burst into tears.

Careless of their safety, all the women huddled around the thin body on the sand. They sobbed as they held his still-warm hands and kissed them. They stroked his hair, they kissed his face, they begged him not to leave them. They sorrowed until

Suzy threw back her head and howled to the sky, swearing to
God that she'd never believed in Him and now she knew she
was right—He didn't exist, there was *nothing* up there.

In that case, Annie wondered, to whom did Suzy think she
was shouting? She said, "We've got to get him off the beach
or they'll know that we've lost our man."

"How can you be so goddamn brisk and practical when he's
only just died?" Suzy cried.

"Because he wouldn't want anyone else to die," Annie said.

With difficulty, they heaved Jonathan onto Carey's back,
his arms dangling over her shoulders. With a strength she
hadn't realized she possessed, Carey pulled him up the cliff,
while Silvana pushed from behind.

They took him to his hut and laid him on the bamboo bed.
Jonathan's blue eyes stared upward—they couldn't make the
eyelids stay shut.

As soon as it was light enough to see, they lugged the stores
back up the cliff, then gathered yellow orchids and arranged
them around Jonathan's body, carefully heaping the blossoms
over the muscular brown arms which now lay folded upon his
breast. The flowers heaped around his bearded face had
looked ludicrously unsuitable, so they removed them.

Eventually Annie wiped her nose on the back of her hand
and said, "We'll have to bury him quickly. You know what the
meat smells like if we leave it for a day. Otherwise the rats
will get him."

"He'd want to be buried at sea," Suzy said.

"We've nothing to bury him in," said Annie. "I think you
have to sew a body up in a bag and weight it down, or it
floats. The lagoon's too shallow, and they'd see us doing it.
We'll come back later and bury him at sea, properly."

Silvana nodded. "A Viking funeral."

They considered burning him on a funeral pyre, but nobody
could bring herself to do it—to light the fire and watch him
burn, and risk the fire going out and having to start it again,
and feeling Jonathan's ashes blowing in their faces. So they
decided to hollow out a grave with coconut shells and bury

him with his clothes on, because they couldn't bear to take them off.

They chose a small grove of evergreen canaga trees, because it was near Annie's prayer place and Jonathan had loved the strong fragrance of the slim, long-petaled yellow blossoms, which flowered for most of the year.

Annie knelt by the grave and crossed herself, trying to fight down the sorrow and bitterness that welled once again in her heart as she remembered the past few days.

At the graveside, Annie emptied Jonathan's pockets. She handed the key ring with the carved shark's tooth to Suzy, who also got the tiny compass on a thong that he'd worn around his neck. Silvana was given Jonathan's fish knife. His underwater watch went to Carey. Annie said, "I'll take his Swiss army knife. Patty can have his cigarette lighter and the rifle."

Then they lowered him into the grave. There was a fresh outbreak of crying, for nobody wanted to cover him with earth. They all knew what would happen to the decomposing body. Once it was buried, it would quickly be consumed.

Afterward, as they stumbled back to the camp, the women realized for the first time that now they had only themselves to depend upon.

Annie insisted that they eat, so Silvana quickly made a soup of dried fish boiled in water and they forced it down. It tasted disgusting.

That night they all slept in the first hut because nobody wanted to sleep in the hut where Jonathan had lain.

Silvana slept with her arms around Annie. They clung to each other out of loneliness.

Annie thrust her hand in her pocket and felt Jonathan's knife. She felt his strength as she touched his possession, and it comforted her. She whispered, "Please help us, Jonathan. Please tell us what to do."

She seemed to hear a voice at the back of her head say, "You ain't had the benefit of my lack of education, but by now

465

I expect you to think for yourselves. *You* know what I want you to do. Make another raft, fast."

Two mornings after Jonathan's death, Annie woke feeling as if a heavy weight lay on her chest. Sleepily she thought, You really *do* feel emotion physically in the area of your heart.

The weight shifted slightly. Annie felt the warm, furry body through her shirt, followed by a sharp bite on her left breast.

There was a scrabble of claws, a sharp yelp and the furry weight—all twelve pounds of it—lay limp on her stomach.

Annie screamed and leaped from her bamboo bed.

"Got it!" Patty said triumphantly. "The rats were under your bed all night. Must have been a wedding."

Annie said crossly, "You might have hit *me* with that stone."

"These days I don't miss," Patty said smugly. She flung another stone at the corner of the hut, stood up and pulled on her fishing gloves. She picked up a knife and swiftly slit the throat of the stunned rat.

"Where is everyone?" Annie asked. The sun was up. She had overslept.

"Carey's on guard and Suzy's weeping away by the fire. I told her it's no use crying, we're on our own." Patty scowled to fight her tears. "Silvana's gone tide-pooling for crabs and oysters. It's low tide and we have no fresh food, only goddamned dried fish slivers." She wiped the blood from her knife. "Rat stew this evening!"

Since the rats had become so aggressive, Annie slept in all her clothes, even her sneakers. She rolled up her bed and hurried outside, where she found Suzy squatting before the fire, her head in her hands.

Big, green, red-rimmed eyes looked up at Annie. "I feel so frightened," Suzy said. "Much more than before."

"We all do. It's not surprising. But nothing's changed in the jungle. It's no more frightening than it was a couple of days ago. You only *feel* that it is." Annie patted Suzy's shoulder.

"Look around. Everything's the same. The fear is imaginary, it's in your head, Suzy. Don't allow it to grow."

To the north of the lagoon, the sea drew back from the black mangrove roots to reveal a black, bubbling slime, from which small crabs scuttled toward the receding safety of the water. To the south of the lagoon, Silvana waded beneath the morning sun, moving carefully around the glistening rocks, thrusting her three-foot-wide, wooden-ended net downward. This was the best time to catch shrimp, during the last couple of hours of the ebb tide when the shrimp were trapped in small rock pools and it was simple to scoop them up with the hand net.

Following the tide out, Silvana pushed the net beneath the clumps of submerged seaweed that clung to the rocks. With a quick up-and-back shaking movement she would pull the net from the water, inspect it, then transfer the shrimp to the canvas bag hanging from a shoulder strap across her body. It was hard work, but Silvana had acquired the knack of doing it, and it was a good way to get a heap of shrimp not only for supper, but also to use as bait.

The heavy net started to tire her arms, so she headed back to shore and laid it on the beach. She took out Jonathan's stubby-bladed fish knife and started to prize shellfish off the underwater rocks, then drop them into her fish bag. With her right hand, she inserted the thin side of the blade beneath the shell and twisted it around so that the thick, chiseled edge of the blade was uppermost as she prized open the lips of a shell. After rounding the end of the shell, she would suddenly feel the mollusk yield to her knife, and know she had severed the muscle which had been keeping the shell tightly closed, and that it would now be easy to open to get at the flesh.

When her fish bag was nearly full, the tide started to turn. Silvana stood upright, stretched and decided to stop.

Then she spotted, below the surface of the water, a huge shell almost hidden by black seaweed. She had never seen such a big one; it was a meal in itself, she thought, as she knelt down and inserted the end of the knife blade. She'd never met such a stubborn shell either, she decided, after a few minutes.

Suddenly the shell gave way. With her left hand Silvana grasped the upper half to wrench it from the rock. With astonishing speed the shell clamped shut on her index finger.

Silvana jumped and let go of Jonathan's knife, which flew in an arc through the air before splashing into the water. She bent down and tried to reach the knife, but it was about six inches behind her grasp.

The shell hurt Silvana's finger. *Santa Madonna!* With her right hand she felt in her bag and fumbled for a small clam, then groped below the water and tried to lever open the shell that was holding her prisoner, but without success.

Silvana looked out to sea. The tide had now turned and was rushing back into the lagoon. Because she had been kneeling to get her knife under the huge shell, her head was about thirty inches above the water. Quickly, she calculated. The tide rose and fell about three feet in the lagoon. When the water rose, it would close over her head and she would drown unless she could free herself.

She bent down and tried again to reach her knife. She could see it, shimmering silver in the water, and unobtainable. She tried again, with different shells from her bag, to prize open the one that held her prisoner in such pain.

Silvana started to scream.

There was no response and Silvana realized that she was too far down the beach for the camp lookout to hear her, otherwise someone would have come by now. The water reached her clavicle and gently lapped at her throat. She was astonished by the relentless tenacity of the shellfish, which had been gripping her finger for nearly two hours.

She had shouted in bouts, to save her voice. Now, hoarsely, she called once more. She waved her right arm, without much hope.

"Silvana . . . ?" Patty called, puzzled. She couldn't hear

Silvana, but from the cliff she could see the hand waving out of the sea.

Suddenly realizing that Silvana was trapped, Patty flung herself down the cliff path, thinking, Please God, don't let it be an octopus!

By the time Patty reached her, the water was lapping over Silvana's chin. Silvana gasped, "I dropped my knife. Can't get my finger out . . . For God's sake, *don't wait!*"

Patty peered underwater. "I'll fetch a hammer."

"No time. My knife is over there—to the right. Get it!"

Patty waded over and retrieved the knife. "I'm not good at this, but let me try—just once—to open this shell."

She tried to cut the muscle that held the mollusk closed.

Silvana screamed in pain, frustration and terror. Patty again attacked the shell. Surely a good knife ought to open it? But it didn't.

Suddenly, in a calm voice, Silvana said, "Cut the finger off, *fast.*"

Patty looked sick. "I can't."

Silvana said, "I've already figured out how. If you won't do it, give me the knife and I will. Otherwise I'll drown."

"I *can't,*" Patty said miserably.

Silvana pleaded, "For years you played nurse back in Pittsburgh! Now it's *real,* Patty. You can't be a coward now, or I'll die. *Cut it off, Patty!*"

But Patty couldn't.

"You phony Florence Nightingale!" Silvana shrieked. "Give me that knife!"

Patty handed it to her and fled.

Silvana hacked at her finger until the flesh was ragged and bleeding, but because of her awkward position, trapped in a crouch, she had no leverage. Red threads of her blood floated in the water as she sobbed with pain.

She heard cries and looked up. She was not going to die alone. Annie and Patty were running along the sand toward her.

Silvana slipped and for a moment her face went beneath the

water. As the trapped woman regained her balance, Annie whipped out her knife, and peered through the water, trying to remember what to do. It had to be a clean cut; the artery would glue up if it was a clean cut. There would be plenty of blood and Silvana would feel great pain, but Annie knew she had to concentrate on making a fast, clean cut just above the first knuckle. The knife wasn't sterilized, so the wound would have to be cauterized later. She hoped Silvana would faint.

Annie bent down and gripped Silvana's wrist under the water. She gave several taps with her knife to the place on the finger where she was going to cut; she was checking for displacement of water which might make her stroke inaccurate.

Unhurried, concentrating, gazing at the bleeding gash where she intended to cut, Annie lifted her knife and struck down, as hard as she could.

That evening, at sunset, they brought Silvana's bamboo bed out of the hut and laid it beside the campfire. Silvana was pale and clammy, and her breathing was harsh. Her amputated finger had been bandaged with strips of rag, sterilized by boiling them in seawater. The sickening agony had passed, leaving her weak and exhausted, but the pain wouldn't let up, wouldn't allow her to sleep.

Annie lifted Silvana's legs and placed them higher than her head on a pile of firewood. She gave her sips of hot water and gently reassured her.

Two hours later, they were all still arguing about what they should do next. Suzy was scared of putting to sea without Jonathan. She thought it was worth risking one of the group to see if they could bribe the Katanga chief to seek help for them.

Which one?

Draw lots.

Patty said, "If I drew the shortest grass, I still won't go. It's crazy to think of calmly walking into a cannibal village after we've been crashing all over their sacred site and asking them to lend us a couple of dugout canoes in exchange for a pen-knife."

"But they *want* us to leave!" Suzy argued.

Patty said, "Okay, then *you* go ask them for help."

In a weak voice, Silvana pointed out that they were now well organized in the jungle. It was only when they were careless that they found themselves in immediate danger. Sure, they'd had a few problems, but think of all the problems they *hadn't* had.

They all nodded. They knew the dangers that had been avoided. Nobody had been bitten by a snake or paralyzed by a stonefish. Nobody had stood on a stingray and been stabbed by its tail. Nobody had encountered a box jellyfish—although those were responsible for more deaths than the sharks. Nobody had even *seen* a crocodile.

Patty said, "Jonathan taught us how to survive."

"They why don't we stick it out, until after the terrorists have stopped fighting? They can't go on forever," Silvana said. "Why don't we wait until another pleasure boat passes the bay, or comes into it for a picnic the way we did? Then we can ask the captain to take us back to Queenstown. We could telephone the Sydney office, and we might be in Australia within twenty-four hours."

Patty said unhappily, "I don't know what I want to do."

Annie found that hard to believe. Patty just didn't want the responsibility for making a suggestion that might be a failure.

Annie said, "I don't think we should wait for Prince Charming to sail by. I want to build another raft. We've done it before, so we can do it again."

"Sure," said Suzy. "That way, we can become *experts*. We could end up winning prizes for raft-making at this rate."

Carey said, "I agree with Annie. We should build another raft, as fast as we can. Silvana can do full-time lookout duty because she can't do anything else." She tried to keep the resentment from her voice. They were all as angry with Silvana for incapacitating herself as they had been with Suzy, whose carelessness had started the sequence of events that led to Jonathan's death.

Squatting in the firelight, they no longer looked like women but like scrawny scarecrows. Their unkempt hair framed lined, brown faces, in which the eyes stared from sunken sockets; none of them carried a spare ounce of fat. Only Silvana and Suzy still had pronounced breasts, and each woman's skin was now slack. They looked alert, but there was a relaxed air about them.

The metamorphosis from those women in their colorful beach clothes who had climbed onto the spotless deck of the *Louise* was not only physical. Nearly four months of basic survival living had altered their outlook, and none of them would ever be the same again, Annie thought as she looked around the firelit circle.

Four months ago timid, self-effacing Annie could not have voiced and upheld an unpopular opinion, and neither could the passive and permanently depressed Silvana. Patty now had to face the fact that when it came to the crunch, she was a coward, and this had nearly cost Silvana her life. Big, calm Carey was now fiercely protective of Suzy, and was clearly ready to attack Patty physically if she gave any more trouble.

They had all come to understand that Suzy's apparent selfishness had been defensive armor. Looking at scraggy Suzy's dirty face, Annie doubted whether Suzy would ever again attach as much importance to her appearance as before.

Instead of their Pittsburgh surface friendliness, their feelings were now deep and passionate. Silvana, Carey and Suzy would have nothing to do with Patty. Patty pretended not to care; she tried to be pleasant to Annie—helping her with small jobs, offering to take her turn at lookout. Warily, Annie refused her offers. She didn't want the women to allow their emotions to divide them into two factions when they were at their most vulnerable. They now had no man to help them, to fall back on, or to blame.

Crouching, Annie said, "From now on, we can't afford to

quarrel. We must all work as a team, to do what we have to do."

"Well, what *do* we have to do?" Carey said.

Annie said, "Whatever we decide to do, we must *stick* to it. We can't stop and argue all the time, the way we've been doing this evening."

"Maybe we need a leader?" Carey suggested.

The others all immediately disagreed.

"None of *us* are leaders, *we're* not like Isabel," said Suzy, breaking the taboo on mentioning their dead.

Carey said, "I don't mean a president or a gang boss, I don't mean someone who orders us around. I mean someone who clarifies aims and jobs and opinions—a sort of nonvoting chairman."

Patty said nastily, "I suppose *you* want to be leader."

"Hell, no," Carey said. "I don't want you all blaming me whenever things go wrong. *I* don't want to be the fall guy. Maybe we should take turns being leader?"

"For how long?" Silvana asked. "Isn't it a little pointless to take turns, when we're such a small group? When our lives are at stake, surely we should have the most suitable person as our permanent leader."

"Who's suitable?" Patty asked. "Who's got the forceful magnetism, cool courage and that sort of shit to be our Joan of Arc?"

Carey said, "We need someone who can listen to everyone's ideas, summarize the situation and then decide what to do."

Annie nodded. "Someone who can assess our strengths and weaknesses with tact."

"And never insist on more than we're capable of," Suzy suggested.

"Someone who can encourage us," Silvana added. "Someone whom we can all trust."

So they voted. Nobody wanted remote Silvana or sharp-tongued, bitchy Suzy, who was always flying off the handle. Patty was neurotic and too impulsive for safety. She'd certainly make the best fighter, but maybe not the best thinker.

Carey was a possibility, but she still see-sawed between aggressiveness and timidity and you never knew which mood would be next, and her practicality and discipline irritated Silvana and Patty, who interpreted this as bossiness.

The person they all trusted was Annie. Nobody found her threatening, she had a natural caution, she was a nurturer, she was used to organizing things for those four huge sons and a demanding husband. So, much to her surprise, Annie was voted leader.

As the fire died down, Annie summarized their situation. "We can stay here, or we can go to Katanga, or we can build another raft and leave. It's a difficult decision, because there's a lot to be said for each alternative. When that's the case, it generally doesn't matter which decision you make, so let's vote on it."

Patty, Carey and Annie voted to build another raft—which, because of their reduced manpower, would probably take them six days.

"Okay, Mother Bear," Suzy said. She looked glumly at her torn and callused hands. "I swore I was never going to have the sort of hands my ma had, because I wasn't going to lead the sort of life my ma did—scrubbing hospital floors. Once she'd finished, it was time to start again. But now I've got a worse job than she ever had."

Annie said, "We haven't had cave-climbing or self-defense practice for two days. Can you see to that tomorrow, Patty? Silvana will organize the lookout, I'll do the cooking, Carey's responsible for getting our food and Suzy will do water duty as usual."

Suzy said bitterly, "Why can't one of you invent the water wheel?"

Annie said, "There's one other thing. Do you remember that Jonathan wanted us to do loners?"

They nodded. Nobody had previously seen the necessity for spending a night alone in the lean-to. Toughen you up, Jonathan had suggested, but when they all objected, he hadn't pushed the idea. Jonathan had been by no means certain that they would all survive; that was why he had wanted them to learn to be alone.

Annie said, "We're going to practice being alone. We'll put the equipment in Jonathan's hut and take turns spending a night in the lean-to. I'll be first."

She added encouragingly, quoting Jonathan, "It'll be like learning not to be frightened of the dark when we were children."

Suzy said, "I'm still frightened of the dark."

MONDAY, MARCH 4

The next morning after foot inspection, without discussing the matter, all the women except Suzy followed Annie and Silvana to their prayer place. They had made a small altar by pushing shells into the earth to form a mosaic rectangle. When any one of them came to pray, she placed flowers upon the shells.

Each woman gained comfort from the keepsakes that Annie had shared out. Annie felt her Swiss army knife. Carey lightly touched her underwater watch. Silvana stroked the hilt of the fish knife in her belt and felt stronger. Patty rubbed the battered, empty aluminum lighter against her cheek. These things comforted them. They felt that Jonathan was still with them.

Back at the camp, they found Suzy crouched before the fire, scowling. "Mumbo-jumbo," she snapped at Annie. "You won't get *me* up there."

Patty glared at her. "Shut up, Suzy. You're inviting a good crack in the teeth."

Suzy sprang at Patty, clawing at her face.

Caught off-balance Patty fell backward, with Suzy on top of her.

Patty hit out, and felt the crunch of bone beneath her fist.

Annie flung herself into the fray to part the two women before Carey joined the fight. Suzy hit her in the chest.

Annie lashed at Suzy. Carey tugged at one of Annie's legs and received a kick in the stomach; grunting with pain, Carey fell on top of the struggling women.

On the edge of the fight, Silvana clutched her bandaged hand, unable to believe her eyes. How had it happened? Within two minutes they were all behaving like slum kids in a brawl. And for the same reason as slum kids, Silvana realized —to relieve their tension and fury against the impersonal fate that kept kicking them back into the pit they were trying to climb out of.

The fight was over almost as quickly as it had started. As none of the women had ever seriously used her body aggressively, it had been more of a muddled struggle on the dusty ground than a ruthless fight. Except for Suzy, who had been raised with violence, the participants were all horrified by their aggression, none of them had ever attacked, or been attacked by, another person.

Annie burst into tears of remorse.

Patty burst into tears of rage. "You'd think none of us had ever had any self-defense training! We were all *scratching*, not using our hands or our bodies properly. What'll happen to us if we're *really* attacked and everything we've learned flies out of our head?"

Then, even Suzy was silent and ashamed—not of having fought, but of having fought stupidly in spite of Jonathan's careful training.

Patty pulled out her aluminum lighter and rubbed it against her cheek. She stood up and said, in the firm voice of one who had come to a sudden decision, "I'm going back to Annie's prayer place. I want to . . . compose myself."

Annie scrambled to her feet. "I'll go with you."

"Me too," Carey said, fingering her wristwatch as she walked away from the campfire.

Suzy screamed, "Jonathan wouldn't want you to turn him into a god."

476

"Hush," said Silvana, watching the other three disappear. "You're being sacrilegious, Suzy."

"Listen to you!" Suzy yelled. "You're making him into a tin idol! I can see how gods are made."

She's overwrought, Silvana thought, far more upset by Jonathan's death than she'll admit. She would suggest to Annie that she send Suzy out hunting with Carey that afternoon. She'd have to concentrate so hard that she wouldn't have time for tantrums.

In the late afternoon Carey and Suzy set off to check the three animal traps that Jonathan had laid to the east of the camp. They were a simple design; a heavy piece of deadfall was carefully propped up with a light stick, beneath which lay a tempting morsel of meat. When an animal went to eat the meat, it knocked aside the wooden prop and the heavy deadwood fell on its head and either trapped it, knocked it out or killed it.

Before they reached the first trap, Suzy had just missed impaling her foot on a sharp stump. After checking the second trap, she was nearly throttled by an overhanging vine when a rotten deadfall gave way beneath her feet.

Both traps were empty. On their way to the third trap, they followed an overgrown animal track which skirted a bog patch where the grass grew bright green. Unexpectedly, they found themselves wading up to their knees in mud spattered with poisoned brush and rotten pieces of wood, while hanging loops of vine brushed against their faces.

Suzy stumbled and almost fell.

In front of her, Carey turned and said, "What's the *matter* with you today, Stumblefoot?"

Suzy burst into tears and hid her face in two muddy hands. In a muffled voice she said, "I'm pregnant."

Carey gave her a nasty look.

"No, it *wasn't* Jonathan," Suzy protested. "I wanted to, but he wouldn't." She burst out, "I've just missed for the *fourth* time. This is *Brett*'s baby! Jesus, I'm so frightened!"

Carey thought, Well, this is all we need. She said, "Don't worry, we all know what to do if you're pregnant."

"I'm not frightened of *having* a baby, I'm frightened of having to look after it, of being responsible for it in this horrible place. Just the thought makes me panic."

Carey put her arm around Suzy. "You won't feel like that when you have it. Anyway, you probably won't have it here, Suzy. We have five months to get you to a doctor." She hesitated, then said, "And you're probably not pregnant anyway. We've *all* stopped! I thought you realized that. Annie hasn't handed out a grass tampon in months." She gave Suzy a muddy hug. "Don't worry now. Let's check the last trap."

Carey turned and waded ahead, out of the bog and onto the faint grass track.

Behind her, Suzy gave a little yelp and Carey turned around again.

Hopping up and down, Suzy said, "God! My hands and arms are stinging like crazy! *And* my face! I must have touched my face with my hands after I touched a stinging plant!" She waved her hands in impotent rage.

"Don't touch your eyes," Carey warned. "I saw some aloe a ways back on this track. I'll go get some, you wait here." Carey melted back along the track. She clearly remembered having seen earlier a clump of the pointed leaves. The women didn't often see them, and when they did, Annie always wanted to know where it was. The rare leaves were magically soothing when applied to stings of almost any kind. They felt like cool slices of cucumber, and almost immediately drew the itch from the skin.

Carey located the clump of aloe and took a handful of the twelve-inch-long, pointed leaves. Then she headed up the track toward Suzy.

She could hear Suzy giving small cries. She must have been

badly stung, Carey thought—although that was no excuse for making such a noise. Suzy could be very childish.

Carey stopped. There was something odd about the cries.

Carey moved fast but very carefully, parallel to the track, dodging from tree to tree and hiding behind the trunks, until she had nearly reached the spot where she had left Suzy.

Ahead of her, Carey could see Suzy lying on the track and struggling with two almost naked, sweating black men, both of whom were kneeling. One man, with his back to Carey, was holding Suzy down by the shoulders, while the man who faced Carey had his hand over her mouth. Carey saw him jump and throw back his head as Suzy bit his hand. In that one glance Carey saw a black, sweaty face, bright orange hair, a yellow cross smeared on his forehead and a green feather stuck horizontally through the cartilage between his nostrils.

Carey watched in horror as Suzy—whose hands were being held behind her back—kicked the man who faced her. As her foot landed in his stomach, he grunted and punched Suzy in the gut, which abruptly stopped her wriggling and gasping cries.

Neither man made any noise. The one with his back to Carey put his knees on Suzy's shoulders and pulled her arms up and back. Suzy lay with the back of her head toward Carey. Still the man made no sound, but the intentions of the man with the green feather were obvious.

Carey noticed two bows and quivers of arrows lying in the grass at the side of the track. She thought, There's only one reason for them to put down their weapons. You can't rape someone with a bow in your hands.

Carey knew she had to wait for precisely the right moment. She dropped the game bag and moved forward, still hidden by trees. With her right hand she pulled out her knife. She remembered, *Decide on your moment and keep your eye on the spot you're going to strike.*

Hearing Jonathan's instructions clearly in her head, Carey launched herself at the man who knelt with his back to her.

She thought, First action. Jump forward, left hand over his mouth and yank back head; simultaneously swing right hand holding the knife in front of him and *completely* across, over to the left of his neck. Second action. Pull back the knife to the right and toward you in one movement, as *hard* as you can, cutting across the throat.

As Carey attacked, the man with the green feather looked up, startled. Suzy, her hands suddenly free, shoved at him with both her arms. She threw him off balance and managed to bring her right knee back to her stomach, then slam hard and fast with the ball of her foot to his crotch. Swiftly, Suzy kicked again, not a frantic woman's kick but a carefully aimed, steady thrust with her right heel. The man doubled up.

The man Carey had attacked gave a strangled cry and fell forward. Carey fell on top of him. She worked her right arm free and in a trembling frenzy she hacked away at the back of the man's neck, until she felt his body yield beneath her.

Carey started to get to her feet, then she saw that the man with the green feather was bent double, with his fuzzy dark head toward her. She knew that she shouldn't attack him from the front, because then he had two arms and two legs to use against her. On the other hand, his back was now exposed to her. She couldn't remember what to do, they'd never had this situation in practice.

She held her bloody knife in her clenched fist, raised it and lunged as she fell across the head of the second man. She mustn't thrust the knife straight downwards into his back, because the ribs overlapped protectively and the knife might slide off bone. Instead, she thrust from below the ribs, pulling the knife back toward her *under* the man's ribs. The knife hit his kidneys. There was a convulsive movement and a howl from beneath her.

Carey pulled out her knife, fell off the tangle of bodies, scrambled to a crouch and stuck the bloodied knife, as hard as she could, into the right side of the native's neck, hoping to sever the great arteries and nerves on that side, in what Jonathan had called a sheep-butcher's thrust.

Dark red arterial blood spurted out, covering Carey's face, arms and chest. The howling changed to a scream, and then faded to a gurgle.

Frantically, Carey pushed and kicked the bodies—both still jerking—off the dazed and winded Suzy, who was covered with gore. Carey tugged her to her feet.

Frozen in horror, the two women stared at the two bloodied corpses, then Suzy grabbed Carey's hand and they fled back along the track toward their camp.

◄ **24** ►

"I had no choice," wept the blood-stained Carey, dazed and shocked as she stood, still bewildered, in front of the campfire.

"Yes, you *did* have a choice," Annie said. "You could have done nothing. You did the right thing. Patty and I will get rid of the traces, and Suzy will just *have* to take us back to that place."

Stubbornly, Suzy shook her head. "I'll tell you where it is. You've both been there. But I'm *never* going back." She shuddered.

"Okay, okay," Annie said. "We'll find our own way." She turned to Silvana. "You'd better get back up the lookout tree. You want any help with your hand?" Silvana shook her head.

"Good," Annie said. "In the future nobody leaves the camp alone, and nobody leaves without a rifle."

"Which one?" Patty asked.

"Jonathan's M-16," Annie decided. "We were all trained on it. The guard in the lookout tree only needs a gun as a signal if an enemy is approaching, so the lookout can have the terrorist's rifle."

"It all happened so fast," wept Carey through chattering teeth.

"You'll feel better tomorrow," said Patty. "I know I did."

482

"But you killed a terrorist—and he wore clothes. Those men were *naked*. I could feel their bodies." Carey shuddered as she remembered the warm, slippery skin, the unaccustomed musky smell of their sweat, the muscular bodies writhing beneath her, the convulsive jerking of the second man—and then blood *everywhere;* even that horrible green feather had been red with blood.

Carey gulped. "I could *smell* them as I killed them."

"Sure could," said Suzy. "They stank like elephants—terrible B.O."

Annie stood up. "You two, take those clothes off and soak the blood out of them. Clean up *below* the waterfall pool, so that you don't foul it, then lie on your beds quietly." She turned to Patty. "Get the M-16 and a couple of coconut shells."

Annie turned to Carey. "We must have been wrong about the Golden Triangle boundary. It *isn't* bordered by William Penn along to the village in the next bay."

"Looks like it's a smaller area," Carey agreed. "A trapezoid within our Golden Triangle."

"What's that?"

"A four-sided figure with no sides parallel."

"Well, anyway, we're unsure of our southern boundary," said Annie. "So on that side, we stay as close as possible to camp."

Patty returned with the rifle. "Maybe the natives were trespassing. Maybe somehow they know that Jonathan is dead, that we're on our own and . . ."

"Maybe they know about Jonathan, but I reckon they don't dare step on taboo ground," Annie said. "Otherwise, they'd have been around here before now—in droves!" She moved off. "Let's get going."

"Okay, I'll show you the place," Suzy said with reluctance.

Patty and Annie had dragged the corpses back to the bog. They had bound stones to the bodies with rattan, then dragged them into the middle of the bog and let go. Standing thigh deep in brilliant green grass and bubbling muck, they watched the bubbles subside. Then they returned to the track and covered their traces as best they could.

"Not that it will help if someone tracks them," Patty said.

She put down the quiver of arrows that one of the natives had been carrying, which she intended to try out at the first opportunity.

"It's hard to track someone—even with a dog—through all these small streams," Annie pointed out. "Sure, if they hit upon the place where it happened, they'll know immediately that there's been a killing. But the odds are against that. For once, the odds are on our side."

Back at the camp, Carey crouched in front of the fire. She looked up at Patty.

"How did you feel after you'd killed yours?"

"It disgusted me. The stink. Then I felt . . . grim satisfaction."

TUESDAY, MARCH 5

The next day, fear drove the women to work on their third raft with added strength. Annie insisted that Carey return to work rather than brood about what she'd done, but Carey refused to move outside the camp. She stayed by the fire, trimming the bamboo poles that Silvana and Patty dragged from the bamboo grove where Annie and Suzy were cutting them.

They had nearly exhausted the bamboo grove, Annie thought, as she looked around it after the midday break. She wiped the sweat from her eyes and said with tired triumph to Suzy, "We'll have enough by sunset."

Suzy nodded.

Then they both heard a shot.

The report was immediately followed by a cacophony of shrieks and screams from the jungle creatures.

Annie leaped for the M-16, which was propped barrel upwards, against a nearby tree. "Take cover!"

"The shot came from the camp," Suzy whispered from behind Annie.

Annie whispered, "I thought it came from William Penn."

The two crouching women looked around them, deceived by the echoes of the shot, fearful of leaving the bamboo grove and fearful of staying in it.

Annie said, "If the camp is being attacked, then we'd better get there fast."

Cautiously they headed for the camp, not using the regular path that led from the bamboo grove but flitting from tree trunk to tree trunk as they moved along.

The camp was empty. The two fires had been extinguished but were still smoldering.

Annie whispered, "They've gone down the cave shaft." Any shot was a pre-agreed signal for the women to scatter and head for the cave.

Still moving stealthily, Annie and Suzy arrived at the carefully camouflaged top of the shaft. Suzy slid down first, followed fast by Annie, who carefully pulled the camouflage undergrowth back over the hole, before slithering down the rattan rope.

The other three women were already waiting in the dark at the bottom of the shaft. Patty gripped the AK-47, Silvana and Carey each held a wooden club taken from the pile where they lay, part of the cave's permanent stock, along with the rations of smoked fish and water that Patty saw to it were always fresh.

"What happened?" Patty whispered.

"Nothing happened to *us*," Suzy whispered. "What happened to you?"

"Nothing. We just heard a shot and scrambled, thinking that you'd fired it."

They all agreed that they'd heard a shot.

"Jonathan said that a shot could carry many miles even in the jungle," Silvana said. "The shot might have had nothing to do with us. A native might have shot a wild pig miles away."

Patty said, "Only chiefs are allowed a shotgun—and then only as a disciplinary measure of last resort."

Annie said, "We'll wait until three thirty, then Patty can swim out of the cave and check the beach and Carey can climb up and check the camp area."

Carey cursed. "If we have to stay down here, it will hold up the raft." She felt even more nervous than the others as she stood on the soft bat shit listening to the rustling and squeaking at the top of that musty cave. Carey feared the bats; she had already taken off her pants and wound them around her head.

At three thirty, Annie handed Carey the M-16 and said, "Okay, Carey, up you go."

Annie then walked cautiously to the front of the cave with Patty, where she handed over the flashlight. Patty took off her watch with the luminous dial and handed it to Annie.

"If I'm not back in twenty minutes, Annie, you'll know there's something wrong and you'll have to grope your way back along the cave to the others." Patty hesitated, then dug into her pocket and pulled out Jonathan's battered lighter. "Look after this for me, Annie."

Patty got to the edge of the black water and then turned around. "Give me back the lighter, Annie. Guess I'll take it, for luck."

Annie stood alone in the darkness, one hand held protectively over her eyes and the other clutching that blessed little circle of luminous pale green—the Swatchwatch.

It seemed far longer, but it was only fourteen minutes after Patty left that Annie heard a splash and heard someone gasping for breath.

"That you, Patty?" They tended to whisper in the dark, even when there was no reason to do so.

Patty climbed out of the water. "There's nobody on the beach. Not a soul in sight. Let's move back to the shaft and tell the others."

When they reached the faint lessening-of-dark that marked the bottom of the shaft, Carey still hadn't returned.

"But we haven't heard a rifle shot," Silvana reminded them, as they waited anxiously in silence.

Just before five o'clock, as Patty checked her watch again, they heard three short whistles. Their signal was one short whistle for "help," two for "hide" and three for "coast clear."

They heard the slithering and the panting, then the noise of Carey's boots disturbing the bat shit as she jumped off the end of the rattan rope.

"Nothing wrong at the camp," Carey said. "But unless we get up there the campfire will die out."

They decided that the rifle shot must have been farther away than they had thought.

"Damn nuisance," Carey grumbled. "We can't afford any more holdups."

Patty climbed up the rope, taking both the rifles on her back. The rest of them swam out of the cave behind Annie. Except for Suzy, they all hated to climb the sixty-foot rattan rope up the shaft.

By five thirty, they were back at camp. At first they all moved cautiously, and then with increasing confidence, because it was clear that nothing had been disturbed.

Suzy suddenly remembered the machete. "Hey, Annie, you dropped the machete at the bamboo grove, when you jumped for the rifle." The two women looked at each other and for a moment they were tempted to leave it there overnight.

Annie sighed and said, "Okay, let's go get it."

Exasperated, Annie led the way, moving along the little path they had trodden parallel to the riverbank, which led to the bamboo grove.

Annie stopped abruptly.

"Oh, God!" Suzy had seen the same thing.

Ahead, with his back to them, moved a figure in a khaki uniform. He carried a rifle, and moved with stealth.

Annie had left the M-16 in camp. She whispered in Suzy's ear, "Shadow him, to the right." She melted into the trees to the left of the track. Suzy quietly kissed the compass around her neck, then moved off to the right. By the time he reached

William Penn, both women were certain that this man was not used to the jungle, and that he was alone. He kept looking to the left and right, then checking behind him, after which Annie and Suzy immediately moved forward. Had the khaki figure not been alone, the two women would also have seen the others close to him. When moving in a patrol, each member, except the point, who led the way, was careful never to lose sight of the man in front of him.

Having reached Willian Penn Place, the man glanced behind him once again and hurried to the left.

Annie looked across at Suzy and with her right hand made two chops with an imaginary knife. The soldier must have spotted their camp and was going to fetch reinforcements.

Suzy nodded.

By the time the women reached the ropes of the Burma bridge the uniformed man was halfway across. His rifle was slung on his back, the top ropes were under his armpits and each of his hands clung to a rope. As they watched, his feet moved carefully over the single base rope. It was clear that he knew how to place his feet on the knots so that he didn't slip.

Annie nodded to Suzy.

Both women unsheathed their knives and moved silently forward.

The man felt the ropes jerking beneath his arms, causing him to sway and nearly lose his footing. He clung tensely to his handholds and turned his head in a swift, backward glance. He saw two wild, dirty brown savages, each hacking at an arm rope.

The man yelled in terror and clutched the arm ropes.

Within thirty seconds the top ropes had been severed. They sprang free.

The man teetered on the still taut bottom rope, then lost his balance. Sixty feet below, the river wound its way between boulders to the waterfall.

He screamed as he fell into the ravine.

Suzy whispered excitedly, "It worked! It worked! Just like Jonathan said it would."

Annie bit her lip, because it *hadn't* worked as Jonathan had predicted.

The man hadn't fallen straight down, to be smashed on the rocks below. He had lost his footing, but he had clung to the handropes as he fell, so he had been pulled down and forward by the ropes. He had been thrown onto bushes halfway down the opposite side of the ravine. He had bounced off these onto some smaller, scragglier bushes farther down. He now lay on scrub near the bottom of the ravine, screaming in pain.

Suzy said, "He's making an awful noise. We ought to shut him up in case somebody hears him."

"How?"

"With a knife, I suppose," Suzy said reluctantly.

"You do it."

"I can't, I *can't,*" Suzy whimpered.

"Neither can I."

Suzy swore, then shrugged her shoulders, "We'll have to do it together. And we'd better do it fast. We can't leave him there, yelling like that."

Longing to just run away and forget it, Annie said, "Maybe we can hear him because we're looking *into* the ravine. Maybe you wouldn't be able to hear him from farther away."

Suzy looked furious. "Annie, you know we've got to get down there and shut his mouth. Now come *on!*"

Carefully, they descended the steep and tortuous slope of the ravine. Their handholds gave way beneath them, and their footholds started miniature avalanches of pebbles; the earth crumbled away beneath their feet and bounced down the rocky chasm into the bright, flashing water below.

In a splatter of stones, Suzy reached the riverbank first. She looked upward.

Fifteen feet above her, Annie was spread-eagled, frozen against the rock face.

"I . . . can't . . . *move,*" Annie gasped. It was an effort for her to breathe, let alone to talk; she was rigid, almost paralyzed by fear.

Suzy couldn't coax Annie down. She couldn't cuss Annie down. She couldn't get Annie to move or speak.

Annie had vertigo. Her knees were knocking so hard that every time they jerked toward each other the movement was dislodging clumps of earth from below her feet.

Suzy looked across the river; it was deep and narrow, fast-moving and noisy at this point. She'd have to get across the goddamned water before the man recovered enough to reach for his gun.

She considered using her slingshot, aiming at his head, but the torrent was about eighteen feet wide at this point and she was the worst shot in the camp. She was also the worst swimmer, of course, but swimming was the only way to get across, and she *had* to stop that screaming.

Suzy moved upstream about twenty feet in order to correct against the current. She sat on the bank and lowered her legs into the water. She was about to slither over the side into the river when the screaming stopped abruptly.

"Please God, *please* let him be dead," Suzy prayed. She pulled herself back onto the bank and returned to the spot where, above her, Annie was glued to the rock face.

"I'm coming up for you," Suzy called softly, and started to climb. On reaching Annie Suzy said reassuringly, "Put your right hand on my shoulder." The thing was to get Annie moving again.

"I can't," Annie whimpered. "I'm afraid I'll fall."

"Okay, I'll wait. But you can't lose if you try," Suzy said. She resisted explaining that Annie was going to fall anyway. She couldn't hold on forever.

For seven minutes the two women hung there, side by side against the chasm wall.

"You'll have to get down before night falls," Suzy warned, meaning that then Annie, too, would fall.

Slowly, Annie pulled her rigid right arm away from the rock face and grasped Suzy's left shoulder.

"Now put your right foot on my left foot, as a foothold," Suzy encouraged.

This time there was only a two-minute wait before Annie's right leg moved.

Slowly, with Suzy moving down a few inches and then Annie following her, they descended the slope until they reached the bottom.

Looking at Annie's ashen face, Suzy's encouragement stopped abruptly. She said sharply, "You *can't* faint now, Annie. We have to deal with this bastard." She turned her head and glanced across the river at the limp khaki body. "With any luck, we won't have to bother. And we'll have another gun. Let's cross quickly, we want to get back before dark."

They crossed the river, swimming side by side, with Annie, the stronger swimmer, downstream.

As they hauled themselves out, through the undergrowth on the other bank, Annie said, "I *can't* climb up to him."

Suzy could see that there was no point in arguing. Agile as a monkey, she clambered up the cliff face. Carefully, she positioned her feet on a rock about two feet below the man. He was lying on his back with his head lolling over a ledge.

Quickly, Suzy tugged at his rifle and managed to pull it from the limp body. It was another AK-47.

She held her hand over the man's face. Yes, he was still breathing.

"The bastard's alive but unconscious," she called softly down to Annie. Nevertheless, Suzy moved about a yard to her right. He might be faking. He might grab her. She didn't want to find herself used as a hostage.

Pulling herself up by the scrub, Suzy climbed to above the khaki figure. Hanging on with both hands, she roughly kicked him with her left foot, trying to dislodge him and roll him down to Annie.

The man didn't move.

She kicked him under the chin. He slithered a few feet down the precipice, but not to the bottom.

She moved down and gave him another kick. And another.

It was much harder than she'd expected. Repeatedly, her toe encountered limp, yielding flesh.

Suddenly the man slithered down the rocks and landed on his back at Annie's feet.

Swiftly Suzy followed him. "Let's shoot him," she said to Annie, who held the man's gun. "We can use his own rifle."

Annie looked down at the khaki clad figure. His dark face was very young, his nose was bleeding and so were his cheeks where the rocks had scratched them.

Annie said, "He looks about the same age as my Fred."

"Shit, Annie, this is no time for sentiment."

"I *can't* kill him, Suzy."

"Then I will." Suzy snarled, and grabbed the gun and held the barrel against the man's head.

Annie waited, dreading what would follow. That head would explode into a red, dripping, dreadful mess.

Suzy pulled the gun away. "I can't do it either."

They looked at each other. Cowards. Neither of them could.

Suzy said, "Remember what Jonathan once said? That the horror is using your hands to kill? Remember he said that pulling a trigger distances you from the act, and absolves you from that horror?"

Annie nodded.

"He was wrong."

Annie nodded again. "I've got a better idea," she said. "Let's take him prisoner and make him take Silvana's place building the raft. Even with a bad hand, Silvana can cover him with a rifle."

Suzy was relieved. "We'll still take his clothes!" She looked speculatively at the boots, shirt and trousers like a peasant woman eyeing the produce of a market stall. "We'd better tie his hands behind his back."

Using Annie's knife belt, they tightly bound the prisoner's hands. Using his peaked cap, Suzy bailed some water from the river and threw it over the unconscious face.

Eventually the man gave a long sigh, coughed and opened his eyes.

Slowly his eyes focused. He saw two women above him. He grinned.

Suzy kicked him hard in the ribs—not that she was able to kick very hard in sneakers. "Wipe that smile off your face and get up."

"Okay, okay, everything okay," the prisoner said hastily.

Suzy cried, "Hey, the sonofabitch can speak English! *On* your feet."

The prisoner tried to stand up, but was obviously incapable of doing so. Suzy encouraged him by kicking him until, awkwardly, he managed to stand. He stood swaying in front of them.

"What were you doing in this part of the forest?" Annie asked.

The prisoner shrugged. "I go for walk. I lose myself."

"You'd think he could invent a more plausible lie," Suzy said crossly.

The prisoner shrugged again. "Is true."

In fact, his story *was* true. The streams of the forest looped, snakelike, back on themselves. If you waded across one curve of the loop and then across another, it seemed as if you had crossed two streams, but in fact you ended up on the same bank from which you started, only a little farther along. This was what the man had done. He had no idea that he had traveled so far south. Until he arrived at the rope bridge he had thought he was heading back to his barracks.

"Don't get too near him," Suzy warned Annie. She pointed to the riverside track that led toward the sea. *"Move,* mister."

"Okay, okay, everything fine," the prisoner mumbled. He started to limp slowly along the track, stumbling over the pebbles and small boulders.

He stopped and turned to the women. "My leg is hurt."

"Too bad," said Suzy. *"Move!"*

The man limped forward another few steps, buckled at the knees and collapsed in a khaki heap at their feet.

Suzy muttered, "Isn't that unfair? Just when I was being really tough."

"I don't think we can handle this by ourselves," Annie said. "You keep him covered while I fetch Patty and Carey."

Annie returned to the camp and brought Patty and Carey back to help them move their captive. The four women half-carried, half-dragged the prisoner downstream, to the point where the river widened but the banks were only a few feet high.

On the opposite bank, they had cleared away the undergrowth for Suzy to draw water. Here, they all swam across. Carey went over on her back, hauling the terrified man across on her chest, her left hand under his chin.

Back at the camp Suzy quickly recounted the events to Silvana, who was still up the lookout tree.

Annie removed the prisoner's boots and pushed up his trouser leg. After gently feeling his bruised foot, she said, "Nothing really wrong, but he might have a slight concussion."

"Great!" said Patty. "Now we have another mouth to feed, an invalid to look after and a captive to guard."

"You should have killed him," Carey said crossly to Annie. "No man would take a prisoner in that situation."

"Okay, let's kill him now," said Patty.

"No," Annie said hastily. "Let's make him work on the raft. We need physical strength and he's got it."

"What do we do with him when we leave?" Carey asked.

"We'll tie him to a tree." Annie sounded more decisive than she felt, as she enlarged on this idea. "He'll either escape or he'll die. But we'll be gone. And this way we get free labor."

There was a pause, while the women considered this. Building the raft was very hard physical labor; work that might have been relatively easy in a cooler climate was almost unbearably difficult in that humid heat where lethargy was unavoidable, where just taking a few steps required a physical effort that left them streaming with sweat. The temptation of slave labor was great.

Carey said, "Suppose he doesn't overexert himself?"

"We know how fast Jonathan worked," Suzy said. "If this guy doesn't work as hard, we won't give him food."

"But then he won't have the strength to work."

Suzy said, "We'll cut off his ear or shove ants down his shorts to show we mean business."

Carey said, "Where's he going to sleep?"

"Not with us," Patty said sharply.

"If he has the spare bed he might free himself by cutting his rope on the sharp ends of the bamboo," Suzy pointed out.

Annie said, "We could hobble his feet with a rope during the day, then spread-eagle him to two trees at night."

Patty said, "What was he doing around here, anyway?"

Suzy said, "The son of a bitch was shooting birds of paradise; he had a game bag tied around him. Those feathers sell for a fortune. I bought two blue ones on a headband last Christmas and it cost Brett a couple hundred dollars."

"How do we know his friends won't come looking for him?" Patty asked.

Suzy said, "He was alone, which means he probably sneaked out to make a few bucks on the side. Look at his shirt, he's only a private, not a general. They're not going to comb the jungle for one missing man."

"With any luck, they'll think that he's just another deserter, or that he's been bitten by a snake, or captured by one of the fishing tribes who were after his rifle," Annie invented hopefully. "Jonathan said that nobody's surprised around here if you disappear without a trace."

Patty said, "Just in case someone comes looking, we'd better gag him, so he can't yell."

Carey said grimly, "He yells *once*, he gets shot in the stomach."

Silvana hurried down from the lookout post. "What's happening? It's time someone else went up that tree, I've been there for hours."

As Silvana bent to look at him, the prisoner whimpered and opened his eyes. Under straight, thick brows, he had the liquid-brown, reproachful eyes of a puppy sitting by the dinner table pleading for scraps. He's so young, Silvana thought, in his early twenties, and very good-looking. He had a shock of glossy black hair, a straight nose, high cheekbones and a wide, sensual mouth.

Gently Silvana asked, "Where do you come from?" He didn't look like an islander.

"Manila, missus."

So that explained the extraordinary good looks of their prisoner, Silvana thought. The Philippines had been a Spanish colony from 1571 until 1898, and this boy clearly had a lot of Spanish blood.

Further questioning by Silvana revealed that the prisoner's name was Carlos Vergara and he was the eldest son of a minor government official. He had lived with his eight brothers and sisters in an apartment in the old section of Manila and been educated at a Catholic church school. His mother had wanted him to be a priest, but he'd left school at fourteen to work in the kitchen of the Blue Cockatoo restaurant, where he eventually became a waiter. The previous October, in a Manila bar, he had met a group of older, tough mercenary soldiers, none of whom seemed to be short of money. The following morning Carlos had woken up in an army barracks. By the time he had recovered from his hangover, he discovered that he had signed on as a mercenary in General Raki's army and had already spent his first month's wages in advance; not a peso remained in his pocket.

He had quickly decided that he was in no position to argue. In fact, Carlos had accepted his new situation with excitement and anticipation. Being part of a secret invading army was more interesting than waiting on tables. This was a manly adventure.

As he explained to the women how he came to be wandering near their camp, Carlos tried to give the impression that he had been abducted against his will, that he had been out of his depth among the older soldiers of the invading rebel army, that he had been too scared to do anything but obey orders.

Silvana looked sympathetic, but Patty snarled, "Ask him if he helped to shoot our husbands."

The prisoner looked up with sad brown eyes. "Carlos no shoot nobody. Work in cookhouse."

"Patty, don't antagonize him," Annie warned. "We don't want him to clam up. We want to know what's going on in the island."

Half an hour later, they knew what was happening. Carlos told them about the military coup and what had followed. General Raki had assumed power overnight. He was now the President of Paui and had put the country under military rule. The elections that had voted him into power had been supervised by the army and had ostensibly re-established the control of the right-wing Nationalist Party. President Raki wished for no more troubles, he wished for the happiness of everybody. Soon he was going to set up military posts around the southern shoreline of Paui. On the northwest plains, the farmers were not difficult to control, and there were few people in the mountains; but along the southern coast the fishing tribes were more primitive and fierce, so the prisoner's platoon was awaiting orders in the Paradise Bay Hotel, now a temporary army barracks.

The prisoner begged the women to let him go so that he could rejoin his unit. He did not wish to return, but should he be caught with the women in the jungle he would be shot as a deserter. Or they should *all* return in a group to the hotel, no?

Patty shook her head. *"No!"*

He looked puzzled. "Why you American ladies hide here? Why you no come back with me? My sergeant look after you, take you Queenstown. Is not good, American ladies live like *this!*" He nodded his head toward the two thatched huts.

Patty, who seemed to have loathed the prisoner on sight, said, "Remember how they looked after Isabel."

Silvana thought that there was something boyish and appealing about the bewildered look in the prisoner's big, dark eyes. Tentatively she said, "Sounds as if he got in over his head."

"It's a reasonable story," Annie agreed, feeling sorry for his poor mother.

"Look at *this!*" Suzy had just explored the pockets of the prisoner's jacket. She held up the rusting lemon-drop tin in which Jonathan had kept their watches. After Silvana had lost her emerald ring the women had also put their rings in the tin, thinking that they might use the jewelry to trade with—and anyway, their fingers were now so thin that their rings slipped off.

Silvana said, "That tin was with the supplies under the lean-to, in one of my bamboo pots."

"So the bastard *did* find our camp this afternoon," Suzy said, "when we were hiding in the cave." She looked around at the suddenly alert faces. "Now, do we assume he's just a common thief? Or do we figure that he was taking back proof that we're alive and living in a camp in the jungle?"

"You should have shot him." Carey looked at Patty. They had never discussed it, but both women knew that they were killers, that they had both broken the basic women's taboo. Women were supposed to give life, not take it, and whether you called it self-defense, manslaughter or murder, killing is what they had done. Without speaking of it, they each knew the guilt and depression that lay on the other's conscience, which no amount of justification could erase.

"I *know* we should have shot him," Annie said. She understood exactly what Patty meant. "But we *didn't*. I made the wrong decision." She looked at the two unforgiving faces in front of her and added, "I *promise* I won't hesitate next time."

Patty lost her temper. "It's *now* that matters!" she yelled. "And because of this, there may not be a next time. Just because he looks like everybody's favorite brother you've endangered our position, you sentimental wimp."

Silvana said, "We've all made silly mistakes. We aren't superwomen, and we aren't automatons. *You* might make the next mistake, Patty."

Patty scowled. "Let's see what else the bastard's stolen."

She covered the prisoner with the M-16 while Annie untied his hands.

Patty said, "Okay, Get them off. Strip. Don't be shy, we've seen it all before."

He looked bewildered. "What you want I do?"

"Take your clothes off. Slowly," Patty ordered.

He started to unbutton his torn and dirty shirt.

Annie said, "He might have some other weapon. A hidden knife, maybe."

"I've got my finger on the trigger and the safety is off," Patty told her.

"Now your pants," Patty growled.

The prisoner unzipped. His penis curled in its nest of dark hair. Nobody took any notice.

He stood before them naked.

His olive skin glistened with youth; he was muscular and slim-hipped, with the tight, taut buttocks of a bullfighter. He didn't stand in any particular way, he didn't seem aggressive, nor contrite nor sexually aware. He stood naked in front of them and fingered the silver dogtag around his neck.

The eyes of the women focused on only one thing.

Entwining the prisoner's right arm, coiling upward from the wrist, was a black and red snake. The head rested against his smooth, brown bicep, but the tattooed fangs reached up to his throat.

◄ **25** ►

WEDNESDAY, MARCH 6, 1985

Like a huge fiery umbrella, the dense clusters of red and orange blossoms hung above the prisoner's head as he lay tethered to the two flame trees in a feigned sleep. As the dark sky changed to pearl, he decided on his victim. He'd also get that tin of jewelry again. The prisoner had no doubt that he was going to escape. His specialty—one which he had studied for years—was the not-so-young American woman.

In Manila, as he glided over the green tiles of the restaurant floor beneath bedraggled cockatoos in gilded cages, carrying trays of expensive seafood to rich tourists, Carlos had moved with boyish confidence, enthusiasm and charm. His good looks were arresting but not aggressively masculine; there was nothing about his face or manner that might alarm the lonely American ladies off the cruise ships. His charm was on the same order as that of the eager but shy young girl who confesses that, as a matter of fact, this is only her second time. Carlos was always interested in the trips of the American ladies, always eager to suggest outings, to help them enjoy their stay. The ladies found his suggestions both agreeable and reassuring.

Carlos carefully studied the beautifully dressed young men who sometimes accompanied these older women to the Blue Cockatoo. Watching them, he learned to snap forward his gold-plated Dunhill as soon as the lady produced a cigarette and to wave his own little cheroot with carefully careless grace. At the end of the meal he would casually lean in the opposite direction, seemingly absorbed by some incident at a nearby table and brushing the end of his eyebrow with a fore-finger—a mannerism that only appeared as the bill was pre-sented.

Every morning, in the windowless cubicle that he shared with his two younger brothers, Carlos stood before the peeling mirror and practiced lifting one eyebrow (haughtily, inso-lently, provocatively) as he blew imaginary smoke rings at his reflection. He knew—he was absolutely sure—that, one day, one of these American women would take him back to the States with her, whereupon he would immediately leave her and catch the Greyhound bus to Hollywood, where he would get a job as houseboy to some old woman movie star, like Raquel Welch. Once he got his chance, he too would become a movie star. He too would be protected, admired, paid a fortune. He too would have gifts and homage showered upon him. This bottomless cornucopia of delight would include the slim, firm, inner thighs of young girls.

In due course, Carlos acquired an ample wardrobe of cheap, flashily cut clothes. He earned a thin gold-link bracelet, neck chain, cufflinks, watch, the gold-plated lighter and a silver cigarette case. Time after time he'd hinted for a gold cigarette case, but the cruise ships never stayed for more than a few days, and Carlos was well aware that a great deal would be required, for a long time, by the donor of such an expensive trinket. Sadly, all his carefully accumulated treasures had van-ished on the night he joined the Paui army. Nevertheless, he snapped his new aluminum lighter with aplomb, as if it were still his gold-plated, guaranteed-exact Dunhill copy from Hong Kong.

When Carlos heard the footsteps, he cautiously opened one eye. Good, it was the quiet one with the bandaged hand. He gave a soft groan.

"Carlos, I've brought you breakfast." Silvana squatted before him and felt his forehead, which was cool, then fed him hot fish mash, spooning it from the coconut shell with a leaf.

After breakfast, Annie inspected the prisoner's feet and dusted them with charcoal. Patty watched the operation with a sneer, holding the M-16 at the ready. After Annie had finished, Suzy tied the prisoner's leg firmly to a tree and untied his hands. While Patty kept the rifle pointed at him, he washed from an upended turtle shell of water, placed too far from the campfire for him to grab a burning log and use it as a weapon. He was then allowed to put on his boots; everything else had been taken from him. Suzy now wore his pants and Annie his jacket.

Carlos was shown how to lash the rattan around the bamboo poles of the raft. Silvana cautiously stood behind him, with his own AK-47 pointing at him.

He worked as hard as he could, for to appear docile and acquiescent was part of his plan.

When they stopped work at midday, it was agreed that he'd worked well. But Suzy said, "I don't trust that sonofabitch. There's something about his eyes. He reminds me of a cocktail waitress I used to know. She was fired for stealing tips from the staff box."

Carey said grimly, "He's not going to get the chance to try any tricks, and he's going to be too damned tired to move at the end of the day."

Suzy nodded, thinking that Carey no longer looked like Princess Diana; instead, beneath her grime, she looked a bit like the young Clint Eastwood.

As Silvana handed around the baked fish, she said to Patty, "Sinatra's died again. Please get me another."

Sinatra I had eaten a cherry-sized orange fruit and had subsequently been found lying stiff in his cage. Sinatra II had gnawed through his bamboo cage bars one night and escaped. Sinatras III and IV had also died after eating fruit. At the sight of every furry corpse the women felt a chill as they realized how close to death they lived.

Silvana put the remains of the fish into a bamboo jar and picked up her tattered fishing gloves. "I'll bury him. The fleas should have hopped off by now."

"Let *me* bury," Carlos offered.

Patty snapped, "Don't speak unless you're spoken to."

Silvana said mildly, "He was only offering to help. To do a nasty job."

"Sure, a real Boy Scout," Patty said.

Annie looked wary, but said nothing. This squabbling had started yesterday, almost as soon as Carlos had arrived in the camp. If only he had died when he fell from the bridge.

Annie quietly slipped away, to pray for guidance. She held the scarlet Swiss army knife in her hand and looked upward. "What should I do, Jonathan?" she whispered. "What would you do? Please tell me."

She seemed to hear a voice in her head say, "You should've dealt with him as soon as you saw him, Annie. It ain't fair on the others, to land 'em with this worry. But seeing you're stuck with him, then work his ass off. And, like Suzy says, don't trust him."

All afternoon the little party toiled on the raft, except for Silvana.

After the evening meal, Carlos—his arms spread apart—was tied by the hands to two flame trees near the sleeping huts. Before she went to bed, Silvana brought him water in a coconut shell. He looked up at her with sad eyes. He said nothing.

It was difficult for Silvana to think of this boy as their enemy. After all, he'd only been walking through the jungle, he hadn't been shooting his way through it. She had first seen him not as an aggressor but as a semiconscious prisoner with a bruised and bleeding face. Of course, he *had* taken the jewelry tin, but . . . Maybe he had thought the camp was deserted.

No, that wasn't possible. Their equipment was lying around and the fire was burning. He had clearly taken something that did not belong to him. Carlos was undoubtedly a thief.

503

But as she covered him with a rifle all that day, Silvana had watched him. He had worked hard at their raft, she had seen the sweat streaming down his body.

He *was* only a boy, she told herself.

Silvana knew that when they left the island, she wasn't going to let the others leave him tethered to the tree, at the mercy of the jungle. They would simply have to take him with them.

There was consternation around the campfire when Silvana suggested this.

Patty said vehemently, "No way am I going to embark on a raft in a shark-infested sea with that bastard sitting beside me ready to shove me overboard."

That seemed to be the consensus.

Silvana looked at the faces around the campfire and said reproachfully, "It's inhuman to leave him here unless we release him, and you all know that."

"We're *not* releasing him!" Carey shouted. "And if you don't stop feeling sorry for the sonofabitch, we'll leave you here with him."

From where he was tethered, Carlos was able to hear the row that followed. Later, when Silvana brought him water, he said softly, "Thank you, missus." The brown eyes looked up at her with gratitude.

On the following day Carlos also worked well. By evening his face was gray with exhaustion. Nobody could say that he wasn't earning his keep.

That evening, as Silvana walked away from the campfire, carrying food to the prisoner, she told herself that the sympathy she felt for Carlos was only natural. She felt protective toward this youth who was young enough to be her son. She was nurturing him, she was responsible for him. But Silvana was surprised that their prisoner accepted his treatment so stoically. She respected him for that, she thought, as carefully she fed him a mango, held like a hamburger in an elephant's-ear leaf. She wiped the juice from his lips.

Back at the campfire Suzy said to Annie, "Watch out for

Silvana. Carlos is making a pitch for her and she's falling for it. She never takes her eyes off him."

"Well, of *course* she doesn't," Annie said. "He's her prisoner. He's doing her job, and it's her responsibility to watch him all the time and see that he doesn't escape." She added, "Silvana's old enough to be his mother."

"So?"

Annie said sharply, "This guy is driving you all haywire. Silvana is only doing her job. She's his *guard*."

Nevertheless, when Silvana came back to the campfire, Suzy demanded, "Why is this guy getting room service of such a specialized nature?"

"How else could he eat a mango?" Silvana said defensively. "I don't see why we should treat him like an animal. Aren't you supposed to behave decently to prisoners of war?" Seeing Suzy's sneer, she snapped, "You're just irritated, Suzy, because he doesn't look at you the way you like men to look at you."

"Are you crazy?" Suzy yelled.

"You may not realize it, but in only two days you've started to walk the way you used to," Silvana retorted. "Waggling your ass and running with your knees together."

Suzy spat back, "I notice that you've started to fix yourself up. *I* saw you cleaning your nails with a bamboo splinter."

Annie said, *"Stop it!* Stop it, both of you!" That was the sixth little spat of the day, she thought crossly.

Almost overnight, the nonstop bitching had started. Annie didn't understand why. Had they been in a restaurant, this little waiter would not have been noticed by any of them. But now, his mere presence was weakening the comradeship that bound the women together.

"We're all acting different," Annie said in exasperation. "And the only reason is that there's a man around." She thought, Sex! It took you over, it ran your body for you, it dictated to you, it was an invisible bond from which you couldn't escape. It had been four months since any of them had felt the sexual excitement, the comfort and reassurance of a man's arms. Annie realized that they weren't suddenly running around in circles because they all wanted *this* man but because he reminded them of what their healthy bodies yearned for.

Annie said crossly, "Even when you've got your back to a man, you're conscious that he's *there*. Even if you're ignoring a man, you know you're ignoring him."

Carey said, "I saw Patty look in her pocket mirror this morning. Next thing you know, we'll be pulling out our lipsticks."

Suzy laughed. "Mine's a melted mess."

Annie said, "Do you suppose that women only act natural when there *isn't* a man around?"

In the flickering firelight Patty muttered, "We should have killed him."

Her voice was low, flat and absolutely sincere.

FRIDAY, MARCH 8

Carlos was not only young, strong and well fed, but he hadn't been living in the jungle for four months. Even Suzy had to admit that he worked as hard and as fast as Jonathan. None of the women mentioned it, but as the young man hacked away with the ax in the bamboo grove they were all fascinated by that red and black snake quivering and leaping on the olive-skinned arm as the powerful biceps moved in steady rhythm.

Tirelessly their prisoner felled the bamboo, piled the cut bamboo lengths in a neat heap near the waterfall or worked on the raft, pulling the rattan taut with a strength that the women could never hope to achieve.

On the third day after his capture, at Silvana's suggestion, the women allowed Carlos to eat the midday meal with them. He was carefully guarded, and his hobbled feet were tied by a two-foot length of rattan. They were a bit ashamed of the way they had been treating him. He had given no trouble, he had worked hard and he seemed friendly enough—almost docile in fact.

After watching the prisoner scratching, Annie said, "Silvana, you should check his head. He can't kill them himself."

Suzy said, "Cut his hair off."

"Then Carlos look small boy, like you." He gave Suzy a sideways look from beneath his thick black eyelashes.

Suzy giggled.

Silvana suddenly felt a pain in her chest. Indigestion, she thought, putting down her lump of coconut; she hadn't been chewing it properly. But the pain continued. Silvana felt it in her chest, a real pain. She wondered whether it could be a heart attack. Was she old enough for that? She looked down at the chewed piece of coconut in her hand. Somehow, in spite of their rudimentary grooming, Suzy's little brown hands always looked smooth and glossy-skinned. But the back of Silvana's hand showed skin starting to crinkle, upstanding veins, the freckles that come with age. And one finger was missing.

As she listened to the teasing male voice and Suzy's brisk rejoinders, Silvana fiercely reminded herself that he was young enough to be her son. She watched Suzy's hand as Suzy speared a morsel of fish from her coconut shell and popped the fish into her mouth with her smooth little paw. Silvana felt old, and ashamed of being old; she felt humiliated and ugly. She couldn't understand how, from one minute to the next, she could feel so worthless and so sad. She hoped that nobody had noticed.

After the meal Carlos walked slowly, on hobbled feet, toward the pile of logs; as usual, he was carefully covered by Silvana with the M-16.

Afterward, none of them could explain exactly what happened, not even Annie, who had been walking beside Carlos when he stumbled, gave a cry of pain and crashed down against the logs.

The neat pile disintegrated and within seconds the logs were rolling and bouncing down the steep slope toward the waterfall.

The astonished women rushed forward, too late, as the logs flew over the cliff and disappeared from sight.

"It's high tide!" shrieked Suzy. "The sonofabitch did it on purpose!" She rushed at Silvana and tried to grab the rifle from her.

Silvana, correctly assuming that Suzy meant to shoot Carlos, grappled for possession of the rifle.

Carey and Annie leaped forward to pull Suzy away from Silvana.

Lying on the ground, Carlos cried, "I fall because you tie my legs together. Is the *truth*."

As Patty scrambled down from the lookout tree she yelled, "Save those logs!"

The women rushed to stop the slow roll of the remaining logs, the ones from the bottom of the pile.

The moment when all the women started to argue was the logical time for Carlos to make a dash for the freedom of the jungle, but he knew that he couldn't run with his legs hobbled, so he didn't try. He also knew that any one of those women could have shot him. But it had been necessary to sabotage the raft or they might go to sea and leave him tied to a tree. He needed more time.

The following morning, once again, the women trailed back to the bamboo grove. Not all the logs had bounced over the cliff. Carey figured that Carlos could cut down what they needed to complete the half-built raft in a day and a half.

Weary and irritable, they toiled on.

Newly alert, they watched Carlos as he worked. No woman moved too close to him. They were always on their guard for the moment when he might try to grab one of them and either pull the fish knife from her belt or try to use her as a shield to get away. Should that happen, they had already decided that the woman who was grabbed would immediately lift both ankles sideways, so that the lookout could shoot Carlos's feet.

All that day, Silvana felt the pain in her chest. It was years since she had felt such violent emotions. She could no longer tell herself that her feelings for Carlos were maternal. She was ashamed of the turmoil she felt since yesterday's midday break when she had watched him watching Suzy walk across the clearing. She had suddenly been possessed by a fierce sensation of rage, sadness and impotence. She had experienced difficulty breathing and trembled with the violence of her sudden hatred for Suzy.

From that moment, Silvana had watched Carlos with a new and sly alertness. Every time he looked in Suzy's direction Silvana felt a sudden stab of pain. Grimly she thought, It's only natural. Suzy is young and very attractive. Then she thought sadly, When I was her age I was also attractive. *It's not fair!*

Thank God, as his guard, she was not supposed to take her eyes off him. She yearned to touch his smooth, glistening skin, to move closer and smell his musky underarm odor, to wipe the sweat from his naked back, slowly to stroke the long muscles on the back of his thighs. She could almost feel her hand touch his flesh. With the tip of her little finger, she longed to trace the ascent of the red and black snake that climbed so hypnotically up that smooth-muscled right arm. She would stroke it lightly—so lightly—she would hardly disturb a hair on his forearm as her finger, soft as a moth, moved around the coils of the snake that bulged and heaved and writhed with every movement of his beautiful, warm, olive-sheened arm.

Short of breath, feeling the stab of pain again, Silvana wiped her forehead. She was miserably ashamed that she, Silvana Cariotto Graham, was trembling at the knees, her stomach lurching at the sight of a dirty, naked Filipino waiter. She felt as if she had been deprived of some addiction, and now craved it. Thank God no one had noticed.

Carlos knew exactly how Silvana felt. He also knew that that raft would soon be finished.

The next night, as Silvana tethered the spread-eagled prisoner's arms to the two trees, watched by Patty with the rifle,

Shirley Conran

Carlos whispered, "When you leave this island, when you go . . . I pray you leave the knife, so poor Carlos can cut free, so no ants biting, till Carlos dies."

Silvana whispered, "I promise I won't leave you here to die."

"You *will* leave a knife?"

Silvana hesitated.

Carlos looked at her with his big brown, black-fringed eyes. *"Please*. I beg."

Silvana heard herself whisper, "Yes."

Carlos was looking at her with burning intensity.

Magnetized, Silvana slowly moved her face down to his. She must be mad, Patty was watching.

She could say she was tightening his bonds, she thought as softly she brushed his forehead with her lips. Carlos did not move.

As if in a trance, Silvana slowly put the tip of her trembling index finger to his cheek and traced the line of his jaw; she had not touched a man with love for years, and now this long-lost yearning took possession of her body, as if she were under a spell. Again her mouth moved, moth-soft, down his straight nose and then her lips brushed against his full mouth, feeling its warmth. Carlos slowly parted his lips and Silvana felt the moist tip of his tongue on hers. Her body started, as if she'd had an electric shock.

"Are you going to be all night?" Patty called crossly. "I want to climb the lookout tree while I can still see it."

"It's okay. I'm just tying his hands tighter. Go ahead."

Silvana could not help herself. As if hypnotized, she slowly lowered her face to his. Again she felt the insistent, wet tip of his tongue enter her mouth.

She put out her hand and felt his right arm, tethered to the tree. *At last,* although it was now too dark to see it, her fingertips slowly, softly, traced the snake upward, to his hard, warm shoulder.

Silvana's heart was thudding in her breast. Spread-eagled and tied to the tree, Carlos was unable to touch her with his

510

hands. Silvana gasped as she felt his chest rise and fall beneath her while her lips clung to his. She felt as if she were drowning, as if her will had left her, as if she were incapable of independent movement. Carlos softly sucked her underlip into his mouth.

"Anything wrong, Silvana?" It was Carey's voice, calling from their hut.

"Everything's fine," Silvana called back with difficulty and staggered to her feet.

Carlos whispered, "You come back later. When they sleep, we kiss." The last sibilant sounded like the wind in the trees.

"No," whispered Silvana sadly, longing to touch him again but not daring to. With an effort, she turned away and slowly moved toward the dying glow of the campfire.

Yes, he had picked the right one. Carlos smiled with complacent satisfaction. She was one nice woman, she had black hair, like his mother; she was not one tough old bitch. She felt good, her mouth tasted good, the smell of her was good. He suspected that she was one hot pussy.

Although she had promised to do so, Carlos didn't trust Silvana to leave him a knife. Even if she did, he knew that Patty or Carey would double-check his bindings before leaving the island. But that no longer mattered. What mattered right now was that he had Silvana in the palm of his hands.

He yawned sleepily. Better have a nap now, because she would be back.

Silvana lay on her bed, listening to Patty's soft, regular breathing. Silvana usually enjoyed the night, smelling the dry leaves of the eaves and listening to the symphony of the jungle, but tonight it was not soothing, because nothing could soothe her tonight. She felt wide awake, her body hot, taut and trembling on the bamboo bed. She ached with yearning; reason had deserted her; and her brain might as well have been sliced off, for all the control it had over its owner. Sexual tension had been building up all day, and now Silvana was a woman controlled, not by logic, but by passion. She thought it had faded with her youth. She thought that she would never again feel this overwhelming sexual urge that was driving her mad. This primitive compulsion, this suspension of logic, this urge to take insane risks was how she had felt with Arthur when they had first . . . No, this was more powerful.

Was this how men felt? Was this what her mother had warned her about, all those years ago? Was this what it felt like to a man, when he couldn't control himself?

Orgasm alone would not calm this overwhelming sexual insistence. She lay quivering on her bed and longed and longed to touch his young cheek again, feel the softness of his flesh, the harshness of the four-day growth of beard along his jaw. She longed to feel his warm breath on her face in the dark; her nipples ached for him, she swelled and melted and longed to feel his warm body press rhythmically against her.

As she watched the moonlight strike the black foliage in front of the hut, Silvana put both hands to her breasts and rubbed her nipples, but her own touch could not soothe the ache of her desire.

She thought, I am possessed, bewitched. Perhaps there *are* spirits in the forest . . .

She slid from her bed.

Carlos lay asleep, breathing steadily, as Silvana crouched beside him, watching his face in the dim light. She hugged this moment to herself, not knowing what the next would bring.

Silvana touched his cheek with her forefinger. In his sleep, Carlos turned and touched it with his warm lips. As she felt his saliva on her finger, she almost screamed or fainted—she didn't know which.

He started to suck her finger with a steady rhythm. His tongue flicked at the tip of her finger, then his lips gently sucked it into his mouth. He sucked harder and harder, until her whole finger was totally imprisoned in his mouth. His lips encircled her finger, pulling at it in a fierce rhythm. It felt like the insistent, sucking pull of the mouth of the newborn calves on her father's Tuscany farm, Silvana thought fleetingly. She felt his teeth give a little nip. His rough tongue encircled her finger, then gradually slackened. Slowly his tongue pushed her finger from his mouth.

Please don't stop. With a soft groan, Silvana knelt by him and cradled his jaw in her hands, dimly able to perceive the shape of his head, but clearly able to smell the odors of his body, mingled with the scent that rose from the earth upon which he lay.

As she felt with her lips for his, Silvana could hear his breathing and feel the thudding of his naked chest beneath her. Their sweat mingled and their beating hearts were almost touching. He slowly kissed her lips, then her chin. He let his tongue tremble gently down her neck.

With shaking hands Silvana tore at her shirt, then felt his soft mouth touch her nipple.

At last she felt relief start to flood through her.

Carlos turned his full attention to her breast, his lips brushing the soft underside of the fleshy curve. Silvana gasped as she felt his teeth softly touch the nipple, then his wet tongue start to lash it.

Abruptly, he stopped. Her body cried out in protest.

But he was only moving to her other breast. Again he nuzzled the soft underside curve. His lips started to pull in a steady rhythm . . .

Again he stopped.

"Please don't stop. *Please*. Please don't."

He whispered softly, "Untie my hands, so I love you properly."

"No, I can't."

"You say you will let me have this knife when you go, so why not untie just one hand now?"

"I mustn't."

The wet tip of his tongue flicked against her nipple, moved slowly around it, starting again wetly to caress the hard tip. She shuddered with pleasure.

Carlos stopped.

Silvana waited, knowing that he was again teasing her, feeling her desire mount within her body.

But Carlos didn't move. He wasn't teasing. He meant it.

Silvana thought, I *did* promise him the knife. So there's no reason for him to run away. And he *must* know how dangerous the jungle is at night.

Silvana slipped off the young, lean body beneath her. She crawled to the right-hand tree and untied the rattan rope. Knowing the risk, but possessed by desire, Silvana gave the prisoner his freedom.

Fast as a cat, Carlos was tearing at the rattan rope which tethered his left hand, to the second tree.

Miserably, Silvana listened to the sounds of his release. She had been a fool. She knew it. Suddenly she wondered if he was going to kill her. She didn't care.

In the darkness, she felt an unseen hand on the back of her head, then fingertips softly stroking the back of her neck. She felt the tip of his tongue in her ear and then the wet, warm flesh quivering inside it.

Silvana closed her eyes and softly groaned as she felt his hand on her naked breast. They fell back together to the floor of the forest, his hand traveling slowly down her body.

She felt a warm rush of happiness flooding through her body to her tingling fingertips.

Carlos was a pro.

MONDAY, MARCH 11

The explosion of an M-16 rifle made a lot of noise; a crack as the bullet was fired, followed by a thump as it hit.

Patty nearly fell from the lookout tree firing at the naked man in boots who ran into the cover of the jungle.

He swerved but ran on. She had missed him.

Patty slithered down the tree trunk. Rifle in hand, she tore toward the tree where Carlos had been tethered. In the ghost-mist of dawn, she could see a naked figure lying face downward. He had killed her!

"What was that?"

"What happened?"

Carey and Annie, both carrying rifles, came running up, followed by Suzy, who gripped the machete.

Naked and dazed, still half asleep, slowly becoming conscious of the ant bites all over her body, Silvana sat up.

"What did that bastard do to you?" gasped Carey. Then, realizing, she stopped dead and screamed, *"You stupid bitch!"* She raised her rifle to fire. As she did so, Annie leaped forward and clutched at her shoulder. The second rifle explosion was followed by a cacophony of screams and squawks in the jungle beyond the clearing.

Suzy snapped, "Don't waste time on *her*. Let's get out there and kill the bastard, before he can bring anyone back to camp."

Annie thrust her rifle at Silvana. "Stay here. Guard the camp. Guard the raft. Shoot on sight and shoot to kill. If he comes back, kill him. If you don't, I promise we'll kill you." She turned to the others. "He won't head for the Burma bridge, because he knows he won't be able to cross it. So, Suzy, take my rifle and cut through the jungle to William Penn, as far south as you dare so he can't get past you to Katanga village. The rest of us will fan out into a stalking line. We'll keep one another in sight and we'll beat toward William Penn to push him onto the path. Then, with any luck, Suzy can move up the path and take him."

"What if he crosses William Penn and goes into the jungle beyond?" Patty asked.

"He won't last long with no clothes and no gun," Carey said grimly.

Suzy said, "Why don't we just let him go, finish the raft fast and get the hell out of here?"

Annie shook her head. "He could get a helicopter here before we finish the raft. Wherever he is, we have to find him, because he knows our camp and our plans. If he doesn't bring

515

Raki's soldiers, then he might warn the villagers that we've nearly finished the raft. We don't want war canoes waiting for us beyond the reef."

Suzy said, "For God's sake, let's stop talking and go get him." She slipped away.

It was clear daylight as the three other women spread out in a line. Slowly and quietly, they moved through the trees, remembering to look up in case Carlos had climbed a tree either to hide or to jump on Patty and grapple for her gun.

As the women disappeared into the bush, Silvana was conscious of their contempt and fury. She shared their opinion. She'd been fooled. She'd been callously used. She'd been betrayed by her own hungry body. She felt deeply humiliated and ashamed.

Silvana felt like taking her fish knife and slashing at her own belly, in pain, in rage, in self-contempt.

She didn't need to be told to kill on sight.

Inside the twilight of the rain forest, the search party slowed down as it approached William Penn and the boundary line of the taboo area.

A bird of paradise flew past, a flash of blue.

Crack!

It was the report of a rifle, from somewhere ahead.

Cautiously they started to run forward, using the jungle lope that was now second nature to them. It might have been Suzy with the AK-47—they didn't know what it sounded like—but it might also be some other rifle . . . or someone might have grappled the rifle from Suzy.

They reached the narrow jungle track that they had christened William Penn. They could see no one.

Simultaneously, all three heads jerked to the right as they heard a scrabbling noise and saw the naked figure of Carlos running toward them.

He stopped abruptly when he saw the women, then crashed off the track into the jungle beyond William Penn. It happened so quickly that none of them had time to fire before he disappeared.

The women ran along the track to the point where Carlos disappeared. As they reached it they saw Suzy running along the path toward them, clearly out of breath and panting too hard to speak. With her right hand she pointed her rifle toward the spot where Carlos had vanished.

Patty was the first to reach it. She turned to check that the others were following her, then they all melted into the jungle and again spread out in a search line. As they moved grimly forward, each of the four women was conscious that they were moving farther and farther away from safety. Nevertheless, they had caught up with Carlos and were close behind him, so they ignored the dim warnings in the back of their minds as they ignored the briars that scratched them as they ran. They pushed their way forward determined to track down Carlos, but he had disappeared.

Patty looked at her watch. She signaled to Annie, who signaled to the others. The four women gathered together.

Patty said, "It's already nine o'clock, we've been out here three hours. I think we've lost him."

Annie said, "At least we know roughly where he is. He knows we're looking for him, so he might hide out."

Suzy suggested, "If we go back to camp now, we could work all day and through the night. We should be able to finish the raft and leave tomorrow."

Patty nodded. "If we've lost him, we should leave as fast as possible before he brings anyone back to the camp."

"Okay." Annie wiped the sweat from her face with the back of her hand. "We'll take a five-minute break and then get back to camp."

Suzy said, "There's a stream over to the right, let's get a drink. *Just this once, Annie.*"

Annie looked dubious. "We're all thirsty and we're all hungry, but remember the last time we had diarrhea."

Suzy suddenly crumpled to the ground and hung her head

517

with exhaustion. "Listen, I've *gotta* have a drink. What about water vines?" She looked around but couldn't see any.

Carey said gently, "You're not going to die if you don't have a drink, but you don't want diarrhea on the raft. *Please* don't drink, Suzy."

Suzy looked up, exhausted. "Can we just stick our feet in that stream, then?"

"Leeches," Carey reminded her.

"Okay, we don't go near the stream," Suzy sighed, and ran her tongue around the inside of her mouth to summon up saliva.

During the five-minute rest, none of the exhausted women spoke until Patty stood and stretched wearily. "The sooner we're back, the sooner we drink. Let's go." She turned and started to move forward.

Annie said, "No, farther to your left."

Patty half-turned and said, "This is the way we came."

Suzy said, "No, it was over to your right, Annie."

"Did anyone bring a compass?" Carey asked. "Where's the one you wear around your neck, Suzy?"

"I take it off at night to sleep."

The uppermost trees of the rain forest, which reached to sixty feet, were nourished by the sun and the rain. The second layer of canopy trees, reaching as high as thirty feet, formed a dense umbrella, which allowed only a little sunlight to filter down; the lowest trees—which rarely reached higher than ten feet—competed with each other for the few rays of sunlight which penetrated the canopy. In the green gloom of the jungle at ground level, it was not possible to judge direction by the sun.

By eleven o'clock when the women stopped to rest again, they had no idea where they were.

"Wherever we are at four o'clock, we stop for the night by a stream," Annie decided. "Patty and Carey fish, Suzy and I collect boughs for beds."

"Maybe we should follow one of these streams until it joins a river," Carey suggested. "The water must follow the tilt of the land, or run parallel to it. At least we know we won't be going uphill again."

"We *haven't* been going uphill," Suzy said.

"Oh, don't start that again," Patty said wearily. "Carey's right. At least if we follow a stream, we'll move faster. I'm afraid we've only been covering about one mile an hour and, as Suzy said, we might be going around in circles. We haven't come across a path or a game trail, and we can't climb a tree to see where we are because the lower trees get in our way; we can't even reach the *lowest* branches of these tall trees."

"It would be easier if we tried at sunset. Then we'd know which way is best," Carey said.

"But once you came down again, you'd lose your sense of direction within five minutes," Suzy objected.

Carey said, "I'm voting that we follow a stream. Streams always move downhill, as I remember. With any luck we can wade in the water."

"Leeches," Annie said.

"Fuck leeches. They don't hurt anyway," Carey said. "We can de-leech when we get back to camp. Streams lead to rivers, and rivers lead into the sea."

"Sometimes rivers lead to swamps," Patty warned.

Annie said, "Following a stream would make more sense than just wandering around. So let's go. From now on, we take a rest every hour. We've all got knives. We can survive out here so long as we don't exhaust ourselves or panic."

"I haven't got the strength to panic," Suzy said as she got to her feet.

Annie said, "Let's hope that Carlos is in the same fix."

By two o'clock, they seemed to be moving along the bottom of a valley, where many little streams meandered between strips of forest. The endless trees were parted by thin, sparkling threads of water, clear and bright and trickling diamonds. At one point, through the pale green gloom they had a glimpse of a small waterfall, beside which an almost invisible track climbed a steep incline. In the larger streams they glimpsed small bright fish and nearly transparent freshwater shrimp lying close to the stones below the water. At least they wouldn't starve.

By now, the women were frightened. The jungle sounds were so different from those they knew. The brilliant birds flashing high overhead seemed to mock them.

"I want to stop again," Patty said, pulling Jonathan's lighter from her pocket. "I think we should all ask ourselves what Jonathan would have done in this fix." Nervously her hands stroked the lighter.

Annie felt in her pocket for the comforting weight of the Swiss army knife.

Carey said,"You realize what you're doing, don't you? You're using Jonathan's possessions as fetishes."

"I thought those were leather whips and black garters," Suzy said.

"No, it's any object that you become excessively attached to," Carey said, "or irrationally devoted to. Suzy's compass, Patty's lighter, Annie's knife—you're either using them as good luck charms or touching them because you feel it puts you in touch with Jonathan."

Suzy nodded. "What's wrong with that? As a matter of fact, I find it comforting. To me that compass is more than just a keepsake. I only wish to hell I had it with me now."

"Just don't start thinking it has any magical power," Carey said.

"But it *has*," Suzy said. "For me."

By three o'clock, the banks of the river they had been following had deepened into a stony gorge.

When they stopped to rest Annie said, "I don't want to raise false hopes, but is this starting to look familiar to anyone?"

Carey said, "I've been wondering the same thing. Do you really think it's the Allegheny?"

"You mean *our* river? You think we might be above the Burma bridge?" Suzy asked. "How come we got to the other side without crossing water, if it's our river?"

Carey said, "I remember Jonathan saying that these rivers

sometimes run underground for a while. If so, we might have walked over it."

"Or we might have walked around the source," Annie said.

Carey sighed. "We might have traveled for miles, or we might have been moving around in one small area, who knows? But it sure *looks* like our river! On your feet, guys."

With new heart, the tired and thirsty women moved forward again, until Annie, who was in the lead, lifted her head sharply and put up her right hand.

Immediately, they all stopped. Nobody moved or spoke. It was their danger signal.

Annie turned around and beckoned to the other women. They moved up to her.

Annie whispered, "I heard a bark. Listen."

"Sounds like more than one," Carey whispered. "Sounds like several dogs."

Annie nodded. "That means a village."

"That means this *isn't* our river," Suzy said.

"Keep quiet! I can hear something else." Carey strained to hear, then gave a tired grin. "It sounds like the rumble of distant drums."

"The surf!" Suzy beamed. *"The sea!"*

Again they all moved forward, still cautious, but now definitely hopeful.

What Carey had heard *had* been the sound of drums. As the little group drew closer to the noise, they could also hear singing and the excited cries of children.

"They're making a hell of a noise," Suzy whispered to Annie.

Annie nodded. "Must be somebody's birthday. No more talking until we've checked this situation out."

Carey warned, "Remember, if a dog comes up, or barks, or snaps at your ankles, stand *absolutely still.*"

With Annie in the lead, the women moved nearer and nearer to the village. Eventually, Annie could see into the clearing ahead of her. The singers were men, their lean black bodies sleek with pig grease. As they danced, the shells of their necklaces clicked against each other. The faces of the men were smeared with white and yellow-ocher paint; the yellow and scarlet feathers of their elaborate headdresses swayed as they shuffled around in a circle. A singing, swaying chorus, they tossed their heads and stamped their feet to the accompaniment of flute music and the throb of empty oil drums.

Surrounding the singers, a further circle of men squatted. They chewed hunks of meat which was being served from the side of the clearing. Naked women chattered together as they crouched beside a battered, galvanized-iron washtub, dipped coconut-shell cups into the tub and ran to offer the palm beer to their menfolk.

Everyone fell silent as a big, middle-aged man appeared at the edge of the clearing. He wore the white feather headdress of a medicine man, his head was shaven, his face was painted with white horizontal stripes and a pair of false teeth hung from a leather thong around his neck. He was carrying something.

Through the shimmering haze of feathered headdresses, to the thump of a single drum, the medicine man advanced to a rough altar that stood on the left side of the clearing. Abruptly, the music stopped. He bowed before the altar.

The medicine man stepped forward and carefully placed his burden upon the altar. He stepped back and bowed reverently.

"Oh, my God!" gasped Suzy. "The snake tattoo! That's Carlos's arm!"

BOOK SIX

ITAMBU

◄ 26 ►

MONDAY, MARCH 11, 1985

The deeper the dinghy penetrated, the narrower the river became. After five hours of travel in the cramped boat, Harry felt claustrophobically smothered by this dark green, slimy tunnel inexorably lowering over his head.

Sounding like the black flies that clustered around Harry's eyes, the small inflatable craft buzzed through the tunnel of green gloom hanging above the frothing river torrent. Rotting vegetation, dead branches and forest muck swirled along in water the color of milk chocolate. The clammy, midmorning heat enveloped Harry in a suffocating blanket of perspiration, and the cloud of insects that surrounded his head goaded him to silent frenzy.

He reminded himself that any discomfort was worthwhile if—as seemed probable—he was at least following an unequivocal clue to the disappearance of the Nexus party.

Mentally, he reviewed the events of the last ten days.

On March 1, the day after the official end of the cyclone season, Harry had flown up to Queenstown Airport—now fully operational—in the new Nexus Lear 30. He was always amazed by the lack of space in private jets. In movies, a jet interior seems huge but in fact, Harry couldn't even stand upright in most private jets, and the cabins were so small and

525

confined that he felt as if he were sitting in a cigar tube. He was always glad to get out of them.

In the sweltering heat of Queenstown Airport, Kerry had been waiting for him. Two armed guards sat in the back seat of the jeep.

Harry jerked his head toward the guards. "Are they really necessary?"

Kerry said, "Yes. You'll see why if you really insist on staying in Queenstown."

"I don't want to start that argument again, Kerry." Harry felt irritated. "I'm only going to get information if I'm in the town center and easy to contact." As the jeep bounced over the ground toward the helipad, he added, "And if I'm staying with Ma Chang, it's easy for anyone to get a message to me quietly by slipping into Ron Chang's sewing-machine workshop and giving it to him."

The two men continued their conversation as they climbed out of the jeep, walked across the helipad and got into the helicopter.

"I suppose the only way to dissuade you is to show you how things have changed," Kerry said.

"Have Johno and the other pilots arrived?"

"They arrived late yesterday from Moresby. The Piper Cherokees will use the Queenstown strip, because there's no sand gear at Mount Ida."

"Why do we have to fly in pilots? Couldn't we have hired Paui Defense Force aircraft? Surely they'd know the area better than eight Aussie pilots from Moresby?"

Kerry laughed. "The PDF air force is still minimal. And what would they do if the Russians attacked while we were using both their Otters?"

The helicopter dipped over dense green undergrowth, then flew north up the coastline. Harry asked his routine business questions.

"Things are okay at the mine," Kerry told him. "Production on target, no personnel problems. Everything's under control in the Nexus compound, and if things turn nasty, we're prepared. Mount Ida has been quietly turned into a small fortress. Since Raki's takeover there's been a dusk-to-dawn curfew, so we don't allow any of the mine personnel—black or white—into Queenstown after six in the evening."

"If there *is* trouble, what will you do with our personnel?"

"Remember I told you that Mindo had been promoted? He's now in charge of our local labor force. If we have to evacuate, it's his job to get every islander back to their own villages or take them with him up to the Central Mountains. Mindo's father is an important mountain chief, so everyone will be safe there until things quiet down."

"And apart from that?"

"Nothing to report, except the atmosphere gets more unpleasant every day since Raki was elected President for Life. You'll see what I mean when you get into Queenstown. There's been a lot of army looting. The theft and violence are terrifying the civilians, and the rest of this rotten regime is just as corrupt as the army. Raki's sudden power seems to have gone to his head. He's behaving like countless other dictators in emerging Third World nations. He hasn't ordered an ermine-trimmed throne yet, but I wouldn't be surprised if one turned up."

"I thought Raki was smarter than that," Harry said.

"Raki would never have been a chief by birth. Because he grabbed control, he and his ministers now have the sort of power their fathers never dreamed of. It's gone to their heads. The ministers behave more or less as they please." He added, "I reckon that Nexus is going to get a lot of resignations and requests for transfers. The wives are being very supportive, but they won't stand for these conditions much longer."

"Has only four months of Raki made such a big difference?"

Kerry nodded. "Though there's nothing we can't handle. My only worry is that *you* might get into a tough spot. There's no problem about continuing the air search, but if you insist on staying in Queenstown I'd like you to travel with a couple of guards." He looked sideways at Harry and added, rather fast, "*I'll* be the one to take the heat from Pittsburgh if they lose any more personnel."

Johno and the eight Australian pilots were waiting in the air-conditioned comfort of Kerry's office. So was Mindo, who except for his squashed nose looked a bit like the traditional representations of Jesus Christ. He had the same compassionate yet firm expression, long hair and a beard, together with an aura of command. This was not surprising in a man who was the son of a mountain chief, who'd been educated at the Jesuit college in Port Moresby and who had just crossed the line from union leader to management.

On Harry's previous trip to Paui, Mindo had been visiting his tribe, so this was their first meeting. As the two men exchanged greetings, they eyed each other with interest. Mindo was even taller than Harry, and said even less. Because of his knowledge of Paui, he had been asked to attend the search-plan briefings. The plans had been decided weeks beforehand.

"What do you reckon has happened to the missing people?" Harry asked.

Mindo did not soften his words. "If they heard shooting, they may have hidden in the jungle. Whites cannot survive in the jungle. They would have died."

"Do *you* think they're dead?"

"Perhaps," Mindo said. "But Paradise Bay used to be a big crocodile hunting area. Now nobody wants crocodiles, so the village hunters have no money. The whites may have been captured for ransom. That is your hope."

"Then why has there been no ransom demand?"

"It would not be unusual to wait. Months mean nothing to the islanders. The hunters may have been alarmed when they realized the importance of their prisoners. They may have hidden them far from Paradise Bay."

"So what can we do?"

"Search. And wait," Mindo said firmly. "My people can handle the land search. Westerners cannot do this."

"Then let's start," Harry said.

The four twin-engine Piper Cherokees had been hired months earlier from one of the two charter firms at Port Moresby. Harry would have preferred planes with floats, but they weren't available; however, the Cherokees were new aircraft. They would grid-search the island, each towing a hundred-foot banner that read, in black on white, MAKE SMOKE HARRY NEXUS. Harry hoped that if the Nexus party was being held prisoner, the most optimistic of the possibilities, then one of that tough, smart bunch of international executives would surely, somehow, be able to set *something* alight.

Paui measures two hundred and fourteen miles at its longest point and seventy-four miles at its widest point—bigger than Belgium, three times the size of Connecticut. That is a lot of land to search, he told himself.

Each of the four Cherokees was going to search a quadrant of the island and fly over it at normal search speed, which was 60 miles an hour. They would fly to a grid pattern. Each pilot had already marked up his large-scale map into small squares; each square measured 7.5 by 7.5 miles, an area of 56.25 square miles, which would take about an hour to search. To search Paui should take 266 flying hours. Allowing a maximum of ten hours flying time per day, this meant a total of twenty-seven search days—roughly seven days per aircraft; an extra day for insurance meant eight days per aircraft.

They were due to start the search on the following morning, March 2, and finish it on the evening of March 9; the pilots would return to Port Moresby on the morning of March 10.

On March 2 and 3 Johno, in the ungainly Duck, would carry out a coastal search. At search speed, he would slowly fly above the 554 miles of coastline, after which he would stand by as the spare pilot.

On March 2 Harry, in the Nexus helicopter, would travel to the area immediately south of Paradise Bay, where he would start a dinghy search of the coastline. He would be accompanied by an armed interpreter who spoke the local language and

Pidgin. At all times, Harry would be in contact with the helicopter pilot.

After the briefing, Kerry and Harry flew to Queenstown in the Bell.

As the helicopter flew over the endless green carpet of jungle, Kerry said, "You've lost a lot of weight, Harry. Feel all right?"

Harry nodded. Not only was he as lean as a stick, but the skin was drawn taut across his high, flat cheekbones. He looked tense and tired.

Kerry also noticed something else. "You've got another gun. Isn't it a bit small?"

"It's what American cops use," Harry said. "A snub-nosed Thirty-eight Special, Smith and Wesson. If it's big enough for them, it's big enough for me. It's big enough to stop a man, not just nick him."

"Talking of being stopped, the guards on the roadblocks tend to get drunk and they're potentially dangerous from late afternoon onwards," Kerry warned. "Try not to go out alone, and always take plenty of cigarettes with you. Carry your passport too, of course—you've got a permanent visa, haven't you? Good."

Irritably Harry said, "I'm not a child."

"We've had to double security at the mine and at the compound," Kerry said.

"Yeah, I read your report. But nothing has actually happened to warrant any action, right? You're just worried that something *might* happen?"

"Not worried, Harry, *scared*. Things have changed a lot in four months."

The ride from Queenstown Airport to the town was spine-rattling. Harry winced as he said, "I'd have been up here more often if Raki had definitely agreed to negotiate. But he wouldn't arrange a meeting."

"Don't worry. Raki knows the mining concession doesn't

530

run out until the end of June, and he knows that we're ready to talk as soon as he is ready," Kerry said.

"Jerry Pearce thinks the Heads of Agreement should be signed by the first of April, latest. The Legal Department will need at least three months on it. Otherwise, we'll have to close the mine temporarily."

"That gives us only three weeks for discussion, Harry."

"So what? Raki's always been a last-minute negotiator."

"And now he holds all the cards," Kerry said. "Let me tell you how he won the election. To begin with, he held it at the end of December, when much of the island was impassable, due to flooded rivers and landslides."

As they drove through a forest where yellow orchids hung from dark green trees, Harry listened to the long list of blatant fraud and corruption. Kerry concluded, "And in areas known to be unfriendly to Raki, soldiers held target practice outside the polling stations; not surprisingly, few people voted."

"Did *anyone* vote Democratic?" Harry asked.

Kerry laughed. They left the high trees of the jungle behind them and briefly drove past cultivated land. "Also not surprisingly, Raki was elected President for Life."

They could now see ahead of them the forlorn corrugated-tin shacks of Shanty Town.

Harry leaned forward and peered out. "I've never seen so many soldiers in Queenstown!"

Kerry said quietly, "Some people around here still remember a time before 1975, when the island didn't have a rotten army and *did* have a good police force. Now we no longer have a police force, just the new so-called Defense Force, now enlarged by Filipino mercenaries and every young tribesman that Raki could raise."

As they approached Ma Chang's hotel, Harry noticed that a new apple-green board hung above the entrance doors. Bright blue letters read, "Presidential Hotel."

"What's wrong with young tribesmen?" Harry asked.

Kerry said, "At first, the young recruits from outlying tribes behaved reasonably, but now they're hungry, rarely paid and encouraged to steal food and money at the roadblocks."

"Are there many roadblocks?"

"You might pass three within a mile, and they stop every cart and bicycle. If you haven't a ransom, you risk being badly beaten with boots or rifle butts. They spend the money on drink. And you know what they're like when they're drunk."

Harry knew the islanders had very weak heads and were not charming drunks. They were aggressive, boastful bullies and could be very cruel. Ears were cut off, noses slit open and eyes gouged out.

"The fun starts at dusk, Harry," Kerry warned. "You'll hear banging on trash can lids and empty oil drums, and sporadic gunfire from those khaki juvenile delinquents. Don't underestimate them just because they look young. They've got real rifles, and they steal real ammunition from their own armory. Most are very good shots. They're given a few weeks' shooting practice, then they're handed an AK and a pair of boots, told they're soldiers and that it's their job to protect the President and use their wits to feed themselves. So people are killed every night. Dogs start eating the corpses before their families can find them."

"I can see why you didn't put in a full report before I arrived," Harry said. "I'd have found this hard to believe."

He jumped down from the vehicle and looked up and down the unusually quiet road. The town felt sullen; menace hung around the buildings like an invisible thundercloud.

In the hotel foyer, a large, touched-up photograph of President Raki now hung behind the reception desk; tinted pink cheeks curved in a benevolent smile beneath eyes as calmly merciless as those of any Roman emperor.

Harry was greeted by an overpowering whiff of magnolia.

"Welcome back, Mr. Scott." Mrs. Chang looked up from the Monopoly board, where Freddy was reluctantly selling Broadway.

"Any news, Mrs. Chang?" Harry asked.

"I received the insurance lists of the valuables belonging to the missing persons, including watches. I was most interested to notice the value of Mr. Graham's watch. Let me see, ten percent of the value is the usual insurance repayment price, is it not? Minus the hundred and seventy dollars you have already paid me, of course."

"Have you been able to locate any of the other watches?"

"Not yet. As you know, it is unwise to be too specific in our search or to offer too generous a reward. People have been killed for less than a watch. However, they know that my boy Ronnie will pay more than usual for good secondhand watches. So the market price has already risen."

As usual, the bar looked as if it had been the scene of a truly gargantuan drunken brawl. The only occupant was Bill, the retired planter who felt that Robert Louis Stevenson had wrecked his life with false promises of tropical allure.

"So *you're* back," he said to Harry. "Is it true you're going to search again and cover the coastline by yourself?"

Harry nodded.

"You want to be careful," Bill said. "Especially round the southern tip of the island. They've got bloodthirsty bastards with nasty customs down there. Millions of dollars were spent looking for that millionaire's son, the one that disappeared in the sixties. He was never found, and we all know why. I heard that the first search expedition found the villagers still wearing his clothes. So watch out you don't end up an hors d'oeuvre wrapped in banana leaves."

"Thanks for the warning. Care for a beer?"

"Thanks, mate. I know it's not my business, but do you really think there's any chance of finding them out there, after four months? Because nobody else does, chum."

"Nexus doesn't give up easily," Harry said.

"The buzz is, you need legal evidence of their death," Bill said. "Otherwise the life insurance claims of the relatives have to wait seven years."

Harry nodded.

"But why are *you* doing it?"

"This is my area and I'm responsible for it. It's my job," Harry said, thinking of Annie.

The following morning, March 2, Harry started his coastline search in the Nexus helicopter. He couldn't use the Duck because it carried only two people and Harry needed an interpreter. From Paradise Bay he planned to move north and work around the island in a rubber dinghy with an outboard. A search-and-rescue project always starts where the missing persons were last seen.

Allowing for visits to villages, cigarette distribution and chat, Harry could only count on covering fifty miles of coastline a day. He would keep in touch with Roger, the monosyllabic helicopter pilot, by means of a flare launcher pocket pen. When Harry screwed a cartridge into the base and pulled back the firing knob on the side, the launcher shot a small magnesium flare two hundred feet into the air. Harry had nine flares. If a flare was not fired from the jungle below promptly every hour, the pilot was to radio Mount Ida for help.

Harry started his search just south of Katanga village, where his questions were met by blank stares and head shakes.

When the black dinghy puttered past Waterfall Bay the distraught women were burying Jonathan. There was no lookout at the camp during the funeral service. Grief-stricken, the women did not even hear Harry pass.

On March 3, exhausted and covered with insect bites, Harry returned from the second day of his coastline search to be told that President Raki had granted him an interview, for exactly ten minutes at exactly seven o'clock that evening.

Upon his arrival at the palace, Harry was searched, then escorted to the President's office. Harry noticed the forlorn air of the previously immaculate garden. The flowerbeds were bare, bushes and trees had been mutilated to provide fuel for bonfires, which had scarred black patches on the parched lawn. As they passed beneath the trees, bats flew out in a filthy swirling cloud and a yellow splat of bat dung, the color of rotten mango, fell on Harry's forearm.

"Good luck," one of the soldiers said.

The palace had gone from ramshackle to derelict. Along the wide corridor which led to the presidential quarters, a length of fire hose trailed on the soggy, stained purple carpet. The nozzle hung over a red fire bucket. The amiable soldier who believed in good luck said, "Toilet water tap no good, get water in bucket from fire hose."

Raki wore an elaborate white uniform, similar to that of a British Admiral of the Fleet in tropical waters. With what seemed genuine concern, the President inquired about the progress of Harry's search for the missing Nexus group. The President would talk on no other subject and firmly avoided discussing the renewal of the mining concession or even fixing a definite date to discuss it.

Harry left in a rage.

On March 7, after another four fruitless days of coastline search, Harry was again summoned to the palace. For this meeting Raki wore only a scarlet lap-lap around his waist. He was clearly in excellent physical condition, muscular and flat-bellied.

Sitting behind his elaborate desk, the President again firmly refused to discuss the renewal of the mining concession. With every appearance of genuine concern, he said, "The urgency is to find these missing friends of yours, Mr. Scott. Surely this is more important than business? Your friends are not the only missing persons. Our people are also in constant communication with the Japanese and British consulates at Port Moresby, for it appears that four other tourists and a member of the hotel staff are also missing from the Paradise Bay Hotel." He threw the missing person photographs down on his elaborate Louis XVI–style French desk and absentmindedly with a dagger started to gouge bits of inlay from the desktop.

"You have heard no news at all, sir?" Harry asked.

Palms outward, both Raki's hands flew up to shoulder

level. "I wish I could be more helpful, but as you know, our investigations revealed nothing. I hoped that *you* might have some news for *me*, Mr. Scott."

Harry shook his head.

An irritable note crept into the President's voice. "Then life must go on, Mr. Scott, don't you think? The Minister of Tourism—you remember my brother Envo?—is seriously concerned about the attention your search is attracting in the foreign press."

"It's hardly surprising, sir," Harry said.

Raki's eyes, their whites nearly yellow, looked blandly into Harry's. "Sadly, the Minister feels—and I must admit that I agree with him—that some definite date must be put to the end of your search. After all, this disagreeable business has now hung over our fledgling tourist industry for four months. The Minister is most anxious that you make your search as thorough as you wish, but we must agree on a date upon which it ceases. The date agreed is the first day of April, which gives you plenty of time to search our small island with the proverbial toothbrush."

President Raki's reasonable tone of voice suddenly changed. "After that you will search *no more!*" His black eyes looked into Harry's gray ones with all the friendliness of a Highland stag about to dispute territory. "After that, Mr. Scott, your eagerness to seek your friends will be interpreted as an exasperating and aggressive attempt to sabotage our efforts at attracting foreign visitors to Paui both for business and pleasure."

The President stood up and leaned forward with both hands pressed on the desktop. "As to our business negotiations, these will not commence until this search of yours has ended. As I must achieve the best possible price for my country, I intend to discuss the mining concession with other interested parties. I believe you know Mr. Jaime Ongpin, president of the Beguet mining conglomerate? A most charming chap, a skilled economist, a scholar of Ateneo University, Manila, and a most interesting fellow. Goodnight, Mr. Scott."

* * *

On the morning of March 10 the eight pilots of the Cherokees shook hands all around, said they were really sorry that
they'd found nothing, it really was a bloody shame, and flew
back to Port Moresby.

That evening Harry returned, depressed and later than
usual, to Mrs. Chang's hotel. As he entered the lobby, Freddy
sprang out and said excitedly, "Master! Master! Mrs. Chang
want tok-tok you quicktime!"

On enormous splayed feet, Freddy flitted up the wooden
stairs. Harry waited, wondering why Mrs. Chang wanted to
talk to him.

Wearing a triumphant smile, she appeared, clutching the
banister. Moving down like a timorous child, one step at a
time, with the left foot always first, Mrs. Chang lowered her
enormous magenta bulk down the stairs and waddled across
the lobby to Harry. Without a word, she dug her right fist deep
into her pocket and then opened it under Harry's nose.

On her sweaty little palm lay a battered steel watch.

Harry telephoned Kerry and asked him to fly down in the
Bell the next morning. He then waited up to put through a call
to Jerry Pearce in Pittsburgh, where it was seven o'clock in
the morning. Jerry was now Acting President of Nexus as well
as Finance Exec.

Sitting in Mrs. Chang's old-fashioned swivel chair, Harry
sniffed the musky odor of sweat and sandalwood, magnolia
and dust. Through the heavy telephone in his hand, he heard a
click, a pause and then, as clearly as if she were in the next
room, a polite telephone operator who had probably showered
in the last few hours and probably wore a crisp white smile
and a blouse to match. "Your party is on the line, sir. Have a
nice day."

Harry told Jerry that Mrs. Chang had produced a second
watch—an old stainless steel Rolex Oyster, waterproof and
automatic, with a perpetual-date system. The watch didn't fit
any of the seven descriptions of insured watches that Harry

had brought back from Pittsburgh. This watch clearly wasn't valuable enough to be insured—but it *might* be worth millions of dollars because on the back were inscribed the words "Roderick Douglas, December 7, 1965."

"Looks as though Roddy got it for his eighteenth birthday," Harry reported. "It's been wiped clean, but there's still what looks like blood in the bracelet links. . . . No, I don't know what blood type he was, but Roddy's doctor will have a record. . . . No, I know the insurance assessors won't accept it as proof of death, but now we have proof that Roddy *and* Arthur aren't wearing their watches. In other words, Arthur's watch can no longer be considered an accidental theft, unconnected with the disappearances."

"Better send them both to me," Jerry said.

"No, Jerry, I'm not trusting the watches to a courier; they'll both be locked in a bank where they'll be safe until I personally bring them to Pittsburgh. . . . No, Jerry, in my experience, couriers aren't reliable, James Bond types. Couriers sit in airplanes and lose things. . . . *No,* Jerry, to hell with correct procedure and what Washington wants; Washington is very efficient at being inefficient. I expect there's a pile of telexes reaching to the ceiling by now, about why nothing has been achieved."

In Pittsburgh, Jerry winced and clutched at his stomach. Damned if he was going to get an ulcer over this. He asked, "Do you know *where* the watch came from, Harry?"

"Not exactly. Not yet. A local—well, I suppose you'd call him a doctor—took it off a dead soldier near a riverside village called Malong. That's about forty miles south of Queenstown. . . . Yes, I'm going there with an interpreter, tomorrow, by boat. . . . No, it's only about fifteen miles upriver, but it might be in impenetrable jungle or swamp and we'd never get a helicopter in. If I can locate more of this soldier's possessions—a paybook or something like that—it might give us a lead to where the man came from. He might have been billeted in a nearby village; he might be one of Raki's military infiltrators. . . . Sure, as soon as I get identification we'll formally ask the Minister of Defense where the bloke was stationed."

Useless to explain to Jerry what had really happened.

Roddy's watch had been worn on the wrist of a Filipino soldier who had shot a piglet in the bush and roasted it. The nearby villagers, to whom the piglet belonged, hadn't even demanded Payback money for the dead animal. As the soldier left the vicinity of the village, the village *luluai* had simply called for his bow and shot the soldier in the back. That was Payback in action.

The Malong villagers already had a telephone, a twelve-bore shotgun and a Mickey Mouse watch, but they lacked a transistor radio. The village medicine man had taken money and the watch from the dead soldier, then traveled by canoe forty-one miles to Queenstown.

As soon as the Malong medicine man had traded the Rolex, the local cheap-radio dealer had nipped into Ronald Chang's shop—everyone knew that Ronald was offering unusually good money for watches. The radio dealer didn't know what had happened to the dead man, but the villagers wouldn't have wasted a good soldier; they would have roasted him.

From faraway Pittsburgh, Jerry Pearce asked how the concession discussions were proceeding.

Trying not to inhale the magnolia miasma that hung about the mouthpiece of the telephone, Harry said, "Raki won't discuss the concessions until this search is finished, he says it's upsetting their tourist business. By the way, it looks as though we have the competition we expected. . . . Yes, Beguet."

"Raki's dealing with Beguet and you're concentrating on this futile search!" Jerry roared over thousands of miles. "Shit, that's the worst news I've heard all week! You should be concentrating on that deal, instead of taking boat rides. Look, Harry, I'm ordering you to stop the search. We've done everything we can, but it's *over*, Harry."

"But, Jerry," Harry began.

Jerry yelled, "The stock is seventeen points higher than ever before and we're about to announce a dividend that's up six-

Shirley Conran

teen percent from last year. Wall Street is sending us all the right signals—the shareholders have accepted our new management. We don't want to hear any more about the disappearances. It brings the whole subject up again. It creates unnecessary anxiety. It's unsettling for employees *and* for shareholders. Let it die down, Harry. Forget it. *That's an order*, Harry." Jerry slammed down the receiver.

Harry thought, Jerry's been in charge for four months. He's proved he can do the job. He's confident, and sure of his position. Jerry thinks he's safe. And he would be—if I didn't have those watches.

He was damned if he was going to give up.

The following morning, shortly after dawn, the old Duck deposited Harry and his native interpreter at the mouth of the Malong River. It was the tenth day of Harry's coastline search, and the interpreter was the fifth with whom he had traveled during that period. Harry didn't care for these constant changes of interpreter, but they were necessary because his total coastal search would mean asking questions in seventeen different languages, all with their own different dialects, according to the area.

Harry inflated the black dinghy with the foot pump, and slowly the sides swelled into black sausages. The interpreter loaded three cans of special fuel, the five-gallon can of drinking water, the insect repellent and tins of food. Harry straightened the map on his clipboard and whipped the outboard into action.

The little craft headed away from the sandy beaches and lagoons that marked the coastline and started its journey up the wide, muddy river. Purple convolvulus and sword-bean vines grew just above the high-tide mark; they passed sea almonds and salt-tolerant oaks dotted with scarlet hibiscus, then the narrow coastal strip of forest disappeared, the gnarled limbs of mangroves were left behind them and the river started to narrow.

Above the steady chug of the outboard, Harry could hear

540

the pure sound of birdsong. He spotted eagles and kingfishers, and watched a red-eyed, silver-crested ground dove that flew before the dinghy, passing a group of black-beaked herons the same milky-brown color as the water in which they fished.

Soon the three levels of rain-forest tree growth were clearly visible on either bank. Yellow orchids hung from the second, middle layer of trees; there was no getting away from the yellow orchid on Paui, it was the national flower. Harry trailed his finger in the water and it emerged covered in a brown sheen.

The small, skinny interpreter shook his head in warning. "No hand in water, puk-puk in water."

And indeed, within two minutes Harry had also spotted the ugly snouts of crocodiles.

At seven o'clock Harry cut the outboard and fired the first green flare into the sky.

After that, the river gradually narrowed, writhing its way through the forest. Harry quickly realized that the map wasn't much use. The muddy rivers which divided southeastern Paui into isolated areas boiled with turbulence in the rainy season, then meandered, writhed and continually changed direction. Old channels closed and new ones opened. After the Long Wet a river might follow a totally different course from the one it had pursued a few months earlier.

Almost indiscernibly, the vegetation closed in. Through the increasingly thick overhead tangle Harry could still see the sky, but he soon stopped trying to keep track of the route they were taking as the river swayed around bends, snaked back on itself, wound around as if chasing its tail, then suddenly spurted in the opposite direction.

Harry maneuvered the dinghy around dead branches that swirled past it and rotting trees that had been submerged when the river changed course. As they rounded each bend, they saw another bend before them. The bends seemed endless.

The river was running against him, like everything on this island. As he followed the convoluted twists, Harry's mind went around and around with possible explanations for the disappearance of the Nexus group, but he was never able to come to any satisfactory conclusion. It was as if those people had been wiped off the earth.

Just after Harry fired the ten o'clock flare, the river twisted up to the right. The dinghy edged into a narrow channel where the trees on either bank almost met overhead. The current seemed to grow stronger as the banks grew higher and water weeds tore at the little boat. As the river narrowed, it seemed to run faster and deeper and smell worse—a stench of slime and rotting vegetation. The branches overhead now twisted together so that the river became danker and darker.

It was hard to find an opening to the sky in order to fire the eleven o'clock flare. After he had done so, Harry felt increasingly depressed. He punted the dinghy deeper and deeper into the tangle; he felt sucked into this damp, dark, rotting maw, consumed by this river of unmistakable menace.

It had not been possible to find a guide who knew this area well, and they were following directions given by Ronald Chang which were based on information from the medicine man who'd sold him Roddy's watch.

The sluggish brown water swirled against the dinghy. Flotsam bumped continually against the black rubber sides. Insects and unseen creatures rustled in the tall, coarse grass that grew on both banks. Once they heard a high shrill scream, abruptly cut off.

"Snake eat rat," said the interpreter with a grin. Harry immediately thought of Raki. Each time Harry had listened to Raki's disclaimers of responsibility, each time he had agreed with the President that Nexus could complain of nothing, that no stone had been unturned and so forth, Harry had sensed a puzzling gleeful note of menace in the President's voice—a gloating semiquaver of triumph that ran contrary to his words. Why? Harry wondered with increasing irritation. Harry could not bear unsolved problems. He liked to believe that there always was a solution, if you studied a problem carefully enough, long enough.

The dinghy was now entering the mosaic of swampland and

lakes that Harry had been warned to expect. A good sign, he thought, as he gazed up at the twenty-foot-high clumps of wild sugarcane and pitpit grass that lined both banks. The muddy banks were now lower, blacker and stickier. Green scum clung to the water's edge, limp, greasy and rotting, like three-day-old salad. It all smelled vile.

Once, Harry didn't duck fast enough. A swaying branch left a worm of blood on his left cheek. Could have been worse, could have been my eye, Harry thought, as he leaned over the stern and pushed the boat upstream with an oar. Once again they found themselves in a deep green tunnel. It was like sliding down a great, dark, rotten throat, Harry felt as the vegetation closed around him.

But always, just when he was at the point of turning back, the river widened, as if sensing his thoughts. The menacing trees fell back, the air became easier to breathe, and they saw occasional glimpses of blue sky. They halted beneath one of these overhead gaps so that Harry could fire the midday flare.

About ten minutes later, they were stopped by an impenetrable mass of wild sugarcane blocking the stream ahead.

The interpreter sighed. "Wrong feller water, mebbe."

The two men tugged their way to the left bank and with their oars hacked at the grass that bound the propeller, then continued upstream.

It took them nearly an hour to reach relatively clear water where Harry was able to fire the one o'clock flare. He was now left with only two flares. He had expected to be back at the beach by now.

At one thirty Harry realized that the boat could go no farther. They had reached another impenetrable tangle of cane— another dead end.

Harry retraced—or thought he did—the route back to the stream they had left. Wearily, as he looked up and squinted at the overhead branches he blew a cloud of midges and mosquitoes from his nose. He would probably have to climb a tree to fire his two o'clock signal. He wondered whether he could still climb a high tree. The interpreter could probably scramble up easily enough, but he didn't really want the interpreter to fire the flare gun. There were only two flares left and Harry couldn't afford a misfire.

Harry glanced to the left. He gasped.

Two huge black hands jerked the pitpit canes apart and the most terrifying face Harry had ever seen glared at him. The face was painted bright yellow, the eyes and mouth were outlined in scarlet, a scarlet line ran centrally down the forehead and the splayed nose was pierced by a white feather. Hostile black eyes stared from jaundiced eyeballs patterned by red veins.

The terrible mouth opened and said, "Cigarette?"

With a trembling hand, Harry threw a pack of Marlboros, which was caught by one of those enormous hands.

Harry looked at the terrified interpreter. "Offer him more cigarettes, if he'll guide us back to the river."

The interpreter shouted questions in a clacking language that sounded like two wooden paddles being hit together. He turned to Harry. "This feller him i savvy this feller place. This feller him i walk one time you me."

By now Harry knew that "walk one time" meant "not far," but *that* might mean ten minutes or ten hours. Anything under a day's journey seemed to be described as "not far." But what had they to lose?

"Okay. Tell him."

The yellow face disappeared and the pitpit cane sprang back into place.

A few minutes later Yellow-Face appeared in a dugout canoe just ahead of the dinghy. They followed the stone black back, which, Harry noticed, was covered with small welts, cut in the pattern of crocodile skin.

Within minutes the dugout turned to the left, up a trickle of water so narrow that Harry would not have dared to take it. After about two hundred yards of torturous wriggling the dinghy suddenly shot out onto wide, milk-chocolate ripples, which, Harry hoped, meant that they had regained the main channel of the river.

As it was nearly two o'clock, the interpreter called ahead to Yellow-Face to halt. They waited in the stream until it was time to fire the flare.

Yellow-Face was clearly impressed. His mouth hung open and his eyes followed the fizzing balls of incandescent red light as it shot up into the sky.

Farther upstream, a few pink water lilies were seen amid the muck of the swampy channel. Animal life suddenly appeared again. Harry spotted a white heron and a couple of ducks. He could glimpse fish in the water and see frogs on the riverbank. Ahead of him the native poled his dugout silently through narrow waterways between swaying savannas of rice grass. Whichever way Harry looked, the view now appeared unvarying.

Yellow-Face gestured to the right. Although Harry could see nothing, he heard domestic noises: the cries of children at play, the squeal of pigs, the squawk of chickens, women calling shrill commands.

As the dinghy rounded the bend to the right, Harry saw the village. Smoke from cooking fires curled up into the air; dugout canoes were tethered beneath thatched huts on stilts; pigs, dogs and children played in the shade under the huts. Women with sticks the size of baseball bats were whacking sago-palm hearts to a pulp, and two old grannies played with a white bird.

A couple of men clustered around a hidden object that was obviously of absorbing interest to them. Their bodies were cut with the same intricate pattern of welts as Yellow-Face's, and their faces were similarly smeared with bright ocher. Some wore bird-of-paradise plumes in their hair, some had feathers stuck through their noses, but they wore no clothes except a sex gourd. Suddenly the air was rent with an ear-splitting screech of static.

Harry, who had given up hope, incredulously realized that they *had*, perhaps, arrived at the place they sought. For these men were arguing over a transistor radio.

Yellow-Face shouted a greeting. Watched by everyone in

the village, he jumped from his canoe onto a rock. Harry and the interpreter scrambled over the side of the dinghy and found themselves up to their armpits in mud. Everyone yelled with laughter. It had been a most successful debut.

Harry immediately distributed cigarettes while his interpreter located Radio Paui on what was clearly a new transistor.

In the shade beneath a hut, they ate fried catfish and sago pancakes, a dull meal that was eaten quickly, in silence. Afterward, everyone got down to business. The interpreter explained that the white man would pay well for any possession of the Filipino soldier who had been wearing a watch.

Nobody moved, but the atmosphere changed from one of friendliness to wariness.

Hastily, the interpreter explained that neither he nor Harry was a relative of this dead soldier, but that the white man had purchased the watch in Queenstown and now wished to buy the other things of the soldier.

The *luluai* stood and beckoned to his two visitors. They followed him, climbing up the rickety ladder of a hut. Inside the hot, dark, windowless space, stone implements and hatchets stood against the walls and ceremonial masks, striped in white, rust and charcoal, hung from the rafters. They sat cross-legged on the wooden floor. Behind them, men crowded into the hut. As the *luluai* spoke, the stench of unwashed bodies was overwhelming.

The interpreter looked nervously at Harry. "This feller say you me come in their place, so they keep boat."

Harry had been mildly surprised that he had kept his possessions this long. He said, "Tell them that if they give us the possessions of the pig-stealing *kanaka* soldier, we will give them *two* more boats."

The interpreter looked frightened. "Master, this feller say all he keep you me this place, pass time two feller boat, he come up."

So they were prisoners, to be ransomed for two more boats.

Before Harry could reach beneath his safari jacket for the

revolver tucked in his waistband, both he and the interpreter were gripped from behind. They had been caught in a confined space and overcome by sheer numbers. Harry knew that it would have been crazy to try anything clever or even to have made a swift movement.

Since he'd started his search, he had known that there was a risk of being captured or killed, but he also knew that he would find nothing unless *he* searched. He had presented gifts to this tribe and had been given a meal, which is a sure sign of friendship. Harry had no reason to have had his revolver in his hand; in fact, that would definitely have been interpreted as a hostile approach.

Justify it as he might, Harry had let himself be caught off-guard.

After the two prisoners had been stripped of everything, including both their watches and Harry's revolver, their arms and legs were bound with rattan cords. They were then tethered by their necks to the rafters, standing out of reach of each other.

Without another look at either of their prisoners, the village men lowered the ladder, scrambled down it and took it away.

The cord around Harry's neck was unpleasantly tight, and he was soaked in sweat. He thought that if he tried to move and lost his balance or fainted, he would hang himself.

He told himself that a dead Harry was no use to these people and they knew it. This treatment was just to show him they meant business.

"Does this often happen?" Harry asked.

"Kissim ransom," the interpreter said sadly.

"Do you think that ransom money is the only reason?"

"Yes, master. Suppose this feller like kill him, you-me. They kill you-me, quicktime."

"But if they kill us, they can't start the boat engine."

The interpreter nodded. "This feller savvy." He started to sob.

Harry said, "Nexus will come looking for us soon. Probably, they are *already* looking for us because I didn't fire the three o'clock flare. They know where we are. I told the pilot that we were going to the village of Malong."

"No, master." The interpreter sobbed harder. "This feller name no belong this village." "Malong," he explained, was the word for a *type* of land and there were many, many villages in Malong, which meant "swamp."

"We lost, master."

The women, shaking with fear, hearts thudding, melted back
into the jungle twilight, away from that severed arm with its
terrible snake tattoo, away from the kaleidoscopic color and
noise of the native feast.

When they had moved back about a hundred yards, Annie,
now in the rear, whistled. The women halted.

Annie said, "At least now we know where we are. That was
Katanga village, so if we circle around it to the east we'll get
back to William Penn."

Carey whispered, "Not too far to the east. We don't dare get
out of earshot of the village because that's our fix."

They moved on. Every twig that cracked, every rustle,
every birdcall made them thrill to their fingertips with terror.
Panic made them short of breath, but their fear sent adrenaline
coursing through their bloodstreams, giving them new
strength and alertness as they edged around the village. Finally, they reached the familiar narrow track that threaded
northward through the trees.

Gratefully, the women hurried along it, faster and faster,
until their stealthy jungle lope developed into a run, then into
a mad, headlong hurtling. Careless of who or what they might
encounter on the track, all jungle lore forgotten in their panic,
they crashed along as fast as they could. Patty raced ahead,

with Suzy behind her. Nobody checked to see if the woman behind her was following. Annie, in the rear, felt as though her back might at any moment feel the thrust of a poison-tipped arrow.

As soon as they spotted the Burma bridge they veered left into the taboo area. They crashed frantically through the dank bush. Startled parakeets squawked, birds fluttered in alarm.

"Stop! Patty!" Annie screamed, but the racing, ragged figures sped ahead, until finally they came to a quivering halt at the outskirts of their camp.

All day Silvana had been in a purgatory of her own making. Repeatedly she had asked herself how *could* she have endangered all their lives? How could she have endangered her *own* life? She might have been found strangled this morning under that tree. And how could the fastidious Mrs. Graham have writhed with passion, hope and gratitude beneath a greasy, calculating little gigolo whom she'd only known a few days?

Silvana's head angrily asked these questions, but she knew that it wasn't her head that had betrayed her. Silvana had been betrayed by her own starved libido.

When she heard the noise of the other women's crashing return, her first reaction was fear, then overwhelming relief at the distraction from her thoughts. She slung the rifle on her back and quickly slithered down the lookout tree. "What's happened?" she called softly.

Sobbing and shaking, teeth clattering with fear, the women were incoherent.

"Water!" Suzy headed for the bucket.

They all clustered around the bucket, scooping from it with their hands, intent only on slaking their thirst.

Seeing Silvana's questioning face, Annie said, "He's dead."

Silvana's eyes filled with tears. She knew she should be glad to hear this, for it meant that they were no longer in immediate danger. But her heart felt as if it had been physically squeezed.

Annie said softly, "He was a thief, Silvana. He stole our watches. He stole something different from you."

As Annie gently told Silvana what they had seen, Suzy started to scream. "I can't stand this fucking awful place any longer. Do you think we're *ever* going to get off it? Do you think we'll *ever* escape?"

Annie said, "Stop it, Suzy! This is no time to crack. We must think of *nothing* except finishing that raft! Tonight we rest, but as soon as we wake up, we work *nonstop* until it's finished!"

Suzy whimpered, "Couldn't we settle for a smaller raft and leave tomorrow evening?"

"No!" Carey said sharply. "What's the point of going through all this, then setting out to sea on a raft that's too small? We'd slide off as soon as we hit rough water. It'll only take another two days to finish it properly."

Patty nodded. "We've survived here for four months. We can last another couple of days."

Through gritted teeth, Annie said, "We're going to work until we *drop*. We're going to concentrate on that damned raft and *we are going to get off this island!* Now let's have something to eat and get to bed. Silvana, you'll have to keep lookout for as long as you can tonight. We'd only fall asleep."

TUESDAY, MARCH 12

Silvana managed to keep watch until morning. As soon as the trees of the camp were discernible, she woke the other women. They prized their stiff bodies from their beds. They thought only of the raft as they ate bits of cold parrotfish from taro-leaf plates. They decided to try to work through the exhausting midday heat.

They did not talk as they worked. An aura of fear and agitation hung over them, and they worked swiftly, binding the bamboo poles with plaited vines. Their tattered fishing gloves now reeked of mildew and decay. Annie guessed they would not last much longer.

During a five-minute break, Suzy turned to Patty and said with surprising timidity, "Could you maybe check your watch for what the date is today?"

"Who the hell cares?" Patty scowled but checked her watch. "March twelfth."

Suzy burst into tears.

Carey asked, "Is it a birthday?"

Suzy nodded tearfully. "Brett's. Tomorrow."

"*Stop* that!" Annie said crossly. "If you want to cry, go off and do it alone. You know the rules."

They all knew that depression was more contagious than measles, and that it weakened them, as a group.

Abruptly, Patty stopped tugging at the vines. She lifted her head. "What's that noise?"

Carey said wonderingly, "It's an outboard motor. That's what it *sounds* like. Could it be?"

"Keep *working*, everyone," said Annie. "Patty, go see what the noise is."

Within a few minutes Patty returned. "A small dinghy just entered the lagoon," she reported. "There are three men aboard. They look like soldiers."

The women jumped to their feet. Annie asked, "Only three men? You're sure? There are five of us and we have two rifles."

Patty nodded. "Three men."

"You see what happens when we don't have a lookout?" Carey panted crossly as they ran toward the clifftop.

They flung themselves down in the coarse, knee-high grass, snaked up to the edge of the cliff and slowly lifted their heads.

In the center of the lagoon, a small dinghy was approaching the beach. The outboard cut abruptly, and an anchor was thrown over the side.

Annie whispered, "How high's the tide?"

"Coming in," Carey whispered back. "Low tide was at eight o'clock. High tide at around eight this evening."

Cautiously, Suzy lifted her head higher. "They don't seem

to be in a fighting mood. And they're obviously not looking for us, thank God."

The three khaki-clad figures in the boat were laughing and joking as they removed their boots, rolled up their pants, and jumped over the side.

As the last man jumped off, the moored dinghy jerked and swung around. Painted in black on her white transom were the words "Paradise Hotel."

The men waded to shore, carrying bottles and bright orange towels. Patty said, "Those look like the hotel's pool towels."

Annie breathed, "Do they have rifles?"

"If so, they've left them in the boat," Carey whispered. "Get your head *down*, Suzy."

Patty said, "They'd be crazy to move around without rifles, so let's assume they're armed."

Once ashore, the men undressed. Naked, they no longer seemed dangerous. Their black bodies gleamed in the sunlight as they splashed in the water, shouting and laughing, lunging playfully at each other, wrestling on the sand. They looked boyish and innocent.

"They're city guys," Carey whispered. "Fisherfolk wouldn't see the point of spending a day on the beach like tourists."

Two of the men walked to the dark shade of the trees at the back of the beach, where the women could no longer see them. The third man waded out to the dinghy, swigging from a bottle as he went. When he waded back to the beach he was carrying three rifles.

From beneath the palms, the men shot at seashells and rocks. The peaceful bay cracked with noise. Patty was shocked. "What a waste of ammunition! They must have let off at least twenty rounds."

Patty whispered longingly, "Just look at that beautiful boat."

The white fiberglass dinghy was about twelve feet long and had a locker in the bow. It was too far away for the women to see anything else.

Annie whispered, "Why not steal that boat? We don't *know* that the raft is going to float."

Carey nodded thoughtfully. "Even if the raft *does* float, I'm worried about the way she might pitch. We could easily lose someone overboard in the night."

Annie warmed to the idea. "It's got an outboard motor, a can of gas, a rudder and an anchor. We'd be heading to Irian Jaya in a boat we could control."

"They're not going to sit by and let us take it," Suzy pointed out.

"No," Annie agreed.

"Couldn't we somehow get the men out of the way and steal the boat, so that it looks like an accident?" Patty suggested.

"Can you think of a way? I can't," Suzy said.

Annie said, "What would a man do?"

"What would Jonathan do?" Suzy asked.

"A surprise attack would be better than stealing a boat that belongs to three guys with three rifles," Carey said. "The safest thing to do is attack fast—before they decide to climb up the waterfall path just for fun. Once they see our camp, we've had it."

Softly, Annie said, "It looks as though they're going to be on the beach for some time. Let's get back to camp where we can talk. Suzy had better be lookout. Wake Silvana, somebody."

As Suzy climbed the tree, the other women squatted around the base of the eucalyptus. Carey started to outline a plan.

Nobody looked very enthusiastic.

Carey said, "Sure they're armed, but we're armed too—and we've got the element of surprise on our side. We know where they are, but they don't know where we are—or even that we exist. Let's think of a plan that uses surprise, all the way."

Annie said, "Those soldiers will be expecting us to act like women, so we should act like men."

"Why not simply shoot them from the clifftop?" Suzy suggested from the branches above.

"Because we might miss, dummy!" Patty said. "Then they'll either be up here shooting or taking off in the boat at top speed."

"Trouble is, we've never actually *shot* anyone," Annie said. "Only simulated it."

"Okay, what do *you* suggest?" Suzy snapped down from the eucalyptus tree.

"Jonathan always said that before you attack, you should put yourself in the enemy's shoes," Annie said slowly. "Watch their habits and routine. Base your plan on observation."

"So we've observed that they're down there, with the habit of drinking cocktails before lunch," Suzy said. "They're just out for a good time. How does that help *us?*"

"*A good time*." Patty repeated Suzy's words thoughtfully. "What we want to do is to get them out of the way, so that we can get their guns, then we have their boat. I suppose the way to do it is to offer them a *good time*."

"What do you mean?" Annie asked.

"Suzy," Patty said.

There was a shout of indignation from the eucalyptus tree, quickly hushed by Annie.

Patty said, "We can send Suzy down to the beach as a decoy. She can lure the soldiers into the quicksand."

"Why not Silvana?" Suzy hissed down. "She'd probably be *glad* if they caught her and raped her."

"Enough of that," Annie said. "The one we should use as a decoy is the one with the best-looking body."

"No, the biggest tits," Suzy called down. "Silvana."

Except for jungle ulcers, the women were now in first-class physical condition. Tanned and supple, none of them carried any extra weight, and because they were on a permanent diet of protein and fruit and were well exercised, they moved with grace and agility. But undoubtedly, Silvana had the biggest breasts.

Wondering whether it was her punishment or her absolution, Silvana said, "Okay, I'll do it."

"No, Silvana," Annie said. "As she runs away from those guys toward the quicksand, our bait must look enticing from the rear."

"Shit!" A shower of eucalyptus leaves fell to the earth below. *"Seriously,* you guys, what happens if they catch me?" Suzy called down anxiously.

"Carey will be covering you from the clifftop with the M-16," Annie said. "She's got the best eyesight."

"Suppose she accidentally shoots *me?"* Suzy wailed.

Patty said, "That's a risk you'll have to take."

"Suppose only *one* of them follows me?"

Patty said, "Suzy, honey, you remember the way you walked by the pool in that white dress at Silvana's party? Just before you fell in the shallow end? You just walk like that, and they'll *all* follow you. We've seen it work, Suzy."

More leaves fell from the lookout tree. "Okay, okay, I'll do my best. But suppose they're gay? Suppose they're lazy? Suppose that, for some goddamn reason, one of them *stays by the boat?* Then what?"

"Then somebody kills him, of course," Patty said.

"What with?" Suzy wailed.

Patty said, "For God's sake, we've got two rifles, an ax, five fish knives, two bows and arrows, and plenty of rattan rope. We aren't going to throw *stones* at him, Suzy!"

Annie said, "Let's stop talking and get going. I'll think over the plan. Patty had better be lookout while Carey and Silvana run the beauty parlor."

Patty said, *"Beauty parlor?"*

Annie said, "Take a hard look at Suzy."

They all looked at Suzy, who was slithering down the gnarled eucalyptus trunk. Her hair, now dark, had been cut short to keep out the fleas; her face was grimy; she wore a tattered, dirty shirt and khaki combat pants that were several sizes too large for her.

"She sure doesn't look like Dorothy Lamour," Carey admitted.

Patty said gloomily, "Remember that western where they have to sober up the drunken gunman in a hurry? We've got a worse problem."

The sun blazed down, the coconut palms rustled in the slight breeze, and in the shade beneath them, the rum bottle was almost empty. In spite of the heat, one of the naked men was still awake. He yawned, scratched his armpits, dusted gritty coral sand from his belly button and casually glanced up the beach.

From the northern curve of coral sand, Suzy wandered toward him. Her brown limbs glistened with coconut oil and a red hibiscus was tucked behind her left ear. Her eyes seemed enormous thanks to a stick of charcoal and, although their lipsticks had long since melted, Suzy had rubbed the greasy residue from a lipstick tube onto her mouth and cheeks. A length of pink-flowered cotton, draped low on her hips, concealed the hidden fish knife.

The naked man sat up and stared.

Swaying provocatively, Suzy walked slowly toward him.

The man blinked, grinned, leaned over and shook the shoulder of the next man.

He opened his eyes, yawned, slowly turned his head, then sat up.

Suzy turned to the sea and stretched out her arms.

On the clifftop Annie whispered, "But wait till they see her *run!*"

One of the men called out a greeting.

Suzy jumped in simulated surprise. She turned to face the men. She put her hand to her mouth and gave a little giggle.

One man jumped to his feet and sauntered toward her.

In the hot bright sunlight, Suzy giggled again and shyly backed away.

The second man jumped to his feet and called out—a warm, encouraging, flattering welcome by the sound of it.

Suzy covered her breasts with her hands and looked uncertain.

The third man sat up, clearly wanting to know why no one had told *him* what was happening.

Suzy turned away and flaunted her small, high, rounded buttocks as she started to saunter back in the direction from which she'd come. Teasingly, she glanced over her shoulder a couple of times. The hibiscus blossom fell from behind her ear onto the sand.

The third man scrambled to his feet.

Suzy started to run, but languidly, in slow motion, as if her knees were bound together by elastic cord.

Delighted by her inviting glance, the first man ran up the beach. When he reached the red blossom that had fallen from Suzy's ear, he picked it up and ran after her, waving it.

Suzy gave a playful shriek and ran a little faster.

Careless and noisy as schoolboys on an outing, the three men splashed across the knee-deep channel that flowed from the waterfall to the lagoon.

As they raced toward her, Suzy started to increase her speed. She hadn't run in a straight line; she was making a big curve around the back of the beach and then back out again toward the sea. She was running fast now—faster than she had intended. Too fast.

With one smooth, graceful movement, Suzy's pink-flowered sarong suddenly unwound and fell to the sand. Her knife lay hidden in the fold. She was now defenseless.

The men whooped and cheered at the sight of Suzy's naked body. Suddenly, the first man stumbled and nearly fell. He flailed his arms in an effort to regain his balance, but the sand seemed to clutch at the soles of his feet. He floundered and tried to pull his feet clear of the muck. Alarm crossed his face as he fell, half-turning to shout a warning to his friends.

The second man had paused to grab up Suzy's pink cotton sarong. He looked surprised when a sharp, eight-inch knife fell from the folds, but he picked that up as well before running after his friend.

Because of his pause, he was not so close behind the first man as he had been. When he saw his friend fall, then heard his mud-covered face scream a warning, he just managed to stop on the edge of the quicksand.

For a moment it looked as if he was also about to be sucked into the sandy bog, but as his feet started to sink he threw himself backward, arms outspread.

As the second man heaved his feet free of the clutching sand, Carey, standing astride on top of the cliff, took careful aim. She heard a sharp crack when the rifle fired but no thump. Shit, she'd missed.

Again, she aimed carefully and gently squeezed back the trigger.

Nothing happened.

She squeezed harder. She squeezed again. And again and again, as hard as she could.

Nothing happened.

Somewhere in that excellent example of design and engineering, the M-16 had jammed, thus proving that it needs to be cleaned if you want to fire it.

Upon hearing the unmistakable crack of a rifle, the third man, who was well in the rear, abruptly stopped running. He turned in his tracks and sped back along the way he had come, toward the orange towels and the rifles that lay in the shade of the palms.

Two grim, ragged creatures stepped from behind the trees.

Annie lifted her AK-47 and fired at him. The shot missed.

Patty, who had grabbed a rifle from an orange towel, raced toward the boat.

When he heard Annie's shot, the third soldier altered direction, but he was running too fast to stop immediately. He threw a look at the dinghy, riding serene on the aquamarine water, but the boat was anchored a good thirty feet out and a woman with a rifle had already reached the water's edge. He had no chance of getting to the dinghy.

He turned in his tracks and started to run, zigzagging as he went, in the only direction that was left to him. He headed for the little path that wound up beside the waterfall, intending to get up those rocks and hide in the jungle.

Annie fired again and missed.

Gasping for breath, the man flung himself at the cliff path, stones rattling beneath his bare feet. Little puffs of dust marked his steps as he scrambled up the rocks.

Lying on her stomach, hidden behind the black rocks at the waterfall pool, Silvana rested her rifle on one of the big stones as she watched the naked man scramble toward her. Silvana was a steadier shot than Annie. She waited until the man had almost reached her, then gently squeezed the trigger.

The man screamed and clutched his left shoulder. His hand was immediately covered with blood. He half-fell, half-scrabbled back down the cliff.

Wildly, the third man looked around. Annie was below him. Patty, who had been running up the beach from the water's edge, stopped and took aim. Behind him, Silvana stood astride the track, aiming at his back.

Realizing that he was trapped, the man stood still and put up his hands.

"No prisoners this time!" Annie shouted. *"Shoot!"*

Without hesitation, all three women squeezed their triggers.

"Where's the second guy?" Patty cried anxiously.

All three women turned to look up to the north end of the beach.

From the top of the cliff the man should have been an easy shot, but Carey was screaming, "This fucking thing won't work! I don't know how to fix it!"

Annie yelled back at her, "Don't follow him, Carey. You're unarmed and he's got a knife. Get down here and grab one of their rifles." She turned to Silvana. "You and Suzy guard the dinghy and the rifles while Patty and I go after him."

Silvana nodded. As soon as the first man reached the quicksand, Suzy had run into the sea and flung herself into the water; now she was swimming as hard as she could toward the dinghy.

Patty sprinted back to fetch the third rifle, then ran with it toward Carey. Clutching their rifles, Carey, Patty and Annie raced north on the beach to where the second man was moving fast, in a random pattern. He had nearly reached the mangroves on the north horn of the lagoon.

The trees glistened in the sunlight, huge, twisted clumps of dark green foliage, some of them over a hundred feet high. The daily three-foot fall of the tide revealed their thick, gnarled roots, tough enough to withstand the constant battle of the waves and the tearing of the winds. The only way the man could make any progress through the mangroves would be to clamber over the intricate, thick roots where the seawater sucked at their interlocked limbs.

"Shame it isn't high tide," Patty said, panting as they ran. She glanced at her watch. It was only ten forty. High tide wouldn't be until eight o'clock that evening.

As the man neared the mangroves, Patty went down on one knee, lifted her rifle and waited for him to slow down. When he did, she took careful aim and fired.

She missed.

"Hope a crocodile gets him," Carey gasped.

"We can't count on it," Annie said, biting her lip.

The man leaped over the first mangrove roots and disappeared from sight.

The women met at the dinghy. Suzy and Carey were crouched in it on a heap of khaki.

Annie looked doubtfully at the dinghy. "It's not very big."

"It's big enough," Suzy said, firmly. "If it was big enough for three of them, then it's big enough for five of us. Now let's get the hell out of here. We have a rifle each, plus a spare, and plenty of clothes and boots. Let's grab the water, the dried fish, the charts and the compass, and *take off!* It doesn't matter if the Katanga people see us. This motor can outdistance any canoes that might be lurking behind the headland. And we have rifles."

Annie said, "We'd never be able to cover the seventy miles to Irian Jaya before nightfall. If that soldier gets back to his base, they could have a helicopter here before dark. It would be easy to spot this white boat on the blue ocean. They could use us for target practice, like ducks at a fairground."

Suzy screamed, "Annie, we go to *all this trouble* to get a boat, and you make us do these *terrible* things, and then you don't want us to use the boat! Why not?"

Annie said, "The only terrible thing about what we're doing is that it wouldn't be considered terrible if men were doing it."

"Jonathan always planned to escape just after dark," Carey reminded them.

"The faster we get away, the safer we'll be," Suzy argued. "That guy may *never* make it back to camp. I vote we risk being seen in daylight."

Annie said, "Hands up, whoever wants to go in daylight."

Suzy's hand shot out, but hers was the only one.

Suzy looked around and said, "Okay. So what *are* we going to do?"

Carey said, "If we hide the boat and no helicopter turns up, we leave at dusk."

"How do we hide the dinghy? There's nowhere to put it," Patty worried. "And the tide's still going out. Soon that boat will be sitting on sand."

Annie said hesitantly, "Maybe we ought to wait *several* nights before we go."

There was an instant chorus of disagreement.

"What's the point of waiting several nights?" Silvana asked. Having shot a man, she was now back in favor.

Annie said, "It's taken us months to get to this point. We're in the best position yet. Let's not blow it. If the guy doesn't make it back to his base, there's no harm in waiting a few days. Right?"

Reluctantly, they all nodded.

Annie continued, "But if we hide ourselves and the boat, then when they come searching they'll assume we've already left in the dinghy and search for us at sea, not on land. We'll hear aircraft and know what the situation is."

Patty said, "We could provision the boat right away, then

take her south around the headland. Hide her in some creek or behind overhanging foliage on the other side."

Annie nodded. "We could hide the boat, come back overland, then hide in the cave. No one's going to find us there, and we've got plenty of water. It's mucky, but fresh and untainted. The dried fish will last for at least eight days."

"Eight days in the dark?" Suzy said. The battery of the underwater flashlight was long dead.

"People have been imprisoned in the dark for *months* and survived," Annie said.

Suzy said gloomily, "I can think of nothing more unappealing than drinking gritty water from a coconut shell and chewing on lumps of dried fish for a week in the dark, while soldiers with fixed bayonets wander above our heads."

"Jonathan always said that our best chance of escape was when nobody was hunting for us," Carey reminded everyone. "That's why he blew up the *Louise*. So I vote we don't go until we decide that the terrorists are *not* going to look, or until *after* they've looked and left. Even if it takes eight days."

"So that's settled," Annie said. "We'll split into two groups. Patty and Carey, take the dinghy around the point as soon as we've loaded it up. Carey, lend me Jonathan's watch, so the camp group has a watch. Take Suzy's neck-thong compass for the trek back." She looked at Suzy. "You get into the cave. Silvana and I will go back to camp and lower our equipment down the chimney to you."

"You haven't convinced me, but let's get on with it," Suzy said.

By eleven o'clock they had discussed and agreed on their plans. Patty and Carey thought that it was worth taking an hour and a half to equip the dinghy properly. This would give the group two hidden equipment areas—the dinghy and the cave. As they didn't know what trouble they were going to run into when they rounded the headland, Patty wanted to take clothes, rifles, food and water in case they had to stay hidden there.

Besides the weapons and the beach towels, the soldiers had carried three fishing lines, three pocket lighters, three packs of cigarettes, six bottles of orangeade, some fruit, and a bottle of rum, now half-empty.

Listening to their brisk, efficient planning, Silvana suddenly realized how much they had all changed from the terrified women who had originally fled into the jungle. Although they had had nothing much in common, at *this* moment these five women were comrades in arms. They had shared danger, and they all knew that they could rely on one another.

Annie said, "We'd better figure out a rough time plan, and then do the best we can."

Carey calculated. "Assuming that guy hits the jungle path and travels at around three miles an hour, he should arrive back at the hotel five hours after we last saw him. That would be about three forty. Allow them twenty minutes to organize a search party—assuming they have a helicopter immediately available—and another fifteen minutes to get here by air. We should all be hidden by four fifteen this afternoon—at the latest."

Patty said, "Sixteen-fifteen hours."

Suzy rolled her eyes. "*Why* are we suddenly on military time? Next thing, you'll be telling us to synchronize our watches."

"Patty and I have already done that," Carey said. "You're going to be in the cave where it's permanently dark, so you'll have to keep track of whether it's four in the afternoon or four in the morning. You don't want to rendezvous twelve hours late."

"It's eleven twenty now. We'll each do three trips to load the dinghy, with Silvana supervising in camp," Annie said. "Allow thirty minutes for each trip. At twelve fifty the boat takes off. With luck, you should round the headland just after one o'clock, Carey. No need to tell you to try to keep out of sight of Katanga. Once around the headland, allow yourselves an hour to find a hiding place and camouflage the dinghy."

Carey nodded. "That brings us to, say, two fifteen in the

afternoon. If we see natives, then Patty will stay on board with a rifle. If not, we'll both try to get back, overland, to the cave. We'll hope to make it by four."

Patty added, "Of course, if we find that the land around the headland is secondary jungle, we won't have a hope of crossing it. We'll stay with the dinghy."

"How can you possibly tell how long you'll take on a trip you've never done?" Silvana asked dubiously.

"If we start out overland, then find that we can't complete the trip by four o'clock, we'll return to the boat—even if we've nearly arrived at the cave," Carey said. "Because if we're found near the cave it might endanger you guys inside."

Silvana nodded. "So we'll have just over three hours to lower down the cave chimney as much of the camp equipment as possible."

Annie nodded. "At four o'clock, everyone here gets into the cave and stays there. Silvana will camouflage the chimney exit and swim into the cave."

Silvana said, "That's going to be tough without light."

"I'll light one of the soldiers' lighters as soon as you swim inside and call," Annie said, "so you'll be able to scramble out."

"Couldn't we throw some wood down the chimney and have a fire in the cave?" Suzy asked. "So we can see what we're doing?"

Annie looked doubtful. "Someone might see smoke escaping from the chimney."

Suzy said, "Suppose that soldier is a regular four-minute-miler and gets back to his camp in record time?"

"With no boots? And no clothes?" Annie said. "Do you remember what that track was like?"

Suzy shuddered.

◄ **28** ►

Patty and Carey heaved up the anchor and pulled the dinghy into deeper water. The tide had turned at eight o'clock that morning and the best time to load a boat would have been just before then, but the tide was still going out, for which Patty was grateful. Although they had the outboard, it still might have been difficult to leave the lagoon with the tide against them.

Patty checked the engine. She pulled the starter, and to her surprise, the motor turned over. Carey cheered. She was less jubilant when she held up the fuel tank and shook it. "Damn things's nearly empty."

Annie and Silvana had each picked up a warm black ankle and dragged the naked body of the third soldier to the back of the beach. They thought of disposing of it in the quicksand, but they dared not walk into that area. As they buried the body, both women were so depressed by their act that it affected their movements, which visibly slowed down.

"We must stop thinking of him as a person," Annie said. "It'd be asking for trouble to leave a corpse on the beach." She looked down at the lacerated, inverted edges of the shoulder wound, then at the ragged, bloody chest wound, and shuddered. "Let's not waste time. Let's make the grave as

566

shallow as possible and get rid of him fast. We'll heap coco-nut-palm debris on top."

After they buried the soldier, Annie went back and kicked sand over the blood stains. She felt better when no sign of the soldier remained.

Except for Suzy, who was in the lookout tree, all the women staggered down the waterfall path laden with food, water and equipment, including the jammed M-16. "I'll clean it later, then try a couple of rounds when we're out at sea," Carey said.

Instead of their ragged clothes, the women now had four heavy-duty uniforms. They decided to share the clothes out and put them on as soon as they had finished loading the boat in spite of the blasting heat. Also, each woman would carry a rifle slung on her back.

They put the bamboo containers of food and water in the forward locker, which was the safest place on the boat, and kept the compass, the rocket flares and the machete there too. They didn't want that dangerously sharp blade slithering around in the confined quarters of the boat. They stowed the fishing tackle, the rifles, the two spear guns and the snorkel-ing gear in the center of the boat and dumped the yellow life jackets in the stern together with the three buckets, the tool-box, rattan string, a coil of rattan rope and the anchor.

By twelve twenty they had finished.

Carey looked dubiously at the laden dinghy. "You don't think we're taking too much, Patty? I mean, this tub is *full!*"

"We can always throw something overboard. Better than leaving Jonathan's instruments behind."

"What's the point of taking a sextant and a chronometer, when we've no idea how to use them?" Carey asked.

Patty said, "I only wish we still had the canvas awning—we're going to fry out there."

The canvas awning had long since been cut into strips for belts and bags, when Jonathan realized that it wouldn't be long enough to wrap around the second, larger raft.

"We could tow a couple of our bamboo stretcher beds behind us and use them as rafts," Carey suggested. "Maybe we could offload some of this stuff onto them once we see how things go. Use 'em as trailers."

"The main thing is to *go*. Thank God we've got the outboard." Patty patted the gleaming black engine, then wished she hadn't, because the metal was burning hot. "Okay, we're off."

To the surprise of all the women, the ones who were to remain behind grabbed Patty and Carey and hugged them goodbye.

"Take care now," Annie admonished through tears. "And get back as *fast* as you can."

The loaded boat lurched sideways as Patty put a brown, lean leg over the side. Carefully, she climbed in and sat on the aft thwart. In the aquamarine transparency of the lagoon she watched, possibly for the last time, fish of every color flashing past the dinghy like brilliantly colored toy submarines.

Carey took her place on the center thwart, facing Patty in the stern. She fitted the rubber grips of the wooden oars into the oarlocks and gently started to row. As her confidence increased, so did her pulling strength. "Oars okay," she reported.

Excitement showing on her sweaty face, Patty yanked at the cord, and the outboard started right away. The two women felt exhilarated as the dinghy hummed straight for the gap between those two curved lines of white-tipped emerald. Twice every twenty-four hours, the wind and the tide spewed water through that narrow channel into the lagoon, then sucked it back again with the swirling strength of a mill race. Should the dinghy be capsized by those churning waters, both women knew that they would be torn to shreds on the submerged coral.

"Hold on to your hat," Patty warned. "Be prepared to stave the boat off with an oar if we get thrown against the reef."

As the dinghy reached the reef, the little craft surged through the gap in the coral.

The two women found themselves at sea.

As the dinghy bobbed on choppy little waves, they listened, dazed, to the thunder of the surf dashing against the coral. They were hearing it *from the other side*—the side of freedom!

Patty, who had been holding her breath, puffed her cheeks and blew out, like the little cupid winds, drawn on antique maps. The sea, pale and blue, stretched endless, waiting to carry them wherever they wished, away from that beach of death and terror.

Carey stood up.

Patty warned, "You should never stand straight up in a small boat, you might overbalance."

Obediently, Carey sat down again. She grinned. "Don't turn around, but they're waving." She waved back at two tiny figures on the beach.

Patty pushed the tiller, and over the bobbing waves they sped south toward the headland.

Carey warned, "You'll shake those rafts to bits if you don't slow down." The two bamboo-bed rafts jerked in their wake.

"I'm going to cut the engine just before we round the headland because of the noise, so get ready to row," Patty said.

As they approached the headland, Patty knew she must keep the dinghy as close to the jagged cliff as she dared. She nosed the boat around it and once again, she exhaled in relief. Katanga village was not visible. It was probably hidden behind the series of cliffs, overhung with vines and creepers, that slowly dwindled in the distance down to beach level.

Apart from the waves that beat against the cliffs, the scene was silent—almost sleepily so—beneath the harsh burn of the midday sun.

Carey looked up at the cliffs. "We'll never be able to climb those monsters."

"We'll just have to do the best we can," Patty said. "I'm going into the first inlet that looks likely. We want to keep as far as possible from Katanga."

The first inlet had no beach, being only a slit in the black cliffs. The second looked more promising, but when Patty steered toward it she saw the dark teeth of rocks rearing up just below the water. She quickly steered out again.

Pulling on the oars, Carey gasped, "If we don't go into the next inlet it's your turn to row."

A little farther on there was a sudden break in the cliffs. At the back of this inlet the forest dipped down toward the sea.

Patty said, "That looks better. What do you think?"

Wearily, Carey shipped the oars, then turned to look over her shoulder. Under the khaki cap, her face dripped sweat. "It looks fairly easy to climb," she said. "But there's nowhere to hide the boat unless we unload, take the outboard off and sink her."

"We haven't time for that, and we've never tried doing it. It's too big a risk," Patty decided. "Okay, I'll take the oars now."

As Patty rowed around the next cliff, Carey's eyes narrowed. Beyond them was a small, grim inlet. At the back a dark green slope fell bumpily down to the sea, and scrawny vegetation trailed just above the water that slapped against the rocks.

Patty said doubtfully, "There doesn't appear to be a beach."

"So much the better," Carey said.

Patty pulled on the oars with renewed vigor. As the dinghy rode into the V-shaped fissure, the sun caught brilliant flashes from within the green vegetation that covered the steep incline.

"There's a stream," Carey said. "Maybe we'll be able to climb up the sides."

When the dinghy was close enough, Carey reached out and grabbed one of the vines hanging over the water.

As she dropped the anchor, then tugged on the line, Carey said, "It doesn't feel as if it's touching bottom."

"It's only a short beach anchor line," Patty said. "This is deep water. We'll tie the painter to a tree trunk." In answer to Carey's questioning look, she explained, "Those ropes at the back and the front are called painters."

Patty shipped the oars. The two women pulled the dinghy

under the dangling, tough undergrowth that sloped into the sea. Pulling leaves from her hair and ducking to avoid branches, Carey said, "We could cut some of this stuff and drape it all around the dinghy so that you can't see the white paint. Camouflage."

"First, let's tether this beast." Patty threw the painter in a half-hitch around a thick, twisted, overhanging branch. "God knows whether that will hold," she said. "Let's tie the oars and oarlocks to the seats."

"Aye, aye, skipper," Carey jeered. She leaned over to haul the bamboo beds aboard.

In a worried voice, Patty said, "It's crazy to think of leaving this boat. It might come adrift. It might rain and need bailing out. Someone might steal it. I think I'd better stay and guard it while you go back for the others."

Carey nodded. "I was thinking the same thing. We should have thought of it before. Guarding the boat is the soft job, so let's draw straws for it."

Carey lost.

"I've got Suzy's compass," Carey said, "but I'll also need a rifle and the machete."

"Let's have something to eat before you start," Patty suggested. "Leave the camouflage work to me. Hand over the machete and let me hack some greenery before you go."

Shortly afterward, Carey pulled herself up onto the branch of an overhanging tree. Carefully, she leaned down to take the rifle from Patty and slung it over her shoulder. Then she crawled back along the branch until she could prop the rifle safely against the tree trunk. She returned along the branch and leaned down for the machete. "So long, Patty," she said. "I'll be back as fast as I can."

"So long."

Suddenly, both women were near tears. It would be the first time since November 13 that either of them had been entirely alone.

Carey climbed the cliff with care. Brambles and branches scratched at her face, but the incline was not steep and there were plenty of footholds. Nevertheless, she worried about dropping the rifle or machete, because the slope was steep enough for it to slither down and plunge into the sea below.

At the summit, Carey paused to stuff some coarse grass into the sides of her newly acquired khaki cap, which was too big for her head. After that, she loped steadily through the soft green jungle twilight.

Carefully using the compass, it took Carey an hour and a half to cross the headland. That was half an hour more than she had allowed, but she was only twelve minutes behind schedule, and smugly satisfied to find she had emerged at roughly the place she had been aiming for: the top of the dark cliffs on the southern end of Waterfall Bay. In the early morning these cliffs looked like a vast black wall, but toward afternoon, when the sun shone upon them and shadowed the vertical indentations, they looked like enormous sticks of chocolate.

Carey set off along the clifftops at a fast pace, keeping under the cover of trees but always within sight of the transcendently blue sea and the rainbow flash of the spray upon the reef. A slight breeze started up. She moved around the huge, elephant-colored tree trunks and picked her way between green ferns and bracken. All was still except for the rumbling of the surf and the high, pure song of birds, flashing yellow and blue above her.

Above the trill of birdsong, Carey suddenly heard another noise.

Abruptly she stopped and checked her watch. Five minutes to four. Twenty minutes earlier than they had calculated. The noise of helicopter rotors was unmistakable.

Her first impulse was to run back to the dinghy, as they had prearranged, but she realized that the women in the cave would not know where to find it. How *could* they have overlooked such an obvious flaw in their plan?

She calculated quickly. The helicopter would take two minutes to land, and whoever was in it would take at least ten minutes to get to the camp. If she raced, she might just make it to the cave chimney in under twelve minutes.

Moving as fast as she could, heedless of the noise she made, which raised a chorus of ugly protests from a flock of white cockatoos, Carey crashed through the undergrowth toward the camp.

The Huey-Cobra buzzed across Waterfall Bay and made straight for the waterfall. Although the tide had turned, there was plenty of beach.

The American gunship, sent in to clear the area if necessary, was followed by the heavy bulk of a Sikorsky helicopter. Twenty men in olive combat fatigues and helmets jumped out. There was a burst of gunfire as they fanned along the beach, obviously intending to climb the cliff.

The staccato rattle was chillingly audible to Carey, racing along, her face torn by twigs and branches, a stitch in her side and her heart pounding.

The troops immediately found the camp, which had obviously been abandoned only shortly before.

The sergeant reported to the officer in charge. He held out a moldy black patent-leather purse, which still contained Suzy's rusty compact and melted lipstick.

"How many people were here, Sergeant?"

"The tracker reports four bamboo beds, sir, and stakes to support two other beds. He also reports five sets of female footprints leading to the lagoon. The women have each made several recent journeys from this camp—we assume to load the stolen boat, sir. We've found a bamboo container of freshly smoked fish among the rocks on the cliff path, sir."

"When did the women embark, Sergeant?"

"Can't swear, sir, but the tracker says the footsteps were made around noon, and their campfire was extinguished with water at about the same time, sir."

The officer inspected the two huts, the lean-to, a small pile of coconut shells, two turtleshells and a heap of stones. He turned around and stared at the almost completed raft, the neatly piled bamboo lengths and the waiting coils of rattan. He looked at his watch, glanced seaward and said briskly, "We have two hours for a sea search, Sergeant. Fire this camp. Leave two sentries up here and a couple on the beach. We'll collect them tomorrow."

As the sergeant saluted, he added: "And remind the men not to underestimate these women. They have at least three of our rifles."

Carey crouched in the undergrowth, not daring to approach the cave chimney, which she could just see on her left when she put her eye close to the quarter-inch gap in the foliage. She heard men's voices, twigs snapping, then louder cracks. She smelled smoke.

Through the trees ahead, Carey saw a golden glow like an early sunset. The gold quickly changed to red and mingled with thick smoke. A shower of sparks flew upward and a tall tree started to flame. Then the hot, dry forest was alight and blazing.

Carey jumped at the sound of a shot, but realized as a shadow blocked the ominous red glare ahead that the noise must have been made by a falling tree.

She couldn't decide what to do. If she retreated, could she run far enough or fast enough to outdistance the fire? Or should she try to reach the chimney? If the forest burned, the women might have to stay down in the cave for several days. If the foliage around the chimney exit got burned, it would reveal the hole and the rope down the chimney—which was obviously manmade. Swearing under her breath, Carey knew that she would have to cut the rope free and let it drop into the caves. Then she'd try to get back to Patty. That way, two of the group would be free to rescue the others if necessary.

She was just about to crawl to the chimney, when a soldier sauntered into view. As he walked straight toward her, he almost stepped into the chimney shaft. He stopped abruptly. Carey held her breath. Had he seen anything?

The soldier unzipped and relieved himself. Then he pulled

off his floppy jungle hat and wiped the sweat from the back of his thick neck and small, shaven head. As he was pulling on his hat, his head suddenly jerked sideways. His eye had been attracted by something.

Cautiously, the man moved toward the camouflaged rattan rope that trailed on the floor of the forest. He squatted, lifted the rope, tested it with his hand, looked to the left and followed the rope to the tree it was tied around. Then he started to feel his way back along its length toward the cave chimney.

Carey unslung the rifle from her shoulder—but no, she didn't dare shoot because the noise would attract the rest of the men.

Now with his back to Carey, the man squatted, parted the camouflage vines over the shaft and tested the weight of the rope with his hand, as if trying to guess how long it was.

Ten feet away Carey held her rifle by the barrel and prepared to use the butt as a club. She crept forward.

When she came up behind the soldier, she twisted her body and wound both arms back. Her blow would have more strength because of the velocity of the swing behind it. Inside her head, Carey could hear the reassuring voice of Jonathan. "The top of the skull is tough and heavy; the weakest spot is just under the ear, where the bone is thinnest. So never hit a feller over the head, because you'll knock him down, but he'll still be alive. Smash at him sideways, from behind. *Aim at the top of his ear.* This is a good blow, because you've got a *double* chance to do damage, both to the skull and to the neck. You can then, quite easily, garotte him with wire or rattan or strangle him by applying pressure to the throat on either side of his Adam's apple. After that, he shouldn't give you no trouble."

She swung. It was much easier and quicker than she had expected. One minute the guy was squatting in front of her, the next he was slumped on the ground. Trembling from reaction, but also feeling pride and relief surge through her, Carey dragged the limp man a few inches to the edge of the chimney. He wasn't as heavy as she'd feared.

Reaching the shaft, she poked her head down and called urgently, *"Annie!* It's Carey."

Calling out was a calculated risk. Carey hoped the crackling noise of the fire would obscure her voice. The alternative was to take the risk that no one was standing at the bottom of the chimney to get her neck broken. But she thought it highly likely that someone *would* be waiting for her at the bottom of the chimney, so she could not take that risk.

A voice echoed up the shaft. "Are you coming down, Carey?"

"Get out of the way, and keep quiet. I'm throwing something down, then I'm following." She let go of the body.

Feeling surprisingly clear-headed, Carey flung the man's floppy jungle hat down the shaft, then pulled up the rattan rope, working as fast as she could. Although she worked swiftly, it seemed to take forever, as the red glare crept inexorably through the forest toward her.

With relief, she reached the rattan string bag that was permanently attached to the end of the rope. She dumped the two rifles into it, securing the barrels to the rope with rattan. She didn't want two ten-pound rifles upsetting her equilibrium as she descended.

Quickly, with the machete, she hacked the rattan rope free of the tree trunk to which it had been secured. She bound the machete to the rifles as best she could, then lowered the heavy load down the chimney, as slowly as she dared. Shaking with anxiety, Carey again seemed to hear the voice of Jonathan in her head. "When you're in a hurry, do things *slowly.*" Finally, hands trembling, she carefully camouflaged the top of the chimney with sprawling vegetation.

Because of her size, Carey could do something that the other women found difficult: she could keep her elbows on the surface outside the shaft while bracing her feet against the other side. As she did so, she thought, This is the most dangerous thing I've ever done in my life! Her nerve failed and she froze with fear.

For months, the five women had schooled themselves not to

think of their families in Pittsburgh because such thoughts plunged them into instant depression. Now, in order to muster her courage, Carey deliberately thought of her daughters. She had always been convinced that she would put herself in any sort of danger in order to protect her children. So now Carey sternly reminded herself that, more than anything else in the world, Ingrid and Greta needed their mother.

It did no good at all.

She thought again of running back to Patty and the safety of the water, but the flames were leaping toward her, flaring higher, beneath clouds of smoke. Oddly enough, it smelled as good as a log fire in a city apartment.

Carey suddenly realized that if she didn't move fast, she would be burned to a crisp. She could never outrun the flames.

She began to lower herself carefully into the shaft. For a minute she was braced with her behind and her feet against the earthen sides of the shaft and her elbows still above ground, where they seemed glued. She dreaded removing them, but finally the crackle of approaching fire forced her into action. When the top of her head was just below the entrance of the shaft she pulled the concealing creepers back across it.

Slowly, she started to inch her way down the chimney.

She refused to think of landing on that corpse and concentrated on her descent. There were plenty of footholds, but the rock dug into her back and rubbed it raw through the khaki tunic. Her knees had been trembling before she lowered herself into the shaft, and now the only way she kept going was by calmly instructing herself aloud.

As the troops moved away from the burning camp, the sergeant realized that a man was missing. He questioned the others. Nobody volunteered information, but they did not seem surprised that he had disappeared. The man's village was only fourteen miles to the south and for weeks he'd been complaining about barracks life and army discipline, clearly pining for the quiet life and fishing. Every week someone deserted from the barracks, just as they did from the copper mines when they found that the work was worth the money but not worth the loss of their liberty.

The sergeant had to decide whether to stop and search the jungle for his missing man or continue his search for the women at sea. There was little more than an hour before sunset.

Had the man been injured, they would have heard him shouting. More likely at this very moment he was deciding how many *kina* he could get for his rifle and what he would do with his girl tonight.

Their orders had been clear.

"Post Narak missing, suspected deserter," the sergeant said. They could return and search for him the following day, by which time Narak would have had time to reach his village.

They'd pick him up if he was there. Otherwise they'd come back here and comb the jungle. In the meantime, a night out in the jungle never hurt an islander.

Patty peered anxiously through the foliage. Beyond this angular split in the cliff she could only see the sea and the sky. The two translucent blues divided by a thin, darker blue line had recently become two dark grays with a black dividing line.

An hour and a half earlier, Patty had seen a big olive helicopter pass along the coastline going south. It had returned later, northbound, but far out to sea.

Apprehensively, Patty looked again at the sky. There was something odd about it. Low dark clouds had piled up since the helicopter had passed. The sea was now the color of purple slate, and the choppy pattern of the waves had changed to black. The invisible sun, which had slipped behind the headland, was still shining with a fierce but detached clarity. The light was sharp and ominous.

Patty checked the mooring and tugged on the ropes of the two bamboo beds. As thunder rumbled overhead, Patty laid one bed over the stern of the boat and lashed it to the transom.

The storm reached the shore with sudden ferocity. Water crashed through the foliage overhead.

Patty was immediately drenched, as surely as if she'd been standing under the waterfall. She grabbed the tin bailer and started to heave water out as fast as she could. She stopped only to crawl forward to the locker and pull out one of the bamboo water containers to use as a second bailer. Then she hurled water from the boat with both hands.

As the squall shrieked over her head, Patty crouched beneath a torrent of rain, scarcely able to catch her breath in the deluge. Frantically, she tried to empty the water from the boat, until she realized that bailing was almost as futile a gesture as that of King Canute trying to hold back the waves.

Shivering, she wound a length of rattan around the second bed and slid it over her so that two-thirds of the dinghy was covered by a bamboo roof. But the beds were not waterproof, and the rain trickled between the poles like mountain rills.

By nightfall, Patty was as cold and as wet as if she had been swimming in the sea rather than bouncing on top of it. She wondered if the storm was going to last the whole night. It was more than likely. She wondered what would happen if she fell asleep. She wouldn't know if the boat were torn from its moorings. What should she do? Should she abandon ship— jump for the overhead boughs, climb along a branch and down a trunk? Or should she stick to the boat and risk being swept out to sea, risk being waterlogged and sunk?

Reluctantly, Patty reminded herself that all their escape equipment was in the boat. Supine, and with some difficulty, she wriggled into her life jacket.

WEDNESDAY, MARCH 13

Patty opened her eyes. Her first reaction was to wonder why she was soaking wet and what that odd slopping noise was.

Her second reaction was relief. She was still alive, and still in the boat—now half filled with water.

The storm had passed.

Patty could hear comforting little slaps against the hull. She felt the soothing, cradlelike motion of the sea beneath her. With difficulty she moved her left arm, wondering how old you had to be to get rheumatism, and looked at her watch.

Eight o'clock in the morning.

She hadn't been so hungry since that first night in the cave. With stiff fingers, she undid the knotted rattan, lifted the battered bed and looked out. The sea was still somber and the sky looked damp. On both sides of her the black cliffs glistened with water; trees shone and dripped. The creek was still in shadow, but she could see that the sun was lighting up the greenery at the entrance, while beyond it the sky was blue.

Patty took a swig of the soldiers' rum and slowly chewed slivers of smoked fish. Then she peed into the bailer, emptied it and used it for its proper purpose.

She hoped to hell that the other women were on their way.

Katanga village straggled across the north bank of the Katanga river. The thatched huts, which were used only for sleeping, stood on eight-foot poles and were reached by rickety wooden ladders. Within living memory the tidal rise had not been high enough to reach the huts. The inhabitants lived and worked in the shade below them.

At ten in the morning on March 13 most of the village women were either rounding up the pigs or tending the vegetable gardens, which had been devastated by the storm. The village was quiet except for a group of children squabbling beneath the huts. They were occasionally bawled out by one of the gap-toothed grandmothers repairing fishing nets, steaming vegetables in big wooden cooking pots or twisting thin rattan to make nets.

The playful noises of the children didn't seem to disturb the men of the village. They dozed in the shade beneath the huts in company with mongrel dogs, anorexic chickens and a young woman who drowsily suckled a piglet at her breast. Sleepily, the *luluai* shifted his position in the shade. After the storm there was much to repair. He hadn't yet decided where to start. The pig fence definitely needed immediate attention, but it was hard work making a pig fence. On the other hand, if it wasn't mended immediately, the pigs would get into the vegetable garden and make an even worse mess. Perhaps they should start on the pig fence fairly soon. He yawned and slowly scratched his ear.

The silence was broken by a low, distant hum—a buzz like the noise of a mosquito. As it grew louder, heads were raised.

A red Bell 206 helicopter appeared around the headland and headed straight for the village.

The *luluai* called sharply to the other men, who scrambled to their feet. Without being told, the village boys ran into the huts and came back with wooden clubs and spears, which they shoved into their fathers' hands. The children and old women rushed terror-stricken behind the line formed by their armed men standing on either side of their *luluai*. On Paui, the village headman always leads his men in danger or he loses his position. The whole village watched in apprehensive silence as the helicopter dipped toward the beaten mud area on the riverbank where the dugout canoes had been pulled clear of the water.

The wind caused by the rotating blades blasted the leaves and beat back the branches of the eucalyptus trees which edged the clearing. It was as if a cyclone were blowing.

Neatly, the helicopter came to rest and the rotor blades slowed. The three black passengers wore military uniforms. One of them was Colonel Borda.

Clutching a rifle, the colonel jumped down from the machine as soon as the rotor blades stopped. After greetings had been exchanged through an interpreter, Colonel Borda announced the identity of their visitor.

"Raki . . . Raki . . . Raki . . ." The words echoed through the group of villagers. There was excited chatter behind the men with bows and arrows, who did not move and would not do so until instructed by their headman but whose eyes were fixed on the small figure which slowly descended from the machine. Raki stood in its shadow, wiped off his sunglasses, pushed them into the breast pocket of his tunic and advanced toward the headman with majestic dignity in which there was no hint of either arrogance or humility.

Inside the dark, hot guest hut, President Raki dropped his solemnity. Briskly, he barked to the interpreter. His few words were translated by a necessarily long and elaborate speech. During the translation, Raki lost interest and his mind wandered. His firm look of presidential resolve changed swiftly to one of bland boredom, then to the malevolent glare of a clever, spoiled child who has been thwarted. This was replaced by the blank-eyed stare of an unpredictable man of violence who might be thinking of nothing at all or who might be just about to pull a trigger.

Upon hearing the astonishing and exasperating news that some of the Nexus women were still alive, Raki had realized immediately that if the women ever returned to the States he would be in serious political trouble with the USA, Britain, Japan, Australia and the U.N. Nexus International Mining, Inc., as well as the International Mining Federation, would be compelled to reassess the wisdom of doing business in Paui. Other powerful international mining companies would also view him with deep disfavor, to say the least. So long as these women were alive, his hold on the presidency was at risk.

They must therefore be found and killed before any news of their reappearance could reach Mount Ida or that overinquisitive Australian with whom he was negotiating the mining concession. The invasion had seriously depleted his bank account, and he was determined that every Swiss franc be replaced. He also needed cash to pay for Cargo Cult junk from Taiwan for the entire population of Paui.

He knew that the quickest, easiest and best mining deal he could make was with Nexus. Undoubtedly, they had already decided the limit to which they would bargain, which limit Raki was grimly determined to reach. He had intended to string out the bargaining. Now, in view of the reappearance of these white women, Raki wished that he had already signed with Nexus.

In the somnolent heat of the guest hut the interpreter nervously repeated the headman's last question. "Mr. President, the *luluai* wishes to know why troops went yesterday to the land above the waterfall which is *itambu?*"

The President replied smoothly, "Those were Filipino troops, who sadly did not know that they were in a forbidden place. They sought the white women who had already desecrated the spot and thus aroused the malevolence of the dead."

Barely an hour before, President Raki had stood on the forbidden land himself. He had glanced contemptuously at the sheet of tin nailed to a tree, painted with the sign of a black hand above the roughly printed words, ITAMBU.

The President had surveyed the smashed, burned-out huts. With one ostrichskin-shod toe he had prodded a bamboo pot into the scattered remains of the campfire, then turned to Colonel Borda. "Does the tracker's information agree with the story from the soldier who escaped from these women?"

Colonel Borda had nodded.

"This *hero*, who let women steal his clothes, must be severely punished. We do not wish him to speak further of the women. National security is involved. Take out his tongue."

"I will see to it, Excellency."

"The women cannot have gone very far, Colonel."

"We are searching the entire coast, Excellency, in case they have not headed for Irian Jaya but are traveling up the coast. If so, we shall quickly hear of this."

"So we are bound to find them?"

The colonel had hesitated. "A twelve-foot dinghy is not easy to spot from the air, sir." He looked at Raki's eyes and sighed. "Of course, we shall do our best, Excellency. Our *very* best!"

Now, sitting cross-legged in the heat of the village guest hut, Raki found it almost impossible to breathe.

The interpreter said, "The headman wishes to know when the soldiers who guard the *itambu* area will depart."

The President leaned toward Colonel Borda. "No point in leaving sentries, is there, Colonel?"

"The sentries must stay until the women are found, Excellency. They might return or be forced back to the area around their camp. This is the area they know. I respectfully suggest that we offer this village a sacrificial feast as soon as our men depart."

The interpreter said, "They would also like to have a rope bridge repaired. It was apparently damaged by the women."

Irritably the President said, "Yes, yes, tell them yes, for God's sake! Then ask them what they know about these women." He knew that the headman was all-powerful in a village, and that information had to be paid for or the headman would lose face—and his position.

"The headman says five women and one man were on the sacred site throughout the cyclone season but the man died," the interpreter reported. "Sometimes they fished and swam in the lagoon. That is all they know. The villagers do not go on ground that is *itambu*."

The President raised his voice. "Tell them that I have not visited this place to learn *nothing*."

Colonel Borda hastily leaned toward the President and said reassuringly, "Sir, I feel confident that these women will be found."

"I do not want the women found, Colonel. I want their *bodies* found."

Silvana and Annie took turns swimming through the underground passage, to check that the sentry hadn't moved from the beach. The women were unaware of the storm until they saw the beach at dawn on the following morning. There was a lot of debris at the high-tide line, but a saffron sun had risen, tinting the sky with sulphur and with rose.

"It looks as if it was a bad storm," Annie reported to the other women in the cave. "I'm worried about Patty."

"I'm worried about the boat," Suzy said.

"Let's try to reach it tonight," Carey suggested. "Any time will probably be bad. I can't stand this place much longer."

Annie nodded. "If we leave this afternoon shortly after three o'clock, we have a good chance of reaching the boat before sunset."

"Three hours should do it," Carey agreed. "It only took me two hours to get back here. We'll travel along the shore, on the fringe of the jungle, then strike out overland for the last part of the journey. I couldn't find my way through that in the dark, so we shouldn't leave later than three o'clock. And I'll need more time to climb up the chimney because of my back."

Carey's back was raw and bleeding after her descent. Nevertheless, it had been decided that she should be the one to climb the chimney to carry up the rope. Suzy was too short for her legs to reach the other side of the shaft. Because Annie was afraid of heights, it had long ago been decided not to use her in any emergency where her fear might endanger their safety. Silvana still had a bandaged hand. And, as Suzy unfairly pointed out, it was Carey who had cut the fucking rope.

All the women were irritable, unreasonable and tense—the more so because of the presence of a corpse. The dead soldier had been dragged away from the bottom of the shaft and stripped by the light of one of their sixteen yard-long dried coconut-fiber torches, lit with one of their new army-issue lighters. Each woman would now have a uniform to provide protective clothing.

In that damp and humid atmosphere, the corpse was decomposing quickly. The smell was like rotten meat, only stronger, with an added sickly-sweet odor. At first the smell had not been unpleasant, but as the body putrefied the stink gradually grew nauseating, partly because the sphincters had relaxed and urine and feces had escaped from the body. Carey had always wondered why corpses needed washing. Now she knew.

The putrefactive gases of decomposition accumulated in the intestines, grossly distending the black abdomen, and the black glistening mess that had been a head crawled with insects and buzzed with flies. Death had an awful, weird smell, thought Carey as she shifted the body to climb the chimney. How strange it was to be so frightened by a dead body when it was exactly at that point that it could no longer be a threat to you.

She started to climb up the cave shaft.

When Carey's head finally poked up above the ground she could see nothing alarming. With an effort, she threw herself sideways out of the hole. Now that the tension of the climb was over, she relaxed her iron concentration and started to shake all over. It was at least ten minutes before she could unfurl the rattan rope that was slung around her waist.

Carefully getting up from her crouch and taking cover at every move, she melted from tree to tree, conscious that she had no weapon but her knife.

When she spotted the charred area that had been their camp, she stopped and waited. At first she saw nobody, but then a sentry appeared. He sauntered from the area at the top of the waterfall, strolling back toward the camp. His relaxed walk told her that he didn't really expect to see anyone. She watched him walk through the blackened grass and turn toward William Penn. Shortly afterward he returned along the same path, turned at the waterfall and again slowly walked east, back toward William Penn.

Carey watched him for ten minutes, then returned to the cave shaft.

The fire had stopped just short of this part of the forest. She needn't have bothered to cut the goddamn rope, Carey thought crossly as she tied the rope around the usual tree and flung it down the shaft. She waited until she felt three tugs, then gave two answering tugs, which meant, "Okay, now I know you have the rope." This was immediately answered by another four tugs, which meant that Annie was coming up.

The little group was delayed by Silvana, who had difficulty climbing up the rope because of her amputated finger. As soon as all four women had climbed out of the shaft, Suzy handed

Carey her rifle. Carey camouflaged the cave chimney, then led the way as the women slipped through the jungle, always keeping the shoreline in view, always following the compass.

Nobody said a word, but only followed Carey's gesture until, on the southern headland, they reached the trail that Carey had hacked with the machete. This led over the final area of bumpy terrain to the cliff above the inlet in which the dinghy was hidden.

Exhausted, they paused for breath before the final descent. To their right, the setting sun tinted the entire sky in chrome yellow and scarlet. Already they could see the fat crescent of the moon. Behind them, the darkening forest was shrill with comforting evening noises, the rhythm of the jungle. Briefly, Carey remembered how frightened they'd been on their first night in the forest, when every night creature had seemed ominous.

As if echoing her thoughts, Suzy whispered, "Why aren't I scared anymore?"

Annie said, "Not enough time to be scared."

Silvana said, "Too many other things to think about."

"We'll be scared afterward." Carey wriggled her stiff shoulders. "Okay, you guys, on your feet. We're going aboard. Thanks for lending me your compass, Suzy." She handed it back, and Suzy shoved it into her pocket.

Followed by the other women, with Suzy in the rear, Carey started to slither down the mountainside. Stones rattled as they descended.

"Hey, it's *steep!*" squeaked Suzy. Five seconds later she fell.

Annie turned round and frowned. "Shhhh!"

"Sorry!" Suzy scrambled to her feet and hurried on.

She did not notice that the thong with Jonathan's key ring and the compass had fallen from her pocket.

Carey, her rifle. Carey camouflaged the cave chimney, then led the way as the women slipped through the jungle, always keeping the shoreline in view, always following the compass.

Nobody said a word, but only followed Carey's gesture until, on the southern headland, they reached the trail that Carey had hacked with the machete. This led over the final area of bumpy terrain to the cliff above the inlet in which the dinghy was hidden.

Exhausted, they paused for breath before the final descent. To their right, the setting sun tinted the entire sky in chrome yellow and scarlet. Already they could see the fat crescent of the moon. Behind them, the darkening forest was shrill with comforting evening noises, the rhythm of the jungle. Briefly, Carey remembered how frightened they'd been on their first night in the forest, when every night creature had seemed ominous.

As if echoing her thoughts, Suzy whispered, "Why aren't I scared anymore?"

Annie said, "Not enough time to be scared."

Silvana said, "Too many other things to think about."

"We'll be scared afterward.". Carey wriggled her stiff shoulders. "Okay, you guys, on your feet. We're going aboard. Thanks for lending me your compass, Suzy," She handed it back and Suzy shoved it into her pocket.

Followed by the other women, with Suzy in the rear, Carey started to clamber down the mountainside. Stones rattled as they descended.

"Hey, it's steep!" squeaked Suzy. Five seconds later she fell.

Annie turned round and frowned. "Shhhh!"

"Sorry!" Suzy scrambled to her feet and hurried on.

She did not notice that the thong with Jonathan's key ring and the compass had fallen from her pocket.

BOOK SEVEN

SHADOW OF DEATH

◀ 29 ▶

"Take us straight out to sea, Patty," Annie said as soon as it was dusk. "Let's get as far as we can from here, as fast as possible."

The little dinghy nosed out of the narrow creek into sea, the two bamboo bed-rafts tossing in its wake. The women had forgotten what speed felt like! They'd forgotten the luxury of being *carried* instead of having to carry. They felt exultantly proud of themselves. They had done it! They were free! They felt the gloating satisfaction and camaraderie of a job completed, a mission accomplished.

After the hot, thunderous oppression of the day it was a relief to be skimming over the cool sea, Annie thought as she trailed her hand through the water and watched the silvered phosphorescence spurt behind her fingers.

"How fast are we going?" Silvana asked.

Patty said, "Maybe five knots. That means we're traveling just over five miles an hour, so that's fourteen hours, minimum, to Irian Jaya." She didn't like to inject a sour note, but felt she had to add, "Although we don't know how much gas is in the engine. Pity the spare can was empty."

Annie said, "So long as the engine holds out until we hit the current we should be all right. We'll have another look at the

591

charts in daylight." They had been puzzling over the charts since Jonathan's death.

Patty said cheerfully, "Jonathan said it's a one-knot current, so without power the fastest we can get to Irian Jaya is seventy hours—three days."

"But maybe we'll be picked up earlier," Suzy said hopefully.

Patty's voice was confident. "Sure. We aren't stuck in the middle of the Pacific. We're in a relatively narrow channel between Papua New Guinea and Australia."

Carey cried happily, "In a nice safe fiberglass boat, with an anchor and two oars!"

"Not a waterlogged raft with no steering!" Suzy sounded euphoric.

The women in the dinghy were exhausted but lighthearted. As Annie listened to their banter, she found it difficult to remember that these were the grim women who yesterday on the beach had fought for their freedom against the men who had wanted to take it from them. Annie felt a fierce satisfaction as she recalled their determination. Freedom is not given, she realized. You have to take it.

Careful not to upset the equilibrium of the overloaded dinghy, Annie swiveled in her seat to face Patty. She said, "I'd like to check what Jonathan taught us about navigation—because now it's for real."

Patty said complacently, "We have two compasses." She held out the black plastic case. "This one, and Suzy's pocket compass."

Annie twisted around. "Your compass okay, Suzy?"

Silvana said, "She's asleep."

Patty said, "We want to hit the offshore current that runs to the southeast and sweeps around southern Paui. Then there will be seventy miles of ocean to cover before we reach Irian Jaya."

Carey said, "We want to reach that island, the one with the name I can never remember."

"Pulau yos Sudarsa," Annie said. "If we miss it somehow, we'll just go on until we hit northern Australia."

Carey nodded. "During the day we steer by the sun, which passes over us at midday—slightly to the north because we're eight degrees south of the equator."

Patty said, "As a rough guide, I point the hour hand of my watch at the sun. Halfway between the hour hand and twelve o'clock is north."

"On cloudy days?"

"Annie, you're getting to sound like a scoutmaster!" Patty sounded cheerfully confident. "On cloudy days I hold Carey's pencil at the center of the watch so that the faint shadow of the stick falls along the minute hand. Halfway between the shadow and four o'clock is south."

"And at night?"

Patty nodded up at the star-spangled heavens. "If we have compass trouble at night, we'll steer by the stars. I keep the Southern Cross over my right shoulder to steer a southeasterly course."

Carey added, "If the moon rises before the sun sets, the curve of the moon will be to the west. If it rises after the sun sets, the curve will be to the east."

"And if the moon rises at the same time?"

"Then it's a full moon, but I forget how to use it."

"Damnit, so do I," Annie said, cross with herself. "We're all tired, we'd better go through this again in the morning. We all ought to be able to gabble it off by heart. . . . Hey!" Annie lurched sideways as Silvana suddenly slumped against her.

Recovering her balance, Annie said, "She's asleep. Lucky she didn't fall the other way or she'd have gone overboard. We'd better rope ourselves to those rings at the front and back of the boat. Carey, you take first watch."

By the time the dinghy had been at sea for two hours, the shore was no longer visible. The swell had increased, and although the boat was still moving, it didn't seem to be making much progress.

The engine coughed. Patty's heart sank. In spite of her crossed fingers, the engine stopped. There's no point in waking everyone up to tell them we're out of gas, she thought glumly.

Patty found the boat increasingly difficult to steer without power. The swell had become more pronounced and slapped the hull with increasing strength. She couldn't stand the pause which followed the heave upward before the boat dipped down the next oily, black wave. She knew that to avoid seasickness she should not look at the sea, just at the horizon. But since it was dark, she couldn't see the horizon.

Carey suddenly moaned, then grabbed the side and heaved over it. The boat pitched violently, then shot forward. She groaned and felt for the bailer. She dipped it in the sea and started to splash water on her face. Then, dropping the bailer, she held her head over the gunwale again. The stars tilted.

By nine o'clock at night all the women were violently seasick. Annie could now understand something she had read: when you're seasick you lose the will to live. She retched and retched again, although there was nothing left in her stomach to void. It was as if her center of equilibrium had spun loose and was gyrating, like a top, in her stomach.

The moon appeared and the women were able to see one another's faces glistening wet against the black, heaving sea.

As she hung feebly over the side, Suzy's peaked cap was suddenly tugged from her head. In the misty moonlight she grabbed at it, but the cap flew just beyond her reach and settled on the water, where it dipped and bobbed on the foam-crested waves.

The wind strengthened, and raindrops drummed against the fiberglass. Suddenly, a torrent of water lashed the dinghy. The women were immediately soaked to the skin.

The waves grew higher and broke over the dinghy. The seawater seemed cold at first, but as sheets of freezing rain fell from above, the water in the boat felt almost lukewarm.

A dazed Carey handled the bailer with slow, exhausted movements. Silvana was already throwing water out of the boat with her cupped hands, as fast as she could. She managed to bail a surprising amount in this way.

Annie yelled to Suzy, "Get some water jars from the locker, then we can all bail."

As the rain slammed inboard the exhausted, bewildered women hurled it out again. At first they bailed carefully, filling their bamboo containers before flinging the water overboard. But their bailing increased in frenzy with the storm, until they were hurling half as much over the side with twice as much strength as was necessary. Once Suzy unthinkingly threw the water into the howling wind, which simply slammed it back in her face. It took her breath away and left her gasping.

Bruised and out of breath, they had to yell to be heard. Unless one woman bellowed straight into the cold, wet ear of another, their voices were torn away by the gale.

"Carey, which way do you steer an overloaded boat in bad weather?" Patty yelled above the wind. "Into the waves? Side-on to the waves? Or do we run before the damn things?"

Carey shouted back, "I've no idea. Try them all! *Quickly!* I thought you knew how to handle boats. You knew how to start the outboard motor!"

"Only for water skiing, on calm water."

Steering side-on didn't seem to be right, and when the dinghy ran before the waves the water immediately curled over the stern, threatening to swamp the boat. Steering into the waves and meeting the sea head-on seemed best, but it was tough on the stomach, Patty thought.

The brutal wind lashed their faces, tore their breath away and sucked the warmth from their bones. Howling with rage, it tore at their battered bodies and froze their flesh. It blew away their willpower. The women were so wet and stiff and cold that it was too much of an effort to move.

Suzy felt the gripping dread in her heart that she had known as a child. Once again she was helpless and hopeless as random violence lashed about her. Fleetingly she felt again that bewildered guilt—not knowing what she'd done to deserve this, but knowing that she *must* be guilty of some dreadful sin, because otherwise God wouldn't punish her like this. Only when Suzy was terrified did she believe in God, and He was always a wrathful, capricious figure.

A wave crashed over the boat, knocking Suzy off balance to starboard. She screamed. Annie watched in horror as a surge of water heaved up and floated Suzy off the boat.

As Suzy was swept overboard, Silvana managed to grab one of her legs. Silvana hung on and ducked her head to avoid Suzy's other kicking foot. Suzy's head and shoulders were underwater. The sudden weight of the two other women tipped the boat to within three inches of the churning sea.

To compensate, Annie threw herself in the opposite direction. She found herself in the bottom of the boat, sprawled in slopping water. She turned her head and heard Silvana's scream snatched by the wind. Without conscious thought Annie scrambled to her knees, grabbed Silvana by the waist and hauled her backward.

Hanging on to the tiller, Patty was helpless, and Carey, crouched in the stern, dared not move in case she further tipped the boat.

Gradually, the weight of the two other women pulled Suzy back aboard. She collapsed, wet and gasping, into the bottom of the boat as the storm's fury crashed around them.

Annie groped her way forward to the bow. Her numb, wet fingers slowly pried open the catch on the locker. Clumsy with cold, she grabbed the flares and rockets and shoved them into her pockets, then crawled back to the stern over the tangle of wet gear and sodden bodies.

Annie shoved the flares and rockets into Carey's hand. The wind tore the words from her mouth as she screamed, "Share . . . them . . . out!"

Silvana crawled back to the bow of the tossing boat and felt for the water containers. She managed to give one to each woman to shove down their tunic fronts.

With frozen hands, Patty pushed the compass into her button-down breast pocket, but her fingers were too stiff to do up the button.

Annie took off her wet boots—her precious boots—and tied them together by the laces. Then, with a length of rattan, she tied everybody's boots to the center thwart. This took longer than it should have, because her fingers were chilled and clumsy. All the women were shivering uncontrollably. Annie tied the empty jerry can to the center thwart, then she tied one wooden oar to Silvana's waist and one to Suzy's. They all now realized that they might have to swim.

A bolt of lightning snaked, violent white, against the blackness. More lightning flashes followed. Every time they lit the scene like stroboscopic flash, the women saw a frozen, monochromatic snapshot of themselves clinging to the little white boat.

Carey screamed in Patty's ear, "You and I are the best swimmers. Maybe if we jump overboard and swim it'd give the boat more of a chance. She won't be so overloaded and get swamped and sink."

Jagged lightning lit Patty's horrified face.

Carey yelled to Patty, "We've got a better chance . . . if we don't lose the boat . . . if we're roped to it. And we've got life jackets."

"What about sharks?" Patty screamed.

Carey's voice was now almost too hoarse to shout. "I think sharks stay sensibly on the bottom in this sort of weather." She spat out water. "We can survival-float. It looks as if we'll have to do that anyway. This way, we may save the boat."

Patty gasped, "Are you crazy? First, let's ditch the outboard. It's heavy—it might make a lot of difference."

With difficulty, the two women unscrewed the motor from its mount on the thwart, lifted it, then let it go. It fell into the water and disappeared.

Carey crawled forward to Annie and yelled in her ear, "We're going over. It sounds crazy, but if we save the boat, we save ourselves."

Nodding, Annie screamed, "Double your ropes before you jump, and do it fast."

The two terrified women lowered themselves feet first over the stern, and were immediately swept from the dinghy.

Occasionally Annie caught glimpses of the seawater-activated lights of their life jackets jerking up and down in the blackness. She could only see when lightning illuminated the oil-black water for a frozen, bruise-purple moment. The world was a black, wet, starless void and they were being sucked into its violence.

For the first time Annie wondered whether a fiberglass boat could break up. But even if it didn't, one of the three women in the boat might be injured or flung overboard by the motion.

The boat suddenly fell away beneath her and Annie's spine jarred as she crashed down on it.

Annie thought, There's only one way to save this boat and that's to overturn it deliberately before it's swamped. Then there will be an air pocket under the hull, so it will float. We can hang on to the boat from outside, then right it, and bail it out after the storm. Otherwise, we're going to lose the boat anyway.

Annie managed to get her mouth to Silvana's ear. The wind snatched her voice as she spoke, and the effort of screaming exhausted her. A flash of lightning illuminated Silvana's face —her mouth was a black hole of disbelief that Annie should want her to jump overboard.

Annie turned her head and howled instructions into Suzy's ear. In the lightning flashes Annie saw Suzy's look of panic.

Suzy remembered how it had felt when she nearly drowned in the lagoon. She screamed, "How do we know the boat won't go on without us? How do we *know* she'll overturn?"

Annie screamed back, "If we all lean on the same side she'll tip over."

With stiff fingers, the women checked their life jackets and the knots of the rattan ropes around their waists, then tied the ropes to the stern ring. Suzy and Silvana clutched their slippery, wet oars. Clumsily, all three women crawled to the downwind side of the boat.

Almost immediately, before they had time to wonder whether or not it would work, the boat obligingly tipped the three women into the churning water, then capsized.

THURSDAY, MARCH 14

Above the black sea a thin line of primrose extended along the horizon. As Annie bobbed in the water, she could see Patty's face in front of her, white and gaunt as an Edvard Munch painting. Patty was clinging to the ghost-white hull of the upended dinghy. The women were still attached by their ropes to the stern ring.

Although she was less than ten feet away, it took Annie five weary minutes to dog-paddle to Patty.

Annie lifted her whistle and blew it twice.

"Here!" "Over here!" The two voices came from the opposite side of the upended hull.

Patty and Annie paddled around the boat. On the other side, Silvana and Carey bobbed up and down in their bloated yellow life jackets, stamped on the back with the word *Louise*.

"Where's Suzy?" Annie called.

The women looked at one another. Nobody spoke.

"I'll swim all the way around," Patty said, although both she and Annie knew there was no one on the other side of the hull.

Patty swam around the boat and returned, shaking her head. "Her rope must have come undone."

There was no other sign of life upon the surface of the sea. Under a layer of heavy gray cloud it stretched flat and black to a thin band of topaz at the horizon. Behind the clouds, the hidden sun shed weak rays upon the water.

"The sun will soon warm us up," Annie said drearily.

Carey, hanging in the water, started to cry.

About twenty minutes later Patty screamed, "Look!"

The eyes of the women followed her pointing finger. They all saw the glimmer of light that seemed to be moving steadily across the horizon from left to right.

As the glimmer surged onward, it enlarged into a rectangle of lights which flickered like the few stars that still hung in the sky.

"A liner," Patty whispered longingly. In fact it was a container ship.

"Can you reach your flare, Patty?" Annie asked. "Do you think they'll work after they've been wet?"

"Don't know." Patty's stiff fingers fumbled beneath her life jacket. "I can't reach them without taking off my life jacket."

"Take her life jacket," Annie said to Silvana. "If you let go of it, then Patty gets yours."

Patty looked nervous. "I don't want to drop the flares."

"Hang on to Carey for support," Annie said.

Carey swam behind Patty and clutched her around the middle as Silvana helped Patty remove her life jacket.

Briskly, Annie ordered, "Okay. Move fast. That ship isn't going to wait."

The ship in the distance was now a third of the way across the horizon.

Patty held up the six-inch white cylinder with stiff fingers. She unscrewed the cap, which exposed the nose of the rocket, then unscrewed the base and pulled out the length of string coiled within. She unhitched the safety catch, held the rocket in her right hand and wound the string around her left knuckle. Lifting the rocket as high as she could above the water, she tugged sharply with her left hand. Then she screamed in pain.

The rocket soared upward, a bright light upon which their lives depended. The eyes of all the women followed the swift, forty-second, white arc as it soared through the sky.

Patty gasped with pain. *"Fucking glorified firework!"* She held her burned and blackened hand beneath the water.

The ship was now in the center of the horizon.

"Don't they have radar?" Carey asked. "I thought all ships had to have someone monitoring it twenty-four hours a day. I heard you can pick up a seagull on radar."

Annie said bitterly, "It's probably on automatic pilot and they're still asleep in their bunks."

None of the women had much hope that the ship would suddenly turn 90 degrees and head straight for them, but they felt inexpressibly forlorn and abandoned as she moved steadily across the horizon. They stared after it, seeing a cruise ship, representing all the comforts of civilization. They imagined stewards preparing breakfast trays with white linen cloths and sparkling cutlery, chilled orange juice, the heavenly aroma of coffee, croissants and marmalade . . .

The ship dwindled to a small glimmer of light to their right. Nobody spoke as they watched the speck disappear. Eventually Patty said, "It moved so fast. I had no idea a ship could move so fast."

The clouds upon the horizon were tinged with pink, and the pale sky soared above the dusky purple sea.

Annie said, "Put your life jacket back on, Patty, then let's get back in the boat."

Deliberately, nobody had mentioned Suzy.

"How do we turn it right side up?" Carey asked wearily.

They all gazed at the inverted white hull, smoothly riding the water beside them. From the center of the hull the keel stuck up sharply, ten inches high.

Annie said, "We'll crawl up one side, hang on to that thing sticking up and pull it toward us. Our weight should drag it over, and that will right the boat."

Patty gasped, "I don't think . . ."

"She burned her hand," Carey reminded them, and helped Patty back into her life jacket.

Silvana looked at the dinghy. "How are we going to crawl up it?"

Various suggestions were made, and tried, without success.

Shirley Conran

Eventually, Carey ducked her head between Annie's legs so that Annie sat above the water on her shoulders. But when Annie leaned against the hull, her weight pushed the boat away. She tried to stand on Carey's shoulders, but this merely pushed Carey's head underwater.

After several attempts, each more exhausting and exasperating than the last, Carey eventually managed to hang on to the gunwale and Annie managed to stand, more or less upright, on her shoulders. If she stood on tiptoe Annie could just grasp the keel.

Annie slipped and fell into the water.

She surfaced spluttering. "Okay, let's try again."

Carey gasped, "Can't we rest a few minutes?"

"Sharks," Annie reminded her.

This galvanized them into finding the energy for further effort. Again, Annie hauled herself into a sitting position on Carey's shoulders, but this time it was far more difficult for the exhausted Annie to alter her position so that she was crouching on Carey's shoulders. Four times, she fell backward into the water.

Weeping with vexation, Annie tried again.

They never knew what they did right, but suddenly, after about thirty minutes of trying, Annie's numb, wet hands managed to grip the keel. She pulled herself up and threw one leg over it.

Annie sat astride the hull.

As Patty was only able to use one hand, she couldn't hang on to the gunwhale and act as a foothold, so she was the next person to be pushed by Silvana and tugged by Annie up onto the hull.

Then Annie hung over the hull with her feet on one side of it, her arms on the other, and the keel biting into her stomach as she pulled Silvana upward. Heavier and less agile than Patty, Silvana couldn't manage to climb up.

Carey gasped, "Take off your pants and loop the legs together. We could climb up it like a ladder." This worked.

602

After pulling on their clinging, heavy wet pants, the women tried to right the boat by using the weight of their bodies. They experimented shifting their weight around, but nothing seemed to work.

Eventually Annie panted, "We'll just have to sit on the top like this. Ride her like a steer."

"Annie, the keel is *sharp*," Carey protested.

"Okay, let's try *once* more. This time, give it everything you've got, guys."

They spaced out, with the two lighter women on either end and the two heavier in the middle. It was the only combination they hadn't already tried.

Slowly the boat turned over, throwing them into the sea. Bobbing about in the water, the women felt a new vigor.

"We *did* it! We *did* it!" Carey yelled.

"Hi, guys." They heard a shrill voice from the other side of the boat. The women all yelled, *"Suzy!"*

Suzy's head shone in the water like a sleek sea animal. "When the boat overturned and we all went under, I came up underneath it," she explained, paddling over to the other women. "My life-jacket light was on, so I could see where I was. I just grabbed upward and hung on to that center seat. My ears were popping and the waves slapping against the hull were very noisy and ominous. After a while I let go of the seat, but for some reason, I still stayed underneath the boat. I was frightened of running out of air and absolutely terrified alone under there. I had no idea if it was day or night, or whether the storm was over, or whether anyone else was alive."

Then she stopped babbling and burst into tears at the joy of no longer being alone.

"Could they have survived?" Although it was six in the morning, the President was already dressed in an immaculate white uniform trimmed with gold braid. He looked at the cal-

endar on his desk; it was March 14. He repeated his question. "Could they have survived two storms in two days, Colonel?"

Colonel Borda said, "I doubt it, Excellency."

Absentmindedly, the President picked at his desktop with his dagger, gouging out bits of the brass marquetry pattern. He stood up, walked to the window and opened the shutters. Rain driven by a fierce wind slammed into the room.

"Unseasonable weather, but very welcome," the President said. He turned and banged the bell on his desk. A servant entered, and fought to close the shutters that the wind had flattened against the outer wall.

Violent squalls had blown until one A.M. Thick, gray rain still hissed on the palace roof. There was devastation in the courtyard beneath the window—not a leaf remained on a branch, and many branches were downed.

Colonel Borda said, "I doubt a small dinghy could even have survived the first storm. The area has been searched *twice*. After last night's storm it seems pointless to repeat the search or extend it. There is no point in looking for something that is not there."

The President dismissed the colonel and pressed the buzzer for his secretary. The man appeared in an instant. "Find that Nexus *soppo*, Harry Scott. Tell him that I wish to negotiate immediately." He chuckled. "A business breakfast—as they say in the West."

The secretary bowed and left, and once again the President turned his attention to the file before him. It contained complaints concerning Defense Force brutality, theft and terrorism. How did people expect an army to behave? Say "Have a nice day" before pulling the trigger?

The President's secretary re-entered. As always, he felt a sinking sensation in his bowels as he waited to give news that the President would not wish to hear.

The President looked up. "Well?"

"Mr. Scott is not in Queenstown, Excellency. He has not been seen for three days, not since Monday. The Nexus group has requested permission to search the Malong area, but the Minister of the Interior has not yet agreed to this."

"Why not?"

"The President will recall that last December he issued instructions that everyone should be courteous but that nothing should be done to help search for any Nexus survivors."

The President banged his desk. "Tell the Minister that I want Harry Scott. Find him fast!"

◄ **30** ►

THURSDAY, MARCH 14, 1985

If Harry put his eye to a crack he could see his four guards squatting below him, teasing the mongrel in the shade of the hut. Harry thought of clean starched shirts, fresh sheets and cold beer. He dreamed of rainbows and the swimming-pool terrace on top of his apartment building. He imagined ice and snow. He remembered things that were clean and cool, as he lay in the gloom on the rotting sago boards of the native hut in the oppressive afternoon heat.

It was three days since the men had been imprisoned. After the first few hours their neck cords had been lengthened so that they were able to lie down, but their hands were still tied behind their backs and their feet were also bound. Harry's trousers were soiled, and he stank.

The nights had been worse than the days. They were alternately hot and then cold as chill, damp night air seeped through the cracks in the hut.

Every morning and evening, the prisoners were fed by two young warriors, who never met their eyes or spoke to them as they put on the floor two banana leaves containing fried catfish and sago pancakes. Nobody spoke to the prisoners. They were literally treated like tethered animals—except that animals could at least shake the mosquitoes and flies away from their faces.

Harry alternated between feeling like a fool for having allowed himself to be captured so easily and feeling hope because his captivity might mean that the missing Nexus party was being similarly held.

But sometimes frustration overwhelmed Harry and he felt despair when he faced the fact that Annie might be dead. In his heart Harry had always felt that there must have been some mistake, that Annie had been intended by fate for *him;* that she was Harry's woman—his destiny—and that Duke had only accidental, temporary possession of her. During the last four months he had expected his feelings for Annie to weaken, to go fuzzy at the edges. He had expected that, grieving her, he could put her memory to rest. But he hadn't. His longing for Annie was just as raw and sharp as it had ever been.

No one had asked the prisoners any questions, but the interpreter told Harry that this was a good sign. He explained that the longer Harry was absent, the quicker his people would pay up. He had hesitated, then added, "Master like go quicktime, master no eat. These feller think you die, these feller sing out money for you quicktime."

Harry felt it would be no hardship not to eat if that would convince their captors that he was dying, so they would quickly negotiate a ransom.

The interpreter reckoned that the price asked would be three hundred pigs for Harry (the maximum dowry for a bride), but he had no idea what would be asked for himself, or whether Nexus would pay it.

Harry said, "Don't worry. Without a note from me to the mine manager, they won't get a penny from him. Whatever is paid for me will also cover the cost of releasing you."

Harry knew that the ransom messenger hadn't yet set off. He would travel by dugout canoe, and it would take two days nonstop to travel downriver, then cover the sixty-five miles to Mount Ida. After that, it would take him the same amount of time to return. So a minimum of four more days' imprisonment lay ahead of the captives.

Seven wasted days! That would take him to March 18 and

would leave only thirteen days before Raki's deadline for call-ing off the search. Harry banged the dirty floorboards in frus-tration.

A peaked khaki cap appeared above the gap in the floor; beneath it was a thin, intelligent, dark brown face. A Filipino.

"Mr. Harry Scott?"

Harry nodded.

The man climbed a little higher up the ladder. From his shoulder tabs, Harry saw that he was an army captain. He said, "The President of Paui wishes to see you, Mr. Scott. I am your escort."

"Delighted to hear it."

"Now that I have seen you, I will arrange for your release."

Harry had been located within two hours after a call had been put out through the soldier-informer network Raki had established throughout the island.

The captain disappeared. The interpreter rolled over on his stomach, peered through a crack in the floorboards and re-ported to Harry what seemed to be happening below.

The men of the village were gathered in a group around the Filipino captain, who held a two-way radio. With him were four armed soldiers, clearly islanders. Sometimes several peo-ple talked at once, sometimes there was a long silence, some-times a few grunts. The interpreter could not hear what was being said.

After half an hour of negotiation, it was agreed that Harry and the interpreter would be released upon the handing over of two transistor radios and the understanding that the subject of one missing Filipino soldier would not be pursued.

Harry, who had been tied up for four days, could hardly move his arms or legs. Both prisoners had to be helped to the two inflatable dinghies that waited at the edge of the water.

Harry asked, "What about our boat?"

"That was included in their price," the Filipino captain said. "It now belongs to them. Show them how to start the outboard. They don't realize it will run out of gas. Don't mention it."

Nobody said goodbye, nobody waved, as the two dinghies drew away from the shore to background music of Tina Turner blaring "Subway Fix" full blast through three transistors tuned to Radio Paui.

After traveling twenty minutes upstream they arrived at a small lake, where an army helicopter waited.

It was after dark when Harry reached Ma Chang's hotel. He showered his disgusting filth away, threw his soiled clothes down from the veranda onto the kitchen garbage heap below and changed into a clean shirt and pants. While the captain waited at his side, he placed a telephone call to Kerry but couldn't reach him at either his home or the mine.

Harry's military escort then pushed him into an army jeep and drove to the Presidential Palace.

Shortly after six o'clock Harry was received in Raki's office.

"I am truly glad to see you, Mr. Scott." The President's voice sounded concerned, but his eyes contradicted his friendly words as he said, "I'm glad you're safe. I want no more disappearances."

Harry thought, That's genuine. No way could Nexus have persuaded any of their personnel to work on this island, however high the salary offered, had he not returned. He said, "I'm even more relieved than you are. Thank you for helping me."

Raki smiled. "You really mustn't, at the moment, move around the island without an armed escort." He added, "I insist."

Harry said nothing.

The President continued. "The proverbial dust has not yet settled on Paui, and you need protection."

"I appreciate your concern, sir, but I don't require an armed escort. I shall be more careful in the future." He didn't want Raki's spy moving around with him.

The President shrugged. "As you wish. But think about it. Now, I hope you will join me for a meal."

At the mention of food, Harry became aware of his rumbling, empty belly.

It was clear from the meal that had been prepared for him that Harry was the President's honored guest. In a shuttered, thirty-foot dining room six attendants wearing white lap-laps served the two men. The room was hung with curtains of pink silk shot with gold; the dining table, covered in ecru lace, reminded Harry of his mother's Sunday dinners. The food was served on Royal Doulton, patterned with blowsy roses.

All the food came from a can: sardines in tomato sauce, which were followed by game soup, breast of turkey with cranberry sauce, potatoes and beans. Dessert was canned Australian peaches smothered in canned cream. The entire banquet—for imported canned goods cost a fortune on Paui —was accompanied by a bottle of green crème de menthe, which is considered by islanders to be a truly sophisticated drink.

Harry was being softened up.

He watched Raki shovel food into his mouth, sometimes with a knife and fork, sometimes with his fingers. He never took his eyes off his plate. Raki was greedy, Harry thought— and really greedy people can never be satisfied. They always want more—more food, more drink, more women, more children, more flatterers, more followers, more power, more money . . . Better than anyone, Harry knew what wealth Raki had amassed in the past ten years. He had a fortune large enough to enable him to leave Paui and enjoy life somewhere far more comfortable—California, Florida, Switzerland, the Riviera. But Raki was clever enough to know that once he left Paui he would be nobody, so he stayed on the island, preferring to be the biggest fish in a small pond.

After the meal, Harry was offered a Romeo y Julieta Havana, doubtless a gift from the Cuban diplomat's pouch. Fragrant smoke filled the room.

"And now to business." Raki leaned back in his chair. "You know my terms. I'm not going to alter them. I want a decision tomorrow."

Harry knew that Third World leaders were notorious for their cat-and-mouse negotiating, their changes of mind and their mercurial decisions, so he was not surprised by this sudden ultimatum. Smoothly, he stalled. "I'm unable to give you an instant answer, sir. I have to refer to Pittsburgh."

Raki looked contemptuously at Harry. "We both know that if we don't have an agreement by the first of April, copper production will halt—and so will your revenue and my taxes."

Harry said, "My company prefers not to sign until we've located our missing personnel."

Raki said smugly, "It's a pity that you're so obsessed by this hopeless search."

"I don't think it's hopeless," Harry said firmly, thinking of the two watches locked in the safe at Barclays Bank.

"Your competitors from Manila will arrive on April second, Mr. Scott." Raki blew a hazy gray smoke ring toward the ceiling. "The longer you search, the less time you will have for business. The choice is yours, Mr. Scott."

Back at Ma Chang's, Harry headed for the bar, where he called for a cold beer to wash away the sickly, peppermint taste of the crème de menthe. As he waited for his can of Fosters, Harry listened to the nightly tintinnabulation of rhythmically banged oil drums and garbage can lids, transistors turned up full blast, the occasional gunshot.

"Thought we'd seen the last of you," called Sandy the journalist. There was nobody else in the bar, and he sat at his usual dark corner table.

Harry carried his beer over and sat down.

Sandy said, "Hear you had a spot of bother upriver."

Shirley Conran

Harry nodded. "Raki sent a khaki nursemaid for me. I was bloody glad to see him."

"You've missed a new black market scandal. Tons of raisins in wooden boxes stenciled 'Gift of the American People to the Children of Paui' were suddenly being sold by street vendors. There was also a similar deluge of cooking oil and powdered milk."

"What's new about that?"

"A lot of mission-educated islanders could read those stenciled words. One of your blokes from Mount Ida called a meeting about it. Fellow called Mindo."

"He's a decent bloke," Harry said.

"His meeting was busted by the military, and he was thrown into jail. Without a trial, of course. Accused of conspiracy against the government, if you please."

Harry put down his beer. "I'd better telephone Kerry."

"Aw, finish your drink, mate. There's nothing you can do."

Harry downed his drink and then telephoned Kerry, who was relieved to hear Harry's voice.

When the helicopter pilot reported that Harry hadn't fired his final flare, Kerry had immediately ordered a river search. His men had found themselves lost in a spiderweb of waterways, and Kerry had been ordered by the Minister of the Interior to stop searching. Kerry had ignored the order, but was relieved that now he no longer needed to defy the Paui government.

"I'll need another gun," Harry said apologetically.

"I'll get you one tomorrow," Kerry said, wondering how many pistols Harry was planning to go through before he fired one.

Briefly, Harry explained what had happened to him, then asked, "Is it true they've jailed Mindo?"

"Yes." Kerry was clearly furious and unusually indiscreet on the telephone. "Raki made a big mistake there. Our men at the mine have already shown that they can organize themselves. They acted with considerable force in last year's strike.

612

They're not scattered, ignorant natives. Mindo is their leader, and there's going to be trouble about putting him in jail. Mindo's father is an important tribal chief—with a lot of warriors. I reckon the lid is about to blow off the kettle. In fact, I'm thinking of sending Betty to Sydney."

Harry said, "Raki didn't look as if he was expecting trouble."

"No, Raki doesn't seem to notice. But then, he's preoccupied. You wouldn't have heard, but he suddenly married again. She's not yet fourteen years old, a hot little number from one of the hill tribes. The celebrations took place the day before yesterday. We had fireworks, pig feasts, palm wine, the works. Haven't you noticed that everyone still has a hangover today?"

"What about his other young wife?"

"Ah. She died of blood poisoning, just before Christmas."

At eleven o'clock that night, Harry's call came through from Pittsburgh. Harry told his news and added, "Jerry, I believe the disappearance of our people is somehow linked to this deal. That's why I don't want to close."

"Bullshit!" Jerry shouted. "You're supposed to wrap up that deal as fast as possible. Don't let Raki get cold again." He didn't give Harry a chance to speak again, but ranted on. "What the *hell* do you think you're doing, Harry? Three months ago, before Christmas, there might have been a slight chance of finding some trace of our missing party. But now, any further searching is an obsessional waste of the company's money! In fact, if you're not back here in Pittsburgh exactly one week from today, with a good explanation of why you wasted a quarter of a million dollars this month on something I ordered you *not* to do, you're *through*, Harry."

The line went dead. Harry decided to have another beer.

The next morning, wakening, Harry first wondered why he felt so terrible. Then to his great joy he remembered that *he was free!* He started to sit up in bed but fell back with a groan. He winced as someone tapped on his door.

Mrs. Chang wobbled in. She wore a furtive expression and blue cotton coolie pajamas. She whispered, "I am so sorry to compromise you, Mr. Scott, but I thought it best not to talk to you last night." Primly, she sat upright on the scarred bentwood chair at the end of Harry's bed. "I have top-rate, top-price information, Mr. Scott. On Wednesday last, President Raki visited a village about twenty miles south of Paradise Bay. The day before, a group of white women had killed some soldiers near this place. They also stole the soldiers' boat, their guns and their uniforms."

Harry jerked upright. The bedsprings protested. Mrs. Chang girlishly covered her face with her hands, to hide the sight of Harry's bare chest.

"What's the name of the village? How do you know? When did you hear?"

"This story comes to me from barracks talk, Mr. Scott. There was also an air search for the women, but they did not find them. *Mr. Scott!*"

Harry had leaped naked from his bed. He grabbed the threadbare towel and twisted it around his hips.

Mrs. Chang said sharply, "You are not to check this story or the President will hear of it. My source will be tracked down and beheaded."

Harry wound his arms around Mrs. Chang, squeezing her in a mighty hug. His towel fell to the floor.

Mrs. Chang cried, "Mr. Scott, *you* are compromising *me*."

As the helicopter started its descent, agonized squeals came from the two shackled piglets in the rear. A misty-gray veil subdued the irregular blurs of black, olive and emerald on either side of the sump-colored river on which Katanga village lay.

Stepping from the helicopter, Harry was greeted by the *luluai* of Katanga. The cigarette ceremony took place and the piglets were presented, one to the village and the other as a sacrifice for the spirits by the waterfall. Both animals were graciously received.

Harry's interpreter then confirmed that white women had been in the area. Tentatively, he suggested an immediate appeasement of the spirits. The medicine man was consulted, but shook his head. Such ceremonies took time to prepare. Tense with anxiety, Harry found it hard to control his impatience. He *had* to see if there were any traces of the Nexus party at Waterfall Bay. Somewhat nervously, the interpreter explained that before he left Paui this white master wished, in person, to appease the spirits of the *itambu* area.

Harry's trump card—a transistor radio—was fetched from the helicopter. Harry demonstrated it, with an appropriate blast of "Banana Revolution."

The medicine man delicately touched the tuner, and Madonna was displaced by slightly more melodic static. The medicine man scratched his head and agreed that it might be in order for the white man to make a sacrifice, then with great bravery he offered to travel in the rear of the helicopter, in the space vacated by the piglets.

Ten minutes later Harry jumped from the helicopter onto the sandy curve of the beach. A few moments later, laden with yellow orchids, he scrambled up the cliff path and followed the river upstream until he spotted the ravaged, burned-out camp.

He looked around the silent clearing and carefully laid the orchids on the ground, then moved slowly around the blackened grass and the charred stumps of the huts. He picked up an empty cigarette pack and a couple of spent cartridges. He could find no trace of the women.

As the helicopter droned back over the headland, the medicine man crouched, terrified but triumphant, in the rear. At the village he descended from the machine with the slow dignity of one who had just visited the gods.

Instructed by Harry, the interpreter asked when the white women had left.

Harry waited, holding his breath. Did they know anything? Would they tell him?

The *luluai* spoke and pointed to the headland.

The interpreter reported. "The women had left in one small boat for an inlet on the headland, just before moonrise two night's previously.

Harry had missed them by less than two days.

Simultaneously overjoyed and disappointed, Harry asked, "How can this be proven?"

The *luluai* clacked an instruction. A youth hurried to his hut. He returned with a small bit of lacy black cloth.

Triumphantly the *luluai* held it up. "Banis b'long susu white missus."

Harry grabbed the tattered black rag.

The interpreter explained that the women had left the bra as a sacrifice for their gods in a sea engine, but their gods had no power to raise the sea engine from the water for them.

Harry reckoned that a tattered, black bra wouldn't be sufficient proof of identity for a hard-nosed insurance assessor.

All right, Harry thought, here goes another one. He unstrapped the plastic digital watch that Mrs. Chang had sold him that morning and said, "I offer this watch for any other thing that belonged to these women."

The watch was passed around the men of the village. The flashing green numbers were much admired. A loud argument followed.

The interpreter murmured, "Man have magic something, no want give you me."

Harry asked for the return of his watch.

More heated discussion followed.

Harry dug in his pocket and held up a pack of playing cards. He flipped the cards from one hand to the other.

The men fell silent. The medicine man held out his hand for the cards.

Harry shook his head.

It was no contest. The medicine man gave an order and a youth ran off. When he returned, he handed something to the headman, who gravely held out two objects in the palm of his hand.

Harry saw an ordinary chrome key ring. Attached to it was a shark's tooth and two rusted keys. One was a door key and one an ignition key. He turned his attention to the other object in the *luluai*'s palm. It was a leather thong with a compass attached. It might have belonged to anybody.

The interpreter pointed to the headland and explained that the women had dropped these articles when they departed.

"Let's get out of here as fast as possible," Harry said. His impatience was great, but he knew the importance of making proper thanks before they departed.

After the interpreter's droning speech, the *luluai* shyly asked if he too could travel in the mixmaster b'long Jesus Christ. Harry knew that if he agreed, the whole village would want a joyride. Apart from precious time lost, the pilot's face had been sour enough when he smelled the medicine man, after the pigs. Harry told the *luluai* that there wasn't enough time to give him a ride now, but perhaps if he visited the village again. . . .

And, showering cigarettes like confetti, the helicopter took off.

"Right," said the jubilant Harry. "Get Mount Ida on the radio. They can plot the area the women could have covered in two days. Head straight out to sea."

"Can't do that, sir," the pilot said. It's breaking the air regulations of every country in the world to go beyond gliding distance of land in a single-engine aircraft with no fixed floats."

"I'm *ordering* you to do it!"

"Sorry, sir. Against regulations."

"Look, this could mean the difference between life and death to those women!"

"Me too, sir. This is a shark-infested sea."

"Get me Mount Ida on the radio!"

Harry took over the headphones to tell Kerry his news. He ordered him to get the Cherokees back and reactivate the air search immediately. Harry added, "Raki didn't tell us this news. Obviously, he doesn't want us to find our people."

"Careful what you say on the air, Harry," Kerry warned. "There's no reason why our friend should report a rumor that may or may not be true."

"To hell with that. God knows how long those women can last in a dinghy. But I'm not making any deal until they're found!"

THURSDAY, MARCH 14, 1985

The rising sun gilded the white dinghy; it smiled upon their pinched faces and thawed their cold bodies inside the soggy khaki uniforms. Nobody spoke until Annie said, "At least we still have some water."

"Four pints isn't going to last long," Patty said. She glared at Silvana. In the darkness of the previous night's storm, Silvana had lost her bailer overboard. She had crawled forward to get another water container from the locker in the bow, and hadn't properly secured the catch. When the women had clambered back into the boat, they saw the locker door hanging open. All the contents of the locker had vanished except a small mirror that had once been in the cluttered junk of Annie's purse—they'd intended to use it for signaling or as a cutting tool—a bamboo container of smoked fish slivers and one coconut.

Annie immediately took an inventory of what remained of their equipment. Everything that had been tied to the thwart had survived; the two flimsy bamboo beds had disappeared, although the ropes that had held them were still attached to the transom. So were the ropes that had bound the rifles—all now missing. The women still had their boots, the oarlocks, the oars, the tin bailer, the empty jerry can and the anchor. They had lost the coils of rattan rope and string but still had plenty left, which had been used to tether objects and people to the boat. All their caps had been lost, but they still had their uniforms. All objects that had been stuffed in their pockets or thrust down their tunics had also survived, including the waterproof rocket flares, but the compass glass had smashed in Patty's hip pocket. Gloomily Patty said, "Probably happened as I left the boat—I remember cracking my hip against the outboard."

"It's not important," Annie said. "Suzy has her neck-thong compass."

But Suzy couldn't find it.

Carey looked at her wrist. Jonathan's watch was still ticking away. She said, "Your Swatchwatch still working, Patty?"

Patty nodded and looked at the dial. "Thursday, March fourteenth, five past six." She shook her right hand. Burned by the rocket, it throbbed painfully. "But we have no idea where we are."

Annie said, "We can steer by the sun, our watches and the stars."

"We *can't* steer," Patty said crossly. "When you dumped the outboard, you also dumped our rudder. We're drifting. We're helpless." She blew on her burned hand, which seemed to soothe it.

"We can tie an oar to that ring on the back of the boat," Annie suggested, "and use it as a rudder."

From her pocket Suzy pulled off the lid of the lemon-drop tin and reported, "We also have two gold watches that don't work, three engagement rings and five wedding rings."

"Maybe we can use them as bait," Patty said.

"After breakfast," Annie decided. "Use the rifle butt to smash the coconut, Silvana. Suzy, collect the milk in the bailer."

Having swallowed a great deal of saltwater during the night, the women were very thirsty. One water container was quickly emptied, as they ate the coconut. They all knew that anyone stranded with only a little water should immediately ration it and drink nothing for the first day while the body lived off the water stored in its tissues.

"Four pints isn't going to last long," Patty said again. Jonathan had told them that a healthy person could live up to thirty days without food, but without water he or she could only live a maximum of ten days, in ideal conditions—and far less in the tropics. "After two or three days without water, we'll become delirious, then die," she said flatly.

"Cheerful, aren't you?" Suzy said. "We do have *some* water." She looked down at her fingers, the tips of which were wrinkled like walnuts.

"We needn't worry about it for four days," Suzy said. They each needed a pint of water a day to keep fit—but they could *survive* on a total of one pint a day, rationed among the five of them. As there had always been plenty of fresh water at the camp, the discipline of water rationing had not been imposed on them.

"You mustn't move about much," Suzy warned, "or you'll lose sweat. Douse your clothes with seawater to keep cool and avoid sunburn, but don't hang your legs overboard because of sharks and barracuda. Let your clothes dry before sunset or you'll catch a chill. Sleep as much as you can."

"Didn't Jonathan also say something about food?" Carey asked.

Suzy nodded. "Digestion uses water, so the less drinking water you have, the less you should eat. Count two parts food to one part water."

"That's fairly easy to arrange," Carey said bitterly.

Nobody laughed. Nobody had said anything to Silvan about leaving the locker catch undone. They all remembere how difficult it had been to move during that raging blac storm. Nevertheless, each woman felt that, had *she* shut th locker, the catch would not have come undone. They als remembered that Silvana had been responsible for lettin Carlos escape. They conveniently forgot the mistakes and wrong decisions that each of them had made during the las four months.

"You mustn't drink urine," Suzy continued, "because it makes you more thirsty. So does seawater. Seawater aggravates your thirst and dehydrates you. You get delirious, then you die."

Carey said, "If you get thirsty, suck a button; it makes you salivate."

They sat in glum silence, until Annie said brusquely, "Two-hour watches, southeast course. Patty takes first watch. Suzy and Carey, start fishing, fast."

"We lost the tackle overboard," Suzy said.

"Unravel the boot laces," Annie suggested. "Make a line of them. Try smoked fish for bait. Or a diamond engagement ring—the sparkle might attract something."

Patty said, "Hey, we need the smoked fish."

"Not unless we have a pint of water each," Suzy said. "So it's best to use it as bait—fast, before we're forced to eat it."

Suzy was soon fishing from the bow, using two hooks improvised out of sharp slivers from the empty bamboo containers. One was tied to a diamond ring, the other was concealed in a bit of smoked fish.

Crouched in the middle of the boat, Annie and Silvana made head coverings, to shield them from the sun. Each woman hacked off the bottom of her tunic, then Annie carefully pulled threads from the fabric to sew with. Silvana made needles by piercing slivers of bamboo with a knife tip to form the eye. Each three-foot length of khaki cotton was cut in half, sewn together so that it was eighteen inches wide—about the size of a hand towel, then halved and sewn into a bag. Annie draped each hood over Silvana's head, to position the eye slits and attach rattan ties. "We look like the Ku Klux Klan," Suzy said.

As the day grew hotter, the glare from the sea gave them all a headache, and they were grateful for the head hoods. Carey appointed herself in charge of the bailer and regularly doused everybody with seawater. The sea was no cooler than lukewarm—sluggish, not very refreshing, and smelling strangely stale. The humidity was over 80 percent. There was no wind and no movement around the exhausted occupants of the tiny dinghy, only that searing arc of orange overhead, indifferent to their misery.

Carey supposed that the boat moved, but it made no discernible progress; it seemed to hang, helpless, on the motionless, silent blue ocean.

By midday Carey's eyes hurt badly. She felt nauseous and the jungle ulcers on her legs were throbbing more than usual, perhaps because of their prolonged immersion in seawater during the night.

"Got a bite!" Suzy reeled in and landed a nine-inch dark brown sea snake.

"Watch out!" Patty warned. "They're dangerous." In silence they all watched the repulsive, wriggling beast.

"I'll use it as bait," Suzy said. With her fish knife, she briskly sliced the snake. "Now you can have your engagement ring back, Carey."

Shortly afterward, Suzy directed Patty toward a patch of seaweed. When they reached it, she carefully hauled every scrap aboard, saying, "You'll have to imagine that you're in a sushi bar."

Annie said, "Check that it's fresh. If it's slimy or limp or smells fishy, we shouldn't eat it. Rub a little between your fingers, to check that it doesn't smell of acid."

Suzy inspected the seaweed and shook a few small creatures from it. "More bait! I'll cut it into strips."

Annie said, "We should try to trap a bird, if we see one. With a snare."

Suzy looked dubious. "Do you think any bird would be crazy enough to get near enough for us to slip a noose over its head?"

Carey held her head in both hands. She gasped, "God, it's hot! I have to lie down, Annie, just for ten minutes. Will you take my line, Silvana?"

Carefully, Carey positioned herself full length in the boat, with her body under the center seat and her head in the shade under the stern transom, between Patty's feet. Silvana and

Annie hunched on the center transom. Suzy leaned with her
back against the forward locker. The clothes, boots and weird
headhoods of the women made them hotter, but protected
them from the glare of the sun and the reflected glare off the
water. Annie wouldn't allow anyone to remove her life jacket.

The heat, Annie thought, was like opening a stove with
your face too close to the door. They huddled in the boat,
longing for dusk when the merciless sun would drop out of
sight behind the horizon and release them from that torturous
white glare.

Suzy said, "Imagine, last night we were throwing rainwater
out of this boat as fast as we could. Do you think it'll rain
again tonight?"

"There's a good chance," said Carey. "We've had two
storms in two days. Why should tonight be different?"

Each woman slept fitfully in the early morning, a brief
escape from the relentless sun. That afternoon Silvana caught
three small, flat white fish. The women wolfed them down
raw, including scales and slime. They kept the bones to suck,
the eyes and entrails to use as bait.

The sea and the sky remained empty.

At four o'clock, each woman drank a single mouthful of
water. Carey still lay, apologetically, in the bottom of the boat,
where she was damped regularly by Suzy.

In the bow, Silvana jumped. *"Filio di putona!* A shark just
pulled the line from my hand!" She looked ruefully at the burn
mark on her palm. "It was so unexpected! And quick!"

"He's not alone." Annie nodded at the sea behind them.
Three large, black, triangular fins could be seen above the
water.

Suzy said, "We've got ourselves an escort."

Annie sighed. "No hands over the side. We'd better stop
fishing."

On the still sea, the boat lay motionless and helpless. Nothing moved. Not the slightest breath of wind ruffled the surface
of the ocean, which shone like a gun barrel in the glare. There

was nothing in sight, just that white-hot circle overhead, burning slowly from one side to the other of the flat, black, glittering ocean, broken only by the sharks' fins cutting lazily through the water.

Suzy asked, "What time is it?"

Patty snapped, "It's ten minutes later than the last time you asked. What the hell does it matter? You can watch the sun, can't you? Knowing what time it is won't make the sun go down faster."

Huddled in the dinghy, the women moved as little as possible, because the gunwales of the now-lightened boat were still only six inches above the water.

The sun beat orange-red through Carey's closed eyelids, and her temples throbbed to a steady beat. There was no sound except that of the sea gently slapping the hull.

"Carey, it's your turn on watch," Annie said. She'd considered letting Carey off, but had a nasty feeling that they might all be similarly inert within twenty-four hours and she didn't want to set a precedent.

Carey pulled herself up with difficulty and stared at the water. "They're waiting for the picnic," she said thickly.

Seven dorsal fins now surrounded the boat, all swimming at the same slow, steady speed.

"That one to the left must be twenty feet long, maybe more," Carey said. "He's easily twice as long as this boat."

"They won't bother us if we don't do anything." Annie sounded more sure than she felt. "They're just curious. They won't attack us if we don't provoke them, and if there's no blood."

All the women knew their shark drill. If you found yourself in the water with a shark, you didn't splash and you moved as slowly as possible or your vibrations would attract the shark's attention. You didn't try to swim away, because you'd never move fast enough to escape a shark; a shark's top speed was over sixty-three feet a *second*. Jonathan had drilled them never to evacuate in the sea, and never to enter the water if they were bleeding from any cuts or at the time of their menstrual cycle—because sharks love blood. They can scent it from a great distance, and their blood lust drives them to a feeding frenzy.

The boat suddenly jerked into the air.

"The bastard bumped us!" Carey yelled.

The stern jerked up again. As the boat tipped to starboard, Carey grabbed the top of the oar with both hands and rammed it down over the stern as hard as she could.

"Ha! I hit the bastard!"

"Carey, put down that oar!" Annie called out sharply. "Sit down here with us, or they'll *all* bump us. *Carey!* . . . Suzy, stop her!"

Suzy scrambled to the stern, grabbed Carey around the waist and pulled her backward. As Carey crashed down on top of Suzy, the oar flew over the back of her head, hit Annie, then went flying overboard.

"Leave it!" Annie yelled, clapping her hand to her eye. The oar was tethered to the dinghy.

Carey started to cry.

Suzy said, "Annie, is your eye . . .?"

Annie said, "It doesn't matter, really."

Carey snapped, "Oh, stop being so *saintly*, Annie. It's driving me crazy."

Annie said, "It's all right, I understand."

Carey burst out, "And stop being so goddamned *understanding!*"

"*Stop this!*" Silvana cried, so loudly that they all turned in surprise. "We're all on edge, because of our thirst, because of this dreadful sun and those *villiaccos*." She swore again as she pointed to the glistening black fins stalking the dinghy. "We all know how to survive in the jungle, but we know nothing about the sea. *So we must learn*. We've done so much already. We must now do a little bit *more*."

"We'll have another sip of water," Annie decided. "Let's try to hang on—and shut up—until sunset. Then we'll be able to think better, decide what to do."

"Do we have any choice?" Patty said.

"You know there's always a choice," Annie said shortly.

After sunset, in the few minutes before dark, the women drank a little more water.

They all knew what it's like to feel thirsty, but they had never imagined the physical agony of dying of thirst. It was a raging, maddening desire that consumed the mind. The pain of hunger had passed, but the agony of thirst got steadily worse. On the tropical sea, they breathed in hot air, and as their faces were covered with hoods, they breathed out *hotter* air. Their throats were dry, their swelling tongues were thick in their mouths, their lips started to crack and so did their voices. The merciless sun slowly robbed them of their will and their humanity, leaving them nothing but an exhausted body that longed only for water: they could—literally—think about nothing else. Worse still, they were surrounded by temptation, but they knew that the punishment was absolute and inexorable. If you drink saltwater, you die fairly fast and in agony.

Annie saw to it that they drank their water ration very slowly, using the water only to moisten their lips and throats, then gargling it before swallowing.

The ate a little fish, then they lay inert in the boat and stared up at the moon.

"Maybe we should keep ourselves awake as long as possible at night," Silvana suggested. "Then we will sleep by day, and avoid the torture of the sun."

In an effort to distract themselves, they recalled their favorite smells. This started off well enough with pinewoods, wet roses and mown hay, but when Annie wistfully said "baby hair," Silvana started to cry.

Patty flung a sinewy arm around Silvana, and the silence was broken only by the gentle lap of the waves, as the women fought back tears. They had set out so well equipped, and with such high hopes. Now they had next to nothing—hardly even hope.

Crouching in the stern, Carey felt ashamed. She burst out, "How did this happen? How *can* we have fallen apart in only twenty-four hours?"

FRIDAY, MARCH 15

At sunrise on their second day at sea, there were only three pints of water left. The day followed the same pattern as the previous one, except that Annie kept to their strict ration of water.

Suddenly Suzy screamed, "I can't stand this anymore! I can't stand this stiff-upper-lip stuff! Don't you all realize that *this* time, we really *are* going to die? We're going to be eaten by those goddamn sharks!" She pointed wildly to the black fins that surrounded the dinghy.

"She's right," Silvana sobbed. "I can't take any more either! I just want to go to sleep and never wake up!" She shook her fists at the sky and shrieked, "How much *more* can we take? How much *more* do we have to suffer? *Why?*"

"Shut up!" Carey croaked. "Save your strength. Save your voice. Don't waste your saliva."

"Carey's right," Patty gasped. "Every move you make now will shorten your life."

"Think about your children," Annie urged. "Think of your families. *Don't give up!*"

All day they sweltered, becalmed under a blazing sun. As they grew weaker and more enervated, they were all also plagued by throbbing headaches and waves of nausea.

They ate the last of the fish and most of the seaweed. They dared not fish again, for fear of attracting the closer attention of the sharks that swam beside the boat. They huddled together, waiting only for the sun to drop out of sight. Heat had driven the life from their bones.

Below the boat, the sea looked green and blue, deep and cool, inviting as an April stream. With her chin on the gunwale, Suzy gazed into the depths of the ocean.

"Don't look down," Carey said, tugging at Suzy's pants. "Your turn to lie flat."

Suzy took her turn in the bottom of the boat, while Carey listlessly replaced Patty. There was no need to steer; the boat floated obediently on the flat water. Occasionally Carey skulled over the stern to get it moving slightly and correct their course. Disturbing its own reflection, the boat glided through the water and its image broke into a thousand pieces.

The women waited for sunset, the dark, and their water ration.

Blood orange, the sun fell toward the horizon. A glittering crimson path shimmered from it to the dinghy across the mirrored surface of the sea.

That evening, it was harder for them to talk. They wanted to talk in order to keep awake, but their lips were cracked and bleeding, and anyway they had nothing to say to each other.

Talk petered out half an hour after sunset.

Patty said bitterly, "Well, Carey, now we're totally self-reliant. How do you like it?"

"You know this isn't what I meant by self-reliance," Carey said.

Patty said tartly, "If this isn't, I don't know what is."

"Go on, Carey," Patty taunted. "Tell us how inner strength and self-confidence are going to help us out of this mess."

Carey said crossly, "Self-confidence is simply knowing what you've been capable of in the past, so you're pretty certain you can deal with that sort of situation in the future. And it's also being prepared to stick your neck out just a bit farther. If you can swim a hundred yards, then you can probably swim much farther, and if it's vital for you to swim half a mile, then you probably will."

"How about seventy miles?" Patty asked.

Suzy scowled and nobody spoke for the next ten minutes.

Suzy broke the silence. "How many minutes are there in a day?"

Immediately Carey responded, "One thousand four hundred and forty."

Silence fell again.

At nine o'clock, in desperation, Annie promised a water ration to those who were still awake at midnight. Everyone immediately grew more alert.

Annie urged, "We *must* keep talking! Think of all those hours we slept this morning, think of the sun we missed!"

Nobody spoke.

Annie said, "We should be thinking positively, and you all know it. *Please* don't lie there like lumps. *Don't* give up. We must keep talking, we mustn't go to sleep! Let's   . let's decide what we're going to do when we get home."

Carey immediately stirred. She said, "I'll never be a Mies van der Rohe, but I'm an architect like a gardener is a gardener." She had always been secretly amazed that she got paid for doing something that she loved. "I just want to get back to my job." And family, she added silently, for family talk was forbidden.

Suzy said, "If I can persuade Brett to try . . ." It was a slip of the tongue, and they all winced. She continued hurriedly, "I thought maybe I'd start a fashion-sportswear boutique. How about you, Annie?"

"You'll laugh when I tell you," Annie said. "I'd like to study nutrition. . . . There, I knew you'd laugh. Seriously, I've seen what mileage we got out of our bodies once we no longer took them for granted. Until three days ago we were all in better shape than we'd been for years."

"Speak for yourself," Patty said.

"You've always been fit," Annie agreed. "But that's what interests me now. Looking after the body."

Patty said, "I'd like to use my sports ability." She had thought of starting a small athletics school for handicapped children. If Silvana could open a hospital in Fiji, why couldn't Patty do something equally useful, but closer to home.

Silvana said, "If we get out of this alive, I swear I'll never let anyone else make me miserable. Arthur used to say that dependency destroys you, and now I see what he meant. You can't have your own identity if you're dependent, if you're part of someone else's identity."

Carey sat up. "We've all got a new identity. Whether we like it or not, nothing's going to be the same when they find out, back in Pittsburgh, that we're killers. Can you imagine how they'll behave to us at parties? At charity committee meetings? Church gatherings?"

Annie said, "No one back home will ever know. We'll *never* tell. It'll be like Alcoholics Anonymous. We *all* have everything to lose if anyone tells."

Patty said, "Suzy didn't kill anyone, so *she* won't have anything to lose. But the rest of us will always be frightened that someone will tell. We'll *always* live with that anxiety! We'll never be able to escape from it, not for the *whole of our lives*. We'll *always* have it around our necks!"

"It's bound to get out," Carey agreed wearily. She was staring up to the sky, where huge, tropical stars were scattered like daisies on a black field. She added, "For a start, how do we explain these uniforms? The Waterfall Bay Army Surplus Store?"

"We couldn't avoid doing what we did," Annie reminded them.

"Carey's right," Silvana sobbed. "They'll hate us."

"Only because we're a *female* gang of killers," Annie said bitterly. "Men kill people all the time."

Patty sat up. "Okay, so we killed some people who were trying to kill us. In *self-defense!* What we *should* be worrying about is how we're going to survive, not what they're going to say about us at the coffee klatches back in Pittsburgh."

"It's not up to us anymore," Suzy said. "What else *can* we do? We can't produce food or water out of thin air."

"What do sailors do if their ship sinks?" Carey asked.

"At least we're in a boat, not hanging on to a plank in the water," Annie said.

"Sometimes sailors survive in lifeboats for weeks," Patty said.

"Well, how do they *do* it?" Carey asked.

"You don't want to know," Patty said.

"Don't be stupid, of course we do."

"Cannibalism," Patty said.

"For God's sake, be serious," Carey said irritably.

Patty spoke faster than usual. "Sailors have *always* done it. It's *still* legal at sea. Apparently, you get used to the idea very fast. The little cabin boy always gets eaten first—even if they have to kill him—and the huge, beefy first mate survives to the last."

"You're not *serious?*" Carey asked, though she did not believe for one moment that Patty was.

"How come you know all that stuff?" Suzy asked.

"Charley told me," Patty said. "Nexus had a problem, a few years back, with a prospecting team in some Australian desert . . . Gibson, I think. Seven Nexus guys got lost in the desert and only two came out."

"I remember that," Carey said.

Patty said, "What you don't know is that a rescue team found five bodies buried in the sand; they still had their heads, hands and feet—all the skinny parts." In spite of the steaming heat, Patty shivered in the dark. "Charley had to hush it up. He had a lot of legal stuff to read up on, over one weekend. There was a book on some British sailors who survived by cannibalism. That fascinated Charley. He read some of it out loud to me. I thought it sounded pretty repulsive at the time."

"I find it pretty repulsive now," Carey said. "And I don't *believe* it's legal. You misunderstood what Charley said."

"Cannibalism certainly *is* legal," Patty insisted. "And not only at sea, Charley said."

"Yes," Silvana agreed. "Napoleon's soldiers ate each other in the retreat from Moscow in 1812, and there have always been rumors about Stalingrad in 1940."

"And starvation situations on polar expeditions," Patty added.

"Prospectors did it in the West," Carey said. "During the gold rush, some guy called the Colorado Man Eater ate five of his friends in a blizzard."

Suzy yawned. "I hope he had indigestion afterward."

"That's right!" Annie said. "Remember those early settlers going West who were snowed in at the Donner Pass and had to eat their dead to live through the winter?"

"Suzy, sit up!" Carey said. "Keep awake or I'll pinch you. We must sleep in the daytime or that heat will drive us crazy."

Silvana said, "Remember when that plane carrying a South American soccer team crashed in the Andes? To save their lives, the survivors ate the corpses of their friends."

Annie nodded. "They were given Communion as soon as they were rescued."

"What's so terrible about being eaten, once you're dead?" Patty asked quietly.

"But none of *us* is dead," Suzy said. "So why are *we* talking about cannibalism?" She yawned again.

SATURDAY, MARCH 16

The sun peered above the black horizon, casting a faint light on the white shell floating on the dark water, still encircled by twenty-foot sharks.

Cautiously, Annie sat up, very stiff after a third restless night at sea. Suzy was talking loudly in her sleep, barking disjointed words. The women had taken off their hoods to sleep, but maybe they should have left them on, Annie thought, maybe then they wouldn't wake at sunrise.

Annie stared out at the glittering water. They had two pint containers of water and a bit of dried fish. They had no idea of their position. They were lost at sea. She thought of the interminable hours that lay ahead, of the suffocating heat, of the enervating humidity so high that it was like trying to breathe in a steam-filled bathroom.

All day, they suffered under that inexorable glare.

At sundown, the suffering merely changed.

The yellow moon illuminated water that shone like black oil, endless to the horizon whichever way they looked. The only sound was the soft murmur of the water under the keel and an occasional soft splash as one of the sharks rolled.

"I can't stand much more of this," gasped Silvana.

"Just a little longer," Annie urged. "By now we *must* be clear of the southern tip of Paui. We *must* have covered, say, thirty miles in three days."

Lethargically steering with the oar, Patty said, "We've got to keep ourselves occupied or we'll just pass out. We should be thinking what we'll do if . . . Okay, Annie, *when* we get back."

Huddled in the bottom of the boat, Carey said, "We're going to get revenge. We're going to see that that bastard Raki is punished for what he's done."

"But we have no proof," Silvana said. "It will be our word against his."

"They'll have to listen to the wives of *five* Nexus executives—all with the same story," Patty said.

Suzy said, "The media will do all the work for us. Just wait till I get in front of all those mikes—ABC, CBS, NBC . . ."

Silvana wasn't convinced. "Even if the whole world knows, it won't make any difference. There'll perhaps be some political argument, but nothing will alter on Paui—not where business is concerned. We'll just be an embarrassment to Nexus. Nexus won't be able to do business on Paui anymore."

"To hell with Nexus," Carey said.

"Maybe Nexus already knows what happened," Suzy said optimistically. In her heart, she *knew* Brett had escaped, but she didn't like to mention this to the other women, who had all seen their men brutally killed. Suzy nursed her hope to her heart. She was going to make it up to Brett. She'd even give him kids. Maybe the steady, reliable, boring sort made the best fathers . . .

"If Nexus knew what happened, they would have found us by now," Patty said.

They all fell silent, each remembering the reality of their position. They had no food left and only one pint of water. That would only last them one more day.

Patty croaked, "We're going to die tonight. All of us. I can feel it. The boat will overturn while we're asleep."

Suzy started to cry. "I don't care," she whimpered. "I *want* to die. I can't stand this thirst any longer. We're going to die of thirst before morning."

Carey was too exhausted to cry, but she was thinking she couldn't stand the pain in her legs much longer. Her deep jungle ulcers now smelled offensive as well as being painful.

Silvana said, "Nothing seems real anymore. The night isn't real and the sun isn't real. It's like a nightmare. None of *you* seem real. How do I know those sharks are real?" She, too, started to sob.

In spite of all their efforts, shortly after midnight all the women were asleep except for Annie, who was on watch and steering. But was there any point to being on watch? As Annie pinched her arms to keep awake, she felt the same desperate despair as the other women. Suddenly, she knew that they *wouldn't* survive.

In the dim starshine, Annie could just see the darker outline of somebody moving in the boat, but even though the boat was so small she couldn't see who it was.

Annie heard the unmistakable sound of somebody drinking, somebody lapping water like a dog.

Someone was stealing the last container of water.

Annie yelled, *"Stop that!"* She prodded Patty, asleep at her feet.

Patty sat up.

"Go check the water container in the locker, Patty, and bring it to me," Annie said.

Without a word, Patty crawled forward.

Annie thought, She's taking a long time to grab it. Why?

Again, Annie heard the sound of someone lapping water.

"*Patty!*" she yelled.

Patty crawled back over the sleeping bodies and handed Annie the container. She said, "For God's sake, hang on to that thing, Annie. I don't trust myself with it."

"I heard you drink!" Annie said sharply, shaking the container. It seemed to feel a little lighter than it should.

"Well, I didn't!" snapped Patty. "But may I ask why *you* want it?"

"I'm responsible for the water," Annie snapped back. Two weeks of responsibility suddenly seemed enough. She said, "Look, I'm fed up with being leader. Why don't *you* take a turn? See what it feels like."

"Oh, shut up. Don't wake me up again." Patty settled down, licking her dry, cracked lips with her dry tongue. Her throat felt like sandpaper; her last sip of water had been at sundown.

Annie felt her resolution sway slightly. Would it matter? Who would know? She deserved it, didn't she? *She* was on watch, while they were sleeping. Inside Annie's head, a friendly, comforting voice agreed with her. Annie felt reassured, she felt a little light-headed, as if an invisible power were gently soothing her conscience, absolving her.

Annie shipped the oar with care. With both hands, she clutched the bamboo container to her breast. Stealthily, she prized off the top of the container and tilted it to her lips. Just one sip . . .

She couldn't stop. Panting for breath, she realized what she had done.

Again, she lifted the container to her burning mouth. She'd say that it had only been half-full.

Sharply, Annie lifted her head.

Someone else was awake.

Someone was moving.

That someone might see Annie, silhouetted against the sky, drinking from the container.

Annie waited. Again, she heard the lapping sound of someone drinking.

But Annie had the only container of water . . . *so someone must be drinking seawater from the bailer!*

"Wake up, everyone!" Annie slammed the top back on the water container and kicked Patty, hard.

A groan was followed by a sleepy "Wassa matter?"

"Get forward and check, Patty! Someone's drinking seawater!" Annie croaked. *"Stop her! Quickly!"*

Patty moved to the next figure curled in the bottom of the dinghy. The head turned away as Patty's fingers touched her cheek, but not before Patty had felt wet lips.

Quickly, Patty shook the shoulder. She yelled, *"Suzy! Sit up! Stop that!"*

Huddled in the fetal position, Suzy refused to budge. She pretended to be asleep even when Patty kicked her.

Patty crawled back to Annie. "It was Suzy."

Annie was astonished. "But she knows how dangerous it is to drink seawater!"

Patty shrugged her shoulders.

Both women again heard the lapping noise.

Patty yelled, "Put that bailer *down*, Suzy."

A small voice wailed, "I couldn't help it, you guys."

In the dark, Patty crawled forward and tried to wrench the bailer from Suzy's hands. Suzy put up a struggle.

Patty yelled, *"Carey!* Suzy's drinking seawater. And I think Annie's stealing our water ration. *Wake up!"*

Carey quickly woke.

The boat was rocking. Annie and Suzy were both crying.

Carey yelled, "Give it to me, Annie! Or I'll shove you overboard!"

Whimpering, guilty, as obedient as a child who's caught with his hand in the cookie jar, Annie handed over the water container.

Carey groped for some rattan; she bound it round and round the container, then knotted it tightly. She said, "Nobody will be able to open this without our being able to see it. Annie, you bitch, you'll get no water tomorrow."

Annie wept with mortification. She thought of middle-aged shoplifters saying in court, "I don't know what came over me." Annie knew how they felt.

She was bitterly ashamed of herself.

SUNDAY, MARCH 17

At the end of their fourth night in the dinghy, the blood-red sun slowly crept over the edge of the black sea.

Everyone in the little boat was already awake. Nobody was speaking to Annie. Carey was still trying to find out how much seawater Suzy had drunk, but Suzy only whimpered incoherently.

Tolerance and friendship had vanished overnight, with the water drunk by Annie. Now distrust was clearly visible in their weary, sunken eyes.

Tormented by thirst and raw, open sores, crammed into a tiny space, unable to move without rocking the boat, adrift on the empty sea under the searing sun, the women faced a slow, agonizing death from thirst and exposure, or a relatively quick but revolting death if a shark overturned the boat.

They sat in silence, listening to the faint sounds of the glassy water.

Patty gasped, "For God's sake, Carey, don't tap on the side of the boat, it's driving me crazy."

Carey took no notice; dull-eyed, she was watching Suzy, who lay moaning in the bottom of the boat. They were all condemned to listen to Suzy's monotonous babble.

". . . She must have been asking for it. No, no, no! . . . If she doesn't like it, she can always leave . . . No, no, no! . . . They all like a little rough stuff . . . What's sexy about . . . Ruptured liver . . . Broken nose . . ."

Patty rasped, *"Carey, stop her or I'll gag her."*

638

Carey turned to look with hatred at Patty. "I'll kick you out of this boat, if you try."

They glared at each other, then Patty backed down. "Sorry," she muttered.

Annie caught Patty's eye and realized that Patty also knew that the exhausted, half-dead women in the boat now had very little chance.

Patty looked away from Annie. Every woman in the boat was deliberately ignoring Annie.

Another day of unendurable heat and thirst.

After the midday sip of water, Patty looked at Suzy, curled up in the bow babbling.

Patty croaked to Annie, "Those boys in the Andes. How did they justify it?"

"They felt they had a moral duty to stay alive, by any means at their disposal," Annie said. "They argued that once one of them was dead the soul had left his body and was in heaven with God. The body, which the soul had discarded, was consequently just a carcass—just meat, like steak in a supermarket."

"So that was their moral let-out." Patty nodded wearily.

Annie added, "They believed God wanted them to live or they would have been killed in the accident. They believed that God had provided them with means to stay alive—the bodies of their friends."

Patty said, "Didn't the priest say afterward that they hadn't sinned?"

Silvana nodded.

"They went to Communion without confessing, didn't they?" Patty asked. "Because *in extremis,* the Church allows it."

Silvana nodded. "But I can't." Slowly, she shook her hooded head.

Patty said, "If I died, I'd *want* you to eat me. I wouldn't want you to waste my body on the goddamn sharks."

Silvana said, "I won't do it. And Carey won't let you."

Patty whispered, "You have to do it *fast.* As soon as the

639

person dies, you have to drink the blood before it congeals. So you *must* make up your mind beforehand."

Suzy was mumbling to herself; she had been violently sick, so now she was dehydrated, babbling nonstop and no longer capable of understanding what was happening. They were all surprised that Suzy's deterioration had been so rapid.

Hours passed. The women lay beneath the white, burning sun and it sucked them dry.

As Suzy groaned and gasped for breath, Carey stroked her forehead, gently and protectively. Carey glared at the other women. She was still the strongest woman in the dinghy.

Their tongues were swollen, protruding from black, cracked lips, their eyes were sunken in their gaunt and haggard faces, the backs of their hands were blistered, their feet and legs were red and swollen.

They had all developed saltwater sores on the backsides, and found it painful to sit or to move. After excessive exposure to that relentless glare from sky and sea, their eyes were red and sore. They were all constipated and found it painful to urinate. They no longer had the strength to use the bailer.

Twilight brought a slight relief, but the air remained hot and close. The women gasped for each breath as if they had been running a race.

A few words were exchanged at sundown as they wetted their lips for the last time.

Annie was not allowed to share the last of the water.

The stars hung low in the velvet-black tropical sky. Below them the women sprawled in the dinghy, sucking buttons from their uniforms to stimulate saliva.

For four months these women had struggled to survive. They had been inventive, resourceful and brave. They had learned to use their strength, and found new strengths. They had come to support and rely on each other as they faced their common dangers. Patiently, they had fought hunger, sickness and fatigue. With determination, they had battled against panic, fear and stress. They had endured their ordeals with toughness and resilience.

Now, each woman thought only of herself—and it was difficult to overcome inertia and indifference to do even that. In only a few days, their little group had disintegrated.

Annie had broken down morally. Nobody was sure whether Patty's suggestion was sensible, wicked or mad. Suzy was mentally finished and near death.

And as the white stars blinked down from the black sky, they all realized that, at some point, one of them was going to be left alive—and alone—in this boat.

Patty waited until darkness. She couldn't bring herself to suggest it in daylight. But then, through cracked and bleeding lips, she whispered again, hoarsely and urgently, in Silvana's ear. "It's better than letting the sharks eat us. This way, some of us will *still* have a chance. Soon, we'll all be too weak to move. We *must* decide now."

Silvana looked at Patty. "How *could* you?"

Patty whispered, "At least I'm not suggesting . . ."

"Just *what* are you *not* suggesting?" Silvana hissed.

Patty whispered, "They used to . . . help someone to die. If one of the sailors in a lifeboat was obviously dying . . . if he was going to die anyway . . . then they helped him to die. It stopped that person's suffering, and meant that the others could live."

"What if nobody was obviously dying?" Silvana asked.

"Then they all drew lots. One sacrificed himself for the rest."

Silvana whispered, "I'm never going to kill anyone, *ever again*, and I don't want anyone else to kill me."

Patty croaked, "How can it be wrong if it's legal? And I promise you it's legal—if everyone agrees, and lots are fairly drawn. The guy who draws the shortest straw is the one who dies, and the longest straw is the executioner."

Carey said, "Suzy's in no condition to agree to anything, let alone draw straws."

Patty jumped. She had thought Carey was asleep.

In desperation, Patty persisted. "It's almost painless. In that English case that Charley studied, the captain did it with his penknife. He slit the cabin boy's jugular vein, then caught the blood in a bailer. It's the blood that saves you from dying of thirst, although it's salty. The first mate had been going to hold the cabin boy's feet if he struggled, but he didn't struggle or even cry out. And he didn't seem to suffer. He just died quietly, in five seconds. And so the rest of them lived." She paused, then said quietly, "Suzy's going to die soon."

642

FRIDAY, MARCH 15, 1985

"Radio message for you, Harry," the helicopter pilot said, and handed him the headphones.

Harry heard a tinny version of Kerry's voice. "Harry? We've got visitors. Raki wants to see you. There's a captain waiting here, to escort you to the palace. He's got a letter for you. Won't let me open it."

"Can he hear what you're saying, Kerry?"

"No, he's in my office. I'm in the radio room," Kerry said.

"I'm not coming back, Kerry," Harry said firmly. "I'm not going to stop this search. Every minute is vital. I'm going to tell the pilot to take me back to Paradise Bay. You can send Johno there to pick me up. I should have thought of that in the first place."

"What's got into you, Harry?" Kerry sounded anxious. "You know we can't ignore a summons from Raki at this point. He's got the power to kick us out, remember? You can talk to him about this news of the women. But what do you suppose they'll say back in Pittsburgh if Jerry hears that you refused to visit the President?"

"Raki already knows about the women, but doesn't want *us* to know about the women, so I don't suppose he'll want to discuss it," Harry said tersely. "But I'm going to find those

643

women before I do anything else—no matter who tries to stand in my way."

"I *strongly* suggest that you don't make trouble for yourself, Harry."

"Look, we've just gotten proof that the Nexus women took to sea in a dinghy two days ago from the Paradise Bay area," Harry said firmly. "So I'm going back there."

Kerry's voice in Harry's earphone said, "That's wonderful news, Harry. But we don't need you *personally* to go on with the search. You're not a pilot. Your absence won't hold it up."

The pilot said laconically, "Not enough fuel to get back to Paradise Bay. We're only seven minutes' flying time from the Ida strip."

"Have Johno waiting at the airstrip with maps and charts," Harry said to Kerry, "and keep Raki's captain away from me until the three of us have decided on the search plan. I'm not going to leave this aircraft until that's finalized."

He was about to sign off, when he added, "By the way, Kerry, please immediately announce a one-hundred-thousand-dollar reward for the women in the dinghy—*alive*. They're at sea now, so Raki *can't* stop us from offering a reward. I want it broadcast as quickly and as widely as possible, giving Johno's calculated search area. Put it out on commercial stations and shortwave, on shipping and local frequencies, throughout the area, in English and in Pidgin."

Kerry said, "I can't do that! That will have to be authorized by Jerry Pearce."

"Okay," Harry said, "call him up. You have seven minutes to get Jerry's answer."

Kerry said, "You'll have another Dunkirk out there—an army of small craft with hopeful treasure hunters, fishermen and tourists."

"That's what I'm counting on "

When the Bell landed on the Mount Ida airstrip, Kerry and Johno were waiting. As soon as the rotors stopped, they ran out to the helicopter. The pilot jumped down. Kerry and Johno jumped in.

Johno said, "What's Roger looking so sour about?"

"I'm pissed off with him for refusing to sea-search," Harry said. "Which means we only have one aircraft available."

"He's within his rights," Kerry said.

"Did you talk to Jerry Pearce?" Harry asked.

"Yes," Kerry said. "He told me on no account to offer a reward. Those were his instructions. I'm sorry." Kerry didn't add that Jerry had yelled, "Can't that jackass Scott just *drop* it? I told him to get back here right away! As far as we're concerned, the search is *over!* What Harry Scott should be asking us for at this moment is a letter of reference!"

"Okay, Kerry," Harry said. "I'll pay the reward with my own money. I'll put a call through to Al Kinsman, the manager of Barclays main branch in Sydney. It'll only take two minutes to fix it. Meanwhile, Johno can figure out where to search."

Johno unrolled the chart on his knees and looked at Harry. "Frankly, I don't think there's much hope of finding these women. You just can't cover that much area with any success. You know a sea search is much tougher than it sounds. The sea is fluid, so the search grid area on your chart is always moving—and expanding." Johno shook his head. "Every day you don't find your missing people, the search grid has to be enlarged to allow for winds and currents, as well as the distance that the missing people might have traveled on that day."

He pointed at the chart. "I reckon they couldn't have gone further than fifteen miles west of Paradise Bay, but it's very difficult to forecast accurately the position of a dinghy after a tropical storm, because the strength and direction of the wind alters in an unpredictable manner. So I've allowed a hundred percent safety margin; the search grid will extend thirty miles west and a hundred miles south of Paradise Bay. Allowing for the current, the search area is three thousand square miles. That's a lot of sea. And all of it is constantly moving."

"And remember, the boat itself is only twelve foot. Easy to

miss," Kerry added, "and a white dinghy can easily look like the crest of a wave.

Johno said, "You're a sailor, Harry, right? So you know about currents."

Harry nodded.

"I don't," said Kerry. "What do we need to know?"

Johno stabbed a finger at the chart, to an area south of Paradise Bay. "They're drifting in a southeast, one-knot current, which means they'll travel twenty-six miles every twenty-four hours. That second storm probably blew them an extra ten miles or so down the coast. If I were to guess, I'd say they were about fifty miles southeast of Paradise Bay at the moment. Unless for some reason they've been deliberately rowing against the current or keeping to the coastline."

Johno placed the grid—a sheet of transparent plastic divided into squares—over his chart. "That grid follows the southeast current, and each of those little squares represents one hour's flying time—that's around fifty-five flying hours minimum search time." He looked at Harry. "I'd say we have about a thirty percent chance of success. But the more people out looking, the more chance there is of finding them, no doubt about that."

"How are you going to start?" Harry asked.

"I'll spend this afternoon doing an overview at two thousand feet."

"I'll get the Cherokees back," Harry said.

As Johno had no means of knowing that the dinghy had an outboard motor, he had not allowed for that in his calculations. The outboard had taken the dinghy eight miles due west, then the boat had been carried a further twenty-eight miles west by the four-hour storm, making her subsequent position thirty-six miles west of Paradise Bay—six miles further west of Johno's search area.

He was about to search in the wrong place.

* * *

The sun hammered down on the back of their heads as Harry and Kerry walked toward the mine offices, where the Paui army captain stood, waiting to escort Harry to the Presidential Palace.

Kerry pulled a sheet of cheap tan paper from his pocket, and said, "By the way, Harry, I've got something that you ought to look at. That union leader, Mindo, broke out of jail last night. Or, more accurately, his jailers unlocked him, then disappeared with him."

"Where did they go?"

"He's thought to have escaped to the Central Mountains with twenty-nine armed men. Remember, Mindo's father is a powerful chief, so no doubt he's waiting for him, with more fighting men. It's rumored that some of Raki's lower ranks have defected too."

"Good for them," Harry said. "Mindo's a born leader."

Kerry held out the flimsy sheet of paper. "This is Mindo's manifesto, printed while he was in jail. Although God knows who's going to read it, when only fourteen percent of the population is literate."

"It's in English," Harry said, surprised.

"A smart propaganda move for the U.N. and the Australians," Kerry said. "There's also a Pidgin version, of course."

Harry quickly read Mindo's proposed policy. "Most of this is reasonable, Kerry. Mindo clearly realizes that there will be no foreign investment in Paui if foreign technicians are too frightened to live here," Harry said. "I'm glad he says why the hostage and ransom business must be stopped immediately."

"It's going to be more difficult to stop the inter-tribal captures," Kerry said.

"Do you reckon that's what happened to our lot, Kerry?"

"They aren't the first whites to disappear in a Third World country. But if *our* people are hostages, they were probably kidnapped for cash. Then maybe something went wrong."

As Kerry opened the door to the office, Harry handed back the crumpled manifesto.

The waiting army captain stepped forward, saluted and handed over a letter. With some reluctance, he prepared to leave Kerry's air-conditioned outer office.

Harry said, "I have to make a short telephone call before we leave. Okay?"

The captain nodded and gratefully returned to his chair.

When he got through to his bank manager in Sydney, Harry explained what he wanted, then said, "Kerry's not authorized to handle this. Mind you, Kerry's the salt of the earth."

"So he's the salt of the earth?" Al Kinsman repeated.

"Yeah, salt of the earth," Harry said, "but he can't do this, Al, so I want you to handle it for me."

Satisfied that their password 'salt of the earth,' had been spoken, challenged and repeated, Al Kinsman immediately agreed that the bank would call the press services right away and announce the reward from their Sydney office.

Seeing Kerry's alarmed face, Harry said grimly, "It's okay, they can't fire me." Mentally he added, And as long as I have Arthur and Roddy's watches Jerry Pearce won't dare to do a quick deal with Raki behind my back.

But from now on Jerry was clearly going to be in charge of Nexus—and Jerry would always see Harry as the man who had openly challenged his authority and then flouted it. There was no future for Harry at Nexus. But Harry had already decided that he didn't want Nexus in *his* future. What he wanted right now was Annie, and the rest of his life could wait.

When Harry arrived at the palace he was taken once again to the dark, overfurnished room where he had witnessed the unpleasant accident suffered by Raki's late wife.

Upon the Persian carpet stood an ornate, nineteenth-century gilt trimmed French sofa. Directly in front of it was an old-fashioned plate camera on a tripod. The photographer's head was hidden beneath the black cloth and only his outdated flared slacks could be seen.

President Raki, splendid in a scarlet military uniform, sat on the sofa. Beside him wriggled a plump young girl with frizzy hair. She wore a long blue satin dress with puffed sleeves. In one hand she held a bottle of Coca-Cola, an expensive luxury on Paui, and with the other she popped peanuts into the President's mouth. As he caught a peanut, Raki's pink, gleaming, wide-open mouth reminded Harry of a hippo's.

The obsequious photographer finished changing his plate, but Raki waved him aside, saying, "You've shot quite enough film for one official photograph." Raki had a surprisingly high, abrupt laugh.

The little black sex kitten continued to eat peanuts and ignore Harry, but Raki nodded to him. "They should have shown you to my office, Mr. Scott, not here." Raki picked up a pair of dark glasses from a table. Harry noticed that one of the side pieces contained a miniature transistor radio. Raki liked his toys. Harry knew that Westerners underestimated Raki because of these exuberant, childlike, vulgar touches, but to Harry they conveyed a sense of ludicrous menace.

As he followed Raki over the stained bright purple carpet in the corridor, Harry noticed that the diamond-laced ostrichskin shoes had lifts. Once in his office, Raki sat behind his desk with his hands clasped. He did not ask Harry to sit, so Harry stood, knowing that he was supposed to feel like a small boy quivering before the principal.

Raki said, "I hear you visited Katanga this morning."

Harry nodded. He knew that he was now being watched at all times.

"And what did you learn?"

"I learned that five white women left two days ago in a dinghy, Mr. President."

Harry was careful not to appear sarcastic or angry. His tone of voice was neutral and respectful. He knew how quickly the President's mood could turn from affability to irritation, to paranoid suspicion, to violent rage.

"There was proof only that outlaws had camped in a sacred

place," Raki said. "There was no proof that the outlaws were white or female. False rumors circulate constantly on this island. It's a terrible thing."

Harry didn't ask what sort of outlaw wore a black lace bra.

"I've called you here to finalize the date for signing the Heads of Agreement," the President said.

Harry said, "We have not yet agreed to the contract terms, or the details of the special arrangements. As you know, my colleagues in Pittsburgh are not used to this type of negotiation. It takes time for them to arrange such payments. Our laws are strict."

For half an hour Harry smoothly stalled the negotiations, without seeming to do so. It was finally agreed that the two men would next meet in two days' time, on March 17, which would give the Pittsburgh people plenty of time to make up their minds. It also gave Harry plenty of time to think up other reasons to stall signing the contract, which would legally commit Nexus for the next ten years.

The President stood up to indicate that the interview was over. He said, "Oh, by the way, we don't want you to disappear again, Mr. Scott. You'd better have a military escort until you leave the island."

Harry said politely, "Thank you, but I have two armed Nexus bodyguards."

The President knew that this stubborn Australian idiot could not move either far or fast without his being aware of it, so he shrugged. "As you wish."

Harry's latest Smith and Wesson was returned to him as he left the palace.

Rather than ask for an escort back to his hotel, since he'd just refused one, Harry decided to walk back. It was broad daylight and he was armed.

As he headed toward town, Harry pondered the meaning of Raki's recent behavior. Raki had made it clear from the beginning that the Nexus disappearances were not his responsibility because they occurred on the day before Raki returned to power. But why had Raki not told Harry that traces of the women had been found? Presumably because, *if* the women were alive, then it *would* become Raki's responsibility to find them. If the women had escaped from imprisonment in some secret jungle camp, then perhaps the Nexus men were still there. So it would also become Raki's responsibility to search for them.

Why hadn't he? Why had the sighting of the women been dismissed as a rumor?

There was another puzzle. Why had Raki played hard-to-get from November until early March, then suddenly wanted to negotiate immediately on March 15—three days after the women were reported alive? Any fool could see that the incidents were related, but Harry couldn't figure out how.

As he trudged down the tree-lined avenue toward town, the burning sun caused Harry to regret his decision to walk. By the time he had passed the last barbed-wire-encircled Colonial house and approached the rundown buildings of the town, his safari jacket and trousers were soaked with perspiration. He wished that he had telephoned for a car, but that would have meant hanging around that sinister mauve palace until the vehicle arrived from Mount Ida.

Harry rounded a bend in the road and found himself staring into the eyes of a group of khaki-clad soldiers. Their brutal eyes looked back at Harry, not with hatred but with blank stares that were more frightening. It was, of course, a ransom roadblock.

Surrounded by at least a dozen young thugs, Harry dared not to draw his gun.

One man, taller than the rest, stepped forward and grunted, "Money."

Harry remembered that he'd spent all his cash on those two bloody expensive pigs that morning, and that he'd given all his cigarettes and his watch to the Katanga tribesmen.

He said, "I have nothing. But I can get money. You come with me to my hotel. I give you plenty money quick."

"You no money? You white man, no *money?*"

"No."

Harry felt a violent pain in the kidney. A rifle butt hit the side of his head. Somebody punched him in the stomach.

Then he was lying in the filth of the street, his knees drawn up to protect his belly and his arms over his head as they started to kick him.

Harry couldn't open his eyes properly. Through swollen slits he could see dirty, whitewashed bricks. His gun had disappeared, of course. His clothes had been stripped from his body. When he tried to lift his hand to his nose, which was bleeding, it felt as if his fingers had been broken.

Harry forced his eyes open. The light was dim, but he saw excrement-smeared concrete before him. He decided not to move just yet. He would concentrate on breathing. He would try to ignore the overpowering musky smell of closely packed human bodies and ordure.

When he had his breathing under control, more or less, he made an effort to sit up. This was difficult, because a naked body lay slumped across his legs. Harry could also feel, and smell, another dank, warm body beneath him.

He recognized his surroundings. He was in one of the cage-like cells in the Queenstown police station. Three naked black men shared the cell with him. Two were unconscious, and an old man crouched in a corner in a kind of stupor. In other cells, people were groaning and someone was crying. Harry felt the unseen presence of many beaten, broken bodies.

Harry tried again, and eventually succeeded in sitting up. Painfully, he eased his legs from beneath the man who lay across them. Crawling on one hand only, he moved around until he faced the black bars, beyond which he could see the police sergeant's desk. The light outside was fading fast, so it must be about six o'clock.

Harry felt his nose. Yes, they'd broken it.

The door opened. Two men, wearing khaki, dragged in another man, groaning, his ragged shirt covered in blood. Someone shouted. The soldier who sat behind the police sergeant's desk stepped to the right, beyond Harry's line of vision.

Harry heard a key scrape in a lock and hinges creak. The man with the bloody shirt was dragged across the floor like a sack of garbage and heaved inside a cell. He heard a shriek, the sound of a snapping bone, a howl, then abrupt silence.

Harry sat slumped with his head hidden on his knees. He didn't want them to realize that he was conscious. He reckoned that, for the moment, he should be as near invisible as possible. He was very thirsty, but he felt far too ill to feel hungry.

As it was now dark outside, Harry figured he had been missing for about three hours. He wondered when his absence would be noticed. Probably not until the following morning, when Ron Chang was to drive Harry to the airport, where the helicopter would be waiting for him.

At that point, Mrs. Chang would telephone Kerry, who would telephone the palace, who would report the time he had left and that he had refused a military escort. Shit, how could he have been so stupid? Whereupon Kerry would probably tear down to the central police station—here—to report that Harry was missing.

It would take Kerry ten minutes to get to the Mount Ida airstrip. No, damnit! The Bell would be at Queenstown Airport waiting for Harry, and Johno would have taken off at first light, so Kerry would have to drive in. On that road, it might take over an hour to cover the twenty-seven miles to town, so the earliest he could hope to see Kerry was after eight o'clock tomorrow morning.

It seemed a long time to wait.

In one of the adjoining cells, Harry could hear groans and odd thumping, squelching noises. Someone was being systematically beaten.

Fourteen hours to go, thought Harry. The man who had been lying in front of him groaned, recovered consciousness, vomited over Harry's feet and collapsed back on the concrete.

The groans next door stopped abruptly. Were they beating prisoners at random, just for the hell of it? Very possible.

Peeping under his arm, Harry had previously counted four soldiers moving in the front area of the police station, but now he could only see the one hunched over the desk, drumming the heels of his boots on the decrepit chair and paying absolutely no attention to what was going on behind him.

Two hours passed.

The front door opened. In the light of a naked lightbulb, Harry saw the captain who had been waiting for him earlier that day at the Mount Ida office. Trimly dressed, the officer stepped forward, pointed his swagger stick at the man behind the desk and spoke sharply. The soldier didn't stand up but nodded in reply, then jerked his thumb over his shoulder toward Harry's cell.

The officer walked over and looked down between the bars. Politely he said, "Mr. Scott?"

Through swollen lips Harry said, "Glad to see you again."

"Can you stand up?"

"I don't think so."

The captain called sharply over his shoulder. The soldier at the desk sauntered over with a bunch of keys. Slowly, casually, he unlocked one section of the bars. The officer spoke brusquely and pointed his swagger stick at Harry. The soldier entered the cell and kicked one of the unconscious blacks out of his way.

Suddenly Harry found the strength to stand unaided.

Not quite. He fell forward, clutched at the bars for support, then winced as pain shot through his left hand and arm.

The captain said, "The President was informed that you had been arrested for failing to produce your passport when requested. He sent me to take you back to your hotel. I have a jeep outside."

Thank God Raki had been tailing him, Harry thought. Slowly and with great concentration, he walked up the wooden steps of the veranda toward the warm glow of light behind the windows of the Presidential Hotel. The captain did not assist him, but stood waiting until Harry had staggered through the front door.

"Mr. Scott!" Mrs. Chang stood up and shrieked, "Bobby! Freddy! Towels!"

Through split lips, Harry mumbled, "Do you think the boys could help me to shower? Please call Mount Ida. And call a doctor."

SATURDAY, MARCH 16

There was a knock, and Mrs. Chang's secretary, Freddy, appeared in the doorway of Harry's room. Behind him were the first rays of the morning sun. Turning his head, Harry winced in pain.

Freddy proffered a red plastic tray, upon which was a glass of vile strong tea, the medicine prescribed by the doctor, and a bill. Freddy rubbed one big toe against the other and looked apologetic. "New house rule. All guest pay bill every morning or bugger off."

Harry thought, If you're the only hotel in town, nobody can argue your terms. With difficulty, he wrapped a towel around his waist and headed for the outside bathroom. Harry's nose and his left hand were in plaster casts, and he was in considerable pain.

On the veranda, Harry almost collided with Bill, the retired planter. Bill was clutching two opened cans of beer.

"I say, old man, lost your pajamas?" Bill asked. "Good God, have you had an accident?"

"Sort of," Harry said.

"Have you heard the news? For the first time in living memory, old man, this hotel is *closing!* I don't know where I'll go. Ronald Chang is already bolting the top-floor shutters. No breakfast was served this morning. I've just grabbed a couple of beers and some peanuts from the bar. Can I get anything for you? Are you *sure* you're all right?"

"I'm fine. Had a spot of trouble at a roadblock, but there's a good Chinese doctor at St. Mary's Hospital. Why is the hotel closing so suddenly?"

"Because of yesterday's commotion. Haven't you heard?"

Harry shook his head.

"Some drunken soldier shot a priest in St. Mary's Cathedral. One of the congregation bellowed out, 'Soldier *go!* Raki *go!*' Within minutes the whole congregation was shouting and stamping." Bill took another swallow of beer. "Army troops from the barracks were sent to the church to empty it. Apparently they didn't have much respect for religion."

"Anyone hurt?"

"One or two. Then the entire congregation rose up and either took to the bush, went home to mother or headed for the Central Mountains.

"And Sandy left when he heard that other people were joining the group along the way. They're avoiding the roads, of course. Don't want to be machine-gunned from above or shot by armed madmen in military trucks."

He emptied the beer can, aimed it at a chicken in the backyard below, then said, "Bless my soul, look down there!"

From the river, a small boy was running up the muddy garden path. He cried excitedly, "Misis Chang! Misis boat b'long you i come long warra bilong kisimu long carim you feller i go long place b'long you long hill."

Bill said, "Good God! Ma Chang's doing a bunk to her house in the Central Mountains. She's got a coffee plantation up there." He leaned over the veranda and stared down.

Beyond the depressed bougainvillea and straggling plants that surrounded the bald back lawn of the Presidential Hotel, a small crimson motorboat appeared on the river. It drew up to the rickety wooden landing stage of the garden.

From the back door, below the veranda, the majestic bulk of Mrs. Chang appeared. She wore purple satin pajamas, wraparound dark glasses and a large straw sun hat with a green silk bow. In either hand, she carried a red leather attaché case.

Slowly, Mrs. Chang waddled down to the landing stage, followed by Freddy and Bobby, who were laden with luggage.

With some difficulty, Mrs. Chang was lowered into the front seat of the crimson launch. Freddy fitted a green silk parasol into a slot behind Mrs. Chang's seat, so that she sat in its shade, and the fringe kept away the flies. The back seat of the little launch was quickly piled high with two wicker picnic baskets, a hat box and some very old, expensive luggage, pasted with labels of ancient steamers and world-renowned hotels.

Having seated Mrs. Chang beside the driver of the launch, her two secretaries then settled themselves, cross-legged and holding hands, in the stern. The heavily laden little vessel slowly set off upstream.

On the veranda, the scarecrow night watchman had appeared. He grinned at Harry. "Misis Chang go walkabout. Big trouble quicktime Queenstown, master."

Harry nodded. He reckoned that Mrs. Chang was a more reliable barometer of trouble than the head of the CIA.

The crimson launch disappeared behind a bend in the river.

"Didn't you say you had a plane?" the old planter asked Harry. "Would there be room for me? It looks as if trouble is about to start."

"Or end?" Harry suggested.

"It might be the end for Raki."

"But the beginning for Mindo, and for Paui," Harry said.

The old planter said sadly, "There'll always be another Raki."

"And there will always be another Mindo," Harry said, firmly.

"How will this affect you blokes up at Mount Ida?"

"If Mindo is going to head a revolution, we'd be delighted," Harry said. "He's a straight shooter. He knows what we want and *we* know what *he* wants, so we should be able to agree to a simple, straightforward deal." Harry added to himself, But this time with no special arrangements. Harry guessed that Mindo would refuse an all-rights deal and would insist on a top Australian mining lawyer to handle his negotiations.

The hotel name board that usually hung above the front door was now propped against the wooden railing at the end of the veranda. Painted upon it in apple-green on blue was "Freedom Hotel."

The night watchman saw Harry looking at it. He said, "New name belong hotel today."

Beyond the name board, at the end of the veranda, Ronald Chang appeared. He started to supervise a couple of boys who were fitting shutters to the windows as fast as they could.

The watchman nodded upriver. "Good time go walkabout," he said.

WEDNESDAY, MARCH 20, 1985

The ominous blood-red streak on the horizon softened into pink, then blue, as the sky lit up. Annie wanted to shut her eyes. She didn't want to wake up. It was their eighth day at sea, and for the last two the women had been without water.

She didn't want to see Suzy curled up in the bottom of the dinghy, babbling and defenseless, nor the faces of the other women before the sun forced them to put on their khaki hoods. She couldn't bear the sight of the emaciated, sunken flesh, the jutting cheekbones, the expressionless, bloodshot eyes, the twitching, split, swollen lips.

They had drawn lots for the job, and Annie had drawn the longest piece of rattan. She had no choice, she knew that. They had all agreed that if the executioner couldn't do her job, she would become the victim. During her sleepless night Annie had considered accepting the sentence of death instead, but then remembered her four children. Suzy had no children. And anyway, they all doubted that she would ever recover.

A bony foot prodded Annie's thin back. Patty croaked, "Annie, you're the goddamn leader. Do it! The sooner you do, the sooner you'll be through with it. I'll help you."

Annie pulled herself up to a sitting position and looked at the other women, slumped against the sides of the dinghy. She saw running sores and blisters on claw-thin hands, where the flesh had been exposed to the roasting sun. Their uniforms hung over shrunken breasts and shriveled skin, the cloth draped over protruding pelvic bones.

Patty tied Suzy's hands and feet with rattan. She met with no resistance. As Suzy mumbled to herself, Carey looked on and wept.

"Get your fish knife out and get it over with," Patty urged Annie, as she picked up the bailer. "Concentrate on a fast, clean jugular cut, and she'll never feel it."

With dread, Annie pulled out her long bladed fish knife.

But Suzy *did* feel it. She arched her back and screamed, a high, thin shriek.

Patty knelt beside Suzy to catch the dark red blood that spouted from her neck. Thirst was more acute than hunger and had to be satisfied first, before they could eat.

Suzy flopped, then lay still in the bottom of the boat.

Patty plunged her face in the bailer and drank deeply. Annie expected her to be nauseated. Patty wasn't. Dripping blood from her chin, she passed the bailer to Annie.

Looking down and avoiding each other's eyes, the four women drank the blood fast, before it congealed. There wasn't as much as they had expected. They swallowed it as best they could, drinking what they could first, then taking turns to lick the clots from the bailer.

Patty cut Suzy's wrists free; her arms flopped by her sides like a Raggedy Ann doll's. Then Patty freed her feet.

"Help me," Patty croaked to Silvana.

With shaking hands the two women undressed Suzy, then Patty looked up at Annie and snapped, "Now the flesh. Quick!"

Annie looked around at the three other blood-smeared faces. They all realized how she was suffering at that moment —but Annie had drawn the longest piece of rattan. She had no choice. If she waited, it would get worse. Trying to help, Silvana encouraged her, "Do it like you cut my finger off."

Annie thought, How frightening Suzy had become now that

she was no longer alive. She picked up Suzy's limp hand, shuddering as she did.

Patty shook her head. "Fingers have no flesh." She pointed to Suzy's naked buttocks, covered with saltwater sores.

Annie shook her head.

"Get on with it," Patty snarled.

Forcing her fingers to do it, Annie plunged the knife, cutting deeply into Suzy's left thigh. The blood oozed over her hands as she hacked off a three-inch cube of raw flesh. Using the center seat as a chopping block, she cut it into four pieces, then grimly impaled the first one on the blunted end of her fish knife. She offered it to Patty.

Patty took the piece of flesh, but hesitated.

"Go on. *Eat it!*" Annie was shaking with resentment as she said it.

Patty finally took a bite. Before she was able to chew it, she vomited. Pink froth dripped from her mouth.

The other women waited.

Patty took another bite. This time, she was able to keep it down.

With slowly grinding jaws, unable to look at each other, the women chewed the small chunks, which tasted like uncooked pork. They ate very little. The thought of what they were doing was almost as bad as death itself.

Patty croaked, "Sailors eat the heart and liver first—eat them warm. Then they dress the body like a deer."

With what strength she had left, Annie shrieked, "I'm *not* going to disembowel her!" She threw down her knife.

Carey started to weep. "I can't stand her staring eyes."

None of them could.

"Sailors usually cut the head off," Patty said.

Two hours later, this is what Annie did. Patty put the head in the forward locker, because if it were thrown overboard, the excited sharks might overturn the boat in their feeding frenzy.

"Let's put it *all* in the locker," Patty said. "So we can't see it."

As Annie hacked at the body and dismembered it, Patty

pushed each bloody limb into the locker. The dinghy was left in a ghastly condition, covered in glistening black blood that had already started to stink.

"We don't dare wash the boat down. Sharks," Patty said.

The women were all relieved that they no longer had to look at Suzy's body. That afternoon they cut the raw meat into strips. They put the strips to dry on the seats in the sun. Dried, it would last longer. The women moved very slowly. Their unwilling arms seemed heavily weighted as they reluctantly prepared their food. Each woman's unspoken thought was, *Who will be next?* Will somebody kill me in the night? Will three of them overpower *me?*

Later, an even worse thought occurred to Annie: Will I be the last survivor? Will I rock in this terrible blood-blackened boat, roasting to death in the sun, surrounded by dead, swelling, decomposing bodies like the body of the soldier who had reeked of the sweet, foul odor of death at the bottom of the cave shaft?

Hardly anyone spoke that day. Annie could see that they were nervous and on edge. Through the slits in her hood she watched the others. She was afraid to sleep. Suzy had not known what was going to happen to her. Her fate had been decided by whispers in the dark.

The red sun glared down on the little white, bloodstained boat.

Eventually, worn out, Annie could no longer keep awake. Her head lolled sideways. She was asleep.

"Wake up! Wake *up!*"

Someone was shaking Annie's shoulder. She opened her eyes.

In the pearly light of dawn Carey was pointing. "Turtles. *Quick!*"

Annie shook her head clear and sat up. Her mouth fell open. Incredulously she whispered, *"Suzy!"*

Carey glanced at the little figure asleep in the bow.

"Suzy had quite a good night. I don't want to wake her. Take the other oar, Annie. We've *got* to catch one of those turtles! For God's sake, Annie, *move!*"

A hundred yards distant, three turtle heads protruded from the water.

"But Suzy is *alive*," Annie gasped.

"Of *course* Suzy is alive," Carey said irritably. "Quick, take the other oar and row with me to the turtles."

Crouched in the center of the boat, Patty and Silvana were hastily twisting all their pieces of rattan into one long length.

Annie started to tremble. *Her dream had been so vivid!* Since they had been in the dinghy, all the women had slept badly. Restlessly, they gabbled nonsense in their sleep. They all had terrifying nightmares.

Carey croaked, "Grab an oar. Hurry up! Patty has a plan!"

"Where have all the sharks gone?" Annie asked, looking around.

"Don't know. Found a better picnic. Pull *hard!*" Carey gasped.

As the dinghy drew alongside the first turtle, it turned its head and looked disdainfully at the anxious, gaunt faces peering over the gunwale. Turtles are very clever creatures, and it is almost impossible to catch a turtle from a dinghy. On a beach, as Jonathan had demonstrated, you can simply turn a turtle on its back—hence the expression "turned turtle"—but in the water, turtles are agile, swift and difficult to struggle with. In a fight, their horny claws are vicious.

The turtle dived out of sight, with a beautiful, energetic swoop into the deep blue water, until it was invisible in the dark depths of the ocean.

"No use trying to hit them on the head with the anchor, because they would simply swim away," Patty explained to Annie. "So we're going to lasso one."

They approached the second turtle.

As it swam, the women rowed alongside the creature. Patty

and Silvana, both roped by the waist to the center thwart, leaned over the side.

It took only two attempts before they managed to fling the loop of their lasso over the turtle's rear end. They pulled the rope tight.

Leaning dangerously over the side, Silvana pulled the turtle toward the dinghy while Patty started to wind the line around its dangerously powerful rear flippers, working as fast as she could.

Like rolling wool into a ball, Patty wound the line around the turtle's rear flippers. Then she wound it around the front flippers. Eventually, the creature was immobilized.

Wincing with the pain of the saltwater on her raw left hand, Patty helped Silvana slowly drag the turtle into the dinghy, avoiding all its attempts to bite them. Carey counterbalanced the boat by leaning against the opposite side.

The turtle fell into the boat, and Patty and Silvana collapsed, exhausted. With Annie's help, Carey quickly turned the creature on its back. As Carey cut the throat, Annie caught the blood in their bailer. With horror, she again remembered her nightmare.

"Suzy first," Patty said, carefully ladling a little blood into an inverted bamboo stopper. She handed it to Carey. "Don't look so nauseated. Think of it as gravy that hasn't been cooked. Drinking that blood may save Suzy's life."

"Weighs about thirty-five pounds," Silvana guessed, looking at the turtle. "Lucky it isn't bigger, or we wouldn't have had the strength to heave it aboard."

Using the anchor, Silvana and Carey broke open the turtle shell.

As they forced down shreds of raw meat, Patty croaked, "I can't understand how I could *ever* have eaten steak tartare."

"It's disgusting," Silvana agreed.

Annie said, "I'm not complaining; it's the first real food we've had for seven days."

Carey said nothing. Kneeling in the bow, she was trying to

push some of the flesh past Suzy's clenched teeth and into her mouth.

"We'd better cut the turtle up fast and dry it before dark," Patty suggested. "We can stow it in the locker."

Annie shuddered.

The meat instantly gave new mental strength to the women. At last, something had improved. They now had enough food for days.

Just after midday, Annie nudged Patty and pointed to the horizon on their left. "Is it? *Is it?*"

"*Yes!*"

They all gazed at the small, low cumulus cloud.

Annie hardly dared to breathe. "It could be land. And it's only a few miles away."

They all knew that low, small clouds which don't appear to move often surround the summit of a hill-topped island.

Carey peered ahead. "Can anyone see driftwood or seaweed?"

"If that's land, we'll see seabirds at dusk," Patty said. Few birds sleep upon the water.

"More rowing," Carey sighed. "Thank God we've at least had something to eat."

Patty couldn't row because of her burned hand. So while the other women struggled with the oars, she doused them with seawater. She also looked after Suzy, who was lying with her head under the stern seat where there was a little shade.

In the blazing sun of early afternoon they rowed due north.

Almost exhausted, Carey gasped, "If there had been an island under that damn cloud, we'd have seen it by now."

"Don't waste your breath," Annie grunted. "Keep rowing!"

It was almost dusk when, having rowed three miles, they reached the little cloud. It hung motionless above them, as though painted on a school-play backdrop. Each woman had been daring the little cloud to move, and not daring to hope that it wouldn't.

Silvana prayed aloud for rain.

Almost imperceptibly, the little cloud started to float farther north.

"It can't *do* that, there's no wind," Patty gasped.

"I can't row any more. I really can't," said Carey, who had rowed far harder than the other two. The palms of both her hands were now blistered and bloody, and her back felt as if somebody was trying to tear out her ribs. She stared in despair at the empty ocean. "If only we knew where we were."

"We're not far off-course," Annie reassured her. "We're going in the right direction."

Patty said, "Better correct now, back to southeast."

The correction was unfortunate. At that point, the women were nine miles due south of Tanjung Vals, on the southernmost tip of Pulau yos Sudarsa, the island which Jonathan had chosen as their goal. Had they rowed a couple more miles north instead of southeast, they might have sighted a native fishing canoe within striking distance of land.

In the dark, Annie felt a fly on her cheek . . . No, it couldn't be a fly out here . . . She felt another one . . . But if it wasn't a fly?

Incredulously, she brushed two huge drops from her cheek. She rasped, *"Rain!"*

For days they'd been planning what to do if it rained, but for a few minutes nobody did anything except lick the water from their hands. They couldn't believe it.

At last Annie said, "For God's sake, catch it."

In the dark, they hurriedly set out the five bamboo containers and their upended lids, together with the bailer and the turtle shell. They crouched around the turtle shell, holding their hoods up-ended. They hoped to catch the rain in them and dribble it into the shell, from which they planned to tip it into the jerry can.

"Drink all you can," Annie urged. "Your body can store all the water it can get."

"You're supposed to drink it slowly," Carey reminded, "or it'll just be flushed out by your kidneys."

"Oh, God, I hope it rains all night. I hope this is another storm," Patty said fervently.

The rain stopped as quickly as it started.

Hope flared in their hearts like a flame. They now had a little food and half a jerry can of water.

In the pale dawn, Annie gazed fondly into the turtle shell. "Well over four pints. That will last us four days. Maybe five."

MONDAY, MARCH 25

White-faced and weary, Harry sat in President Raki's office. Once again he said, "I've already made our terms clear, Mr. President. Our lawyers in Pittsburgh have told us that they need five more working days on the documentation, before they can get them out here for signature."

Raki frowned. "As today is March twenty-fifth, that means we can't sign until the first of April."

"Yes, sir." Harry knew that he could not delay the signing beyond April 1 without good reason, or copper production would suffer. And the Nexus competitors would be in town.

April 1 seemed to be everybody's deadline, Harry thought, angry with frustration. He still had the impression that the answer to his riddle was very close, and that it was being deliberately withheld from him.

"Very well," Raki said. "April first seems a very suitable date, Mr. Scott. April Fool's Day, is it not?"

TUESDAY, MARCH 26

"Any news?" Harry asked as usual, as he stepped down from the plane into the glare of the early morning sun.

Johno shook his head. "For once, the answer's no."

After the reward offer had been broadcast, Kerry had received hundreds of reported sightings of the lost dinghy. He now spent his days following up telephone and radio reports and sorting them out. Every night, he prepared a list of the reported sightings, all of which were checked by Johno. They were often confusing, if not contradictory.

Harry burst out, *"I can't understand it!* People don't just disappear these days! You can find *anything* with modern technology. They can fish small airplane wheels up from the bottom of the Atlantic, for God's sake!"

"But lots of big ships still disappear without a trace," Johno said. "Think of the Bermuda Triangle. You mostly hear about the *successful* rescues. Those pictures in the newspapers are of the guys who *have* been found. You don't hear so much about the guys who are never seen again." He looked at Harry's thin, tired face and said, "The Cherokee chief pilot is in Kerry's office. He wants to know if they can leave tomorrow."

"No," Harry said. *"Tomorrow we start again."*

"You mean cover the *whole* area again?"

"Yes," Harry said. "Allowing for the current, of course, and moving the grid daily."

"You really *mean* it?"

"Yes. Please try again."

"You sure are determined."

"You mean stubborn," Harry said.

Nobody contradicted him.

Kerry was at his desk, sorting out reported sightings. As with road accidents, the moment a Mayday call is put out over the radio everyone in the area with nothing better to do seems to gravitate to the spot—especially if a reward is involved.

Kerry looked up. "Same as usual, I'm afraid. Some of the amateur search craft have been reporting other search craft. We've had six vessels run out of fuel, one collision and a

sixteen-foot dinghy capsized—with no loss of life, luckily.
Some of the Australian coast guard have officially complained
that we're adding to their work, but they *have* joined the
search." He nodded at the piles of paper on his desk. "To add
to the confusion, a lot of gawking tourists are now out there
—incompetent idiots who should never have been allowed in
the search area."

Johno said, "It's March twenty-sixth. We only have four
more days to search."

Harry said firmly, "The Katanga headman told me that the
women had plenty of stores aboard. They could still be alive.
Maybe they're sitting out there somewhere enjoying the
voyage."

The boat stank of dried blood and putrid turtle. They had
run out of drinking water the day before.

Carey, who was steering, looked sadly beyond the sleeping women to Suzy, whom Carey nursed, fed and guarded
fiercely.

Even after drinking rainwater, Suzy had not recovered her
sanity. Crouched in the bow, she crooned to herself in a
hoarse, cracked voice. The only person who wasn't distressed
by Suzy's plight was Suzy herself. Her face glistened, her
purple-black mouth was flecked with foam, her blank eyes
were turned upward, her teeth chattered when she spoke, and
although the tone of her voice sounded reasonable, everything
she said was merely a jumble of disconnected phrases.

Suddenly a strange, fierce look came over Suzy's face. She
screamed, "I'm saved!"

She started to clamber over the side.

Carey lunged across the tiny boat and threw herself on top
of Suzy, who fell beneath the bundle of bones that Carey had
become.

"Wassamatta?" Annie looked up, dulled by sleep and too
lethargic to move.

Carey croaked, "We'll have to tie Suzy up. She just tried to
jump overboard again."

The other two women roused themselves. Silvana and Annie slowly tied Suzy's wrists together, then roped them to the center thwart. Then they bound her ankles.

The sight of Suzy, her skeleton-thin hands covered with wizened skin, tethered like an animal, distressed them more than anything else had in the twelve days since they had embarked in the dinghy. But she had to be prevented from throwing herself overboard—and possibly pulling somebody else over with her. The sharks, which still accompanied the boat, would attack her within seconds, before she could be hauled back aboard.

Six hours later Carey said, "I'm going to untie Suzy; now she's too weak to move." Cradling Suzy's head in her lap, Carey was reminded of the two babies she had nursed.

As Suzy's limbs twitched and jerked, involuntarily, they realized that they were watching Suzy die.

All day they watched in silence.

WEDNESDAY, MARCH 27

As the sun rose, the fishing vessel *Anna*, with a good catch aboard, was clearly going to be late back to harbor. A bad lead and the failure of her bilge pumps meant that she would miss the morning market in Merauke.

The crew of the *Anna* were intent on getting their boat back to harbor by hand-pumping, when they spotted what appeared to be a empty white dinghy about five miles to the west. Even with binoculars, the skipper couldn't be sure that it wasn't just flotsam, because the slight swell interrupted his view and the dawn mist created a mirage effect.

Because of her own problems, the *Anna* wasn't able to investigate the dinghy. Nor could she radio for help, since her radio was out of action too. So—although the skipper was obliged by law to radio a report of the sighting—he was not able to.

When he finally returned to port, the skipper leaped off his boat and ran to claim the reward in the harbor master's office.

The harbor master laughed. "You're the three hundred and seventeenth claimant," he said. "Lots of luck!"

Harry was used to disappointment now, but he couldn't help feeling depressed by the thought that he had only five more days to search.

In front of him, Johno was silhouetted against the blue sky. The Duck droned on a northwest course back to Paui, after yet another false report.

Well, he'd given it his best try, he told himself.

Johno half-turned and shouted, "Kerry's on the radio. He's just had another dinghy reported by the coast guard; it's eighteen miles southwest of Merauke."

"That coastal town on Irian Jaya, about two hundred miles east of Tanjung Vals?"

"That's the one, Harry."

"How long will it take us to get there?"

"If we turn back straight away it'll take about an hour and a half. I'll tell you exactly in a couple of minutes."

"Okay, Johno, let's go."

"Kerry wants to talk to you, Harry."

Harry took the headphones. Kerry's tinny voice said, "Looks as if we've hit something interesting at last. Theoretically they could be in this area if they'd hit the coastal current and been swept east around the tip of Pulau yos Sudarsa into this bay."

"We'll do a grid search from the southern point and follow the current," Johno called out, tracing the area on the chart with his finger.

Ahead of them the sea stretched empty and flat.

Harry said to Kerry, "Keep your fingers crossed."

Kerry's voice was hesitant. "If you find them, Harry, remember they've been at sea a long time. If you see any, uh, *unusual* remains, the medics always tell the survivors not to

671

mention a word to anyone, to *forget* it. You get my meaning?"

"Don't think I haven't thought about it," Harry said.

The midday sky was the usual brilliant light blue. The blinding glare from the water was as painful to their eyes as looking directly into the overhead sun.

"Are you sure she's dead?" Carey croaked. She had only just woken.

Crouched over the limp, shapeless bundle of clothes, Annie nodded. Silvana's face had the translucency of flesh beneath which blood no longer pumped. Her sightless eyes looked up, without blinking, at the sky.

"I think Silvana has been dead for several hours," Annie moaned. She would never forget Carey's eyes at that moment.

"I can't believe it," Carey whimpered. "Somehow, I thought we'd all make it."

Annie gently stroked Silvana's hair. She said, "Now that it's started to happen, I hope we all go fast."

"Of course we won't do it," Carey croaked.

"Of course not," Annie said, firmly.

"We gave it a good try," said Carey.

"Fourteen days," Annie said.

"Don't wake the others yet," Carey said, looking away from Silvana.

Gleaming black fins surrounded the boat.

Carey whispered, "Nine of those bastards out there now. We can't let them get her."

"I hope they never get *any* of us," Annie said. "I hope we all drift until we dry to skeletons."

Annie's choking sobs woke Patty from a hideous nightmare in which she kept trying to eat Suzy's eyeballs. Her teeth couldn't bite on them, they bounced off like rubber. Her mouth was too dry to swallow the globes. An eyeball was stuck in her throat. Patty couldn't breathe, the thing was choking her . . . .

Patty blinked and sat up. She really *couldn't* swallow, because her throat was too dry. But, thank God, there was nothing in her mouth.

"Silvana's dead," Annie sobbed.

Patty croaked, "Why are you crying? *That means that we can live!* Quick, cut her throat. Where's the bailer?"

Annie gasped, "You can't do it, Patty!"

Patty, on her knees, ignored Annie as she leaned a trembling hand forward to pick up the bailer. "Silvana is dead and *I* am alive—and I'm going to stay alive as long as possible."

Patty's knife was out, and her eyes looked as fierce and determined as those of a wolf at bay.

"Take away her knife, Carey!" Annie ordered.

"She'd only knife me," Carey whispered. "And a fight might upset the boat."

"Don't you *see?*" Patty asked wildly. "God has given us this gift. Now we don't have to do anything terrible to stay alive."

"For heaven's sake!" Annie gasped. "It's cannibalism! Don't you call that terrible?"

"Are you going to let a primitive taboo kill you?" Patty shrieked with what strength remained to her. "Can't you accept a gift from your God? That's food and drink!" She pointed down at Silvana's scrawny corpse. "Just believing what you're told is *dumb!* It's also going to kill you. But *not me!*"

Carey glimpsed the flash as Patty lifted her knife. She turned away because she hadn't the strength to stop her and she couldn't bear to witness what was going to happen.

And then she saw it.

"*Patty!*" Carey rasped. "Look over the back, to the left."

Annie and Patty both looked. Her knife upraised, Patty paused. "It's a *plane!*" she cried, squinting at the black speck that had appeared over the horizon to the northwest.

Steadily, the speck traveled across the sky to the east.

"*Carey!* The flares!" Annie whispered hoarsely.

Slowly and painfully, Carey crouched to open the locker and felt inside for the flares. Both her palms were covered with broken blisters. Patty's left hand was raw, stinking and unusable, so Carey handed the flares to Annie.

"Careful!" Patty croaked as Annie, legs trembling, clambered onto the center thwart and stood there.

"Don't! You might fall," Carey implored. "Get down."

With shaking hands, Annie held up the flare in her left hand, hoping that she wouldn't get burned the way Patty had. Her fingers were clumsy and slow as she unscrewed the base of the flare with her right hand, unraveled the string from the base, gave it a couple of turns around her right hand, then yanked hard.

The dinghy rocked violently, but nothing else happened.

"Try another one!" Patty urged.

The plane was nearer, they could now hear a faint buzz. But it was flying almost due east on a course that would take it away from the dinghy.

The second flare lit with a roar, but it rocketed sideways into the water without rising more than twenty feet.

Nobody in the boat moved as Annie tried again. She was almost too weak to stand.

The flare rose in a twenty-second arc of light, then fell into the water and disappeared.

The plane flew on.

"It didn't see us," Patty croaked.

They all gazed at the moving black speck.

"Keep trying," Patty urged. "Quick, while it's still in sight."

As Carey handed another flare up to Annie, Patty shrieked, *"Look!"*

The white-hot circle of the sun flashed silver on the metallic, pale blue wings of the Grumman Duck as it altered course and headed straight toward the dinghy.

Mesmerized, not daring to hope, the forlorn women in the little boat watched the silvery blue dot grow larger.

The aircraft flew steadily nearer and lower. It passed the dinghy about fifty yards to starboard. As it swung in a turn and circled back toward the boat, clearly preparing to land on the ocean, the women saw the strange, ungainly silhouette